The
Future
Burns Bright

Book Four : *The Future Alight*

(First Edition)

by

Marcus B. Shields

ISBN : (978-1-926515-17-5)

For additional information about *The Future Burns Bright*, surf to :

http://abfbook.telostic.com

For human generations yet to come
For whom a vast, strange universe beckons...
May you be up to the task

And...
May this beautiful, life-giving, blue and green planet
Still be there for you

Table of Contents

Prologue

Since this book is the fourth and final volume of the sequel to a predecessor series, it is strongly suggested that you should enjoy...

Angel of Mailànkh (Book One)
Doubt Me Not (Book Two)
Angel and The Empire (Book Three)
Children of The Fire (Book Four)

Of *The Angel Brings Fire* series, and then...

Storm In The North (Book One)
The Race (Book Two)
Against Time (Book Three)

Of *The Future Burns Bright* series...

Before starting to read *The Future Alight*.

With that said, it is recognized that for various reasons, some readers will have happened upon *The Future Alight*, without having convenient access to the preceding books of the series.

We have therefore provided the following brief synopsis of the events of *Against Time*, so that the reader can make sense of some of the characters and themes involved.

Marcus Shields

Author

The Future Burns Bright (Book Three) – Against Time begins with the former (legitimate) President and his family, protected by Sylvia Abruzzio and her dog, Jerry Kaysten and the Storied Watcher's animate arm-shield, narrowly escaping capture while fleeing his house-arrest at Arnold Air Force Base. The group is crammed into Sullivan's car as they head to Washington, D.C., hoping to re-establish the ex-President's authority over the U.S. government.

Leveraging various alien-powers on the part of Abruzzio, Kaysten and the Storied Watcher's arm-shield, the former U.S. leader manages to tunnel directly into the basement of the White House, and – after a stand-off with suspicious Secret Service Agents – he delivers an impromptu, televised address to the nation, in which he defies the Mars Gang (and the Storied Watcher, who he incorrectly thinks is planning to make good on earlier threats to destroy the United States), to call off their campaign of destruction and to instead negotiate with him, in person.

The broadcast is met with dismay and hostility by the imposter-President from his airborne vantage-point in the Airborne Command Post, because it effectively establishes *two different* "Presidents", each competing for the loyalty of – and control over – the U.S. federal government and its military.

Meanwhile, Jacobson and the main part of the Mars Gang travel across the southern United States in their stolen V-37 vertical-take-off transport-plane, fighting off repeated attacks by the U.S. Air Force all along the way. Aided by information from the "NRA" hacker group, the Mars Gang arrives at their destination with only minutes to spare, rescuing the former Mars mission commander's wife Yvonne and his family, along with several other "civilians" unlucky enough to have been caught in the cross-fire.

Jacobson and his group re-direct the V-37 eastward, but they are again pursued by the U.S. military, which comes out on the losing end of several engagements with the Mars Gang's super-powered team-members.

The former Vice-President – hunting the Mars Gang with a cold fury from his vantage-point aboard the Airborne Command-Post aircraft – soon has far more pressing issues to deal with. After unsuccessfully trying to force the captive Minnie Chu to surrender data that would allow the tracking and defeat of the Jacobson team, the *faux*-President tires of Chu's obstructionism and orders her murdered. This savagery backfires; the cornered and desperate ex-FBI-team-leader – fighting for her life – unleashes her deadly *Gaze of the Khùl-Algrenàthi'i* death-ray against her captors and tormentors. When the brief, unequal fire-fight is over with, Chu is now in partial command of the aircraft (although she cannot control its direction of flight) and has the faux-President and several of his sycophants, as hostages.

While Jacobson and the core of the Mars Gang are far to the west, Brent Boyd has flown to West Virginia, planning to meet up with his wife Laura and children, in the small town of Fayetteville. However, as he calls her from a bed-and-breakfast hotel in the town, to his dismay he overhears the sounds of a pursuit, because Laura and her children are being hunted by malevolent, murderous CIA-agents.

The former Mars mission pilot is able to track his wife's car to where it is hiding on a highway in West Virginia, and as the Agency assassins close in, Brent Boyd arrives on scene. His alien-powers make short work of the CIA-men and – after a joyful reunion with a family from which he has been separated, since he first set out on the trip to Mars – the consolidated Boyd clan goes into hiding until they can meet up with the larger Mars Gang.

Shortly thereafter, Boyd and his family have a chance encounter with the two ex-FBI-agents – Hendricks and Boatman – who are now themselves fugitives, after having used their supernatural powers to prevent arrest by a posse of local police, albeit only at the cost of several human lives. The combined Boyd-Hendricks-Boatman group head for Fayetteville, to *rendez-vous* with the rest of the Mars Gang.

After more mishaps – including an airborne "friendly-fire" incident in which Brent Boyd badly wounds Cherie Tanaka, after mistaking her for a hostile aircraft – the Jacobson team meets the others waiting in Fayetteville. They hear the President's challenge and decide to head for Washington, D.C., to settle their issues with the American government, once and for all.

Other events are unfolding out west in the Greater Los Angeles area. The Aryan Brotherhood's two most vicious, skilled skinhead warriors are hunting for Sebastiàn and his gangster-army, who are, in turn (separately from a group of Muslim fanatics and various other local street-gangs, who are in pursuit of the same goal), approaching ever-nearer to where the Brotherhood has hidden its stolen, ex-Pakistani nuclear weapon. There are several pitched battles, with many killed on every side.

Karéin-Mayréij, meanwhile – having left the most-part of her followers in the relative safety of the cavern she hewed from the rock of Bouvet Island in the South Atlantic – has now returned, along with a small number of friends and family, with the *Mailànkh Express* air-ship in tow.

She keeps a very low profile while approaching and over-flying the United States, as she does not want to interfere in what she (incorrectly) believes to be the progress of the Mars Gang and the Chu / Abruzzio group, toward the tests upon which they latterly embarked.

Despite her best efforts – the Storied Watcher and her air-ship are ambushed by marauding U.S. Air Force fighter-planes; these meet the fate of all who are foolish enough to tangle with the alien-girl (not to mention Melissa Claremont, who has gained formidable alien-powers of her own), but the air-ship is damaged in the encounter, and Karéin-Mayréij is forced to land the vessel to effect temporary repairs.

However, her choice of landing-area is indiscreet and a crowd forms. The onlookers ask the alien-girl if she plans to take the President up on his challenge to come to the White House and take up her issues with him, there. Caught somewhat at a loss, the Storied Watcher agrees to do this, and, unaware that the Mars Gang is planning to do the same thing, she soon sets out for Washington, D.C.. She arrives at the White House shortly thereafter and is immediately embroiled in a tense (and long-awaited) confrontation.

Matters rapidly degenerate into violence as Bob Billings and Tommy George attempt to kill the President, as revenge from the atrocities inflicted upon themselves and others, by the U.S. government; but they are opposed by Jerry Kaysten and Sylvia Abruzzio, along with some desperate, last-minute maneuvers on the part of Karéin-Mayréij herself.

Miraculously – although several are wounded – no-one is killed in this encounter, but the Storied Watcher warns that the President's transgressions cannot go unpunished, and she stages a simulated execution of the horrified U.S. leader's two children (Matt and Clairie). In fact, however, the alien-girl's plan is merciful; all she actually does is to impart the Holy *Fire* of *Amaiish* upon them.

Matters take a deadly turn on board the Airborne Command-Post aircraft, which is on a slow course heading for Washington, D.C.. Minnie Chu, who is – along with her hostages the *faux*-President and several of his advisers – ensconced in the Command-Post's central communications-room, is informed by (Brother) Harold Crowford, that he has smuggled a live nuclear weapon on board the aircraft, as part of a deranged, religiously-motivated plan to lure the Storied Watcher close enough to the plane to kill her when the bomb is detonated.

But worse still is yet to come. From his secret underground bunker, the malevolent CIA-director – who has his own, paranoid fantasies of murdering the Mars Gang, Karéin-Mayréij and the President – has used the spy-tricks of his Agency, to commandeer control of the government's single operational nuclear weapon, which is integrated with a cruise missile located on a stealth-bomber, flying over the east-central United States.

Acting on his own authority, "Top Dog" unleashes the missile on a high trajectory against the Airborne Command-Post; so now, the unfortunate Minnie Chu, on that aircraft, is not only riding a flying bomb that may detonate at any minute, but is also the target of a *second* nuclear weapon hurtling at her.

The aircraft's systems detect the missile-launch and estimate that its flight-path will intercept the Command-Post, over downtown Washington, D.C... that is, right over the 1600 Pennsylvania Avenue, from which the President is now attempting to restore his authority over the government.

These developments are communicated to the White House, where they are received with dismay not only by the U.S. leader, but also by the nonplussed Storied Watcher, who at first argues that she has no responsibility to save the United States or its leadership, from the two nuclear weapons, whose appearance on the scene, she had nothing to do with.

Eventually, however, age-old feelings of duty and honor change Karéin-Mayréij's mind, and she reluctantly agrees to organize and lead a rescue-party composed of the "New People" to save Chu and the inhabitants of the D.C. area, by leading the Airborne Command-Post out to sea, away from populated areas. Upward they climb, and soon, Abruzzio is able to create a massive illusion that fools Crowford, from his vantage-point in the aircraft's control-cabin. He forces the co-pilot to head for what looks like downtown D.C.; but in fact, the image is just a "mirage". He, is in fact, flying the Command-Post out to sea.

But almost from the start, other events have overtaken these finely-laid plans, as the Storied Watcher notices Top Dog's cruise-missile descending on Chu's aircraft. Racing skyward at maximum speed, the wary alien-girl dreads the risks that she may have to accept, to deal with this sinister weapon. While this is going on, Minnie Chu receives some terrifying news : the suicidally-crazed Harold Crawford, believing that Karéin-Mayréij is now aboard the Command-Post to rescue Chu (when, in fact, the alien-girl is many kilometers away, chasing the nuclear cruise missile), has set the timer to detonate the first H-bomb, on board the aircraft.

Not knowing how long the count-down will last but expecting to be immolated in nuclear fire at any second, the terrified Minnie Chu uses her *Gaze* to blast open one of the Airborne Command-Post's entrance-hatches and dives out into the cold night air beyond.

Washington, D.C. now faces imminent destruction by no less than *two* nuclear bombs : one on-board the Command-Post, as it flies toward the Atlantic Coast; and a second one, aboard a plummeting cruise-missile.

The lives of millions of helpless people lie in the balance, as the Storied Watcher and her "New People", try to bring about a *miracle!*

The Devil's Hat-Trick

A Second Shot, Courtesy Of The Gods

Karéin-Mayréij was aware – both from the real-time, *Makailkh*-language-and-script-display on her visor, and from centuries of personal experience – that she had passed above the troposphere.

The more rarefied, much colder air up here provided less resistance, so to avoid over-shooting the target, the alien-girl checked her speed to well less than a fifth of what she knew she was otherwise capable.

In the darkness far below and slightly ahead, she perceived the sprawling shape of Minnie Chu's aircraft, going in and out of the cloud-banks.

In front of the Airborne Command-Post – indistinguishable to human eyes, but easy to discern for the Storied Watcher – was a shimmering, translucent pocket of compressed, distorted air. This somehow was keeping its station in front of the aircraft's cockpit, despite the the plane's several-hundred-miles-per-hour forward-speed.

Furthermore, forming a couple thousand feet below the airplane, was an odd-looking, hurricane-mimicking cloud-level. This was burgeoning outward; it was already about three times the size of the ACP and it was rapidly expanding.

Suddenly, Chu's aircraft banked slightly to the right and began to level out of the gradual decline that it had previously been maintaining.

That vessel is a doomed ship... why do you not jump clear of it? anxiously reflected the alien-girl.

Noble Hector's arts will cushion your descent!

I cannot hurry thither and save you – to do so, even if our plan to thwart the bomb aboard works perfectly – that would leave death from above, to claim us both, equally brave Sylvia, stalwart Hector, and possibly all those in the Express!

May the Fates and Gods keep you safe this night, little sister!

As to the missile, the damnable thing was clear in her senses, now; but much about it, made little sense.

It resembles the one that exploded, near to that island, over the northern sea, on the other side of this continent, mused the Storied Watcher.

But its course was not set to intercept Min-ee's airplane in the most efficient manner.

Most odd... it is as if the foul thing was meant to impact with something on the ground – alas, there must be many thousands of these 'humans' down there – rather than with that big airplane, which is just 'in the way'... in that, at least, perhaps do the Weavers of Fate show us some fortune, today.

The distance was closing rapidly now, and again the fast-thinking-skill charged her faculties.

A killing-burst of the little-particle-shine? As I informed dear Bob back in bed, in Tucson – that could unstring its bow, yet... some of the com-pu-ters said that that might set it off, a "rad-haz fuse"...

Oh-kay then, the Gaze... *but that I know,* surely *will detonate the devilish thing... or the blazing fire of mine ancestors, or of* Væran Ksé'l'ch' *– yes, I hear thee, little one... but* never *would I task thee with such a fatal peril!*

We must use something that the humans would never have expected... what, among our array of war-tools, can do this?

Venerable One... thy help, I beg!

Quest lend weirding-arts my to will, came back the amulet's voice, its timbre and tone exotic-sounding, with accents of languages long-lost, even to the likes of Karéin-Mayréij herself.

Slow but down it afar from craft-magic with can I.

Delay within gears the evil their do to... to try fixes it warn when to hellfire its light.

Again – eternally do I live in thy debt, noble clan-mother! returned a grateful Storied Watcher.

We shall need every last morsel of spy-craft and trickery... which of our war-arts, do those of this world, use not yet against each other?

Hmm – no poison, however lethal, shall plague such a techno-bomb – but in looking at the com-pu-ters, never have I seen reference to their knowing of the Ways of Winter-Deep... nor of the mind-push-and-pull-skill... those at least, we can *deploy – no time in which to ponder others!*

Let us turn those to our use... and pray mightily that they fail us not!

Again, she turned her sensory-abilities to the target in front (and still ahead) of her.

Behold! It arcs and now begins a dive!

More haste, children – turn thy efforts foremost to protection, and not just from our quarry, but from the direction of Min-ee's air-ship... for that may also *shortly burn as do the Eighteen Hells of Dreaded* Væran Bssìro!

Invisible shield of my ancestors – come thee now, to full potency!

Venerable One – turn thy witchcraft against its techno-brain!

Warnings of some kind – telling of "something large approaching the airplane, from the southern direction" – reached her psyche; but the alien-girl, preoccupied with the task-at-hand, suppressed these.

We must freeze this accursed missile first – one shot only – then gently reverse its course; we cannot do so abruptly, lest that make it think that it has struck a solid object, thus to detonate...

The reading-sources tell of a "bare-oh-metric fuse being triggered if the weapon falls too far down, into this planet's sea of air... pray we that forcing it back upward, will not do the same...

The cruise-missile was gradually accelerating; faster and faster it fell.

As near as Karéin-Mayréij could remember from precedent over the seas surrounding Amchitka, she had about ten seconds before the missile would descend to an altitude guaranteed to completely vaporize the ACP.

I must freeze it and turn it back in no more than five ticks of the clock, she resolved. Any more and the air-plane will be crushed by the blast!

The inner voice of *Vìrya Quü'j* notified her,

Goddess young can I done all.

Slowly brain its thinks; intent deadly with still thinking though is.

I bless thee, Venerable Mother! quickly responded the Storied Watcher.

Curse it, she inwardly muttered, *even though it falls on a steady course – it evades only in a minor way – the techno-stealth of the missile confounds my aim... steady, Storied One, lock on to its little particle-shine, it cannot fully cloak that... estimate the lead-distance...*

With her war-song echoing across the heavens, she cried,

Come to mine arms, Frigid Blast of the Osda-Osdéam – come, *with savage hibernal arts, yea, to freeze even an* ocean – **come!**

With a forward-thrusting-motion of clenched-fists, she unleashed a jet of near-invisible, supernatural cold, expertly targeted at the precise point in the stratosphere, where the missile was set to reach in another second.

Her attack looked to be flying true; but without warning, the American weapon abruptly changed course. It deviated a few degrees from its original trajectory, slowing slightly as well.

The cold-bolt flew harmlessly off into the distance, its frigid essence slowly dissipating into nothingness.

Her attack had *missed!*

A momentarily-stunned, horrified Karéin-Mayréij – keeping the fast-thinking-thing going dangerously overlong, as evidenced by a painful headache – tried to react.

She cast her telekinetic tractor-beam against the missile, but the combination of the distance between herself and the weapon (several kilometers), its unanticipated course-change, plus its stealth-coating, seemed to shrug off her grasp.

I never miss, when the hour is thus dire! she panicked.

What could have –

Now *something* – an aircraft of some type, much smaller than the ACP but still at least the size of two or three city-buses next to each other, propelled by four large engine-nacelles, with long jets of flame blazing from the rear of each – appeared just underneath Chu's airplane.

The intruder was on an east-by-north course, gradually climbing at a decent speed (though slightly less than that of the ACP itself). In a second or two it had ascended to above the ACP's current altitude.

The missile began to change course even more radically; its path curved away from the ACP.

It is homing in on the fire coming from the second airplane! realized the Storied Watcher.

Gods be kind to whomever is on-board this latterly-appearing air-ship!

Another shot – ancestors, bless me with fortune on this day!

Bolt of Deepest Winter – fail me not now!

Again, Karéin-Mayréij did some desperately-forced firing-calculations, adjusting for the flight-paths of both the missile and its new-found quarry, and let loose with her cold-bolt.

The attack took a half-second or two to travel to the target point; this time, her aim was true, and the frigid-shot struck, dead-on.

The missile – its exterior frosted with condensed oxygen- and nitrogen-molecules – wobbled in flight for a second. The alien-girl winced and braced herself, expecting a deadly burst of light, heat and radiation to come at any second.

But instead, the missile just began to turn, still tracking toward the new aircraft.

Wait... praised be – the Gods do open a door! she exclaimed to her war-children.

Accelerating beyond the ability of any lesser being so to do, the Storied Watcher rocketed to a point about a kilometer ahead of the new airplane, keeping careful track of the missile, which was gradually closing the distance with the former.

She cast her telekinesis on the second airplane, pulling it toward her and forcing its speed to increase, while changing its course to an eastward, slightly-ascending heading. She tried to fly into the relatively darker area between the bright lights of Baltimore to the north and Washington, D.C., to the south, changing the direction of the entire aerial group slowly, by a degree or two per second.

The missile seemed to be flying faster as well, perhaps to compensate with the velocity of its target.

Ahead of Karéin-Mayréij lay the reaches of the ocean, no more than a minute or two distant, at these greater speeds.

If I can just keep the new air-ship between us and that damnable missile, she mused.

As long as the weapon's brain remains frozen, and remains befuddled by Venerable One's witch-trickery... those engine-flames may limit how long...

And with the shield of my ancestors at full-flower, even if the weapon explodes, with a kil-o-meter between us and the airplane, and another one or two between the 'plane and the missile... yes, we might survive that!

Wait!

Those who are on the airplane... I cannot leave them to such a fate!

Yet... if we approach close enough to save them – and the missile then detonates –

Relief came to her mind when she heard, by the voice of *Vîrya Ahn'jë,*

Dear there mother descry I none people living air-plane on.
Force-life none within.

My conscience sighs in thankfulness! answered a gratified Storied Watcher, as the ancient greatness and confidence, rushed back to her.

But how would an air-plane be set on such a course, without any humans aboard, thus to travel through the skies?

It is most peculiar... something to be inquired after, when the battle is done... but for now, we question not this good fortune!

Now let us complete a quest... and lead an Ark of Death out to sea!

As she led the second airplane – and its deadly follower – out over the dark, cloud-enshrouded Atlantic, another thought occurred to the alien-girl.

O Sylvia... O Hector – may thine own ancestors, also bestow ye a generous second chance!

Steer The Jet Clear; Then... Steer Clear Of The Jet

Like some others on this night, former JPL scientist Sylvia Abruzzio tried not to look down; after all, she had only taken to the skies within the last week.

It had been hard to say "goodbye" to little "Rainbow"; but the *tristesse* had been tempered by the knowledge that the puppy would have a much better chance of surviving the night, than would the more-than-a-woman, herself.

Abruzzio had never flown this high before, and she found it very difficult to synchronize her altitude and forward-velocity with that of the huge, intimidating Aerial Command-Post.

The latter of these two attributes, in fact, she was only able to achieve, by locking her telekinesis on to the starboard side of the lumbering 747-derivative's fuselage, near the bow, and then allowing the aircraft to put her in its tow. This was much easier said than done, because at first her aim was off, and she had mistakenly tried to lock on to the compressor-face of the ACP's outboard starboard engine; as she began to be thrown around in a circular motion, at several thousand revolutions per minute, Abruzzio instantly and wisely broke her grasp and instead redirected it to a more stable part of her quarry.

Luckily – as far as she could tell – she hadn't done any permanent damage to the engine.

But I bet if I had forced it, she confidently noted, *I could have shredded that thing.*

Pratt and Whitney take notice...

Thus, the former JPL scientist had decided to take a position somewhat below and ahead of the aircraft's main row of view-ports, while still blurring her image so she could remain here, undetected from inside the plane.

Having to do these airborne maneuvers, while concentrating on a maintaining a substantial-sized lens-refracting illusion – causing, she hoped, the scene in front of the ACP to appear further away and on a steep downward angle – in front of the airplane, was not any easier. She was frankly amazed that her skin was neither being shredded nor frost-bitten, given the speeds at which the Command-Post was flying through the frigid Atlantic Seaboard night air.

Yet it seemed that her personal force-field was holding these dangers at bay, with consummate ease; the only reminder of what would actually have confronted a normal member of the *Homo Sapiens* species, in the same situation, had occurred when – out of idle curiosity – Abruzzio had willed her protective-shield to temporarily reduce, so she could hear all the sounds of what was going on, in the area.

The experiment was a short-lived one, as the icy blast of the near-stratospheric outside-air, almost knocked her completely out of breath.

Remind me to dress more warmly next time, ha ha, ruefully noted the former scientist.

But even "buttoned-up"... I can still hear my war-song... and a while back, I could hear Hector's, too.

Another one to add to the experimentation-list, should I live past this night, she reflected.

That other missile – shouldn't it have hit by now?

Abruzzio looked up at the ACP, using her enhanced senses – especially, the heat-seeing-one – trying as hard as she could, to glean some trace of information as to what was happening within the aircraft.

Wait – what's that! she inwardly exclaimed, with a double-take to something approaching *fast*, from below the command-post.

She caught a fleeting glimpse of something – an airplane, or some other kind of aerial contraption – rocketing through the local airspace, below and just ahead of the ACP. Abruzzio's infra-red vision was temporarily overwhelmed by this other craft's four engines, which were blazing out long tongues of flame – and a trail of vaporized elements, intermixed with larger metal-parts, as well – behind. But then the interloper vanished behind the command-post, flying to the north and east.

A few seconds later, Abruzzio thought she heard the Storied Watcher's tell-tale war-song, and believed that she felt the discharge of the alien-girl's weirding-powers, from somewhere above and to the north.

I should go and figure out what that's all about, she thought, *but I can't leave this ship, and keep my illusion still going in front of it.*

If that's you, Karéin – my trust's in you, for good, this time!

And the fact that I'm not yet dead, suggests that my trust is well-founded... I hope...

Again turning her attention to the ACP, Abruzzio noted with interest that one of its main-floor windows, a bit forward of amidships, had sustained signs of obvious damage; it was patched up in jury-rigged fashion, but looked like it might not survive a hard turn or even severe turbulence.

Unfortunately, the blinds over many of the other windows were drawn, and there were long stretches of them that were completely opaque to Abruzzio's scrutiny.

Come on, Minnie... I know you're in there! she broadcasted. *Answer me!*

But there was no response.

Fucking metal – or maybe it's the damn thing's EMP-shielding (sorry, God), mused the ex-scientist.

I can still dimly make out Hector's presence, back with the Express *– and he's at least a thousand feet below.*

"Remind self to ask Karéin why her bloody telepathy is like a ten-dollar walkie-talkie with a nearly-dead battery", yes, next up for discussion...

However, Abruzzio was now confronted with evidence of things very definitely going on, inside the ACP. Her infra-red sight detected movement within one of the main-deck corridors, and then – somehow, even though her force-field was still blocking the onrushing air outside it – she perceived the staccato sounds and muzzle-flashes of gunfire.

With alarm, she noted that one of the shots seemed to have punctured the aircraft's fuselage above the window-line; the hole did not seem to be a very large one, as near as she could tell.

A gunfight! realized the immediately-shocked ex-scientist.

From what Minnie said, if that gets out of control and the airplane crashes, the bomb might get triggered... and where I am now, I might as well be standing right on top of Ground Zero.

Hail Mary, Mother of God, Full of Grace – protect me this night; and if it's thy will that it be my last... consider this my confession of sins.

Yes... I Moira and I did some, uhh, "things" while we were in Mother Theresa Academy... but I tried not to, and I went to Mass, most Sundays!

And as for waking up in bed with Chris O'Bannon from Father Gregor Boy's School... we were both drunk, all three times... but he said he loved me, and besides, I promise... nothing like that will happen again!

Oh-kay... I can say that, because booze is now being neutered the moment it hits my lips... but shouldn't I still get credit for the effort?

After crossing herself, Abruzzio scanned in every direction, determinedly using her supposed "enhanced noggin-power" to figure out alternative situational strategies and tactics.

For a moment or two, she was thrown off-track by the amazing, otherwise-invisible detail about the aircraft, as revealed to her mind by the heat-seeing, the star-light-seeing and all the other "special senses".

Human-figures, wraith-like in the infra-red sight mode, went back and forth inside the ACP's main corridor-level; but as yet, the tell-tale signature of a "more-than-human" such as Chu, was nowhere to be seen.

Where is the bloody thing?

The glow of ionizing radiation leakage, I should easily be able to detect – lots of experience with that over Amchitka – but... nothing!

What if that preacher-guy was lying about it, all along?

What if he... wasn't?

If I could just get a fix on it, I could try a targeted burst of microwaves and hard X-Rays, transmute enough U-235 or Pu-239 to non-fissionable isotopes, to inert the accursed thing... oh yeah, but didn't Minnie warn that it might have a radiometric fuse?

And, of course... doing the radiation-burst would insta-kill everybody anywhere nearby, when I let fly. Minnie might survive, but it wouldn't be very pleasant for her.

They're likely doomed anyway – but let that not be on my account, O Lord!

So much for that idea...

Should calculate how far I've got to get away and how fast I have to fly, to have a chance of surviving the damn thing – sorry for the cursing there God, but with things being the way they are – I don't even know how big a bomb it is, exactly!

Too many variables!

Let's suppose it's the same as the one that blew just south of the island... good an assumption as anything.

I figure, to be on the safe side... five kilometers minimum, preferably ten or more – if I can get below that cloud-deck that Hector's working on to soak up some of the initial energy-output... how far's that? Maybe one kilometer or so?

And how am I going to fly properly, anyway? Ground-level's a long way away, I've got minimal ability at this altitude to use it to push off from...

I'm locked-on to the aircraft now, and I used that to equalize airspeed with it earlier... but doing that when it explodes could be a fatal mistake... what if the thermonuclear plasma can somehow ride up my tractor-beam, or if it creates a weakness in my force-field?

I have no idea, scientifically, about how my telekinetic power works, or what it's actually made up by, Abruzzio ruefully admitted to herself.

If it's charged-particles, or subatomic particles... the plasma might find that the path of least resistance...

Gee, Karéin – there's a use case that you never tutored us about...

And also... how come the damn – err, darn – plane's still on a gentle climb? she pondered.

It should be going down, to get to breathable air... oh, wait... that's what we wanted it to do – to go upward, stop it from crashing into downtown D.C. – right?

A wry smile came to her face.

Forgot...

Speaking of that... where are we? Abruzzio asked herself.

She cast her special senses downward and ahead, below the kaleidoscopic deception in front of the aircraft. Ramirez' cloud-tricks obscured some of her sight-abilities but it did not stop all of them.

It's working! she gratefully realized. *It must have completely fooled them!*

Not only are we ascending... but we're now steering well clear of the built-up area!

There's the Atlantic... should be only a minute or so before we hit the coast...

But at this juncture, the sounds and feelings of more gun-shots – this time, coming from almost at the tail-end of the ACP, in an area that didn't have any windows to show the battle – intervened to interrupt Abruzzio's calculations.

Then there were at least three more bullet-puncture-shots that perforated the aircraft's skin. It was leaking air at a steady rate because of all this.

Ugh – despite that good news, there's some bad sh... going on, inside there.

The question is... "who and where are the good guys".

Minnie could be up front – or she could be in the back, where that latest gun-fight was coming from. She doesn't know how to fly, which is probably why she hasn't bailed... which leaves it to me and Hector to get her the H out of here.

Oops... sorry again, Lord.

Can we just keep a running total and work it out in Purgatory, if You don't mind?

Well, I can't just sit around out here, ad infinitum; I'm just as much at risk from the bomb, as if I were actually inside the airplane.

Maybe if I get closer, I can look inside the windows on this side, then if necessary, sneak above the plane and rotate over to the other side, check to see if anything is happening on the port-side... try to locate Minnie, if she's even still aboard...

I can use the blurring-thing to avoid being too obvious about it, in case somebody's looking out, while I'm looking in... somehow I can see through it... thanks for that, Storied Watcher...

So Abruzzio re-empowered her telekinetic grasp, and began to edge backward and upward, still marveling that she could do any of this in the face of a jet-speed wind-stream and an oxygen-deficient surrounding environment. Many of the view-ports were closed and she could only see inside every fifth one or so, but she could still make out the tell-tale signs of gunfire and damage to the aircraft's interior.

Subtle vibrations from inside the hull told of some kind of commotion going on just inside and toward the bow, relative to where she was hanging on.

Wait... what's that... hearing something... feeling it, too – whoa, no doubt now – that's Minnie's song!

Abruzzio put her ear to the ACP's fuselage and concentrated.

Too late to really do any good, her senses somehow picked up the sounds of human-talk, from within the aircraft, in whatever area was on the other side of the starboard bow, main-level access-door. But she could only make out perhaps each fifth or sixth word. Still, the more-than-a-woman could tell that some kind of heated discussion – or argument – was ongoing.

Sounds like Minnie... I think, she mused.

So difficult to tell, through all this blasted metal –

The latter words proved coincidental, because at that exact moment, a shower of sparks flew outward from the access-door, at approximately where its activating-handle was recessed into its left-hand side.

The portal was now no longer fully flush with the aircraft's fuselage, but neither was it open.

Somebody's shooting *at it, from the inside!* realized Abruzzio.

That could be my chance to get in there – but if it opens, it'll depressurize the plane... and do I want to waltz right into a gunfight?

Suddenly, a voice that could *only* have been that of Minnie Chu – accompanied by her buzzing, entrancing, siren-calling war-song – began to shriek an impassioned warning; though the exact message was hard to interpret, its ominous import carried forth not just through the atmosphere and aircraft-structure but also within Abruzzio's very psyche.

And now, there was no doubt that Chu herself, *was* close-by. The access-door was now struck, obviously from the inside, by a blazing laser-beam, which, in the first half-second, shot the portal's locking-mechanism clean through. In the next half-second, the door itself was sent flying off into the night sky by some tremendously-powerful force – capable of ripping metal retaining-clamps in half – again projected from the inside-out.

The tell-tale signs of explosive decompression, evidenced by air carrying debris from inside the aircraft, now grimly manifested themselves. The ACP's starboard wing dropped and it began to bank at a shallow angle.

Minnie's blasting *her way out!*

*She'd only be doing that if... O My **Lord**!*

I'll get one chance at this! resolved Abruzzio.

Grace Of The Angel... Of Almighty God! her mind cried out, while her war-song waxed, her eyes glowed and the enervating, thrilling touch of *Amaiish* played over every molecule in her body.

*Full **power**!*

She tried to emulate the "fast-thinking" instructions that the Storied Watcher had imparted to all of them, back at the camp; but she had no idea at all as to whether the lessons had sunk in, or if the ability was even present in her.

A human figure – in almost fetal-position, with its face obscured by hands placed tightly over the eyes and nose – shot out of the doorway. It flew straight out for a split-second and then was caught in the slip-stream, being rapidly carried aftward.

Reflexively, Abruzzio cast her telekinetic tractor-beam at this forlorn creature. She hit dead-on, then pushed off as hard as she could from the ACP, careening into the darkness, not trying in any way to retard her fall, while using her mind-pull-skills to reel in the refugee from the aircraft closer to her.

This feat was accomplished in no more than a couple of seconds; oddly, whoever it was, did not seem to be resisting Abruzzio's mental lock-on.

Hmm, she thought, *heavier than I recall... maybe Minnie has been enjoying a little too much of that fine Air Force One cuisine?*

Now, the jumper was close enough for the more-than-a-woman to physically reach out and grasp.

"*Minnie!*" she shouted, while dropping just enough of her force-field to let the words and sounds, through. "I'm *so* glad that I –"

Her jaw dropped, as a horrified, astonished look showed on her face.

The man – because, it *was* a man, in fact, as his ruddy, clean-shaven, young-20's face revealed upon the partial removal of his hands from it – who she had captured, shouted back, as they both plummeted downward,

"Lady – where's Minnie – and who the hell are *you?*"

Let 'Em Have It, Kid

The boy had been alternating between moods of well-hidden fear about being on top of the air-ship (he had, after all, been subjected to a nuclear explosion over Alaskan skies, and was not eager to repeat the experience), and elation at just being part of everything that was going on.

Mom told me to hide my eyes and put all my power into the safety-shield, when it goes off, he mused.

But how am I supposed to know when that is?

He scanned with his alien-senses enabled, in every direction that he could so do, considering how tightly-strapped-in he was, relative to the *Mailànkh Express.*

The intermittent clouds made doing so difficult, however, and the picture was not complete.

Thankfully – despite his earlier boasting – there had been no sign of either the Air Force's fighter-planes, or their lethal missiles, in his immediate vicinity; he had thus been escaped of the responsibility of shooting them down.

Not like a video-game, Tommy reminded himself. *No "replays".*

Kind of lonely and scary up here... I miss Melissa and Miz Sylvia, he thought.

Even though she almost killed me, back at the White House.

That radiation of hers – talk about nasty!

Felt like the worst "flu" I've ever had... combined with the worst sunburn I've ever had!

And that was with my safety-shield almost on full power!

Ugh!

And her dog's almost as bad.

Cute... but almost as bad, anyway.

And about the missiles, I don't think they could blow me up – Mom says I have a real good safety-shield – but those guys inside the ship... that would suck, if any of them got killed, because I missed my shots at one or two missiles, and Miz Sylvia and Melissa aren't here to get the ones that I miss.

And I'm awfully far up, he reflected.

Mom says I could easily fly down.

Yeah... but it's scary.

Like a lot of stuff that's happening, tonight.

But there were still many things apparently going on, in the airspace over the greater Washington, D.C. area, that the boy couldn't make any sense of.

Far to the south and west, there had been booming-sounds and brief flashes in the sky, as if a big air-battle was going on over there; but it was so distant that none of the details were discernible. Then, somewhat closer, but lower in altitude and so far back over the aft of the *Mailànkh Express* that Tommy couldn't bend all the way over to get a good look, there were more battle-sounds, including multiple explosions that *had* to be missiles, or bombs, or something of that sort.

He had held his breath, anticipating having to shoot down a volley of missiles coming at him from the air-ship's rear-flanks; but even after several minutes, none came and he was able to momentarily relax.

Shortly after this, and well after Abruzzio had gone off to find the ACP, there had been a startling and unexpected development : some kind of medium-sized airplane, or missile (the boy couldn't quite tell what it actually was), had passed to the right and below of the *Express*.

This object – seemingly propelled by four brightly-burning rockets – appeared to be hurtling on a collision-course with the lumbering 747-derivative, but the expected collision (and the dreaded nuclear explosion that had been expected to inevitably follow, seconds thereafter) was somehow avoided; the ACP started gently climbing and the second aircraft streaked past, heading off into the dark airspace to the north.

I don't understand why we don't turn around, unhappily thought Tommy.

With each second, we're getting closer to that plane with the bomb on it.

I can even see it, way far away ahead, with my Mars eyes.

And Mom said, "if you can see it, my son... you are much too close".

And, we're getting close to the ocean, which is wicked cold this time of year. And there are those big white sharks in it!

Mom says my safety-shield will protect me from all that... "*if I can plunge safe and sound to the very depths of the seas, young prince, surely you can do so, right at the surface*"...

But will my Fire-shot *work underwater?*

So dark down there, I couldn't even aim *it!*

No way *do I want to test that out!*

But his self-referential complaining was abruptly interrupted by the appearance of his adoptive father's head and shoulders, appearing through one of the vessel's emergency access-hatches in the top of its alien-constructed hull, slightly down and behind where the boy was secured into his seat.

"Mr. *Billings!*" shouted Tommy, over the din of the couple-hundred-mile-per-hour headwind. "Mom said not to *open* that! She said –"

"Stow it, kid!" answered the ex-salesman, his voice straining as well. "I can hardly fit through this thing anyway, so only a bit of air's getting out... or in... or, whatever. And I need to –"

Mind-talk... oh-kay? sent the boy.

Don't have to drop our safe-shields or shout so much.

Fine, then – I never really got the hang of this mental mumbo-jumbo, responded Billings, *but I guess I can use the practice.*

Tommy remarked,

Remember, Mom said –

Yeah, silently responded Billings,

She told us to do a lot *of stuff, half of which I pay no attention to... but you'll have to get hitched up to a woman before you understand that.*

So what did you want to say, Mr. Billings? asked the boy.

Well, explained the ex-salesman, *down there in Steerage, the cheap seats on this tour-bus I mean, we noticed Sylvia going off on her way – that was part of the plan, I guess – but then Melissa's theme-song sounded as if it was receding, too?*

Immediately, a tone of alarm roiled over Billings' mental transmissions.

Hey... where the hell's Sari? *What* gives? *Where'd she* go?

Didn't you hear her message, Mr. Billings? the boy inquired.

I heard... I heard something, came back the rueful response.

Maybe it didn't all get through...

Mom had to go off *up there, to shoot down a nuclear missile,* sent Tommy.

It's falling out of the sky, and she has to catch it before it hits Miz Chu's airplane.

Mom said she loves us.

Billings didn't have to be a mind-reader to note the gut-wrenching apprehension in his adopted son's demeanor.

Yeah... okay, the ex-salesman tried to reassure.

She's doing what she's good at, kid. Best in the universe at, I'd wager.

I'm sure she'll be alright.

We've both seen one of those things go off, Mr. Billings, countered Tommy. *And we've both felt what it's like.*

I'm not just scared for Mom... I'm scared for Væran Ss'éth'ch', Væran Ksé'l'ch' *and the rest of my brothers and sisters. They're my friends now, you know, Mr. Billings. They told me that they're scared, too. But they know they have to be brave, to fight alongside Mom. They're alive too, you know!*

Yeah... I guess they are, helplessly confirmed the ex-salesman.

He tried to change the subject.

I see Hector back there, asked Billings, *but he looks like he's really straining to keep the* Express *airborne, with all that jiggery-pokery that Sari asked him to do, below us –*

At this moment, the attention of the two was redirected by a brilliant flash. Both Tommy and Billings instinctively cringed, believing one or more nuclear bombs to have detonated. But instinctively, something didn't make sense; there was little to no heat-pulse, and the light was coming from below and to the right – not from above and ahead, as they would have expected.

Then, in the next couple of seconds, something looking very much like a high-intensity searchlight started washing over the *Mailànkh Express,* going back and forth as if intensely examining the air-ship. Curiously, there was next to no sound coming from it.

That's gotta be the Air Force! mentally yelled an alarmed Billings.

Some kind of super-secret, silent helicopter, come to either force us down and imprison us... or just to shoot us down!

Tommy turned, and, with red-glowing devil-eyes accompanied by his sinister, foreboding war-song, began to power up his attack.

I'll blast 'em!

Go for it, kid! came Billings' nervous assent.

I'll lightening-bolt 'em... if I can get my arms free of this damn hatch!

Hey, Ramirez – what's the matter with you, man – hit 'em with all you've got, before they shoot us out of the skies!

There was a muted, scrambled, ambiguous response from Ramirez, who obviously had his hands full with the multiple tasks assigned to him, not least of which was, "keeping the large and heavy air-ship, airborne and moving forward".

Tommy tried to aim for the center of the shine, but its intensity was ramping up rapidly in all visible wavelengths of the electromagnetic spectrum. The light's cone of coverage was also increasing, covering almost the entire air-ship. .

It was, in fact, next to impossible for Tommy to get a clean fix on whatever was bedeviling the *Mailànkh Express,* despite the more-than-a-boy calling on all of his enhanced senses.

Mr. Billings, he warned, *I'll have to do a lot of little shots – weaker ones, not as much* Fire *behind each one – if I want to hit anything – I can't see what I'm shooting at –*

Less talk – more bang-bang, kid! came back the panicked response.

Here goes! exclaimed Tommy.

The boy's claw-like hands let loose a barrage of between six and ten shining, screeching, energy-discharges, in the general direction of the burgeoning light. These flew in an irregular pattern, the paths of several interleaving with the others, as they streaked outward and downward.

At first, a crestfallen Billings and Tommy believed that their attack had wholly missed; but then, there were two obvious "hits", as showers of sparks, accompanied by the satisfying cracking-sounds and pressure-waves of projectile-impacts, struck something perhaps fifty or sixty feet to the right of them, in the darkness.

Along with the sounds and the impact-reverberations, there were momentary glimpses of something transparent, or at least translucent, being hit; but these lasted only a split-second, and the image was almost overwhelmed by the damnable flood-lights, in any case.

*Mother*fucker! came a first thought, from out of the blue.

Who the fuck! came another.

You okay? came a third.

Machine-guns? again broadcast the second one.

No – not like guns, the first one commented.

Whatever that was... hurt like hell... but I'm functional... I think, it added.

Return fire? the third one ominously suggested.

Just a second – came an idea from the second one.

Tommy... is that you? demanded Billings.

No, Mr. Billings, came back the answer.

Just a sec – I'll give 'em another shot –

Now a new mind-talking source – it sounded like Ramirez – appeared.

Bob... Tommy... don't... think I see... Madre de Dìos!

Hold your damn fire! added a very upset-sounding, external thought.

But Mr. Billings – I thought you wanted me to – offered Tommy.

That wasn't me, kid! the ex-salesman tried to broadcast.

Well then... who is it? Tommy asked.

Didn't Mom say that only we could –

Air Force got somebody who can listen in on us? offered Billings.

There was a long pause.

Tommy...? probed the ex-salesman.

Ready to give 'em another –

He's got the kid firing those damn Fire-*shots at us!* claimed the third entity.

Bob... you idiot! called out the first mental voice.

Cease your fire!

Who the hell's that? broadcasted a perplexed Billings.

You Air Force assholes don't scare me!

Just wait *until I get my hands free, and...*

I knew *we should have left him in that jail down in Amchitka, Commander,* grumbled the second voice, as the light began to wane, and the war-song of Brent Boyd, began to serenade the inhabitants of the *Mailànkh Express.*

To Remember The Heart Of A Star

By now – thankfully – the Storied Watcher had been able to lead the Air Force's accursed multi-purpose, stealth-technology cruise missile, via its machine-brain fascination with the second airplane's flame-bedecked engines – well out over the Atlantic Ocean.

At the same time, she had tried to induce an increase in altitude as well; the effort had been moderately-successful, and the three members of this sinister air-convoy were about a thousand meters above where they had started.

However, repeated sensory-scans of the area revealed that to get the weapon to climb appreciably while being so led, would take many more minutes than likely could be safely gambled upon.

At least, now, the little-particle-shine is clear from within it, noted Karéin-Mayréij.

So we know that we have the right one... oh, how fortunate *are we... think ye not?*

Dear Bob would have something amusing to add to this, no doubt, she ruefully acknowledged.

But soon, children... we come to the time of reckoning!

Prepare ye for a soul-crushing-fast retreat, a quicker-start than ever have we done... and when the moment comes, make for our weirding-shield to be proof, yea, against even the burning heart of a star!

Venerable One... I place mine life in thy hands; for this dread quest may require faster responses, than my weaker, human-side will allow.

Take control of my safety-powers – and use them in the fraction-of-a-clock-tick, when needs be.

Do will Mistress can I best, responded the ancient-crafted living-amulet.

And the Storied Watcher's counsel proved prescient.

The jury-rigged afterburners on the V-37 – first, the rear two, then the forward ones – began to flicker and fail. One by one, over a space of no more than two or three seconds, they were extinguished altogether, and the transport, now with no thrust at all, began to careen toward the dark waves far below.

At first, the missile seemed to continue on a straight line toward the point in space that the V-37 had last occupied, as if on inertial-guidance; but then – suddenly – its engine fired at what must have been full power, and it changed its heading to that of a collision-course with the alien-girl.

Evidently, the thing was homing in on the infernal, infra-red-rich essence of *Vîrya Ahn'jë*. It began to rapidly close the distance, which was already too meager for comfort.

Karéin-Mayréij realized that she was now being directly targeted by a missile with a powerful nuclear warhead; but where lesser creatures would have quailed with fear, *this* being – the proud, noble victor of hundreds of battles, over ages unremembered – resolved... and *acted*.

We could confound its Um'nàhr'é-sight with thy frigid arts, brave Væran Ss'éth'ch', she quickly sent to her weirding-companions.

But then it might reverse and again vex the cities below and to the west.

Such must not come to pass!

Let it approach, so it fixes its hateful gaze upon us... but not too close... Okt'á... Ym'ë... Zjù!

To the heavens – we **soar***!*

Her war-song resounded through the skies, and – unafraid of the beckoning target that so doing would provide for her tormentor – the Storied Watcher caused her *Fire*, both mundane and supernatural, to surge to an incandescent, brilliant fury.

She accelerated at a fantastic rate that would surely have killed even one of the so-called "New People", putting a space of perhaps five kilometers on a thirty-degree upward-incline, between herself and the missile, then slowing abruptly to just over the sound-barrier, to match the weapon's apparent maximum speed.

The alien-girl intentionally weakened the top-facing side of her force-field to the minimum needed to deflect the increasingly-sparse air-molecules, so she could correspondingly reinforce the side that faced downward, in the direction of the missile.

Upward went Karéin-Mayréij and her deadly pursuer, by a thousand meters... then another... then another. The distance between herself and the missile was gradually being increased.

Good... it is working... *just another minute or two, and we should be –*

All of a sudden, from far to the south and much lower in altitude (but not too far away to the west, judging by longitude), came a brilliant, sensory-overwhelming flash, sinister in its portent. An accompanying burst of heat – enough to bedevil a human being, even at this substantial range – also was instantly evident.

Min-nie! howled the anguished spirit of the Storied Watcher.

An impassioned warning came from *Vîrya* Quü'j.

Other shine-particle detonates one this!

Goddess young... now!

With her arms and legs in braced-position, the alien-girl reinforced her force-field with enough power to resist a collapsing mountain, jump-started upward at a yet more brutal rate than before, shut down her sensory-scans and closed her eyes tight.

And as the molten, radiating embrace of the second nuclear weapon to detonate over Atlantic skies on this night, caught up with her, Karéin-Mayréij tried to recall how – only a few short weeks before – she had survived the raging essence of this planet's home-star.

A Note To Say "Goodbye"

He had heard the sounds of mayhem coming from a floor below him and behind him. He had also seen the cockpit warning-lights, telling of a "major atmospheric pressure breach" in exactly the same area.

It's time, he realized, after screaming a challenge into the intercom.

She's here!

Martin my boy – I'm hopin' you've done your job... because the fate of the world, rests on you havin' done so.

Thus – knowing, in his heart of hearts, that he likely had nothing to lose except a life already lost – Former Spiritual Adviser to the President of the United States, Harold Crowford left the almost-unconscious co-pilot strapped into his seat, downed a handful of his special "personal-confidence-pills", quickly unlocked the cockpit access-door and dashed outside.

Onward Christian Soldiers, going as to war...

Crowford had expected a fusillade of bullets to greet him – and was perfectly ready for such a fate – but much to his surprise, not only were there no Secret Service or Marine guards immediately outside the aircraft's cockpit, but, in fact, there was nobody at all in the top-section of the plane.

The reason for this was clear when he took his next breath; the amount of oxygen in the air around here was already low enough to have him reflexively gasping, though he was able to overcome this and was able to move in determined fashion toward the spiral staircase leading to the aircraft's main deck.

With his well-memorized ultimate unction being muttered with each set of strides, the Spiritual Adviser dashed down the stairway, again steeling himself for the deadly impact of gun-shots... or from some other-worldly attack, whose effects could be yet more painful.

When he had but one or two rungs to go, he saw why his former assailants were in no shape to oppose him; most were either gasping for air, or were holding on for dear life, to the nearest solid object that they could find. But there were only three or four human beings here, far fewer than he had expected.

And there was – to Crowford's shock – no alien-girl.

Well... she's probably hidin', waitin' to ambush me, he considered.

Devil's a coward... afraid to square off against a soldier of the Lord, straight-up.

But where'd all the other Marines and Service agents go, anyway? he wondered.

Under a steadily-flashing red alarm-light, the ACP's port-side access-door had been torn from its hinges and was nowhere to be seen. The dark void opened up by the door's absence, was still greedily swallowing small objects and the occasional large one, as the inside atmosphere of the aircraft continued to escape, hurricane-fashion, to the outside night sky.

It all makes sense *now!* he realized.

Alarms went off in the cockpit when the Devil-Girl ripped the door off – that's how she got aboard. She'd have to do that, because to cut the hull open elsewhere, would probably weaken the structure, crash us right there – and that would mean that her whore harlot lover would go down with it. But gettin' rid of the door, sucked half them soldiers off the plane.

Lord... remember their souls!

At least, for those of 'em who believe in You.

But back to business... after she tracks down that sinful "Chu" bitch... she'll be comin' for me!

If I can just get down there – lead her to it – make sure that Martin did his duty, can't take the chance that he maybe got shot by the guards on the way in... by the time she figures out what's goin' on, she'll have no time to get away...

Lord – guide my steps!

Now, two Service agents noticed Crowford. One, on the opposite side of the area – though weakened and nowhere near optimum fighting-form – raised a semi-automatic pistol in the Spiritual Adviser's direction. Crowford ran for it, going down the port-side of the airplane.

He heard the "crack"-sound of a gun-shot, which narrowly missed the back of his head and shattered the glass of a view-port, causing air to vent out of the ACP on the opposite side from the missing access-port.

Calling on all his Army track-and-field training to make speed, the former Spiritual Adviser sprinted down the port-side corridor, to the entrance to the rear access-ramp, leading to the aft cargo-hold.

He ran the distance in record time, considering the need to jump over debris left over from earlier battles, at various intervals along the way.

If the bitch is in there chattin' with Chu, he considered, *that door's on the starboard side.*

If I can stay on the port, I can get right past 'em – make sure that the key's in, and we're on the count-down...

He looked back, once or twice, counting the each second as he ran. For better or worse, nobody seemed to be following him, although he noted with disgust that discipline aboard the aircraft had broken down; several crewmembers in the intermediate seating-sections were either "fornicating" with little regard for privacy, or were obviously intoxicated, or both.

Don't the fools know that they're gonna be meetin' Jesus Himself, in less than a minute? Crowford furiously reflected.

No... they don't, he unhappily realized.

Lord – forgive 'em – at least the Christians... they know not what they do!

I'll even beg You to accept the Catholics... how merciful Thou art, even toward liars and apostates!

Upon reaching the door leading to the cargo-hold, he allowed himself a precious second or two to catch his breath; ordinarily, a man as spare and fit as was he wouldn't have needed to do this, but the depleted oxygen of the local atmosphere was affecting him badly.

The Spiritual Adviser noted that the cargo-bay-door was – counter-intuitively – open by a crack, and its digital locking-mechanism was disengaged.

"Here I *am!*" he taunted, shouting backwards into the aircraft's main-level corridors. "Come and *get* me, witch!"

Again throwing caution to the winds, and expecting to be assaulted by an enraged alien-girl at any second, he barged through the entrance-way, into the dimly-lit cargo-hold.

But there was nobody down here, either.

The floor was strewn about with random objects, ranging from suitcases to eating-utensils, that had either come loose in the airplane's previous maneuvers, or – for a large portion of it – that seemed as if it had been deliberately but hap-hazardly *thrown* off the storage-shelves.

Despite the clutter all about, in a few seconds Crowford managed to position himself right in front of the wooden crate that had originally housed his special toy, when first it was brought aboard the ACP.

"Well... what're you *waiting* for, Spawn of Satan!" he shouted, to no-one in particular. "You too busy fornicatin' with your whore, Chu? Come on *down!*"

He used up another few seconds waiting for a reply, or for movement.

None came.

A flashlight lay by the Spiritual Adviser's feet. He picked it up and verified that it worked, turning its beam toward the damaged crate and its contents.

He noticed that the side of the crate facing him, had been badly damaged; it looked as if someone had laid into it with an axe or hatchet, because many of its slats had been either cut right through or had been torn away, leaving a large hole where the device could be directly accessed.

"Grassleigh! *Grassleigh!*" he called.

Other than for the pervasive background engine-noise – and for an odd-sounding "hum", reminiscent of the 60-kilohertz "buzz" of a florescent light, coming from the object inside the crate – there was no answer.

"Oh, Tarnation – hang that!" muttered Brother Harold.

"Martin! Where *are* you, boy?"

Again, only engine-noise – and the slowly-burgeoning humming-sound – met his ears.

Now the Spiritual Adviser, fumbling all the while to locate his precious key, leaned over and got as close as he could do, to the cylindrical, metal-clad device. It resembled nothing so much as an old-school hot-water tank.

Upon approaching to about a foot away, he felt the skin on his face warming, as if it were exposed to a well-lit fireplace; or perhaps it was more like having stayed overlong at the beach, on an especially sunny day.

I know what that *means... but I'm one foot away from bein' with my precious Savior, anyhow,* he mused.

It's all the same to me... my die is cast, and the story of my life is complete... I seek to shower and bathe in the holy blood of my precious Savior!

I'm ready... bring her hither, Father God!

The key was now in his hand.

He looked a little closer, but – much to his surprise – there was an identical one already in the device's activating-slot. It was sunk in to the device's external shell so deeply that pulling it out was effectively impossible. The second key appeared to have been inserted into a position lined up with the left-most tick-mark in a semi-circle of similar marks at intervals like the measurements on a watch-dial, extending all the way to a final tick-mark on the right.

Hallelujah! he joyfully mused.

Count-down's already goin'!

She ain't gonna get away now!

"I'm *here*, whore!" he bellowed. "Afraid of God's judgment?"

The top-end of the other key was now pointing in a direction just a couple of tick-marks above the right-most one. It was moving to the right, in a small, but perceptible, manner. Crowford guessed that the last position would be reached in, perhaps, another eighteen to twenty-four seconds.

Lord... summon the both of 'em, to stand before me, thus to receive thy harsh judgment, he prayed.

Hold on... what's that?

He bent further forward, and now the feeling of heat on his face was actually painful. The outer layer of his skin was starting to peel away. He suppressed a rush of nausea in his throat and behind his jaw.

But something else caught his attention. There was a hand-written note, its strokes and lines done in narrow-tipped black magic-marker, affixed to the top of the device with several strips of masking-tape.

Quickly, the former Spiritual Adviser tore it off and began to read it, with the help of illumination from the flashlight.

The note said,

> *TO DEAR ELDER BROTHER HAROLD*
> *Sir :*
> *I followed your orders... the key is in, and there's no stopping it now.*
> *But, my weak human flesh has betrayed me!*
> *I was in one of the Secret Service rooms in the back of the plane.*
> *I tried to get forward to be with you, but they wouldn't let me.*
> *They had CCTV cameras, so I saw what happened.*
> *That "Chu" woman you told me about, some Service guys told me,*
> *She was communicating with somebody at the White House.*
> *They think it might have been the Devil-Girl. Nothing adds up!*
> *Then Chu went forward. She shot out the door in the front.*
> *Then she jumped ship – she's either dead now, or with the Devil-Girl.*
> *I have FAILED, sir!!!*
> *I'm afraid of facing the Lord!*
> *Especially after having done all that I've done!*
> *I need more TIME, to repent and prepare myself!*
> *A Service Agent told me that there are parachutes back here.*
> *If you are reading this... I'm already gone from the plane.*
> *I'll be praying for you, sir!*
> *YOUR LOYAL SERVANT*
> *MARTIN*

A sickened feeling washed over Crowford; and it was not from anything in the immediate environment.

He fell to his knees, with his head thrown back on his shoulders, as if staring up at an imaginary sky.

"*No... no... NO!*" he shouted out loud.

The device was now enshrouded by a translucent blue haze. The feeling of heat was near-overpowering; but the Spiritual Adviser was made of sterner stuff.

He yelled at the top of his lungs,

"**Lord... what more could I have *done*?**"

"**Thy Cleansing Fire – it was for *her* – the Devil-Girl – for traitors like Minnie Chu and Martin – not for th –**"

None would know – nor would any techno-system ever record – what the last words uttered by the Spiritual Adviser, were meant to be.

For, at that precise moment, it was proved that the late "Brother Lazlo's" artifice, had worked perfectly; its implosion-mechanism, its "primary", and then – in tiny micro-fractions of a second, its "secondary", executed their sinister nuclear-physics magic-tricks, in precisely-planned sequence.

Thus, no-one – in *this* reality, at least – would ever know if the flames that Brother Harold, Most High of the Klan of Jesus Christ, had spent so much effort in bringing about, would be there to greet him, in the next one.

That knowledge, was to be his... and his, alone.

Dive, Minnie... *Dive!*

A second or so after leaping out the torn-off access-portal, Minnie Chu collided with the frigid night sky's slip-stream, and – despite her pretensions of executing a graceful swan-dive pose – began tumbling, head-over-heels, flying backward, narrowly clearing the top-surface of the ACP's starboard wing.

She instantly experienced the frigid touch of the outside-air, but strangely, it just felt, well, *cold*... not, "unpleasant".

Thinking faster than she could ever remember herself having done before, her Mars-senses warned that she was hurtling straight at the knife-edge of the aircraft's tail-wing.

Using a fraction of the mind-pushing-skills that the Storied Watcher had tried to impart up at the Canadian forest camp, Chu somehow bounced her telekinesis off the aircraft's rear fuselage, and in so doing, propelled herself downward and to her left, clearing the area of the ACP after being subjected to an unpleasant taste of jet-engine-exhaust from the aircraft's outboard engine (somehow, this made its presence known, even though Chu's force-field stopped its momentary, several hundred-degree heat).

Warden, she sent, *keep track of how many seconds are passing by; for, each passing one makes it more likely that the bomb will go off.*

Silver big four from we when bird left, came back the answer.

Five... six... the count continued, in some partitioned-off recess of her mind.

She closed her eyes, concentrated and tried to energize the flying-ability that her alien mentor had, weeks ago, informed her was "latent within".

Yeah, well, Karéin, sourly reflected the more-than-a-woman,

Didn't you mention something about "you should learn this slowly, Min-ee – like from a height of four meters, over a swimming-pool, at first"?

Sorry... but the hotels they had me staying in, weren't a good fit for all that.

The effort was only partially-successful; Chu was still in free-fall, but, to her immense satisfaction, she found that she could stabilize her motion, so as to maintain a consistent attitude. She was no longer tumbling or rotating.

Well... I'm at least falling upright – and I'm heading away from the damn plane, she considered.

But likely not fast enough, and... where the hell's Mooney?

I probably can't save him – for that matter, can't save me *– but I owe it to the poor guy to at least* try.

Frantically – not even trying to retard her fall, on the theory that she would thus match the Air Force guy's rate of descent – the former FBI team-leader began to frantically scan the airspace around her, in all forward directions, with the enhanced heat-seeing and star-light-seeing abilities.

And, indeed, many falling objects were immediately revealed to her; but little of what she saw, gave her any solace.

To her right, Chu saw a mixed collection of hapless, tumbling, human figures – perhaps sixteen to twenty of them – plus five more suspended on parachutes, descending much more slowly. The latter were quickly moving out of her field of view, as her airspeed exceeded their own.

A quick glance backward added the grim realization that four of the aircraft's former staff, passengers, guards or crew had elected for "slower suicide"; they had jumped out the portal just after her, and were a few seconds behind on the free-fall descent. (More had jumped; but one hit the wing and was no longer showing life-signs, while another must have fallen into the ACP's inside starboard turbofan, meeting a fate that Chu didn't want to dwell on.)

The infra-red signatures of the people falling immediately behind Chu was not the only attribute that she detected.

A stench of gut-wrenching fear – akin to what she was feeling herself, but on several orders of magnitude greater – assaulted her psyche.

Seconds ten bird silver from, came Warden's dutiful count.

I probably can't rescue you folks, grimly reflected the more-than-a-woman, *but perhaps I* can *draw you nearer, so we call all say "goodbye" together.*

My wannabe lover – my angel *– if you're listening – help me learn how to fly, now... help me to* save *these people!*

Chu wheeled in position, so that although she was still descending as she had been doing, she was now facing backward. She cast her telekinetic powers in a wide-area net, and – surprisingly – had no trouble at all, in locking on collectively, to the others who had bailed out behind her.

Fear's crippled their natural resistance to being tractor-beamed, she realized.

Can't blame 'em...

The former team-leader caused the falling-crew's motion to gently accelerate, relative to her own; she also induced the group to come closer to each other, so that there was no more than a foot or two between each of them.

As they came near, she tightened her grasp, rotating her quarry – now visible as a twenty-something, blond Caucasian woman in civilian-clothing (a business-dress and urine-stained hosiery), a Latino or mulatto guy wearing combat-fatigues, a short, squat, older Italian-Caucasian guy in Air Force working-overalls and a short, middle-aged African-American woman wearing more formal Air Force blue clothing – so that they were all descending upright, facing forward.

Chu could see looks of inchoate terror on the faces of all except the black woman, who seemed to be repeating a prayer. It was hard to tell if the ashen expressions were solely caused by fear of impending death, or by alarm at Chu's glowing eyes, or some combination of both.

The FBI team-leader strained to scan in her front-flank, for any sign of the young Air Force technician who had entrusted her with his life. The effort was complicated by the intermittent clouds that appeared at different altitudes, and by an odd-looking, more substantial lower cloud-layer that, she noted with interest, seemed to be exactly in parallel with the flight-path of the now-departing ACP.

None the less, after again rotating so as to face forward (although, to her immense satisfaction, Chu could somehow tell that her telekinetic grasp was still holding firm, on the escapees plummeting behind her) and with a determined effort, she identified a figure, falling downward about two hundred meters ahead, whose dimensions almost exactly matched what she would have expected of the unfortunate Mooney.

That's got to be him! she declared.

Seconds fourteen, advised Warden's ethereal little voice.

Up at the campsite, Cherie said, "imagine that there's a wind at your back" – that's what did it for her... right?

Oh-kay Karéin – you said, back in L.A., "if the hour is dire and if you truly believe, *blessed* Amaiish *shall empower you in exact measure to what is needful to win the battle"...*

I really need *it now – I* believe, *Storied Watcher – show me how to fly!*

Holy Fire *– be thou my* wings!

Her eyes were now glowing brightly.

Her war-song echoed, even above the rushing winds.

And, to the former FBI team-leader's joy and utter astonishment, she felt herself moving, and not just under the force of gravity; slowly at first – but then with such intensity that she feared overshooting her target – she began to rocket forward, still with her four telekinetically-linked captives trailing behind her.

She experimented with moving side to side, and up and down, and happily discovered that these maneuvers – at least at moderate speeds – seemed quite easy to do.

As Chu closed to perhaps half the distance to the other falling figure, the gap between herself and the presumed Mooney started closing much faster than what her forward-motion could possibly have accounted for.

Then, she heard the unmistakable, rhythmic sounds of a familiar war-song; and she did not resist, when she felt the powerful telekinesis of a sister *Fire*-warrior, closing on her body.

I'm slowing – how the hell is Sylvia *up here – who cares... I'll* take *it! Gotta slow down those people up there, though... here goes...*

Chu – partly under Abruzzio's telekinesis – came to almost a dead stop in mid-air. The four former ACP-staff who she had been dragging behind, continued their downward-motion for a heart-wrenching second or two; but then the team-leader was able to reassert her tractor-beam-hold upon them, and they were reeled in to stop, almost level with everyone else.

Seconds twenty, Warden counted off.

Both war-songs abated but were still playing in the background.

Sylvia? Sylvia! sent Chu, not knowing if the mind-talking-skill had also graced her.

Minnie! came back the thrilled-sounding, relieved response. *Thank God! I was afraid you were still on the plane!*

That asshole Crowford set the fuse on the bomb! communicated Chu.

A completely-befuddled-looking, oxygen-deprived Mooney shouted out loud from behind chattering teeth, "Why doesn't somebody *say* something, for God's sake!"

"Sorry, Stephen," apologized Chu. "Sylvia and I can communicate telepathically – I'll speak out loud. Sylvia – bomb on the plane's going to *blow!* We've got to get *out* of here!"

"I've figured out how to fly at this altitude – but limited airspeed," noted the former JPL scientist. "And you?"

"I can... I *think*," offered Chu. "Just came to me. Not sure how fast, either."

"Are there any more from the plane?" asked Abruzzio.

"Some back there, jumped out the back," replied the team-leader. "I'll find 'em – every second we waste, they're getting closer to the ground – but I need your protection, Sylvia!"

"You've *got* it, sister!" cried Abruzzio. "Lock on me and fly – I'll grab these people, and any others who we find! Take my *hand!*"

Their hands, and then arms, were now tightly-entwined.

Seconds forty, warned Warden's dutiful voice.

Chu felt Abruzzio's potent telekinetic abilities locking on to the group of dumbfounded-but-relieved humans, floating in the vicinity.

"Let's *go!*" exclaimed Minnie Chu – as both she, and her weirding-sister, powered up their flying-skills, and – with both war-songs howling across the Eastern Seaboard night-skies – accelerated with brutal rapidity.

There were cries of alarm from Mooney and from the four escapees as they reacted to the sudden G-forces, but as far as either of the more-than-women could tell, nobody was seriously hurt.

They were now streaking across the night sky, dodging in and out of thin clouds, descending on a highly-oblique angle toward the much thicker layer of coverage that had, oddly, formed below the ACP's track. Both Chu and

Abruzzio had their alien-senses set to maximum-scan-ability, at least for the airspace ahead of them.

Omigod, Karéin, reflected the team-leader, *no* wonder *you're so at home up here!*

Flying like this – faster than the swiftest bird – it's thrilling*!*

Sylvia, she silently communicated – the message being transmitted and received much faster than human lips could have formed conventional syllables – *it's been forty seconds or more, since Warden warned me of radiation surging on the aircraft.*

How long before –

Got no idea, responded Abruzzio, *it's instantaneous with a military weapon... but for a jury-rigged bomb that might have a mechanical fuse, one that has to do manual tritium or deuterium injection around the primary... maybe one minute, or a bit more?*

Omigod... gulped the former FBI team-leader. *We got twenty seconds...*

I'll raise my rainbow over our top-right flank, pledged the ex-JPL scientist.

And her promise was true; above and to the right of the group – covering an area at least the size of an Olympic swimming-pool – appeared a translucent, shimmering, multi-colored shroud, through which the now-far-off shape of the ACP was only barely visible. It extended at least ten meters forward of the group of seven air-travelers (Chu, Abruzzio, Mooney and four terrified, shivering escapees) as well as the same distance to the rear.

There they are! announced Chu, both mentally and verbally, though the shouted verbal message was likely difficult for human.

Seconds fifty, ominously counted Warden.

Tell me when we're at sixty, little one, requested Chu.

Remember we're out over the ocean, added Abruzzio. *We can't just put down. I'll ask who "little one" is, later, but whoever you are... thanks!*

Sylvia auntie mother of noble kin, greetings Warden from, came a thought.

Both of the Storied Watcher's acolytes cast their senses forward.

Far below – dangerously close to sea-level, and under the strange cloud-layer – Chu and Abruzzio detected seventeen faint human-like heat-signatures. Above, and to the east, were five parachutes; of these, one was almost at the lower cloud-deck, while the other four were a long way above it. It looked as if the leading parachute must have jumped before the other ones had left the ACP.

We don't have time to go back and get those four 'chutes up there, advised Abruzzio.

If we do – the ones below, will be killed when they hit the water!

"Then, sister... we *dive!*" cried Chu; and indeed she and Abruzzio so did, rocketing downward at a speed that must have been in the high hundreds of miles per hour. This caused immediate howls of terror and discomfort among the escapees (though, Mooney retained a stoic silence throughout), but in no more than a couple of long seconds, they had reached the cloud-layer.

Abruzzio locked her telekinesis on to the lower-most parachuter – a spare, tallish guy in an ill-fitting Air Force crew-suit, not very different-looking, as near as anyone could tell, from Mooney himself – who reacted with an anguished yell, as the man felt his parachute's canvas folding and being pulled downward, along with himself. The additional drag of this guy's chute was noticed by Chu, although she was able to compensate for a couple of seconds; then she sliced it away from him with a quick shot of her *Gaze*.

They were now below the strange, ACP-following cloud-deck. In no more than two or three seconds more, the plummeting refugees would certainly hit the cold Atlantic waves.

Get low enough to drive them upward, from below – resolved Chu, as she led the group into a near-vertical descent at terrifying speed; yet, the former team-leader herself seemed absolutely certain of her ability to pull out of the dive.

Seconds fifty-seven... fifty-eight...

I'll grab the six over here, she communicated to Abruzzio.

Got the rest, sister! came back the confirmation.

Bitterly-cold, damp maritime winds plagued the human-passengers, as – with no more than thirty feet or so to spare – Chu pulled up over the dark ocean surface and locked her telekinetic grasp on six mortified, one-second-to-death refugees from the ACP; Abruzzio did the same, with the other eleven.

As near as could be determined, everyone (with the exception of the parachuters, above the cloud-layer) who had been falling from the sky – at least, those who had been doing so anywhere near Chu and Abruzzio – had been caught.

The escapees' plunge came to a gradual, if unpleasant, deceleration and halt, about fifteen feet above the waves; then, they were put in tow by the two more-than-women. At least five of the former airplane-dwellers seemed to be unconscious.

"Coast's over *there!*" shouted and sent the former FBI team-leader. "Maybe a kilometer – look – neon lights, big buildings –"

The group now flew at flank-speed to the west, at a very low altitude, perhaps ten feet over the wave-tops..

Now count sixty... sixty-one... sixty-two, unhelpfully mentioned Warden.

They were flying toward a sandy beach, with moderately-large ocean-waves breaking upon it. Ahead, was some kind of high-class resort-town, with large, gaudily-bedecked hotels, all – apparently despite curfew-regulations – lit up brilliantly with flashing signs advertising floor-shows and "guaranteed winnings". Just to the south, on the left, extending a few hundred feet into the Atlantic, was a large, fully-enclosed pier of some kind, big enough to accommodate a good-size hotel all on its own.

"Almost there – some kind of sidewalk – no, a *board*walk – see if we can make it to –" called Chu, with a quick glance back across her shoulder, to validate that the humans were all still securely in tow.

She turned her head to again face forward, just as they cleared the edge of the beach.

Then – from behind, far out to sea – a hatefully-brilliant light illuminated the entire area, as if it were suddenly noon in a Saharan hot-house. Its dazzling, cruel rays evaporated the lower cloud-deck, striking Abruzzio's rainbow, which – thankfully – did not seem to be inordinately-strained by the assault. Screams of fear emanated from the human-refugees, although nobody seemed to be on fire. Steam started rising from the surface of the ocean and from water-deposits on surrounding buildings and edifices.

The group crashed into the sand, with Chu and Abruzzio furthest-inland and a few of the rescued escapees landing nearer to the surf.

"Sylvia – are you –" inquired the former team-leader, just as a *second*, wickedly-bright surbrilliance, further away still but just as frightening, added to the terror of the already-shocked escapees. Abruzzio's rainbow-shield held up easily against this one, however.

"Everybody stay where you are!" she yelled. "Shock-wave's coming!"

To the accompaniment of multiple moans and groans, someone called out, "I'm hurt... I need help... help... *help!*"

The rumble of displaced, compressed air from above, roared at them, out of the skies. As the sounds of shattering glass came from all directions, the shock-wave from the first explosion, hit the surface of the water.

A huge wave, at least seven feet high, rushed toward the beach. Its dark, foaming expanse, loomed over the quavering group.

"Brace yourselves – sister – *lock on!*" shrieked Sylvia Abruzzio.

Somehow, We're Still Here

The President and the First Lady had been down to their knees and back up again, three or four times, by now; and even for a man raised as a devout Missouri Synod Lutheran – who was expecting to take his last breath at any second – the novelty and utility of the exercise was starting to wear thin.

He stood up and leaned against the side of the Resolution Desk facing inward into the Oval Office and called out to the Secret Service agents who were manning the communications-room.

"Any news?" he demanded. "Anything at all?"

"Sorry... nothing, Mr. President sir," came back Kortish's voice.

"Well, how the hell can it *be*, that we can't even get the military to tell us where all these planes and missiles are, right now?" complained the U.S. leader.

"I'm trying to raise the Secretary of Defense, sir," Kortish explained, "But the channels were being maintained by Blanshard, who's out of contact right now. I'm told we should be able to get Secretary DeWitt shortly."

The President nervously pounded his right fist into his flattened, outstretched left hand.

"Fine... but the moment that you –" he started to reply; but his commentary was pre-empted by a suddenly-appearing, unnaturally-brilliant light, coming from the Oval Office windows, behind the President's right shoulder, apparently from the east (or, perhaps, the north-east). It lit up the entire room as if it were broad daylight.

In much less than half of a second, the U.S. leader was face-down into the carpet, with Kaysten's body – and, some kind of odd-looking, barely-visible, yellow-white glow, above – positioned over top of him.

"This is *it*, sir!" loudly proclaimed the Chief of Staff. "Been a pleasure working with you, sir! It'll hit me first – an honor –"

"*Clark!*" screamed the terrified First Lady, as she crawled over to where her husband was being covered and restrained.

"Wait," whispered the President. "That... that *can't* have been right overhead – if it was, we'd be dead already... we're still here! It might have –"

But again, he spoke too soon.

Yet *another* sinister, far-too-brilliant light, bathed the Oval Office in incandescent fury, before the first one had even faded away.

For perhaps ten seconds, the U.S. leader, his wife and Chief of Staff just lay there, afraid to speculate about what might happen next.

There were the thumping-sounds of helicopter-blades, off in the distance. Then there was a far-off "booming"-noise. Sirens – both from air-raid gear, and from mundane police-cars – wailed throughout the streets of downtown Washington, D.C..

As near as could be told from this limited vantage-point, it appeared as if a number of street-lights and other electronic-gear-trappings of modern society – including the small television-screen that the Service had set up in one of the Oval Office wall-shelves – had gone dead.

"Mr. *President!*" shouted Kortish. "Crawl to me! Shock-waves are coming, and if they blow out the windows –"

"Yeah... okay!" managed a shaken President.

Accompanied by Kaysten and the First Lady, he moved as quickly as he could, to the communications-room.

"Can you raise the airplane.. that 'Chu' woman?" he demanded.

"Sir," protested the Secret Service agent, "We've *got* to get you and the First Lady – Mr. Kaysten, as well – to the *bunker!*"

The "thump-thump-thump" sounds of a helicopter landing in the South Lawn became manifest.

"Those must be the evac-birds," observed Kortish. "About *time!* Sir, after we ride out the shock-waves, we can get you up to Andrews, or to the secondary or tertiary refuges. We'll need your direction as to which one –"

"I *hear* you, Curt... but if the Lord wanted to call Kathy and I home, he just had two shots at it, and I've got to assume that now's not the time," countered the U.S. leader. "If you or any of the other agents want to head down there – either to the bunker or the evacuation-sites – you have my permission to do so. As long as you teach me how to run this control-panel."

A look of weary resignation was on Kortish's face, as he said, "Mr. President... you *know* I can't do such thing. Very well, sir – but can I at least ask you to remain in here with me, until we're sure that the shock-waves have –"

Just then, an ominous rumbling-sound, almost like an earthquake, shook the White House. Paintings fell from the wall, curios toppled from the side-shelves and one Oval Office window developed a hairline crack, though – thankfully – none of the expected, lethally-flying glass-shards, materialized.

The crashing-sounds of metal tearing and glass-shattering, came from outside on the lawn, somewhere. An orange-red glow showed in the windows facing out into the South Lawn.

About five or six breathless seconds later, a second such tremor – lower-frequency and less powerful, as if it had originated further away – added a little more chaos to that imparted by the first.

"That's two of them," remarked the President. "Curt – what about fallout? How long do we have?"

"Not sure, sir," stated the Service agent. "Depends on where they went off, and if it was an air-burst or a ground-burst. If they were to the west of us – hard to tell from what information we have – we might only have a half-hour or so, maybe less, to avoid flying right upward into it. *Sir –*"

"Understood," spoke the President. "We've done our duty here. Being taken to the Lord in a blaze of glory, that I can *handle*... dying of radiation-sickness – well, from what Ms. Abruzzio told us – I think I can explain to the people, why that's not a reasonable 'ask'. Kathy – grab whatever you can in the next minute, and let's get to the helicopters –"

Either bravely or in fool-hardy manner, Kaysten had darted over to the Oval Office's south-east-facing window.

His voice interrupted, "I don't think you'll be doing that, Mr. President."

"What..." stammered the U.S. leader.

"Have a look," the Chief of Staff proposed.

His tone was regretful.

The President hurried over to the window, and it was immediately apparent what Kaysten had been referring to. An evacuation-helicopter *had*, indeed, landed on the South Lawn; but it had been hit by the first shock-wave and had flipped over on to its dorsal-surfaces. The impact had shredded its propeller-blades and started fires, which were in the process of consuming the machine.

"Lord in *heaven!*" gasped the aghast President. "Curt – see if you and the team can help any of the people who might have been in that 'copter. We'll be okay in here, for a few minutes."

"Didn't they say there were *two* helicopters on their way here?" inquired the First Lady.

"Yes ma'am," commented Kaysten, "But my Mars ears heard an explosion off in the distance – but not *too* too far – when the first bomb went off. It sounded a bit like a plane-crash. I'm afraid that might have been the second 'copter. Anyway... there's only one out there now... and it's in no shape to get us *anywhere*."

"Affirmative, sir," complied Kortish, "But that means you'll be right here, when and if the fallout hits. Sir – you've *got* to get to the bunker!"

"No argument there," retreated the President. "Try to re-establish our links to the military, Chu's plane and everything else, in that order, and then re-route our communications – such as they are – to where we're hiding, if you don't mind. I'd like to have *some* idea what's going on, topside. And then get yourself and the rest of the Service guys, down there."

"Mr. President... our place is up *here*, guarding the White House," argued Kortish.

"That's an *order*, Curt!" repeated the President.

The Service leader threw up his hands in resignation.

"Any other variations from the rule-book that you'd like me to know about, sir?" he asked.

"Yeah," answered the President. "Namely... 'how the hell do we *govern*, on the bloody morning after'?"

Lend Me Your Telekinesis

"Where's Mom – I want to go find *Mom!* Turn us *around!*" shouted an upset Tommy, from his perch on top of the slowly-descending *Mailànkh Express*.

"You *know* why we can't do that, son," Jacobson – also on top of the airship, along with Boyd, White and the just-appearing Russian (Wolf was still far off in the distance to the south, although his infra-red signature was easy for them to track) – tried to cajole. "Those two explosions almost knocked us out of the sky and almost knocked me off the ship – which may still be damaged; I don't have any idea if your 'Mom' fully shielded it against electro-magnetic pulse. And Bob told us that you have civilians – humans – down there in the hold. If we head out to where those bombs went off, we might be flying right into a fallout-cloud. You, I and the rest of Karéin's people might live through that; the humans likely won't. Doing so would be *extremely* irresponsible."

"Yeah... and there's no guarantee that the Air Force won't target us again," commented the subdued-glowing Brent Boyd. "Fighting those AAM's isn't as bad as dealing with a nuke, but it's still damn dangerous."

"He is right, Tommy," added Misha. "Your 'Mom' bestowed upon me, advanced abilities to deflect missile-attacks – or to force them to reverse course back against whomever launched them – and these may have saved my life, in the battle that I just returned from. But it is not an experience that I care to repeat, if I can avoid it. Neither should you."

This got nothing more than a hostile stare from the boy.

"By the way," asked Ramirez, "Has anyone seen Melissa, recently? I tried to track her for a short while, but I got preoccupied with other things."

Nobody answered.

"There's nothing more that we can accomplish while we're up here, son," continued Boyd. "We need to land, assess if the *Express* is still safe to fly and find out what the media's saying about what's been happening tonight. If your Mom's still alive – which I hope and pray – she'll find *us*, eventually."

"Easy for *you* to say," grumbled the head and shoulders of Bob Billings, showing through the opened dorsal escape-hatch. "She's not *your* wife... okay, she's not *mine* either... but I like to think of her that way."

"I *still* want to go find Mom!" pressed Tommy. "And I'm ready to fly off by *myself*, if I have to!"

"Look, you two –" Boyd was going to argue; but he was interrupted by a shout from the aft-quarters of the alien air-ship.

"Hey, you guys!" called a frustrated Ramirez. "I could use a little *help* here! This is getting *awfully* tiring – I burned through a lot of *Amaiish* trying to build that cloud-deck under that 747 with the bomb, so it would abate the heat-flash... another ten minutes or so and I might not be able to keep this ship airborne!"

The more-than-humans camped out on the upper hull of the *Mailànkh Express* stared back and forth at each other.

"Love to help," snidely offered Jacobson, "But I have this little issue with flying."

"I just learned, don't you know," deflected White. "And if Bob would get his ass out of that hatch, I could get down there to say 'hi' to my own wife."

"So did I only recently develop this ability," noted the Russian, "But I am willing to try, I suppose. I am not sure of the asymmetric effect if I assisted on one side of the vessel, with no-one on the other, though."

"I'll help Hector at the back of the bus," volunteered Boyd.

"Yeah, okay... fine," unhappily replied White. "Don't want to be the only flyin'-slacker 'round here, I guess. Bob – y'all tell Saquina that Lover-Boy gonna be by, presently. And I'm only doin' this shit until Mr. Gas Barbecue gets his flamin' butt back here. Deal?"

"Agreed," said Misha. "I will ask *Væran Ivan* and *Væran Pyotr*, to fly a defensive-pattern above and below the *Express*... this will hopefully give us some additional warning of any attack, and some terminal defense. I only hope that we will not have to deal with any more nuclear detonations. Two of these were *quite* enough – I only just closed my eyes in time... and that second one caught me by surprise."

"No shit," supported the black ex-astronaut. "'Least my ice-curtain didn't melt straight off, this time 'round. Y'all ready?"

"As you Americans say... 'as I will ever be'," confirmed the Russian.

With three war-songs playing at low volume, White and Misha energized their *Fire*-powers, jumped off the *Mailànkh Express*, and assumed cruising-stations to the port and starboard of the air-ship respectively. Boyd, for his part, levitated up by about two meters and then darted to a point about ten meters behind the *Express*, joining the former JPL scientist in another second or two. The telekinetic grasp of the three newcomers locked on to the hull of the ship, and they began to lend their propulsive-powers to its forward-motion.

The two dull-glowing Russian living-daggers took up their escort-positions, about five meters above and below the air-ship.

"Wow... I felt that immediately!" called Ramirez. "Thanks!"

"No problem, man," shouted White, to the back of the ship. "But we got no idea where the hell we're s'posed to be flyin' *to*..."

For a moment, Billings looked as if he was retreating back into the hull of the air-ship; but in fact, he was just communicating with unknown parties within it. His head and shoulders again popped up through the hatch and he announced, "Those two, uhh, 'Presidential' kids are sort of with it now... and they're asking if there even *is* still a 'Washington, D.C.'. What you want me to tell them?"

"Hold on a sec," replied Jacobson. "I'll have a look."

Using his mind-pulling-skill to anchor himself, and with his diamond-armor powered-up to protect against unanticipated nuclear misadventures, the former Mars mission commander stood upright on the top of the *Express*, in between Tommy in front and Billings behind. He carefully scanned the airspace and terrain-features first to the west, sweeping his gaze dead ahead and then to the east. The intermittent cloud-layers made this challenging, but he was able to cycle through different alien-powered vision-modes to compensate.

To the far north-west, Jacobson saw the lights of a distant metropolis – Columbus or Pittsburgh, maybe? – and a quick glace downward over his right shoulder confirmed that Richmond and Norfolk were still there, looking no different than usual, at the bottom of the Chesapeake Estuary.

Yet, when he scanned directly ahead, the former Mars mission-leader saw things that disturbed him. Far off to the north-east, where Philadelphia should have been, there was nothing but darkness; and Baltimore was much less luminous than usual, with only a few lights showing anywhere in its vicinity. A scan in infra-red revealed the signs of numerous small fires, especially in the area along the Interstate going north to Wilmington. The same syndrome seemed to be playing out closer to the Atlantic coast, with most of the city-lights in this region having been extinguished, and fires appearing spottily here and there.

As for the D.C. metropolitan area, it seemed less badly-affected, but its north-east quarter was dark, with a few fires burning out of control. As near as Jacobson could tell, the downtown Capitol Region seemed only lightly-damaged.

Jacobson now turned his attention to the east. He looked out over the ocean, scanning first in *Um'nàhr'é* and then again in *Um'b'as'ài*, repeating the process several times just to validate the observations. He saw two huge 'balloons' of super-heated air inside the trademark mushroom-clouds, still dimly-glowing in the infra-red band, slowly rising; one was lower – between five and fifteen thousand feet above sea-level – and was approximately twenty kilometers offshore, while the other – larger and hotter, despite its greater distance – was further to the north, almost parallel with Philadelphia (Jacobson figured), and was much higher in the atmosphere.

My God, he reflected, *so that's where the damn things blew.*

If Karéin went after either or both of those, like Tommy and Bob mentioned... or if Chu was on-board the command-post when...

Don't want to think about it. Not going to!

He turned to address Billings.

"So here's what I'm seeing," he carefully related. "It looks like both of the bombs went off over water – thank God for small blessings, *that* could have been a lot worse – quite a long way to the north and east of us. I think the EMP knocked all of Philadelphia, most of Baltimore and some of northern D.C., but – and don't quote me on this – I'm betting that the White House and central Washington are intact. If the President's still down there, like you told us, then he's likely alive."

"I'll *tell* them," said Billings.

He disappeared down the hatch for a moment or two, and then came back up.

"You aren't going to *believe* this, Jacobson," he remarked.

"Bob... by now, I'd have thought you'd have got religion, about the 'believing crazy stuff' thing," smartly responded the former Mars mission leader. "What *is* it?"

"Their names are 'Matt' – that's the boy – and 'Clairie' – that's the girl," started the ex-salesman.

"Yeah... I remember," confirmed Jacobson.

"Well... they want us to fly down to the White House," relayed Billings. "'Be back with Mom and Dad', kinda thing. I think it's a bogus idea, by the way. How many H-bombs do they have to *throw* at the place, before we get smart and vacation somewhere else?"

"So far as we knew," noted Jacobson, "There were only two of those... and both are accounted-for. It's true that we might run into defensive-fire if we went back there, but we could probably avoid it by engaging the cloak and doing a little dodging... as you did the first time, right?"

"Yeah, but Commander, they had the Storied Watcher with them – " argued Boyd.

Ramirez interrupted.

"I'm not going *anywhere* until I find Sylvia!" he declared. "I owe it to her. *Si Dios lo quiere*, she's still alive... but she might be hurt or something. I won't stop until I know for sure."

"Hector – I hate to be the bearer of bad news," unhelpfully remarked Billings, "But she went right up next to that plane that just nuked itself into ratshit... remember? She was a damn brave woman, but –"

"I don't want to *hear* it, Bob!" shouted the Tex-Mex ex-scientist. "You don't want to help me look, that's *your* business – but you can fly this ship all by yourself, in that case!"

"For what it's worth," commented White in a loud voice, from his side of the air-ship, "I didn't feel no psychic scream – like, when one of us 'super-humans' gets beat up, or worse. 'Member, Angel Lady said that thing's fickle as a first date... but maybe it's a good sign – like, 'they ain't dead yet'. 'Least, that's what *I* like to think."

Boyd – who was right beside Ramirez, pushing the *Mailànkh Express* forward, asked, "I *hear* you, Hector, and the last thing in the world that I want to do is 'leave a wounded buddy behind'... but even if she survived the explosion and then the fall to earth afterwards... how would we *find* her? All this has been going on, over an airspace of hundreds of miles in every direction. Searching could take *weeks!*"

"Before she left, she said something about, 'Rainbow will know when you get close to me'," answered Ramirez. "We were very short of time and I forgot to ask her, 'how close, is 'close', here?'"

"I guess we put her mutt on top of the ship and hope for the best," opined White. "'Less y'all got a better idea."

"How come you're willing to search for Miz Sylvia... but not Mom?" peevishly interjected Tommy.

"Kid's got a *point*," agreed Billings.

"I could argue that Karéin is much less likely to have been hurt or killed by these explosions, than Sylvia," evenly remarked Boyd, "But... point taken. Same really goes for Minnie, too. I'm not optimistic, but... look, here's *another* idea. Even with Sylvia's dog, searching like this – in the dark, on top of everything else – isn't likely to produce a lot of quick results. And furthermore, if they're alive, but badly-wounded, they might be no match for the military, if it happens on them first and things get out of hand."

"So what are you proposing, Major?" came the voice of the Russian, calling at high volume to be heard over the airstream.

"Well," said the former Mars mission pilot, "Why don't we do what these kids in the hold want – that is, proceed to the White House – and demand that the President organize search-parties of his own, with strict 'rescue-only' rules of engagement? That'd be *much* more likely to find Sylvia, Minnie or maybe even Karéin herself... and it would be a sign of good-will on his part. If he turns us down flat, we trash the place – optionally, trash *him* – and then resume the search ourselves. What about it?"

"I don't think you'll have to search for Chu," mordantly stated Billings. "She was certainly on that plane... the one carrying the nuke. Which, went off. I don't think even *Sari* could survive something like that –"

"Don't *say* things like that, Mr. Billings!" complained Tommy.

"I haven't given up on your Mom... my girlfriend, or wife, or whatever," answered the former salesman. "I'm betting that she kept her distance, before those bombs did their stuff. But Minnie was was practically sitting on *top* of one of 'em. She *knew* what she was doing, kid; she told us so, in so many words. I *respect* her for that. You should too."

"Yeah," sadly admitted the boy. "But Mom told me, 'a prince of the *Khul-Algr*... uhh... the... 'whatever-it-is', never gives up on a friend, even when all seems lost, and the night-sky is dark and starless'. It's like with Miz Sylvia. We've got to find out what happened... you know?"

"Yeah... I know," nodded Billings.

There was a long silence, but eventually, Jacobson spoke up.

"You tell those two kids that we've, uhh... got *business* with the President?" he asked the ex-salesman. "I mean... we mean them no harm, but beyond that, if we go for Brent's plan, I simply can't give any guarantees. About their *father*, that is."

"Oh... I doubt he's that worried about you, Jacobson," teased the ex-salesman.

"Why would *that* be, Bob?" countered the former Mars commander.

"Well," diffidently offered Billings, "After the number that Sari, Tommy and I did on him, earlier tonight – and on that snob wife of his, not to mention Kaysten – there's not much you can do for an encore."

Two Victories And A Broken Heart

By now – in addition to uncounted dozens knocked out of the skies, in battles recently past – *Vîrya* Cherie Tanaka, First of the *Fire*, had notched up another six or seven fighter-planes to her score.

The attacks had started at an alarmingly-close distance to the moonshine-hideout where she had left Hendricks and Boatman in charge of the refugees, who had been collected on the "Mars Gang's" cross-country tours. She had been climbing and picking up speed over one of the east-most West Virginia mountain-ridges, over State Route 33 at the Virginia border, when *Vìrya Sài'ymë* had warned her of "birds-war, many, fast coming above left behind and".

The weirding-armor's mind was bombarded by curse-words that were (mostly) as yet unfamiliar, as the more-than-a-woman fumed at having to waste many minutes of precious time, on this distraction.

But Tanaka's powers were returning – even, increasing – rapidly; and by now she had the benefit of experience with many such engagements, so the battle was a short and decisive one.

Another advantage soon became apparent : of the twelve fighter-planes that had bounced her, only three turned out to be the high-tech F-32E's that had been dogging the "Mars-Gang" in earlier contests.

They're running out of stealth-fighters, she mused, with satisfaction.

Those ones are at least a challenge... hard – but not impossible – to track, especially at long range.

The ordinary ones, well... can we say, "sitting duck"?

More durable than the stealth-fighters – but they didn't maneuver worth a damn... wonder if they're starting to run out of trained pilots, too?

Dodging the obligatory barrage of air-to-air missiles with repeated, high-G turns that no human pilot could have imitated and lived to tell about, the former Mars mission science officer streaked skyward – well above the highest cloud-level – and then, with the advantage of altitude, dove like an avenging hawk scattering a flock of intruding crows, blasting her quarry to pieces with cruelly-powerful, expertly-targeted lightening-bolt-shots. She noticed that, for the first time, she was able to accelerate past the maximum speed of the stealth-fighters (although not the other ones).

Her force-field was grazed a couple of times by auto-cannon-shells, but otherwise, Tanaka came through this engagement practically unscathed.

Excellent, mused Tanaka, *now I only have about fifty thousand miles per hour more to go, before I can have a race with Karéin, and hope to win it...*

The battle drew to a one-sided close, as the former Mars science officer tried not to aim for cockpits... but did not try very hard. When all was said and done, she only noticed five parachutes floating downward to the Allegheny Mountains.

Serves 'em right... but dare I keep heading north-east? she wondered.

I've wasted at least ten minutes – maybe more, hard to tell when you're fighting for your life – and if the damn Air Force saw where I lifted off from... they might carpet-bomb the hideout!

Vìrya Sài'ymë – can thou tell me... do any more war-birds approach the mountain, whereupon we left the others?

There was a short delay, and then the living-armor replied,

More twenty fly none but do east by north, us below sea toward the and; war-arrows their fired just have not we see target that.

But you believe the Cass Mountain refuge to be safe, for the time being?

Mother honored do I yes, came back the answer.

Good enough for me, I guess... thank you, dear.

Tanaka now cast her senses to the north-east. Through the clouds, she detected exactly what *Vìrya Sài'ymë* had been describing.

A larger Air Force formation than she had just scattered – a mixed one that appeared to contain five F-32Es, thirteen older fighter-planes and at least six smaller IR-signatures that she guessed would have to have been armed drones, were proceeding at increasing speed toward some as-yet-invisible destination that must have been slightly east of a due-north heading.

Then, events started to unfold at a rapid pace.

First, the fighters fired a barrage of missiles at their closest target – to Tanaka's enhanced sight, this was an insignificant heat-signature, not much bigger than a large bird – perhaps five or six miles to the north, on a collision course with the aircraft-formation.

What the hell are they targeting? she thought.

That can't be a plane, or even a missile – and it can't be Brent Boyd – he'd dazzle everything in twenty miles – nor can it be Wolf... I see his IR-sig clear as day, below me and far off to the east – no way I can be wrong, I've flown with him too long, I can tell his signature from everything else, easily; big guy's flying north to "I know not where"...

Hmm, looks like he's been in a battle too, judging from those burning planes that are spiraling down, behind him... good job there man... but the Air Force must know that he's in the area – why are they firing at that tiny target, and not Wolf?

Makes no sense!

Well... could it be Misha, maybe?

No... doesn't fit him, either, unless he's figured out some advanced way to hide...

Well, resolved the more-than-a-woman, *I have to get out of here... if I follow Wolf, I can meet up with him and maybe he'll lead me to the V-37 and the rest of our benighted "Gang"...*

Cruising at relatively high altitude, Tanaka began to accelerate, reveling in her new-found speed. But just as she was about to really hit a torrid pace, the missiles below – as well as the vanguard-aircraft of the fighter-formation – were disintegrated by a tremendously-powerful, but peculiar-looking, explosion. Its thundering, almost-invisible shock-wave echoed throughout the heavens, displacing the air as far up as the former Mars science officer, was flying; but unlike what would have been expected from a conventional blast, there was no fireball, only a weakly-manifested heat-flash.

Immediately, she slowed, reinforced her shielding and tried to engage some of the "cloaking"-tricks that the Storied Watcher had, altogether too briefly, tried to impart, earlier.

Holy Jehoshaphat*!* mused a duly-impressed Tanaka.

I don't want to tangle with whatever that *was!*

A frenzied air-battle broke out, just to the south of where the explosion had occurred. But little of what was going on, added up. Many of the surviving aircraft and drones seemed to be flying routine defensive-patterns, with two or three fighters providing cover to one in the lead of the sub-formation, while a larger number – four fighters along with three drones – started chasing the small heat-signature, up into the stratosphere.

The quarry, and its pursuers, were nearing Tanaka's own altitude, albeit at a distance of maybe six to eight miles to the east. The fighters and drones began to fire auto-cannons at the heat-signature. It was struck several times, and its vertical motion abated noticeably – but it remained airborne.

No human-built plane, drone or missile, could take that *kind of pounding, and live to tell about it – that's got to be one of "us"!* realized the former Mars science officer, with rage surging in her breast.

The heat-signature wobbled and then began to slowly fall backwards.

Tanaka's war-song echoed through the skies as she raced toward the battle-scene, at break-neck speed. Within no more than five seconds she was within accurate firing-range. She unleashed a well-aimed barrage of lightening-bolts, apportioned at the drones and the solitary stealth-fighter of the enemy-group. The attack struck dead-on – except for one drone that was badly-damaged and that fell, trailing smoke, out of the scene of battle.

The F-32E that Tanaka had targeted was blown completely in two, but – despite its forward-section cork-screwing downward – its pilot somehow managed to pop his 'chute.

You're very lucky that you didn't kill whomever it was of my kin-folk, who you were shooting at, mused Tanaka.

Otherwise... I'd have seen how well you fly without that parachute holding you up.

Three fighters – older, non-stealth-models – executed high-G turns in the stratosphere and the dived on the descending, enigmatic heat-signature. Again, Tanaka blasted two of these out of the sky, with one pilot surviving and the other one being killed instantly when his aircraft exploded; but she missed the hard-maneuvering third one, which ignored her and began firing an auto-cannon at its original target.

Muttering an oath, the former Mars science officer prepared to launch another lightening-bolt; but just before she was about to fire, the same invisible explosion that she had seen from afar a few seconds earlier, ballooned from the heat-signature outward. Its roiling, translucent forward-edge hit the last fighter-plane, which simply *disintegrated* on contact.

Needless to say... no ejection-seat, nor parachute, was observed.

Though she was at least a kilometer away by the time the back-wash of the expanding-blast reached her, Tanaka cringed at its impact on her own personal force-field.

Holy Toledo, she grimly reflected, *if it's like most blast-waves, and degrades in energy at the third power to distance... I don't want to imagine what it must be like, being hit by this terrible thing, up close...*

Oh-kay... I'm not going to get into another "friendly fire" incident...

She slowed to a complete stop, threw most of her *Fire* into her defensive-screen and caused her war-song to sound at the highest-volume that she could manage.

The IR-source slowed to a stand-still, as well. And a different war-song was heard coming from it. The tune was somehow familiar.

Where have I heard that before... oh, wait –

The other flying-being slowly drifted closer. Tanaka could see an indistinct, slim, female-proportioned figure, with glowing eyes.

Now an external thought appeared in her mind.

Miz Cherie? That y'all?

First Of The Fire! the former science officer sent back, while both war-songs receded to the background.

Melissa? Melissa Claremont*? But... how? Karéin said that she was staying out of all this... right? What are* you *doing here?*

That a long story, Miz Cherie, came the mental answer.

We was chillin' in th' cut, but then Angel Lady got a bit restless just standin' round watchin' th'action, I reckon – she took some of us back here, an', well, Air Force and guv'ment been makin' it some hot for us, since we got here...

She done hauled th'Express – y'all knows, that bein' our corolla – long way up here, an' we was fixin' to do some shit wid th' plane that Miz Minnie bein' on – but then we see all these fighters, an' ah had to keep 'em off our butts... y'understand?

Anyways... thank y'all for the help... they was layin' the smack-down on me damn hard! Funny how every time ah gets mah ass in trouble, y'all show up right on time!

My pleasure, little sister! sent back the former Mars mission science officer.

It was at this point that Tanaka realized that a giggle could be communicated telepathically.

And she also reflected,

So I'm hovering here, at around 20,000 feet in the night sky, exchanging telepathic "how'd-you-do's" with a godly African-American teenager from Detroit's ghettos... who just blew half an entire Air Force fighter-plane-squadron out of the sky, all by herself.

What else is new, Cherie?

Not something you had counted on, when you suited up for the Mars mission?

But she forced her mind to return to the matters-at-hand.

If you don't mind my asking... that, uhh, thing that you did to the fighter-planes... what is it? I felt its after-effects at a distance of miles, and, well... at close range, it must be lethal...

Oh... that called "Th' Shatterin' Shield", Miz Cherie, explained Melissa.

A

Angel Lady done teached it to me, back aways. She say that it jus' like turnin' mah force-field, which is for defendin' me, into a major wicked WMD. An' she say, "'Lissa, y'all only doin' this bad thang if'n yo' own life's in danger."

Ah figures, "if ten or so of them fighter-planes don' count there... what does... y'know?"

You'll get no argument from me *on that point, honey,* sympathetically responded Tanaka.

And... congratulations on your mighty powers, Melissa – may you ever use them wisely!

Thanks, ma'am, came back the polite-feeling reply.

Listen, continued Tanaka, *I've been tracking a strong signature in* Um'b'as'ài *that I'm almost certain is Wolf – you know, the big guy, the bounty-hunter – who's heading almost due north... I can still just see him. Is he with you? Is he going back to Karéin's air-ship? I was thinking we could follow him, and –*

Umba... what? Oh, yeah – th' heat-seein' thang, offered Melissa.

Weren't he with y'all, Miz Cherie? Ah ain't seen him since we's all back in that camp up Canada. Wid us – ah means, Angel Lady 'n she homies, on 'th Express – we gots Miz Sylvia, Mista Hector, Bob Billins, Tommy, Miz Saquina, 'n two of th' Pres'dent's kids –

Did I hear you say – uhh, think *– that you and Karéin have the* President's *children with you? The President of the* United States, *I mean?* inquired a befuddled Tanaka.

Why... yes'm, answered the teenager.

See... they cackalackin' in she pimpmobile, 'cuz th' Pres'dent ridin' the walrus when –

But at this moment, both of the more-than-human women, instinctively shut their eyes and poured whatever *Fire* they had at their disposal – all except the absolute minimum to offset the pull of the planet's gravity – to reinforce their defensive-shields.

Oh mah Gawd! psychically shrieked Melissa.

It done blew!

In the next half-second, she felt Tanaka's vice-like telekinetic-forces, closing on her.

Cast your own one on me, Melissa! the former science officer, demanded.

If one of us loses our ability to fly –

What's that – Lawd in Heaven – another one! came the panicked message from the teenager.

They waited for untold seconds.

Vìrya *Sài'ymë – count thee the time as it passes –*

Who that? asked a perplexed Melissa.

Then she began to cry.

She is a sister to Karéin's war-children, explained Tanaka.

I consider her my daughter. I'll introduce you better, when we get a minute...

Vìrya *Sài'ymë's telling me that these explosions were very far away – over the Atlantic, to the north and east of us... thank God for* that, *at least they weren't over a city or something.*

The blast-wave will be very weak when it hits us here.

That's good *news!*

Why are you crying, Melissa?

'Cuz, sobbed the teenager's thoughts, *Miz Minnie was on th' plane, that had one of them bombs, on it!*

After an aghast silence, with Tanaka's shoulders slumping as if a ton of lead had suddenly been loaded upon them, the little, as-yet-innocent voice her intelligent-armor, spoke up.

Mother blessed, asked Vìrya Sài'ymë, *break heart why thou do?*

Stand-Off On The South Lawn

As the *Mailànkh Express* cruised in full stealth-mode at roof-top altitude over 17th Street N.W. in central Washington, D.C., even those inside the air-ship – staring out through the vessel's few, small windows – could see that something was wrong, below them. Entire city-blocks were pitch-black, without street-lights of any kind – and there were small fires burning unattended, here and there. The signs of damage were becoming more frequently-encountered, as Jacobson and his crew proceeded from the city's southern suburbs on a north-bound course.

Though the air-ship flew too fast to get a clear picture (this problem was compounded by its hull's weirding-defenses, which blurred and refracted light-waves both inbound and outbound), it also seemed that the downtown streets were littered with car-crashes and broken glass; the latter might have been caused by the two nuclear shock-waves, but more likely was the result of widespread looting, which seemed mostly out of control. Crowds of rioters were milling about, unchecked by the few available policemen who were still on duty.

"There it *is!*" yelled Tommy, rather more loudly than would have been advisable, though the cloaked-and-almost-invisible *Mailànkh Express* was flying fast enough so that his voice wouldn't have been easily-identifiable at any one location. "I see that thing that Mom dropped in the lawn!"

Jacobson was frankly amazed that they hadn't encountered any opposition this far on the way in; but his apprehensions were, at that precise moment, validated with the worst kind of proof.

As the air-ship turned north-east and cut across the north-west corner of the Ellipse, heading towards President's Park, a flurry of ten man-portable surface-to-air missiles popped up out of nowhere, hurtling at frightening speed toward the *Express*.

Three of the missiles were fooled by the vessel's impromptu stealth-technology, and veered off harmlessly to either flank ("harmless" was a relative term, as the weapons crashed into office-buildings on the other side of the street, exploding and causing severe damage, killing several bystanders and starting large fires). Neither Boyd nor Ramirez had a clean line of sight, but the Russian's war-daggers each accounted for one more and White was able to freeze two solid. However, the other three tracked the *Mailànkh Express* cleanly.

Tommy had been alert to the danger and he fired a fusillade of his screeching, glowing *Fire*-shots at the missiles. Two of these sinister projectiles struck dead-on and detonated their prey at a safe distance; but one only narrowly-grazed its target, wrecking the weapon's tail-wings and causing it to career crazily through the air, on a collision-course with the air-ship.

At the same split-second, the *Express* was targeted by hidden machine-guns which appeared in four different pop-up turrets previously hidden in the south White House lawn. These sprayed bullets wildly, again killing many innocent bystanders in the area, but they also struck the air-ship all over its forward-quarter.

Tommy was hit repeatedly, being knocked back so he was facing to the sky, as Jacobson rocketed off the vessel. The former Mars mission commander aimed his leap perfectly, intercepting and smashing the remaining missile into pieces. He was rewarded for this act of valor, by being right next to the weapon when it blew up with tremendous force.

Jacobson was sent flying dozens of feet upwards and backwards; but – to his satisfaction – the detonation, which certainly would have killed a normal human-being and in fact would have blown most small aircraft, clean out of the sky – proved amazingly easy to shrug off. He then proceeded to land on the South Lawn – noting, in passing, the mine-fields that had been hidden in several belts protecting ingress-routes to the White House – then lept again, methodically landing on top of the gun-turrets and crushing each one in turn, with deadly-powerful, diamond-encased fist-strikes.

Behind him, the stricken *Mailànkh Express*, its fore-quarters flickering with flames from missile-shrapnel and bullet-strikes, came a-crashing-down on the South Lawn, just to the western side of the gigantic top of the

Washington Monument, thence deposited much earlier by the Storied Watcher herself.

While Boyd, the Russian and White powered up their war-songs and alien-abilities, with the two former Mars mission astronauts assuming defensive-positions above the air-ship (this – particularly Boyd's glowing presence, which lit up the entire grassy area like the floodlights at a sports-stadium – attracted unwelcome attention from crowds milling several blocks away, in the surrounding, cordoned-off streets), Jacobson hurled himself back on top of the *Express* and tended to the boy.

"Tommy... *Tommy!*" he shouted. "*Speak* to me, son!"

The dazed youngster slowly came up to a sitting-position.

"*Wow*, Major Sam," he managed to say. "That... *hurt!*"

"Are you wounded?" demanded Jacobson.

Tommy coughed, but – mercifully, as near as the ex-Mars mission commander could tell – no blood could be seen coming out of the boy's mouth.

"I... I got the wind knocked out of me, Mister Jacobson," remarked Tommy. "Hit the back of my head on the ship, too, because I was strapped in when those, uhh, *things* hit me... couldn't move. Feels like I got punched really hard, right in the middle of my chest. Don't think anything's broken, though. Oww!"

Jacobson embraced the boy.

"Thank God," he breathed. "That's all I need... a dead, or badly-injured, Number One Son of the most powerful being on the planet. Alright –"

White interrupted.

"You, Captain," he called out, "We got company, don't y'all know."

He was right. From all directions of the compass except south, the newly-arrived air-ship, and its inhabitants and escorts, were being approached by dark-suited, gun-toting Secret Service agents, accompanied by a skeleton-force of perhaps four or five Marine guards.

Billings' head popped up, through the escape-hatch.

"What *gives!*" he protested. "That was a damn hard landing, Jacobson – Moira hit her head, one of those GrayWar jerks lost his lunch, and we got nothing to clean it w... *oh...*"

The former salesman stopped in mid-complaint, upon seeing the White House guard-contingent.

One of these – a portly, heavy-set and tough-looking Caucasian Secret Service agent – yelled in the direction of the *Mailànkh Express*.

"I'm now addressing the terrorists over there – you are in violation of *numerous* Federal laws, by landing here!" he accosted. "Lay down your arms, put your hands on top of your heads, and –"

They probably couldn't see Jacobson rolling his eyes, underneath his self-projected crystalline armor-suit; but they certainly *did* see him raise his hands, to about shoulder-height.

"*Look*, assholes," he shouted back, "You're extremely lucky that you're still alive – because if you had really *hurt* Tommy here, we'd have drawn straws, to see which one of us gets to splatter you all over the landscape! If you hadn't noticed, I got three guys flying CAP over this ship, and any one of them can grease you with a wave of his hand. Put down those fucking toy guns of yours and call the President... tell him that the Mars Gang, is here to pay him a little social-visit. You *hear* that?"

"The... uhh... *Mars Gang?*" repeated the lead-agent, with an obvious tone of fear in his voice.

"Well who y'all *think* we was... maybe the fuckin' Presidential Pizza-Delivery Corps?" taunted the floating, ice-enshrouded Devon White, from above.

A malicious laugh came from both the airborne Brent Boyd and from Tommy.

Just then, the egress-door in the middle of the air-ship, opened. A groggy Matt appeared in it.

"Is that... Mr... Kortish..." he mumbled.

"Yes," the agent responded. "You're the President's son... right?"

"Yeah... Matt here," weakly stated the teenage boy. "Clairie's just waking up, too. We're... uhh... back at the White House? But there was a *bomb* – hey, we've got to get *out* of here –"

Jacobson called down to the young man, "Both of the nuclear weapons have already detonated... they tell me that you and your sister were 'out', when it happened. As far as we know it's safe here now... at least from *that* kind of threat."

Matt stared upward at the diamond-encased, glowing-eyed, intimidating figure of Sam Jacobson.

"Who the hell... are *you*, Mister?" asked the teenager.

"Sam Jacobson, official leader of the *Eagle / Infinity* mission to Mars, and *de facto* leader of the Mars Gang, at your service," came back the smug-sounding answer. "My associates, up there, Majors Brent Boyd and Devon White, along with 'Misha' our representative from the Russian Federation, as well. We also have some other members of our team unaccounted-for... but presumably out there, somewhere."

"The... uhh... *Mars Gang?*" nervously echoed Matt. "But you guys are, uhh..."

"'*Criminals*'? the shining, godlike presence of Brent Boyd, interrupted, from on high, with a laugh. "Well, son... 'who's a criminal', depends on 'who makes the laws'... and, 'who enforces them'."

"We had an agreement with... the... uhh... *alien*," countered the teenager. "She made up with Dad... or hadn't they told you?"

"So I've heard," evenly observed Jacobson. "Don't know if they mentioned this... but, we don't answer to her."

The face of the other Presidential offspring – the girl – now appeared beside that of her brother.

"I... *heard*... all that," she groggily commented. "Whoever you are – what are you here to... do? Why'd you come back here?"

"You can't remain here," interjected the lead Secret Service agent. "Get back in that, uhh, ship, and get out of here, *immediately!*"

"Or you'll, 'what'?" challenged Billings, from his hatch-perch on the *Express'* dorsal hull.

"I'll have no choice to use lethal force, which is duly authorized," threatened the Service guy.

As if to reinforce the point, a number of the other agents and guards removed the safeties from their guns.

"Remember *me?*" spoke Hector Ramirez, from the rear-part of the airship. He had levitated himself so as to stand on the rear of its hull, just back from where Billings was.

"So... let's assess this situation realistically... shall we?" offered the Tex-Mex scientist. "I see in front of me about eight Secret Service agents and four Marine-guards. Each of you has a conventional gun. You are opposed by a group of so-called 'terrorists' who have successfully fought off *the entire United States military*, for days or weeks. The 'Mars Gang' includes flying, super-human beings who can, respectively, freeze you into a solid, dead mass, drive daggers of poison or lightening through your bodies at high velocity, or simply vaporize you with a photonic death-ray. This is on top of Commander Jacobson, who is invulnerable to all your attacks and who can crush a tank with his bare hands –"

A smirking Jacobson interrupted, "That's not *completely* true, Hector; the most I've been able to do so far, is twist a tank's cannon into a pretzel... and to rip its turret off. But I'm getting better at it, every day!"

"I stand *corrected*," wryly allowed Ramirez. "And I should add that you have two members of the Presidential family standing right here, and who could be shot dead in the crossfire, if you start firing at our ship. I doubt that your boss would be very pleased, with such an outcome –"

"Get to the *point!*" demanded the Service guy.

"Well," suggested Ramirez, "If I were you... I would put away those guns, usher those of us who wish to go, into the White House, call the President, and tell him that Commander Jacobson is here to talk to him. Leave the decision about what to do, to the President. Why isn't that acceptable?"

"Because you're a mortal threat to the President's safety and security," riposted Kortish. "That's not a serious proposal... and you *know* it!"

In the blink of an eye – showing up as if from nowhere, although Jacobson and the other 'more-than-humans' thought that he had been detected a split-second beforehand – the figure of Jerry Kaysten, appeared next to the Service agent.

"Hi there, Commander!" he greeted. "What brings *you* here? And I don't see Cherie Tanaka, or Wolf... where are they? Oh... and what about Melissa... the Claremont girl, I mean?"

"The Professor and our friend Wolf have been, uhh, *delayed*, doing other things," evaded Jacobson. "I'm sure they send you their regards."

"Melissa flew to the south, to defend us against fighter-planes that were approaching from that direction," explained Ramirez. "We don't know where she is. We hope she's okay..."

"As if you don't *know* why we're here, Jerry!" chided the hovering Brent Boyd. "We got *business* with your boss. Why don't you call him out here, so we can have a nice friendly chat?"

"What makes you think he's even still *here*?" bluffed the Chief of Staff. "We had two H-bombs aimed at us... need I remind you?"

"If that's you using your alien-power... boy, did you ever get the short end of the stick," snorted Jacobson. "We have several people aboard the *Express*, attesting to the fact that he's here. Come *on*, Jerry – I give you full marks for doing your duty – that goes for you too, agent whomever-you-are – but cut the bullshit! You *know* you can't face off against one of us... never mind, *all* of us!"

I'd still be careful, Jacobson, sent Billings.

He may be a pencil-necked geek, but once he gets going – let me assure you – being hit by a geek who's traveling at a couple thousand miles per hour... that ain't fun.

Jacobson nodded but continued to accost Kaysten.

"Jerry," said the Mars mission commander, "Just tell the S.O.B. that we're here, that we intend to talk to him and call him to account, one way or the other – and we'd prefer to do that without having to level the place; but if it *comes* down to that – *you* get the idea."

Kaysten looked at Billings and Tommy.

"We had an *agreement*, you know!" complained the Chief of Staff. "Mr. Bunny-Hopping Diamond Chandelier here – as well as you, Hector, Saquina, Tommy and the rest of 'em – *have* to be aware of that! Is that all your word means? Or... *hers*?"

"Your White House missiles, and those gun-things, *shot* me, Mister Kaysten!" countered Tommy. "How *come!* We just wanted to *talk!*"

"Good point," added Billings. "I heard the bullets hitting the hull. We didn't get this kind of reception when Sari first dropped the *Express* down here. Why all the hostility this time?"

"Service has been getting the defenses back on-line," offered Kaysten. "But you *should* have been, uhh, 'engaged', the first time that Karéin landed you here. I suppose she's got some advanced way of faking out our systems. Have to work on that... right, Curt?"

"Definitely... yeah," agreed Kortish.

"By the way, Tommy," mentioned the Chief of Staff, "For what it's worth... I'm sorry about that – just like the President and I are really, truly sorry about everything else that's been done to you and your family, up to now. You gotta *understand*, these things – what fired at you, I mean – they weren't meant for you; they were meant for all the crazy people who try to break in here and hurt the President or his family. You stumbled in here and they went off, automatically – not, *intentionally*. Like your mom said, 'there's been way too much violence going on... let's not make a bad situation, worse'. Remember what she said, kid?"

"Yeah... she *did* say that, I guess," retreated Tommy, his eyes temporarily looking downward.

Watch out, son, Tommy received.

That son of a bitch has some kind of 'magic silver tongue', bestowed upon him by your mother.

You can't be sure that he isn't using it, right now.

Tommy silently nodded in Billings' direction.

A tense silence descended on the scene for three or four long seconds, and then Kaysten volunteered, "Tell you what – why don't you let me skedaddle back to the President, and see what his P.O.V. is on all this. If he's agreeable, fine, you can come in to the Oval Office and have your little chat with him, there. If not – then you get your asses out of here, on the double. Fair?"

"No!" called Boyd. "You're bluffing with deuces here, Jerry. Nice *try*."

The previously-silent Russian spoke up. He had to speak relatively loudly, to be heard over the sirens of ambulances that had arrived in the area, to deal with the many civilian collateral damage casualties that had occurred when the *Mailànkh Express* was attacked on its way in.

"Mr. Kaysten," he politely intoned, "Every member of the group who you call the 'Mars Gang', here in front of you, has come a very long way, to arrive here; and every one of us has been repeatedly subjected to determined efforts, on the part of your government, to kill us. It is hardly rational for you to expect us to simply abandon our quest and to go home with the basic issues, still unresolved. The President surely knows this, and he must have been preparing for it. The 'race' between Commander Jacobson and Ms. Chu has been decided in his favor. So –"

"I wouldn't quite put it that way, Misha," coldly responded Kaysten. "The only reason that you can say that, is because Minnie – God rest her brave soul – was on the Vice-President's airborne command-post, when the nuke aboard it, went off. She stayed aboard and sacrificed her *life* so that this disaster could end without millions of dead, here in D.C.. Have a little *respect*, if you don't mind!"

"Is that... *true?*" gasped Saquina White, who had somehow managed to edge past the two Presidential teenagers in the air-ship doorway.

Kaysten grimly nodded acknowledgment.

"We have one hundred per cent verified communications from Minnie, aboard the 'plane, less than five minutes before it blew," he observed. "*Nobody* could have survived something like that. I've only known her for a few weeks... but it felt like I've known her for a *lifetime*. She was my *sister*, you know. Just like she was yours."

Jacobson sent to Boyd,

You get any, uhh, bad feelings, recently?

Like, 'one of us has died', kind of thing?

That's a 'negative', responded the former Mars mission pilot.

Same here, added Devon White.

"And Sylvia went off to help Minnie, to divert the airplane's flight-path," sadly added Ramirez. "We haven't seen her since..."

And where's Mom? whimpered Tommy, into Billings' psyche.

Stay strong, kid, responded the ex-salesman.

Something in me says, "she'll be back".

Your Mom's on a whole different level, compared even to us "post-humans".

Saquina White started crying. Her husband flew down to comfort her.

A stony silence enveloped Boyd, Misha and Jacobson.

"So you see," continued the Chief of Staff, "We can duke it out here, in front of the TV-cameras, and maybe leave Karéin with more of us to mourn... or we can try to work it out, peacefully, between us. I'm for doing the latter. If only in Minnie's memory. And Sylvia's."

This could be his alien-tongued trickery, kid, warned Billings.

If I were you, I wouldn't believe a word *he says!*

But Mister Billings... we knew *Miz Chu was on that airplane,* silently replied Tommy.

Mom was real scared for her. And she was nice to me. She went with Mom up to that island, looking for us. I really liked Miz Chu!

And even though she almost killed me... I liked Miz Sylvia, too.

I feel... awful!

Billings was only able to console the boy with,

Remember how Jacobson and I told you – when we were way down there in that dungeon below Amchitka – that this ain't a game... and you don't get second chances?

Well, son... there you are.

Damn hard lesson – I'll admit as much.

I didn't always agree with Minnie, but I respected her. She was a straight-shooter, God rest her soul. I guess that's true of Abruzzio, too.

Though I won't miss being in her sights... that was one hell of an attack she had...

A familiar, fatherly-sounding voice called out from the distance, by the outside-entrance to the Oval Office.

"Mr. *President!*" shouted a horrified Agent Kortish, "Get back inside! This area is *extremely dangerous!*"

"It's alright, Curt," deflected the President. "I've been watching what's been going on. There's no need to do this in public. Show them in."

Tested

Saquina White – for her part – had insisted on accompanying her husband into the Oval Office, on the grounds that "I missed all the action, first time 'round, and I ain't gonna do no such thing, again."

This was only one instance of many such bartered comings-and-goings, since the President had similarly insisted on his children re-joining him and the First Lady. The First Lady had ushered them away from the scene, but Matt and Clairie returned shortly thereafter. They parked themselves just outside their father's office and looked in at the goings-on.

Except for Kortish and one other Secret Service agent, the U.S. leader had retained only a small number of White House bureaucrats and waiters in the immediate vicinity of the Oval Office; much to their displeasure, the other Service agents and Marine guards had been dispatched to the South Lawn and the periphery of the White House grounds, to reinforce the D.C. Capitol Police.

In fact, the President really had little discretion in the matter; after the excessive use of force against the Storied Watcher's air-ship, scores of Washingtonians in the line of fire had been either killed or seriously-wounded, and something approaching a near-riot had been developing on the surrounding streets. The crowds were swelling, media-helicopters and -drones were hovering nearby, and several networks were apparently providing live, minute-by-minute news-coverage of the unfolding events (a replacement TV had been brought into one corner of the Oval Office; it was tuned to the Disney channel, albeit with the sound muted).

Along with the affable Ramirez – who extracted a promise for a full tour of the White House with his family, "if it's still standing, after all this is over with" – Moira Sullivan and the two GrayWar mercenaries had been detailed to stand guard over the *Mailànkh Express*, to prevent incursions from overly-curious agents of the U.S. Federal government.

Sullivan had asked, "Exactly how am I supposed to stop men with guns, if they try to climb aboard?", to which Kaysten had replied, "try telling them a really funny joke... tie 'em up in knots... it works for *me*".

The joke was, however, lost on Abruzzio's childhood friend, as she nervously settled down in the air-ship. It did not help very much, that the first thing she overheard from Maloney and Rizzo was, "how much you think we could get for this thing, on NeoNet?"

But eventually, Billings and Tommy also returned to the *Mailànkh Express,* and they made it abundantly clear to the GrayWar types that "she has counted every last finishing-nail on this crate, and heaven help *you* if she finds one of them missing."

This reassured Sullivan, immensely.

Now the President had sat down on his chair behind the Resolution Desk. Arrayed in front of him – standing, after having declined an offer to take a seat – were, from the U.S. leader's left to his right, Devon and Saquina White, the Russian, Jacobson and Brent Boyd. Kaysten was leaning up against one of the office's inside walls, to the President's left.

The more-than-humans had tamped down the external manifestations of their alien-powers, with the exception of a subtle, almost-invisible back-glow in each of their eyes.

"You all know why we're having this discussion," started the President. "But before I begin... there's one of you – I believe that's Professor Tanaka – who's missing? Is that right?"

"Yes," answered Jacobson. "Cherie was injured, some time ago. She's in what we believe to be a safe location. We're hoping that she'll make a swift recovery. There's also one other member of our group – 'Wolf' by name – who's as yet unaccounted-for."

"I see," said the President. "If you don't mind... who is this gentleman over here, next to Major White and his wife? I'm sorry, but I'm not familiar with you..."

"My name is Misha Grishin, sir," answered the Russian. "I was a field operative of my country's SVR – roughly the equivalent of your CIA – who was assigned to locate and track the Storied Watcher, after our space-defense systems discovered that she had fallen to Earth, in the United States."

"And did you succeed in that?" idly inquired the U.S. leader.

"Only too well," replied Misha. "You might say that at a certain point... *she,* discovered, *'me'.* Karéin is a difficult person to resist, when she resolves to do something. As a result of this encounter, I seem to have ended up with the same kinds of unusual alien-powers, as are evident with the rest of our, uhh, 'gang'. It has certainly been a unique experience."

This brought a snicker from Devon White, which was in turn rewarded by an elbow in his ribs, courtesy of his better half.

"Incidentally," added Misha, "I believe that my life is now at risk, given that I have deviated from the orders given me, when this all started. If you ever again end up speaking with Russia's *Presidient,* I would appreciate a request for clemency."

"That," neutrally offered the President, "Will depend on subsequent events."

"Of course," politely stated the Russian.

Jacobson interjected, "All of this information is being provided to you out of courtesy, on the assumption that it won't be used against us. Do I have your assurance of that?"

"Yes," agreed the President. "You have my word. Everything you say to me here is in strict confidence – unless and until you specifically allow otherwise."

"Well... that's 'progress'... of a sort," coolly observed Jacobson. "And I have a favor to ask myself, as a confidence-building measure on your part."

"Really?" said the President. "What is it?"

"Well, sir," explained the former Mars mission commander, "As you're no doubt aware, two nuclear explosions have recently occurred, somewhere over the Atlantic Ocean – and we believe that two of the Storied Watcher's close friends, specifically Minnie Chu and Sylvia Abruzzio, may have been either killed or badly-wounded, as a result of those events. We're also unaware of the location or status of Karéin-Mayréij herself. She might need help as well. We can try to find them ourselves, but we have a finite number of personnel; so we're asking you to order a search-and-rescue operation, using whatever government resources may be available, to find Minnie, Sylvia and Karéin, and to return them safely to us, or to the nearest hospital. This necessarily means that the Armed Forces will not engage in any hostile action towards any of our friends. Do you understand what's being requested here, sir?"

"Indeed," confirmed the President. "Curt – contact Homeland Security and get the search going, please. I think we already have profile pictures of all three of these people... correct?"

"Yeah, we do, Mr. President, sir... but I'm hearing from Homeland that their SAR-resources are already heavily-tasked with the after-effects of the bomb-detonations," answered Kortish. "I'll ask them to make this a priority."

"Please do," ordered the President. "And make it clear that there is to be no shooting at these people – under *any* circumstances!"

"Yes, sir," stolidly replied the Secret Service leader.

Kortish disappeared into the communications-shack and began to make calls using the gear within that room.

"Thanks," evenly stated Jacobson.

"So... I assume you heard my address to the nation, in which I invited you here?" remarked the U.S. leader.

"Yeah... we got the gist of it," confirmed Boyd.

"And...?" asked the President.

"And... *what?*" responded the former Mars mission pilot.

"As you'll recall," explained the President, "What I proposed, in that speech, was that we establish what would in effect be, a 'Truth and Reconciliation Commission' – or something of the sort, that could get to the bottom of the grievances that set you off on this campaign of wanton destruction, that you've seen fit to unleash against your own government. In the speech, I also promised to be held to account for my own actions, or failures to act. But I need a commitment from each of you, that you'll do the same."

There was a tense silence, and then Jacobson countered with,

"With all due respect, Mr. President – and I'll leave it to the historians to decide how much 'respect' that is – my team and I have next to *nothing* to answer for... as opposed to your side of the table, which is responsible for a long list of abuses of power and war-crimes, starting with our unjustified imprisonment after first arriving back on Earth, then including attempts to have us tortured to death, along with Karéin's family-members, in an Agency dungeon underneath Amchitka, and extending to multiple attempts on the part of the government to *kill* us and our families, ever since we escaped the torture-chambers and made our way back to the continental United States. There's no excuse for any of this, sir – none at *all!*"

"I *know*," calmly acknowledged the U.S. leader.

"No... you *don't!*" challenged Boyd, who was obviously trying to keep his own anger under control. "The Agency's goons came within a couple of minutes of murdering my family – including my three kids, the eldest of whom is ten years old, for God's sake – and had I not showed up right at that time, I'd have lost *all* of them, along with my *wife!* I can show you several other families in our company, who weren't nearly as lucky... who had loved ones murdered by the government, who had houses destroyed – the list goes on and on, for no reason other than 'being in the wrong place at the wrong time'. You expect us to just 'forgive and forget', about bullshit like that – well, don't excuse my French, but 'go fuck yourself'!"

"Major Boyd," the President argued, while trying to maintain his composure, "I've already admitted that there's no excuse at all, for what's been done to everyone who's in some way been associated with the alien. I'm taking full responsibility for it, but you should be aware, most of these atrocities occurred in my absence – *after* I had been illegally-removed from this office. The government has been developing these patterns of behavior for *years*, and when George staged his *coup* against me a few weeks ago, it looks like he removed the few checks and balances that were left. I *still* don't have complete control over what the military and the intelligence-agencies do – as the rough ride that you encountered on your way in here, should attest. I'm not perfect and I've made some terrible mistakes, for which I'm prepared to be punished if a court of law, so decides. What would you have me *say?* What would you have me *do?*"

"Yeah, well, Mr. President *sir*," grumbled Devon White, "Always seems to be some fuckin' smart-ass reason why y'all get to shoot at *us*... and *we*, don't get to shoot back. 'Case y'all hadn't noticed... since our last meetin' – back in that nice little jail we got dropped into, as a 'thank-you' for freein' Karéin and savin' the whole damn world from that comet – tables been turned a bit. Y'all bein' mighty apologetic right now... but it don't take a genius to figure out what'd be goin' down, way of 'attitude', if we didn't have a gun at your head. Why should we believe a word y'all say? Y'all done reneged on just about everythin' that's been promised to us, so far. Why break a perfect record – y'understand what I'm sayin'?"

"A-*men* to *that!*" chimed in Saquina White. "I saw first-hand what th'Army was doin' to my neighbors, down Compton way. If it hadn't been for Minnie, and Angel Lady herself, we'd likely all be *daid!* And that's on *top* of all the shit – non-stop lyin', keepin' us from votin', throwin' black folk out of the guv'ment and such – that y'all been dumpin' on us, over the past Lawd knows how many years. Y'all got some kind of nerve, accusin' the Commander here, of bein' some kind of 'criminal'. Y'all want to see a 'criminal'... look in the *mirror!*"

"They speak the *truth*, sir," noted the Russian. "I have lost count of the number of times when your armed forces tried to kill us, and, in fact, everyone *around* us. We have used lethal force only in self-defense, and then, as sparingly as possible. There is simply no legitimate comparison between your behavior, and our own."

"The President's already *had* this kind of conversation, with Karéin herself, you know," interjected Kaysten. "She was pissed with the government, and can't say I blame her... but after an, uhh, 'vigorous debate' –"

"I *bet*," interrupted Jacobson, pointing to the damaged Oval Office couch and the indentation in the wall, where Billings and the Chief of Staff had fought.

"Yeah... well, let's just say that opinions were expressed forcefully," responded the Chief of Staff, with a slight grimace. "But the point is, the outcome – and the decisions – were basically inevitable. As, I'd submit, they will be with you, Commander... whether or not you want to admit it."

An irritated Jacobson shot back, "And how do you figure *that*, Jerry? What's to say that we don't just reduce this whole damn mansion to rubble? Who or what's going to *stop* us?"

"*You* are," evenly replied Kaysten.

"I'm not *following* you," countered the former Mars mission commander.

"Jerry – let me –" the President tried to assert; but Kaysten – in a way that none in the room had ever previously seen him do – just continued to talk, over his boss.

There was an odd, far-off look in his eyes.

"Sir," persisted the Chief of Staff, walking forward as he spoke, "This is the first and last time that you'll ever see me speaking out of turn, where you're concerned... but please trust me. Let me say my piece... and then our friend Mr. Jacobson here, can do whatever the hell he wants to. He's probably right that he can beat the ratshit out of me, although for the record, if it comes to that, I'll give him a good run for his money."

"Aptly put, Mr. Kaysten," remarked Misha.

"Go ahead then," allowed the President. "I trust you, Jerry."

"*Clark...*" called a frightened First Lady, who had joined her two offspring at the doorway leading to the interior of the White House.

The President sent her a sympathetic glance, accompanied with a head-shake and a "back-off" finger-gesture.

"So, Jacobson!" accosted Kaysten.

"Yeah, Jerry?" answered Jacobson.

"You *still* don't get it... *do* you?" said the Chief of Staff.

"You're pushing your luck!" growled the Mars mission commander. "What aren't I getting? And no *Fire*-bullshit, if you don't mind. I see it coming out your mouth, and you'll be spitting out teeth, a half-second later."

"Thanks for the kind words," parried Kaysten. "I promise I won't tell any jokes. But anyway... when we were all back there in Canada – in the camp, that is – the fact that Her Nuclear Highness was so hot to trot with this idea you had of going on a 'quest' – her words, not mine – to slay the evil dragon called 'The President of The United States'... didn't that strike you as a little, uhh, 'odd'?"

"What y'all gettin' at?" inquired Devon White. "We were all there, too. She just didn't stop us, from doin' what we figured we had to do."

"Is that *right*, Devon?" contested Kaysten. "She didn't just 'go along' with it... she actually *delivered* you guys to, well, wherever she dropped you off... and she did the exact same thing for Minnie, Sylvia and the rest of us. You may have thought that the plan was yours – and maybe in some sense it was – that's certainly what *I* thought, but the truth is... it was *hers*, all along. She set you *up*, Jacobson! She did it to *all* of us! You being here, her having come here beforehand, with Tommy, Billings and the rest of 'em – you too, Mrs. White – it's all part of the *plan!* Don't you *see?*"

"Well, that's a wonderful theory," argued Boyd, "But you're missing just one little ol' thing : namely – if this was all the 'plan'... what would the Storied Watcher hope to accomplish, *by* it? Letting us wander most of the way across the country, being shot at at nearly every stop, while Minnie ends up getting herself blown to bits, on an airplane carrying a nuke – that doesn't sound like a 'plan' devised by a goddess... it sounds much more like a 'plan' thought up by a *moron*... or by nobody at all. Ever heard of the 'Watchmaker Analogy', Jerry?"

"Sorry... guess I must have missed that college class," deflected the Chief of Staff. "But as to the plan... I'm really astounded that you haven't figured it out."

"Stop playing *games* with us, Jerry," demanded Jacobson.

"Okay, then," retreated Kaysten. "What you don't understand – what's been her objective, all along, I mean – is... it's a *test*, Jacobson!" he exclaimed. "It's a test of you. Of *all* of you. Of me, Sylvia, Minnie, God rest her soul... of all of *us*. Angel Lady had this figured out, right from the start. I'm an *idiot –*"

"Hooray! Now we *agree* on something!" sourly jested Boyd.

"What I *meant*, Major," smoothly continued Kaysten, "Is that I'm an idiot, for not having seen this much, *much* earlier. All along the way, I was asking myself, 'why the hell is Karéin hanging back, not intervening on one side or another'; it didn't add up. But then, I had the chance to listen to what she said to her son, right here in this room, earlier today... and it all started to make *sense*."

"What *did* she say to Tommy?" asked Misha.

"Of *course*," breathed the President. "Of *course!* My *God*... she *couldn't* have planned all this out... *could* she? But that's *impossible*, Jerry! How could she have figured on all this, happening –"

"Mr. *President*," phlegmatically remarked the Chief of Staff, "Remember who we're *talking* about? You know? 'Comet', 'end of the world', 'three hundred thousand-year-old guardian-angel', 'on a different plane of reality', 'comes from worlds of goblins, wizards, demons and magic', kind of thing? You *really* want to question whether doing something like I'm describing, is beyond her?"

Less self-righteously – he had obviously been thrown off-guard – Jacobson requested, "Jerry... you owe it to all of us, to explain yourself. What *did* Karéin say to her son?"

"Well," Kaysten offered, with a mischievous shrug, "Even with this 'silver tongue' that I've supposedly got, I couldn't really do it justice... but from what I remember – and Mr. President sir, correct me if I get any of it wrong – it came down to, 'Angel Lady herself decided to refrain from going after my boss, but she left it up to Tommy and our friend Bob, to either let him live, or die'. She said something about 'quests', and also about 'coming to a fork in the road'. As I'm sure you're aware, either of those two could quite easily kill the President, all by themselves. Tommy, for reasons that we all understand, wanted to pull the trigger... but he couldn't. And when he admitted that he couldn't, Karéin congratulated him for 'passing the test of nobility'."

Boyd, the two White spouses, the Russian and Jacobson, exchanged bewildered glances.

"So you *see*, my friend," claimed the Chief of Staff, "*That's*, the 'test'. She wanted each one of us, to get into a position where we could act 'nobly'... or, I guess, 'not, nobly'. Tommy, Bob and Karéin herself, passed the test. So did Minnie and Sylvia, in their own ways. I'll leave it to others to pronounce on me, but the President clearly passed, too. Now... it's *your* turn. I'll just repeat what she said... 'choose wisely'."

A clearly-frustrated Boyd took a random walk backward, slamming his fist into his other hand's palm.

"*Fuck you*, Karéin!" he swore. "*Please* don't tell me..."

"Wait a minute... *wait* a minute!" desperately argued Jacobson. "She couldn't have *possibly* planned all this out! There are too many variables... too many of these 'forks in the road'! At any time, we could have just been captured and killed... in which case this wonderful 'plan' comes to an abrupt, undignified end! She'd have to be stupidly-optimistic – or just insane – to have set us up with an open-ended 'quest' like what you're describing! The chances of it turning out in the exact way that she had intended –"

"Ahh... but I must, at this point, echo what Mr. Kaysten said earlier," offered the Russian. "Remember who we are *dealing* with, Commander Jacobson! As you know, I – uhh – got to know Karéin, better than perhaps anyone except for Bob Billings, or, arguably, Ms. Chu. At that time I was becoming 'superhuman' myself; but it was obvious how utterly inferior I was to the Storied Watcher. I would agree with you that no human being – however Machiavellian – could contrive such a scheme... but we are – to put it mildly – *not* talking about a human being here. Perhaps she has some kind of 'questing-power' that she has never revealed to us. Is this not at least *possible*?"

"But y'all sayin' she done *tricked* us, all th'way through," disputed Saquina White. "I *know* Karéin! She just wouldn't *do* nothin' like that to us! We're her kinfolk – she said so, in so many *words!* Is sendin' her family on some damn wild-goose-chase, all 'cross the country, gettin' shot at every five seconds – is *that* what she'd do to her kin? Talk about not 'makin' no sense', Jerry!"

"Mrs. White," spoke up the President, "For what it's worth... the Storied Watcher repeatedly told me, in those conversations that we had, before most of this happened, 'you must understand, sir... I do not *think* like you do'. She went out of her way to inform me that "human-reasoning" meant little to nothing, to her. That mentality was very apparent when she was here earlier today – for example what she did to Matt and Clairie. She even had Ms. Abruzzio – who, I gather, is supposed to have some kind of 'sixth sense' of her own – completely fooled as to what her real plans were. No... I'd say that both Jerry and your friend 'Misha' over there, are almost certainly right. This whole thing... it's been *her* plan, from start to finish –"

"Oh... shove it up your *ass!*" angrily exclaimed Boyd. "I know Karéin too – and you keep claiming that she somehow engineered the cruel torture of her own *son*, not to mention multiple other atrocities, all of which were undertaken not by her, or by anyone under her control, but by the government, and I'll –"

"I do not think that anyone is making such an assertion, Major Boyd," the Russian stepped in to say. "Only that the Storied Watcher may have – in some way that we can only guess at – set the basic patterns of these 'quests', in motion. She probably does not have the ability to micro-manage each and every exact event that occurs, along the way. Nor does she likely *want* to... doing so would invalidate the entire point of the exercise. And perhaps our ability to navigate past or overcome all the challenges that we encountered prior to arriving here, was in *itself* a 'test' of some kind. The only way to know for sure, would simply be to ask her."

"Well... for all we know... she ate one of them nukes up there, over the Atlantic," unhappily commented Devon White. "So we might not get a chance."

Another silence fell over the group.

"Don't think this lets you off the hook!" growled Jacobson, pointing his finger at the President. "We're not here just representing ourselves; there are many other innocent victims of the government who are looking to us to deliver justice. You have a hell of a lot to answer for – 'test', or 'no test'."

The U.S. leader was about to reply, but he was interrupted by a shout from Agent Kortish, in the communications-room.

"Mr. President," he said, "I've got a phone-call that you need to take!"

"I'm *very* busy, Curt," argued the President. "Our discussions are at a critical stage!"

"Should I tell Ms. Chu and Ms. Abruzzio, that they should call back later, sir?" pleasantly replied the Secret Service agent. "They say they've tried to get through six times already."

Sorry... No Bubble-Bath, No Romance-Novel

The President pressed a button hidden underneath the Resolution Desk, over which he supported his fore-body with two outstretched arms on the desk-surface.

A familiar woman's voice sounded from speakers recessed into strategic locations all around the Oval Office.

"This is Minnie Chu," it announced. "May I speak with the President, please?"

Grins and gasps of relief – along with whispered prayers of thanks, from both sides of the White family – were evident with everyone except, perhaps, the dour Secret Service leader-agent.

"Speaking!" responded the President. "Ms. Chu... it's *wonderful* to hear from you... but we thought you were –"

"*Dead?*" interrupted the voice on the speakers. "Sir – if you *only* knew, or could possibly appreciate, how close Sylvia and I have come to that, over the last hour –"

"Ms. *Abruzzio's* there too?" asked the astonished U.S. leader.

"Ah, sir," came another voice, clearly that of the former JPL scientist, "To paraphrase a famous writer, 'reports of our demise have been somewhat exaggerated'. Minnie's right, though – you aren't going to *believe* what we've both just been through. It starts with, 'jumping out of a flying bomb, at twenty thousand feet or so, without a plan or a parachute'... and it goes downhill, pun intended, rapidly from there. We had just landed on a beach, when the overpressure from the bomb – the *first* one, that is – hit the surface of the ocean. We almost got washed out to sea by an instant *tsunami* caused by the shock-wave. Minnie and I had to use our telekinetic abilities to fish out people from the water. It was a very near thing."

Devon and Saquina White sat together on the arm of one of the Oval Office couches. The former Mars mission communications-officer put his arm around his wife, as a crying Saquina White bowed her head and prayed in a low voice, "Thank y'all, *Jaysus*..."

"Saquina," requested Abruzzio, "Would you mind mentioning to Moira, that I'm still alive?"

"Of *course*," complied the former Compton-native.

Migod, silently sent Boyd to Jacobson.

She made *it!*

Yeah, agreed the former Mars mission commander, *that's great news. Honest it is.*

I got no idea how she did it... but she must *have learned how to fly – we can be sure of* that.

Though I'm happy to know that Minnie's alive... it does *change the picture.*

It gives us a lot less time to decide to do whatever we're going to do with the man in front of us, with the government, with... everything.

If Minnie shows up here – especially if Sylvia and Jerry back her up – things could get ugly, real fast. The President might believe that he can violently resist us.

We'd win... but the cost in lives and collateral damage could be disastrous.

We had better be able to press our case before any of that happens... you agree?

I got your back, came Boyd's response.

I'm not for letting the son of a bitch off, scot-free... 'test' or 'no test'.

"I feel the same way, Mrs. White," nodded the President. "*Surely* the Lord's with us tonight."

He again spoke upward and outward.

"Any sign of the alien, Ms. Chu... Ms. Abruzzio?" he asked.

"Unfortunately not, Mr. President," came the former FBI team-leader's voice. "Contrary to Mr. Crowford's expectations, Karéin never even came aboard my aircraft... at least not that I was aware of. Nor – for the record – did I ever call for her to do so. I have no idea what happened to her."

Joy turned quickly to groans of deflated sadness, among the group.

"I believe that I saw Karéin – or manifestations of her powers – in the same general airspace as the Airborne Command-Post, just before it became too dangerous to stick around... that is, before I jumped clear of the airplane and flew back to Earth, along with Minnie," recounted Abruzzio. "I lost track of the Storied Watcher, after that."

"We *do*, however," continued Chu, "Have a number of refugees from the aircraft, who we were able to bring safely down with us. Unfortunately, this amounts to only a small fraction of those who were on the Airborne Command-Post. I'd have to assume, sir, that General Blanshard, the Vice-President, Warnock, Crowford and most of the others who were on the plane... didn't make it. They're certainly not with *us*."

"You don't know for sure?" pressed the President.

"No sir," answered Chu. "But you have to understand – we only barely got far enough away from the ACP to survive when it blew... and we had alien-powers to help protect us. A human being any closer would have had no chance."

"Well... there *were* a few parachutes, who we simply didn't have time to rescue," noted Abruzzio. "But they were popped out too early – so close to Ground – err, Air – Zero – that the heat-rays would have likely set them afire. The only relief, if you can call it that, would have been when the parachutes burned through and then these people would have plummeted down into the Atlantic. A terrible way to die... no doubt about *that*."

"Curt," directed the President, "Re-direct the search-parties who were looking for Chu and Abruzzio, to search for survivors from the Command-Post – special priority on locating the Vice-President, the FBI Director, General Blanshard and Harold Crowford... or their remains. We need positive identification if possible. Keep looking for the alien, as before. Understood?"

"Understood, sir," acknowledged Kortish, who again started working the communications-gear.

"So," inquired the U.S. leader, "What's your situation now, Ms. Chu... Ms. Abruzzio? What are your immediate plans?"

"I'll let Sylvia speak for herself, Mr. President," spoke the team-leader's voice, "But honestly... I'm *exhausted*. I just jumped out a plane going five hundred miles per hour, at twenty thousand feet, and had to learn how to breathe without oxygen and how to fly, all by myself, on the way down. Then I had two hydrogen bombs, set off over my head. That's on top of having been in multiple fire-fights while on the plane, and I could easily have been killed in any one of those. I'd just like the opportunity to *relax*... bubble-bath, hot meal, sit in bed reading a romance-novel... that kind of thing. You know, Karéin's *Fire* is weird; I somehow know that if I call on it, I can keep going indefinitely... but the human side of me is just completely zonked, mentally. If that makes any sense."

"Minnie's pretty much summed up how I feel too, sir," added Abruzzio's voice. "We're stuck down here in Atlantic City – we're using a communicator belonging to an ambulance-attendant – hey *you* there! Yeah, *you!* You're gonna be *famous*, now... so, *thanks!* But, uhh, anyway, Mr. President... I'd like some time off, too, honestly. My rainbow-shield just absorbed enough fast neutrons to kill you seventeen times over – and that's kind of *draining*, if you know what I mean. At least there seems to be no fallout coming back on land; Minnie and I would have sensed it, if so. The winds are blowing to the east so in the short term it's not going to be a serious threat to places like

Philadelphia and New York. But as to our immediate situation... we're completely out of money, I left my credit-cards back in the *Mailànkh Express*, and they confiscated Minnie's I.D. the first day that she was on the airplane... isn't that right?"

"Yeah," confirmed Chu. "Not that having it would be of much help, anyway; most of the hotels around here have their reservation-systems down, because of the bombs' EMP-effects, and Warnock seems to have rescinded my Bureau standing expense-account-privileges, when he imprisoned me on the plane. Incidentally, there's a lot of other damage down here – broken windows, fires, downed power-lines, car-accidents, *et cetera* – would probably have been much worse if it hadn't been raining here, just before the bombs detonated. We've heard rumors from the ambulance-guys – they've got a pulse-resistant radio-system – that Philadelphia and New York City got hit pretty hard, especially by the second weapon... electrical-grids are almost completely down and there's chaos breaking out everywhere. I'm just glad the damn things went off, way out to sea. This could have been a *disaster*, Mr. President!"

"You'll get no argument from me on that subject, Ms. Chu," the President agreed. "Curt... you got a fix on her signal yet?"

"I've looped in the auto-locators, sir," responded the Service agent. "They're acting up, but the hardened secondaries are still on-line... wait a second... yeah, okay, Mr. President sir, I think I've got them. Yeah... *there* they are. We got map-coordinates, locked in."

"Can we get a helicopter out there?" requested the President.

"I can *try*, sir," Kortish obliged, "But the resources are heavily-committed already... looks like a lot of our non-combat air assets are grounded for reasons of 'systems-failures'... probably EMP. I'll see if I can divert one of the operational ones, from the nearby airbases."

"Good... keep working on it," said the President. "Let me know when it's on its way. Anyway, Ms. Chu... Ms. Abruzzio... I'll take this opportunity to thank you, both on my behalf and that of the nation, for the bravery that you've shown in this matter. I'm sure I'll be seeing you here in the Oval Office for an award-ceremony, when all this is over with and we return to normalcy."

"Can we speak with her, please?" asked Jacobson.

"Who's that?" instantly queried Chu's worried voice. "It sounds like –"

"Yeah... you *got* it," the former Mars mission commander confirmed. "Good to hear from you, Minnie. Until a few minutes ago, everybody here thought you and probably Sylvia too, didn't make it. That's great news, of course... but we're still terribly worried about Karéin."

"So are we, Commander," observed Abruzzio. "She *must* have had something to do with the second nuke having been diverted away from Minnie's plane... and from D.C.. My mind has been searching for her... but nothing so far. Oh – how's Rainbow?"

"She's fine," noted Jacobson. "She's in the *Express* with Hector."

"Make sure you tell her that Mommy's oh-kay... will you? Tell Hector too, please."

"Of *course*," politely agreed the former Mars mission commander.

"Listen, Commander," spoke Chu, "I realize that this might not be a good time, but... I take it you're there along with the rest of your team... in the Oval Office... is that right?"

"Definitely," said Jacobson. "Cherie was hurt earlier and is recovering; Wolf and Melissa are AWOL – we're hoping they're alright. Devon, Saquina, Brent, Misha and I are here with the President and Jerry Kaysten... also the First Lady and the President's two kids."

"So... what's the situation?" carefully inquired the former FBI team-leader.

"Hi, Minnie – welcome back," interjected Boyd. "I don't want to speak for anyone else... but from my POV, I'd say that the situation's 'unresolved', as of yet. Anybody want to dispute that?"

"Nope... I'd say y'all bang-on there, my man," observed Devon White. "We were prayin' for y'all – Sylvia too, Minnie."

"Thanks," said Chu.

"Ms. Chu," offered the Russian, "We only just arrived here in the White House, after being subjected to a determined attack by local armed forces, on the way in. Fortunately this did not result in any casualties on our side, but the *Mailànkh Express* may have been damaged. Frankly – as you can probably imagine – our discussions with the President did not get off to the best start."

"Forgive me for being so blunt then," stated Abruzzio, "But I think you owe it to Minnie and I, to know the truth. Commander – should we expect to see news-reports about a *second* dead President... and a wrecked White House?"

"I'd say those outcomes are still a possibility," ominously remarked Jacobson, "But after what our friend Jerry just explained to us... they're an increasingly remote one."

"What do you *mean*, Sam?" asked Chu. "You've got a basically-helpless President in front of you – Jerry certainly can't stop you all by himself, and from what I heard from Sylvia, neither Bob nor Tommy nor Hector are going to intervene... what are you *waiting* for? Isn't, 'kicking the President's head in', what you were out to accomplish, right from the start?"

"Minnie," they heard Abruzzio's voice cautioning, "I don't think it's a good idea to challenge him like that –"

"She's not telling me anything I don't already know," Jacobson pointed out. "But the situation – some of the basic assumptions behind it, anyway – has *changed*. In a very frustrating and unfair way, I'd add."

"I'm not following you," said a confused Chu.

"Jerry... what's going *on*?" demanded Abruzzio.

"Why don't you come down here and find out?" teased Kaysten.

"Jerry – if you're going to play games, I'll just tell her myself!" warned Jacobson.

Those with "Mars Ears" heard Abruzzio whispering, "what's going *on*, over there?"

Then they heard Chu say – just before she cut the connection – "Mr. President, you can cancel the helicopter... Sylvia and I will be there in a few minutes."

"But how are you going to – oh... *right*," the President started.

"Just don't shoot at us, when we get there," requested the former team-leader. "That goes for you *too*, Sam!"

The line went dead.

"I guess we've got one more 'copter available now, Curt," observed the U.S. leader.

He'll Fit Nicely In An Urn

Jacobson, Boyd, the two Whites and Misha had been vociferously arguing with both the President and Kaysten for several minutes, with each side sticking obstinately to its parochial perspective and not much being accomplished in terms of progress toward an agreement.

At this point, various pairs of "Mars Ears" took note of on-coming war-songs. This was in spite of the fact that the approaching beings involved, had intentionally suppressed this awkward manifestation of their alien-powers, in hopes of approaching the White House relatively undetected.

Something looking like a self-propelled meteor – a flame-enshrouded, brutally-hot, glowing, *something* – did several passes over the Presidential palace, flying in a circular motion, cautiously descending a little more with each transit, as if it were trying to test out defenses.

He's trying to tease out their IR-seekers, silently sent Boyd to Jacobson.

Two other such entities – much less spectacular, but foreboding none the less, flew irregular, slower patterns in the darkness further above, in classic "top-cover" fashion.

Finally, the fireball started to descend, almost vertically, with an intended landing-spot on the South Lawn, about fifty feet distant from the Oval Office door. It reached an altitude about twenty feet above the roof of the White House, when three man-portable missiles streaked in its direction.

One was blown out of the sky, by a smaller fireball, that shot outward from the larger one; a second missile fell to one of the alert Tommy's screaming *Fire*-shots; but the third – perhaps thrown off by some unknown homing-failure – curved upward and detonated within ten feet or so of one of the other interlopers, about a hundred feet above the White House. The missile flew so quickly that whatever got hit, had little to no time to maneuver away.

A powerful explosion rocked the Oval Office.

"Mr. *President* – get *down!*" yelled Kortish, as he rushed from the communications-shack.

Kaysten, of course, had beaten the Secret Service agent to it; the Chief of Staff was already draped all over his boss.

"*Damn it!*" cursed the U.S. leader. "I gave *orders* to hold our fire! I want whoever disobeyed me, court-marshaled and thrown in the brig, on the *spot!* If we've hurt Chu, or Abruzzio –"

The aerial-intruder that had suffered the missile-impact, crashed to the South Lawn. As it fell into a lighted area, even the President and the humans in the vicinity could make out that this was a dark-skinned, slim female figure. She lay prone on the ground, moaning and spitting up blood.

Ramirez was the first to get to her side.

"*Melissa!*" he cried. "*Dios mio!* Somebody come and *help!*"

Saquina White broke contact with her husband, and, though moving at lightening-speed out the door toward the fallen-teenager, managed to spit a warning to the President.

"I *swear* if she daid – I'm gonna fuckin' sink this whole house in the Potomac... with y'all *in* it!"

Devon White followed her out the door.

"Y'all really pushin' your *luck*, slick!" he spat. "Y'all gonna *float* when my wife does that... 'cause y'all gonna be in the middle of an *iceberg!*"

He dashed over to where Melissa had fallen.

An upset Jacobson added, "You wanted an explanation of why we're here, Mr. President? Well... there's your example! It's what we've been facing since we damn well landed here. And it's going to *stop* – one way or another! Of that, I *assure* you!"

"Curt," demanded the flustered, frightened President, "Issue an order – on my personal authority – for the Service and the military, to *stand down!* We can't afford any more fuck-ups like what we just saw happening! The fate of the *Republic* may depend on it!"

"I'll of course do that, sir," responded Kortish, "But remember that we have a lot of GrayWar around here – they were subcontracted to run the White House's perimeter defenses. They answer to *their* leadership... not to us. We may have to forcibly disarm them. Do I have your authorization to do that, sir?"

"You *bet* you do!" quickly agreed the President. "And if they resist, tell them that you're authorized to use whatever level of force is necessary!"

In another couple of seconds, many of the more-than-humans had clustered around the wounded teenager.

The fireball dropped down on to the South Lawn grass and revealed a sinister-looking, crimson-eyed Wolf within it.

They heard Melissa groaning, "Wasn't 'spectin' no such thang... didn't have mah shield up all th'ways..."

Saquina White's voice spoke, "Take it easy, child – lookin' like y'all got a broken arm... we'll tend to y'all in the ship."

It appeared that they were taking her back into the *Mailànkh Express*. Sullivan appeared at the air-ship's entrance-hatch and ushered them in.

From high above, the angry voice of Cherie Tanaka – it was artificially-boosted in some weird way – broadcast a warning to everyone in a wide radius.

"The next government employee who lifts so much as a *finger* against us," it boomed, "Will be *destroyed* – along with everything within twenty feet of him! And if I see any vehicles leaving the building, they'll be *vaporized!*"

Wolf just stood in place for a short while, looking around carefully, as if he was anticipating another attack. Then he wheeled in place, and – with the red glow in his eyes making him look every bit the part of a devil – began moving slowly and methodically in the direction of the Oval Office.

He stopped about twenty feet away from the door separating the office from the South Lawn outside and bellowed, "I know you're *in* there, fucker – and thanks for makin' what comes next, an easy decision! Come a *long* way for this. You can run... but there'll be no hidin'!"

"Who's... who's *that?*" stammered a fearful President.

"That'd be Wolf," evenly noted Jacobson. "About 50,000 degrees of real bad attitude."

"Commander," quickly mentioned Boyd, "What you want to do? You *know* what he's capable of!"

"I'll give you ten seconds to show your sorry ass, before I burn this whole place to the ground!" growled the voice of the bounty-hunter, from outside.

"Sir... we've got to get you down to the bunker, *now!*" shouted Kortish.

"Yes... I think you're right... let's go," agreed the President. "We'll issue the stand-down orders from down there."

"I'll see what I can do up here," said Kaysten. "I'll be better off if I have some room to maneuver."

"Don't *bother*," called Boyd, to the President and the Service-agent, as they were about to reach the inside-door heading to the rest of the White House, in the company of the First Lady and the two Presidential children. "Wherever you end up, Wolf will eventually find you.. and he'll simply burn through any wall you put between 'you', and 'him'. He can melt tungsten steel like it's warm butter; I saw him *do* it, at Fort Knox. If you try to fly away you'll be blown to bits by that guy, or by Cherie Tanaka, or by both. *That's* what you're up against."

"You will note, sir," dryly added the Russian, "That Major Boyd said, 'you'... not, 'we'."

"Fine, then!" sighed the U.S. leader.

He whispered something to the First Lady and his children. A lively dispute seemed to be breaking out, but at length, the rest of the First Family – escorted by Kortish – disappeared into the interior recesses of the White House. The President and Kaysten stayed just inside the Oval Office, hovering around the door leading to the rest of the West Wing.

"You try to escape, and I'll do you *myself!*" warned Boyd.

"There's no need for that, Major Boyd," called back the President. "I'm not going anywhere. I mean to see all this *resolved*, once and for all... whatever it takes."

"Let's try to talk with Wolf," proposed Jacobson. "We got nothing to lose."

Both Misha and Boyd nodded affirmatively and they followed the former Mars mission commander out the Oval Office door, into the South Lawn area.

"Well, well... if it ain't my bestest *amigos*," snickered the bounty-hunter, upon seeing the three arrayed in front of him, about ten feet away. "See you all beat me too it. Or... *did* you?"

The heat from his presence was oppressive, even at this distance.

"How'd you figure we'd headed back here?" inquired Jacobson.

"That always *was* the plan... wasn't it?" Wolf replied. "Anyways... met up with Cherie – she's still flyin' round up there, deal with any other little surprises that get thrown our way – and Melissa... put down in some little place, walked in to a bar, watched the TV-reports, saw that somethin' big's goin' down here, and, well – can't expect us to miss the party... now *can* you?"

"For sure," deflected Jacobson. "Thanks for the help against the interceptors, back there over Virginia."

"Oh... I'm gettin' better at *that*, all the time," boasted the bounty-hunter. "Another six or seven to my credit, at the very least."

There was an awkward silence, and then he again spoke up.

"So... where *is* he?" he demanded. "Anything *left* of him? You want me to dispose of the 'mortal remains'... I'm up for that."

"If what you mean by that is the President," remarked Jacobson, "The answer is, 'he's very much still alive'... probably hiding somewhere in the White House. Listen, Wolf... we've got to talk about what we do, here –"

"Maybe we're not *communicatin'* very well," challenged the heat-emanating bounty-hunter. "If you ain't taken the first shot at the fucker, yet... that's *your* decision. I got my own. I ask only one thing of you, Mr. Space Man – and that is, 'stand aside'."

"Wolf," spoke Misha, "Every one of us – as you know – is anything *but* sympathetic to the American President, as well as the mendacity and indiscriminate use of violence, that we have come to expect from his Administration –"

"There you go again, usin' them fancy-ass words, pardner," quipped the bounty-hunter. "Thought we had an *agreement* about that. What exactly is a 'mendacity'?"

"It means, 'he lies through his teeth all the time'," explained Boyd.

"Anyway," said the Russian, "Neither Commander Jacobson, nor I, nor – correct me if I am wrong – Major Boyd here, has anything invested in his survival –"

"You got *that* right!" tersely opined Boyd. "I'd even draw straws with Mr. Flying Gas Barbecue there, for 'who gets to disintegrate him first'."

"Well then... what the fuck we *waitin'* for?" asked Wolf.

"While you were away, much has happened to complicate the situation," continued Misha. "Jerry Kaysten is in there and he is claiming that he will defend the President, should we attack. Obviously, Jerry can likely not resist us for long – but he could potentially injure one of us or give the President a chance to escape, if he has not already done so. Secondly, we have just discovered that Minnie Chu and Sylvia Abruzzio survived the two nuclear explosions – albeit only narrowly – and they are now on their way here, using their own abilities. In other words... they have both learned how to fly, and, apparently, the potency of their alien-powers has been increasing *rapidly*. This would greatly increase the risk factor if we they were to join Jerry in defending the President. So –"

"All this just says to me, 'we'd better grease the fucker, while we've still got *time!*'" retorted the bounty-hunter.

They could feel the terrible heat (though, it was invisible) surging from him.

"Wait... *wait*, for *God's* sake, man!" loudly protested Jacobson. "Wolf, you *know* that I don't give a rat's ass whether this guy lives or dies... I've hated his guts since he imprisoned my team and I, just after landing back on Earth. Him trying to kidnap and torture my family, hasn't endeared him to me, either. But something else has happened while we were on our way here, and I honestly don't know what to make of it. Before we do something that can't be reversed, we need to think it through."

"I'll give you a minute or two to say your piece, Mr. Space Man," growled Wolf, "And then I'm goin' in there, 'risk factors' or not. I didn't come *this* far, to let that fucker get away!"

"Okay... *okay!*" stammered a clearly-worried Jacobson. "So here it is. We don't know where Karéin is – she might have survived the nukes, she might not have – but apparently while she was here, before she and the rest of them set off in the *Express* to divert Minnie's airplane away from D.C. and also to deal with the second H-bomb, she said that bringing her family, that is Tommy, Bob and so on – and us – that was some kind of 'test' or something. That is... 'you can either act with vengeance, and fail the test... or act with mercy, and *pass* the test' –"

"What a pile of horse-shit!" snorted Wolf. "Who *told* you all this, Jacobson? Don't tell me... let me guess – Mr. President's bum-boy –"

"Yeah, it *was* Jerry... and we know all *about* his silver tongue, and that he has an obvious reason to lie to us, or stall for time," spoke Boyd. "The problem is that Billings and Tommy sort of confirmed what had happened, in the short time that we had to discuss it with them, prior to getting here. Jerry's claiming that this entire exercise – that is, Karéin dropping us off in Florida, and doing the same thing for Minnie and her team, up in the Northwest – it's some kind of 'quest', possibly involving the use of alien-powers on the Storied Watcher's part, that we know nothing about and that she never revealed to us. Personally, I think it *is* bullshit... but I *could* be wrong. And if *that's* the case –"

"What's all that to *me?*" contemptuously argued the former bounty-hunter. "I flunked out of school in, like, sixth-grade. Never *could* do tests... never cared about it, either."

"Oh – use your *brains*, man... if you've *got* any!" shot back Jacobson. "If it *is* some kind of contrived 'alien-quest' – and we abjectly flunk it, by slaughtering the President out of hand – we'd likely have to kill or injuring his wife and kids too, as they'd *certainly* stand in our way – we might be seriously pissing of Karéin *herself! If*, that is... she's still alive, and *if* she'd hold it against us. Neither of which we know for sure."

"What we are saying, my friend," added the Russian, "Is... 'do you want to run the risk of antagonizing the most powerful being in the Solar System, just to be able to kill the American President now – as opposed to, later'? We have already proved that his defenses are useless against us. The only rational thing to do is simply to wait until we can find out what the Storied Watcher really *meant*, by what she is alleged to have said, earlier. *Then* – not now – we can act."

The bounty-hunter – unlike himself – seemed genuinely nonplussed.

Then he countered, "What if Little Miss Comet-Whacker never comes back at all? Or what if she's takin' a nice little three-week vacation on some beach somewhere? We just gonna sit here suckin' our thumbs? Then why'd we fly all over the fuckin' *country*, gettin' our asses shot off? Then it's all for fuckin' *nothin'*, Jacobson! *You* can show up here all dressed up in a suit of diamonds with nowhere to go, for all *I* care – but I ain't leavin' here without finishin' what we *started!*"

"Or, 'what if she shows up in the next five minutes, and tells us to leave the bastard alone'?" unhelpfully added Boyd. "Commander – we've got a narrow window of opportunity, here. Wolf may not be articulating this elegantly but I think he's right. We *know* that Minnie and Sylvia are on their way here. We have to move, or possibly forever lose our *chance!*"

"I *hear* you... both of you," muttered Jacobson, "But, we also got to live with the consequences... *forever*. There's another factor here, that you haven't yet heard about, Wolf. Minnie and Sylvia mentioned that the former Vice-

President – who took over some time ago – is now probably dead; he got wasted, along with the FBI director, when Minnie's airplane blew up. That means, if we grease the guy behind us in the White House, the country effectively has no President *at all* –"

"Why's that *my* problem?" shrugged the bounty-hunter.

"Because we have no idea where the Speaker of the House of Representatives is," explained the former Mars mission commander. "He's theoretically next in the line of succession, when the Vice-President isn't available. And whoever he is... I very much doubt he'd accept the job, with us floating around here, able to kill him the moment that he pisses us off. It would be the same situation as we face now with the existing guy."

"A society this complicated cannot function without a visible, effective leader," opined Misha. "The U.S. government might degenerate into chaos, as different factions fight for control – and that struggle could take a long time to be sorted out, with severe economic consequences while it was going on. You could destabilize the entire world economy. The American people would blame *us*, for having brought about this state of affairs, without having a viable plan about how to manage it. We could become very unpopular here... we might have to flee the United States, once and for all."

"This all sounds like a bunch of fuckin' *cowards*, thinkin' up lame excuses why they got cold feet, at the last minute!" contested Wolf, his infernal aura waxing yet again. You jokers want to plead innocence and pin it all on *my* ass when Mr. President goes up in smoke, I'm good with that!"

"Wolf – listen to *reason* – I'm not arguing with you – he *deserves* whatever he gets... but we have to have a *plan* for what comes next!" pleaded Jacobson.

A small ring of fire appeared at the bounty-hunter's feet. It was slowly proceeding to envelop his ankles, and was advancing up his legs.

Boyd, Misha and Jacobson could not understand how Wolf's clothes were not charred to a crisp; the heat was *murderous*, and already almost at the limit of their force-field-reinforced ability to tolerate. It certainly would have inflicted serious burns on a normal human being standing this close. The three more-than humans in front of the bounty-hunter reflexively took a step back.

The grass under his feet was sizzling, blackening and starting to smoke.

"I don't want a fight," ominously remarked Wolf, "But you better not stand in my way!"

"Okay... *okay!*" desperately retreated Jacobson. "I *get* it! Just answer me this *one* thing... will you?"

"*What?*" growled an irritated Wolf.

"The moment after you vaporize the bastard," challenged the former Mars mission-leader, "Are you ready to stand in front of the TV-cameras, proudly declare, 'I just murdered the President of the United States – and his whole family – and I'm your new President... two cheers for *me*'?"

"It would be more like, 'I am your new *king*,'" mordantly observed the Russian.

"I just *told* you, Jacobson," the bounty-hunter countered, "That's somebody else's problem! Like... *yours!*"

"Oh, *no,* you don't!" shot back Jacobson. "I'm telling you now, man, that if you go off half-cocked and do this – my next move is to blame *you* for everything and then get my family down to an airport, hijack a plane and get my butt as far away from the United States as I can –"

"That idea is *wildly* unrealistic and optimistic, Commander Jacobson," interrupted Misha. "After matters settled down and a stable government again took control here in Washington, there would be nowhere on the *planet* that anyone associated with this – including myself – could find a safe refuge. We would be 'the worst terrorists in human history'; we would be hunted and attacked anywhere we went. Perhaps, if she is still alive, we could ask Karéin to transport us to Mars. But even *there*, we would be vulnerable to a nuclear sneak attack, delivered by long-range space-rocket. We would have precisely two options : one, to try to rule the United States as dictators; two, to surrender and face life in prison... or worse."

"But they already think of us as 'terrorists', anyway," commented Boyd. "We've just *shot* our way in here, after all! The government probably has a rescue-force on its way, as we speak –"

His words were prescient; a large contingent of mixed law enforcement elements and military troops started ringing the three sides of the White House grounds that were immediately visible. They began to deploy machine-guns and other heavy weaponry in strategic locations and seemed to be forcing the burgeoning civilian-crowds in the area, back to further-off parts of central D.C..

"And we've got to assume that we might shortly come under counter-attack by Special Forces," the former Mars mission pilot warned. "We had better get the rest of our people inside either the White House, or in the *Mailànkh Express*. They'll be positioning sharp-shooters all over the place."

"Cherie," Jacobson called up to the hovering Tanaka, "Brent's advising us that the military may be planning an attack. Do you see any signs of that? Or any signs of the President trying to escape?"

A quick scan by the former Mars science officer's enhanced alien-senses revealed that this was indeed likely the case.

"No vehicles coming or going... I see guys with high-powered rifles – snipers, obviously – on three buildings on the other side of the streets," she informed. "And two of them have partners carrying... let's see... those look like man-portable missiles. You want me to vaporize 'em?"

"No... hold off on that for a minute or two – but be ready to go," requested Jacobson. "Nice to see you back in fighting-form, Cherie."

"Thank God you're feeling better," observed a relieved Boyd.

As a determined half-smile appeared on Tanaka's face, a carpet of fire began to spread outward from Wolf's boots. His own flame-shroud was now level with his belt.

"I hear it's a nice carpet he's got in there," hissed the bounty-hunter. "Too bad about that."

"And there's your final reason not to smoke him just yet," claimed Jacobson. "Namely... 'we need him, as a hostage'."

"I got no problem with that," responded Wolf, "But your 'hostage' is gonna fit in an urn."

He bellowed, in the direction of the Oval Office, "You better be sayin' your prayers, fucker – because if there's a God, you're about to *meet* him!"

Despite the threat, Jacobson, Boyd and Misha could tell that the President had not moved from where he had been standing.

You got to admit... the asshole has balls, sent Jacobson.

If I were him, I'd have made a run for it, out one of those escape-tunnels we've always heard about.

You have a point, Commander, silently remarked Boyd.

But where would he run to?

He probably thinks – and he may be right – that we could eventually track and intercept him, if he were to jump on another one of those airborne command-posts. So that's out.

If he tries to hide somewhere on the ground, well... long-term, he'd just be postponing the inevitable. We've proved that the military can't effectively defend him. Not that they'd want to, since it would be suicide on their part.

If he's going to go down in a blaze of glory – bad pun intended – it might as well be here.

Wolf stepped to the right and was heading for the outside door between the Oval Office and the South Lawn. He was walking slowly and deliberately. In two seconds he would have a clear shot at anyone inside that room.

"Back *off!*" they heard Kaysten's voice shout. "Wolf – I love you as a brother, man... don't *do* this! Don't make me sacrifice my *life*, defending the President!"

The bounty-hunter stopped for a second and retorted, "I got nothin' against you, Jerry – but if you're in the way, that's on *you* – not me! He ain't worth wastin' your life for! *Amscray, amigo!*"

"Wolf – I *beg* you, sir!" exclaimed the Russian, "Do you wish to be remembered as the *murderer* of the only man who can hold your country together?"

What we gonna do? sent an anxious, immensely-frustrated Jacobson.

Even with my force-field fully up – trying to hold him back would be like wrestling with a blast-furnace!

Boyd silently replied,

If you're asking me, "Should I show him what noon on the surface of the Sun feels like", Commander – that'd be a "negative" – I don't give a rat's ass if the President –

Wolf shot a very small fireball at the Oval Office door, whose handle charred instantly. The door flew wide-open, revealing a rapidly-vibrating, glowing-eyed Kaysten, in front of a grim-faced President.

It was at that exact moment, that two familiar war-songs were heard. Their exciting, susurrating beat combined into something whose whole was much more than the sum of its parts.

Those responsible had been flying very low, following the patterns of the streets of downtown Washington, D.C.. They did a slight "pop-up" maneuver to clear the fences separating the South Lawn from the narrow street to the east of the Treasury Building, and then streaked past the upended top of the former Washington Monument, landing just to the east of the Oval Office, behind Wolf, who immediately wheeled in place to observe what was going on.

"Hello, brother!" hailed the loud, proud, clear, defiant voice of Minnie Chu, in the direction of the bounty-hunter.

"Let's *talk!*" she announced.

Family Reunion; Family Feud

"Well, well – if it ain't Little Miss FBI," taunted the flame-enshrouded Wolf. "'Fraid you're a bit on the *late* side, though!"

Though his burning screen protected him from almost every direction, they could still see his sinister, crimson-glowing eyes from inside the infernal surroundings. His feet had started a small grass-fire.

Devon White and his wife had walked away from tending to Melissa, who was ensconced inside the *Mailànkh Express*, apparently with Hector Ramirez and the two GrayWar guys. Billings and Tommy were parked inside the side-portal of the air-ship, watching the goings-on with intense interest. The former Mars mission communications-specialist and his spouse were closer to the White House than the rest. They were about halfway between Chu and Abruzzio, and Wolf, with a clear line of sight to all of them.

The former JPL scientist's little dog raced out of the air-ship, despite best efforts among Billings, Ramirez and several others, to catch it (or, rather, to catch a mirage that they had incorrectly believed to be "Rainbow"). The animal dashed across the lawn, hopping into the air at random intervals, and eventually coming to Abruzzio's side, where it was greeted with the inevitable baby-talk.

Somewhere behind the President, there were the sounds of a commotion. The U.S. leader looked behind him. A few of the others heard him arguing loudly to unknown parties inside the inner reaches of the White House, to the effect of, "I *trusted* you to follow my orders and go with your mother –"

"What are you *saying?*" demanded Chu. "Where's the *President?* You'd better not have –"

"He's in here with me," came Kaysten's voice from just inside the Oval Office. "Mr. Gas Barbecue here is threatening to *kill* him. Since getting to the President means, 'getting past me first', that means, 'he'll have to kill *me*, too'."

He, too, did a double-take to his rear-flank.

"Holy crow – *that* was fast!" Jacobson and few others heard the Chief of Staff say.

"This is no place for kids," mentioned Kaysten, to someone behind him.

"Wolf – is that *true?*" challenged Abruzzio, who had floated down to be at Chu's side.

She saw an overjoyed Moira Sullivan, in the entrance-way to the *Mailànkh Express*, waving to her. Abruzzio returned the gesture.

"*Will* be, in about two seconds... if you fuckers just get out of my *way!*" shouted the bounty-hunter. "I'm makin' no promises about people gettin' hurt, if they act *stupid!*"

"Stand *down!*" shouted Chu. "Wolf – you *know* I can't let you do that!" she added. "My powers have increased *substantially* since you last met me! Let's neither one of us do something that we'll regret later!"

"Yeah, well, Minnie," growled Wolf, "So have *mine!*"

As if to emphasize the point, he lifted off the ground, until he was about eight feet into the air. He looked like a floating fireball. The brilliance of his aura lit up half the South Lawn.

Devon White accosted the bounty-hunter.

"Y'all out of *line* there, jack!" shouted the former Mars mission astronaut. "I hate the man's fuckin' guts too... but 'less y'all want to find out if 'ice' ranks 'fire' – cool yo' jets, slick!"

All around, could feel a sudden chill in the air.

Sparkles of frost were appearing all over White's body.

Saquina White – who had a doughnut-shaped cloud of condensing droplets ringing her and her spouse – added, "Y'all don' listen to my husband... we gonna see how well them fires of yours burn, under ten feet of *water!*"

A bright-eyed Cherie Tanaka called down from above.

"Minnie – you're my sister in the *Fire*... but I owe the big guy more than one," she countered. "He risked his *life* for me! You can't fight *both* of us!"

Abruzzio – with her war-song humming – levitated until she was roughly the same altitude as Tanaka, albeit over a hundred feet away in horizontal separation.

"She *won't* be alone," warned the former JPL scientist, as her dog somehow vanished from sight below. "Cherie – this is the wrong *way!* Nobody should be fighting *anybody!*"

"Sylvia," argued the former Mars mission science officer, "The man down there in that office has been trying to kill us since the moment we started out, down here – and his goons have got my *mother!* You expect me or Wolf to just sit back and let him get away with it, when we've come *this* far?"

"No, I *don't!*" allowed Abruzzio. "What Minnie's saying is, 'threatening the President's life, is backing her into a corner'. She *can't* let Mr. Dumpster-Fire down there, try to kill her Commander-In-Chief... and you *know* it! What the hell's the *matter* with all of you? Where's the *harm*, in waiting a few minutes and *talking*, before somebody pulls the trigger?"

Again, words were prescient. From across the South Lawn in the direction of the Treasury Building, a loud voice sounded over a bull-horn or some similar voice-amplification device.

"This is a first and last warning to the terrorists now intruding on the grounds of the White House!" it bellowed. "Law enforcement has every one of you in the cross-hairs of our sharp-shooters! Get down on your knees with your hands behind your heads, in the next ten seconds... or we'll use lethal force!"

Tanaka – her own voice supernaturally-boosted – angrily answered back, "This is Cherie Tanaka, First of the Holy *Fire*! Take one shot... and I will *personally* vaporize you, as well as everyone and everything within twenty meters of you! We've defeated the entire U.S. Air Force on our way in here – or hadn't your idiot officers, informed you of that?"

"Hold your fire, Cherie!" shouted Chu. "You *know* they can't pierce our force-fields with rifle-bullets!"

They heard the voice of the President, inside the Oval Office, yelling at the top of his lungs, to some unknown persons further inside the residence.

"*Damnit!*" he shrieked, "Is there *anybody* in the government who understands how to follow *orders!* Whoever those guys out there are, I want them relieved of duty, or shot on the spot –"

Another voice – probably that of Kortish, although audible only to Jacobson, Kaysten, Boyd, Misha and Wolf – was heard to say, "GrayWar, sir, nothing we can do –"

"Five *seconds!*" came the amplified voice, from its hidden speaking-location, across the street.

"Four," it counted.

Then, all of a sudden... the count stopped.

Another voice – this one apparently from the southern end of the Eisenhower Building, on the south-west corner of the South Lawn – picked up the narrative.

"Surrender *immediately*, or we'll –" it demanded; but then this putative protagonist, as well, suddenly went silent.

The more-than-humans stood alert, for a few seconds, waiting for more hails from the government's forces. But instead, all that occurred – this time, further away, near the tops of buildings on 17th Street and 15th Street, to the south, were the sounds of some kind of commotion.

From their aerial vantage-points, both Tanaka and Abruzzio were just able to make out soldiers being forcibly ejected through third- or fourth-story windows, then falling – albeit, oddly slowly – to the streets below.

The same thing happened in at least four other buildings, including two that were to the north, on the other, unseen face of the White House.

"What the..." exclaimed the perplexed former Mars science officer.

"Sam... do we have anyone, unaccounted-for, down there?"

"We know where Hendricks and Boatman are," interjected Boyd, "So unless either or both of them learned how to fly –"

Chu looked like she had been punched in the gut; she fell to her knees.

"Major Boyd – what... what do you *mean?*" she stammered. "They were thrown out of the plane – *murdered* – by that bastard, the Vice-President –"

"As they explained to us, Madam," broke in the Russian, "You are half-right... they *were*, indeed, thrown out of your aircraft, without parachutes. But somehow they managed to, ahh, improvise a solution, on the way down. As, indeed, it appears that you have done yourself. They are in what we believe to be a safe location, along with several others."

"*Alive?*" gasped the instantly-crying former team-leader. "*Alive?* Thank *God*... oh my dear Lord..."

She managed to upright herself, while wiping tears of joy and gratitude.

"Damn amazing story... I'll grant you *that*," offered Jacobson. "I don't blame you for how you feel right now, Minnie."

He looked around, doing a quick mental count of his team, and then addressed Billings.

"Bob... who's in there with you?" requested the former Mars mission commander.

"Ain't nobody here but us chickens," quipped the ex-salesman. "Just Tommy, these two GrayWar jerks –"

He turned his head and spoke to unseen parties, "Hey, *you!* Yes... *you* idiots! I don't care if I don't get a buzz, but that's *my* booze – get your hands *off* it!"

Billings now turned outward again and said, "But anyway... Hector's in here too, along with Melissa. Kid's still pretty banged-up but she's recovering damn fast, I'd say. What's this about?"

"Someone – or something – seems to be attacking some of the government's sniper-positions," observed Abruzzio. "Not one of us, as far as I can tell..."

"Tommy and I have been enjoying watching the fireworks, from here," insouciantly mentioned Billings. "My head says 'Minnie'... but my heart says 'Wolf'."

"Thanks for the support... I *think*," offered a still-shaken Chu.

"Did I tell you that I usually don't do what my head says?" the salesman replied.

"You didn't *have* to," sarcastically parried the former FBI team-leader.

"Well, Bob," offered Wolf, "You get your ass out here and help me do the fucker – I'll even give you the first shot. Or at Jerry, if that's more to your likin'."

"I *heard* that," came Kaysten's voice, from inside the Oval Office. "I love *you*, too!"

"A second chance to..." Billings started to say; but then he did a double-take at the severed top-half of the former Washington Monument, at rest in its upside-down indentation in the South Lawn.

The side of the vandalized thing was more directly in his line of sight than for others in the area, though it was in fact visible to two or three of those milling about.

"Hey... did any of you notice *that*?" called out the ex-salesman.

"What, Bob?" demanded Devon White. "More of them military guys?"

"No – something written – no, uhh, *inscribed*, it more looks like – on the side of this damn big thing that Sari dropped down as a lawn ornament," noted Billings.

Immediately, both Abruzzio and Tanaka abandoned their positions and flew downward, hovering about five feet off the lawn in front of the side of the Monument, to which the ex-salesman had directed them.

"Wow!" spoke the former JPL scientist, "He's right about the 'inscribing' thing – this is deeper than any chisel could do – looks like it's *melted*, in fact. And –"

"Yeah... okay," shouted Jacobson, who had – along with the Russian – taken the opportunity to quietly move directly in front of the Oval Office door, so as to block the line of fire from outside to inside the White House. "But what does it *say*?"

"You're not going to *believe* this," relayed Abruzzio, "It says,

'*A stone rolls downward;*
The gods of the mountain, can either...
Make war amongst themselves, and see the village-folk be crushed...
OR...
They can work together, as brothers and sisters, to stop a needless doom...
Before all is too late'."

"Well... what the fuck's *that* mean?" demanded the hovering, flaming Wolf, from behind his meteor-like fire-shield. "Riddles ain't my thing,"

"Riddle me *this!*" a smiling Abruzzio called back. "*Who*, do you suppose, could sneak in here – while all this is going on, and we're all a half-second from pulling the trigger on each other – and not be noticed, at all?"

A broad smile appeared on Billings face, as the rest of them heard Tommy shrieking at the top of his lungs, "Mister Billings – you *mean* –"

"You *bet*, kid!" answered the gratified ex-salesman.

Ooo – Oooo – Ooooo – wailed an enticing, surreal-sounding war-song, its subtle, pulsating back-beat issuing simultaneously from every direction.

A slim female figure with weird-looking sunglasses and flowing blond hair under a black skull-cap, appeared as if from nowhere, standing on top of the White House, over the Diplomatic Room out-jut.

She was clad in a blue-flame-flickering fortress of ebon armor, with a buckler and flaming sword in hand.

Her dark cape billowed out like a spinnaker.

All In A (Hard) Day's Work

"There goes our shot at him!" glumly muttered Boyd, *sotto voce*.

"Not *necessarily*," countered Jacobson. "We have to figure out what her *game* is, here."

"I shall be most interested to see," commented the Russian.

Despite Billings attempts to restrain him, Tommy rocketed out of the airship, flying through the air to meet the descending Storied Watcher, about fifty feet off the ground.

The two slowly came to earth, still embracing.

The weirding-sunglasses disappeared, revealing the alien-girl's face and shining eyes.

"*Karéin!*" shouted Tanaka, Chu, Abruzzio and Saquina White, almost in unison. In less than a full second they had all joined her in front of the South Portico. Multiple, tearful hugs – given and taken despite the flaming defenses of *Virya Ahn'jë* – followed in rapid succession.

Abruzzio's dog appeared out of nowhere and received a friendly head-pat from the alien-girl.

Many others, from Ramirez to Devon White, waved welcome-signs to the Storied Watcher.

A visibly-deflated Wolf dropped down from the sky as well; his fire-shroud waned away.

"Couldn't you have waited, say, just ten minutes longer, or somethin'?" he complained. "President and me... not to mention Mr. Space Man over there... we had *business!*"

"So do *I*, noble Brother of the *Fires* – both types thereof," offered Karéin-Mayréij, with a pleasant, saturnine smile on her face. "It is fortunate that your 'business', has not yet precluded my own."

She looked around, in several directions.

"Bob... where is *Bob?*" demanded the alien-girl.

Billings sprinted out of the air-ship and charged up to the Storied Watcher. He, too, embraced her, while suffering no ill-effects from the flame-flicks on her body-armor.

"Welcome home, honey," he gratefully greeted. "Some of these guys were worried, but not ol' Bob – I've learned my lesson about doubting you!"

"Your love has kept me *so* strong," she responded. "How can I tell you?"

Devon White, Boyd, Jacobson and Hector Ramirez had also drawn near, by now.

"Karéin," cautioned Abruzzio, "The 'particle-shine'... it's *on* you... I can sense it..."

"Wow... yeah," added Tanaka. "You're *radioactive!* If you got too close to a human being –"

"I... oops!" admitted the abashed alien-girl. "I tried to suppress it... but this was difficult, as I feel it not inside me, as you would from outside. Sylvia – I pray you, sister – draw it forth from me... take it into yourself, as I instructed up at the northern camp. Are you ready?"

"Yes... sure," replied the former JPL scientist.

Abruzzio extended her forearms, as the rest stepped back from close proximity to Karéin-Mayréij. A "rainbow" emanated from the former JPL scientist's arms, enveloping the Storied Watcher for a second or two. Abruzzio winced, shook her head as if trying to recover from a hangover, and then pulled back, causing the rainbow to disappear.

"Whew!" she gasped. "That was a... *lot*... like I'd expect to get from a dozen reactor fuel-rods. Where the H *were* you, Karéin?"

"I was far *too* close to one of those accursed 'atom-smashing bombs' when it worked its sinister wrath," explained the Storied Watcher. "But I survived... after a long fall, and, uhh, what one might call, a 'deep dive' – at quite a depth, the underwater pressure becomes oppressive enough to awaken even one who has earlier been knocked senseless. At that juncture I decided that I fancied your planet's upper-atmosphere more than I did its cold, ocean-abyss... so upward I went. Then I came here."

Stunned looks showed on several surrounding faces.

"So, honey... you played footsie with an H-bomb, laughed at several jillion degrees of nuclear heat, fell, like, ten thousand feet straight down, sank halfway to the bottom of the ocean... all in a day's work – right?" quipped a bemused Billings.

"How to say – oh, yes... 'pretty much so'," confirmed the alien-girl, with an insouciant shrug. "Only... may I not have many more 'days of work', such as this, Bob... one was more than enough! May I ask you something, my love?"

"*Go* for it!" said the grinning ex-salesman.

"How many is a 'jillion'?" she inquired, with a quizzical look; and none could tell if she was really joking. "That is a really big number... is it not?"

The crowd laughed with a mixture of awe, hysteria and relief.

"Listen... all of you," requested Karéin-Mayréij, "It is *wonderful* to see you arrayed here – I feared the worst for you, Min-nie, and equally for Sylvia – my heart leaps with joy at seeing you oh-kay... but some are missing. What of Jerr-ee Kaysten, Will Hendricks, Otis Boatman and Melissa Claremont? I pray that they are not –"

"Boatman and Hendricks are at a 'safe location', protecting our families," interjected Jacobson. "Melissa's inside the *Express* – she took a missile on the way in here. Hurt pretty badly but now recovering satisfactorily, we're told; Sylvia's friend and the GrayWar guys are standing by her. By the way, the President's two kids, who we're told you had some kind of interaction with... they skedaddled into the White House to stay with him. Jerry's in there, too."

"Oh... well *that* is truly a relief!" breathed the Storied Watcher. "Quests such as these, they often do not turn out..."

Her voice trailed off.

"Odd that you'd call it a 'quest'," observed Boyd. "Anything you've got to fill us in on, there, Karéin?"

She cast a gaze into the Oval Office.

"In there," she directed.

Airing Our Little Differences

There had been a couple of slight delays.

First, the Storied Watcher insisted on entering the *Mailànkh Express* to review Melissa's condition. Happily – although the flying-teenager had suffered a broken forearm, numerous cuts and abrasions and two cracked ribs – she was reassured that "this shall pass by, brave little sister, in a fortnight".

Apparently the healing-process was to be hastened by the magic of the Storied Watcher's weirding-amulet, which was affixed to Melissa's neck for a few minutes. The improvement was immediately visible.

A request was made to Sullivan and the GrayWar duo, to stay in the airship along with the Claremont teenager. This was accepted, as was – with somewhat more paw-dragging – Abruzzio's instruction to little "Rainbow" to "make these nice people look like something else, if the bad guys try to come in and hurt them".

The dog had repeatedly tried to go with its master, but had finally been bribed with a piece of Billings' precious, earlier-acquired beef-jerky strips.

Secondly, a request was made for "who will stand watch outside, guarding against aggression on the part of those who encircle this palace"; after some unhappiness, it was decided that Devon White – and the ever-faithful Hector Ramirez – would see to this vital task, with the former Mars mission communications-expert and the Tex-Mex scientist both maintaining hovering-positions over the residence.

"Y'all owe me *big-time*, Karéin," grumbled White. "Trip to Jupiter, at least."

The repartee came back quickly : "Of *course*, noble brother... but have you yet figured out what you will do, when you will arrive there?"

Hopefully, the situation would be made safer by the warning that the Storied Watcher's fire-dagger, *Væran Ksé'l'ch'*, inscribed in the night-sky, over the White House : *"Do not attack – the President and his family are safe – talks continue"*.

White and Ramirez had reinforced the message by flying concentric patterns of steadily-increasing diameter around the White House, yelling the same caution to the cowed National Guardsmen and other assorted LEA-forces who were arrayed in a perimeter around central D.C..

They were not immediately shot at, which both took as a positive sign.

To their mutual satisfaction, the President and Kaysten, regarding the TV-screen set up in his office, noted that Disney News Network was playing this for all it was worth; there was a panel of "experts" busily discussing – in between incessant commercials for diet-pills and "miracle male potency cures" – the import of each of the flaming-weapon's incandescent words.

Now Karéin-Mayréij, in the vanguard of a flying-wedge of super-human beings, with Jacobson and Tanaka on her right and Chu and Abruzzio on her left (others followed further behind, on both sides), approached the damaged outside-door of the Oval Office.

The eyes of all involved held a dim glow, though they had been instructed to tamp down the other external manifestations of their alien-powers; the Storied Watcher had changed back to her stylish mufti, in a flash that was (to Wolf's salacious disappointment), too fast for even the more-than-humans to track the progress of her disrobing, within.

Kaysten was there in the doorway. He rushed forward to embrace his alien mentor, planting a friendly kiss on her cheek. This was rewarded by another hug.

"Damn good to see you back here again!" he gushed. "And not a *moment* too soon, I'd add. Things were getting, uhh, a little *hot* around here."

"*Could* have been a fuckin' *lot* hotter!" unhappily whispered Wolf.

"Well, Jerr-ee," observed the alien-girl, "One could say the same, of events measurably above the surface of this planet, over yonder ocean – by a few million of your 'degrees' – as Venerable One and my war-children, will personally attest. I salute your bravery in standing forthrightly here, in the face of these terrible weapons, whose infernal kiss is now all too familiar to me. May we enter this royal-chamber, to parley with the President?"

"Welcome back, Karéin," called out the voice of the U.S. leader. "Come on in... we obviously have some things to talk about."

Kaysten stood aside and the alien-girl, along with Chu, Jacobson, Abruzzio, Boyd, Saquina White, Tommy, Billings, Misha and Wolf, entered the Oval Office.

"We may be here for a while," observed the President. "Anybody need to use the washroom? And pull up a chair."

Gratefully, a wincing Sabrina White, as well as the Russian, were ushered by Curt Kordish, to the "Presidential Facilities", just past the communications-room. Meanwhile, Abruzzio – working on the left, while the Storied Watcher worked on the right – telekinetically-pulled the Oval Office sitting-couches forward, so that those seated upon them, would directly face the Resolution Desk.

"*Much* easier than trying to latch on to a 747, at twenty thousand feet and five hundred miles per hour," commented the ex-scientist.

Most of those around took a seat, facing the President who again sat behind his desk, with Kaysten standing just behind him and to his right.

Matt and Clairie entered the room through the door to the rest of the White House.

"Hello, new brother and sister of the Immortal *Fire*," greeted Karéin-Mayréij. "We meet again, under – I hope and pray – more positive circumstances. How are you feeling?"

"Tired," offered Matt. "I keep seeing these, uhh, weird-ass *colors*... like really deep purple and red... hard to explain. But, yeah, I'm doing a bit better... I *guess*."

"Very good," pleasantly offered the Storied Watcher.

"*That* guy there," accused Clairie, pointing at the bounty-hunter, "Threatened to *kill* my Dad – not to mention Matt, myself, Mr. Kaysten and Mr. Kortish – not fifteen minutes ago! When you did that, uhh, *thing* to Matt and me... you never told us that these other guys would be showing up, with so much hostility!"

"She didn't know – at least not precisely – how and when we'd arrive here," Jacobson pointed out. "Isn't that right, Karéin?"

The Storied Watcher evaded with an ambiguous shrug.

It is... complicated, brave Sam, she sent.

Jacobson stared stolidly forward.

"You're the guys who trashed Fort Knox – right?" challenged Matt.

"You *got* it," confirmed Boyd. "We could have flattened this place, instead... would you have preferred that?"

"You look *cute*," taunted Wolf, with a misogynist faked kiss, in the Presidential daughter's direction. "Wanna *hot* date?"

"Just a hunka-hunka burning *love*," maliciously cackled a winking Billings, to Tommy's obvious delight.

"*Ewww!*" winced a disgusted Clairie.

"Young prince and princess," explained the Storied Watcher, "*Many* hard words and feelings have gone back and forth, since I fell upon this planet, on both sides – though I constrain to say, that the fault in this matter, is not equally-shared. Loyalty compels you to defend your father, and by so doing, you demonstrate your burgeoning nobility; but I ask you to refrain for the time being, until we – hopefully – work out our differences."

"Easy for *you* to say," argued Clairie, "He isn't threatening to kill *your*, Dad!"

"Well," offered Karéin-Mayréij, "Not an hour ago, I, uhh, 'ate' a hydrogen-melting bomb, on behalf of your 'Dad'... do I merit no credit for thus having done?"

The Presidential daughter maintained a sullen silence, as Saquina White and Misha returned into the Oval Office.

"Thanks, Matt... Clairie," stated the U.S. leader, "You *know* how much I love you and how much I value your support. But, Karéin – before we try to work out our differences, I think we owe it to each other to reconstruct what has happened, earlier tonight. If only because, assuming of course that I'm alive to do it, I will have to inform the country. What did you *do* up there? And by the way – I give you fair notice – everything that goes on in this office, is being recorded."

"Good," grumbled Billings. "I hope you're not 'bleeping' out the swear-words."

"That's only done in post-production, Bob," dryly commented Kaysten.

"I can only tell you what I experienced, from my perspective, sir," offered the Storied Watcher, to the President. "I flew upward at a rapid pace, with the *Mailànkh Express* in tow, though also propelled by my friends Hector, Melissa and Sylvia; I had planned to assist them in pulling Min-ee's doomed airplane away from its course to crash upon and destroy, this palace in which we now parley. But as I approached, my war-children and I detected a missile with one of those atom-smashing bombs, hurtling down upon Min-ee's aircraft. I had but a few seconds in which to deal with this – and had planned to use my war-arts to stop the damnable thing – but at the last moment, another airplane, its four engines trailing bright-fire, flew past, and thus distracted the missile –"

"Well... Sombitch *Pierre!*" an amazed, but proud, Boyd interjected. "Karéin – that was the V-37 transport that the Commander, Devon, Misha, Wolf and I, decided to abandon in mid-air and put on a collision-course with the ACP. Obviously... we missed."

"As did I," confirmed the alien-girl, "The advent of your own airplane threw off my aim, but the weapon followed the four-engine-craft away from the larger airplane, and I was able to use my mind-push-and-pull to position myself on the other side of the newcomer, so as to lead the missile out to sea... away from imperiling either Min-ee, or from the cities below. All was going well, when another one of these 'bombs' exploded below and to the south. This, in turn, set off the missile that I had indirectly in tow... and I was much too close to the latter, at the time – probably between one and three of your 'kil-o-meters', I believe. Thus I fell and only later awoke from the ordeal of facing nuclear hell-fires. Ahh... I have two such, to my credit, by now. Though not by choice."

"Let's not make it a 'hat-trick'... shall we, honey?" remarked Billings.

"May the Gods and Fates so grant," said Karéin-Mayréij, with a deep breath. "Two were *more* than enough!"

"Or... 'three strikes, you're out'," mentioned Boyd. "Mr. President – do you *understand*, what she's just been describing? Do you have any *idea*, of what kind of energy, she just withstood... what kind of *power*, is sitting there on the couch, in front of you? I can't *imagine...*"

"Nor can *I*," gravely observed the President. "I have the feeling of addressing a *goddess*... Karéin, I hope you understand how this is a humbling experience – and how it makes me uncertain about how to proceed."

"Indeed... but you should consider me a 'goddess', compared to yourself, only physically – not 'morally'... not, 'ethically'. I am not perfect, sir – I just have many weirding-powers of great potency, and the experience of many years," demurely replied the Storied Watcher. "And I am not the *only* one, who lately has faced – and survived – these terrible weapons. Min-ee – Sylvia – sisters – how is it that you are here, alive, with us, this day?"

"I guess I'll go first," said Chu. "I got invited on to the Airborne Command Post by the former Vice-President as well as his hangers-on – apparently it was Crowford's idea... he had it in his head to use me to get at both yourself, Karéin, and at Sam's team. Crowford had this nutzoid idea of putting me at risk and having Karéin ride to my rescue – I tried to tell him that I didn't even know where she *was*... but he wouldn't listen. Then the Vice-President ordered the murder of Will and Otis by throwing them out of the plane at thirty thousand feet – for the *longest* time I thought they were dead, but just now, I've learned, thank *God*, that they somehow managed to land safely – and that left me alone with the Vice-President, Warnock, Blanshard, Crowford and a bunch of the rest of them. They tried to get me to tell them how to kill Sam, Brent, Cherie and so on; of course I dragged my feet as much as I could –"

"Thanks, Minnie," acknowledged Jacobson. "It's truly appreciated."

"Yeah... owe you one, sister," added Tanaka.

"Least I could do," replied the former FBI team-leader. "The 'thanks' I got from the Vice-President for protecting you, by the way, was, he ordered me taken outside the ACP communications-room, to be summarily executed, on the spot. At this point I figured I had nothing left to lose, and, well... I gave them a nice hot 'gaze', if you know what I mean –"

"*Ouch*," winced Kaysten, from behind the President. "Sir... I've *seen* her do that. Not a good idea to be anywhere in front of her – I can *assure* you of that!"

"So I've *heard*," evenly remarked the U.S. leader.

"I want you to understand, sir," elaborated Chu, "That I used lethal force only as an *absolute* last resort, and only when my life was *immediately* in jeopardy. I sincerely regret these actions and the loss of life that they inevitably caused – but there was no other way. No way at all. If I hadn't defended myself, I'd be long-dead by now."

"You made the right choice, Min-ee... as I tried to demonstrate, down on that city-street, many weeks ago," declared the Storied Watcher. "To refrain from needless violence is noble; to refrain from righteous combat, is a fool's false conceit. I am glad that you have come to realize this."

"I wish I hadn't *had* to," sadly noted Chu.

"I accept your observations," offered the President. "All that I ask is that if you're called to testify about these events, that you tell the whole truth about what happened. As will I."

"Of *course*, sir," agreed the team-leader. "May I continue?"

"Go ahead," the U.S. leader requested.

"So after that," Chu explained, "There was a stand-off, with me holding the Vice-President and Warnock hostage... then I found out that Mr. Spiritual Adviser had upped the ante with Karéin by – and don't ask me *how* he accomplished this, it escapes me – having smuggled a hydrogen bomb on-board the Command Post. It was at *this* point, I believe, that he decided to crash the airplane into downtown D.C., in a kind of insane last effort at attracting the Storied Watcher before I went 'boom' along with the plane. He shot his way into the cockpit and hijacked the ACP and set it on a course to crash into the White House. I went forward intending to zap him and regain control of the aircraft and warned the Marine guards about what was going on, but they refused to let me get at Crowford. At that point, my little *alter ego* warned me –"

"You said, 'alter ego'?" interrupted the President. "You mean some kind of alien-power?"

"No... his name is 'Warden'," spoke Chu.

She grasped the locket from her upper-chest, held it up for all to see and addressed it.

The Storied Watcher was beaming.

"See, Warden," said the former team-leader, "This man is the 'President', who I have told you about. He runs this kingdom called, 'United States'. Can you introduce yourself, son?"

Many in the room – including the Presidential children but not the President himself – heard a thought in their heads,

Son War-den me Mother Minnie Blessed is.

All Fire-*brothers*, Fire-*sisters*, *greetings you to.*

Suddenly, *another* "unseen voice" sent out psychic-messages of its own.

Joyful Sài'ymë Vìrya *Warden brother* Væran *rejoins!* it happily broadcast.

Double-takes were seen all over the room, with the exception of the members of the "Mars Gang".

"What... who..." stammered a befuddled Clairie. "Matt – you *hear* that?"

"Yeah – no – holy *crap*, that's *weirdo*," the brother replied. "I *sort* of did..."

"Welcome to our world, princelings," called the Storied Watcher, back to the two Presidential teenagers.

"Cherie – yours?" asked Chu.

"Seems we both were given a 'companion', when this all started," observed Tanaka.

"Actually, I got Warden from Will," the team-leader corrected. "Just before he... anyway."

"This is fascinating, Ms. Chu – Ms. Tanaka," the President remarked, "But... so... what, again, did this 'Warden' tell you?"

"He warned me of a rapid increase in radioactivity, somewhere else on the plane," explained Chu. "I interpreted this as Crowford having triggered the bomb – an assumption that unfortunately turned out to be true – so I shot out the side-door on the ACP and jumped for it. I met Sylvia on the way down, we saved as many others who had also bailed, as we could. We were almost at the shoreline when the first bomb blew... followed in quick succession by the one that Karéin was shepherding out to sea. That's about it. Frankly, sir... I'm still amazed to be *alive*. If Crowford's bomb had a faster fuse..."

She shuddered.

"Help me out, here," inquired the President. "You said, 'you jumped for it'? Without a parachute?"

"That's right, sir," answered the team-leader.

"Well then... how did you..." he pressed.

"Oh... *that's* easy," breezily replied Chu. "I learned how to fly."

"You learned how to... 'fly'... just like *that?*" incredulously responded the President.

"Like riding a bicycle," Chu happily remarked. "Oh-kay... maybe more like learning how to swim, except it's in the air, as opposed to in water. How did you think that Sylvia and I *got* here, starting from Atlantic City, sir? Matter of fact... we kind of paced ourselves, to see how fast we could go. I figure, 'several hundred miles per hour'."

"*Amazing*," offered the President. "On many levels. Ms. Abruzzio – can you verify Ms. Chu's account of what happened up there?"

"*Definitely*," confirmed the former JPL scientist. "As Karéin mentioned, and as you saw yourself, I accompanied her, Melissa and Hector in lifting the *Mailànkh Express* upward towards the Airborne Command Post, with the intent of diverting the airplane away from its collision-course with Washington, D.C.. We got close enough to conclusively identify the ACP and I cast my telekinesis at it; with some difficulty I locked on and pulled up to it, while the *Express* and the rest of those on her, turned back. Around this time, Karéin warned us that she had seen the second nuke – the one on the missile, that is – and she blasted off into the stratosphere in chase of it. This threw our plans into disarray as I now had to figure out how to divert Minnie's aircraft without Karéin's help. With me so far?"

"I *think* so," confirmed the U.S. leader, "Although all this talk of 'alien-powers', 'telekinesis', and so on... I can just imagine how it's going to sound, in a report to Congress..."

Tommy extended his left arm, pointing at the Resolution Desk. The entire thing began to lift off the floor.

"Now, *now*, son," tut-tutted the Storied Watcher, "That is an *expensive* piece of furniture, with – so I am told – much history undertaken, upon it. I think that you should put it down."

"Okay," complied the boy.

The Resolution Desk came crashing down, landing with a solid "thud".

Fortunately, it did not appear to have been seriously damaged.

"See?" illustrated Abruzzio. "If they don't believe you, well... I'm sure we can convince them."

Smirks and chuckles broke out around the room.

"Okay," continued the former JPL scientist, "So the rest of the story is, I did my best to create an illusion in front of the ACP, to make those inside think that it was off-track – the 'track', of course, being 'landing on top of the White House' – so that it would change its flight-path away from the city. I thought this couldn't *possibly* work, because the flight-crew would just rely on their instruments... but, somehow... it *did!* I tried to find Minnie but it was very difficult, due to the mayhem going on inside the aircraft –"

"You can say *that* again, sister!" ruefully interjected Chu. "I've been shot at more times in the past twenty-four hours, than most soldiers have done to them in five tours of duty... it's almost becoming old hat to me, actually."

"*Tell* me," agreed Abruzzio. "To close out the story, Mr. President... I was clinging on to the outside hull of the Airborne Command Post for dear life – remember, we're talking, 'twenty thousand feet, low oxygen-count in the air, freezing cold and five hundred miles per hour airspeed' – and then I saw Minnie's 'deadly stare' shoot the airplane's forward access-door straight through; it flew completely off in the next second, and at this point, I figured that she wouldn't do that unless things had gone *seriously* wrong inside –"

"I don't *know*, Sylvia," quipped the former FBI team-leader, "Would you say that being on-board a plane with a H-bomb about to go off under your feet, at any second, would count as 'seriously wrong'?"

"Y'all try to *find* me somethin' that's more 'seriously wrong' than *that*," added Saquina White, to more laughter.

"So then," continued the ex-JPL-scientist, "I saw a figure flying out of the ACP – keep in mind, all this happened in a couple of seconds, there was virtually no time to think things through – and I let go, flying downwards and backwards to catch up with what I thought was Minnie. It turned out, however, to be a young Air Force guy who she had entrusted just before they both had to bail. I ran into Minnie further on the way down, we used our telekinesis to save as many other refugees from the aircraft as we could... and then the bombs exploded. Incidentally... the guy who I intercepted in mid-air goes by the name of 'Stephen Mooney'; he's down in Atlantic City. He's obviously a bit shaken up but otherwise he's oh-kay."

"If you need someone to corroborate my testimony, sir," mentioned Chu, "You can speak to Stephen. He was there in the ACP communications-room with me, the Vice-President and Warnock, all the way through. Go *easy* on him, sir; he's a good kid... he's been through *a lot* lately."

"As have we *all*, Madam," echoed the Russian.

They noticed that the Storied Watcher was wiping a tear.

"Don't blame you, hun," offered Billings. "What a damn ordeal... unbelievable that these two are still alive."

"Not just that, my love," Karéin-Mayréij replied, "But also thus have you all been tested... and you have passed, though perhaps," – she shot a friendly glance in Chu's and Abruzzio's direction – "Some, with a higher ess-ay-tee score, than others."

The bounty-hunter threw up his hands and defensively remarked, "Yeah, well, Little Miss Nuclear Angel... *some* of us, don't take so good to havin' *bombs* dropped on 'em, every time they try to hide behind a tree and take a shit... you know? If that's a test... then I guess I flunked with flyin' colors. Not that I *care*."

"Surviving – and defending oneself and others less powerful – in the face of murderous onslaught – *that, too*, is a test, brother," observed the alien-girl. "Do not think so ill of yourself. I do not."

"Yeah, well, Karéin," answered Wolf, his tone unusually subdued, "Even by *that* standard – some of us are comin' up short, I reckon. What the fuck are we s'posed to *do*, when there's bombs fallin' all over Hell's Half Acre, and we can barely save *ourselves* – not them civilians who just happen to get caught in the crossfire?"

He glanced at Tanaka.

"*You* know what I mean," he said.

The former Mars mission science officer explained, "When we were in Texas – chasing Sam's kidnapped family, incidentally, but I'll let him fill you in on *that* – the Air Force must have tracked us down; they carpet-bombed the area. In so doing they murdered the father of a farm-family who came outdoors to see Wolf, who was recovering from a battle overhead. We took the survivors under our wing... but you can imagine how we felt about it. *Still* feel about it, Mr. *President*. These people are only a few of the many who have been cruelly-affected just by being around us, at the wrong time."

The U.S. leader carefully responded, "There will be an accounting for that, just like there will be for everything that has transpired up to this point – although again I have to point out, this was likely undertaken under *George's* orders, not mine; I *repeatedly* warned him that the indiscriminate use of violence was likely to make things worse, not better. Unfortunately... it looks like I was right, on that issue. Anyway... this brings us to Mr. Jacobson, and *his* story. What do *you* have to say?"

Jacobson began by stating, "First of all, Mr. President, I want you to know that Karéin or no Karéin sitting here, from my point of view, you're just as much on trial by *me*, as I may be, by you – my team and I didn't come *this* far, and didn't risk this much, to just walk away with a smile and a handshake, or with vague promises on your part. Even if Minnie insists on us leaving you alone personally –"

"At this point, Mr. President," Chu interrupted, "I need to make my own position on this matter, absolutely clear; again, I'll let Sylvia speak for herself. But for the record, sir... I'm here to defend the integrity of the office of the President, of the rule of law, of due process, *et cetera* – not any one particular person. As much as Sam has valid reasons for hating both you and the government – and I *saw* the government's behavior against Commander Jacobson and his team, first-hand, while I was on the Command Post, and the use of force was absolutely *inexcusable* – if he, or any member of his team, tries to use violence here, today... I want everyone in this room to know that I will do my best to stop him or her. Beyond that... all bets are off."

"Pretty much *my* position too," commented Abruzzio. "The military tried to kill me, on multiple occasions, including when we rescued you out of that gilded cage that you had been confined to, Mr. President. Saying, 'we're not into murder', is a different thing from saying, 'and there doesn't have to be a reckoning for past injustices'. Just as saying, 'I don't want to make an already bad situation, worse', is different from 'I don't want to make a bad situation, better'."

"Thus I'll explain what our experiences have been, up to this point," mentioned Jacobson, "And the rest of my team can jump in if they so desire. Basically, Karéin dropped us off in the southern U.S. and we tried to stay moving after that point, since we knew that the government was likely to be hunting us. Unfortunately that assumption proved all too true. We were repeatedly attacked, both by local law enforcement and by the military, all the way up to waves of fighter-planes with missiles and the bombing-raids that Wolf has referred to –"

"Again... I'd point out that the government was, at that time, under control of an illegally-appointed President," the U.S. leader argued. "Go on."

The former Mars mission commander – his voice becoming more and more agitated with each passing word – elaborated, "Mid-way through our travels we challenged the government to come to terms and answer for the atrocities that we uncovered it doing up on Amchitka; we were answered by even more violence. We invaded Fort Knox to send the government a clear message of what we were capable of doing, and that we wouldn't stop until we got justice; we were answered by yet more attacks, including – we found out – attempts to kidnap our *families*, undoubtedly so they could be held hostage and tortured or killed, like we had seen the government already do in the prison in the Aleutians. Apparently this despicable tactic wasn't just confined to the 'Mars Gang' but in fact it was targeted at *everyone* who had been associated with the Storied Watcher. At this point our mission changed radically because we had to protect our own loved-ones. This objective was only narrowly-achieved –"

"*Except*," angrily interjected a glowing-eyed Tanaka, "For my *mother...* who, I've been told, was seized by government agents, some days ago. I swear to *God*, Mr. President, that if she's been harmed in any way, it won't *matter* what deals you make with Sam, Karéin or anyone else – I will *personally* track down everyone and anyone associated with her abduction, including yourself if the evidence leads there, and blow them to Kingdom *Come!* If I have to knock down skyscrapers and set *cities* on fire – that's what I'll *do!*"

"Never doubt," evenly remarked Jacobson, "That she's capable of doing that. It would take me longer, I assume... but the outcome would be the same."

"And she'll have some *help*, fucker!" cursed Wolf. "'Specially with the 'cities on fire' thing."

"From me too," committed Boyd. "As Cherie knows... I *owe* her one. And I've seen what the government was planning to do to my family... Commander Jacobson's, too. You may remember, Mr. President, that I gave you, or your successor, several public warnings about 'keep your fucking hands off my wife and kids'. These warnings were apparently all ignored. There will be *consequences* for that!"

"Can't say I *blame* you," unhelpfully cackled Billings. "Tanaka's seen, first-hand, what kinds of things your lovely government does to people like Tommy, Elissha... or me. Ms. Thunder-Thighs goes and does that... I'll be watching the gory details on TV with popcorn and a beer or two. Shit *happens*, you know."

A grave-faced President looked over his shoulder to Kaysten and quietly ordered, "Jerry – please get to work right now with Curt, and locate Ms. Tanaka's mother, as well as all other extended family-members associated with Jacobson and his group. I want anyone who the government has already seized, flown to here, the White House, to be rendered to my personal custody, *immediately!* This is a top-priority assignment and anyone who resists or has been involved in the kinds of abuses just described, is to be arrested – if they resist, the use of force is hereby authorized. Please get on this, now!"

"You can be *sure* of it, Mr. President!" obliged the Chief of Staff. "We'll do our best... but you *know* how little control we have over some of these guys. If any of them were loyal to George... she might be as much a hostage against *us*, as against Cherie."

"We'll have to take that chance," replied the President.

"Understood, sir," said Kaysten, as he moved with unnatural speed to consult with Kortish. The two disappeared into the inner recesses of the White House.

"Finally," spoke Jacobson, "We were able to round up all of the family-members who we believed were unaccounted-for –"

"Just a *minute*," interrupted an alarmed Chu. "Commander... did you say that the government's attempts to kidnap family-members, might have been directed at *all* of Karéin's followers? Including, potentially, Sylvia or myself?"

"Or Hector? Or Otis... or Will?" chimed in Abruzzio.

"That's our understanding," confirmed the former Mars mission commander.

"Who told you this?" asked Chu.

"A reliable, 'inside' source," cryptically stated Jacobson. "We found that the information provided by this source, was usually highly accurate."

"Mr. President," the team-leader requested, "I hope you realize the implications of this – the government might have gone after *everyone's* families, including, for example, my fiancée – he's a software-analyst in New York. You *know* that I'm pledged to defend you... but my first loyalty *has* to be to Kaiser –"

"I have some bad news for you, Minnie," offered Tanaka, "But we heard specific references to the government looking for him. I'd have to assume that he's already rotting in some dungeon, somewhere. Welcome to *my* world!"

Chu's face lost its color.

"And my parents – my *brothers!*" added a frightened Abruzzio. "We have no idea of how far afield the government might have gone, here. What if they're arresting grandparents... cousins... nephews and nieces?"

"Anything *goes*," observed Billings. "'Long as you can record their screams, for a few shits and giggles... right?"

"Yeah," added an angry-looking Tommy.

The President called out to his offspring.

"Matt... Clairie," he directed, "Can you please go locate Jerry and Curt and inform them of all this, *immediately?* Tell them that I want the scope of our rescue efforts to include all extended-family members of anyone associated with Karéin. Come back here when you've done that... okay?"

"Sure, Dad!" answered the Presidential children, who rapidly exited the Oval Office, in the direction that Kaysten and Kortish had gone.

"Puts a whole new *perspective* on our little grievances with the man in that chair... doesn't it, Minnie?" complained Boyd.

"I... yeah," admitted the team-leader. "Mr. President... there is absolutely *no* excuse for this kind of thing. I'm letting you know now – if I find out that Kai has been hurt, or worse... you can bloody well defend *yourself*, against Commander Jacobson and his 'Gang'! You *got* me on this, sir?"

"Count *me* out, too," mentioned Abruzzio.

"Loud and clear, Ms. Chu... Ms. Abruzzio," the U.S. leader replied. "Assuming that we can determine the extent of these illegal actions on the part of the state intelligence agencies – and I have to warn you that given my limited control over the government right now, there's a real possibility that we can't easily do that – the next issue will likely become, 'how do we free hostages in these circumstances, if those holding them, refuse an order to release them'. I may need to call upon all of your help."

The Storied Watcher disappeared for a second or two, then re-appeared.

"I can help, sir," she pledged. "Bob?"

"I thought we were *done* with the whole 'risking our life in a noble cause' kind of thing," Billings said, with a sigh and a roll of the eyes.

Yet he, too, temporarily vanished from view, then again became visible.

"Don't count on too many of these 'abductors' being in one piece, when the rescue's over with," threatened the ex-salesman. "I got some *scores* to settle!"

"I'll just ask you to keep the use of lethal force to a minimum, if and when it becomes necessary for you to participate in a rescue-operation," said the President.

Abruzzio got up from the couch and started to pace around.

"Mr. *President*," the distraught ex-scientist exclaimed, "Why didn't you *tell* us about this? Before!"

"I *had* heard rumors," he tried to say. "But what George told me was that the efforts were directed *exclusively* at the 'Mars Gang'. I *warned* him that doing this was just going to unnecessarily antagonize Commander Jacobson and his team yet more... but he didn't listen to me, and the government was answering exclusively to *him*, at the time. I –"

"Get them *back!*" cried an increasingly-angry Abruzzio.

Her eyes were glowing with rainbow-*Amaiish*. "Get them *back*, right *now!* Or – as God's my witness – I *swear* – after Cherie and Wolf get finished with setting every city in this country on fire, I'll make sure that the rubble's radioactive for the next ten thousand *years!*"

"Why don't we start in D.C., and work outward?" growled Boyd.

"Nice to see you on board," observed the bounty-hunter, with an evil grin in Abruzzio's direction. "Never *seen* a radioactive bonfire before. Sure it'll be a 'thing'."

"Just a *minute!*" the desperate President pleaded.

He reached under the Resolution Desk and evidently activated some other button or toggle-switch.

He spoke forward, apparently to no-one.

"This is the President here, calling the bunker," he said. "Jerry – Curt – are you there? Have Matt and Clairie showed up yet?"

The answers came back all at once.

"Affirmative, Mr. President sir," sounded the voices of the Chief of Staff and the Secret Service agent.

"Yep... we're here, Dad," they heard the two Presidential offspring say. "Mom's down here too."

"Listen very carefully, all of you," the U.S. leader directed, "We have a potentially-explosive situation up here; Jerry, Curt, as we discussed earlier, we knew that George had ordered the illegal abduction and imprisonment of the families of Commander Jacobson and the rest of his team... but we've just now found out that the exercise might have actually extended to target not just *them*, but also the families of *anyone* else known to have been associated with the Storied Watcher. We don't know how far back these efforts go and they might involve grandparents, aunts and uncles and so on. Specifically, the government might be after – or might already have seized – the families of Ms. Abruzzio, Ms. Chu, Mr. Ramirez, or –"

"Or *my* Dad... or my *sister*," Kaysten broke in. "*Fuck* George... wherever he is! Excuse my language, sir."

"Well," ruefully noted the President, "Your feelings are about the same as I've just observed, from Ms. Abruzzio and others here. Curt, Jerry – we need to understand the scope of George's operation, and then we need to locate each and every one of these people, and ensure that we get to them, before forces loyal to George, or the conspiracy, do. I need a report and an action-plan on my desk in the next hour, as to their whereabouts. Is that clear?"

"Understood, sir," came Kortish's voice. "We had profiles on pretty much all of 'em already in the database... but I don't know if we had real-time tracking enabled for them, like we did for Commander Jacobson and those directly associated with this 'alien' who you've got up there –"

The Storied Watcher said out loud,

"As I have noted before, sir... you may have only one 'alien' to deal with; I have an entire *planet-full* of them. Perhaps when this is all done, we can, ahh, 'do lunch', some time. I have been impressed by the loyalty to your 'boss' that you have demonstrated."

"Thanks... I *think*," replied the Service agent. "Before we 'do lunch', ma'am, I'll just ask you not to blow my whole *country* to bits. Is that all, sir?"

"Get *working!* Matt, Clairie – assist as best you can," demanded the President. "Things were tense enough up here, before this new factor came out into the open. C-In-C, out."

"Not *me* who now warns of a doom," offered Karéin-Mayréij, with a flippant shrug and a serious-looking half-smile. "Perhaps this 'George' should have considered upon whom he was, ahh, 'picking'... ere he ordered these atrocities."

"*Now* you're talkin'!" congratulated Wolf.

"Well," observed the Russian, "I *do* remember a scene, not too long ago, in which you and I tried to counsel her out of pursuing a similar path."

"Aye," acknowledged the Storied Watcher.

"So where that leaves us, Mr. President," offered Jacobson, "Is – to be very clear – if I don't hear what I want to hear out of your mouth, my *next* recommendation to my team is going to be to simply leave here and tear the country *apart*, brick by brick. This is independent of – though related to – any differences that Sylvia, Minnie or the others may have with the government. We have already proved that the military won't be able to stop us. You and your family can stay here safely if you want to; and you'll be presiding over a *wasteland*. Do you understand what I'm saying?"

"I don't take kindly to *threats*, Mr. Jacobson," shot back the President. "Karéin... what do you have to say about all this?"

"I would say, two things," diffidently replied the Storied Watcher. "First, it is a test both of those who negotiate from a position of strength – and those who do so from a position of weakness – to acknowledge the same, neither 'bluffing' nor seeking to humiliate; for a fork in the road again approaches, and those who would be wise, and those who would be king, should know which path to take. Second... I have already announced forbearance in what your government has done to me and my family; yet my love and loyalty comes first to all those upon whom I have bestowed the Holy *Fire* – whose divine name is '*Amaiish*' – and thus, sir, if your negotiations break down... I will mourn this, and the destruction that will follow it... but I will *not* defend you, or your kingdom! Not after what was done to me, when first I tried to live at peace, among you."

"About what I'd *expect*," sourly offered the President. "Alright, then."

"But I would ask, on the other hand, Sam... is 'searching for kinfolk", not something upon which both you and the President can agree?" suggested the Storied Watcher.

"I suppose," grudgingly allowed Jacobson.

"Then it is a start... is it not?" said Karéin-Mayréij.

"I think what she's saying, Commander," offered the President, "Is that perhaps this can be the start of an agreement between us... a 'negotiated settlement', as it were."

"Work together on *something*, before you have agreed on *everything*," advised the alien-girl. "No 'promises' on either side. If a war there will be, between you, certainly there is ample time in which to do it... though I suspect it would be quickly over with. Do you understand?"

"The *quid pro quo* could be, that the American government undertakes to find those responsible for the abductions, and other crimes, while trying to secure the safety of the remaining family-members," proposed Misha. "While Commander Jacobson's team – including myself – refrain from hostilities, until we ascertain that these third parties are known to be safe. Other, long-term negotiations, proceed while this is underway. Is that what you meant, Karéin?"

"Yes," she confirmed. "The details are up to all of you."

"What the hell's a 'quid pro quo', pardner?" interrogated Wolf. "That Russian for something?"

"Why, yes," deadpanned Misha. "It means – roughly translated – 'five dollars for a table-dance'. In a risqué bar, that is."

Abruzzio and Tanaka bent over, teary-eyed with mirth.

"What's a 'risqué'?" pressed the bounty-hunter.

"That is Russian too," Misha went on, trying hard not to laugh out loud. "It means... oh, *forget* it."

"You mean to say that you took him with you... put up with him... all across the U.S.?" incredulously observed Abruzzio.

"A bit rough round the edges – but a good guy, none the less," said Tanaka, regaining her composure. "Wolf... don't take it too hard. We *mean* well. It's just, I guess.... everybody's a bit *tense*, right now – we need a little comedy here and there, to lighten things up."

"Then you ain't gonna zap me, if I call you 'Thunder-Thighs'?" he asked.

"Not at all, brother... not at *all*," the former Mars mission science officer answered, with a kindly, sympathetic glance in the bounty-hunter's direction.

"Sari," proposed Billings, "Why the hell don't you just... *you* know... get inside his *head?* You can make him do anything you *want!* Sure – *I* can probably resist you, and maybe all us other 'post-humans' can – but he's, well, just a 'human'. He'd be your *puppet* –"

The President reflexively moved back slightly from the Resolution Desk. His face was ashen.

"Same reason that I haven't done the same thing, Bob," said Chu. "Though both you and Karéin know, that I can do it as well."

"And why would *that* be?" idly inquired the former salesman.

"Because... it would be *wrong*," the team-leader answered.

"He'd surely do it to *you*, if he had the chance," countered Billings.

"Tommy... do you remember what we discussed, when last we were here?" cajoled the Storied Watcher.

"Yeah," the boy repeated, "You said... you said that I – we – had to be better than him... that if we wanted to be, uhh, 'noble' – whatever *that* is – we couldn't use our powers against him, because he'd be helpless... and it's, uhh, 'bad' to pick on somebody who can't fight back. Is that right?"

This got Tommy an immediate alien-girl hug.

"Indeed, young prince," she gushed. "*Indeed!*"

"How do I know that you're not trying to control my mind right now?" anxiously demanded the President.

"We're *not*, sir," reassured Chu. "If any of us were... I'd tell you."

"Ha, ha," maliciously disputed Billings. "If either Sari or Minnie were doing that, you wouldn't know it in the first place. They could tell you, 'oh, no, my friend, you're *fine*... just, *fine*' – and, know *what?* It'd be so *convincing*... you'd *believe* it, hook, line, and sinker! How you like *them* apples?"

"I... I don't know what to *say*," gulped the U.S. leader. "If what you say is true – how do I know –"

"I assure you that Min-ee speaks the truth, sir," declared Karéin-Mayréij, "And that no 'mind-fuckery' – as Bob has inelegantly branded this ancient and subtle art – is going on, here and now; nor have I so done, in any of our earlier encounters. But all of this *does* illustrate a point."

"And *that* would be..." cautiously asked the U.S. leader.

"Sir... this is the same thing about which I assailed you, in that brief conversation that we had many days ago," insisted the alien-girl. "That is, when forcibly I entered that big air-plane – the one with the powerful laser-gun in front. Do you remember?"

"Uhh... yeah," he admitted.

"As you will recall, sir," pressed the Storied Watcher, "You said that you were 'too busy' to speak with me... even though at that point, I myself threatened to lay waste to this kingdom, unless you freed Bob, Tommy, Whitney, Melissa and Curtis."

"Karéin, you must *understand* – at the time, I was –" the President tried to argue.

"*Listen*, for once – *would* you!" interrupted the alien-girl. "The point was – then as now – you were, and are, *badly* over-matched; yet... you refuse to *acknowledge* this! You bargain as if *you* – as opposed to Sam Jacobson – were 'in charge' of the situation. As I remarked at the time to the crew aboard that air-plane... this is the mark of an inexperienced, fool-hardy or reckless leader... not a wise one! Sir, it is no shame to strike the best bargain that you can do, when faced with an overwhelmingly more powerful opponent – particularly, one who has already proved his superiority-of-arms. Many times earlier in my own life, have I, had to do *exactly* this! And though the price was sometimes bitter... I came to understand, over many long centuries, that an uncertain future is far preferable to a present, in which one faces disaster by puffed-up rigidity. Why can you not *learn* this lesson?"

"Were you expecting an answer to that?" evaded the U.S. leader.

"No – I was expecting an answer to Sam and his team," stated Karéin-Mayréij. "*Work* with him! Make *concessions* to him! Give him some *reason* not to walk out of this room and begin wrecking your entire *country!* This 'stone-walling', refusing-to-bargain tactic that I have heard of – and have personally experienced – it is *lunacy!* The main reason why I did not carry out my own pledge to wreak havoc in the defense of Bob, Tommy and Whitney's family, was simply that I was perplexed... I thought to myself, 'well, he *must* have some kind of secret weapon... otherwise he would not bargain with such absurd over-confidence' –"

"Don't forget," reminded Tanaka, "That by hurting all these people, it certainly inflicted pain, vicariously, on yourself... I felt it too. Maybe *that's* what made the fucker so sure of himself –"

"This I concede," stated the alien-girl, "But even after being used repeatedly... it merely *hurt* me terribly – it did not stop my campaign. It will not stop Sam and his team, either! Mr. President – if you would be a wise leader... I should not have to explain this, to you."

"Couldn't have said it better myself," smugly commented Jacobson.

"And to *you*, brother," came the counsel from the Storied Watcher, "I urge you not to abandon subtlety, state-craft and guile, simply because you can – as we all know – simply crush this 'man' in front of you... his entire army, too. Let the President come away from these discussions, with a measure of dignity. Unless, of course, you plan to kill him and then declare yourself 'king' of this 'America' – for I will not do so myself; I make a poor queen, unfortunately. I have tried before, long ago, and found the role most unsatisfying. Let me ask you something."

"Sure... what, Karéin?" the former Mars mission commander replied.

"Did the action of this 'American' government, cause the death of any member of your family... did it hurt any of these, beyond any recovery?" asked the alien-girl.

"As for my family – Brent's and Devon's too, from what I know – the answer is 'no'," said Jacobson. "But it wasn't for lack of *trying*... and we have the examples of Minnie's fiancée and Cherie's mother... maybe many more."

"Don't ask me to forgive them, Karéin," warned Tanaka. "Or to lay off them, if they've harmed my mother. I *won't!*"

"Kin-folk are special," observed the alien-girl, "Wrongs done to the likes of dear Elissha's brother *must* be brought to justice; if you did not insist on it... I, would. But if we are to wreak a terrible vengeance for such, we must first be absolutely sure that we smite he or she who, in fact, bears primary responsibility for the crime. The 'President' states that he failed in his duty to prevent this savagery, but that he did not intend it to unfold in the way that it did. I believe him – if this assertion was a lie, my arts would so inform me. And *that* means, inevitably, that someone *else* ordered, or implemented, all this. That person, or persons, could still be out there, devising yet more calumnies and treachery."

"For what it's worth," observed Chu, "I believe the former Vice-President – also Warnock, Blanchard, Crowford and most of their entourage, to be dead... that is, killed when, or shortly after, the first nuke went off. DeWitt is somewhere else, as are many other senior government officials, including the CIA director, who in my opinion certainly had a hand in all of this –"

"You're absolutely right about that, Ms. Chu," interjected the President. "As God's my witness – and go ahead and use all these 'alien-powers' to detect if I'm lying in saying this, because I'm *not* – the plans to abuse Karéin and her family were *his* idea, initially. To my everlasting shame... I didn't put a stop to it, right then and there. I've already admitted as much to Ms. Abruzzio."

"That *right*, Sylvia?" suspiciously asked Boyd.

"Yes," confirmed the former JPL scientist. "Both Karéin and I had it out with him over this, earlier on."

"Because of this grave injustice," added the Storied Watcher, "I forever with-hold the Holy *Fire* from him – though not from Matt and Clairie, since never do I lay the guilt of the father, on the children. Some 'wrongs' can *never* be made 'right', sir! This *is*, one of them. You will live your life out, and eventually will die, as a normal human being. Perhaps, in time, you will come to understand what a severe punishment I do thus inflict upon you."

"I accept that, Karéin," responded the President. "All things considered, I can't reasonably dispute you."

"Mr. President," Chu continued, "The fact that these many senior officials have likely been killed, raises another issue. Namely – we've heard that while George was in charge of the government, he ordered large-scale purges, including the arrest of people like Fred McPherson and my former Bureau director, Cesar Ochoa. I also heard that later on, the National Security Adviser, Mr. Bezomorton, had been abruptly fired, so perhaps he's in jail somewhere as well. These people all might be subject to the same kinds of abuses that were inflicted on Karéin's family. What can you do to have them released?"

"Jerry and I were working on that," mentioned the U.S. leader, "When all *this*, started to happen. George seems to have sacked and imprisoned anybody in the Executive Branch and military – for example, General Anderson – who had any loyalty to myself. In so doing, incidentally, he crippled much of our command-structure, which is one reason why the military was never able to co-ordinate a major attack on Commander Jacobson's group –"

"You could have fooled *me!*" griped Tanaka. "We *routinely* got jumped by twenty or more fighter-planes, at a time!"

"Would you have preferred, say, 'two hundred', Ms. Tanaka?" challenged the President.

"Just more aluminum-debris all over the landscape... more dead pilots," shrugged the former Mars science officer. "For the record – I regret the latter, obviously; but it was either *them*, or *me*. Blame the stupid sons of bitches who continued to send them up into battle with a greatly-superior opponent, like they used to send soldiers into No Man's Land in the First World War. Blame the generals – not the guys with the machine-guns."

"I got a few to my credit, too," reinforced Wolf. "And you don't cut a deal with Mr. Space Man there, you can be *sure* that Ms. Thunder-Thighs there and me... we'll be runnin' up our score a mite further."

You going to let him call you that? sent Boyd to Tanaka.

He is what he is, she silently answered.

I got bigger fish to fry here, than 'nomenclature'.

"Well, Wolf – I hope you don't mind me referring to you like that," politely replied the U.S. leader, "What we're trying to do here, is to avoid putting anyone like yourself or Ms. Tanaka, in a position where you feel you have to do something like that, ever again. Use a little common *sense*... what did you *expect*, after little incidents like you and your team-mates pulled off, at Fort Knox? I *saw* the casualty-reports from the local Army and National Guard forces, who tried to take back the facility – our losses in life and limb, were *horrendous! No* political leader – certainly not one who wanted to stay in elective office – could fail to strike back, after something like *that!*"

"Well," drawled the bounty-hunter, "Like Mr. Floor-Tile said, back aways... 'shit *happens*'. I'd remind you that the government started shootin' at us long *before* we paid our friendly visit to that-there bank-vault. Came away nicely richer, though; kind of a shame that a lot of it went down with the 'plane we, uhh, 'hot-wired', back at Fort Knox. 'Easy come... easy go', I guess. By the way... go ahead and call me 'Wolf', by all means. Just as long as you don't mind when, after you and Mr. Space Man here end up at each others' throats again, I have to make a bonfire out of your sorry ass... you know?"

"You certainly have a unique way of introducing yourself to someone," stiffly noted the President.

"They tell me, 'tact ain't my strong suit'," reparteed the bounty-hunter. "'Spose that's right."

"Wolf's challenges in etiquette aside, Mr. President," resumed Chu, "I'd like to request that you ensure the immediate release of these other abductees –"

"*Especially* Fred McPherson!" interrupted Tanaka. "His only 'crime' was to have spoken to us, and to Karéin."

"*All* of them," continued the team-leader. "Commander – this could be another 'confidence-building measure'... do you agree?"

"Possibly," mentioned Jacobson. "Provided that it isn't just lip-service, and if risks have to be accepted in so doing, the safety of those in the government's custody, is paramount."

"You have my assurance of that, Commander," committed the President.

"And there are still others," demanded the Storied Watcher. "I have prepared a list... just a moment, if you please..."

She retrieved a sheet of paper from a hidden pocket within her clothes and put it in front of the President, on top of the Resolution Desk.

The writing on the message-paper, though burned in as opposed to being inscribed with ink, was easily-legible; however, the edges of the sheet were badly-charred and there were other signs of fire-damage all over it.

"*That* looks like it's seen better days," commented Billings.

"Well... it *has* just been inside a 'hy-dro-gen bomb'," matter-of-factually noted Karéin-Mayréij. "Several hundred thousand of your 'degrees', a hands-width away, you know."

The U.S. leader gingerly touched the document and then quickly withdrew his hand.

"It isn't... *radioactive*... is it?" he worried.

"Not any more, after the application of Sylvia's arts," airily responded the alien-girl. "Quite safe, even for 'hoo-mans'... I *assure* you!"

"Would we lie to you about something that doesn't involve money?" maliciously added the former salesman.

"*Right*, then," nervously offered the President, as he grabbed the bottom-edge of the message with the tips of his index finger and thumb and quickly dragged it within viewing-distance. He released his grasp just as expeditiously.

"Hmm," mused the U.S. leader, as he surveyed the document. "A lot of names here... not ones with which I'm familiar... who *are* these people? Like, for example, this one – 'Juanita Losada' – a child – and her father, 'Freddie', in Tucson? Or this 'Serena Nicandro's father, Enriqué Nicandro', also of Tucson? And who's *this*... a waitress and restaurant-owner, up in Idaho? A short-order cook from Pascagoula? Or –"

"These are all people who I have met or befriended, in my travels," explained the Storied Watcher. "Some are known to have been thrown in your dungeons; others may or may not have been... but all require safety, until the current uncertainty has been dealt with."

"We'll do our best," stated the President. "But some of these may be difficult to get to... all you've given me is a name. And others – like for example this 'Donny' guy, who you describe as a 'big-truck-driver' – you don't even have a last name for him, and given the nature of his job, he could be anywhere –"

"He is dear to me!" interrupted Karéin-Mayréij. "I had intended to search for him myself, as for the others... and would you rather having me doing that, than helping you mediate –"

"His last name's 'Wade'," offered Jacobson. "And don't worry, Karéin – he's safe and sound. He has been traveling with us for some time, and – for the record – he's given a good account of himself, when called upon to do so. We've got him with our families... with Will and Otis, as well."

The Storied Watcher's face looked thunder-struck and overjoyed, at the same time.

"But... how is this *possible?*" she stuttered. "Oh... such *wonderful* news!"

"Ran across the man on the Interstate, down south," said Wolf. "He was handlin' fires from a car-crash, almost as well as I can. Said he hadn't been the same since... well, I'm sure *you* know about that."

"Yes – I gave Don-nie love and pleasure, and took some in return," the alien-girl replied. "Where I come from, this is what friends do for and with, each other. And in so doing, undoubtedly bestowed the Holy *Fire* upon him... though at the time, I knew it not. I *so* desire to give him a hug and to thank him for the warm kindness that he showed me!"

"She *does* come from a rather different culture, compared to our own," observed Abruzzio. "Karéin... the difference between you and us Catholic girls is, 'we do the same things – but we don't admit to it, except in Confession'."

"When one is fancied a 'goddess'," haughtily stated the Storied Watcher, "One is often confessed 'to' *by* others... as opposed to confessing *to* other, higher powers."

Billings looked green with jealousy, though he wisely said nothing.

"I can see that there is a, uhh, 'back-story' to much of this," noted the President. "Just a minute, please."

Again, he activated the communications-link to the White House bunker.

"This is the President, calling, once more," he said, out loud. "Please acknowledge."

Kaysten's voice sounded.

"Go ahead, sir," he replied. "Curt's trying to get through to the LEA and military who we think are on our side. Matt and Clairie are handling the database searches – man, sir, you should *see* how fast they're working! Kind of like when we were down in Compton and Sylvia picked out one address out of a whole *page* of 'em –"

A few in the room noted a broad smile on the face of the Storied Watcher.

"You *know*, sir," she offered, "You will die a human... but your *children* – long-lived and mighty, indeed shall they be."

"Something to be glad about, I'm *sure*," agreed the U.S. leader, "But right now... Jerry – we have another high-priority task. Specifically – as you know – right after George staged his *coup*, he and the Agency started arresting senior officials suspected of loyalty to myself. We need to add all of these to the list of people who we need to locate and free. Please start with Cesar Ochoa and others who can help us re-establish our control over the government. The one exception to this is my former Science Adviser – Fred McPherson – as he's a personal priority for Commander Jacobson and his team. Understood?"

"Got you loud and clear, sir," pledged the Chief of Staff. "We were already partly pursing this, but we'll push it to one place below 'finding these extended family-members'. Matt – Clairie – did you hear what he said?"

"Yes, Mr. Kaysten," came the girl's voice. "*Too* well, in fact. Dad – Matt and I are hearing a lot of crazy sounds – like, 'people's hearts beating', 'people walking in rooms three doors down' and stuff – and it's getting *lame*, like, 'too much information, too fast'. We can barely shut it out... it's driving me *crazy!*"

"I will teach you how to do this, next time you come up here," reassured the Storied Watcher. "This is all part of becoming a young *Vîrya* or *Væran*, of the Holy *Fire*. Your powers wax, young princess – be proud... but not *too* proud."

"I'd settle for a good pair of earplugs," ruefully remarked the male teenager.

"Now there's one other thing," added the President. "Karéin has given me a paper list of other people, across the United States, who she also wants rescued. These appear to be mostly from ordinary walks of life, and she doesn't have a lot of details on some of them, so we may only be able to do a positive ID on them with her help. Matt, can you please get up here ASAP to take physical possession of the document that she's recorded the names on... then add the people referenced, to our search?"

"Leaving now," came the response.

"Remember – report within an *hour!*" said the President. "Over and out." He cut the connection.

"So if it's permitted... I'll cross this 'Donny Wade' guy off the list," he said.

"Of course," agreed the Storied Watcher.

"One down... about twenty-three to go," glumly remarked the U.S. leader. "Before Matt gets up here – are we sure that's all of them? I mean... it's inefficient to be constantly revising the list. Is there anyone else who you want us to look for, Karéin?"

"What I have inscribed represents the totality of those who I believe, require our protection, sir," answered Karéin-Mayréij. "This is, of course, to some degree dependent on how far that your government has, ahh, 'cast its net', if you know what I mean. If it is anyone with whom I have simply talked, then, indeed, we could be looking at hundreds or thousands. Frankly, I would be more worried about Sam, Min-ee, Sylvia, Bob and so on... they may have many kin in this kingdom, who could be at risk."

Just then, the Presidential son arrived at the door leading from the Oval Office to the rest of the White House.

"*That* was fast," observed his father.

"I seem to be running with the wind at my feet, lately, Dad," remarked Matt. "Not as fast as Mr. Kaysten, but, hey! I'll *take* it. Now if she could just teach me how to turn down the *volume...*"

"Here's the list," stated the U.S. leader, as he handed the Storied Watcher's document to Matt.

"Try saying 'silence' to yourself, five times in quick succession, with your eyes closed," advised Karéin-Mayréij, "And relate this to your sister as well. It is not as effective as techniques that I will teach you later... but it will provide *some* relief."

"Thanks," the teenager replied. "You know... you never *told* Clairie and I, about this kind of thing."

"Hah!" interjected Billings. "Did she mention to you, kid, that you'll never get a buzz from a beer – or a fifth of Jim Beam – ever again? You can taste the booze, but it's got no punch... not like old times, I'm afraid."

A crestfallen Matt asked the Storied Watcher, "Karéin... is that *true?*"

"Alcohol is a *poison*," she explained. "Your body will now neutralize it... as it will so do to almost all other ones, venoms and drugs included. This is a *gift* – not a curse!"

"*That*, my dear," grumbled the ex-salesman, "Is a matter of opinion."

"Damn right," agreed Wolf. "I can drink anybody under the table... but no fuckin' *point* in doin' it. Still gotta piss like a race-horse afterwards, by the way."

"Hmmph," pouted the alien-girl. "Such *ingratitude*, for a subtle and vital immunity!"

"You should get going, son," requested the President.

"Yeah... sure, Dad," complied Matt.

As he exited through the door to the White House interior, they heard him muttering about "Damn voodoo magic..."

"Ahh," remarked Karéin-Mayréij with a wan smile, "A young prince takes his halting first steps, along the blessed paṭh of the Holy *Fire*. Surely has he, and his sister, yet much to learn."

This got the expected chuckles from everyone in the Oval Office, except for the politely-taciturn President.

"So where does all this leave us?" asked Jacobson. "As of now."

"I've been *thinking* about that, Commander," answered the President. "And in that respect, I have a proposition for you."

"Yeah?" the former Mars mission commander replied, with a stone face.

"Well," carefully explained the U.S. leader, "As those of you who are familiar with the political process are aware, given all that's transpired over the past few hours, I have a responsibility to inform the country – the people, that is – about what's been going on, and in particular the fact that the danger posed by those nuclear weapons, seems to be over and done with. I'd obviously also like to be able to say that the danger posed by the 'Mars Gang' is over with –"

"It *isn't!*" interrupted a hard-staring Boyd.

"I *know* that, Major," evaded the President, "But can't we, uhh, 'park' it, for a few hours – days, maybe? I had invited all of you to the White House on the assumption that if you agreed to submit to the rule of law, I'd do that too –"

"Oh, *puh-lease!*" contemptuously barked Billings. "*Some* of us, have seen what your 'rule of law', looks – and *feels* – like. Ever been injected with battery-acid, Mr. President? I can give you the instant play-back, if you're up for that."

"Your 'laws' ain't worth the used ass-wipe they're printed on," growled a crimson-eyed Wolf. "Mostly they say, 'government can do whatever the fuck it wants to'. Well – guess *what?* Now *we* can do whatever the fuck, *we* want to. You can like it or hate it, fucker – but you can't ignore it!"

"My mate and brother may not be the most tactful in so stating," added the Storied Watcher, "But still do they speak the *truth!* Sir, you *pose* as being the 'disinterested enforcer' of a code of law; but in fact, these laws are drafted by, of, and for, the wealthy, powerful and well-connected, and are interpreted in the exclusive interests of these oppressors of the meek and weak. I, myself, have experienced as much. No doubt, your court-tricksters could bring you a 'legal ruling' that would obligate Sam Jacobson and his team to commit suicide... or some other contrived outcome, equally perverse and unjust. For you to expect them to willingly bind themselves to such, betrays contempt both for their intelligence – and for their dread powers. If I were Sam, I *certainly* would not agree to what you propose."

"No offense meant, Karéin," sourly commented Jacobson, "But... *duh!*"

"This 'duh'... I presume that it means, 'one states the obvious'?" inquired Karéin-Mayréij.

"You *got* it," said Boyd. "Teach me the equivalent in *Makailkh* one of these days... okay?"

The alien-girl sent him a friendly nod.

"I had expected you to say that," continued the President, "And given what you've all been through, I can't reasonably argue against it. For the record, many of the things that you've described about the government, I knew about – I'll be honest about that – but outside of a crisis atmosphere like the one we're now in, it was next to impossible to shake the system out of its complacency and make effective changes –"

"As if you ever *tried!*" accused Boyd.

"You're right, Major," conceded the U.S. leader, "I *didn't* try hard enough; particularly, I *way* over-estimated the amount of control that I actually had over the military and the intelligence agencies. I *thought* they'd do what I told them to do – but going right back to that disaster with Karéin in the Tucson hotel-room, it became all too apparent that they simply don't think they have to listen to my orders. That's going to *change – believe* me when I say it!"

"One could legitimately ask," remarked the Russian, "Why you did not come to this conclusion, far earlier, sir. Right from the beginning you must have had reliable reports from your intelligence agencies that the Storied Watcher's powers were increasing much faster than the American government could cope with. Why did you not –"

"I was *going* to, Mr. Grishin!" countered the President. "And then I was *deposed! You* know – that lovely traditional scene when you're escorted out of your office at *gunpoint!* I *tried* to warn George that the whole 'alien' business – no offense, Karéin, but that's how the government regarded you – was getting out of control, and that we had to try to talk it out with her... Ms. Abruzzio *witnessed* one of these conversations! If it had been up to *me* –"

"That right, Sylvia?" asked Tanaka.

"Yes," confirmed the former JPL scientist. "It happened when Jerry and I, along with *Vîrya I'ëà'b'* incidentally, visited the President at the residence where he'd been confined under house-arrest. He called the former Vice-

President and it was very apparent that George simply believed in using violent force... full stop. I tried to reason with him myself, and it was a total waste of time. The guy was simply a jerk."

"Hopefully... a *dead* jerk," muttered the former Mars science officer.

"So," elaborated the President, "Reference your concerns about the impartiality, or lack thereof, of the justice system that I think should rule on all that's happened up to this point... I've been thinking of some way that we – collective 'we' – could restore some trust, here. Clearly – while it's vital that justice not only be done, but that it be *seen* to be done – we need to avoid personnel, in senior positions of responsibility, whose objectivity might reasonably be questioned, by either side."

A beaming Abruzzio interrupted, "Mr. President... what a *great* idea!"

"*Please* don't tell me that this 'mind-reading' thing's –" he started to protest.

"Karéin told me that it's one of my powers, sir," stated the former JPL scientist, "But it's not *that* one. Go ahead and say what you were going to say... and I'll tell you if I guessed right."

"Uhh... okay, I guess," the spooked U.S. leader uneasily responded. "To get to the point... one of the most important positions in a process like this, from an 'administration of justice' point of view, would be the 'Director of the Federal Bureau of Investigation'. That person is in charge of all findings of fact and of criminal investigations, at this level. While we're of course looking for Cesar Ochoa – the former Director – we have no assurance that he's either alive, or capable of executing the duties of his office. Thus, effectively, we have a vacancy in that office. Anyone nominated for the position – even in 'acting' capacity – would have to have extensive previous knowledge of FBI procedures, would need appropriate security clearances, as well as would have to have demonstrated, proven, loyalty to the chain of command and to the rule of law."

"Ha... ha," chuckled a knowing Tanaka, casting a glance at Chu.

"Looking around the room," diffidently offered the President, "I *wonder*... who do you think could assume this position?"

"Congratulations on the promotion!" quipped Boyd.

"Sylvia," said a smiling Storied Watcher, "*Indeed* do your arts inerrantly flourish."

"Sir," asked a flabbergasted Minnie Chu, "What are you *talking* about?"

"Ms. Chu," the President stated, looking deliberately at the former team-leader, "Will you agree to serve your country as Acting Director of the FBI... with the understanding that should Cesar Ochoa not be able or willing to resume his tenancy of this position... you'll undergo formal confirmation-hearings, in front of the Congress, as permanent FBI Director?"

A wide-eyed, bewildered Chu, her jaw dropping all the while, looked back and forth within the Oval Office, searching for something-or-other.

Finally she said, "But... sir... I'm just a *team-leader*, after all! I mean – this would be a promotion by about ten ranks, within the Bureau hierarchy! What about seniority – precedent –"

"This is fundamentally *my* decision, Madam," countered the President. "For which I'm accountable. And as to 'precedent', well, let's see... so far, we've had our entire planet almost destroyed by a comet – thank God for you, Karéin – we've had two hydrogen-bombs almost go off right over our heads, and I have a crew of nearly a dozen angry, godlike, post-human beings sitting in front of me, threatening to either vaporize me, or to wreck the whole country, or both. I believe I can make a convincing case to the Congress, that 'precedent' isn't a particularly applicable concept, under the current circumstances."

He paused for a second, and then repeated,

"Ms. Minnie Chu... will you serve your country as Director of the Federal Bureau of Investigation... so help you God?"

Tears – and a glow, not from *Amaiish*, but from simple pride – were welling in the team-leader's eyes as she replied, loud and clear, "Yes, sir, so help me God... I *will!*"

"Maybe there's some hope for this damn government, after all," observed Saquina White. "Can't wait 'till Otis 'n Will hear 'bout *this!*"

The U.S. leader pressed his under-the-desk communications-button.

"Jerry," he requested, "Are you finished down there?"

"Pretty much, sir," he answered. "Curt's just printing the report. A lot of gaps but best we can do, this fast. What's up?"

"I need you up here in the Oval Office, as soon as possible," said the President. "Can you bring that Bible that's down in the bunker, please?"

There was a pause; then Kaysten replied,

"Sir... is something *wrong*? If any of them think they can get away with –"

"No... nothing like that," reassured the U.S. leader. "Something a lot better, in fact. You know how to work the video-recorders... right? You know – the ones that we use to document state functions. Get up here and I'll explain."

"Yes, I do... and on my way, sir," committed the Chief of Staff, as the connection dropped.

The President arose from his chair.

"Ms. Chu," he directed, "Please step over there – behind the couches, by the back wall. We'll need to clear some space."

The team-leader had survived perils that would have terrified or killed any ordinary human being; but this was the first time that any in the Oval Office, had seen her visibly tremble.

As she got up and slowly stepped past the Storied Watcher, she heard,

"Behold... how the tides of history do change, in front of our very eyes."

Not Just Your Daughter, Anymore

Jacobson, Boyd, Wolf and Tanaka had maintained a polite, if icy, silence (the Russian was somewhat more forthcoming) in front of the cameras, as a proud – but still half-disbelieving – Minnie Chu stepped forward, placed her hand on the Bible and took the Oath of Office.

The team-leader had lately been in situations more stressful than most people had to deal with, for their entire lives; but despite this, it was the first time that Chu's fellow more-than-humans had seen her nearly overcome with emotion.

"This is for *you*, Otis and Will," she had whispered, as she put her hand down on the book.

"Mr. President... it's a great honor," Chu had tried to say. "I only hope that I'll be able to live up to the expectations..."

"You *will*, having been forged in the flame of adversity," the Storied Watcher had reassured, only to be upstaged by Billings, who quipped, "How could you do any *worse?*"

Meanwhile, matters had been progressing at a rapid rate, downstairs.

Just after the swearing-in ceremony, Matt and Clairie – followed some distance behind by the Secret Service agent, Kortish – had re-appeared, with a couple of e-paper document-readers in hand. Upon explanation, it appeared that only Tanaka's mother and Chu's fiancée were definitely known to have been abducted, probably by the intelligence-agencies that had participated in the *coup*; several other extended family-members – notably those of Ramirez and Abruzzio – were unaccounted-for, while efforts were still underway to get in touch with the others.

Billings – late-comer to the program – had finally thrown his support behind it, when it was pointed out that his elder brother and family, apparently living in Nevada, might also be in jeopardy. The ex-salesman had even given Kaysten and Kortish the last known address of his former girlfriend, in Arizona.

"I would like to meet her, you know," the Storied Watcher had offered. "One who has loved you – I would love her as a sister, if she would have me."

"Fine... as long as you don't expect me to explain what the hell's been going on, to her," harrumphed Billings. "She *already* thinks I'm a liar... and a story like *this* isn't going to do anything to change that opinion."

In general, the efforts had been greatly complicated by Kaysten and Kortish having to use only "loyalist" elements of the government that were known to be reliable; all were aware that to mention who was being sought, to the wrong forces, could easily backfire badly.

So far, there were six search-parties dispatched out to various parts of the continental United States, with others being organized. However, nobody had yet been rescued.

After the alien-girl had relented and allowed her adoptive son to use his telekinesis on the two Oval Office couches – Tommy had to be reminded, "son, you must lift them before pulling, or this nice carpet will show spurious wounds of war" – they had resumed their former positions in front of the President, who was again in his chair behind the Resolution Desk.

With one exception – this time, Chu stood, along with Kaysten, behind the U.S. leader.

"Just remember, Minnie," Kaysten said with a smile, "Technically, I out-rank you."

"Ah, but Jerry," reparteed the former team-leader with the wink of an eye, "I can now have you *arrested*."

"All you got to do is *catch* me," came back the inevitable response.

"So," began the President, "We have the search-parties out and about, although obviously it will probably take some time before we start to see results, which we hope and pray will be good news. Which leads us to the next issue... namely, 'how we're going to handle what's gone on, up to this point'. What I'm proposing is –"

The communicator-console below the desk began to sound a ring-tone.

"Just a second," said the U.S. leader.

He hit some buttons and engaged the speaker-driven communications-link.

"This is the President," he announced. "I'm in the middle of an *extremely* sensitive meeting – what's the *reason* for this? I gave very clear instructions not to be interrupted –"

"Ahh," wryly observed the Storied Watcher, *sotto voce*, "At least *this* time, it is not some annoying 'alien' having blasted her way upon an air-plane, who interrupts such an important meeting. As I recall... 'any good books to read'?"

Several on the couches, smiled and suppressed giggles, at hearing this.

"Very sorry, sir," came a previously-unfamiliar, female voice, "But we have a *critical* situation down here, with the press! They're demanding *answers* –"

"We don't have any... at least not yet, Susan," argued the U.S. leader.

"Can I at least tell them you and the First Family are safe, sir?" persisted the voice. "Are there any more nukes? When can we expect a statement? Sir, the networks are going *crazy*, here – conspiracy-theories –"

"We believe that the immediate threats to the D.C. area have now been dealt with; Kathy's safe, and I'd assume I am too... at least for the time being," evaded the President. "As for Matt and Clairie – hey, you two! Speak up!"

"Hi, Ms. Feldner," said the male teenager, who was standing in the back of the Oval Office. "Thanks for hanging in there, for us."

"Thanks," the voice replied. "It's *great* having you back, Mr. President, sir. It was, uhh, *difficult*, working for George. I was *so* scared about those 'bombs'... but he told me that if I left the White House, he'd... well, I'm *sure* you know."

"Indeed I do, Susan," offered the President. "I'm very glad you stayed."

"We're *fine*," added Clairie, who had taken a seat in a single chair, considerably behind the couches that were up at the front, facing the Resolution Desk. "Maybe a bit *too* 'fine', as a matter of fact."

"Uhh... Mr. President... what's *that* mean?" asked the remote voice.

"We'll provide more details, shortly," he stated. "Look – I've got to go, but you're right... we'll have to explain the situation to the country and to the press – I'm not disputing that. Give me ninety minutes – then have the reporters assembled in the Press Briefing Room. Okay?"

"I'll have to coördinate that with the Service and the Capitol Police, sir," answered the voice. "They've got access totally locked-down. Do I have your personal go-ahead to let the press in here?"

"You do," authorized the U.S. leader. "Talk more later. C-In-C, out."

He dropped the connection.

"An hour and a *half?*" exclaimed a nonplussed Jacobson. "You think that's enough time to work out all the issues between us?"

"No – of *course* I don't, Commander!" replied the President. "Doing that will take days... weeks... potentially, *months*. As I said in my earlier address to the nation, I've committed to submit myself to the rule of law, and to be judged by the same, with respect to what's happened up to this point – including my role in it, the decisions I've taken... the works. If that means that I get thrown in jail – so *be* it. I intend to stick to my side of the bargain, whether or not you do; and that's exactly what I'm going to tell the press and the people, in a few minutes."

"I'm not *following* this, sir," inquired Abruzzio. "What exactly do you propose to tell the press, about Commander Jacobson and his team, here?"

"I'll tell them the *truth*," phlegmatically offered the President. "Just like Karéin insists that I do. Namely, 'I've got a crew of enraged super-beings in the Oval Office, ready to kill me at the drop of a hat, I might not last the rest of the night... and have a nice day'. What else am I *supposed* to say?"

"That may not be what your citizens want to hear," observed the Russian, "However much that it may be accurate."

"Why don't you just put them off... tell them to *wait* for their damn stories?" challenged Boyd.

"*Because*," interrupted Kaysten, "He has a *job* to do, and a *responsibility* to inform the public, before the whole damn country disintegrates into total chaos. If, that is, it hasn't already. Remember when I told you guys – up at the camp, I mean – that, 'all due respect' – you just don't understand what it's like, to sit in that chair? Well... now, you're getting a ring-side seat about what it *is* like. He can't use any of these ass-kicking 'alien-powers' that Ms. Angelic

Excellence over there bestowed on us... he has to manage by his wits, along with gut instinct. Always has been that way in politics... always *will* be."

"Thanks, Jerry," appreciatively mentioned the U.S. leader. "And that illustrates the next decision that you – Commander Jacobson, Major Boyd, Ms. Tanaka, all of you – have to make, in the next few minutes. I'll be blunt about it; you can either *kill* me, and try to run the government by yourselves – best of luck to you – or you can work *with* me, on the difficult task of sorting out what the hell has gone wrong, up to this time... and in trying to restore trust, not just in the government but also in the justice system, the economy... all of it."

"Why's all that important to *me?*" argued Jacobson.

"Because," said the President, leaning forward with a deliberate, focused stare, "What I see in front of me, is a man who feels personally-responsible for setting wrongs, right – who's very suspicious of being cheated out of the justice that he came here to see done. I'm betting on the hunch that you're a guy who, deep down, is still a loyal American... a guy who understands how much easier it is to destroy, than it is to rebuild. Above all else, Commander, I think you're someone with some common *sense*. If I'm wrong, well... I guess I won't be around to worry about it."

"Don't *say* stuff like that, Dad!" protested an anguished Clairie.

"It's okay, dear," he tried to reassure. "Remember... in this family, we believe in God. Your Dad's good with whatever fate He has for me. Just tell Mom that I love you and Matt very much."

"You could have said all these nice words when you had us in that jail you put us in, the moment we got back to Earth," countered Tanaka. "You're only saying this because your back's to the wall! The moment you think you can turn on us – you *will!* Don't think we don't know what's motivating you!"

"You know what, Ms. Tanaka?" argued the President. "You're *half*-right about that. If you were just a bunch of – excuse my language, but it's appropriate – 'ass-out-of-space-suits astronauts', standing in front of me, without any bargaining-power, my attitude probably *would* be a lot less forthcoming. I'll admit that. Like Jerry said... 'that's politics'. But like Karéin said – I screwed up on this front, *big-time*. I refused to acknowledge the bargaining-power that you, and she, obviously *do* have... I'll regret that for the rest of my life, however long that is... but I won't make *that* mistake again. And if you, Commander Jacobson, Wolf, Major Boyd, Major White out there and Mr. Grishin had just meekly sat back and surrendered when the government ordered you to – you're right, I *wouldn't* have respected you. That's politics too; it's a rough business."

"You're damn right about *that!*" accused Boyd, "As in, 'trying to kidnap and likely, torture, my wife and young children'!"

"You're right," acknowledged the U.S. leader, "Sometimes it gets far *too* rough. Remember that saying about 'absolute power, corrupts absolutely'? If you decide to depose me or contest how I run the country – or just keep it simple and kill me outright – you'll find out how that feels like. I can *assure* you, it's not what it's made out to be. You say that you're outraged and horrified at what might have happened to your families, had you not intervened in time? I don't blame you... don't blame you a *bit!* Now... try to imagine what it's like to be responsible for the safety not just of one or two families, but for a whole *country-full* of them. I guess if you get completely drunk on these 'alien-powers' of yours, maybe you won't care. I can tell you... I, *do*."

"So where does this leave us, sir?" inquired the Russian. "Even if Commander Jacobson and his team – including myself – accept all that you have stated about the challenges of running your country... what is your 'ask', of him? That he just stand there and smile, while you reassure that United States that 'everything is back to normal'?"

"Problem is," sourly commented Saquina White, "Your idea of 'normal', ain't anythin' like what we poor folk think of as, 'fair'. Y'all just tryin' to smart-talk him into givin' up, without a fight!"

"No... of course not!" argued the President. "What I'm asking for is, 'give me a little *time*, for God's sake!' Real change *is* needed, at every level – I *acknowledge* that. I'll warn you ahead of time that doing it won't be easy... the government has developed bad habits over *decades* and rolling them back *will* encounter deeply-entrenched resistance. I'm willing to stake what's left of my political career, in spear-heading efforts to reform the system. But ask yourselves – is it more likely that's going to be done with something resembling a stable government having been restored... or after I"m gone, with a bunch of super-human beings, with no legal justification at all, other than brute force power that is, in charge, here? This is what I meant about 'common sense', in addressing you, Commander –"

"So you expect us just to stand around, smiling sweetly, while you 'restore normalcy'... is that right?" complained Jacobson.

"No!" shot back the U.S. leader. "I'm not proposing that you folks just fold your tents and slink back home, with your tails between your legs. Were I sitting where you are, if I heard that from this chair, I'd probably kick the 'President' into next week... and he'd *deserve* it. I'm simply asking you to hold back – let me try to put the pieces back together as best I can, hopefully with your assistance where it's necessary – and if at any time during that process, I do something to seriously antagonize you, we'll be back where we are right now. Meanwhile we will engage the Justice Department, with Ms. Chu there ensuring that there's no favoritism on either side, to decide 'who's accountable for what'. If you have a better idea of how to move forward... now's the time to let us know what it is."

"I don't know much of this damn 'government' stuff," sullenly replied the astronaut's-wife. "So don't ask *me!*"

The President looked from face to face.

What confronted him – particularly among the "Mars Gang" membership – was a combination of frustration, thinly-suppressed anger, and suspicion.

"Karéin... Bob... Tommy," asked Chu, from her vantage-point behind the President, "How does this all sound to *you*? After all... it was *your* family, who the government initially targeted; and as we all know, many of the worst crimes were done to Elissha, to her late brother, and to Tommy."

"Mom told me to be *nice* to him," pouted the boy. "Besides... if I try to blow him up – *she* might get hit, like the last time. I don't want *that* to happen! I don't know about the other stuff. I was going to take Civics next year... but I ran away from the reservation, so I missed those classes."

"Well, kid," offered Billings, with his usual cynicism, "I don't think they'd have taught you about how the government pulls peoples' fingernails out, when they get slapped with a parking-ticket... so you didn't miss much. As for what he's saying, my only comment would be, 'you got him by the balls... so I'd make him agree, ahead of time, to anything and everything that you ask of him later'. Like, for example, 'I don't want to pay any taxes again... *ever*'. Or, 'I get to pop in here – to the White House – and use the Executive Washroom, whenever I've been doing the bar-circuit in D.C. and I'm about to burst. *That* kind of thing."

"Really?" pressed Chu. "I mean... you *know* about the 'alcohol' thing."

"I'm a 'practical' kind of guy," claimed the ex-salesman. "I might be out with friends, who haven't yet turned into space-aliens. Buzz or no buzz... I might still knock a few back, just to be one of the crowd, you know?"

The former team-leader let out a sigh and said, "Karéin... ?"

"I refrain from intervening in a test of judgment," diffidently responded the alien-girl, "Except to say... 'those who would depose a ruler, should be prepared to rule in their own right'. I can attest that it is a, ahh, 'full-time job'. Prepare to devote much of your time to signing scrolls of acknowledgment, when the peasants bring sacks of grain as tax-payments, to the king. Not to mention, 'for hearing complaints made by one of the high-born against another, over breaches in etiquette, and other slights, real or imagined'."

"Were you a *queen*, Mom?" whispered an enthralled Tommy.

"Yes, young prince," she confirmed. "But not a very *wise* one, I must confess. And the crown was too big for my head. It kept falling down."

The boy giggled intensively.

"So what's *your* POV on this, Minnie?" asked Boyd. "You've taken an oath of loyalty to him –"

"Not true," quickly retorted Chu. "I've pledged my loyalty to the Constitution, to the United States... not to a specific individual. That's what I intend to do."

"Well *that's* nice to know," continued the former Mars mission pilot. "But what's your answer?"

"I'm honestly not sure, Major," replied Chu, "It will depend on the testimony and the evidence, as it's presented to me and, I presume, the Attorney-General. Based on what I know of the law – unless there's something like a Presidential pardon involved – I *do* have to state that you guys are up to your *necks* in it... I mean, that business at Fort Knox... the list of felonies just there, would probably fill a good-sized book. Of course, you'd have many potential defenses, in particular 'necessity', 'self-defense' and 'government misconduct', as mitigating factors."

"What about all the shit that *he* done to *them?*" complained Saquina White. "Or to everybody else? Down Compton way, the Army was shootin' folks in the *street*, by the *dozens*, with them helicopter-gunships! Or don't y'all remember how y'all handled *that* situation, *yourself,* Minnie*?*"

"What's she referring to?" requested the President.

"Along with many of us, Karéin was rescuing school-children, and their families, in urban L.A., because we were afraid – and I'm *still* afraid, incidentally – that there may be a loose nuclear weapon in that area," uncomfortably related the former team-leader.

"For reasons that are still unclear – I'd assume it was that they were hunting the Storied Watcher herself," continued Chu, "The military sent a large strike-force into the area. Unfortunately, sir, I personally witnessed the use of *wildly*-unnecessary lethal force at that time, including the indiscriminate use of machine-cannons against innocent civilians in the vicinity. While Karéin was otherwise occupied, I was put in a predicament where either I could use my alien-powers to defend some of the refugees that she was trying to save, or just stand by and watch these people get *slaughtered*. I chose the former, and in so doing, I... uhh... shot down a gunship. I don't know if the pilot survived but I'd have to assume that he didn't. If I was placed in that situation again I'd do exactly the same thing. That's about 'it', sir."

"You know," quietly observed the President, "An incident like *that*, might well disqualify you for holding the position that you've just been sworn in to."

"So would, 'slicing several Secret Service agents in half, with the *Gaze of the Khùl-Algrenàthi'i*, sir," argued Chu, "But –"

"The 'what' of the 'what'?" interjected the U.S. leader.

"It is one of noble Min-ee's most dread powers of the *Fire*... akin to mine own, sir," explained Karéin-Mayréij. "This skill projects a beam of directed energy from one's eyes; anything directly in one's core line of sight – unless it be greatly-robust, such as mighty Sam's diamond-fortress – will be cleft in twain, or set ablaze from end to end... or, may it just be disintegrated in its entirety. Either of us can show it to you, right here. Would you like us to do so?"

To the President's panic, her eyes were suddenly glowing with a brilliant golden-hue.

"Yeah, Mom – *show* him!" enthusiastically demanded Tommy.

"No... no!" back-pedaled the President, "That's quite alright... I'll take your *word* for it. "

"Why are you *threatening* him!" called Clairie, from the back of the room.

"Young princess... come here," directed the Storied Watcher.

The teenager, with her brother in her tow, advanced to stand over the couch upon which the alien-girl was sitting.

Karéin-Mayréij – her eyes still glowing – turned her head to look directly at the Presidential teenage daughter.

"Does this," said the Storied Watcher, pointing with both index fingers at her eyes, "Affright you, Clairie?"

"Y – *yes!*" stammered the girl.

"But it is... *you*," offered Karéin-Mayréij. "It is who you now... *are*."

"I don't *want* it!" protested the teenager. "Make it go *away!* Stop scaring my Dad!"

"Clairie," purred the alien-girl, "I want to show you something."

The Storied Watcher – with the shine in her eyes still visible, but somewhat more subdued – stood up and advanced until she was right in front of the Resolution Desk.

She pointed at one of the President's exquisitely-crafted, gold-encased document-signing-pens.

"May I borrow this for a minute or two, sir?" she asked.

"Yes, I suppose," agreed the U.S. leader, "But don't take too long – remember, I have a press-conference coming up shortly."

"This will only take a moment," assured the alien-girl. "Clairie... come up to the desk, if you please."

Nervously, the teenager complied, with her ever-faithful brother just behind, looking over her shoulder. She stood next to Karéin-Mayréij.

"Good luck, sister," said a knowingly-smiling Cherie Tanaka.

"Ha... just like up on ISS2," observed Boyd.

The Storied Watcher laid the pen on the desk, about two feet in front of both her and the female teenager.

"I have a test for you," stated the alien-girl. "See that pen, yonder on the desk?"

"Sure," confirmed Clairie.

"Move it toward me, to place it within reach," directed the Storied Watcher.

Clairie bent forward and extended her hand to grasp the pen; but this was rewarded with a quick, light slap-on-the-wrist, from her alien mentor.

"Did I say that you could use your *hands*, child?" she remonstrated.

"Well how else am I *supposed* to do it, Karéin?" protested the teenager.

"With your *mind*, stupid!" taunted Tommy.

"Son," corrected Karéin-Mayréij, "That is *not* appropriate language to use, with your new sister. Are you not regretful for having said that?"

"Yeah... I guess, Mom," sulked the boy. "Sorry, Clairie."

"No problemo," answered the teenaged girl, "But Karéin... really! I don't know –"

"Yes... you *do*," interrupted the Storied Watcher. "Now heed my counsel : stare deliberately at the pen. Clear your mind of thinking to any person or thing, except this object. Close your eyes briefly, then open them, and when you do, focus all of your attention upon the pen; then, imagine that you are pulling it toward you, as you were about to do... but do *not* extend your arms. Go ahead."

"This is ridiculous... but okay... just to get it over with," grumbled Clairie.

She followed the alien-girl's instructions.

Clairie's eyelids closed and re-opened, staring at the writing-instrument. She stared straight forward for one second... then another... and on the third clock-tick, her shocked father – who had been carefully observing the experiment – reflexively pushed his chair back from the Resolution Desk, as the pen began rolling, all on its own, toward the alien-girl and her new student.

"D... Dad?" uneasily spoke Clairie. "What's *wrong?*"

"Sweetheart... your *eyes!*" he managed.

The teenager turned to face those on the couches.

There was a dull – but definitely-visible – cerulean glow within her eyes; this faded from sight, in the next two seconds.

"Holy *shit!*" exclaimed Matt. "Sis... it really *is* happening to us, you know!"

"Karéin," quietly demanded the President, "Is she still my... *daughter?*"

"No," plainly responded the Storied Watcher.

"*Damn* you!" the U.S. leader cursed.

"That's not *true!*" cried an upset, tearful Clairie. "Dad – I'm still the same person that I *always* was! I still *love* you! *You* know that... don't you?"

"No... you are *not*," contradicted Karéin-Mayréij. "You are now someone much more noble... more powerful. You will live many times the life-span of your father and mother. Will you inherit the deadly *Gaze* which empowers Min-ee and myself, child? Or will your mind crush army-tanks and uproot trees? None shall know, except the Weavers of Time-To-Come."

"What's the *point* of all this, Karéin?" challenged Matt. "Just to scare the shit out of Dad? Not to mention, 'out of both Clairie and me'."

"That is a fair question, young prince," answered the Storied Watcher. "The answer is, 'it is for two reasons'. First off, to make the two of you understand, that to fear *me* – or to fear those others of the Holy *Fire* who you see arrayed in this room – is, to fear *yourselves*. Doing so makes no sense! It is rational to fear and distrust an enemy against whom one is hopelessly outmatched... not one whose abilities are, or shortly will be, akin to one's own."

She paused briefly, then continued, "For second... it is to show both your father – and certain others here in this room – how much that things have lately... *changed*. The old ways no longer stand; their days are gone, their times are past, no matter how some would use guile, to restore them. The test – for all who hear these words – is to navigate as best they can through this situation, hoping for the best, ever while guarding against the worst. Do you understand?"

"Yeah... *sort* of," muttered the Presidential son. "Listen, Dad... I'm feeling the same way that Clairie is. I guess we really *aren't* the same any more... but that doesn't make us any the less your son and daughter... you know?"

"I'm glad to hear that, son," offered the President. "This is going to take some getting used to, I'm afraid."

"A *lot* of 'getting used to'," noted Abruzzio. "Both for you... and for them."

After a couple of seconds of silence, the U.S. leader announced, "Well. It's getting near time... I have to address the country. You already *know* what I'm going to say. Is anybody going to stop me, when I leave for the Press Gallery?"

There was more silence.

The President arose.

"Jerry – Ms. Chu – I'd like you to accompany me," he said. "There's a makeup-room on the way."

He straightened his tie, walked around the Resolution Desk and stopped briefly in front of Jacobson.

"Thank you," offered the President.

The former Mars mission commander looked up, with a wary look on his face. But he said nothing.

As the President, with Chu and Kaysten alongside him, exited the Oval Office, Jacobson sent,

What do we do now, team?

Show-Time

Kortish had been dispatched to the bunker, to assist the few remaining Marines monitoring the defensive-systems. He had been given instructions to alert immediately, if any other attacks were detected inbound towards 1600 Pennsylvania Avenue.

After Chu had taken a few minutes in one of the communications-rooms to interact with the Bureau, there was a stop-over in the White House "Presentation Preparation Facility" – an amazingly well-equipped place, easily the equal of any makeup-room on any TV production-stage, despite its relatively constrained dimensions – and then the U.S. leader and his entourage were declared "ready to face the cameras".

Somehow, most of the staff of the facility hadn't bolted the White House earlier on (actually, as was divulged during quick conversations, they *had* tried to leave, but all the exit-doors had been auto-locked); this was much to Chu's relief, as they had actually been able to find her a decent-looking change of clothes, complete with new shoes. These, in fact, belonged to the Press Secretary – Susan Feldner – whose height and build closely approximated the former team-leader's own.

Chu had even found five minutes in which to take a *blitz*-shower and to dry and brush her hair, prior to being made up to make a good impression under the bright lights. She had to take turns with both the President and Kaysten, who cycled in and out of the washroom to shave themselves and wash faces.

"No rings under my eyes?" anxiously worried the former team-leader, as she, the President and the Chief of Staff queued up, outside the entrance to the Brady Press Briefing Room, waiting for Feldner's signal to enter.

"I've lost track of how long I've been up, without any sleep," Chu warned.

"You look *great*, Minnie!" deflected Kaysten. "Uhh... but maybe – note to myself, as well as to you – no *Amaiish* in there... okay? They get a look at the eyes – like back in the Oval Office with Clairie, a few minutes ago – and they'll go *apeshit*. We already *got* conspiracy-theories... just imagine if..."

"Right, then," ruefully acknowledged the ex-team-leader. "No 'being lit up from inside', no glowing eyes... no death-rays projected from them. Gotcha."

She whispered, "That goes for you *too*, Warden."

A small mind-voice replied that it had understood.

"Let's not be too hasty, Ms. Chu," mordantly joked the President. "I can name for you several reporters who I think would be better off with a taste of this '*Gaze*' of yours."

"I'll take that as general as opposed to specific guidance, sir," she smartly replied. "But Jerry... you *know* this is my first public press-conference... don't you? Unless you count that fiasco down in Tucson, by Bob's former residence."

"Relax!" he counseled. "Just be yourself – you'll do *fine*. Let the Old Man do most of the talking, and if they ask you something, try to answer as tersely as you can – just address the question... you don't owe them a full explanation. *You* know these guys – they're always looking for an angle... something that they can spin as a 'crisis' or whatever."

"Not that they're short of 'crises' to report on, these days," sighed the President. "I've no idea how I'm going to credibly reassure the people, with

Mr. Jacobson and his crew in the next room, capable of leveling this place in a fit of pique... but I'll think of *something*... I always do."

Feldner's pleasant-looking, New York elite face appeared in the doorway. "It's time," she said.

A voice inside the room announced, "The President of the United States!"

The President nodded affirmatively, as he straightened his tie one last time (a move mimicked by Kaysten) and strode confidently, followed by his Chief of Staff and then the "Acting FBI Director", into the Press Room.

The overhead-lights were harsh in their intensity; but for her part, Chu noticed that they hardly bothered her.

Immediately, there was a commotion, as several in the crowd cast stares of disbelief at Kaysten.

"It's okay, folks," reassured the Chief of Staff, with a polite smile and the wink of an eye. "Rumors of my demise have been greatly-exaggerated."

The U.S. leader engaged in a little banter with some of the senior TV-network White House correspondents, pointing and smiling at one or two of them. Then he advanced to the Blue Goose lectern, paused for a second or two to collect his thoughts, and then – in his best fatherly, dignified tone – began to speak.

"Good evening, ladies and gentlemen... members of the press," he started. "I'd like to thank all of you for coming here on such short notice, under what as we all know have been very trying circumstances – arguably, even, at great personal risk to your own life and safety, given what's been going on around here, lately. And regarding the latter, I'm immensely grateful to report to you now, that – thanks to the help of Almighty God and of some new-found friends, who I'll say more about, in a few minutes – *the danger is over. The D.C. region is safe.*"

Gasps, sighs of relief and murmured prayers were easy to detect, even among the hardened reporters in the audience.

"Let me say this again... lest there be any mistake," confidently announced the President. "Though we came far too close to a disaster of catastrophic proportions – specifically, a despicable terrorist attack using no less than *two* nuclear weapons – as many of you have already been reporting, both of these weapons did not detonate close to centers of population, but rather did so far out over the Atlantic Ocean, where the damage that they could inflict was, relatively speaking, 'minor' – at least compared to what *might* have happened, otherwise."

He continued, "None the less... we *do* have reports of some damage along the Eastern Seaboard from at least the Chesapeake Bay area to Long Island, including power-outages in much of New York and Philadelphia, likely due to the bombs' electro-magnetic pulse or 'EMP' effects. Both federal and state governments are now assisting with these situations. We urge all citizens of the affected areas to remain at home unless you absolutely *must* travel, and to obey the instructions of the police and other public safety authorities. As usual, crimes such as rioting and disorder will be swiftly and effectively dealt with. We all need to pull together, to recover as quickly as possible from this near-disaster."

He paused for a second or two, and then said, "Now... I know that what will be foremost in the minds of most Americans watching this tonight, is the 'why' question – specifically, 'how could all of this been allowed to come about... and how did the government successfully deal with the situation, albeit at the last moment'. I'll try to provide a summary – as best we currently understand it – here and now; but I also have to advise you all that some details, particularly concerning national security methods and resources, will have to remain classified; also, some of the information that I've been provided with, is as yet unverified or incomplete. To avoid saying something that later turns out to be misleading or untrue, I'll have to ask you all to wait, until I'm sure of what I'm saying, when all the facts become known."

"So," explained the President, "With that in mind, here is what we know now : the Capitol Region was threatened by attack by two *different* nuclear weapons. One was stolen by terrorists, from our military near Barksdale Air Force Base in Louisiana, some time ago; this one was somehow smuggled on-board the National Airborne Command Post or 'ACP', which as some of you know is often used as personal transport for the President and the Cabinet. The second bomb was on a stealth cruise-missile – a standard military weapon – which was then launched, without legal authorization, with its intended target either being the ACP or Washington, D.C., itself. While many of the details involved in these crimes are still awaiting verification, we *can* tell you that we believe that two *separate* groups of terrorists, were responsible for each of these threats. We believe that the leadership of the first group, perished with the detonation of the bomb on-board the ACP, over the Atlantic. The leadership of the second group *may* still be at large, and obviously, we're now engaging in intensive efforts to locate and apprehend, or eliminate, these criminals. However, we have also done an inventory of the military's remaining nuclear weapons, and we have,"

He reflexively coughed, then went on,

"A high degree of confidence that all of these are accounted-for. Thus, we do not believe that any more incidents of the type that I've just described, will be forthcoming."

A cacophony of anxious, shouted questions erupted from the press gallery. The President motioned for calm, with outstretched hands.

"Please... *please!*" he demanded. "I'll take your questions later. Let me provide the rest of the explanation, for now. There's much you don't yet know."

Slowly, the crowd quieted down.

"We believe," said the President, "Based upon the first-hand testimony of a witness who's here with me today – that the former Vice-President, who among others was involved in an illegal *coup* against me as the legitimate President of the United States – was killed in the first nuclear explosion, that is, the one that destroyed the Airborne Command Post. Furthermore, we believe that my former Spiritual Adviser, Harold Crowford, the former, illegally-appointed 'Director' of the FBI, William Warnock, and General Blanshard of the U.S. Army, were also among the victims of this event. Former National Security Adviser John Bezomorton is, as yet, unaccounted-for. Sadly, to the best of our current knowledge, all of these individuals – with the possible exception of Blanshard – were also involved in the *coup*. Of course, we mourn the loss of the many other government staff, who likely had no personal involvement in these illegal activities, aboard this aircraft. I'll be calling for a Congressional Commission of Inquiry to review the evidence, as soon as possible."

"Now," he elaborated, "As to the second nuclear device, as I've said, we believe that *it*, too, was launched by disloyal elements within the government. We are not sure of the relationship – if any – between this group, and the conspirators who were involved in the plot that originally removed me from my legitimate office as President. Investigations are continuing, and let me assure the nation, that those involved in this *will* be swiftly apprehended and brought to justice."

The President said, "But this brings me to the question that no doubt all of you have on your minds, which is... 'how is it, that we managed to avoid having these two weapons going off, directly above Washington, D.C.' – which, God forbid, had it happened, would undoubtedly have caused *unimaginable* destruction, leading to the deaths of *millions* of our fellow Americans. I *did* order the Armed Forces to do their best to prevent this; but a number of factors – in particular, the short notice that we received about the threat – made it impossible for our brave Air Force pilots to satisfactorily intercept and destroy the ACP and the other missile."

He paused, looked directly at the front rank reporters within the Press Gallery, and announced, "However difficult it may be to believe what I'm next going to say... it is, as the Lord is my witness... the *truth*. My fellow Americans, I can report to you now, that it was only by the grace of Almighty God Himself, and with the extraordinary efforts of the alien Karéin-Mayréij, also known as the 'Storied Watcher' – as well as those of her followers, many of whom have some of the same super-powers as she does – that we were spared from disaster."

More gasps of shock and disbelief, came from the audience.

"While some of the details are still unclear," continued the President, "What we *do* know is, the Airborne Command Post was lured away from its intended target – that is, 'the White House' – by the use of these 'alien-powers', by Karéin's friends, at great personal risk. The Storied Watcher herself – again, at significant risk – was responsible for diverting the second weapon, that is, the one on the cruise missile, far enough offshore to detonate it relatively safely. She apparently was very close to this bomb when it went off, and was wounded in so doing... although she *did* survive. Had these people not intervened, it's likely that the First Lady and myself would be among millions dead or dying, due to the likely impact of either or both of these terrible weapons. I literally owe these people my *life*... as do, many of you listening to these words, right now."

"And," he stated, "In that respect... I have someone here with me today, who I'd like to introduce. This woman – a seasoned veteran of the Federal Bureau of Investigation, who also has first-hand experience with the alien, Karéin-Mayréij – was on the Airborne Command Post, just before it was destroyed by the first nuclear detonation; she only escaped by the narrowest of margins. She also fought against the *coup* conspirators and was instrumental in the efforts to divert the ACP away from D.C. and out to sea. Her actions – along with those of another very brave, loyal person who you will see later – bought us the time that we needed, to get the Command Post away from the city."

"And," continued the U.S. leader, "As we believe that former Director Warnock, who had been illegally-appointed in any event, perished along with everyone else in the aircraft involved – and as we believe the earlier Director, Cesar Ochoa, isn't able to execute his duties, I'm pleased and very proud to announce today that I have – under my authority as Commander-In-Chief – provisionally sworn in Ms. Minnie Chu, as Acting Director of the FBI. With years of experience with the Bureau, Ms. Chu has already demonstrated a professional commitment to law enforcement as well as loyalty to the United States, far above and beyond the call of duty. It's probably not an exaggeration to say that many of you in the room here tonight, owe her your *lives*. She will be – in my opinion – an *outstanding* choice as Director. Minnie... would you please step forward and say a few words?"

For a second or two, Chu was transfixed by the sheer enormity of what was going on, and – to her inner (but carefully-disguised) embarrassment – she froze. But then something from deep inside re-motivated her, and she walked straight up to the podium, which Kaysten quickly adjusted to fit her height.

"Thanks," she whispered in his direction.

He nodded supportively.

Then she turned to face the crowd, and said,

"Thank you, sir, for the kind words of support."

"First of all," Chu declared, "I'd like to say that I can confirm your account of recent events... especially those having to do with the Airborne Command Post. Like you, I deplore the loss of life aboard that airplane. I did all that I could to save those who I could. My only consolation, obviously, is that it *could* have been worse... much, *much* worse."

Gestures of acknowledgment. and appreciation came from both the President and Kaysten.

"Mr. President," continued the former team-leader, "You have my word that I'll do everything within my power to faithfully and completely execute the duties of the office to which I've been nominated. To everyone listening – both in this room at at home – I'd like you to know how deeply-committed I am to the Constitution, to the rule of law and to the safety of the American people. You know, sir... lately, we've all been through a *lot*. Some of those responsible for the recent, nearly-disastrous events in the skies overhead, may still be at large; and as you're already aware, law enforcement is also following up on a despicable terrorist bombing against the FBI regional headquarters in Chicago – a cowardly act of violence that's left *dozens* dead and many more seriously wounded."

"I promise," she vowed, looking straight at the cameras, "That I'll leave no stone unturned, in bringing those responsible for all these crimes, to justice. To the staff of the Bureau... I'm counting on *your* help and support, too. I'll try to provide good leadership, but it's *you* – individual field-agents and folks on the inside, doing the tough work, behind the scenes, day in day out – that keep this country safe. I hope to earn your trust... and to deserve it when and if I do."

"That's it, sir," she concluded.

"*Excellent*, Minnie!" whispered Kaysten.

A barrage of questions erupted from the crowd of reporters.

"Please – hold the questions for now," demanded the President. "We'll give you plenty of time for them later... and I have more to say."

The Chief of Staff re-adjusted the podium, increasing its height substantially.

"Now," spoke the U.S. leader, "There are also some other recent events that have happened in and around the White House, that you and the American people, deserve an explanation for. Around an hour or so ago, an, uhh, 'airship' – that's the best way that I can describe it – originally built by the alien, Karéin-Mayréij – attempted to land in the South Lawn, just outside the Oval Office. As this visit wasn't anticipated or pre-cleared, our local defenses reacted automatically against it, and, unfortunately, during that engagement, a number of casualties resulted within crowds that were in too-close proximity to the White House. We sincerely regret this tragedy, and I have instructed the government to ensure that those who were wounded, will get the best medical care. To avoid a repeat, however, I'd ask tourists and other onlookers not to approach closer than one city block away, until further notice, when we've stabilized the situation. We don't need a repeat of what happened in this case."

"Now," the President continued, "After the 'air-ship' – which was not seriously-damaged, by the way – actually landed, we discovered that it was carrying – *ahem* – the so-called 'Mars Gang' –"

Yet another gasp of shock mixed with fear emanated from the audience.

"That is, Commander Sam Jacobson, Majors Brent Boyd and Devon White, of the *Eagle / Infinity* Mars mission, as well as several more followers and friends of the Storied Watcher... Ms. Cherie Tanaka, also of the Mars mission, and certain others, arrived here, shortly thereafter," described the President. "Some of these people may already be familiar to the media; others, I'd assume, are not... at least, 'not yet'. And – except for a couple who I have been told, are maintaining defensive-positions outside, on the White House grounds – most of them, including the 'Mars Gang' and Karéin-Mayréij herself, are now – *ahem* – in the Oval Office."

Panic broke out, as several from the audience started heading for the exits.

"Please – please stay at your *seats!*" pleaded the U.S. leader.

The demand was mostly complied with, although a few reporters insisted on remaining on their feet, near the doorways.

"There's much that you don't know about this situation, which admittedly *is* rapidly-evolving," the President quickly remarked, "Starting with the obvious factor that if these 'more-than-humans' wanted to do anyone around here, serious harm... we'd all be standing in a pile of rubble, as opposed to in a functioning White House. As you'll recall from one of my recent speeches from the Oval Office, I had invited the 'Mars Gang' here to discuss their grievances against the government, in the hopes of reaching an agreement with them. While these discussions are ongoing, I believe that we have been making progress, and –"

There was a knock on the door.

"Susan... deal with that, *would* you?" requested Kaysten, *sotto voce*. "Don't whoever that is, know we've got a press-conference going on?"

"Of *course*," she complied.

Feldner hurried off to the door. She opened it, and a few in the audience with a good line-of-sight, saw her jaw drop with wary astonishment.

"Wait – you *can't* –" the Press Secretary tried to argue; but it was too late.

Into the Presidential Press Gallery – led by a cleaned- and tidied-up Sam Jacobson – walked the 'Mars Gang', with yet more of the 'more-than-humans', following right behind. Jacobson, Boyd, Devon White, Tanaka, the Russian and Sylvia Abruzzio had somehow each been given a TV-makeup-job and had been provided with formal business-attire (down to shiny black, lace-up shoes), and a couple of them were actually wearing ties, although Wolf was his usual, scruffy-denim self. Saquina White was absent. Bob Billings – somewhat cleaned-up himself, but less so than the Jacobson group – came in next.

The last two to enter the room, were a pretty, teenager-slim-looking female with striking green eyes and blond hair cut into a bang on her forehead, wearing attractive, flowing, California- or Florida-style night-time casual clothing... and her young, wide-eyed, tan-skinned son, holding her hand.

A Bananas Republic

The President – looking quickly over his shoulder – did a double-take. He did an expert job of masking his surprise (verging on "shock"), however.

"I'd... uhh... like to introduce Commander Sam Jacobson and his Mars mission team," he announced, with feigned composure. "And I'll say 'hello' and 'thank you' again', to our alien-friend – Karéin-Mayréij – over there."

The Storied Watcher – instantly the center of rapt attention, from the press-crew – did a demure curtsy. Tommy also did an obviously-rehearsed slight, Little Lord Fauntleroy bow.

"As there are quite a few of you here," proposed the U.S. leader, "It may make sense for some to come around the back, so we can have somewhat equal numbers on either side of the podium."

"Thank you, Mr. President," politely responded Jacobson. "We'll do that."

He motioned to the far side of the speaking-area, next to the outside-wall, and Devon White, followed by the Russian, Boyd and Wolf, took positions to the President's right. Jacobson, Tanaka and Abruzzio stood to the U.S. leader's left, while the Storied Watcher, Billings and their adoptive son were further back, nearer to the door leading to the inside of the White House. Kaysten, Chu and Feldner were behind the President, up on the demi-stage.

Even with the White House press corps being under-strength due to many correspondents having decamped for safer locations, it was crowded in here, particularly at the front of the room.

"Mr. Jacobson," carefully offered the President, "I'm assuming that you came here with something to say? This is being carried live, around the world, by the way."

"So I had assumed," answered the former Mars mission commander. "And yes... *we*, do. May I?"

"There you go," obliged the President, as he ceded the podium.

"Thank you, Mr. President," smoothly stated Jacobson. "First, I'd like to introduce those who are here with us tonight; going from right to left, behind me, are my former Mars mission communications-officer, Major Devon White; Special Agent of the Russian Federation, Misha Grishin, Major Brent Boyd, also of the Mars mission; and our friend 'Wolf', from Tucson, Arizona."

He turned to face behind and to his left.

"We already of course know Jerry Kaysten and Minnie Chu – I'm sorry but I'm not familiar with –"

"Susan Feldner," she whispered. "I'm the Press Secretary."

"Thanks," said Jacobson, with an even smile. "To my left, are Science Officer Cherie Tanaka, of the *Eagle / Infinity* Mars mission, and Sylvia Abruzzio, of Jet Propulsion Labs Ground Control, also in support of our trip to Mars. Hector Ramirez, who worked alongside Sylvia at JPL, is outside, along with Devon's wife, Saquina White, and with Melissa Claremont, who's wounded but who is recovering on-board our air-ship. And finally – behind, nearer to the door – we have Bob Billings, of the Tucson floor-tile business –"

"We also do 'custom kitchens and appliances'," inopportunely interrupted Billings, while his alien better half sighed and rolled her eyes.

"I stand corrected... 'floor-tiles and custom kitchen appliances'," patiently repeated Jacobson. "Beside Bob, is our youngest team-member, Tommy Singing-Bird George... and his adoptive mother, who should need no introduction, by now. Hi, Karéin."

The Storied Watcher crossed her arms upon her chest, did a slight forward-bow and batted her eyes.

"Collectively, we are all friends and followers of Karéin-Mayréij," explained Jacobson, "And there are many more of us, other than those who you see now. We have all endured tremendous risks and great personal hardship, in order to get here. We were on a mission... and we mean to see it through to its successful conclusion."

The President bit his lip.

"There's *so* much to relate," continued the former Mars mission commander, "I'll have to skip the details – which I'm sure will come out later – and instead just concentrate on what needs to be said here, tonight. I'll start by addressing what's likely to be the Number One thought on your minds... which is, 'but I thought they were *criminals*'. No... we aren't! We're just a bunch of Americans – and, a few non-Americans – who were illegally-imprisoned, without due process of any kind, and who were then repeatedly attacked – almost killed, on several occasions – by the government. The difference between what happens to hundreds of thousands of the government's ordinary victims, and us, is that we inherited some of Karéin's 'alien-powers'. These kept us alive, even in the face of *murderous* attacks, including for example guided missiles fired by fighter-planes, that would have defeated small armies."

He paused and said, "The bottom line is... the fact that you see us here talking to you tonight, is *in spite of* what the government wanted to do to us. Particularly at the start of the misadventure... it was a very near thing. We could all *easily* have died! That factor colors much of our thinking."

Jacobson took a deep breath, and went on, "As the President surely knows, we have it within our power to do anything we want here, and, in fact, almost anywhere on the planet, in the fullness of time. We could lay the entire *country* to waste, if we wanted to. But that has never been our objective. Rather, it has been to get *justice* – not just for ourselves, and for all the wrongs that have been done to us – including, for example, the attempted kidnapping and torture of our families – but also for all the *other* helpless victims who the government has been abusing, over the past decades. We'll settle for no less, and there are many other structural reforms that we have come to understand are necessary, if this country is to return to anything even vaguely *resembling* a real democracy."

The crowd was very quiet, now. They hung on his every word.

"But," offered Jacobson, "The question comes down to, 'when you have ultimate power... how do you use it to make things *better*... as opposed to just 'making a mess". Had this country still been under the control of the former Vice-President – a man who'll live in infamy for his illegal seizure of power, his cruelty, deceitfulness and bigotry, particularly toward Karéin and anyone in any way associated with her – the discussions would have been over, we'd have violently overthrown him and that would have been that. But fortunately... it appears that events have taken care of *that* situation, all on their own. So we're left with a flawed government that we hope, is reformable... and a sort of duly-elected President, with whom we *hope* we can work."

"That's what I hope too," added the President, loudly enough to be heard elsewhere in the room.

"My team and I – and I should point out that the 'Mars Gang', as it has been so identified by the media, does *not* include all of Karéin's friends and followers – it is limited to myself, Majors White and Boyd, Wolf, Agent Grishin, Cherie Tanaka and one other individual who's not here with us tonight," explained the Mars mission commander, "Have been in intensive and, frankly, difficult discussions with the President, since we arrived here, and I'd further point out that we were 'greeted' with a missile-barrage and machine-gun-fire... not something that gets one off to the best of starts... you know?"

There was a little forced laughing from the press corps.

"I'm gratified to report, however, that except for one person – Melissa Claremont, who is not part of our group but who was quite seriously wounded in this latest, treacherous attack, she is now recovering – the government's latest attempts to kill us have failed, just like all the previous ones did," Jacobson stated. "However this was pretty much what we have come to expect from the government, over the past few weeks... and it's *intolerable!"*

Jacobson paused for a second or two for effect and then declared, "Therefore – with the full support of my team – I'm announcing tonight that further attacks on any member of the 'Mars Gang', or on any other followers of the Storied Watcher, or on our families or other loved-ones, or against those who we designate as being under our protection, *will* result in the immediate, *total* destruction of whatever and whoever tries to injure or kill us. We *will* use indiscriminate force in retaliating for these types of attacks and we *will not* be held responsible for any loss of life and property that may result. There will be *no* exceptions to this policy – *none!* Mr. President, we *can* not and *will* not negotiate in good faith, with someone whose forces are trying to *murder* us! Is anything unclear about what I have just said?"

"Mr. Jacobson," replied the President, "May I take the podium for a minute, please?"

"Sure," replied the Mars mission commander.

The President took a couple of steps forward and, while standing next to Jacobson, spoke into the microphone.

"This next directive is from myself, the President of the United States, acting in my capacity as Commander-In-Chief," he loudly proclaimed. "I'm going to end this fiasco, right here and now! On my personal authority, until further notice, I'm hereby ordering all government forces, including but not limited to the Armed Forces, the intelligence agencies, the Secret Service, the FBI, the Coast Guard, local, state and federal law enforcement authorities, and in particular the GrayWar Corporation, to *stand down* with respect not only to the 'Mars Gang'... but in fact to all followers, friends and family of Karéin-Mayréij, including extended families of anyone within that scope. They are *not* to be apprehended, attacked or harmed in *any* way! Any of these people who are currently being held by agencies of the government, are to be *immediately* released, to my personal custody, within the next *hour*. If they require medical treatment I expect it to be given to them *en route* to the White House. Enforcement actions of *any* type involving the followers of Karéin-Mayréij, must be *personally* cleared by myself, beforehand. I'm further ordering the immediate arrest, detention and court-martial of anyone who attempts to organize activities against this group of people, outside the parameters of the orders just described."

His voice lowered, into a more subdued, counseling mode. He added, "Let me be clear about something, to our Armed Forces, law enforcement agencies and intelligence agencies : *this situation is beyond your effective control.* I *know* that being told to 'just leave them alone' is contrary to your instincts, your rule-books and your training... but it's absolutely *essential*, in this case. Leave dealing with these 'post-humans', exclusively to myself and the Executive Office staff. If and when it is appropriate to change the rules, this will be communicated to you through the normal channels. If anything's unclear about the rules, please contact the White House Staff Secretary or Chief of Staff, for an explanation. I'll conclude by repeating, 'this is a direct order from your Commander-In-Chief'. I'll expect it to be obeyed, without *exception!*"

He turned to Jacobson, "I trust that will be sufficient, Commander?"

"Well," smugly offered Jacobson, "It *does* appear that we're making some progress here. So with your permission, Mr. President... I'll continue on with explaining our position."

"Please do," obliged the U.S. leader.

"So... here's the rest of it," elaborated the Mars mission commander. "My team and I – and I believe we have the support both of Karéin herself and most of her other followers, in saying this – have decided upon these principles, in guidance of further negotiations with the government. First of all, while in the long run we acknowledge the supremacy of the rule of law, we have severe doubts as to the impartiality, objectivity and fairness of how the law is currently implemented and interpreted. With this in mind – while we will make ourselves freely available to legal institutions that are making good-faith efforts to uncover the truth about recent events – we *will not* agree to any legal or government order, that would imprison us or otherwise constrain our personal freedom of movement. We will testify in court or in front of Congress, if called upon to do so, and we *will* tell the truth – as best we understand it – in those cases."

"Second," Jacobson went on, "We will *not* accept responsibility or punishment for, actions that we took in self-defense, after the point at which we were first illegally-detained by the government. So everyone watching tonight knows what I'm referring to, my team and I – before our current 'alien-powers' had fully developed – were abducted and sent to an underground prison, on the Alaskan island of Amchitka, where it became clear that the government – specifically the CIA – intended to torture us to *death*, in hopes of inflicting long-term pain on the Storied Watcher... or possibly even *killing* her. These same atrocities had already been inflicted on some others, notably Tommy and Bob Billings, as well as others who aren't here right now. For example, one of the people who we rescued, had the tongue cut out of her head – no anesthetic, of course. Much worse was done to others. The activities were diabolical, inhuman... words simply fail."

"And all too closely, did they almost succeed in their foul plan," called out Karéin-Mayréij, from her vantage-point in the rear. "It plagued me *grievously!*"

"But – thank God," resumed Jacobson, "You *survived*... as did my team and I, though not for lack of trying, on the part of the government. The point is... my team and I *did* use lethal force to survive that situation, and many other ones like it, or worse, subsequently. By no reasonable principle of justice, can people who are acting in self-defense, or who are acting to save others from these kinds of criminal acts, be punished for fighting back just to stay alive. We *do* agree to be accountable for anything that we do past today, subject to the prohibition on the government undertaking further aggressive actions against ourselves or our families – in which case, we accept no responsibility for what may happen, to anyone who is trying to hurt our loved-ones."

"Sam," interrupted Tanaka, "May I speak for a minute, please?"

"Of course," he agreed, handing the microphone to her.

"For those of you who don't know me... my name is Cherie Tanaka; I was the Science Officer on the mission to Mars. My title is 'First of the Holy

Fire' – that's Karéin's supernatural energy, by the way – and I can assure you... it's aptly-named. Like some others here, but lesser than none of them, I have the power within me to... well, let's just say, 'to do a *lot* of damage'."

Tanaka was clearly struggling to avoid having outward manifestations of the *Fire* from surfacing, as her voice rose with undisguised fury.

"I've been told," she angrily exclaimed, "That as-yet-unidentified agents of the government, are holding my only remaining close family-member – my elderly mother – hostage, right now. Now... let me say something *very* clearly, to whomever may be involved in this despicable crime, as well as to anyone who is in any way associated with it. *If* you release her in good health, right now – as the President has ordered you to do – I *might* just spare your life. But if you have harmed her in *any* way – I will not *only* kill you, but I *will* disintegrate anyone and everyone within a *mile* of you! There is no hiding-place so remote – no bunker so strong and deep – anywhere on the face of this *planet*, that will keep you safe from me! As God's my witness – I *will* hunt you down... and I will crush you like the *insects* you are!"

"And," warned Brent Boyd, from the sidelines, "She'll have a lot of *help*, in doing that!"

"Damn right!" solemnly added White, while Wolf glowered and the Russian nodded in agreement. "Whoever y'all is... your ass is *grass*, fuckers!"

The former Science Officer hung her head. She was sobbing openly, now.

"That... that's *it*," she managed.

Jacobson embraced her, as she retreated. He whispered a few words of support.

"Majors White and Boyd speak for all of us," he confirmed. "We've all had our families threatened like this. It's a *disgrace* – and we will *not* stand for it!"

"If you please," requested the President.

He again took over the lectern.

"Let me just reinforce something that I said earlier," he declared. "This next message is for GrayWar and certain staff within some of the intelligence-agencies. I have been extremely disturbed and disappointed to have seen numerous instances of insubordination within these institutions – some of which acts, may have contributed to indefensible and illegal activities, which Ms. Tanaka has so eloquently denounced."

"To every member of the intelligence community as well as to GrayWar Corporation," stated the President, "Your first loyalty is to *myself*, as your Commander-In-Chief. You are hereby directed to refuse any orders from your nominal superiors, that do not conform with the parameters that I stated earlier tonight. This directive over-rides *every* other rule of conduct, chain-of-command or internal regulation that your organization may have. Thus, you are hereby ordered to *immediately* release Ms. Tanaka's relatives, and all others held in similar circumstances, to my personal control, as noted earlier.

You are further directed to *immediately* report any such insubordination or variance from my orders, to the White House Chief of Staff, and to place those involved in this insubordination, under arrest. Lethal force is hereby authorized, as a last resort, if these orders are disobeyed or are not fully implemented, by others within your organizations. Failure to faithfully and completely execute these directions will result in personal liability on your part, including but not limited to dismissal from your jobs and potential criminal prosecution. There will be *no* exceptions granted to these rules! I hope I've made myself clear."

Chu advanced and said, projecting her voice to the microphone, "Mr. President, in my capacity as Acting Director, I'd like to add to that. Effective as of now, I'm ordering the Bureau to undertake all possible measures to locate and effect the timely, safe release of Cherie Tanaka's mother, as well as – as the President has stated – all other detainees associated with this situation. I'll need a status-report on the investigations and rescue-activities, from Bureau H.Q., within the next three hours. Please communicate this to the White House Chief of Staff – Mr. Kaysten here, behind me – until I can get back to a Bureau office and manage operations from there. As the President has stated, this operation has the *highest* level of priority! Back to you, sir."

"Ms. Chu's directives have my full personal endorsement and support," remarked the U.S. leader. "I'm also ordering all government institutions to coöperate with the Bureau's investigations, in every possible way. If you have information relevant to this operation, you need to communicate it to FBI headquarters, immediately. As usual... failure to comply will be considered a dismissal offense."

"That's encouraging... as far as it goes," offered Jacobson, as he took over the podium again. "But it brings me to the final part of what my team and I have decided, in our deliberations, earlier tonight. We didn't just battle our way to the White House, only to protect and avenge our families and friends... though doing so obviously proved to be necessary. We've come here to force real, structural change in how the country is governed, particularly in terms of civil liberties, the administration of justice, how elections are conducted, and a wide range of other topics."

The President looked worried and annoyed, but he said nothing.

"If we fail to do this," asserted the former Mars mission commander, "Not only will much of our march across America to this point, have been for nothing... but there's a high likelihood that the country will simply revert to the way it was – that is, as a corrupt kleptocracy, kept in power by cruelty, dishonesty, lying and brute force – beforehand. That's unacceptable and I"m telling you now, Mr. President – we will not *stand* for it! Our intention is to work with you – inside the system if possible – but I'm putting you, the Congress, the Supreme Court and everyone else listening to this tonight, that the moment that we believe that the system is trying to silence us, or sideline us, or pay us off – all bets are off, as well."

"Mr. Jacobson," protested the President, "I *know* I shouldn't be debating or negotiating with you in public... but given the, uhh, singular irregularity of everything that has gone on thus far, I suppose neither I – nor the country – has much left to lose, by doing so. The United States can only have *one* President, and *one* government. It sounds to me, like you're proposing to set up an alternate one – presumably with you in charge of it. If that's the case... consider this my resignation, effective immediately!"

A shocked, frightened gasp came from the audience.

"No sir!" quickly countered Jacobson, "That's absolutely *not* what the 'Mars Gang' – or any of Karéin's followers – have in mind!"

"Well then... what *do* you have in mind?" the perplexed U.S. leader shot back.

"This was originally Karéin's idea," stated Jacobson. "Karéin... would you like to explain it?"

By now, almost every waking human being on the planet was watching the events unfold, as the Storied Watcher – her divine grace and poise, waxing with every step – slowly walked toward the podium, leaving Tommy in Billings' care.

She stopped halfway, lifted her left hand, and caused the microphone to be telekinetically-pulled into her grasp.

Her pleasant, supernaturally-elegant voice spoke, "Indeed this is the truth, Mr. President; it is a form of rulership that I have seen work successfully many times before, on worlds far away and lost in the mists of time. Verily, I say to you : there are many forms of power that may co-exist within the halls of a king's-castle. Some of these are compatible, and can work together easily; others are naturally in opposition, and need to be balanced, lest the one overwhelm the other. Foremost among these, are the ability to say "yes, go and do something," and the power to say, "no... this shall not *be*". The former is what empowers a ruler to go out and do *good* things; the latter is what *prevents* him, from doing *bad* things. At least... this is how it appears, to my way of thinking."

The President listened intently, with an equally-rapt Kaysten by his side.

"Right now," claimed the alien-girl, "Both these powers reside in your office – in fact, in yourself – and, well... the results, are plain for all who listen to my words, to see. So what we propose, is simply that you go back to running this 'America' empire as you see fit – nothing will change, in that respect – except that, Commander Jacobson and his team will be there to, ahh, 'call you back', if you – or your government – tries to do evil, or does so, by blunder or ignorance. For the record, sir... I have read these 'Con-stee-too-shon' documents that are your country's sacred texts, and if you faithfully abide by them – as opposed to twisting their words into self-serving parodies – none of this should be difficult; it is what these holy books require, in any event. And I also have confidence in you, personally. You have risked your life, to guide your kingdom through the crisis that – the Gods and Fates willing – is now behind us. *Believe* in yourself, sir! You can make this work... if only you would try."

She did a slight bow and sent the microphone back to the podium.

"Let me clarify something here," mentioned Jacobson. "I want everyone listening tonight to understand that – as he said – there is only *one* President, and only *one* Commander-In-Chief. That's not me – it's *him*. Neither I nor any member of my team has any intention of intervening in the normal functioning of the government, or of unilaterally re-writing laws. That we will leave to the existing system, although we do expect to see forward movement, as opposed to foot-dragging and back-sliding. We're simply putting the government, and the system, on notice that if we see it going off the rails – for example, rigging election-results, or keeping innocent people locked up in concentration-camps – we reserve the right to step in and put a *stop* to it. Which – be assured – we *will* do. That's all."

"Commander," challenged Kaysten, "I know I'm speaking out of turn here, particularly on national television, but – to put it bluntly... 'who voted for *you?*' *Millions* of people voted for the President, you know."

"'Who voted for us', you say, Jerry?" coldly retorted Jacobson. "I'll tell you... Tommy did... Elissha did... Korey did... Bob did... with every one of their agonized screams. As do the *thousands* of others, who are, no doubt, suffering the same, as we speak!"

The audience fell silent.

A thought surfaced in Jacobson's mind. It sounded like Abruzzio.

For God's *sake, Sam,* it implored,

Give the President a little political cover!

If he looks like he's taking orders from you... he's toast!

Sure, you can humiliate him in front of the voters – the world...

And then *what?*

"The old order has only the legitimacy of what it advertised itself to be, Mr. President... Jerr-ee," offered the Storied Watcher. "Not what it has revealed itself to be, in such terrible manner, as Sam Jacobson has referenced. But what was, need not be, what *will* be. Now comes the test – there is a *choice*... a different path to take, one that was not there, before. I believe that you and all the common-folk in this 'America' kingdom, will be far better-off, in the long run, if you seek the counsel of Sam and his team, where it is appropriate... and if you do not assume that 'the way in which we did this, in the old days... that is how we *should* do it, henceforth'. Give it a *try*, sir! What do you have to lose?"

Millions around the world, watched with bated breath, as the U.S. leader considered his options.

Then, he slowly stated, "You must understand, Karéin – Commander Jacobson – that our system of government is based not only on elections, but also tradition... the law... our written Constitution... many other things, which distinguish a real republic – which I'd still claim, we are – from a 'banana republic' –"

"A 'bananas republic', sir?" interrupted an off-put alien-girl. "Is that a kingdom, built upon tree-fruit? I do not understand the –"

Inevitably, Billings loudly joked, "It's one with mass appeal, honey."

The crowd, including many of those up at the front, collapsed in paroxysms of laughter, while a wide-eyed and slightly-blushing Karéin-Mayréij cringed.

"No, Karéin," explained the President with a slight, forced chuckle, "A 'banana republic' is one with weak laws and traditions of governance, in which rulers can do whatever they want, so long as they have military power behind them. The point is... I have no intention of dignifying this government with my presence or support, if that's how it's going to work. Our system has no provision for an unofficial, un-elected shadow government... which is what I think Commander Jacobson has in mind."

"But, sir," interjected Abruzzio, "As you know... we *do* have the concept of a 'veto'. That's basically what he's saying. I don't think Sam intends to start writing laws, issuing National Security Orders, holding cabinet-meetings or, in fact, trying to run the government, at all. Am I right, Commander?"

"Very definitely not," confirmed Jacobson. "All that we're asserting, is the right to say 'no'."

"Forgive me, Commander," demanded the President, "But where in the Constitution, does it say that an insubordinate Air Force officer, has a 'veto'?"

"Where in the Constitution does it say that the 'President' can order the large-scale, arbitrary detention, torture and murder of American citizens?" countered Jacobson. "You talk of the Constitution, of the rule of law... okay, then! I think the record will show that we in the 'Mars Gang', are much more on the right side of *that* argument, than *you* are – that is, if anything like an objective third party, is judging us both. As of somewhat earlier tonight, I believe *that* piece of the puzzle has now been put into place. Like Karéin said... what've you got to *lose?*"

The former Mars mission commander turned to directly address the audience and the press.

"Ladies and gentlemen – people of the United States," he called out, "The 'Mars Gang' and I didn't come here tonight to *negotiate*... we came to *communicate*. And what I'd like to communicate is, we will not stand in the way of any *legal, ethical* action undertaken by the government. We aren't going to knock over skyscrapers, just because we got a parking-ticket –"

"Does that include parking our ship in the Rose Garden?" Billings broke in.

"Well... I haven't seen any traffic-enforcement agents out there, if *that's* what you mean, Bob," parried Jacobson, to the crowd's enjoyment. "The point is, however... provided that the government doesn't do stupid and offensive things – like, 'trying to arrest us', 'threatening the safety of our loved ones', or 'preventing certain citizens from voting in the next election' – nobody has anything to be afraid of, from us... *and*, our war against the government ends, here and now. I'm just describing the situation as it *is*, Mr. President. I'm describing *reality.*"

"Best deal you're gonna get tonight, pardner," commented a stony-faced Wolf. "You *know* what some of the rest of us, wanted to do!"

The former Mars mission commander stepped away from the podium.

Again, millions of eyes looked to the U.S. leader, trying to guess what he would do.

After a second or two, he came forward, adjusted the microphone and said,

"At this point, Commander – Karéin – and others, I have to be guided by what I believe is best for the country under the circumstances, within the confines of the Constitution and the rule of law, as I understand it. So I'll make you the following offer : as long as you and your team understand that you have *no* official status within the government – none at all – and that we – including myself – are all subject to the truth and reconciliation process, as discussed earlier tonight in the Oval Office... I see no reason to resign the office to which I've been duly elected. For the record, while I'm open to enacting the reforms that you speak of – some of them are long-overdue – these will need to go forward, through the normal legislative process. I will *not* be party to rule by decree – either from the elected President... or from anybody else! If you can't agree to that... now's the time to let us know."

"I have no problem with that, Mr. President," answered Jacobson. "But I won't presume to speak for my brothers and sisters on that subject. Devon?"

"Fine by me," said White. "Sure took some *doin'!*"

"Misha?" asked the former Mars mission commander.

"I do not think it would be appropriate for me to pronounce on matters of American self-governance," sniffed the Russian. "Except to say that I hope that the political authorities of my own country, are observing this situation closely. Who *knows* where else, a similar scene may play out, in the future?"

His face wore a sly smile.

"Wolf?" cycled Jacobson, out of turn.

"I wanted to put this whole damn place in my pipe and smoke it... but I got out-bullshitted, and out-voted," bluntly grumbled the bounty-hunter. "Just don't *push* me, if you know what's good for you, pardner."

"I'll make a point *not* to," politely stated the U.S. leader.

"Brent?" inquired Jacobson.

"I'm willing to give it a try," responded Boyd, "But, Mr. President... Wolf's right. This is a *very* big climb-down, on our part. Implementing it will require complete good faith on both sides... and if that's not forthcoming, as the Commander stated... 'all bets are off'. I've already prevented, only by the narrowest margins, *one* attempt by the government to kidnap, torture and murder my family, and – like Cherie has said – I won't *tolerate* another! If I have to melt *mountains* to deal with anyone who tries this kind of garbage again... I can and *will* do that! I hope you understand."

"I *do*, Major Boyd," quickly replied the President.

The U.S. leader looked at the press-gallery and observed, "The press, and the American people, should know that Major Boyd's description of his abilities is – unfortunately – *not* an exaggeration. When he says, 'melt a mountain'... he definitely *is* capable of doing that. And his supernatural powers are similar to those of the rest of the Storied Watcher's followers. Karéin's own powers are yet more unbelievably potent. She just shook off a hydrogen bomb, at very close range. Just so you all *know*."

Heads were shaking and gasps were heard within the crowd of journalists.

There was a proudly-defiant look on Boyd's face, and it was shared by many of the "New People".

The Storied Watcher stepped forward.

"American peasants, townspeople and gentry... your leader speaks the truth," she declared, "But the wise and noble measure their powers by how much they can build – by who they can help – by who they can defend – not by how quickly and easily they can kill and destroy. Those who inherit the Holy *Fire*, they are called to a higher purpose... they must commit to a vow of charity, morality and the use of violence only as a last resort. I pray that all who hear these words, have taken this pledge fully to heart."

She crossed her arms in front again, bowed her head and then stepped back.

Jacobson now looked backward over his left shoulder.

"Cherie? Do you endorse the President's offer?" he asked.

"I'm like Karéin... I hope," said the former Mars mission science officer. "In that I think I'd make a poor queen, or dictatress. So... 'yes'. But remember what I said about my mother. Don't tell me to 'leave it to the government'! You *know* what kind of answer you'll get."

"Ms. Tanaka," promised the President, "We'll support you however we can."

"That goes for me too, Cherie," added Chu. "We'll *find* her! You *know* why this is a priority for me, as well. By the way, Commander... given my position, I don't think it would be proper for me to voice an opinion on the proposal. If Will and Otis want to vote later, that will be up to them."

"Just to pre-empt the inevitable speculation, I'd like the press and the population to know," disclosed the President, "That yes, Ms. Chu *also* has inherited some of the Storied Watcher's alien-powers – the same ones that I described while speaking with Major Boyd. Her abilities are – well – *devastating*... that's the best way I can find to characterize them."

"Oh, well, Mr. President," demurely teased the former team-leader, with a raised eyebrow and a wan smirk, "All I can do, is give people a 'dirty look'. *Surely* that's not so special?"

Giggles broke out within the company of Storied Watcher-followers, as members of the press predictably began typing speculative guesses into their communicators, about what was being referred to (the most common idea to appear in the media, perhaps inevitably, ended up as, "HAS THE PRESIDENT BEEN HYPNOTIZED BY HALF-ALIEN FBI CONSPIRATOR?").

"Sylvia?" addressed Jacobson.

"I support the proposal," mentioned Abruzzio. "It's a reasonable compromise between your quest for justice, Commander, and the need to keep a functional, stable government in existence. We can ask him later... but I'm pretty sure that Hector will feel the same way."

"Bob?" asked the former Mars mission commander.

"You know me... I'm a nihilist," shrugged Billings. "But I won't stand in your way. This is *your* fight, after all! But, folks – for the record – all of you out there in TV-land, don't realize how much you owe Mr. Jacobson. I just hope when it all comes out, you'll give him and his team the credit they're due."

Finally, Jacobson's gaze fell on the Storied Watcher herself.

"Karéin?" he requested. "Do you approve of all this?"

She stepped forward.

"This is neither my world, nor my kingdom, nor my quest," she deflected, "Thus, it would be ignoble for me to stand in judgment of what you and your 'President', propose to undertake. I *will* say, to the many people of Earth who now are watching, that I aim *not* to rule – either in America, or elsewhere. I am your planet's protector – your guardian – *not* your queen or despot, and I will refuse a position of political leadership, if it is offered to me. I say this because many of you who do not know us personally, may be suspicious that we are somehow trying to 'take over' the American government, either directly, or by proxy. I can assure you all that if either Commander Jacobson or I had wanted to do so, this, ahh, 'press-meeting' would have been a much shorter one, with a much more simple message. My kingdom... uhh, 'queendom'... is not of this world. It is... *elsewhere*."

More than a few heads turned, upon hearing this. But Jacobson went on,

"We'll of course need to find out how Hector Ramirez and Melissa Claremont – and some other members of our group, who aren't here tonight – cast their votes, but based on the count as I've heard it... I think we have an *agreement*, Mr. President."

The U.S. leader stepped forward and extended a hand.

Jacobson shook it.

"Trust... but verify," he mentioned, below his voice.

The President nodded in acknowledgment.

Cheers of relief and thanksgiving were heard from the normally-professional press gallery.

He stepped in front of the podium and then said,

"And with that, ladies and gentlemen... we'll open it up for questions."

Mingling And Mole-Hills

It seemed as if every single member of the press corps. had jumped to his or her feet, and was shouting questions at the top of his or her lungs.

The President motioned for calm two or three times, but it proved utterly impossible to contain the pent-up curiosity and emotion within the audience.

He found the petite figure (she came up perhaps to his chin) of the Storied Watcher, suddenly by his side, and – though he was well past his prime – he struggled to resist her feminine charms, which were unnervingly-potent at this close range. The movement of the alien-girl did, however, seem to momentarily abate the shouting, and the Press Room quieted down to hear what she was saying to him.

"Sir," suggested Karéin-Mayréij, loudly enough to be heard at least in the front ranks of the press-gallery, "There is very much that we both – along with Commander Sam – should inform these people about. Rather than standing up here and answering questions one-by-one... would it not make more sense for us to just, ahh, 'mingle' with yonder crowd, thereby to parley with each of them, as they best see fit so to do?"

"Yeah, but Karéin, the idea of a 'press conference' is to only give them the... oh, *forget* it," Kaysten tried to interrupt. "Who *cares* about the rule-book, any more?"

The alien-girl mischievously winked at him.

"Well... I don't...." the President tried to say.

Then he faced the audience and announced, "Ladies and gentlemen of the press... we have decided on a variation in the format. Instead of taking questions from you in the normal manner, what we'll be doing instead, is giving you the ability to speak, one-on-one, on the record, with both the Storied Watcher and Commander Jacobson's team."

He quickly looked down at the alien-girl and quietly mentioned, "Karéin – you *do* know what 'on the record' means... don't you?"

"Does it not mean, 'do not be forthcoming', sir?" she replied.

"Yeah... *something* like that," he confirmed. "Like, 'don't say things to the press, that they can make a mountain out of a mole-hill, about'."

"'Mountains'... 'mole-hills'... more idiom," she complained.

"Well," she airily added, "I *do* have several thousands of your years of having learned, how to flatter and cajole, while still saying precious little. Would *that* do, do you think?"

"It'll *have* to," he reluctantly agreed.

The Storied Watcher turned to face her more-than-human followers.

"Everyone!" she called. "Shall we go and speak with these 're-porters'? The President advises us to be judicious in what we say – and there is no harm in that – but never shall we say an untruth, or seek to mislead by silence... is that oh-kay with all of you? Oh, and to start the party... I see a table at the back, with some nice things to eat and drink, thereupon, behind the techno-gear for the tee-vee networks –"

"They got beer?" interrupted Wolf.

A second later, a downtrodden look came to his face.

"Shit... *forgot*," he glumly added. "Couldn't you have, like, let us turn it off, just for Happy Hour?"

"It does not come with an, ahh, 'on-off switch', my brother," she pleasantly replied. "If it did, enemies would just convince one to do so, and then land an en-venomed arrow. And in any event, no, I do not see any 'booze' back there. But take heart – there are many sweets. *Surely* these are preferable?"

"Yeah... *sure* they is," commented White. "Anything you *say*, Angel Lady."

"Then let us go!" she instructed. "Oh... but one teensy, little thing."

"Yeah?" asked Boyd.

"I get that nice, icing-frosted pastry on the left-side of the table... the one with the little candied red fruit on top," she happily demanded. "You all can pick any *other* one."

You know, Abruzzio sent to a nodding Tanaka and a bemused Chu,

I'll never really understand her.

A being with the power of a goddess – who can shatter comets and withstand an H-bomb –

Whose Number One Motivation, is 'getting to a frosted Danish, before everyone else'.

A second later, they all received,

I feel that being awarded the first pick among sugar-confections, is the least of rewards for dealing with an 'atom-smashing bomb'... do you not?

Abruzzio's eyes were tearing as she said, out loud, "Just don't tell us what you're prepared to do, for a layer-cake."

The alien-girl again wheeled in place and walked down the side of the room (this would normally have been difficult to do without running into people, but the White House press-corps was below its usual complement of staff, given that many of its members had left the downtown D.C. area earlier in the evening), right beside a number of astonished, disbelieving reporters and press-correspondents.

Behind Karéin-Mayréij came her more-than-human troupe, with the exception of Chu, who stayed behind and spent her time intensively working a mobile-communicator. The post-humans lined up at the refreshment-table near the far end of the press-room, and began to partake of the casual food and drink found there.

As they fanned back out into the main part of the room, everyone – including Tommy – was pressed to "make a statement" or to "give your account of what's happened tonight".

Members of the Mars Gang, in particular, were singled out for special attention. Though repeatedly pressed for this information, most of the post-humans – especially Abruzzio, Chu and the Russian – were very close-mouthed about the details of their alien-powers, or those of the others. Despite this, altogether too much uncomplimentary information was volunteered – especially by Wolf and Billings – but on the whole, Jacobson and his team stuck to the script and did an admirable job of defending and promoting their arguments against the government and its behavior.

More than that; at least three provisional contracts for "tattle-tale" book-deals were tentatively agreed-to. (Wolf had to reluctantly agree to have his own, ghost-written by the Russian and Abruzzio, given that, by his own words, 'I ain't too good with writing stuff down, and I never *could* figure out that damn spell-checker thing on the computer'.)

As for the Storied Watcher herself, the alien-girl was the natural star of the show; reporter after reporter openly marveled at the simple fact of being in close proximity to a creature of her ilk. But after a few words of introduction, in each case, Karéin-Mayréij displayed her disarming innate friendliness (enhanced by freely-handed-out hugs and some supernatural trickery, such as "knowing the first and last name of every reporter, before he or she volunteered it") and she quickly established a strong personal *rapport* with each of her interrogators.

The charm-offensive extended past this, in fact; two of the reporters had close family members with serious diseases, which resulted in promises by the Storied Watcher for a personal curative visit "as soon as possible, when I am sure that no more death-bombs are about to be dropped on our heads".

For his part, the President – with Kaysten's silver tongue assisting throughout – managed what was going on, as best he could. The U.S. leader tried to stick to the line that "I'm still in charge... and *only* I am in charge," but this was repeatedly challenged by skeptical members of the press.

Still, it did appear that he was being given the benefit of the doubt; the reporters were all too aware that they were participating in a get-to-know-you party with beings that could vaporize any one of them, at will. This *did* tend to reinforce the message, "what did you *expect* us to do... use harsh language on Mr. Jacobson?"

The chaotic, *ad hoc* "mingling-event" went on for almost two hours, with various sub-sets of it being broadcast, all over the world, in real-time. Finally, Jerry Kaysten, along with Minnie Chu (who had taken a few questions, but who had held back as much as possible) and Susan Feldner, advanced to the Blue Goose lectern and spoke into the microphone.

"Okay, ladies and gentlemen," announced the Chief of Staff, "Like you, we'd love to keep this going all night, but a lot of us have been up for a long time by now, and we really need some rest... so we're going to end it here. We'll of course be making ourselves available for extended questions, later this week, as circumstances befit. We'd like to thank all of you for showing up for what's obviously been a historic occasion."

"I'll be providing you all with the schedule for press-conferences, tomorrow," added Feldner. "Our staff will show you out. Thanks, everyone!"

There were a few grumbles from the hardier members of the press corps; but every one of them had also been continuously on the go for many hours, so there was little organized resistance.

Finally, the last of the reporters and press correspondents had been ushered out the door, leaving the President (and his two newly-superhuman offspring, who had been watching the goings-on in the outside-hall, and who had now entered the Brady Press Room) and Feldner, in the press room with the Storied Watcher and her family, friends and followers.

A weary Abruzzio slumped into one of the front-row chairs. She said,

"You know... apart from having been 'up' and going continuously – I figure for the better part of a full day or more– and risking our lives almost every moment of that... we never figured out where we'd be sleeping, tonight, or this morning, or whatever it is. Karéin, the *Fire* is keeping me going... but mentally, I'm nearing total burn-out. As soon as I track down Rainbow – or she tracks down me – I really need to get some rest."

As if on cue, they heard a friendly "yip", and saw the puppy's comical face, peeking out from behind the doorway.

"You little *twerp!*" called the former JPL scientist, as the dog jumped into her arms. "This is supposed to be one of the most 'secure' places in the country, you know!"

The dog gave another happy bark and licked her face.

"Well... it – she, I mean – can do pretty much everything you can, Sylvia," mentioned Kaysten. "Like that 'illusion' trick."

"You got any dog-food around here?" asked Abruzzio, in Kaysten's direction.

"*Used* to have," he confirmed. "The best kind possible, for visiting foreign dignitaries. When we figure out what we're doing, I'll find it."

"Yeah," agreed Billings, with a yawn. "All this 'having H-bombs dropped on my head' stuff... it tires you out... you know?"

"Well," patiently offered Karéin-Mayréij, "One such, was dropped rather more closely on mine own head... more than enough to give one a, uhh, 'Ek-say-drinn head-ache'."

Even the President joined in the laughter that followed. Then he said,

"You know, Karéin... intellectually, I understand what you're saying, but... somehow, the rest of me just can't *accept* it. How in the Lord's name could you *survive* something like that? I mean... wouldn't it, uhh, 'vaporize' a human being at that close range?"

"Yes... it *would* have so done... many thousands of times over," she quietly replied. "You know... what is, ahh, 'funny' about it is... I was somewhat further away from the first one that I encountered... over the northern sea island, I mean. *That* one was a rude awakening, for sure. I resolved not to try it again. And yet... here we are... here, I am. I am almost, 'getting used to it'. Note how I said, 'almost'."

After a few more chuckles, he asked, "How did you *do* it, then?"

The alien-girl looked straight at the U.S. leader and replied, "Honestly, sir... you will never know. You will *never* understand what it is to reach deep down inside of oneself and call upon mighty, weirding powers of protection, of defense, or of war-skills, the likes of which one never dared to presume to have, before... but now, one *must*... and so... one *does*. There is nothing within the normal human realm of experience, to which I could make a valid comparison. But take heart."

"What do you mean?" he asked.

"*You*, will never understand, sir," stated the Storied Watcher. "You simply... *cannot*. Nor will your human wife. You are limited by the circumstances of your species. But *they*," – she pointed to Matt and Clairie – "*They, will* know this, in time. *They* will know what it is, to have the power of life and death, over beings who resemble themselves... but whose abilities are inferior in every possible way. I pray that they will use this gift wisely. Perhaps great challenges await *them*, as well. Who among us, can foretell the future?"

Her face wore a far-off look.

The President silently nodded.

His daughter and son came to his side and embraced him.

"I love you, Daddy," breathed Clairie.

"I know," he wearily responded.

"Well, look," offered the President, "There are plenty of bedrooms here in this house – obviously, we have to entertain state guests all the time. If you need a place to rest, I'll make the White House available to you."

"Thanks, sir," said Chu. "Given all that's going on, I think it's preferable that I stay here until things settle down. Nothing fancy, please – just a clean bed and somewhere to wash up in. Oh... and would it be possible for me to get access to a room where I can do tele-conferences? With Bureau staff, that is."

"Of course," agreed the U.S. leader. "Talk to Curt... he'll set you up."

"Just one rule," flippantly mentioned Kaysten. "Namely : 'no death-rays, lightening-bolts, photon-beams, fire-storms, ice-castles or suits of flaming armor, on the carpets or furniture', if you don't mind."

"You didn't mention the walls or windows," joked a clearly-very-tired Tommy. "So –"

"Yeah, kid... no shooting holes in the walls, the floor or the ceiling... or blowing out windows, either," the Chief of Staff requested. "And speaking of vandalism, Karéin... about the top of the Monument out there..."

"Oh... I shall put it back... when I have a little spare time," diffidently chirped the Storied Watcher. "Did you not think that it adds something to the decor of yonder grass-park?"

"Just needs a little cleaning-up... you could turn it into a water-fountain," maliciously echoed Tanaka.

"Or modern art," suggested Boyd. "If you'd like, I can melt down the sharp edges, so it looks more 'organic'."

This got him a high-five from a wearily-bemused Devon White.

"Only lettin' you do that, Mr. Space Cadet," added Wolf, "If I can burn a message on the side. 'Member what I wanted to put there?"

"I fear," wryly stated the Storied Watcher, "That writing such things, would likely result in your invitation to stay in this fine palace, being rescinded."

"I still can't believe that you *did* that, all by yourself," remarked Feldner.

The alien-girl shrugged and, without looking directly at the Press Secretary, calmly extended one arm and engaged a hand-gesture. Feldner began to float upward, to her obvious discomfort; but before she was two feet off the floor, Karéin-Mayréij had gently let her down again.

"See?" chided the Storied Watcher. "Just like that, my sister... give or take a few ten-thousand of your 'tons'."

A flustered Feldner had no idea what to say back.

"Well... what about it, folks?" inquired Abruzzio. "Are we going to crash, here?"

"Mr. President, surely do I appreciate the kind offer of accommodations in your palace," said the Storied Watcher, "But I would prefer to lift the *Mailànkh Express* to a hopefully-safe location elsewhere, thence to take Bob and Tommy, if they will go with me. And any others who care to accompany us."

And also, she sent to Jacobson,

Many of those who were at the Council of the Woods with all of us – including for example Hugo Szabo, Whitney Claremont and many more – now languish in the hollowed-out bosom of a desolate, remote island, in the southern polar sea of this planet.

They were carried hence to keep them as safe as possible, from the attentions of this empire or others, until the matters-at-hand are dealt with.

They knew that I would leave for some days... but I cannot keep them there, unattended, forever.

Their food will run out shortly... not to mention, their patience.

The former Mars mission pilot stared forward and nodded acknowledgment.

So as soon as I will meet with your family, continued the Storied Watcher,

And those of my other friends – I must away to tend to them, and determine how they would proceed.

While I am here, I must ensure that they will be safe, if they elect to come back to this 'America' place.

"Aww... don't I get to use the Presidential rest-rooms?" *faux*-complained Billings.

"We will presumably be returning here later, my love," parried the alien-girl. "You can so indulge, then. If – that is – we are welcome."

"Any time," politely pledged the President, "Although, to avoid any more 'misunderstandings' such as the one that occurred earlier tonight, I'd appreciate a little advance-notice, before you fly in."

"We will do our best to provide it, sir," she answered.

"As a matter of fact, Karéin," commented Jacobson, "If you were planning on heading off with the *Express*, we have somewhere we'd like you to go."

"Where is that?" asked Karéin-Mayréij.

It's in West Virginia... a mountain-top where we had to leave Donny, Will, Otis and our families, he sent.

I'm 'thinking' to you as, it might be reckless to divulge this information to the President.

Even if he doesn't actually intend to attack us again... he may not be in charge of significant parts of the military.

We can't take chances with something this important.

"Aye," she stated, out loud.

"It's like... like I'm hearing something... like every fifth word of a conversation... but I'm *not* hearing it," Clairie mentioned, with a bewildered head-shake.

"Yeah... *wicked* weird," agreed Matt.

"Just keep whatever you heard, to yourselves... if you don't mind?" demanded Jacobson.

"Well... considering I have no idea what you're– was that *you?* Are saying," dodged Clairie, "I don't think you have anything to worry about, Commander Jacobson."

"What's going on here?" demanded the President.

"Didn't we explain the mind-talking to you?" teased Abruzzio.

"You're... telepathic... mind-reading... right?" he mumbled.

The former JPL scientist just smiled.

"You know... when all of this gets out – as inevitably it will – it will be next to impossible to convince the public that I'm still actually in charge of the government," unhappily commented the President. "I believe you when you say that you aren't manipulating me like a puppet... but *they* – the people – *won't.*"

"Well, 'scuse my French, sir," mentioned Devon White, "But maybe if the government hadn't been talkin' shit for so long... folks'd believe y'all a bit more."

"You're probably right about that, Major White," conceded the U.S. leader. "Another one of those 'bad habits' that I acknowledged, earlier tonight. But we can't un-make the past, unfortunately."

"One *can*, change the future," observed the Storied Watcher. "That, at least, is within your grasp, sir... but it will take humility, mixed with perseverance. Ever so have been the ingredients of changing one's destiny."

"We'll see how practical all this is to implement," deflected the President. "But Ms. Abruzzio is right – this has been a *very* long day, and we all need to get to bed."

"Who's for a night in the White House?" cajoled Kaysten. "A once-in-a-*lifetime* opportunity!"

"You should have been in sales," said Billings.

"I sort of *am*," replied the Chief of Staff. "Who's staying?"

"We should bring Melissa in here, so she can get whatever medical attention's appropriate, for one of us 'post-humans'," noted Tanaka.

"There is little that your 'human-medicine' can do for her," mentioned the Storied Watcher, "But indeed, perhaps a nice, warm, soft bed will be of use, compared to the poor accommodations that I was able to craft into our air-ship."

"I'll help you with Melissa," volunteered Abruzzio. "And, Mr. President, if I'm welcome, I'll take Jerry up on the offer. Let me see if I can convince Hector, as well. Just one thing... I'll need to take Rainbow outside in a few minutes, if you know what I mean. Don't worry about any messes, though... it dries out, when microwaved."

The dog let out another cute "yip!".

"I'll take your word for it, Ms. Abruzzio, and of course you're welcome," obliged the President. "Anyone else?"

"I'd like to invite Moira," requested Abruzzio.

"That's fine," agreed the President.

"What do you want to do with those two GrayWar jokers, Mr. President?" asked Kaysten. "What were their names again... oh yeah, 'Rizzo'... 'Maloney'..."

"I think one of them is actually U.S. Army," observed Abruzzio.

"The Service can find some barracks-accommodation for them, I'm sure," commented the U.S. leader.

"Since I know our family's okay," spoke White, "I hope y'all don't mind if I skip goin' back to, uhh, well... you know where. I'll head out in a minute and see if I can get the Missus to join me. Figure this is kind of payback, y'know?"

"I suppose we have to limit the number of people who end up in the *Express*, anyway," opined Jacobson. "We were straining the capacity of the V-37 as it was... and that aircraft is – uhh – no longer available."

"That airplane was probably worth a several tens of millions of dollars, you know," commented Chu. "Hijacking it – using it to commit numerous Federal crimes – well, I'm sure you know where I'm going, Commander."

"So *sue* me!" pleasantly responded Jacobson.

"Yeah... and then try to *collect*, when and if you win," taunted Boyd.

"I only ask that you think up some way that I can explain this, and still maintain a *shred* of credibility as a law enforcement official," complained Chu.

"Perhaps you should put us on trial," offered the Russian, "But – as your standards of justice require one to be tried by a 'jury of one's peers' – and as our 'peers' are, arguably, only us 'post-humans'... I would presume that the pool of potential jurors would be somewhat limited, and would thus be likely to acquit."

"There you *go!*" joked a grinning Boyd. "Logical as ever, that man is."

"Thank you," said Misha.

Chu sighed and shook her head.

"We're going to have to strategize about this, Mr. President," she declared.

"Yeah," he agreed.

"I'm goin' back with you folks... in the *Express*, that is," said Wolf. "Don't feel quite at home in here."

"No hard feelings... right?" advanced Kaysten.

The bounty-hunter shrugged, ambiguously.

"Mr. President," spoke Tanaka, "I have serious misgivings about parking myself in this residence, given that it's still possible it might again come under attack; remember – whomever launched the second nuke is still out there... I don't think it's likely, but what if he – or she – has *another* one?"

"Min-ee," interjected the Storied Watcher, "My intuition says that this is not the case. What does yours say?"

"Just a second," requested the former team-leader.

She closed her eyes and seemed to be meditating. Then she opened them again and said, "I don't see anything... certainly not like the terrible scenes I saw, when dealing with Crowford. That's good news... I *hope*."

"'Aye," offered Karéin-Mayréij.

"If that's the case," continued Tanaka, "I'd like the chance to stay here for a few days, so that I can be as close as possible to the operations searching for my mother. As long as it's understood that I need to be given full access to the information involved, as it comes in."

"That won't be a problem," complied the President. "But before you, uhh, fly off and do something that you might regret later... can you please first consult with myself?"

"That's my intention," the former Mars mission science officer stated. "With that said... I'm not agreeing to *any* limitations on my personal freedom of action. Please don't try to order me to leave whomever has kidnapped my mother, alone."

"Cherie... we'd only ask you to do that temporarily, so as not to compromise a rescue-operation," promised Chu. "The same goes for me and Kai, of course."

"I think we understand each other, then," mentioned Tanaka.

"As you know... I'm going on the *Express*," declared Jacobson. "Brent... you coming along?"

"As if you had to *ask*," the former Mars mission pilot confirmed. "I'm not leaving Laura and the kids, out 'there', one *minute* longer than I have to. But we should figure out what we're doing after we get back. Mr. President, what we're referring to here is, our families – plus a lot of other people who we had to pick up along the way, to keep them safe from the government – are being hidden in a safe place... or at least one that we *believe* to be safe. But obviously we can't leave them there forever. If – hopefully – the war between 'us', and 'you', is over – or if at least we have a working truce – it leaves open the question of, 'what do we do with them, now'. Do you have a position on this?"

"Frankly, Major Boyd... I hadn't given that much thought," admitted the President. "How many people are we talking about?"

"About twenty, if my count's accurate," said Jacobson. "Around ten adults and ten or so teens and children."

"And my two pups," added Wolf. "You'd better leave 'em outside, pardner... 'less you're good with burn-marks on this pricey furniture you got in here."

"I'm sure we can find some good kennel-facilities for them," predicted the President.

"Y'all ain't never dealt with dogs like *this*, Mr. President, sir," quipped Devon White. "Damn things start a fire every time they, uhh, 'do their business'. They're actually not too hard to get used to – I'm all 'ice' and I did okay with 'em – but if I was y'all, I'd bring a fire-extinguisher first time they size y'all up."

"Make a point of that," the U.S. leader directed to Kaysten.

"Oh yeah," mordantly agreed the Chief of Staff, while Feldner shook her head in amazement.

"Well, they could simply all just go home," proposed the President. "Wouldn't *that* work?"

"Some of them – you know the ones I'm referring to, Commander – don't have a home left to go *to*," argued Tanaka. "And if I were Brent – or Sam – I'd be very worried about the intelligence-agencies trying to be 'second time lucky', in another abduction-attempt."

"*Definitely* so!" supported Jacobson. "Before I'd even *entertain* such an idea, Mr. President, you'd have to demonstrate that you had complete, unchallenged control over all the government's intelligence-agencies – particularly 'The Agency' but also the other 'black' ones, as well as the military – and that they were likely to follow your orders. To put it mildly... we're nowhere *near* there, yet. Our families, and other refugees traveling with them, will be much easier to protect, if they're in one, reasonably well-defended location... I think I'd also like it to be somewhere that it's not easy for the press to get at them. They've been through a great deal... they deserve a little privacy. What could we do, given all that?"

"Hmm... other than putting them up here, or maybe in the Blair House... I'm honestly not sure, Commander," offered the President. "Jerry... any ideas?"

"Yeah... that's a 'toughie', for sure," said Kaysten. "The issue is, if it looks like a prison, they probably won't react well to that... and who can *blame* them? How about Andrews... Camp David... something like that? It'd be out of the way, the creature-comforts are top-notch, and as long as we make sure that only 'our' people in the military are in charge there, they should be reasonably safe."

"I'll authorize that," said the President. "I'd prefer them to stay at Camp David; from what I've been told over the past few hours, it looks like that the staff in that location are almost all on 'our' side. Obviously there are secure areas in there that we'd not make available, but the general guest-quarters should be fine. Jerry, you and Curt can make the arrangements."

"I'd imagine that we could have our families and the others ready by approximately noon tomorrow... or today, or whatever it is," mentioned Jacobson. "Assuming, of course, that they don't balk at the idea of getting anywhere near somewhere that the government runs. Is that too early?"

"Shouldn't be," promised the Chief of Staff. "All those evac-sites are already ready to go, given what – uhh – has been happening around here. I just have to give the word. Would I be right in assuming that you'll be arriving via the *Express*?"

"I don't know... Karéin – *are* we?" asked Jacobson.

"Well... yes," agreed the Storied Watcher. "Just as long as you know that after this trip – assuming that we can safely fit all these people into our air-ship, and that might be challenging, even though it would presumably be a short ride – I will need to take the *Mailànkh Express*, ahh, *elsewhere*. I do not know how long I will be away, because that depends on decisions made by our other brothers and sisters. So you will need to find your own transportation, should you need to leave this 'Camp David', after I leave –"

Feldner broke in, "Ms., uhh, 'Storied Watcher' –"

"Just 'Karéin' to you, friend," obligingly corrected Karéin-Mayréij.

"Okay... 'Karéin'," continued the Press Secretary, "I've seen that, uhh, thing, that these folks," – she waved her hand to indicate all the 'more-than-humans' – "Arrived here in. It's *huge!* Are you telling me that you're just going to drag that into the air, behind you? How's that *possible?*"

"Actually... I am told that the primary propulsion for our air-ship was provided by stalwart Hector, who is now outside," offered the Storied Watcher. "But you are *partly*-right. When the time is nigh, I will have the *Express* in tow, and she and I will fly at some thousands of your kil-o-meters per hour, to our destination... which is rather distant. I intend to cruise, under mine own power of course, in the 'strat-o-sphere'... that is to say, 'far higher than your tallest mountain-peaks'. Why is this such a surprise to you, Susan?"

"Are you... *real?*" said the awed woman.

"Very," replied Karéin-Mayréij, with a sympathetic smile. "I know that our weirding-powers may seem overwhelming to you; but perhaps, in time... you will come to understand them better... one way or another. The first step to availing oneself of something, is 'being interested in it'."

"Karéin," protested Chu, "You can't *do* that!"

"'Cannot do'... *what?*" replied the alien-girl.

"*Leave... that's* what!" implored the former team-leader.

"*Why* not?" inquired a perplexed Storied Watcher.

"Because we still have *another* loose nuke to deal with... *that's* why!" reminded Chu. "Specifically – the one out in the Greater Los Angeles Area. *You* know... the one that made you show up with the rest of us, down in Compton, to evacuate the kids from that school!"

"And why is that one, *my* problem?" challenged the alien-girl. "For stars' sake, my sister... I have already helped with making us safe from one 'nuke' and nearly spent my own life, in saving these cities around us, from the second! Is there not a 'vay-cay-shun' from, 'being blown up by atom-smashing bombs', offered to your 'Guardian Angel'?"

"Angels don't *get* vacations," quipped Abruzzio. "At least that's what they told us in Catholic girl's school. Honest! If you don't believe me... just ask Moira... she took the classes too."

"Ms. Chu is absolutely right, you know," commented the President. "Jerry – did we get any status-updates on this situation, lately?"

"I can ask Curt... but the short answer as far as I know, sir, is 'no'," replied Kaysten. "I think I saw a message about 'we've got the thing tracked as far as the L.A. 'Inland Empire' area'... but that's about it. Frankly – given all the other stuff that's been going on, around here I mean – we've kind of put that one on the back-burner."

"Well, we need to get back on the ball here," ordered the U.S. leader. "I obviously don't have to explain why having a nuclear weapon outside of the government's control, in the middle of an American city, is unacceptable. Have we got back in touch with Arthur yet?"

"'Got' this... 'get' that," groused the Storied Watcher. "Do you people *ever* use the correct verbs, even in your own language? Why not just say, 'have we yet contacted this man'?"

"English-lessons from an alien space-hottie, who speaks some kind of weirdo language that none of us can say a *word* of, to her walkin', talkin' space-armor and swords and shields," joked Wolf. "Okay, then."

"*One* of us does... *sort* of," corrected Boyd.

"I love you too, dear brothers," smartly answered Karéin-Mayréij.

"Not recently, sir," stated the Chief of Staff.

"I've been *trying*, Mr. President," announced Chu. "But it seems that there's still some kind of jamming going on... or perhaps recent events have damaged the communication-networks. Maybe the military can set up a secured channel? The point is – particularly given that General Blanshard is probably now dead – we'll need a reliable liaison with the Department of Defense, to coördinate operations in L.A.. Do you know if Secretary DeWitt is on your side, sir?"

"He was more or less neutral during the *coup*," observed the President. "I'm not sure if we can rely on him... but I suppose we'll have to take the chance, assuming that we can make contact."

"Well," noted Kaysten, "If George, Warnock and the rest of that crew have gotten what they so richly deserved... anybody else who was part of the conspiracy, are likely feeling pretty lonely right now. We can use that as leverage, Mr. President."

"Definitely," agreed the U.S. leader. "It would sure help if I had a few super-humans on my side, to drive home the message that 'resistance is futile'."

"You've got at least one, sir," volunteered Minnie Chu.

"Two!" jumped in Kaysten. "What am I... chopped liver?"

"No offense meant, Jerry," said the former team-leader, with a smile.

"Three," mentioned Matt. "Dad, I'm not sure which of these funky 'alien-powers' that I've got – other than for 'seeing a few dark reds and purples that I must have missed before' – but I'll fight by your side however I can."

"Four," added Clairie. "Same diff. I guess if you need someone to roll a pen across a table... I'm your girl."

"Karéin," dryly remarked the President, "Maybe I *was* a bit hasty in condemning what you did to my children."

"Nothing she didn't do to her own... or to *me*," commented Billings.

This got him a kiss from his alien better-half.

By now, Tommy had fallen asleep; he was curled up in one of the chairs.

"Commander?" said the President, in Jacobson's direction.

"I have to hand it to you in the 'chutzpah' department, Mr. President," objected the former Mars mission commander. "Not two hours ago we were one inch away from killing you, as just desserts for the government torturing kids and trying to murder our families... and now you're asking us to meddle in the government's internal power-struggles, with what in it for *us*, I have no idea. I can only speak for myself – but I think you *know* what the answer's going to be."

"That goes for *all* of us, I'd wager," added Boyd. "Fight your *own* damn battles! I'll help Cherie find her mother... that's the extent of it."

"Yeah... we've got enough of our own," complained Tanaka. "As in, 'stopping the government from torturing and kidnapping our loved-ones.'"

"You *know* I'm trying to put a stop to that, Ms. Tanaka!" argued the President. "I'd do that whether or not you were here reminding me of the issue. I want a clean break from the misconduct of the past, and so help me God I'll do it... or die trying."

"Then *do* it... and we'll talk!" shot back the former Mars science officer.

"Rainbow and I will defend you against attack, Mr. President," pledged Abruzzio, "But it's not appropriate for us to get involved in the rest of this. Doing so might later on lead to questions about 'are *we* working for *you*... or, are *you*, working for *us*'. We intervened in the ACP situation because of an imminent threat to millions of innocent lives, that could not be dealt with in any other way. I don't think it's a good idea to be maneuvered into potentially using lethal force against one part of the government, at the behest of the *other* half of the government. At least that's how *I* feel."

"Karéin?" asked the President.

"My sister Sylvia speaks with wisdom," deflected the Storied Watcher. "You know... many here, have been tested in different ways, over the past fortnight; and to one extent or another – my heart sings with joy as I do say – 'all have passed'. Now comes another test for *yourself*, sir. I wish you all success in accomplishing it – but I must be neutral in this, and I would advise the same of all those who know the *Fire*... at least, those who owe you not a natural oath of personal loyalty. Ours is to see that the king does no evil; but we do not care *which* king, that is."

"Alright," noted the President, "I suppose we all know where we stand, then. All I'll ask of you and your team, Commander Jacobson, is simply to stay out of our way as much as is possible, while we try to deal with this remaining dangerous situation in L.A., and while I try to regain control over the government –"

"It's not in our interest to intervene in either of those, sir," interrupted the former Mars mission commander. "But again... I won't presume to speak for all of us. Do any of you disagree?"

Most remained silent; but eventually, White spoke up.

"With all due respect, Captain," he said, "I can't go with that. The 'L.A.' part of it, I mean. I got no skin in his game – like, 'who gets to run this sorry-ass country' – but them folks down in Compton... they're *my* folks – y'understand what I'm sayin'? So, Mr. President... yeah, I'm 'in' on lendin' a hand in L.A., if necessary, and if y'all think it'd help. Prolly get my ass fried – 'three nuke strikes you're out', kinda thing – but down where I come from, and that's pretty much *exactly* where that last nuke's s'posed to be hidin' out – y'all don't just run when your homies takin' it some hot. I *owe* those folks! Pretty sure Saquina feels the same way. Only thing is... I don't fly nowhere *near* as fast as Angel Lady here – so y'all gonna have to get me there the old-fashioned way. I'm good for sleepin' on the plane... if *that* helps."

"Thank you very much, Major White," replied the President, "I'm sure your country can use you on this mission. For what it's worth – seeing you, or your wife, ending up hurt or worse, is the *last* thing that I'd want to see happen. On top of everything else... getting the first man to set foot on Mars, killed in an operation like this – especially after how you've been treated thus far – well, that wouldn't look too good on *my* record, either."

"Yeah, well," mordantly offered White, "Steppin' out on Mars... that was damn easy, compared to the shit that's gone on since we got back to Earth. *Sir.*"

"Listen, man," sympathetically stated Boyd, "I totally get how you feel, and I'd go with you... but I have to help Cherie, then get back to Laura and the kids... you know?"

"Same here," added Jacobson.

"The moment I find my Mom," pledged Tanaka, "I'll be there by your side."

"No problem," agreeably answered White. "Y'all take a rain-check on the next H-bomb."

"I figure," he sighed, "There's *always* gonna be another one."

The Storied Watcher looked upset and at odds; but she said nothing.

"Major White," spoke Chu, "Could you – and your wife if she chooses to accompany you – help us devise plans to deal with this weapon? If you're 'in' on the operation, it would make sense for everyone to cöordinate roles and responsibilities, as closely as possible."

"Sure... I can do that," agreed the former Mars mission communications officer.

"That means you and your wife will be staying here – in the White House, I mean?" suggested Kaysten.

"'Least until we can get on a plane headin' west," replied White. "Funny, y'know – not the way I figured it'd all end up, when we started this damn thing. I mean... 'Devon and Saquina White gettin' a night in the White House'... somehow, seems kinda poetic."

"That it *does*," murmured Abruzzio.

"We can probably get a transport-plane for you," proposed Kaysten. "There should be a few available, since a lot of them were grounded recently, given the – *ahem* – problems with 'unsafe airspace' over the central part of the country. Devon... are you and Saquina ready to go immediately, if necessary?"

"Yeah... I s'pose," reluctantly replied the former Mars mission officer. "But if we get back here in one piece... I'm knockin' on the door with a reservation in my hand, and I ain't walkin' away until I've cashed in my hotel points, y'understand what I'm sayin?"

"You and your wife – your children too – are welcome any time you want to call, Major White," assured the President. "Listen... it's been incredibly stressful over the past few hours, and I'm *terribly* beat. Can we conclude at this point? If there's anything left unresolved, we can re-open the discussions at a later date."

"Yeah... fine," agreed Jacobson.

Karéin-Mayréij stood up.

"In that case," she said, "I believe that it is time for those of us who will go in the *Mailànkh Express*, to Commander Sam's place of refuge, to make way to the air-ship. Now is the final call... should any of you prefer the luxurious accommodation of this palace, to the mean comforts of the *Express* – now is your time thus to declare."

"So the count is," repeated Kaysten, "Karéin... you, Bob, Tommy, Misha, Wolf, Brent and Commander Jacobson, are flying out to – uhh, *somewhere* – in the *Mailànkh Express*, while Minnie, Cherie, Devon, Saquina, Melissa, Sylvia and her mutt of course, plus hopefully Hector and Moira, will be hanging out with us here in the White House, for the duration – at least until we can get Major White and his wife into a transport for points west. Oh... and we'll find somewhere to put those two GrayWar guys, where they can't get themselves into trouble... but they've got to disembark from the air-ship. Am I missing anybody?"

"I'd like to stay here for the time being, Mr. President," requested Feldner. "I need to be close to the goings-on... for handling the press, I mean."

"Of course," agreed the U.S. leader.

"May I invite my former team-members – specifically, Otis Boatman and Will Hendricks – to rejoin me here, sir?" asked Chu.

"Certainly," said the President.

"Commander... when you get back to wherever you're going – would you mind conveying my request?" asked the *nouvelle*-Director.

"Sure," complied Jacobson, "But I'm not sure how they'll get here, once they're told? I mean – is Karéin dragging the *Express* back here, after she re-unites us with our families?"

"I had not intended so to do," noted the Storied Watcher. "I do not fancy any more, ahh, 'warm welcomes', of the sort that apparently Commander Sam encountered, upon arriving here."

"You'll have none... I *promise*," pledged the President. "Anyway... don't worry about that. We can arrange a helicopter to take them from Camp David."

"Verily, sir," warned the alien-girl, "May we hope that your orders to your warriors shall be obeyed – since, undoubtedly you know what will become of them, should they attack us, *en route* to our destination. We *will* defend ourselves... is this clearly understood?"

"Fuckin' *ay!*" grunted Wolf.

"Karéin – please delay your departure until we've had a chance to send my orders to the military, to stand down, out on all the internal government communications-channels," requested the U.S. leader. "I'll make the situation as clear as I possibly can, to Arthur – that's Secretary of Defense DeWitt, by the way – and to the armed forces. There still may be some units that either haven't gotten the message, or that still believe George to be in charge... they may be working under obsolete orders. As I don't believe you're disposed to just sit around and wait until everything is completely under control, all I can ask is for you to use minimum force in defending yourself against the Air Force. Remember... these are loyal soldiers and airmen, who are just doing their duty, as they interpret it. Spare their lives if you possibly can. *Please*."

"Yeah, Karéin," spoke up Clairie. "It's not *fair* for you to blow them to bits, if they were told to shoot at you, by George. How's that *their* fault?"

"How's it *her* fault, when she shoots back, after being shot at first, kid?" countered Billings. "You and your brother there... you need to spend a little more time on the poor side of town. That'd teach you all about, 'I'm from the government and I'm here to help you'."

"Well that may be, Mr. Billings," said the teenaged girl, "But it's still *wrong* to hurt people who can't fight back!"

"Even if they don't *know* that... and they had every intention of killing you?" argued Boyd. "We got a quick lesson about all that, when they dropped us off in that dungeon the government had set up, underneath Amchitka. It went badly for them... but not for lack of *trying*."

"Had Karéin's powers not flowered in us, at that very moment," added Tanaka, "We'd likely all be *dead* – that includes Bob and Tommy, and other helpless victims who you've not yet seen, as well. We had a very hard lesson in 'survival ethics'. We *killed* a bunch of vicious scum, who were about five seconds away from killing *us*, for no defensible reason at all. I sure hope you never have to learn the same way, Clairie. I really *do*."

"You have had a very sheltered existence," observed Misha. "Your father – understandably – has hidden from you, the methods of coercion and violence that are used on a routine basis, by the American government. As you become more conversant with what we have been talking about tonight, perhaps your views on this will... *change*."

"I will do my best to be merciful, young princess," pledged the Storied Watcher, "But my first duty is to protect my family, my friends... and, 'you'. Soon, this solemn task will fall equally to you and your brother... and you both will understand how challenging it is, to execute. It is a thing of mists and guesses, not clarity and certainty, and one is never sure if one has done the right thing. When I leave, your duty to defend your father and his kingship – using the Holy *Fire* with which you have latterly been entrusted – that, will begin. I pray that you will act wisely."

Clairie – more than a bit intimidated by her mentor's regal demeanor, and by the stories related by the others – just mutely nodded acknowledgment.

There was a moment of silence, and then Kaysten advanced, "It's been a long night."

"Aye," agreed Karéin-Mayréij. "A day for the ages. Let us end it now. Who shall follow me to the *Mailànkh Express?*"

She looked downward – with a mother's kindly regard – at her somnolent son, who she lifted with her arms (they could not tell if she was using telekinesis) and carried, while he was still asleep.

His head rested over her left shoulder, though Tommy was in fact too big for an equivalent-sized human woman to attempt this with.

"Do you see, sister Susan?," she offered.

"Some burdens, however weighty," she reflected, "Burden one not."

Check The Belts

Since the débacle at the house back to the northwest of where the *Mujaheddin* were now, things had gone steadily from bad to worse, for Qusay-al-Sabah, Waqas-al-Nusri and those few who remained of the South California *Shaheed* Strike Group.

After wasting more than a full day fruitlessly searching both for their original "objective" and for the Satanic buzzing-terror – the presence of the latter having been confirmed, under torture, by a couple of infidel gang-bangers briefly taken captive, before being ritually beheaded – they had finally decided to rest and take overnight refuge in what must, at some time in the recent past, have been a general-goods corner-store.

The choice was fortunate, as it had proved possible to scrounge various necessary items, such as disinfectants, painkillers and bandages, from the shelves.

Lamentably, most of the available foodstuffs weren't *halal*; thus, these had to be passed-by, something that did nothing for morale.

But this was the least of the group's problems. Repeated encounters with local black and Latino gangs had inflicted severe attrition; two more of the faithful had been martyred in recent fire-fights, and two others had been so badly-wounded that – after the necessary purification-rites – they had to be left behind.

Each man had been given one hand-grenade; and the grim sounds of the corresponding explosions had been evident within five to ten minutes after the *Mujaheddin* had vacated the area.

But these latest of our martyrs, no doubt took many infidels with them, silently noted al-Sabah.

Surely... this is most pleasing, in the eyes of the Almighty!

None the less, al-Sabah was forced to evaluate the situation : his force had lost *so* many Muslim warriors that encounters with groups of more than three or four hostile local gangsters, had to be avoided at all costs. He now had few enough remaining *shaheed*, that one bad fire-fight could easily put a permanent end to the mission. His group had been – due to repeated run-ins with the Bloods, Crips, El-Rukns, 18th Streeters, *Maras*, Mexican Mafia and a seemingly-infinite collection of other, less easily-recognizable gangs – moving rapidly; but now, the utmost caution had to be maintained... at least, until al-Sabah could be sure that the objective of the quest, was within sight.

The objective – yes... that is all that matters, now!

Dawn was breaking.

"Brother," al-Sabah softly called out to his second-in-command, "Let us consult the map... where are we, now?"

He noticed that Waqas-al-Nusri had mimicked his own violation of group rules, and had the beginnings of a beard on his rounded, forgettable, brown-to-tan face.

The shorter man – smelling of the sweat produced by days in 100-degree heat, never with a shower or a bath – rapidly advanced and unfolded a detailed map on a table-top.

"We are... *here*," indicated al-Nusri. "Eighth Street and... uhh... 'Her'... 'Her-mosa'... yes, that is it."

"Did you check the apparatus?" demanded al-Sabah.

"Yes – about ten minutes ago," declared al-Nusri. "Finally, we now have a much better fix, than we had even an hour past. It is showing a signal in the south-east direction'."

"But how far, exactly?" pressed the *Mujaheddin* leader.

"Alas... it is not showing that precisely, brother," the shorter man parried. "Only, that it is close. Within one to two kilometers – I am almost certain of that, judging from what we were taught, when we trained on the device, at home. As of right now, I cannot use the remote trigger. But if it comes within a hundred meters behind cover, or if within visual-range – that is, we have a clear line of sight – *then*, I can try. Of course... only on your specific orders."

"Well, as you know," evenly mentioned al-Sabah, "What *cannot* happen, at all costs, is for it to fall into the hands of the U.S. infidel government. If this appears to be imminent – for example if we see it being transported away from us – then we must act, *immediately*. Is that clear?"

"Of course," confirmed al-Nusri. "And may the Almighty steady our hands, in this hour of trial. You know, brother... I crave to join the martyrs, and somehow, I know that my wish will shortly be granted. When the time comes... I will not hesitate!"

"Allah be praised," reflexively repeated al-Sabah. Then his voice trailed off as he stared out into space.

"Yes?" asked the other man, after a second or two.

"So far," explained the *Shaheed* commander, "To maximize speed to the objective, so far, we have been going down the main streets... and we have lost many martyrs, by doing this. You say that we are now close?"

"Indeed," confirmed al-Nusri. "It cannot be more than five or six, uhh, 'long blocks', from where we are now."

"Look yonder," directed al-Sabah, pointing his finger to the south-east, at what appeared to have been, at some time in the past, a low-rise set of storage-rental units. "Unless it was abandoned – and common sense and intuition suggest otherwise – then the device will likely be well-defended. It would be most unwise to approach down a main street... snipers would send us quickly to Merciful Allah, from far off. We must now proceed cautiously through these buildings, making the best use that we can, of terrain-cover. When we strike for the final time, we must do so by complete surprise... so that the enemy is overtaken, before he can react. Do you understand?"

"Perfectly," complied the shorter man. "I will organize our brothers... and I will lead the way."

Al-Nusri turned and waved to the other men, who recognized the "break-camp" hand-signal.

Just as the group was about to leave its temporary bivouac and proceed across Hermosa Avenue, toward the industrial buildings on the eastern side of the street, al-Sabah went over to tap his understudy on the shoulder.

"Brother," said the leader, "There is one more thing."

"Yes?" asked the shorter man.

"How many of the special belts do we have left?" asked the commanding *Mujaheddin* warrior.

"Five," replied al-Nusri, with an phlegmatic shrug.

My Plans For Valhalla

The hulking, bulging muscles of the Lictor General strained, along with those of the other five Aryan warriors – all who could be spared from his bodyguard, given the on-going contingencies on at least three battle-fronts in the immediate vicinity.

"Mother*fucker!*" he involuntarily inveighed, while trying to man-handle the iron-bound *thing* – its form-factor reminiscent of an old-style hot-water-heater-tank, hence its *nom-de-guerre* of "the Heater" – up the stairs leading up to the golf-chalet's main level.

"Fuckin' thing weighs a *ton!*", he complained.

"Six hundred and twenty-three pounds, after they ripped some of that electronic shit out and put the extra shielding, back on it," corrected one of the few AB'ers on the crew, who really knew what was going on. "Hey – don't *bump* it, boss!"

"Why's that?" grunted the leader.

"One of them Latrino scientists... he told me, '*bad* shit might happen, if you drop it'," explained the subordinate. "Said something about the impact-fuses being, uhh... 'sensitive'."

"Same shit in the long run," parried the Aryan commander. "Come on, you fuckers – put your *backs* into it! We only got to get it to the 'copter, you know. Any of you hold back, I'll tie your asses to the bottom of the 'copter and drop you one second before, well... *you* know!"

So – with that "encouragement" to remind them of their sacred duties – the whitemen did, indeed, pull together as one team; and soon, the Heater had been hauled up to the landing at the top of the stairs. The rays of the dawning sun illuminated the interior of the former golf chalet, from the east.

The Lictor General cast his gaze in all directions. What confronted his eyes was not what he had intended to see.

He had been mostly living in the basement for the past few days, spending his time alternatively rape-murdering young Latinas and overseeing the project to bring the Heater up to full capability; he had been told of the savagery of the fighting going on topside, but *this* was an unpleasant half-surprise.

Stray bullet-rounds had shattered – or, at least, perforated – every one of the chalet's original, man-height plate-glass windows, and the subsequent impact of the projectiles had wrecked or seriously damaged almost everything else of functional utility, on the main level. This was a very near and real issue; the sounds of intermittent gunfire echoed through the streets outside, no more than a few blocks distant in any direction.

Piles of rotting trash, half-eaten food and buckets filled with stinking excrement were distributed at random intervals throughout the area – the chalet's only remaining working toilet was located in the basement, and the General had reserved it for himself – and, worse still, the place was near-deserted. Only six Aryan warriors, three of them obviously seriously-wounded, seemed to be present.

One guy who seemed combat-ready – a tall, wiry whiteman with unusually long, black hair, a goatee beard and a prominent scar across his right cheek – stood quickly to attention. The other two slowly got up.

"Heil *Hitler!*" he correctly barked, with the familiar stiff-arm salute.

"Heil to our Immortal *Fuhrer*," amiably responded the Lictor General. "I'm up here for the 'copter. You got it ready?"

"*Think* it's flyable," offered the warrior. "But that ain't for lack of *tryin'* on the part of them niggers on the south flank. They put two long-range rounds into it when we left it out in the parkin'-lot – fuckers got a sniper-rifle I guess – don' t think they hit anything important... we had to fold the rotors and move it back into the garage. Didn't take no more shots overnight, luckily. You want us to haul 'er out and get 'er set up?"

"Right away," directed the Aryan leader.

The huge, battle-scarred form of the east-front lieutenant, appeared in the exit-way leading to the outside parking-lot behind the chalet. He had to duck, being so tall as to hardly fit under the top of the doorway.

"Already done," interjected the warrior. "Patched 'er up as best I could – brackets and winches on the underside, too – and we'll get off the ground good enough... how far we'll get past *that*, it's anybody's guess. Been trackin' the Army and they got that motherfuckin' air-defense pretty close by – no more than a mile back from the front, and that's about four or five blocks from here, no further than I-15. If they get a clear line of sight, they might cap us, if we get much higher than them warehouses back down Sixth. 'Least that's *my* opinion."

"You said we could fly low... right?" queried the Lictor General.

"Yeah... gotta watch out for power-lines... shit like that," confirmed the east-front captain. "'I wouldn't want to try it at night. Specially with *that* damn thing hangin' below us– can't drop it or have it bang up against a wall, or whatever. They're tellin' me it weighs about a ton or so?"

"More or less," claimed the Aryan leader. "We can lift that?"

"Yeah," grudgingly acknowledged the other whiteman, "We got two turbines on the rig, and theoretically, even one's enough. Should be okay with you and me in the cabin, maybe one or two other guys too. Just don't ask me to fly too high – not that we *want* to, of course."

"Silk purse out of a fuckin' nigger's lips and a Jew's nose," quipped the Lictor General, to a chorus of laughter among those arrayed around him.

"Okay... so gather around and listen *up!*" he continued, standing tall and addressing the crowd.

He went over to an open area that must have been used for karaoke or perhaps casual dancing, in an earlier time. The Public Address microphone was still operational. The Lictor General activated it and spoke.

"This is an announcement from your leader!" he intoned. "Come to *attention!*"

Idle banter quickly ebbed away, as a number of other skinheads and AB'ers, who had previously been elsewhere in the facility, gathered around. There were now about thirty big, Caucasian street-fighters in and around the room.

"Fellow Aryan warriors," said the Lictor General, "The time of blood and glory, has *come!* As you know... we've been at war to preserve the future of the white race for weeks now, against the conspiracy of the Jew-run government, along with its hordes of niggers, beaners and other polluted-race swine, all around here. You've been fightin' like the noble Viking berserkers that you are; and I want each and every one of you to know, how much I appreciate that... and how much future historians, will marvel at your tenacity, your courage and at the massive body-count you've run up. I've personally seen the results, first-hand – and I can assure you – gonna be a lot of nigger mamas and taco-shitter bitches missin' their filthy offspring, on account of your merciless good shootin'!"

This brought a friendly cheer of appreciation from the crowd.

"I'll bring you all up to date on the situation," the Aryan leader continued, "And about what we intend to do with it. It ain't too good... that's the bottom line. History's repeatin' itself, and it seems that our blood spilled on the ground, will be what gives life to a new generation of pure, white citizens and warriors. The Jew-Army's closin' in on us from the east, there's a bunch of chili-shitter gangs comin' at us from the west – they got some fuckin' voodoo 'insect-swarm' shit that's eatin' our soldiers up bad – and the south's blocked off by millions of niggers... Bloods, Crips, 18th Streeters and other mongrels. We *could* all make for the mountains to the north; but runnin' ain't the white-man's style, and besides, they'd just pick us off one by one up there, eventually."

The whiteman leader stopped to take a long breath, and then he declared, "Our Lord and Savior, Adolf Hitler, taught us how to deal with situations like this – namely, to go out fightin' to the last bullet, to the last grenade... not *fearin'* death– but rather, *welcomin'* it! We will *not* dishonor our Aryan blood by surrenderin' – but by leavin' a legacy of blood that will last ten thousand *years!* For every white man who dies with his boots on, in the final battle... a *thousand* niggers, Jews and wetbacks, gonna go down beforehand!"

There was another cheer, although it appeared somewhat less enthusiastic than before.

"As some of you know," he stated, "But as many more don't – some time back, we, uhh, 'inherited' a nice big atomic surprise, from a bunch of them *Maras*. We surprised them *pollos* at the perimeter, shot the fuck out of 'em – to this day, we got no idea what they planned to *do* with it... but they're probably too stupid to even know how to throw the switch. Anyway... over the past few weeks, we've been workin' hard to get it into shape... and we just did."

There were some gasps from the audience.

"I've been thinkin' about where best to set it off," he remarked. "At first I figured that was right here in 'Cucamonga; but problem is, there's a lot of fine Aryan warriors here, and we might take a few niggers or Army soldiers with us, but, *nah!* That ain't *dramatic* enough! What *we* need to do, my friends, is to make this city as Jew-free as we can... and there simply ain't nowhere better to do that, than... *Hollywood!*"

This time, the applause was whole-hearted, with stiff-arm salutes clearly evident everywhere.

"Now," the Lictor General elaborated, "Our intel says that there's a few W.A.R. boys up in Beverly Hills, which ain't too far from there... but they're not directly under our leadership, and it'll teach 'em for playin' around in places tainted by Jewishness, anyway. But *you* know – and *I* know – that Hollywood's a cesspool of race-corruption, liberalism and Yid bullshit... always *has* been, always *will* be. It's *crawlin'* with smart-ass Jews, drivin' their luxury-cars in their Gucci suits and havin' a grand old time whorin' out *real* white women, pollutin' them with their diseased body-essences... world will be better off *without* 'em!"

"Oo-*rah!*" bellowed the crowd.

He went on, "I expect every Aryan warrior hearin' my voice to fight to the death, for the honor of the white race; and 'every Aryan warrior', includes, *me*. I ain't expectin' anything of you, that I don't expect of myself. That's why I'm gonna set the time-fuse on our little present to the kikes up there in their lovely mansions, before I take off in the 'copter... I'm gonna give it just a bit more time than it should take to get us there," – he turned his head to interrogate the east-front lieutenant – "How long's that, you think?"

The big guy in the doorway replied, "Oh, I don't know – it's like, just under fifty miles, and normally, the 'copter could make it there in, say, fifteen, twenty minutes... but we're weighed down, and we gotta fly low, so we can't just take a straight-line route. I'd say, 'give it forty minutes, or an hour if you don't mind waitin' around a bit'."

"It's got a command-fuse, too," the Aryan leader pointed out. "Real short delay. But make it an hour... okay? Before we get to Jew-land, we're goin' huntin' for that motherfuckin' 'insect' thing that probably got Clay. If we find it, we're gonna lead it right to the Yids, so maybe a few of 'em experience the fun of bein' eaten up, before they get vaporized. How fast you think we can fly, with the 'present', underneath us?"

"She can do over a hundred and eighty knots, clean," offered the east-front lieutenant. "But with *that* weight, and the two of us, or even one other... I dunno, boss. Maybe a hundred and ten at full-throttle – and we'll burn out the turbines if we do it for more than a few minutes. Seventy to ninety's more realistic, I'd say."

"Good enough for *me*," assented the Lictor General. "Get a map and draw out our flight-path."

"Yeah," acknowledged the east-front commander. He disappeared out the door.

"So – with that in mind... here's the plan," announced the Aryan leader. "None of us should be surprised that there's a price on *all* our heads... but *I* ain't bein' taken alive – not by the Jews in the government, not by the spooks, not by the *chicos*, not by *nobody* – no, Viking whitemen; just like our Lord and Savior Adolf Hitler did, I'm ridin' that bomb all the way to the end... I'm goin' Odin-speed straight to *Valhalla!*"

The room burst out with stiff-arm salutes, with howls of "Heil *Hitler!*" and "Glory Of The White *Race!*", echoing all around.

After the commotion had died down, the Lictor General pronounced, "As to every one of you... you've got a decision to make : either hold out here – make sure you leave at least one round or grenade for yourselves, because you *know* what them niggers and beaners are gonna do with you, if they take you alive – or, you can head out on your own, groups of no more than three per team – and see if you can make it past the Army and them mongrel-gangs that's everywhere else. After that, you'll be on your own."

"But ain't that... *desertin'?*" asked a voice from the throng.

"Only if you don't kill any niggers or spics, as you go," contested the Lictor General. "I assume you know what's the right thing to do. Look... if I was any one of you, I'd want to stay here and die with my boots on, just like our mighty Fuehrer did, back in – when was it –"

"'Forty-four," somebody said.

"Forty-five," called out another.

"*Whenever* the fuck it was," the Aryan leader commented. "Anyway... I believe that the *true* glory, is in goin' out in savage combat against the agents of the accursed Zionist Occupational Government... and thus in settin' an example for the next generations of the white race. But we gotta be *realistic* here – *someone* has to live through it, to tell the story to white kids, everywhere else, and inspire 'em to fight another day. So you have my permission to make your own decisions. All I ask is that you do honor to your Aryan blood and take as many kikes, niggers and beaners with you, as you can, along the way. I'll be looking down from Valhalla... and I'll be smilin', fellow-warriors."

"We *know* you will, boss!" came a supportive shout from the crowd.

"Say 'hi' to our Immortal Father, Adolf Hitler!" added another.

"I'll *do* that," pledged the Lictor General.

Cheers and more stiff-arm salutes came from almost all around.

The whiteman leader cast a glance to the team that had been man-handling the Heater.

"Let's get her out and under the 'copter," he ordered.

Leadin' It On

At daybreak, Clayton Lomass' eyes came into focus, staring at a multi-perforated drop-ceiling, which – at some time in the not-too-recent past – must have been part of a low-rise, white-collar office-complex.

As a matter of fact, the ceiling was practically *all* that he could see. His body – almost all of it except his boots and a small gap through which he could see – seemed to be covered in a pile of printed paperwork, loose-leaf notes and other random, business-office-style *bric-a-brac*, as if he had fallen against a paper-laden table or some other such furniture, before hitting the floor.

Remembering his training about "not letting on that you ain't dead", he didn't arise right away; instead, the Aryan warrior slowly and carefully moved his head to the left, and then again to the right, validating that the place in which he had come to reside was, in fact, deserted.

A few sheets of paperwork were thus dislodged, giving him a wider field of vision.

Cursing the pathetic, atypical weakness that plagued his entire body, he slowly sat up, ruefully coming to terms with the fact that he could no longer use both arms to prop himself up.

The rest of the junk covering his body began to slide off.

Fuck... he realized, *I passed out!*

Sure glad none of the other guys were around to see it.

For how long?

Not wanting so to do – but knowing that he had to, at some point – Lomass forced himself to look at what remained of his right arm. There was an ugly, congealed, reddish-brown welt covering the stump of it, which had been severed at the elbow-joint; but the pain had receded to something manageable, if certainly not "pleasant".

Another bout of physical nausea – quickly-suppressed and followed immediately by a sense of pride – assaulted his being, upon seeing what his battle-knife handicraft had wrought.

Doesn't the Bible say somethin' about, "if your arm pisses you off... get rid of it"?

Well... I just did!

Passed the test!

And, Whiteman... "that which does not destroy me... only makes me stronger"!

He managed to come to a cautious crouch, retrieving his auto-rifle with his one remaining good hand.

It was now obvious what must have happened; he had become unconscious right next to an office-desk that was, at the time, covered with paperwork, had tried to reach out with his good arm to stabilize himself, but had instead grabbed the stack of paper, which had covered him when he fell to the floor. He took only a perfunctory glance at it, but the writing on the stuff seemed to be about "polished metals and custom assembly-coatings", with enthusiastic-sounding language making claims about "two-day delivery" and the like.

Unwelcome, Hispanic voices sounded, far-off and apparently to the south. Lomass scanned in every direction, and discovered – partly to his relief, though he longed for more kills – that no opponents were in the immediate vicinity. He was about in the middle of this large, open-concept office-space, with the windows – which enclosed the office on three sides – at least twenty feet away.

The place had the usual accouterments of 2040s white-collar business-affairs, including dirty coffee-cups in a nearby kitchenette (disappointingly, the refrigerator had already been looted; its door swung open to the elements), wall-posters exhorting staff to "fire 'em, don't hire 'em, when you see an 'illegal'", powered-down computer-keyboards with matching, paper-thin video-displays and inoperative interior lighting.

Overall, it gave the impression of having been quickly-abandoned, as if the order to evacuate had been given with little or no advance notice.

Too fuckin' bad I don't have more time, he mused, *'cause if I did... maybe I'd find a safe or some cash lyin' around.*

Again blessing his years of training from the Army and from the traditions of the Aryan Brotherhood, Lomass used his one good hand and some of his camping-rope to tie his hunting-knife, to what remained of his right arm, so the blade faced forward.

Well... probably won't help much in a fight... but better than nothin', he resolved.

And damn good I learned how to fire the rifle, left-handed, years ago.

Anyway... back to business... none of them beaner cunt-muffins close-by...

Good – I don't get capped just for standin' up.

Okay, then... recce time.

Still taking no chances, he came to a fully-upright position and slowly advanced to the set of windows facing west. The streets in this direction – and, as he discovered in the next minute or so, to the north – were deserted. However, when the Aryan warrior inched toward the south-facing window-array, he had to suppress an urge to exclaim.

Far away to the south-east, he saw a burst of star-shell – or, maybe, just multiple flare-gun-discharges – blazing across the early morning sky.

It's ready, he grimly reflected.

Meanwhile, there were more pressing military considerations, closer to his current location.

Lomass' field of vision to the south was relatively narrow due to being partly-blocked by the hulks of decrepit cars; despite this, ahead of him, just short of a full long-block away, he could see a crowd of perhaps a hundred or more Latino gang-bangers, complete with various souped-up automobiles and trucks (the sides of which were, of course, covered with gang-colored graffiti, though Lomass didn't recognize this particular set of symbols) and the obligatory, foolishly-loud *mariachi*-music.

Holy fuckin' Hitler's balls! he noted.

Stupid chili-shitters must have gone down the street, right past *me!*

Either they never even checked in here... or they did, but they somehow missed me...

Well, Clay... there's your lucky break on this mission...

If you can call anythin' that's gone down so far, "lucky"...

And there was something else.

At the edge of his visual-abilities to the far south, he observed an ever-changing, fifty-foot-high *thing* – it looked sort of like a Southwestern dust-devil, but it was different, moving and recomposing every second as if made up of a million, too-small-to-see constituent parts, like a cloud of starlings are wont to do – towering over the crowd.

Someone – or perhaps multiple people, to whom Lomass did not have a line of sight – were yelling something at the throng; whomever it was, must have been using a bull-horn or other audio amplification device, given how far away the scene was from where the whiteman was hiding. It almost looked like some kind of perverse religious ceremony, with the Latinos in the crowd worshiping the whatever-it-was.

The whiteman had never learned how to speak Spanish – doing so was beneath him – but none the less, he still was able to pick out a few words.

Hmm... "destiny"... "your leader"... "golf course, ahead"... wait – what the fuck!

"The golf course?" Motherfucker!

That's where he's going – and that's where the boss, has got the bunker!

Whiteman – if ever there's been a time for blood and honor... now's it!

I'm gonna take out that fucker... or die tryin'!

And who cares about livin' – when you hear that German music, Clay... it'll be time, either way.

Lictor General sees that fuckin' insect-thing, he'll be comin' straight for it...

Time for a last meal, I guess.

Lomass took out the last of his carefully-husbanded, amphetamine-boosted beef-jerky, and helped himself to all of it.

Next taste in my mouth gonna be beaner blood... as befits a savage, white predator! he resolved.

He re-scanned the area.

There was the set of doors through whose plate-glass he had smashed to gain entrance to the building, far off down the entry-hall, but there was no other apparent path of egress. The doorway faced south, but it was hidden from the street to the west by several stands of trees and from the south by a collection of wrecked cars and more trees.

Lomass looked around very carefully, searching for hidden assailants or a rear-guard, but he found none.

Fuckers are too busy havin' a fiesta, than in guardin' their rear-flank, he amused himself by realizing.

Good, then... there's my opening!

Quickly collecting his gear (and finding, to his relief, that he was adjusting to having only one usable hand), the whiteman crouched below the window-line and moved as noiselessly as he could, down the entry-hall to the doorway.

Again he checked for Latino stragglers, but nobody at all seemed to be in the vicinity. Staying as low as he could to the ground, and ensuring that he made as little noise as possible, Lomass exited the building through the smashed-in doorway and then immediately dashed to the west, hiding in the tree-complex on the east side of the narrow, back-street just beyond.

The Aryan warrior ran a temporary retrograde course to the north, moving far enough in that direction to ensure that he couldn't be seen by the party-goers far down the street to the south.

He reached a tree-lined intersection and looked at a couple of faded, dust-covered street-signs, which said "Center Ave." and "7th Street" respectively. Scanning all around and almost on his knees, he sprinted across the north-south street to a tall stand of pine-trees on its west side.

Keeping his right flank to wall-side while using his left arm to wield his auto-rifle, Lomass crept forward in classic ambush fashion, advancing quickly to covering-terrain, then halting to survey the surroundings, thus to ensure that the hunter hadn't become the hunted. This side of the street was better than the other one, for the purpose of sneaking up on one's enemies; there were more trees and fewer open driveways and parking-lots.

He proceeded south by a couple hundred feet and then had to stop, as by now he could clearly see the tail-end of the Latino gang-convention, only a small part of which was actually on or around Center Avenue; instead, a much larger portion appeared to be fanning out into an open area just south and east of the last large factory-complex that he could see in that direction.

Now I'll get... uhh... where'd the fuck it go?

He searched as hard as he could, but the twisting, multipartite tower of doom had vanished; or at least, its top-parts had descended to below the roof-levels of the industrial-buildings all around.

Far-off, in the distance to the south-east, he heard more noises of mayhem; but these were different; they were deeper and more concussive, as if powerful explosives were going off.

Didn't know the Army was this close, he ruminated.

Be quite a show to see 'em run up against that fuckin' weirdo thing that got Little Joe... if, of course, I live that long...

Looking out of the corner of his eye, Lomass' danger-senses were alerted immediately upon seeing movement to the east, across a parking-lot on the other side of the street. He saw a group of perhaps eight to ten olive-skinned, mostly-bearded, dark-haired and exclusively male gangsters – some of whom were unusually-dressed in a kind of white smock with matching skull-cap and a heavy-looking belt weighing them down at the midriff – proceeding rapidly to the south-east.

Shit! he inwardly cursed.

Fuckers are tryin' to flank me – wait *a minute* –

He took another long glance, doing his best to remain hidden in the tree-stand.

Can't be that – *they* couldn't *have seen me, and anyway... they're headin' away, through them factories and shit.*

Almost looks like they're tryin' to flank them chili-shitters who's havin' a fiesta down there... maybe they're some other kind of beaner-gang?

But there's hundreds of wetbacks in the gang just past where it opens up, at the end of the street!

How the fuck is another posse of ten guys, gonna take 'em out – or even last more than five minutes when everythin' gets off the gate?

He had been unable to reason this out, when more unexpected developments came from the same direction. The first, strangely-dressed gang had almost exited his field of view, when – from approximately same location – a second group of potential "hostiles", appeared.

These were more familiar to Lomass' eyes; they were clearly heavily-armed, tough-muscled, black, male ghetto-dwellers dressed in sport-pants, brand-name sneakers, polished gold chains and other gang-regalia (he noted that neither red nor blue showed prominently on their attire, so whatever they were, they probably weren't mainstream Crips or Bloods), and they were moving very rapidly, as if trying to overtake the first gang.

A repetitive, "thump-thump-thump" sound now came from the south-east. Whatever was making it was not visible, as it was undoubtedly blocked by the buildings of the industrial-park.

A shot – then several more – rang out, from some point in the same direction, out of the Aryan warrior's field of view. One of the black gangsters immediately dropped, his head and upper-body pulped by multiple bullet-strikes. As their fallen comrade lay bleeding out on the parking-lot pavement, the other posse-members stopped and returned fire from whatever terrain-cover that was immediately at hand. Curses bellowed from the black gang; they were matched by some kind of incomprehensible shouting from further to the south-east.

As the gunfight escalated, Lomass again looked due south. The fracas had an immediate effect; the *fiesta* – or whatever it was – amongst the original Latino gang-army, came to an abrupt end.

He caught wind of frenzied exclamations in Spanish, and could make out words to the effect of, "behind us – kill them all, *muchachos!*"

To his dismay, these instructions were matched, a second or two later, by a significant number of Latino gang-warriors charging northward up the street – and they were heading directly for where he was hiding.

They're tryin' to west-flank whoever's closin' on them, he realized.

They'll shoot first and ask questions later – I got maybe six or seven seconds, but if I break cover, they'll see me for sure –

Okay then... I'm good with it – this Aryan warrior's goin' with his boots on!

With grim determination, he ensured that his auto-rifle had a full clip (plus "one in the chamber"), while doing preliminary targeting so as to drop the highest number of opponents in the least possible time.

Two grenades left, he remembered.

One for them… one for me.
Lots of rounds left for the rifle and the pistol.
Heil Hitler – *all the way to Valhalla!*

He unengaged the safety, and lifted the barrel of his gun to draw a bead on his first target. The Latinos were within fifty feet by now, and even if they *were* charging ahead with little caution, in another couple of seconds even the least-attentive of them would have to notice where he was inadequately-secreted.

Suddenly, the onrushing gangsters stopped in their tracks, shrieking Spanish invective. They seemed to be staring up into the sky, above and behind them.

A quick glance showed Lomass what the commotion was all about. A turbine-driven helicopter was flying very low – almost at roof-height, in fact – and it was *also* heading almost straight at where he was hiding. However, something was wrong with the 'copter; it was trailing smoke and seemed to be looking for a place to land.

Shit, he observed, *that looks like the one from back in the –*

Utter pandemonium broke out.

From an unseen location ahead and to the south-east, the sinister "insect-cloud" issued upwards, but not on a course to intercept the airborne craft. At the near, visible end of this hideous thing, there was a white-robed figure completely enveloped in the cloud, screaming out his last living seconds in agony as the very flesh from his bones was being quickly consumed.

The victim's shrieks were immediately followed by the fireball of a huge, tremendously-powerful explosion, very similar to the one that Lomass had almost fallen to, back up at Sierra Madre.

The detonation vaporized the visible-end of the death-cloud, which disappeared below the roof-line (this was accompanied by a somehow-audible, subconscious howl of pain, the likes of which the whiteman had never before encountered), and it also sent the helicopter careening sideways, toward the side of a building.

The pilot – who Lomass noted must have been a damn good one to have coped with what had just occurred – fought desperately to regain control, and only just succeeded, being able to right the 'copter just before it would have crashed; he managed to clear the roof of the building in front of him, then roared almost right over Lomass' head, coming to a controlled descent in the open field to the north-east of 7th and Center, to the north of the whiteman.

He allowed himself a quick glance in that direction. His suspicions were confirmed; indeed it was the Lictor General's personal craft, and as the 'copter's doors opened he saw his old boss, accompanied by another dark-haired, heavy-set Aryan warrior who Lomass recognized as "Growlin' Jim Jemriah" (an especially-violent and sadistic – if intelligent and resourceful – ex-biker-gang-member with a "thing" for wearing German World War 2 army-helmets), quickly disembark.

Unusually, they didn't seem to be paying much attention to the surroundings – or the threat of being ambushed – but rather, they were preoccupied in examining some kind of payload that must have been suspended underneath the helicopter. This was only dimly-visible, as its shape was obscured by the craft's undercarriage.

The pilot – for his part – seemed to be trying to re-start the engines, but the latter were responding fitfully, with the rotor-blades spinning in a slow and halting fashion. A second glance at the pilot revealed that he was in fact the former east-front commander.

Lomass again turned to deal with the immediate situation. The Latino gangsters were almost upon him, and though he would get the first shot, there were far too many of them for one warrior – however skilled – to deal with.

Yet, if he just sat there – and by some miracle went un-noticed – in the next twenty to thirty seconds, the "wetbacks" would *certainly* have a clear line of sight to the damaged helicopter, which would be within easy firing-range. The Lictor General, his bodyguard and the pilot, would last no more than a few seconds, particularly if taken by surprise.

Now, the old, cherished race-rage, came back to the Aryan warrior's blood. He knew what had to be done... and he did it : breaking cover, and standing tall as he unloaded his auto-rifle with controlled, short bursts at the Latinos, Lomass – his face wearing a proudly-defiant scowl – bellowed,

"Fuck The *Untermenschen! Yaaaaaaaaa!"*

His ambush was almost perfectly-executed; one, two, three, then a fourth Latino gangster dropped in quick succession. But after their initial shock, his adversaries reacted in expected fashion, diving for cover and unleashing a barrage of menacing – though poorly-aimed – gunfire in his direction.

Figuring that he had only seconds left to live, Lomass groped for his grenade and resolved to go out in a blaze of glory; but – to his astonishment – he saw the two "wetback" gunmen closest to him, shot dead in front of his eyes. The bullets that felled these unfortunates, however, didn't come from the whiteman's own guns; rather, they were fired from the area where the black gangsters had taken up positions, after their pursuit of the strangely-attired first gang had been stopped in its tracks.

A shot – issuing from the same place – whizzed dangerously close to his head. Another would have hit his right arm, had it still been part of his body. It appeared as if the black gang ensconced in the industrial-park, was shooting indiscriminately at anyone or anything that they detected to their west-flank.

Reflexively, the Aryan warrior dove backwards, to the north, into marginally-deeper cover, while the sounds of gangland gunfire raged just to the south of him.

Niggers are takin' on the chili-shitters! he realized.

Surely – a sign from our immortal Fuehrer!

Crawling as quickly as he could on his knees and one good hand – since, to have raised his head any further than this, would have incurred a grave risk of having it shot off – Lomass retreated as rapidly could, towards the intersection of the two streets. He reached the street-corner in a few seconds and then allowed himself to go up to a crouch and review his south flank. He could clearly see that the Latinos were fully-engaged in the fire-fight with the black gang, with dozens of gunshots ringing out from second to second, as the two groups bogged down in static warfare.

Still in a low crouch, the Aryan warrior dashed eastward across Center Avenue; for this, he was rewarded by being the target of at least two poorly-aimed gun-shots, each of which missed by a large margin. He got to his feet and sprinted toward the helicopter, which had crash-landed almost in the middle of the open area to the north-east of the road-intersection.

For a second, Lomass worried about being offed by "friendly fire", as he saw both the Lictor General and his bodyguard – now identifiable as the east-front commander from back in the bunker – raising their rifles. However, in the next second, he saw these being lowered, while both of the other whitemen raised stiff-arm, Nazi salutes.

"Heil *Hitler!*" sounded two gruff voices.

Lomass approached to within about fifteen feet.

The Lictor General said, in an annoyed tone of voice,

"Clay… *Clay?* That *you?* Why ain't you salutin'?"

The Aryan leader took another glance.

"Oh… holy *shit!*" he offered, upon seeing the stump of Lomass' right arm.

"Okay – so I *see* why not," said the leader, "Good to see you… but what *happened?* Where's Buzz and Little Joe?"

"They're *dead*," responded the Aryan warrior. "Buzz got smoked by a bomb back aways… set off by some fuckin' posse I ain't never seen before that, but they're around here now – so watch out. As for Joe… you don't want to *know* what happened to him. I *saw* it. It was the *thing* – the *bugs*, I mean. And as for me, I got bit by one of them taco-shitter gang-bangers, while the *thing* was eatin' Joe alive. Some kind of fuckin' poison… would have done the rest of me once and for all – but I *dealt* with it... you know?"

"Just like a tough-ass warrior of the master-race *should* do!" congratulated the Lictor General. "Honor to *you*, whiteman! Listen… you got a clean track on that fuckin' 'insect' thing yet? Because we thought we saw, just back there –"

"Yeah – it's just to the south of us – but but no time for that now, boss," countered Lomass. "I'll explain later. We gotta take cover – other side of that intersection, 7th and Center, back behind me – there's a fuckin' *huge* posse of wetbacks comin' up the street. They got tied up with a bunch of niggers further into the industrial-park… but there's too many wetbacks... jungle-bunnies won't last long. If we head into them buildings over there, we can –"

"Out of the *question!*" contradicted the Lictor General.

"But boss... we'll get cut to *pieces* out in the open here, if we –" Lomass started to argue; but then, he was able to get a clear look at what was underneath the helicopter.

Jemriah was on the other side of the craft. He seemed to be manipulating something on the opposite side of whatever was suspended below the 'copter.

"That... what I *think* it is?" inquired Lomass.

"You bet," started the Aryan leader. "And it's –"

"Boss – you better have a *look* at this – right *now!*" interrupted the hulking, Wehrmacht-helmeted white warrior, from behind the helicopter.

"Watch out for anybody comin' from south of us," the leader demanded of the pilot, who was fiddling with the cockpit-controls in his continuing attempts to re-start the engines.

Lomass and the Lictor General rushed around to where Jemriah was crouching.

"What's the *matter?*" demanded the white leader.

"Look at the *display!*" advised the panicked AB'er, pointing to a recessed, red-glowing LED maintenance-panel on the side of the Heater. "Fuckin' thing's been *triggered* – and we got eighteen *minutes!*"

"Eighteen... *minutes?*" stammered a shocked Lictor General. "What the *fuck?* I didn't activate –"

"I *know* you didn't, boss!" interrupted Jemriah. "I first saw the warnin'-light back there, just before we went down... maybe whatever the fuck *that* was, fucked up the electronics? No, wait – don't make no sense neither, 'cause the warnin'-light went on just *before* that explosion blew under us, when we flew over them Latinos wearin' them pansy white dresses. Anyway... either we drop it here and fuck off right now, or..."

The three stared mutely back and forth at each other.

"I'm not runnin'," pledged Lomass. "Not as long as I have one bullet left... and I got plenty, still."

"Neither am I," echoed Jemriah. "I just said that, so you know what the *situation*, is. Anyway... I doubt we'd get far enough away, 'specially on foot."

"I told the boys back at the golf-course... my fate is sealed, too," remarked the Lictor General. "My only objective is to take as many mongrels with me, as I can. So –"

His voice was drowned out by the welcome sound of the turbines firing up, and of the rotor-blades beginning to move faster and faster, over their heads.

"Got her runnin' again," shouted the east-front lieutenant, "But I had to enable 'Emergency Over-ride Mode' for everythin' – won't hold up more than fifteen to twenty minutes at eighty-five knots... then we go straight down."

"That'll do just *fine*," the Lictor General answered back. "Clay – you –" he started, only to be cut off by yells of alarm from the other three.

"*Wetbacks, at the junction!*" yelled Lomass, pointing to 7th and Center.

The Latino gangsters had, indeed, reached this crossroads. They immediately began firing at the helicopter; however, their aim was wild, probably due to using pistols and submachine-guns instead of rifles.

"Holy shit – what's *that!*" shrieked Jemriah, who was gesturing towards the roof-level of the building closest to the street-junction, to the south.

Above this roof, was the now-familiar, malevolently-buzzing "cloud of death", rapidly advancing upon them. In its approximate center was the dimly-visible image of a human, or humanoid, figure. This had an eerie, greenish glow all around it. A sinister-sounding, other-worldly kind of electric *mariachi*-music, accompanied the harbinger of doom and destruction.

Two more powerful explosions reverberated to the south-east, breaking glass windows, assaulting eardrums and almost tipping the helicopter over on its side. Smoke from not-too-distant fires, poured into the sky. There were the sounds of high-intensity gunfights from the same direction.

"*Into the 'copter!*" bellowed the Lictor General, as he dodged several incoming gunshots (a few of these hit the 'copter, but did not seem to do any significant amount of damage).

The Aryan leader's order was immediately obeyed by both Lomass and the other AB'er, as the east-front lieutenant gunned the turbines and the helicopter – though now burdened by the weight of four big men, as well as the "Heater" below it – staggered into the air, picking up speed as rapidly as possible.

Both the Lictor General, looking out the craft's right-hand side, and Lomass, who was doing the same out the left, tracked the progress of their weirding assailant. It was now almost a perfect sphere, perhaps eight to ten feet in diameter; and it was matching – or, even, slowly-overtaking – the forward-motion of the helicopter, on a north-west course toward central Los Angeles.

"Bring us up, 'much as you can," ordered the Aryan leader, to the pilot.

"Tryin'," replied the pilot. "She's fightin' me... bet I can get us up to twenty-five hundred feet – maybe three thousand – and hold there... not much more. Go above that, rotors will lose too much lift – they'll stall and then we go down *fast!*"

"It'll have to do," grunted the Lictor General.

Lomass unleashed two or three shots from his auto-rifle, striking the insect-cloud dead-on, although he seemed to miss its central-parts. But the gunshots did no apparent damage.

"Hey, Clay!" admonished the Lictor General, "Lay *off* it!"

"What the *fuck*... boss, you *know* what that fuckin' thing will *do* to us, if it catches up?" argued the whiteman.

"*Sure* I do," the Aryan leader replied, with smug satisfaction on his face.

"Well then?" pressed Lomass.

"I *plan* to have it catch up," said the white leader with a Cheshire Cat smile, "Right over them kikes in Hollywood!"

He leaned forward to tap the pilot in the shoulder.

"Make sure we don't outrun the fucker... until I tell you to stop and hover," demanded the Lictor General. "And one other thing."

"Yeah?" asked the pilot.

"Get that Wagner music, cued up on the speakers!" ordered the Aryan leader.

White Men Can't Jump

"How close *are* we now?" demanded Devon White over the poorly-suppressed, constant background whine of the aircraft's four big turbines, as he stared out one of the rearmost, porthole-like windows – of which there were few indeed, in the cavernous cargo-hold of the lumbering, heavy-load V-40 high-speed Air Force transport-plane. "Been flyin' for *hours!*"

He took another look.

"Sun's comin' up," he noted. "Light enough so I can see what's goin' on down there."

One of the three Air Force staff who were accompanying the former astronaut, entered some commands into a portable tablet PC, and responded, "Another... uhh... fifteen to twenty minutes, sir. That's to the nearest provisional military airbase, of course, which is about twenty-five miles back of the front. Then there's the escorted convoy to where you'll be briefed. After that, it's in the hands of local ground commanders."

The brush-cut Caucasian soldier paused for a second and then said,

"Uhh, Major White, sir... we're at twenty-five thousand... even without cloud-cover and in broad daylight, *nobody* could see..."

White smiled and interrupted, pointing at his eyes with both fingers, "*Mars* eyes, don't y'all know. See all *sorts* of shit, 'cludin' lots that I really don't need to, or want to. And for the record – that's quite a change of attitude, my man!"

"Sorry, sir – I'm not following you," politely responded the Air Force guy.

"The 'sir' stuff, I mean," teased the former Mars mission communications-officer. "Weren't two days ago, only 'word' I got from the Air Force, was them tryin' to shove a missile or two, up my ass. How things *do* change..."

"President says 'you're on *our* side now', you know, sir," offered the Air Force guy. "I hope that's so."

"So do I," elliptically commented White.

"Devon, why don't y'all come back here and lay *down*," requested his wife, from her vantage-point on a group of four folded-together bench-seats on the port interior side of the aircraft. "We be there when we be there... ain't nothin' more that anybody here can do 'bout it."

"Yeah, fine, okay... whatever," grumbled the ex-astronaut, as he rejoined the more-than-a-woman on the bench. "It's just that, well... just hate sittin' 'round, don't you know?"

"Well, 'Amen' to *that!*" said Saquina White. "'Get it over with', kind of thing. Y'all want more blankets? It's *cold* in here."

A bemused look came to her face; then she sheepishly added, "Oh... *right*. Guess I *forgot*."

"Trade it all for bein' able to really taste a beer again... cold or not," quipped Devon White.

"'Angel Lady giveth... 'Angel Lady taketh away'," the wife observed. "I just wish she'd told us beforehand, so we could maybe have one last –"

A warning-buzzer-like sound started issuing from the Air Force guy's tablet PC. This commanded his immediate attention for a second or two, but he was distracted by Devon White, who darted over to sit beside the soldier.

"What's goin' down?" demanded the ex-astronaut.

"Checking, sir... hold on... priority message... holy *shit!*" exclaimed the Air Force guy. "Sir... we have *contact!*"

White peered over the man's shoulder and intensely stared at the information displayed on the tablet.

"I'm seein' a map of L.A., here," he announced. "That purple dot what I *think* it is?"

"Yes – sure *is*, sir!" confirmed the soldier. "It just surfaced, about three minutes ago... OPEVAL's saying that they waited to confirm that it wasn't a false positive, but their confidence is high. Clean track via neutron-emission – what you're seeing here is relayed from a high-altitude drone we have deployed over the Greater Los Angeles area. Remember the briefing from back in D.C.?"

The ex-astronaut's wife was now also looking at the computer-display.

"Yeah," muttered White, "They figured the fuckin' thing was hidden – encased in lead or whatever – so they couldn't bingo it before... had to wait 'till it got out in the open, and they got the trackin'-gear closer. Well, 'thank the Lord for small blessins'... 'cept now, we got to figure out what to *do* with it."

"Major White, sir," remarked the Air Force guy, "Look at *that* – it's *moving!*"

"What... oh, yeah... *now* I see it," confirmed White. "Looks like the fucker's goin' west – not too damn fast, though, hardly movin' on the map – y'all got a speed-track?"

"Checking, sir," said the soldier. "Yeah, *there* it is... hmm, *interesting...* about seventy to eighty miles per hour or so. Heading slightly south of west."

"That mean they got it on a truck or something?" asked Saquina White.

"Well, if they *do*, Ma'am," observed the Air Force guy, "They must have the best driver in California, or maybe anywhere – we've got overhead recon showing most of the streets, even some of the major roads and highways, littered with debris or with roadblocks on 'em. It would be like an obstacle-course even if you were driving, say, forty miles per hour... never mind, eighty."

"What *is* it, then?" demanded the more-than-a-woman.

"Honestly don't know," said the soldier. "We'll have to get closer – okay, looks like local forces are sending out drones to recce it out – holy *crap!*"

"What?" pressed Saquina White.

"Those marks there – that's gunfire, issuing from our drones," he explained. "Also seems to be taking big-time damage from local explosions... maybe a grenade-launcher or an IED – but *that* makes no sense... I mean, who'd have –"

"They *shootin'* at it?" the alarmed wife half-shouted. "They fuckin' *crazy?* Don't they *know* what it is? What if they hit it and it goes off –"

"No *shit!*" ruefully mentioned Devon White. "Ain't nothin' they ain't done to y'all and me, repeatedly... 'cept *this* time, they're gonna get more than just a few fighter-planes with their wings clipped. Fuckin' left hand not knowin' what the right one's doin' –"

"Oh, thank God... look at *that*... shooting's stopped," proclaimed the Air Force guy. "They must have gotten the word from H.Q... *uh-oh...*"

"That up there in the right... that's the speed-track... right?" inquired the former Mars mission communications-officer.

"Yeah – and as you can see, sir... it's slowing down," stated the soldier. "If it really is a ground-borne transport, maybe its drivers are wounded, or... *Jesus!*"

"What's *that* mean?" asked Saquina White. "That little dot – it's, like, changed to bright orange –"

"That's code for 'surging neutron output', Ma'am," ominously described the Air Force guy. "It could mean that the primary – or the primary injection system – has been triggered."

"How the hell would *that* happen?" angrily demanded Devon White.

"And why in the Lord's name, *now?*" added his wife. "Damn thing been just sittin' there for days, *weeks* – and now it fixin' to go off, soon as we get near to it? That's sure some damn *coincidence*, wouldn't y'all say?"

"Don't know, sir... ma'am," replied the Air Force guy. "I only did one year in SAC, and I didn't get the full training... but from what I remember, we were told that terrorist nukes are primitive – they aren't like ours – they might need a lengthy activation-sequence to get the weapon to actually fire properly, especially if it's an H-bomb as opposed to just an A-bomb. As to why it got triggered, ma'am – your guess is as good as mine. Maybe someone rigged a contact-fuse and it got hit by shrapnel? All I can tell you is... the instruments don't lie."

"They tell you how long, that 'lengthy' shit, might happen to be?" pressed the ex-astronaut.

"Honestly got no idea, sir," deflected the soldier. "Could be one minute, could be an hour... depending on how sophisticated the device's fusing is, although from what I remember of my training, an hour's about the maximum, and it's usually a lot less than that except for really crude weapons. What I *can* tell you is... once it gets to the stage we're now seeing – if it doesn't misfire, it *will* go off, eventually. You can be pretty sure of *that*."

Saquina White – the color in her face now eponymous – shot a horrified stare at her husband.

"Well... Lord forgive me for sayin' so... but that seals the deal!" she offered. "Devon – we *can't* go down there, no more! Y'all *know* why! It could go off any *second!* We owe it to our *kids* to turn back!"

The ex-astronaut got up and restlessly strode back and forth.

"Minnie said that the one she had to deal with... it took some *time*," he noted. "And it *ain't* just our kids – I figure there's a *million* or so of 'em, down there... an' they *all* our homies. How far away are we from this fuckin' thing?"

"Uhh... sir... we can't *possibly* land near –" the soldier tried to say.

"I ain't talkin' 'bout landin' the *plane!*" shot back Devon White. "How far – right *now!*"

The Air Force guy quickly entered some commands and replied, "We're now over Yucca Valley... let me see... yeah... about a hundred kilometers or so, give or take a few. Sir – if you don't mind me asking – what on *Earth* are you planning to do? Sure – we got parachutes on this rig, but we're already *dangerously* close, if the bomb goes off while we're in the air... overflying Ground Zero in a transport like this would be *suicide!* We've only got minimum EMP-shielding on the V-40, and even at our altitude, the blast would –"

"Ain't plannin' on no such *thing!*" countered White. "Don't *need* no parachutes! I'm gonna suit up with Karéin's Spandex fashion-statement underneath, and Minnie's rad-haz battle-suit over top of it. Just hope I don't die of overheatin' down there... and I *don't* mean from no bomb!"

A chill went through the air, as the ex-astronaut's demeanor became more dignified – intimidating, even – as his eyes revealed a dim, blue glow.

He somehow looked about an inch taller, as he pronounced, "Saquina... I'm goin' down there. If y'all ain't comin'... I'll understand."

His wife left her station beside the Air Force guy, who nervously observed much the same alien-powered transformation, forthcoming from the more-than-a-woman.

Her eyes bore an aquamarine glow, as she replied, "'For richer or poorer, in sickness and in health... 'till death do us part' – that's what I signed up for. Devon – y'all *know* that if your stubborn ass is set on doin' this... I'm with y'all. But the *kids*, man! What gonna happen if –"

With a "calm down" hand-gesture, Devon White quietly offered, "Already thought 'bout that. Got an arrangement with both Whitney and Angel Lady. Honey... if the worst happens, y'all and I, we'll walk hand in hand through them pearly gates... and our kids gonna be well cared-for. We don't have to worry. This is a time to trust in the Lord... and to do what He wants us to. Which *I* intend, to do."

Saquina White – her eyes full of tears, though they were still glowing – did not verbally respond; but she nodded affirmatively, and the look on her face was unmistakable.

The unbelieving Air Force attendant regarded the two.

"Sir," he managed, "What are you... uhh... proposing to *do*?"

"Easy," explained Devon White. "The missus 'n me, we gonna jump out the back of this rig and fly down there, under our own power – given how far we are away, I figure that gonna take about ten minutes or so at most, if we push our airspeed as much as we can – then we gonna grab it, drag it out to sea, make a fuckin' *iceberg* out of it... let it float away to 'wherever', 'long as that ain't 'L.A.'. *If*, of course... it don't vaporize us, first."

"Sir," protested the soldier, "We had reports that it's a ex-Pakistani weapon... yield might be as much as four or five hundred *kilotons!* Something *that* powerful could vaporize the biggest iceberg in the *world*, and several more besides! I see these 'alien-powers' of yours – damn impressive, sir, if you don't mind me saying – but even at that, this plan can't possibly *succeed* –"

"Y'all got a *better* one, slick?" riposted the ex-astronaut. "One that don't leave a million or more poor black and Latino folk down L.A. way, blown to Kingdom Come?"

"No, sir... I'd have to admit... I don't," retreated the Air Force guy.

"Okay, then," directed Devon White, his voice noble, majestic and commanding. "Get Minnie's gear for both my wife 'n me, 'cept for that trackin'-bug and the walkie-talkie, I don't need nobody back home tellin' us how to tie our shoes – Saquina, y'all pull up a fog so's we can change without them peeps gettin' a nice strip-tease show – then open up that ramp at the back end of the plane, when I tell y'all to. Shot-clock's tickin' down... and I'll be *fucked* if Saquina and me don't get our last toss in, before they call the game!"

The Air Force guy dashed for the equipment-locker.

As he did, he heard, from behind his back,

"Oh, and by the way... if y'all wonderin' why they sent the two of us, and not all them other 'post-humans' back East... well, 'white men can't jump', don't you know."

Pick Up The Pace, *Mis Pequeños*

Ese es lo que estamos persiguiendo, pequeños, Sebastiàn sent to the thousands of individually-indistinct – but collectively-sentient – little minds, that enveloped him in every direction, as the weirding-cloud of insects and more-than-a-human, raced across the morning skies of Los Angeles.

He tried to shut out the after-effects of what had happened, just a few miles behind.

He had just completed a portentous address to his *camaradas de armas* and he was feeling good, *gracias al Señor Yayo* (a big stash of half-coke, half-synth that the scouts had discovered – enough to keep him on top for *days*, in fact), when *something* from deep inside– he knew not what, or how – had alerted him to the rapidly-increasing proximity of the "prize".

Then, the shooting re-started, not that it had really ever completely ended; it seemed that *El Ejército Del Nuevo Diablo* was besieged on at least two flanks. After ordering the ever-faithful Ramòn to muster a defense of the western approaches, the more-than-human leader had commanded his sinister insect-cloud to deal with a group of strangely-attired, long-bearded, olive-skinned gangsters who had – perhaps out of bravery, or maybe they were just *loco* – charged right into the open area where *El Ejército* had been celebrating its *fiesta*.

In the pandemonium of the furious fire-fight that immediately ensued, Sebastiàn noticed three of the white-robed gangster-group charging forward, under cover of heavy fire from their comrades, the latter well-secreted under cover to the north. He decided to have his insect-*compañeros* make an example of the second of these crazy-men, who was running well ahead of the other two. Sebastiàn commanded his fearsome swarm to engulf this putative victim.

At almost precisely this point, the *prize* – in the form of a cylinder suspended below a twin-turbine helicopter, flying very low between the buildings of the Rancho Cucamonga industrial-park – appeared over the battlefield. Some inner, poorly-understood sense within Sebastiàn's psyche informed him that, with no doubt… this *was, el verdadero regalo*.

The robed-gangster's tortured death-screams serenaded Sebastiàn's ears like fine music; but, suddenly, the howls were overwhelmed by the thundering blast of an enormous explosion – similar to, but much more powerful than – that of a grenade.

As the damaged helicopter spun out of control, towards imminent collision with the side of one of the nearby buildings, Sebastiàn experienced an overwhelming wave of other-worldly anguish from his miniature army-of-thousands, perhaps a third or more of whose lives were instantly snuffed-out by the blast.

While the *jéfé* was desperately trying to regain control over his insect-cloud – he commanded what was left of it, to come to his self and thus be comforted and consoled – he saw that the helicopter had, against all odds, re-stabilized. Though obviously weighed down by its cargo and by the weight of several passengers (Sebastiàn noticed that they were all big, white, heavily-muscled and -armed), it was slowly gaining altitude. In another few seconds it would likely be too far away to catch up with.

Ahora es el momento de volar, pequeños amigos, he commanded; and – despite their continuing, numbing pain – his miniature army responded magnificently. In only a few seconds – with his senses now extending by proxy, in all directions – Sebastiàn cleared the top of the nearest building, thus gaining a line of sight to what appeared to be a grounded helicopter in a field just to the north. Two more powerful explosions came from behind him, and while these inflicted terrible damage on his *ejército* – thankfully, as far as he could determine, not on Ramòn – by now the *jéfé* could not turn back.

He had only time for the briefest of parting-messages.

¡Debes guiarlos ahora, mi hermano!

¡Para ti... tiro la antorcha!

He hoped that Ramòn had understood.

¡Comamos todos! he directed to his buzzing, humming entourage; but – as Sebastiàn began to descend on a bee-line for the helicopter – to his dismay, he beheld it again getting uneasily skyborne. The machine was picking up speed with every second, heading on an apparent north-west track.

¡Vuela más rápido... más rápido! he demanded; but – despite the best efforts of his insect-army – he seemed to be falling behind.

Somehow, an idea came to the *jéfé's* mind that the loss of a third of the "little soldiers" a few minutes ago, might now be coming back to haunt him.

¡No... no! he furiously inveighed.

¡Es mía! ¡Solo mio! ¡Debemos recuperar, lo que es nuestro!

Far above and to the west, he noticed something unusual occurring; it was like the white contrail of a very large transport-plane, or, perhaps, of an aircraft that was deliberately generating a large smoke-screen behind it. A couple of seconds after this, there were flashes of an unusual-looking, dim blue light within the newly-appearing "cloud", followed by explosions on the ground underneath the cloud, perhaps a couple of seconds yet later.

¿Que se pasa, por alla? he wondered.

Somethin' ain't right 'bout that cloud – hay que ir, y –

He was still pondering this when gunshots crackled out from the auto-rifle of a big, tough-looking white guy, who was hanging out of one of the helicopter's side-windows. These passed harmlessly through Sebastiàn's cloud, though it was arrayed for flying-speed and not defensive-robustness.

I would take a bullet or two, he grimly resolved, *for another fifty miles per hour... wait... ¿que demonios?*

The 'copter was now gaining altitude... but it was also, slowing down!

Quizás la fortuna nos favorece hoy, he mused.

And another thought – this time, from his army of a hundred thousand half-minds – came to him.

Master, they communicated,

In another ten minutes, we will be able to fly much faster, still.

Muy bien, entonces; responded *El Nuevo Diablo de Los Angeles,*

¡En unos minutos… tendremos un pequeño regalo para ellos, también!

The Voices

Their departure had been delayed significantly due to a variety of logistical complications, ranging from prolonged consultations between the two White family-members and Minnie Chu, about "how to deal with the Los Angeles situation", to an impromptu tour of the White House for a few of the "post-humans" (Billings had tried to invisibly steal some of the cutlery, until the Storied Watcher noticed and shamed him into returning it to it place; Tommy was more successful, managing to telekinetically swipe one of George Washington's embroidered handkerchiefs), to frustrating negotiations with GrayWar management about what to do with Mr. Rizzo.

The latter situation had been dealt with by a threat on the part of the President, to send three alien-powered deputies over to GrayWar headquarters, "to personally enlighten you, Mr. Duke, about who is back in charge, over here."

Fortunately, there had been no more encounters with hostile fighter-planes, missiles or other elements of the United States' remaining armed-forces, after the Storied Watcher – to Susan Feldner's slack-jawed amazement – finally lifted the *Mailànkh Express*, complete with its crew of post-humans and other hangers-on, off the White House lawn and thence into the Capitol Region early-morning sky.

This time, the alien-girl had not suppressed any of her war-songs, nor did she engage the air-ship's cloaking-tricks; in fact, she had flown a low, circular course, roaring an "*oo-oo-oo-oo*" melody of might and defiance, right over the throngs of half-terrified, half-thrilled downtown D.C. crowds. In so doing she gave the Washington television Press Corps a good look at both herself – adorned in her trademark, blue-fire-blazing war-garb – and at the *Express*.

Then – as she passed over Pennsylvania Avenue for the third go-around – Karéin-Mayréij rocketed skyward with the air-vessel in tow, disappearing into the clouds, leaving the savants of all the networks (and millions of those less-informed) to speculate on what had just transpired in front of their very eyes.

The consensus, of course – as so detected by the Storied Watcher's innate arts, as well as by the electronics on the air-ship – was that "a conspiracy of space-aliens, Commies and Mars mission astro-zombies, is now firmly in charge of the White House, having replaced the President with a zombie stunt-double."

What does one do, with a kingdom populated by peasants, thus credulous? had communicated a frustrated alien-girl to those inside the *Mailànkh Express.*

Billings had returned the inevitable commentary :

You can be on TV, honey, he sent, i*n your own reality-show : "Alien Princess Does The Ultimate White House Fashion Make-Over".*

You just need the right agent.

I volunteer.

Judging from the guffaws coming from every quarter of the air-ship's interior, evidently at least a few of the other passengers had intercepted the salesman's repartee, while Karéin-Mayréij powered the *Mailànkh Express* on its West Virginia-bound trajectory.

At first at a loss, after a second or two, she responded,

What is that phrase that you taught me?

Ah, yes...

"Hardee har har"... is that not how it goes, my love?

After leveling out at around fifteen thousand feet, the airship – along with its super-human propulsive-force – was now on a straight track to the place that the humans had named, "Cass Mountain".

We fly at about – how do you humans reckon it... ah, yes, so my war-children say – four hundred kil-o-meters per hour, sent Karéin-Mayréij, to her erstwhile mate and lover.

A nice, gentle speed... the better to give comfort to those of you who are inside.

She tried to make the communication-session a private one, though she knew that this was an inexact art.

I calculate, "fifteen minutes or so, until we should descend towards the hiding-place, of which Commander Sam informed us", she added.

Eventually – Billings had apparently fallen asleep, in the interim – she received the reply,

Take your word for it, sweetheart... but so what*?*

There was a long pause, and then the Storied Watcher sent,

I cannot take you all the way there, Bob.

I have other duties, to which I must attend.

Can you ask Wolf and Brent to come outside, then to use their arts so the Express *can remain airborne, and can land as we had planned?*

Billings' mind revealed sudden confusion, mixed with panic.

Now what the hell's this all about, Sari? he answered.

We had it all worked out at the White House... or had you forgotten?

You take the space-boys to this "mountain hideout", they catch a 'copter ride back to the President's nice little Camp David chalet... then we all leave

for that Godforsaken rock in the middle of Nowhere, South Atlantic, and hope Hugo and Whitney don't strangle us the moment we show up inside that big rock-tomb that you hollowed out, a few weeks ago... for being so late.

I rarely "forget" things, Bob, she argued,
And now is not one of those times.

The refugees in Bouvet will be oh-kay for a bit longer – I left them with much food and they have plentiful supplies of fresh water.

With careful distribution and rationing, they could survive for many weeks yet... perhaps, even for months.

And that is without any fishing-catches from the central reservoir, nor with vegetables grown in those "hy-dro-pon-ic" things that I brought to the redoubt, from the southern continent.

Look, honey, the salesman protested, *I can tell when you're cooking up some cockamamie new "save-the-world" plan –*

Do you remember how, when we were in bed together, back in your "Too-sawn" home, interrupted Karéin-Mayréij, *you asked me, "are you an 'angel'?"*

Yeah, Billings responded.

Do you remember how I replied, Bob? she elaborated.

You said that you "hear voices"... or some-such mumbo-jumbo, he sent.

You may call it "mumbo-jumbo", or "hokey-pokey", or... whatever, communicated the Storied Watcher,

But now do they speak again to me... and they command me to fly west.

Oh... shit! complained a panicking Billings,

You're going off to deal with that last bomb – the L.A. one – aren't you?
Please tell me I can talk you out of it!

Brave Devon and Saquina – though their powers do wax mightily – they cannot deal with this weapon, themselves, she explained.

If they approach this dreadful thing close-on enough to take hold of it and lead it away from the city, they will be overwhelmed if it detonates.

And there is another of our brothers – who you never met, and whose essence of the Holy Fire *is much different from that imparted to the rest of you – who – my arts do inform – he is also thus imperiled.*

Notwithstanding what I told this "President" back in his House of White... I cannot stand idly by while my three kin, set out on a death-quest!

But, Sari! he tried to plead,
Think of Elissha – Sayuri – Tommy – me!
What's to become of us, if you –

I know, dearest, she sent back,
Though I will be careful... whatever becomes, my love is always with you.

That is... all four of you, not just "you"... accursed Eng-lish pronouns!

Oh for God's sake, Sari, complained Billings,
Enough with the language-lessons... okay?

And you waited for weeks, while this damn thing was sitting in L.A., fixing to go off!

Why the hurry now?

Because I had two more to deal with over the "White House", Bob, *and two atom-smashing-bombs, outrank one*, she offered,

And because, it was not until now, that the voices have told me... "Karéin... this is the right time."

There was a long pause, and then eventually, *Billings ventured,*

Sari... just what do these bloody "voices" sound like, anyway?

How do you know what they tell you to do, is the right thing?

They are the spirits of Light and Grace, who have guided me ere I was born, so many long eons past, explained the Storied Watcher.

Only with my most close and dear, may I share their song–

Oo-oo-oo-oo-oo...

And in the next moment, the ex-salesman's mind was overwhelmed with an alien symphony of surpassing majesty and wisdom, akin to Beethoven's Fifth boosted by electric-rock guitars, but enhanced in some indescribable way that– though it swamped Billings' limited psyche– to his immense inward pride and satisfaction, still revealed perhaps a quarter-part of what the original totality of the melody, must have been.

The music (and the mental imagery that accompanied it) was simultaneously subtle and clashing, delicate and thunderous, familiar and alien; yet, carrying through all its hundreds of inter-mixed chords and notes, there was a commandment of purpose, quest and duty.

Billings was too busy maintaining his sanity, to attempt to comprehend the specifics of what his alien lover's "voices" were saying; none the less, he was still enough in control to wonder if the words "H-bomb" really *were* in the stream-of-consciousness, in which he had been immersed.

She allowed him a few seconds to recover, and then communicated,

I will *survive, Bob... if only to teach you, Tommy, Elissha and Sayuri, how to understand the Immortal Great Ones... to heed their inerrant counsel.*

By so doing, do mortal people – only a very few, in each age – become akin to the Gods, Themselves.

Do you trust me, my love?

Do you believe me?

Do you believe... in me?

The sweating, half-dazed– but proud and smitten– salesman spoke vacantly out loud,

"Of *course* I do, Sari."

Then he said, "I take that back... I believe in you, *Karéin-Mayréij...* who lifted this Average Joe up, since Day One. You go and do what you've gotta do."

Instantly, he was the focal-point of at least four-pair of staring eyes.

"She's heading west... isn't she?" remarked Jacobson.

Billings just nodded.

Boyd addressed the Russian.

"We'd better get outside, then," he said.

Thirty Seconds To Meet And Say Goodbye

Neither Saquina nor Devon White– the former partly in the latter's tow, due to the husband's better-practiced flying-skills– allowed themselves to dwell upon what they were now doing; namely, "streaking across the dawn Greater Los Angeles skies, entirely under their own propulsion, with tens of thousands of feet between them and the hard surface of southern California".

This – and the fact that they were heading toward a nuclear weapon, by all accounts a few minutes– or possibly only a few seconds– away from detonation, was an issue to be "overlooked", if possible.

Y'all better with navigation than I am, sent the wife.

We still on track?

Well… considerin' that I had to get the Eagle *and* Infinity *all the way from here to Mars and back, I'd have to have learned how to read a damn map,* responded the husband.

Yeah – far as I can tell. Last look we got at the display had the fuckin' thing in Rancho Cucamonga – y'all remember we did some golf over there with them folks from NASA, just after I got accepted into the space program– and I think I recognize it down there.

Looks pretty dead though… hardly any cars goin' nowhere, and the Interstates ain't got nothin' *on 'em.*

Shouldn't be a surprise, I guess, if the only "law and order" in your hood, happens to be the Bloods, the Crips and the Maras…

We close 'nough to use the – oh, damn! called the wife.

Look out, Devon – we got trouble, *comin' up from below –*

He cast his enhanced senses downward, and determined that Saquina's warning was, indeed, well-founded.

From an area halfway between San Bernardino and Rancho Cucamonga, he saw three small points of heat-energy flying upward, straight at the two.

Them's missiles! he sent.

Fuck th' Army – don't them mothers ever listen to orders?

Get ready – gonna maneuver away from 'em – but gotta keep flyin' west – can't afford to lose time, and can't waste too much Fire *on 'em, neither!*

Ain't hardly no clouds over L.A. this morning, remarked the wife, *but I can make some if y'all want… just pull the moisture in the air together, easy as shit. That throw 'em off?*

Might fuck up their heat-seekers, answered Devon White as he started a zoom-climb, picking up altitude rapidly as his war-song began to sound.

But they might have active radar, too.

I got some English on makin' chaff out of ice-crystals – fuck up their radar – but just to be sure, I'll have to freeze 'em – but they're comin' fast enough, gonna only get one shot.

Y'all better hope I don't miss –

Y'all won't, reassured Saquina.

In the next five to six seconds, the wife's guarantee, thankfully, proved to be correct. Inhabitants of eastern Los Angeles (those few who dared venture outside, in the presence of uncontrolled gang-activity) looked skyward with amazement, as a thick, contrail-like, white-colored billowing-cloud issued behind an invisibly-small *something*, cutting a swathe across the otherwise nearly-pristine southern California early-morning sky.

Then – dimly-visible in the center of the *nuage* – there appeared deep-blue flashes of some sort, causing part of the cloud to fall as snow. A second later, three tiny-looking metal devices fell Earthward, tumbling end-over-end from the interior of the cloud. As they hit the ground, they detonated with powerful-sounding explosions, causing many of the onlookers to immediately head back to their hiding-places.

Now very high – almost in the stratosphere – Devon White sent glumly to his wife,

There goes our "element of surprise", don't y'all know.

Whoever got the fuckin' thing, if they got a brain in their head... they gotta know some weird shit goin' down, up here.

I'd fly down to them missile-launchers and make Popsicles out of them fuckers that fired on us... but every second we waste, might be one we ain't got.

Let's go!

Let's go! echoed Saquina White.

Downward they hurtled, their flight-path bending slightly south-west. The buildings and criss-crossing freeways of Greater Los Angeles came rapidly into clear view, as did the metropolis' central business district slightly south of west, and as did the Santa Monica and Malibu coastal-beaches, further to the west.

The two stopped and hovered at medium-altitude – probably around five or six thousand feet based on previous experience of landmark-sizes per distance – and intensely scanned the subdivisions of eastern Los Angeles.

Y'all check where we last saw it, back on the plane, sent the wife.

Yeah, hold on, he replied, *I got Minnie's "magic wand" here... hopin' that –*

The former Mars Mission communications-specialist pulled out a small, plastic-and-metal box about the size of an old-style smartphone (it had a tiny LCD screen divided into sectors, as would the "bulls-eye" of a primitive radar-scope), extended its telescoping antenna and pointed the latter downward and to the west.

Using key-sequences taught to him by FBI and Secret Service agents back in D.C., Devon White activated the device.

Immediately, a bright point of light appeared on the tracking-display. The former Mars astronaut moved the box, changing the direction of its antenna slightly, until the indicator-light was right in the middle of the scope-display.

Okay... sayin' "distance 11.465 kilometers", communicated Devon White. Neutron-flux goin' up slowly and steadily. Now ain't that just fuckin' wonderful.

Least we got a fix on the damn thing –

That don't make no sense! protested the wife. *It* can't *be that far!*

Y'all forgettin', it's countin' in our altitude-differential, too, the husband pointed out.

Fucker can't *be more than about 6 clicks away now... horizontally, I mean.*

Devon, nervously sent the wife,

What happens if it blows, while we this close?

It means, darlin', he replied, *we both pour every last ounce of* Fire *into them force-fields that Angel Lady claimed we have... and then y'all'n me promise to hold up in front of Saint Pete, 'till the other one gets there... y'understand?*

Yes, Saquina sent back.

I love you, man.

In this life, and the next one.

Okay, communicated Devon White, *now let's see if we can see... let's descend on the track, get within visual-range... and y'all know, if we can see it, and it goes off, well...*

I know, she confirmed.

Again, the duo resumed a downward course, flying as rapidly as they dared do, while still keeping the tracking-device pointed at the sinister quarry of their quest. With each passing second, the relative sizes of the ground-landmarks increased, and as they arrived at an altitude of perhaps three to four thousand feet, the former Mars mission crewmember called an abrupt halt, coming again to a hover.

Saquina, he sent, *y'all see that?*

I got the box pointed right at that thing there – movin' fast and it ain't followin' the streets, it's gotta be a 'copter, rotors on top – don't see the bomb, maybe it's aboard or underneath – but it's definitely trackin' on the 'copter...

Yeah, she responded,

And... y'all remember how Sylvia tried to teach us 'bout that "little-shiny-particle" thing?

I can feel *it, Devon! I* feel *it!*

Jus' like she said, and she showed us... like 'moonbeams' bouncin' off y'all... Sweet Baby Jaysus...

The real deal now, missus, he reflected, while drifting north-west to keep station with their newfound quarry.

Y'all feel them "moonbeams" rampin' up too fast... it's time to do the jet, fast as we can go.

Yeah, she agreed.

Okay – should have it down by heart, but just to be sure, one more time, to account for changed tactical-situation...

Y'all cloud everythin' up as much as y'all can – confuse whoever's flyin' that 'copter, and we'd better hope he don't have no "instant-bang" trigger on it – I find the damn thing, freeze it solid... hopefully that'll fuck up its firin'-mechanism, or at least slow it down some – 'member, Karéin mentioned that was her idea, with the second bomb, back East?

Sure do, replied Saquina, *'cept I don't got to tell y'all – y'all chillin'... but she chillin' more...*

No shit, he admitted.

Her husband allowed himself a brief glance at the terrain-features.

Hmm, he communicated,

If I'm judgin' it right, we just passed 605... we're between State Route 60 and I-10... maybe over El Monte?

'Far as I can tell we're trackin' to the Business District, and we sure don't want it goin' off over there...

So... like I was sayin', he continued,

I encase our friend the bomb in the toughest ice I got, keep it cold, we lock on and make sure that we can still lift it – carry the fucker ten miles out to sea...

Then I make 'bergs floatin' all over the place, y'all pull as much water as you can do, upward... then we try to link it all together with big sheets of ice formin' the biggest wall y'all ever seen, facin' on an angle to the west.

Don't have to be too thick – we're just tryin' to deflect the heat-rays and the blast-wave a bit... no point it tryin' to stop it... we know that.

We're gonna have to work faster than we ever done, to make this work at all. With any luck, it'll absorb a lot of the initial energy... don't know if it's gonna make much difference from it just goin' off the regular way... but what we got to lose?

Just our lives, *dumb-ass!* mordantly joked the wife.

That's why I love y'all, Saquina, he sent back,

Always on the bright side.

Know what?

No... what? she answered.

Y'all, all wet.

Sure am, she wryly acknowledged.

Y'all want to find out how much... get us out of this alive, *slick!*

Damn straight! he responded.

Okay... no time like the present, I guess... let's do *it – uhh, Saquina hon – what the fuck y'all make of* that?

He pointed to a spot below and to the south-east of the still-climbing helicopter. Both the former Mars astronaut and his wife stared in disbelief, as their enhanced visual-senses focused in on the bizarre entity that Devon White had just warned of.

They beheld an amorphous, continuously-self-reconstituting, translucent, unidentified globular flying object, from which was emanating a sinister-sounding, buzzing, humming melody (or, at least, a complicated succession of sounds), loud enough to be heard even at this distance – although somehow, both the ex-astronaut and his wife could tell that the volume-level of the music, or sound, was actually relatively low.

More fantastic yet was the fact – as both of the more-than-humans could easily perceive – there was a humanoid figure with dimly-glowing, green-tinted eyes, directly in the middle of the cloud. Both the cloud and especially the figure, fairly *reeked* of threat, hazard and... *power.*

The weirding object seemed to be chasing the helicopter, matching its velocity and flight-path almost exactly.

Lord in Heaven, sent Saquina,

Y'all see that?

It's bugs, *Devon... bugs!*

Like, beetles, 'n flies, 'n bees, 'n wasps, 'n moths, 'n I don't know what!

Thousands of 'em, all travellin' together, as if they's all one big happy family... or some-such shit!

This was never in the plan, *man!*

Damn straight – and I got no idea what the hell that is or what it's fixin' to do, communicated the ex-astronaut,

But we gotta assume it might be hostile.

Y'all be ready to soak it big-time if it makes a move against us – bugs don't like water, I reckon.

Keep the fuckin' thing tied up while I get 'hold of the bomb, freeze it up and drag it out to the coast... okay?

Nothin' here's "okay", husband, she replied,

Like, "I'm flyin' like a bird over my old 'hood, without no wings, without the faintest idea how I'm really doin' it in the first place... and chasin' an atom bomb that might go off any minute now.

But I ain't got no better idea, so... "okay".

Welcome to the world of Angel Lady! sent Devon White.

Here I go...

The former Mars communications officer moved away from his wife and fully powered up his ice-screen. This whirled around him, forming a translucent, scintillating bluish-white "bubble" that would have been impossible for anyone with a line of sight to miss in the first place; and to make him unintentionally yet more conspicuous, this was accompanied by

White's burgeoning war-song, whose stirring-yet-languid chords serenaded everyone and everything for (or so it seemed), leagues in every direction.

In an odd simile of the unknown object that he and his wife had just encountered, all that was visible of the ex-astronaut himself, within the ice-bubble, was a dim outline of his body, accentuated by blue-white-glowing eyes.

Accelerating in impressive fashion – while trying, and mostly failing, to tamp down his war-song – Devon White darted downward, passing the insect-cloud at an oblique angle.

He cruised below the helicopter, scanning upward for a couple of seconds, with all his "Mars-senses" fully-enabled. The sinister energy-emanations issuing from the oblong, nondescript cylinder below the 'copter ended any doubt that this was the object of his quest. It seemed to be slung underneath the helicopter by a tight-fitting collection of metal straps and cordage of other types.

To his alarm, White saw a recessed, LED computer-display – much too small to be seen by human eyes, except up very close – on one of the object's sides. The display seemed to be counting down.

The numbers read, "11:02:56", and were rapidly decrementing.

Shit, reasoned the ex-astronaut,

If that means what I think *it does…*

Saquina – y'all hearin' me?

We got eleven minutes… no more!

Loud 'n clear, husband, came the reply.

Devon… we gots to act now!

I know, he sent back,

Give me thirty seconds… then we take matters into our own hands.

I can handle what's here, but y'all keep that "insect-thing" off my back.

Devon White now flew level with the helicopter on its opposite side, noticing as he executed this maneuver that the insect-cloud – which did not seem to have changed its course or its relative distance – was still flying forward in lock-step with the 'copter.

He noticed that the weird formation of the helicopter, the insect-cloud and the two more-than-humans now seemed to be over Montecito Heights; just to the south-west, were the glistening skyscrapers of downtown Los Angeles, while ahead – on the course that they were now following – were Hollywood and Beverly Hills.

Immediately, the ex-astronaut was greeted by a fusillade of automatic-weapons fire, which – as he was completely confident would be the case – simply bounced harmlessly off his own ice-shield.

Inside the helicopter were at least three big, tough-looking, tattooed and heavily-armed white guys, one of whom was wearing a World War Two German helmet. One of these tough folk – in the back-cabin of the aircraft –

seemed to have lost an arm in some past engagement, although his firing-aim with the auto-rifle held in his other hand was dead-on.

Using his arts, White allowed his *Amaiish*-boosted voice to project through his protective-shield, without weakening it sufficiently to risk a bullet-penetration.

"Y'all got somethin' that belongs to *me*... below this 'copter!" bellowed the ex-astronaut.

"I'm *takin'* it – y'all better bail right now!" he added. "Turn your 'copter 'round and land it as far inland as y'all can get in five minutes... then hide somewhere!"

The face of an older, fuller-bearded white man showed up on this side of the helicopter. The pilot had to compensate for the now-unbalanced passenger-load.

"I don't know *who* or *what* the fuck you are," defiantly shouted this guy, "But it's *ours* – a fuckin' nice big nuke, if you hadn't figured that out already – and it's got an impact-fuse on it! Make one move, and we let her go right here and now... and your ass goes up right along with ours! Better fly away home, Tinkerbell – while you still can!"

"*Tinkerbell*", ruefully considered Devon White,

Well now... don't that just take the cake.

'Spose I must look a bit like her, from the outside lookin' in...

"Listen, motherfucker," inveighed the ex-astronaut, "When I let loose on y'all – it ain't gonna be no pixie-dust! I'm with the Mars Gang, not to mention with Karéin-Mayréij – the Storied Watcher – herself, and y'all got no chance *at all* 'gainst me 'n my wife! Y'all got five *seconds*! Four... three... two..."

The count-down was interrupted by a barrage of gun-shots accompanied by every filthy curse-word that White had ever heard before (and then some that he somehow hadn't). The bearded guy withdrew to the other side of the helicopter, and was replaced by a mean-looking thug wearing a German *Wehrmacht* helmet. This man unleashed a steady stream of expletives accompanied by accurate auto-rifle fire. This – fortunately – was no more effective than had been earlier fusillades.

He tried to narrow-cast to his better half,

Saquina... now I got to do somethin' I hate doin'... I can't reason with these peeps – and we're out of time.

Y'all put in a good word with the Lord for me, when I got to 'splain this?

Always, hon, came back the answer.

Okay, then... y'all 'Aryan' motherfucker... here's back for a lifetime *of keepin' my mouth shut, in front of your kind!*

Sno-Kone!

The ex-astronaut's invocation was accompanied by the surging chords of his war-song – and by a dim, blue-colored, arrow-fast jet of terrible, life-consuming cold-combined-with-kinetic-energy. White's attack inerrantly tracked the open door of the helicopter, striking the helmeted-guy dead-on.

With grim resolve, the former Mars communications officer saw an expression of surprise on his victim's frozen-solid face, a split-second before this – and the rest of his body – shattered into a million, red-tinted ice-shards. The ice-jet also sideswiped everyone else in the back of the 'copter, leading to screams of anguish...

...And to the frightening sight of an elongated, cylindrical object dropping rapidly into free-fall, from underneath the helicopter.

Pushing his *Fire*-fueled flight-skills to their limit, as he streaked downward White sent to his wife, not caring to narrow-cast,

Fucker dropped it, Saquina! *Get your ass down here! Forget 'bout everything else!*

On my way, husband, came the instant response.

I'll say it for both of us... "Our Lord In Heaven, Hallowed Be Thy..."

In a second and a half, Saquina White – also on a near-vertical downward-trajectory – was visible, just above and behind the ex-astronaut. Her own war-song reverberated across the skies.

I can lock on... but it's too heavy just for me! he warned.

I'm slowin' it... but it's still gonna hit!

I got it... I got it! she messaged.

They were now at a point about three hundred feet below the helicopter, which – though wobbling erratically – seemed to still be airborne. Its course had not changed significantly, as its crew undoubtedly realized that there was no avoiding what they expected to have exploding below them, any second. The crew was also still hostile, as evidenced by occasional rifle-rounds coming from the 'copter's direction. The shots were badly off-target and all missed.

Yeah... that's it... y'all and me together, Devon – that's enough! sent Saquina.

Thank y'all Karéin, for teachin' us how to do it... never imagined usin' it like this...

Sure is damn heavy, though... can y'all see that "number" thing on its side –

He stared at the display, which was indicating "9:36:29".

Under ten minutes, he advised.

Let's get it goin' westward!

I'll take the front, y'all take the back –

Sure 'nuff, she agreed.

I got a firm lock on it at the rear, I'll push...

Devon White fired one of his cold-bolts (albeit, at much less than full-power) at the weapon. Soon it was encased in super-cold ice, except for a small open spot that had been left to allow checks of the countdown-timer.

Unfortunately, these revealed that the timing of the detonation had not changed.

Well... that's good news... didn't blow the minute I iced it up, he observed.

Lord givin' us a mulligan, responded the wife.

We need to climb as high and as fast as we can, came the husband's suggestion, *so the fucker's on a ballistic trajectory when we let it go... might give us a few seconds more before it hits the water and goes off.*

Let's follow I-10, then head out over the ocean between Santa Monica and Marino Del Rey. We see them nice places in Malibu to the north, I figure we're far enough over the Pacific to give this plan a chance of workin'. Okay?

Roger that, answered the wife.

Oh... and by the way... "Thy Kingdom Come... Thy Will Be Done..."

Yeah... y'all sayin' what I'm thinkin', hon.

The duo – with Devon White about seven feet ahead of and above the weapon, with his wife the same distance above and behind – now guided their deadly, ice-bound cargo towards due west, thus turning away from downtown Los Angeles and cruising over the University of Southern California. To their relief, they realized that they were slowly picking up speed and altitude, although the coastline seemed discouragingly far away.

The helicopter, meanwhile, seemed to have turned away to the northeast, and was declining in altitude.

As they passed over what appeared to be a small recreation-area or public park, with the seacoast clearly visible just ahead, the ex-astronaut – whose perception-senses had been temporarily focused forward – suddenly received a panicked mental-broadcast from his wife.

Devon – right below me! she shrieked.

He cast his gaze backwards, and to his dismay, saw the *thing* – the insect-cloud, with all its buzzing malevolence – less than twenty feet below and behind his flying better half. It was rapidly approaching, and would likely overtake and engulf Saquina White within five seconds or less.

Empowering his voice with alien-energy, the former Mars astronaut bellowed in the direction of the insect-cloud,

"Get *away* from us – before I turn y'all into a fuckin' *Popsicle!* That thing we're carryin's a fuckin' *H-bomb,* peeps! We's *daid already!*"

Don't say things like that, communicated the wife.

Figure of speech, evaded the husband.

¡Esa cosa es mía! interrupted a thought, from the direction of the insect-cloud.

¡Dámela, ahora!

Well... Holy Angelic Strange Company, ruefully acknowledged a half-believing Devon White, *whoever – or whatever – that is in that "insect-plague" down there – it's, like, mind-talkin' to us.*

Saquina... y'all ever learn any Spanish?

The insect-cloud was still approaching, albeit more slowly.

I say in English, then, came a reply from the unknown party,

It is mine! Mine alone!

La Dama de los Cielos gave *it to me... she say it was my "death-quest"!*

Don' make me take it from ustedes, *or* mis pequeños *gonna eat you* alive!

They were now very near to the coastline. Just ahead and below them, both Saquina White and her husband could see the yacht-docks of Marina Del Rey. They could feel their airspeed and altitude increasingly steadily; however, their insectoid pursuer seemed to be matching this, step for step.

Look, hombre – whoever *the fuck y'all is*, Devon White tried to communicate,

Y'all with Karéin, that makes y'all on the same side as Saquina 'n me... but we got work to do here!

We got to get this fuckin' thing out to sea – it's gonna blow in, let me see – shit... five minutes!

It goes off over L.A., millions *of people – Latinos, African-Americans, white folk, all of 'em – they gonna die!*

Anyway... if we gave it to y'all... what y'all gonna do with it?

There was a long pause, during which the ex-astronaut checked carefully for signs that their unrequited guest was actually implementing an attack; but whomever-it-was, continued to keep station at the existing distance.

Finally, the answer came.

I take it out to sea, cholo.

I take it out there... myself.

A stunned Saquina White sent to the unknown party,

We can't aks y'all to do that, man!

Don't y'all understand what that means?

Sí ... lo entiendo muy bien, señora, sent the insect-cloud-guy.

Es usted *who don' understand!*

They were now almost at the coast, with the Venice Beach underneath them.

To the dismay of both the more-than-humans, the beach was already beginning to attract swimmers and surfers, hoping to catch the morning waves.

We can't protect them... realized the distraught wife.

Listen, hombre, interrogated Devon White,

Even assumin' we trusted y'all not to just turn 'round and drop the fucker on the city – and even assumin' y'all could keep it airborne, 'cause it's got an impact-fuse on it, it'll blow the minute it hits a solid object – doin' that's suicide!

Prolly suicide for Saquina 'n me, already, even if we release this damn thing right now and then turn tail to the east, as fast as we can!

What the fuck y'all out to accomplish, *by huggin' an H-bomb and gettin' vaporized?*

What's your game, *hombre?*

I got no time to 'splain, came back the broadcast, *'cept for this...*

If ustedes live through this one...

Tell La Dama de los Cielos que Sebastiàn did the quest that she gave him...

Because, like she tell me... "to die in a noble cause – that, is not 'failure'".

An' tell her, "Sebastiàn sabía desde el principio que ya estaba muerto", *from before she save him...*

And he's glad she give him a few weeks, to know what it's like to be "el Rey de la calle".

Tell her, it's all that su amigo from the other side of town, ever wanted to do... and he's leavin' with no regrets... none at all!

¿Lo entiendes?

Yeah... we do, quietly responded Saquina White.

Lord be with y'all, man.

They were now out over the water, though still worryingly close to the beachfront.

Saquina, asked the husband, his mental-broadcast somehow heavy and full of regret,

Y'all got any objections, if we get the toss-bomb goin' as best we can... then we let him take over?

No, she answered.

Listen, "Sebastiàn", inquired the ex-astronaut, *y'all able to lock on – telekinesis, that is – and hold 'er up, on your own?*

No, came back the answer, *but my little ones will.*

I send them ahora...

And immediately, the still-iced-up nuke was enveloped by perhaps half the insect-cloud, while the other half kept the newcomer airborne. Both Devon and Saquina White felt pangs of other-worldly anguish, as the insects closest to the weapon started to gradually succumb to its rapidly-waxing radiation-output.

Shit... three minutes! warned the former Mars communications-officer, after a quick look at the countdown-display.

We need to do the toss, now!

With the newcomer somehow staying in westward-flying formation, despite the three more-than-humans and their lethal cargo reaching speeds into the hundreds of miles per hour and thousands of feet in altitude, Devon White announced,

I'm givin' a ten-count – then we let go – nine... eight...

As they hurtled upward and to the west, Saquina White sent to the newcomer,

I'd have liked to get to y'all a bit better, Sebastiàn.

I'll be prayin' for y'all.

Six... five... counted the ex-astronaut.

Gracias, came the reply,

But they call me, "El Nuevo Diablo"... an' if that's where I'm goin'... I'm good with it.

Two... one... **release!** cried the mind of Devon White.

As he and his super-human wife turned away and poured as much power as they dared, into reversing course and flying eastward, and as the deadly unpowered-projectile began its final arc to the Pacific Ocean beyond, they perceived a final thought from the weirding newcomer.

Dile a Dios, y a la Dama del Cielo que Sebastian no teme a la muerte – ¡que él está en paz, después de todo!

*¡Fuego sagrado ... **tómame!***

A Forlorn Hat-Trick

Earlier on, the alien-girl had explained to her human paramour, how – in now-lost ages – she had cruised across the skies, "enshrouded in a mantle of white fire".

As she rocketed low over the western slopes of Keller Peak in the San Bernardino Mountains at over four thousand miles per hour, the Storied Watcher knew that this attribute was again hers to claim.

She had, in fact, flown even faster in the outer stratosphere – nearly eleven times the speed of sound – at the apogee of her cross-continent trip. But now, her protective force-field – deliberately deprived of the energy-recycling stealth-tricks that had previously masked her position from the U.S. Air Force's infra-red sensors – glowed incandescently with the murderous, friction-generated heat of the Earth's lower atmosphere.

Truly, I am become the meteor... or the death-missile, grimly mused Karéin-Mayréij, to her war-children.

Scarcely can we see in Um'nàhr'é, *to ahead-quarters, even with the view-clearing eye-spectacles of* Vìrya Ahn'jë; *but set ye together to use all thy arts in marking our quarry, and our brothers and sister... wherever they may be.*

All we glorious queen Watcher do pledge so Mother to! came back the immediate reply.

The Greater Los Angeles metropolitan area lay spread out ahead of her to the west; but the Storied Watcher realized that at speeds like *this*, she was covering a kilometer or more every second. Thus, as the alien-girl streaked over the skies of Chino and Pomona, she applied braking-thrust to slow her to a more sedate velocity.

Ah, reflected Karéin-Mayréij, *just comfortably faster than those "rifle-bullets" that Bob, Whitney, Tommy, Melissa, Curtis and I inquired after, in the Tucson hardware-goods store.*

Whitney... do you remember how you told me to take fright, at the bullets of a gun?

Behold how I outpace these... but who may know, if this speed be enough?

The alien-girl cast her senses westward, and empowered the "little-particle-shine" one as much as she dared; but to her frustration she saw little but interference coming from almost all directions on the ground

This accursed thing should stand out like the proverbial purple coin in a beggar's sack... but I see nothing in such stark clarity, she considered.

Min-nie said that her spy-agency had devices made specifically to track it down... ah, if only I had borrowed one of those!

Surely could I find it, given enough time to home in... but time is something that we have not, children...

Well, mused Karéin-Mayréij, *we still appear to have a city below us.*

In that *at least, may we take temporary solace...*

She came to almost a dead stop, hovering in mid-air, over East Los Angeles.

Where was that place, from which so many of the children who hailed me in my hour of trial? Ah, yes – "Comp-ton"... that is it.

Perhaps I should start there, circling outward – hold – what is that?

The Storied Watcher cast her gaze to the west. Far out in the Pacific Ocean – about ten kilometers or so from the coast (as far as she could tell from this distance) – she saw something bizarre. It looked like a line of four huge white squares, each at least the height of a large office-tower but much broader horizontally, facing outward to sea.

An fifth instance of these unknown things seemed to be under construction, as it was rapidly coming into form from the bottom upwards.

Let us hasten thither, instructed the alien-girl, to her war-children; and so she did, rapidly accelerating at a bone-crushing pace.

Within a few seconds, she was again racing across the Greater Los Angeles sky – this time at more than five thousand miles per hour, shrugging off the blazing friction-heat at the front-end of her force-field as she went, with a loud sonic "boom" (along with her burgeoning war-song) rattling windows and thus announcing her presence to the denizens of the city.

Oo-oo-oo-oo, wailed her war-song, its volume and complexity waxing with each second. As she closed the distance to the coast and again tried to slow to a speed that would allow even crude maneuvers, Karéin-Mayréij now had a clearer look at the strange, off-shore artifices.

The last of these was almost complete, and just behind and below its top-parts were two self-levitating, force-field-enshrouded figures who could only have been members of the "New People". Their arts had apparently caused a reverse-waterfall to arise several hundred feet from the surface of the Pacific, and as this struck the ice-barrier, it, too, was frozen into place as part of the structure.

The Holy *Fire* was strong, here; it was all around, and it flowed from the two silhouettes.

Devon! Saquina! the alien-girl tried to hail them with; but either the distance was still too far, or they were deliberately ignoring her.

She was now almost at the ice-barrier, and lowered her altitude to be almost level with its top-parts.

Let us cast our powers to reinforce that structure and equally our brother and sister, she commanded; and instantly, a wide-angle field of telekinetic force – as well as other, weirding energies, in particular a kind of near-Absolute-Zero cold – did just that.

A half-second later, the little inner voice of *Vîrya I'ëà'b* sounded a warning.

Out kind one a is yonder far out third, Mother Queen!

A third of our kind? responded a shocked and horrified Karéin-Mayréij.

That can only be – we must quickly go to rescue –

The alien-girl was struggling against the crushing G-forces to change course, when a now-familiar, hateful light flared almost at sea-level, perhaps ten kilometers further out to sea than the ice-barrier. Instantly, its surface began to sublimate, as the detonation's hellish thermal-flux began to melt holes all over the structure; this caused a huge fog-cloud to rise above the barrier, scattering the last of the heat-rays in all directions.

Our bubble holds – noble brother, I pray – oh ye Gods! moaned the afflicted Storied Watcher, as a psychic shock of monumental proportions knocked her mind into the black void of unconsciousness.

She was still spiraling downward in the panicked care of those few of her war-children who were still functional, when the shock-wave hit and knocked the lot of them backward on a ballistic trajectory, heading for the ravaged coasts of Los Angeles.

Last one's almost done now – time to do the jet – advised Saquina White to her husband, while the more-than-human couple put the finishing touches to the top-parts of the fifth ice-barrier.

If the Lord take us now, she added, *I'll say, "we done what we could, in a couple of minutes"... these things's amazin'!*

An objective observer – of which there were hundreds on the Los Angeles beaches, plus many more in the downtown office-towers – would undoubtedly have agreed with the astronaut's-wife.

Below her and to her right, they had crafted five huge icebergs, towering over the surface of the Pacific Ocean (although in fact, most of their mass was below the waves); each of these presented an enormous, mostly-flat ice-surface – akin to a giant's skating-rink, stood on one of its short ends – affixed to the 'berg's western side. Each of these reflecting-things was bound to the next in line with more alien-crafted ice, and the 'bergs themselves were similarly-connected.

Though in fact the tall-standing structures were nearly twenty feet thick from front to back, they were so large that ordinary ice would never have remained intact under the gravity-stresses weighing upon them; but Devon White's arts had been able to pack the water-molecules and ice-crystals tightly enough, to make the barriers into something just short of stainless-steel's consistency and durability.

Just a sec, he sent back, if I'm countin' right, we *got six or seven seconds yet –*

They heard the ululating, haunting, *Amaiish*-infused war-song, coming from the east. Its ethereal chords transmitted enervating, adrenaline-enhanced confidence, building exponentially, second by second.

What's that – damn, it's her! he exclaimed.

Contrary to their previous plans and promises, both adult members of the White family reflexively turned their attention to the eastern horizon. Though it was approaching much faster than a rifle-bullet, the Storied Watcher's meteor-like, white-hot-glowing force-field was impossible to miss or mistake.

I can feel *her power, over y'all and me, and them 'bergs we made*, remarked the ex-astronaut.

Hey Angel Lady – we're down here!

She say she wasn't comin' – Saquina White tried to start; but her commentary was suddenly cut short by a terrible light, followed almost instantaneously by blowtorch-like heat seemingly coming from everywhere to the west of them.

The infernal rays struck the ice-barrier and immediately began to melt through it, although somehow they could tell that much of the energy was being reflected backwards and out to sea, as they had hoped it would do. Because Devon and Saquina White were below the crest of the fifth reflecting-surface – and thus did not have a direct line of sight to Ground Zero – they were, mercifully, protected from the worst of the bomb's thermal- and radiation-flux.

Oh oh **oh!** she moaned,

I can feel *Sebastiàn dyin', Devon!*

Lord… I pray Thee to receive his soul!

Hold me! she wailed; and in less than a second, her husband was there, close by her side.

All power to the shields, prayers for our fallen brother, he had the time to communicate,

And all glory to our Lord and Savior, Jesus Christ… **amen!**

A few seconds after its detonation, the nuke's blast-wave hit the ice-barrier and immediately shattered four out of five of the reflective-surfaces, with the third in line – though badly-damaged – miraculously withstanding the stress. The bomb's monstrous pressure-hurricane also sent entire icebergs spinning towards the coastline, while also sending the two Whites eastward, like golf-balls shot out of a cannon.

'Member what she told us, the ex-astronaut sent,

Don't fight it... ain't no problem with ridin' the front 'till it peters out –

As if we could fight it! Saquina White managed.

As they tumbled, bruised and half-conscious, end over end, she caught a glimpse of *another Amaiish*-bubble, careening aimlessly through the plagued Los Angeles skies.

Karéin – we can see y'all – why ain't y'all flyin' – the more-than-human wife tried to send, in the Storied Watcher's direction.

There was no response.

She's hurt! called Saquina White.

Devon – I want to go over to her, but I can't hardly fly no more... my bubble took a beatin' and I had to use all my Fire *just to stay alive!*

Me too... but we're still a few hundred feet up, observed the ever-practical Devon White,

And she's bein' pushed back east, by the same shock-front that we are.

Let's surf it over to her!

As they were propelled over a large cemetery, trying to ignore the signs of devastation arrayed below them (neither one could overlook how aircraft at LAX were being tossed about like the toys of a careless child), the White couple did their best to implement the ex-astronaut's suggestion.

It was challenging, to say the least, since by now the blast-wave's energy was beginning to dissipate. Gravity re-asserted its pull on both the Whites and their super-human quarry, who – worryingly – did not respond at all to numerous psychic entreaties. However, after frantic efforts, they were able to close the distance enough so that a telekinetic "lock-on", was possible.

They were now crashing Earthward, with a few seconds before they would hit. They could see the shock-wave – though its potency was clearly diminishing rapidly as it spread out inland – still doing massive damage on the ground, with plate-glass windows being shattered all over, sending broken glass flying into unsuspecting human victims.

Use your mind-pullin' thing! he requested,

We're comin' down in that parkin'-lot by the shoppin'-center... try to cushion the blow for all of us!

I'm tryin'... but my Fire's *almost all used up, husband!*

I know – we'll get through this thing – it ain't our time, Saquina... and it ain't hers, neither!

I love y'all! was the last thing he heard, before they hit a decrepit, dust-covered, parked car, bounced ten feet back up into the air, and eventually came down, smashing – groggy-headed though still intact – through the front-cab window of a van.

A second later, the still-red-hot protective bubble of Karéin-Mayréij crashed into a nearby sedan, melting its structure into twisted-metal. Then she impacted with the ground, leaving a long furrow, almost like the one that she had made in the Wyoming mountains, scant weeks ago.

Not An Order-Follower

Looking every part the poised, well-dressed professional, Minnie Chu none the less seemed out of sorts, as she paced back and forth in the deep-underground recesses of the White House.

She looked up at the wall-clocks that bedecked the far wall in the Situation Room, on the other side of the long, rectangular meeting-table in the middle of the place.

The *nouvelle* FBI-director had a decent-sized audience, composed of Jerry Kaysten, Sylvia Abruzzio, Hector Ramirez (Cherie Tanaka was preoccupied with tracking down her mother's abductors, and was working elsewhere in the building), various military and Secret Service personnel (including the ever-durable, stolid Curt Kortish), and liaison staff with communications-links to the U.S. Army ground forces in the Greater Los Angeles area.

"We're now at 9:38 a.m. Eastern Time... that's 6:38 Pacific," observed Chu. "They should be there now... don't you think?"

"Yeah – more or less," answered the Chief of Staff. "Give or take a few minutes."

"Well... we can't afford any screw-ups here," cautioned the former team-leader. "Not since the local Rad-Haz drones got a positive track on the damn thing. Mr. Kortish," she requested, "Can you please raise the transport on the video-link? I need to speak with Devon and Saquina White."

"Yes ma'am," the Secret Service agent replied. He went over to one of the communications-consoles and consulted for a few seconds with a young Air Force guy who was managing this equipment.

A worried frown appeared on Kortish's forehead.

"Hmm... some problems with the network... oh wait... *there* it is," he stated. "Okay, Ms. Chu – we've got a visual with the transport. I'll put it on the big screen."

A second or two later, an interference-degraded picture of another twenty-something Air Force staffer (a Caucasian man with a brush-cut), appeared on the big flat-screen display in the middle of the far wall, between the clock-arrays.

"Transport Delta Tango X-Ray 43, responding to your challenge-code... Airman First Class Bill Sandberg here," said the face in the display.

There was a lot of background-noise coming from the audio part of the transmission.

"I'm Acting FBI Director Minnie Chu," announced the former team-leader, "Calling you from the White House, under direct orders from the President. Do you copy?"

"Copy that," obliged the remote Air Force guy. "What can I do for you, ma'am?"

"Can you please locate Major Devon White and his wife Saquina, and put them on so I can talk to them?" requested Chu.

There was a pained look on the staffer's face.

"Didn't you get the bulletin, ma'am?" he said.

"*What* 'bulletin'?" responded the *nouvelle* FBI-director.

"I sent it a minute or two ago, on DoD Channel Number 5241, priority One, ma'am," elaborated the remote Air Force guy. "That was the one assigned for this project... wasn't it? Just a second – confirming that – yes, 5241. Ma'am, you should already have the message, if you're monitoring that channel."

"Okay – let's skip the business about 'what channel should my TV be tuned in to'... shall we, soldier?" demanded Chu. "What was the 'message'?"

"Oh... well, ma'am," evenly repeated the man on the transport-plane, "Major White and his wife, uhh, jumped out the back, a few minutes ago –"

"He... *what?*" stammered a perplexed Chu.

"Doesn't surprise *me*," offered Abruzzio.

"I gave Devon very specific *orders!*" protested the former team-leader. "He and Saquina were supposed to –"

"Well, for what it's worth, Minnie," insouciantly interjected Ramirez, "I seem to recall that he had developed a habit of ignoring – or, at least, 'temporarily overlooking' – orders from home base... like, the ones that Sylvia and I both tried to give him and Major Boyd. Good thing they did, too, or Karéin might still be stuck in that tomb on Mars."

"That may be, but I still have to talk to him so we can coordinate plans," persisted Chu. Mr. Sandberg, can you please patch Devon or Saquina – doesn't matter which one – through on the communications-link, ASAP?"

There was another pained silence.

"I... I don't believe either Major White or his wife, took a communicator *with* them, ma'am," disclosed the Air Force guy.

"For God's *sake!*" exclaimed a visibly angry Minnie Chu. "What did they do – leave it behind by mistake or something? Maybe leave it in their lunch-box? What's the explanation for *this*, mister?"

"Major White said that all he needed was the radiation-tracking box, ma'am," said Sandberg. "His mind was kind of made up about it, and as I'm sure you can appreciate, Ms. Chu... we weren't in much of a position to argue with him. I've read the intel on what he – and you – can do, and –"

"He wouldn't have used violence to resist you," interrupted Chu. "Anyway – this is past history. Can you at least give me an update on where the bomb is?"

"Checking, ma'am," responded the Air Force guy. "Yeah… there it is… we got a triangulated track with back-up low-res video from three drones overhead, neutron-emission signal's steady and clean – whoa – that *can't* be right!"

Consternation showed on the faces of everyone in the Situation Room.

"What do you *mean?*" called out Abruzzio.

"It's showing as being about ten clicks offshore!" explained the remote Air Force guy. "How the *hell* – 'scuse my French, ma'am – did it get out there? And what the H are those humongous things in the water, between Malibu and Palos Verdes… they look almost like – *oh my God!*"

The interference in the video-screen ramped up to the point where it was almost impossible to recognize Sandberg's face, as the audio-channel was simultaneously overwhelmed by background-noise. What little was visible on the video-signal looked like the camera were being bounced around, as if in a car on a bumpy road.

"Airman Sandberg! What's going *on! Respond!*" shouted Chu.

Then the signal dropped altogether.

Kortish – still at the Situation Room's computer-consoles – spoke up.

"We have a *detonation*, ma'am," he said.

A second or two later, he beheld Jerry Kaysten, Minnie Chu, Sylvia Abruzzio, and Hector Ramirez, in various contortions of severe pain, as if each had suddenly sustained an invisible prize-fighter's haymaker to the stomach.

"Someone has… *died!*" they heard Abruzzio say, between gasps of agony.

The Future Alight

But Now I Can Assure You...

"Thank you all for attending this press conference on such short notice, after what was a trying day, yesterday," announced the President, as he walked up to the Blue Goose lectern.

Though the outside-facing windows revealed a sunny, early-morning scene of late-spring manicured-lawn elegance, his tone was somber.

Behind him were arrayed members of the uniformed military (the highest-ranking thereof, a few members of the press were perceptive enough to realized, were approximately at the colonel level) and a very washed-out-looking, dull-eyed Jerry Kaysten. All the other "more-than-humans" seemed to be elsewhere; the President's two offspring were lying around indisposed due to severe headaches and other body-pains, that had somehow afflicted both of them at exactly the same time.

Immediately, the President was besieged by a barrage of impassioned questions, shouted at him from all directions save from behind.

"Please... *please!*" he demanded, with hands in the air. "We need *order* here – there will be time for questions in a few minutes!"

After a few seconds of discontented murmurs, the crowd eventually sat down and – in a loose manner of speaking – complied with the Press Room rules.

"I have to advise the American people, of an unfolding tragedy on the West Coast, specifically in Los Angeles," grimly offered the President. "About ten minutes ago, I was advised that a nuclear weapon – believed to have been one of several stolen from the former government of Pakistan, after the collapse of that country's government some time ago – *ahem* – detonated several miles off the Southern California coast. This was not a small weapon – we estimate its yield at several hundred kilotons, in otherwords, from twenty to thirty times the power of the Hiroshima bomb, or roughly the same explosive power as one of the weapons that were set off yesterday, off the East Coast."

"Unfortunately," he continued, "Initial reports of damage to the Greater Los Angeles area are distressing, with numerous fires, especially in districts nearest to the sea – such as Santa Monica, Manhattan Beach and Torrance – having been started. Apparently many thousands of people both in these areas and further inland, have been severely wounded – or worse – by flying glass, which was propelled by the shock-wave of the explosion. Casualties in and around downtown Los Angeles have been heavy, due to fires and to glass-debris falling from the many office-towers in this area. But at least the weapon didn't go off in the middle of the city. For *that* – at least – we can be grateful."

The press-gallery was silent. Their faces wore the same expression as did the President's.

He went on, "We can take some solace from the fact that, due to the law enforcement issues that have been ongoing in the L.A. area up to now, fewer people were in the streets than would normally have been the case; it appears that many people in Los Angeles have been hiding in their homes for some time, which has helped to reduce casualties somewhat. However, the ongoing gang activity in this area is making it difficult for public safety personnel to reach affected areas. The U.S. Army had already been advancing through San Bernardino to restore law and order prior to the event, and we will be accelerating its timetable; but we need the cooperation of all citizens of Los Angeles to get the gangsters off the streets and allow our paramedics and firemen to help those in need."

Staring straight forward and gesturing forcefully as he spoke, the President added, "Let there be no doubt about this – we will *not* tolerate further criminality or disrespect for the law – not under circumstances like these! The Army and the National Guard in the area have been substantially reinforced and they have my authorization to exercise summary judgment against anyone – especially apparent gang-members – who in any way attempt to impede public safety personnel or emergency responders. Federal and state governments are working around the clock to deal with this very serious situation."

He paused for a second, and then said, "Now… I'll take questions."

There was bedlam in the press-gallery, as all the correspondents shrieked for attention, at the top of their lungs. Eventually, the President was able to calm the crowd and single out a female reporter in the second row.

"Millicent Grabner from Real Live CGI News," he called. "Go ahead."

"Mr. President," asked a past-middle-age, portly Caucasian lady, "Do we have any idea who was behind this attack? Were they the same terrorists that set off the bombs around New York and Philadelphia?"

"I honestly don't have anything to tell you about that, Millicent," responded the U.S. leader. "While it would be premature for me to speculate too much on this subject, I will say that from where we are now, it seems unlikely that the same criminals who were responsible for the outrages of the past twenty-four to thirty-six hours, were behind this one. Beyond this I can't say very much, because, as you can appreciate, we have an ongoing law enforcement investigation underway, which we don't want to jeopardize. Yes? Bob Drake from Disney News?"

An impeccably-dressed Caucasian guy with a blow-dried conservative haircut spoke up from the front row,

"Mr. President... in view of recent events, what should the American people make of your assurance – of only about a day ago – that 'the threat is over'?"

The U.S. leader did the best he could to avoid showing annoyance as he countered, "Bob, I believe if you review the tapes, you'll find that what I said was, 'the danger to the Capitol Region, is over'... or words to that effect. That statement was true then and it remains true now. At the time, because we were still trying to locate and take control of the third bomb – an effort that unfortunately seems to have come up just short – I didn't refer to it, and that's a decision that I'd make again under the same circumstances. What I *can* tell you now, however, is that on the best intelligence data currently available, there are no more bombs unaccounted-for – *none!*"

"But Mr. *President –*" pressed the Disney reporter, to no avail, as the President now pointed to an elderly, white-haired Caucasian in a dated suit, far back in the sixth row.

"Gary? You got a question?" said the President.

The guy stood up and replied, "Gary Fortenot from Traditional News Network... thank you, Mr. President. So my question is... what about fallout, sir? Does everybody in Los Angeles have to dig a shelter?"

The U.S. leader's visage was now even more somber, as he answered,

"The only honest thing I can say about that, Gary... is that we don't know yet. The bomb went off over water and that may mean less fallout depending on how the winds are blowing. After many of them were knocked down by the initial force of the blast, we were able to get a few replacement drones into the air in the area, with radiation-testing equipment; so far, we have no results... but that does not mean there isn't any danger. We're advising all citizens of the Greater Los Angeles area to remain indoors, seeking shelter in basements if they can, until we can give the all-clear over standard radio-channels."

He again turned to the front row, pointing to a youngish, blond Caucasian woman in an expensive-looking blue professional-dress.

"Samantha Day from ENN here... thank you, Mr. President, " she stated. "What I'd like to ask you is, sir... last night many of us were here with you and all these 'super-humans', including the alien herself. If you already knew about the Los Angeles bomb at that time – why didn't you send them out after it?"

Again, the President struggled to keep his composure as he answered, "Well, first of all, Ms. Day... I'd remind you that Karéin-Mayréij and her friends *did* – at very significant risk to their own lives – intercept and neutralize two different nuclear weapons, that very night. They told me," – he tried to feign a chuckle – "That they deserved a little time off, afterwards."

The U.S. leader's laugh was echoed by a few nervous giggles from the crowd.

He went on,

"Notwithstanding the above... I can disclose that indeed we *did* ask some of the Storied Watcher's associates – specifically, Major Devon White and his wife Saquina – to assist with military operations in the Los Angeles area. They should have arrived there by now but I also have to tell you, their current status and whereabouts are unknown. Obviously we hope and pray that they're alright. As for Karéin herself and the rest of her friends – for example Commander Jacobson and his team – we're attempting to get in touch with them... but they don't answer to me and I have to ask – I can't command them to do *anything*. That's really all I have to tell you on that subject."

"Yes? Don, over there in two? Go ahead," he called out.

"Thank you, Mr. President," said a portly, average-looking guy in his late '50s, with thinning hair, bushy black eyebrows and a creased, tired-looking business-suit, "Donald Heenee from KKKL-TV Superstation, New Orleans. Mr. President... what do you make of the reports coming in from some local reporters and voggers, about 'icebergs' just off of Marina Del Rey and Los Angeles International Airport? They're saying that these things showed up out of nowhere... and that they were right in front of the bomb when it went off."

The U.S. leader – caught in the proverbial "deer in the headlights" look – seemed totally at a loss.

"I don't... uhh, just a minute, if you'll allow me," he requested.

"Of course," obliged the reporter.

The President departed the lectern. for a moment or two. He conferred with Kaysten.

"Jerry... what do we know about that?" demanded the U.S. leader. "Could it be Major White or his wife?"

The Chief of Staff seemed dazed; he was most unlike his regular, sharp self.

He mumbled, "Well, sir... remember Minnie was steamed about the fact that Devon and Saquina went their own way, out the back of the transport? Yeah... *could* have been them... I guess... we don't know where they went, after that. It wasn't the Army-base – Minnie called after the bomb blew, and they didn't check in. I mean... who else you got out in L.A., who can whip you up an instant iceberg or two?"

Kaysten tried to force a smile, but it was clear that he was still in a state of shock.

"I suppose we don't know if they're still alive... do we?" cautiously inquired the President.

"Wouldn't bet on it... wouldn't bet against it," offered the Chief of Staff. "If they were the ones who built those 'bergs and they were still at it when the bomb blew, they'd have been closer to it than anybody in L.A... but they *might* have gone and hid somewhere, beforehand. All I know, sir, is that a few minutes ago – when the damn thing went off, I think – it felt like I had the wind knocked out of me, combined with the worst hangover you *ever* had. Something really, really *bad* happened to somebody out there, sir. I can *feel* it."

"I... *see*," acknowledged the U.S. leader. "Okay... when will we know more?"

"Air Force, Navy and Coast Guard are already approaching the harbor, sir," mentioned Kaysten. "Curt told me he'd have better information within the hour, depending on the Rad-Haz situation."

The President nodded, patted Kaysten on the back and strode to the Blue Goose speaking-lectern.

Re-addressing the crowd, the U.S. leader said, "Having consulted with my staff, I can tell you that based on the preponderance of currently-available evidence, we believe that these artifacts – the icebergs, that is – *may* have been the work of Major Devon White. I say this because we have previously seen Major White demonstrate some amazing alien-powers associated with elemental cold, and perhaps these could have built an 'iceberg'. What he was out to accomplish by doing this, I'm not sure... we will just have to wait until, as we all hope, he and his wife are able to explain their actions, in person. We'll provide everyone with more information as soon as we have it."

"So with that, ladies and gentlemen, we'll conclude for now," he declared. "I know that there are many questions still outstanding and rest assured, I want to get to the bottom of this just as much as any of you do; but the government's priority now has to be in getting assistance to the people of Los Angeles, before an already terrible situation becomes that much worse. We'll be holding regular press-conferences every morning for the remainder of the week at least, to keep the American people informed of developments as they occur. Thank you... and God Bless America."

The ritual cries for "one more question, Mr. President" and "what about..." rang out as the U.S. leader, with a rubber-kneed, blanching Kaysten in tow, walked briskly off the podium and into the corridors of the White House.

As they escaped the presence of the reporters, the President mentioned to his Chief of Staff, "Jerrry – whatever that is... you should *do* something about it. You look like death warmed over!"

"Funny you should say that, sir," remarked Kaysten. "You might just be *right*. And you know what else?"

"No... what?" asked the President.

"She claimed, 'you won't get sick anymore'," ruefully commented Kaysten. "Then she told me that *I* was the one with the super-duper forked tongue."

Last Year's Hand-Me-Down Costume

The "first man on Mars" had also been the first to come to his senses, after coming hard to ground. Shaking off the fog of semi-consciousness, he found himself – and his groggy wife – arrayed in awkward contortions in the middle seats of a '30s-style family-van, through whose front windshield both had shattered and crashed through, twenty seconds before.

The driver's and passenger's seats hadn't fared much better; all that remained of them was shredded foam-padding and charred, twisted metal.

Ain't doin' that – I mean, "flyin' through the windshield, with all that busted glass 'n such" – ain't that s'posed to kill *a man?* he idly ruminated.

Oh yeah... I ain't a "man" no more... am I?

Keep forgettin' that, somehow...

He looked to the left and saw his wife's face. Her eyes were closed.

"Saquina," he quietly spoke. "Y'all okay?"

The more-than-a-woman's eyelids fluttered, revealing an absent-minded stare.

"Oh...kay?" she muttered. "Oh, yeah... I'm oh-kay, all right... jus' gots to fix this lil' ol' bomb, and – *bomb? Bomb!* Devon, where *is* y'all –"

"Hey... *hey!*" he quickly responded, while holding her close. "I'm right here, hon. Looks like y'all took quite a knock back there –"

Now apparently conscious, Saquina White looked up at her husband.

"Well... no *shit* I did!" she riposted, with a wan smile.

"Y'all know me, Saquina – *nothin'* gets past yours truly," he quipped.

She steadied herself, sat up in what was left of her seat and looked about, in all directions.

Though the remote part of the parking-lot into which they had fallen was almost deserted – this and most of the other cars in the immediate vicinity looked as if they had been abandoned for months – to her surprise, the wife noted signs of pre-detonation automobile and pedestrian activity (for example, suddenly-abandoned shopping-carts that had been strewn hither and yon, by the just-passed shock-wave), closer to what appeared to be the buildings of a suburban shopping-mall.

The entire area, encompassing several city blocks, was encircled by a fairly tall chain-link fence, and the entrances to major streets had some sort of guard-kiosk inspecting whomever was allowed to enter or egress. This – like many other similar edifices – had some of its windows smashed in, with unknown consequences to those inside.

There appeared to be numerous casualties elsewhere, however, with a group of bloodied, despondent people near to one of the mall's main entrances wailing out for help. Smoke from fires rose above the horizon of nearby buildings, but these must have been caused by the bomb's secondary effects, since there was none of the charring or other thermal-damage that would have been evident, otherwise.

As far as either White or his wife could tell, electrical power was "out", although there must have been a backup-generator in the mall, since some of its interior lights were still functioning.

"Where *is* we, anyways?" she asked.

"Shoppin'-center, somewhere in L.A., I think," offered Devon White. "I thought the whole damn city was closed down tight, what with them gang-bangers all over the place... guess I was wrong. Looks like a lot of folks was caught out here when the bomb blew – see them over there?"

The wife cast her senses outward. Her countenance darkened.

"Oh my sweet *Lord!*" she gasped. "Some of 'em lookin' like they was in a car-accident or somethin'. We gonna help 'em?"

"How your *Fire* doin', babe?" he asked.

"Not too damn good," she disclosed. "Feel it comin' back – but I don' think I can fly yet... maybe in an hour or so? How 'bout y'all, Devon?"

"'Bout the same, I'm 'fraid," he admitted. "Guess neither of us was payin' a lot of attention to what we might want to use it on, after... well, y'all know. I'd say, we'd be better off tryin' to find Angel Lady, first."

A wide-eyed stare met the ex-astronaut's eyes.

"*Karéin!*" exclaimed Saquina White. "I done forgot all *'bout* her! We gots to go *find* her –"

Just then, the van's side-panel door – apparently not damaged beforehand – was torn away from its auto-body and casually discarded, in much the same manner as a person removes a paper-tissue from its holding-box.

"Sister... I will spare you the trouble," sighed a dirty, exhausted- and bedraggled-looking Storied Watcher, who stood just to one side of the van, out of the line of sight of those closer to the shopping-center. Despite them being obviously the worse for wear (the flaming essence of *Vîrya Ahn'jë* had been reduced to a pale, flickering shadow of its former self, and all the other colors of her war-garb seemed oddly subdued and faded), her "war-children" still adorned the alien-girl's frame, giving her a bizarre, almost-pathetic image.

"I hope y'all don't take this the wrong way, Angel Lady," offered Saquina White with a pleasant grin, "But y'all look kind of like some unlucky kid stuck with last year's hand-me-down Hallowe'en costume."

The Storied Watcher's shoulders fell slightly as she replied, "Or some 'disk-oh ball costume', as I recall stalwart Wolf was wont to say. There, *there*, children – sister Saquina means ye well... it is just her cultural way of speaking, as earlier I tutored ye. Oh, my brother – my sister – it is *so* good to see you both alive and, I think, unharmed! What *befell* us back yonder? Too late – too late *again*, was I! And *death* – much death – was the coin that others paid, for this!"

Karéin-Mayréij hung her head, with tears in her eyes.

"Hey, there, Karéin!" consoled Devon White, "Y'all got nothin' to apologize for... I mean, we didn't even think y'all was comin' out here at all! What made y'all change your mind?"

"The voices *told* me," she answered.

"Y'all mean, 'the same ones as y'all were talkin' about, when we was all up in that campground'?" asked Saquina White.

"Even so," confirmed the alien-girl. "I just wish that my guiding-spirits would give me adequate advance-notice, of the advent of such duties; I flew as fast as I could across the continent... and still arrived too late..."

"Sebastiàn," commented the wife.

"You met him?" queried the Storied Watcher.

"Yeah," responded Devon White. "We were carryin' the bomb, which he was lookin' for – we met up with him about one minute before the damn thing was about to blow. That was one weird 'gift' y'all set him up with, Karéin; he was all *covered* with little bugs – a whole *cloud* of 'em, in fact – and they were what kept him flyin' after us –"

"You misunderstand the Gift of *Amaiish*," corrected Karéin-Mayréij. "I am merely the vessel from which the water of nobility and power, flows; I control not how it flowers in a person, once so bestowed. That is the decision of the Gods; or, mayhap, of *your*, 'God'... and thanks be to Him, if appropriate, for bringing you safe through this trial. But as to our brother Sebastiàn... my soul laments, as I already know that he has passed from this world. Yet... I would know how this happened; I would know of his last moments. Please tell me!"

"Well... it's like this," explained the former Mars astronaut. "We didn't get off to the best of starts – man threatened to have them bugs eat us alive, if we didn't give him the bomb. But we could tell that he'd been with y'all at some point, so we figured shootin' at him would be a bad idea, and to tell y'all the truth... findin' *anybody* who wanted to take that fuckin' bomb off our hands – well, that suited Saquina 'n me just fine –"

"'Amen to *that*'," ruefully interjected the wife.

"Yeah," continued Devon White, "So anyway, we made him promise to take the thing as far offshore as he could get, before... well, *y'all* know. Just before he left, he mentioned some stuff that we really couldn't figure... my Spanish ain't that great but I think I got the gist of it – somethin' about, 'tell Angel Lady that I completed my quest', and that 'I knew I was dead already, so goin' out with the bomb's really just makin' things the way they was before', and 'Sebastiàn's leavin' with no regrets, and thank Angel Lady for lettin' him play King For A Day'... 'least, that's what I think I heard. Saquina... that sound right?"

"Pretty much," agreed the more-than-a-woman. "Karéin... what's all that mean, anyways? 'Specially... all this shit 'bout a 'death-quest' 'n such? Why y'all lay that on him?"

The Storied Watcher took a seat on the floor of the van, looking outward.

Though she tried to hide it, both of her interlocutors could still see the crestfallen, despondent look on her face.

"It is... like *this*..." she quietly offered. "The Holy *Fire* chooses her own quests of those who would inherit her blessings. When I dream or, sometimes, when I meditate, I can try to influence these – make them different in a way, change the destination, lengthen or shorten the duration, substitute one challenge for another, enhance a follower's abilities to better withstand the trials – but I cannot change the final outcome, nor what doom that achieving it might ultimately bring to a brother or sister of the *Fire*. I can but do my best to prepare them, beforehand... to give wisdom and insight... to help them on their way."

"Y'all make it sound as if y'all just some kind of passive referee... or maybe the guy with the startin'-pistol," complained Saquina White.

"Or... a *slave* to fate," added her husband.

"Are not we all?" countered Karéin-Mayréij. "Was I not *just* so, when confronted with that comet that your people had named, 'Lucifer'? I, too, had a very dangerous quest laid upon me. Welcome to the world of the *Khùl-Algrenàthi'i*, my sister and brother – you have mighty powers... and thus the Fates and the Gods require great things of you, worthy of a super-hero or of a demi-god. Ever has it been thus, since the first of days."

Neither of the other two could immediately think of something to say, and then after a few seconds, the Storied Watcher intoned,

"But still my heart is heavy for my fallen brother Sebastiàn, who did not turn from his quest... even though he knew it would be the end of him. Did I adequately prepare him, for this terrible duty? All honor and peace to Sebastiàn, Prince of Venom – may the Gods see him safe, on his journey to the Planes Beyond!"

"I asked God to let him into heaven," remarked Saquina White. "Just... *before* it all went down, that is."

Staring reflectively out into the distance, Karéin-Mayréij murmured, "Aye – perhaps that will come to be. None may know where mortals go, ere they leave this reality. I *pretend* to know, to counsel you on this... but it is just a conceit. All that we *do* know, is, 'never again, can we be with the departed, in *this* life... in *this*, reality'. And *that* – whatever may await, elsewhere – *that*, is terribly sad."

"Yeah," said Devon White, with an affirmative nod. "Listen, Karéin... y'all mind if I ask y'all somethin'?"

"Not at all," responded the alien-girl. "Go ahead."

"We had a little chat 'bout this subject, when we was both back on the *Infinity*, just before y'all went off and blew old 'Lucifer' to Kingdom Come," recalled the ex-astronaut. "And both then and now, y'all tellin' us that y'all really don't know about what happens after we, well... after us mortals stop breathin' for the last time... right?"

"I believe that is what I just said... so, 'yes'," answered the Storied Watcher.

"If y'all *did* know... would y'all tell us, then?" pressed Devon White.

"No," obliquely replied Karéin-Mayréij. "I would not."

"So all that stuff 'bout Jaysus 'n such... y'all sayin' it ain't true?" persisted the former Mars communications-officer.

"I did not *say* that," countered the alien-girl. "Is it not possible that I simply do not know?"

"Y'all avoidin' the *question*," complained Devon White.

"Well, Karéin," helpfully interjected the astronaut's-wife, "I s'pose it might take some time for us to make a Christian out of y'all... puttin' that aside for the time bein'... what we gonna do now? Y'all *seen* what's goin' on over there – shoppin'-center, that is. Lots of folk needin' *help*, Angel Lady! Y'all in any shape to lend a hand?"

"Of *course*, my sister!" answered the Storied Watcher. "The events of this young day weigh heavily on my soul – but that is a poor excuse, to stand idly by and see yet worse, to come about. Perhaps by so doing, I can erase some of the shame that I now feel, for having been – ahh, how does dear Bob say it – 'a day late and two bits, short'."

"It's actually 'a *dollar* short'," corrected Saquina White. "But a dollar these days ain't worth more than a quarter was, a few years ago... so I s'pose it kind of makes sense."

The alien-girl looked over her shoulder, nodding affirmatively and casting a sad-looking smile in a backward direction.

Then she stood on her two feet, took a few steps away from the wrecked automobile, reversed direction so as to face them, and the two Whites saw flashes of the old majesty, dignity and power, again issue from the slim – yet, supernaturally-determined and square-shouldered – figure of Karéin-Mayréij, clad resplendent in the blue-flame-flickering fortress of *Vîrya Ahn'jë*.

"I beg the two of you to help our stricken human brothers and sisters, as best your arts will allow," declared the alien-girl. "Lend them a morsel of your life-force – as I so tutored you, back at the forest-camp – if their own is slipping into the abyss... but not too much, lest they pull you in with them. My war-children and I will busy ourselves with extinguishing fires, with clearing rubble which may entrap those in damaged buildings, and with righting what has been knocked down, nearer to yonder coast. No doubt, many in those parts, are in urgent need of assistance."

Her *Fire* was now roaring, radiating an infernal field that began to blister the remaining paint on the van, although neither of the Whites were much affected or concerned.

"I'm almost gettin' *used* to that, y'all know," offered Devon White. "Even though my English's 'ice', and that shit is hotter'n *hell*."

"Do you know what is 'hotter', Devon?" teased the Storied Watcher.

"I can *guess*, don't y'all know," he replied, with a knowing smile.

"That is my way of pleading to the very Gods... 'no more atom-bombs'... *please!*" she said, a second before she rocketed back into the sky, making an impossibly-abrupt turn toward the Pacific Ocean.

Not While We're In This World

They had gathered in the precise middle of an expansive basement – actually, a converted underground parking-garage – under a ring of high-powered florescent lights immediately overhead.

The eleven men, each one dressed in conservative business-attire, each with a small, gold crucifix suspended on a discreet neck-chain, sat three to a table; except for the fourth and last table, which had an empty spot.

One of the attendees – a male Caucasian like all of the others, but somewhat more elderly than the average for this group – spoke up.

"The meeting will come to order," he announced. "Let us bow our heads."

Respectful compliance was immediately evident, as the man intoned,

"Blessed Father God, we give Thee heart-felt thanks for welcoming our fallen leader, Brother Harold, into Thy everlasting glory, to exult with our Lord and Savior, Jesus Christ, and Thy angels and saints. Guide us now, as we pick up the sword of Thy righteous wrath to continue Thy holy war against the forces of – cursed be his foul name – Satan The Deceiver, and his evil, sinister Angel of Death, which calls itself the despicable name of "Karéin-Mayréij". Let all of us here today be as unafraid as Thy faithful servant, Harold Crowford, was, in sacrificin' his dirty, polluted, Jew-tainted, sinful life in this world, to be born again in spiritual purity in Thy endless, sanctified life in Heaven. Lord, this we pray in Thy holy name... Amen."

"Amen!" came a chorus from around the tables.

"Alright," spoke the chairman. "As you all know, by tradition, these meetings are to be kept as short as possible, so I'll get right *to* it."

He cast a glance over to the empty seat.

"Is there any word?" he asked.

One of the other men – a guy with Brylcreemed, dark hair and a severe, clean-shaven face (who could have been mistaken for a younger Harold Crowford), spoke up.

"We've been looking," said the man. "But nothing positive, as yet. When we first heard the intercepts, we got our people over to the beachfront as quickly as we could, hoping against hope to find him –"

"But he was with our late, hallowed Brother Harold on the *plane*," argued the chairman. "We'd have to assume –"

"Forgive me for speaking out of turn, Brother," interjected another man, a jolly-looking, rotund guy at the end of one of the tables, "But *both* of them had the tracking-devices. We checked the time when Brother Harold's stopped transmitting and that was the precise moment when... well, *you* know... he ascended into heaven, to be with our Lord and Savior, Jesus Christ. But Brother Martin's one, on the other hand – it kept going for quite some time thereafter. We eventually tracked it down to a dumpster in Pleasantville, New Jersey – but there's no sign at all of Brother Martin himself. *So...*"

The room fell silent for a couple of seconds and then the chairman continued, "The problem is... he *might* have gone to Jesus on the plane along with Brother Harold, and somehow the trackin'-thing got blown clear or survived the explosion in some other way; or he might have survived the blast – now mind you, I don't know how he'd have *done* that, but the Lord works in mysterious ways – but in *that* case, why wouldn't he return to the fold, to tell us all about it? The thing is... I honestly don't think we can offer final unction for him up to the Lord, without knowin' for sure. Does anyone here disagree?"

His opinion was confirmed by seeing unanimity in shaking heads, around the tables.

"Alright then," declared the chairman, "It will be so recorded, that the matter of Brother Martin must be held in abeyance, until more clear evidence of his fate, becomes available. Of course, that doesn't prevent any of us from prayin' to the Lord for guidance and enlightenment. If any of you hear from the Lord on this or anythin' else, don't hesitate to inform the others. Alright?"

"Amen," came the response from around the tables.

"So with that in mind," said the chairman, "And as you know from church regulations, in the absence of a leader anointed specifically as such – which *would* have been Brother Martin – it falls to this council to collectively make decisions... or to implement tasks left to us, by the former leader. And I think that each and every one of you knows, what *that* means. Brother Leo... what's the state of the preparations? That is, to fulfill Brother Harold's last testament, before he got on the plane."

A thin, spare, brush-cut guy with a small crucifix tattooed on the top of his left hand and a bleeding heart on the right one, stood to attention and spoke up.

"Preparations are almost complete, Brother," he announced. "Given the chaos going on after the recent... *events*, the military and LEA had to abandon a lot of the normal data-security protocols – both physical access and encryption – just to get the clean-up duties going. Our people are still just as 'embedded' as they've *ever* been. We've been watching the FBI starting to clean out the Agency and the Palace... it's all happening in front of our deep-cover folks, but the Bureau seems to have completely missed us. Oh, and our relationships with Mr. Duke and GrayWar are also helping a lot –"

"That's great," interrupted the chairman, "But are we ready to *go* yet?"

"We *will* be, in about another few days," claimed Brother Leo. "Our embeds are tracking the movement of the targets, almost in real-time. It's been much more difficult with the Devil-Girl itself, I'll have to admit, because of its crazy mobility – our DoD agents had it flying from coast to coast at speeds of over four thousand miles per hour. For reasons we aren't sure of, it seems to have left the Western Hemisphere... we've lost track of it, although with God's help and our sources in the military, we'll see it the moment when it reappears. But as for the other ones, it's just a matter of getting the teams in place."

"Excellent!" congratulated the chairman. "As for the other objective – that is, 'punition for the sinful government leaders who opposed Brother Harold's holy mission'; and replacement thereof. I take it that Brother Jethro is standing by? What's the status there?"

"Same," stated Brother Leo. "Initially we encountered some challenges – as I mentioned, the administration and the FBI launched a purge of anyone within the Executive Branch whose loyalty was suspect, and that set us back temporarily – but they missed several of our operatives, including one deep-cover fellow right in the White House. We've got better intel on the President's schedule and plans, than anybody else, including the Bureau by the way... at least that's what I figure. When comes the time... we'll be ready."

"God is *impressed* with your diligence, Brother!" encouraged the chairman. "And so we come to the last question : do any of you in this meeting today, have an objection to acting on our fallen Brother Harold's, last instructions to his followers?"

Silence was the response, until another man – a guy with a slightly more sallow complexion and a lot of five o'clock shadow – said, "I only wish, Brother, that I could be among them. We all know what the odds are. I'd like to end my sinful life here like Harold did. Maybe not with as big a 'bang'... but still with a smile on my face, as I look upward to see our Savior."

"I surely *do* understand," sympathized the chairman. "But each and every one of us has his appointed duty to do. Every army must have its foot-soldiers... and its General Staff. We *are* that. Let us pray, before we conclude the meeting."

Again, heads bowed, as the chairman pronounced, "Blessed Father God, we have come here today to plan the next steps in Thy holy war against polluted, unclean Muslims, Jews, lib-rals, atheists, Democrats, free-thinkers, feminists, vegetarians and those that Thou have cursed with the mark of monkey-black skin; but especially against the Devil-Girl and her legion of Hell-powered bastard children. We beseech Thee to find favor with our poor preparations, and to fix us brave and strong to carry the good fight to the sinister enemy that confronts us. Lord, with Thy terrible swift sword, there is no evil that we cannot overcome! Let us smite the wicked, until their poisoned blood is spread all around, never again to empower them! This we pray, in Thy holy, merciful name. Amen."

"Amen!" came back an enthusiastic reply.

As he looked up, the chairman offered, "And once her offspring have been sent back to Hell... then we finish the job that our great Brother Harold, started on our behalf. The Lord's work is never done... at least not, while we are still in *this* world."

No Straight Story, No New Leaf

There were four different high-definition television-screens arrayed within convenient viewing-distance of the Resolution Desk in the Oval Office, and the restless U.S. leader's attention darted from one to the other and back again, multiple times each minute. He had abandoned his chair and leaned back against the desk.

"Anything new, sir?" asked Kaysten, who stood in the doorway to the inner recesses of the White House.

He was almost himself, again, after a rough half-hour or so.

"Well, we've now got some reports from the ground, inside the city," answered the President. "That's *something*, I suppose. You know – I never really liked reporters... but I've got to admit, some of those guys have got guts. What with the gangs all over the place, I mean."

"Kortish is telling me that the gang-bangers took it harder than everybody else down there, because a lot of them were out in the streets, when it blew," observed the Chief of Staff. "The busted glass from the explosion cut many of 'em to ribbons. Most everybody else was indoors... thank God for small blessings, eh?"

"Yeah," confirmed the U.S. leader, "I suppose we can take some small comfort, in *that*. General Gainmeister – you remember, he's Blanshard's third-in-command – he just sent in a report indicating that the Army's making much better progress than before, in advancing westward. You see that one?"

"Sure *did*, sir," said Kaysten. "But I've been talking with DoD liaison and they've apparently got a different problem, now – they're running out of soldiers to garrison everything with, and on top of that, they're being swarmed by refugees. Some of those places in and around L.A. haven't had food-delivery for six *weeks* or more. There's an impending starvation issue, apparently. Fun times..."

"A lot of catching-up to do, out there," agreed the President, whose attention had seemed to focus on the third television-screen from the left. "Hey, Jerry – have a look at *this*."

Though there was no evidence of a remote-control, something, or someone, immediately dimmed the other three screens and turned up the volume on the third one. It showed a scene from somewhere in urban Los Angeles, with a female, blond-haired, young Caucasian reporter and camera-crew in casual dress, giving a rapid-fire account of the chaotic situation unfolding around them.

The camera pointed at a tall office-building about a block away, from which smoke was profusely issuing in its top four or five floors.

"This is Marjorie Davis of KABC Disney News Two, reporting to you live from the corner of Lucas and Wiltshire," announced the reporter. "We're first to be live on-scene in downtown L.A., after the recent nuclear detonation offshore –"

"Don't they know about fallout?" said the President.

"I'm being told that there wasn't very much – it blew up in the air, not in the water – and the offshore winds are blowing it mostly south and a little east... San Diego might get dusted, and the Army's trying to get everybody down there indoors," noted Kaysten.

"Never thought I'd hear myself saying it, but... 'that's good news'," ruefully admitted the President.

"Did she tell you," proudly mentioned the Chief of Staff, "That I'm basically immune to it? Apparently I can survive enough, uhh, 'rads', to kill off kelp or cockroaches. Just another little fringe-benefit, you know."

"Hmm," murmured the U.S. leader. "Would that be true of Matt and Clairie, too?"

"I *think* so, sir," affirmed Kaysten. "But for the record... the kind of radiation that Sylvia uses – *that's* something else, altogether. When she hit Bob and I with it, somehow I *knew* that it'd kill a human being in a second or two. I only survived because, uhh, 'we', all have this 'force-field', and 'we', all heal damage, really fast. I sure wouldn't want your kids to fight it out with Ms. Abruzzio... *that's* for sure."

"I... see," remarked the President. "Well... let's hope they never *have* to."

"As you can see," continued the reporter, as the camera panned almost 360 degrees, revealing broken windows everywhere, accompanied by dozens of fires smoldering within the nearby city blocks, "The Chase Center's on fire, and we're being told, it's out of control – if the fire keeps growing, the skyscraper's structure will be weakened and there's a chance it will collapse. Also, further to the north along Lucas, Good Samaritan Hospital is trying to deal with spreading chemical fires that are blocking its main entrances, and power's out across the city, so the hospital – which is being overwhelmed by a steady stream of those injured in the explosion – is in a desperate state. We don't see any police or fire department personnel, because they – hold on – what's *that?*"

Ooo-ooo-ooo-ooo, sounded a now-half-familiar, eerie wail, from overhead. Exciting, other-worldly music with an exciting, staccato, pulsating back-beat, seemed to issue from the very air-molecules.

A caped, blue-flame-enshrouded female figure, flying a circular pattern around the top floors of the stricken office-building, burst on to the scene. A second later, two tiny, bright-shining objects – the first glowing bright yellow-orange, the second with a dull, blue hue – were propelled outward from the figure.

The yellow object circumnavigated the building, and as it went, it a trail of fire, smoke and sparks from within the Chase Center seemed to be somehow "pulled" outward, vanishing as soon as it came in contact with the flying yellow-thing. The blue-thing followed its yellow companion at a distance of perhaps two hundred feet behind, and as it passed the areas just denuded of fire, it unleashed a dim, blue-white attack of some kind, which resulted in the areas struck being frosted with a glistening coating of ice. The terrible cold of this, sent a momentary chill even as far down as street-level. Then both of the small objects seemed to return to their owner.

"Uhh – hold on – something's happening," stammered the reporter. "Jim… do you see this, up there at the top of the Chase Center – folks, it looks like the fire's now out, and – oh my *God* – it's coming right *at* us –"

There must have been at least two mobile cameras, since one showed a scene of Marjorie Davis – frozen in place by sheer terror – staring helplessly upward, as something out of the field of vision, descended upon her.

In a half-second, the flame-bedecked, wide-caped, supernaturally-intimidating figure of the Storied Watcher, stood on the pavement, with crossed arms, in front of the reporter.

A crowd started to approach.

"Are you – are you – the *alien?*" pedantically stuttered Davis.

The reporter's knees went to rubber, and it was all she could do to avoid kneeling.

The war-music ebbed, though it was still perceptible. The Storied Watcher's vision-goggles disappeared, revealing her beautiful face and striking green eyes.

The fangs were also there, but were tactfully-retracted.

"Aye… I am Karéin-Mayréij, the Storied Watcher, the Guardian of Earth," declared the alien-girl, in a clear, Stentorian tone, "And, if you are agreeable to doing this… I would like to give a 'status-report' of what now besets your city… and of how I am trying to fix it. I must be brief in this, because much remains yet to be done. May I go ahead, Marjorie?"

"How you… never mind," replied the reporter. "Go ahead. You're on national TV."

"Thank you," said Karéin-Mayréij. She was now staring directly into the camera.

"First of all," explained the alien-girl, "My heart and soul cry at the scenes of destruction that I have so far seen, on this dark day. I tried to stop what has occurred; lamentably, I was too late by a few seconds, and could not effectively protect your city from this accursed weapon's blast. I did not know precisely where the weapon was, and I lost time in searching for it. With that said, everyone should know that these evils would have been *far* worse – that is, the atom-smashing bomb would have gone off right over the city – had it not been for the bravery and arts of three of my followers, specifically Devon White – Prince of Snows, and Saquina White – Queen of The Spring Flood – and, foremost, the late Sebastiàn, Prince of Venom... who sacrificed his very *life*, to carry the bomb offshore, and thus to save millions of people who live within the city. Verily I say to those living in Los Angeles who now hear my voice – you owe your *lives* to these three, and especially to my fallen brother, Sebastiàn. All honor and glory to him! May his memory be venerated, never to be forgotten!"

She bent her head, looked down at the ground, held her hands together in a prayer-gesture, and fell silent for a second or two.

Then she continued,

"Secondly... so far, my war-children and I – ice-bound *Væran Ss'éth'ch'* and infernal *Væran Ksé'l'ch'*, who you have just seen in quenching the blaze upon yonder office-tower over there – we have extinguished over ninety-five major fires and a number of smaller ones; we will attend to those that are in front of the hospital, in a minute or two. We have also tried to help those who are hurt, as we have happened upon them; but we cannot be in more than one place at one time, and there are too many wounded-people everywhere for us to handle by ourselves. I bid your doctors, police and medical-assistants to come hither and tend to your stricken brothers and sisters, wherever they may be – especially the poorest of them, who were in the streets and had nowhere to hide, when the nuclear weapon exploded. I will deal with anyone who tries to impede your way, although from what I see, there will be few who will try to interfere... and woe betide them, should they so to do!"

"That's my *girl*," wryly commented Kaysten, to the President.

"Ms. Mayréij," asked the reporter, "We're receiving reports of forest-fires breaking out in the hills to the north of the city... and downtown, there are apparently a number of other buildings that have suffered structural damage, or that may be on fire. Is there anything you can do –"

"Yes – of *course*," interrupted the Storied Watcher, "As soon as we clear the entrances to yonder hospital. We are working our way in from the seacoast, as the areas nearest to that, suffered the most damage. Remember that the blast-wave from a weapon such as this, weakens quickly, as it goes out. There is a big highway to the east that runs north-south, beside a canyon, and we see only light damage past this point; but to the west of that, there remains much left to do. And I must hasten thence."

"But ma'am, we'd just like to ask –" attempted the reporter, to no avail, as the Storied Watcher – her war-song again waxing in majesty and potency – rocketed upward, executed a right-angle turn to the north and began to suck the energy out of the fires in front of the Good Samaritan Hospital. Onlookers also saw collections of burned-out, piled-up vehicles being moved to one side or another, by some mysterious, unseen force, akin to an invisible lifting-crane.

Temporarily at a loss, Davis eventually regained her composure and, addressing one of the cameramen, spoke,

"There we have it, folks – an exclusive interview with the alien Karéin-Mayréij, the so-called 'Storied Watcher' – who seems to have appeared in the Greater L.A. area, shortly after the bomb's detonation. No doubt the government will have some questions to ask about all of this, what with the proximity of these two events, so close to each other, and with what's just occurred on the East Coast. Okay, Jim – what we're going to do now is, we're going to check out the status of the Chase Center… stay with us as we get in there. Let's go!"

The TV-screen continued to follow the exploits of the reporter and her team, as the President gestured with an index finger and the fourth screen returned to the same status as the other three.

"Here come the conspiracy-theories, Mr. President," glumly commented Kaysten. "I can just *see* it now, on MySpaceTube – 'the sinister alien dropped the bomb on L.A. *herself*, kind of thing. We should get our own story out, first, to pre-empt the rumors and take charge of the situation."

"Agreed. Let's *do* that," requested the U.S. leader.

"How far you want to go?" asked the Chief of Staff. "I got an angle…"

"What's the idea?" inquired the President.

"Why don't we tell the press, that we – sorry, sir, *you* – dispatched her out there, yourself?" mischievously proposed Kaysten.

The U.S. leader paused for a moment, sending his subordinate a long stare.

"Whew," the President expressed, "That's a *stretch*… don't you think? I mean… won't she be pissed off about us – uhh – *exaggerating*, our role in her activities, out West?"

"If she does… I'll handle her, sir," pledged the Chief of Staff.

"*How?*" retorted the perplexed Commander-In-Chief. "We're talking about a creature who can *vaporize* either one of us, with about as much effort as it would take you or me to snap our *fingers!*"

"Well, if she did… I'd like to think that I'd last long enough to tell a 'goodbye'-joke," said Kaysten, with a wan smile. "But I don't think anything like that will happen, sir. What I mean is – look at it from Karéin's point of view. She'll probably be as screwed as we are, once these stories get going, and there were quite a few circulating around beforehand. *Nobody* will trust *anything* she says! Considering that she swore off – right in front of us – what she seems to have decided to go off and do anyway… she'll need some kind of cover-story to explain it. If she buys in to the idea – even if all she does is not completely deny it – then it will be hard for her to walk it back later. It's a great opportunity to get her on our side!"

The President seemed honestly torn.

"Didn't she say something about, 'I was supposed to turn over a new leaf'… or something?"

"I think Oscar Wilde had a snappy comeback about that, sir," cheerily offered Kaysten. "But all I'll say for now is… let's get her barking up *our* tree."

When To Call It "A Day"

It had been two more tumultuous days of frantic effort in the Greater Los Angeles area, before Karéin-Mayréij and the adult members of the White family, felt comfortable with leaving the city's needy to its public-safety personnel.

The metropolis' urban gangs were still there; but for the most part, they (wisely) scurried for cover, upon hearing the war-songs of one or more of the super-powered visitors. Evidently, word had traveled fast in the L.A. underground about what had happened when the Storied Watcher had last visited the city, and few of the gangsters were eager to challenge either her or the two White family members. This, in turn, provided relatively safe ingress for the U.S. Army and various other forces of law and order, though there were still areas of the city that they elected to stay out of.

For their part, Karéin-Mayréij and her two friends had worked 18- to 22-hour shifts, variously extinguishing fires, uncovering the hapless victims of damaged buildings, and – in the case of the Storied Watcher, at least – allowing her very life-force to be drained into the bodies of Angelenos who were *in extremis*, due to the bomb's after-effects.

At one such instance – in which a miraculously-still-barely-alive little child was dragged out from inside a wrecked car, in a partly-collapsed, flame-scorched underground parking-garage – the alien-girl was asked by a rapt emergency-worker, "Miss Angel… why are you takin' such trouble to find out who she is… where she lives?"

The cryptic answer came back, "Who among us knows what the future holds, for those touched by the *Fire?*"

Still – all things considered, after a few days of determined rescue-effort – it became apparent that Los Angeles had, in fact, gotten off relatively lightly, considering what might otherwise have happened. Using her own, ruefully-earned judgment of such matters, the Storied Watcher advised a beaming Devon White and his elated wife that their "ice-war-sculptures", as Karéin-Mayréij termed the structures hastily built offshore, had likely absorbed or mitigated three-quarters of the bomb's thermal-pulse, and at least half of its blast-wave.

"That, and the 'Mars' thing," replied the ex-astronaut, "Gotta get me a high-school or two named after me… don't y'all think?"

"If I were you, my well-accomplished brother," phlegmatically offered the alien-girl, "I should hold out for one of these 'sports-stadiums', such as the ones to which we carried many of these wounded citizens, as a temporary holding-place; or, if not that... perhaps the President would volunteer to rename his own palace, in your honor."

Saquina White actually wanted to try this, but her husband, perhaps wisely, insisted on "not pushin' it... 'least not 'till Angel Lady yanks that damn big 'ornament' she dropped in the lawn".

"It *will* be done," pledged Karéin-Mayréij with an insouciant smile, "But after all – I *was* asleep for very long... was I not? Many things, therefore, can safely be made to wait awhile, until the Gods and Fates deem the time to be just right."

It was late afternoon on the third day in Los Angeles, and the Storied Watcher, along with her two more-than-human acolytes, had stolen away to the top of a steep hillside, overlooking Topanga Canyon and the Pacific Ocean.

Several hundred feet below them and to the south, there were some trendy-looking restaurants, which – despite recent events – seemed to be rapidly filling up with those brave and well-heeled enough to risk the possible dangers and the guaranteed swingeing dining-bills.

They had tried to have this discussion in two other places in the L.A. area, but in each case, had been recognized and hounded into an airborne escape, by the ever-present *paparazzi*.

Saquina White had taken the opportunity to needle her alien mentor with, "How y'all like bein' *famous* now, Karéin?", to which the response came, "About as much as fighting the legions of the dread Black *Væran* of Warlike Devastation... except, when you scatter them, *they* know well enough not to come scurrying right back".

For a moment or two, all three just stared out over the ocean, as Earth's star began to slip below the horizon.

The Pacific was placid today; it was starting to cool off and there was a light breeze. It was a classic, gentle California sunset.

"Beautiful... is it not?" observed Karéin-Mayréij.

"Bet y'all seen better... considerin' where y'all been, before," suggested Saquina White.

"No... not 'better'... just, 'different'," countered the alien-girl. "For example, on my home-world, sometimes there are *two* suns – a big one, whose light is a little less yellow and a little more orange-white, than yonder 'Sun'... and a smaller one, whose light is brilliant and is tinged with blue. It is truly spectacular when they are both in a certain position, but this happens only once in... ah, I am rambling! I beg your leave, for this. It is just that, sometimes... I miss 'home'... you know?"

"Of *course* we do, Karéin," remarked Devon White. "'Cept, these parts – leastaways, Compton 'n such – that's *our* crib... y'all know? I kinda feel guilty leavin' these folks so *soon*."

"This is an art of judgment that you must learn to apply, as each day goes by, Devon," counseled the Storied Watcher. "You – or I – could, and would be called on so to do – to spend literally *every* waking hour, in service to the least among you... and if that were to come to pass, then no-one – certainly not me – would say you nay, for so doing. You – and I – can do *so* much; we can *help* so much – over the last hours, you have seen me bringing many people back from the brink of death, simply by letting them pull my life-force out and take it into their own souls, thus to start recovery where otherwise none could succeed –"

"Yeah... that's damn amazin'," acknowledged an awed Saquina White. "Y'all understand why everyone thinks y'all an 'angel', girl? What y'all been doin', 'front of the TV-cameras sometimes... folks's sayin' them's *'miracles'*, and for the record... I agree. 'Guess what I'm sayin', Karéin is... for folks like Devon 'n me, that is 'Christians'... it's a humblin' experience just chillin' with y'all. Sometimes we feel like we're in the presence of God Himself, frankly."

"Ha!" bemusedly replied the alien-girl, "These poor arts that I employ... yes, they *are* impressive, in the context of people who have never before seen them, up close, but... a 'God'? I would not want to disappoint a friend... but flatter me not with such talk, my sister! I deserve no such accolades, and if people knew what – uhh – 'bad' things that I have done in times long-past... well, they would not be *nearly* so eager to volunteer their worship. But anyway... this was really not what I wanted to talk about."

"If y'all want to change the subject... we're okay with that," retreated the wife.

"Thank you," spoke Karéin-Mayréij. "Because important counsel follows. So... as I was saying... you may ask, 'why provide these services – the ones that bestow health, yea, even life itself, for your unfortunate human brothers and sisters – for five hundred people... but not *six* hundred?' And if for six hundred... then why not for *seven* hundred? There are *always* more such... always, always... *always*. However much we should wish it otherwise, suffering, poverty and deprivation are the natural way of things; and no matter how powerful and wise that we may be... never can we eliminate these evils, entirely."

"So what y'all *sayin'*, Karéin?" challenged Devon White. "That we shouldn't do *nothin*? If that's the rule... then I'd say y'all been breakin' it big-time, over the past couple of days."

"No," argued the alien-girl, "I have been living according to my principles. And in this respect, I would impart some advice to you and your brothers and sisters of the Holy *Fire*, on the subject. Namely : you must give aid when appropriate, but not always give aid, lest those who receive it become over-dependent; you must spend *some* of your time with the hurting and the down-trodden, but not *all* of your time; and most of all, you must apportion time and effort so that helping the needy seems a joy... not a burden. It is shameful to see a throng of the needy, and to do nothing; but it is *not* shameful to do 'something' – as much as your soul bids you to do – and then to politely disengage, leaving the rest to the Gods and the Fates, while encouraging those who are able, to, ahh, 'pick up where you left off'. Only by learning this – and *doing* this – can you avoid becoming just a slave to the world's travails and sorrows. Do you understand?"

"Perfectly," confirmed Saquina White. "Sounds pretty much like what Jaysus say we gots to do, 'cept maybe his Disciples didn't get no holidays. Y'all gonna tell them folks back East 'bout all this?"

"Surely I plan, so to do," answered the Storied Watcher. "Though it strains my imagination to the breaking-point, to envisage dear Wolf, for example, as being easily taught to lend a helping hand, to those who beg in the street for spare change. Still – our kind, must strive for great things... would you not say?"

"Well, Karéin," harrumphed Devon White, "Knowin' the man as I do, I'd say y'all have better luck with him lightin' fires, rather'n puttin' them out... but I'll give y'all full marks for tryin'. Listen – this has been a heavy chat, and I'm gettin' a bit hungry. Y'all want to drop in on one of them restaurants, down by the highway? Bet we can be in and out before them dudes with the cameras show up and make our lives miserable."

"Not 'miserable', brother; just, 'never alone'," responded Karéin-Mayréij. "If you would see it, there is a joy in *that*, as well... as long as you learn to manage it. But nay – you and Saquina go by yourselves, and enjoy what time that you can have with each other. I would advise that you just walk down yonder hill-slope, rather than flying, since the latter would draw much attention. As for me... I have something – rather, some*one* – who I must search out, within the confines of this city, ere I head back east, to the others."

"Who's that?" asked a perplexed Saquina White.

"I will tell you when I am sure," came back the answer.

She extended her arms, hugging both the ex-astronaut and his wife, as only a Storied Watcher could do.

Then she bowed and vanished from sight.

Devon and Saquina White stood side by side for a moment, staring mutely at each other.

"Never *will* understand that girl," said the wife. "'Specially with her comin's and goin's."

"Well," offered the husband, "I don't think 'understandin', is somethin' y'all gonna use a lot, on an 'angel', don't y'all know."

He looked down the steep slope to his left.

"Want to see which of us can get down there, without flappin' their wings?" he teased.

"Y'all *on*," said Saquina White, with a smile and a long bound.

Ramòn Stands Surprised

A disquieted Ramòn sat by himself on the hood of a wrecked car and looked out over the encampment of his restless, at-odds 'army', as he wondered what his next move should be.

He tried to recall what Sebastiàn's last counsel had been; but everything had happened so *fast.*

That helicopter come over, remembered the second-in-command, *then he say to me, "You in charge now... I throw you the torch".*

Then el jéfé, *he just do the jet!*

Last I seen of him... ¡que làstima!

Then... I dunno... the bomb go off, and inmediatamente, *me duele tanto en mi corazón... like I'm dyin' or somethin'... good thing that send me to the ground, doubled-up, 'cause about three or four minutes after that, this big thing, like an earthquake, it come through here, bustin' windows an' knockin' shit down everywhere... lost a few* compañeros *when that goin' down...*

Well... por lo menos, *I'm fully healed up from that hurtin' after the bomb, an' from everything that went before it. I should be dead... but I ain't.*

Somehow.

But I ain't got no skills in leadin' an army! *What I s'posed to do,* ahora?

It's been almost three days since the bomb go off an' he don' come back, unhappily reflected Ramòn.

He cast a sideways glance at the iridescent-colored little beetle (maybe it was a cockroach... maybe it was something else), that had taken up residence on his left shoulder. He had never seen a bug exactly like this; its appearance was unique.

"*Él no regresará ... ¿o sí?*" he softly spoke, in the direction of the insect.

Strangely, the little bug moved its tiny head horizontally back-and-forth, as if to confirm Ramòn's morose assumption.

"*Por lo tanto... te nombraré, "Sebastian", mi pequeño amigo; solo para recordarme a él, todos los días,*" he pledged.

"*¿Eso te agrada, pequeño?*"

A gentle, feminine voice, coming from somewhere behind him, now added,

"I think that our fallen brother would like that very much, Ramòn... New Prince of Venom... heir to the Holy *Fire.*"

In a panic, Ramòn jumped off the car-hood, wheeled in place and stared at the shaded sidewalk from where the dialogue had apparently come. His eyes saw nothing; but *somehow...* he could tell that someone *was* there.

He just didn't know exactly *where.*

"Who... who there?" he challenged. "You don' try nothin' stupid... ¿lo entiende?

"*Ciertamente, lo entiendo, mi hermano recién descubierto. ¿Podemos hablar?*" came back the pleasant-sounding voice.

"Do not worry," it added, in English. "I will not hurt you, Ramòn – the opposite, in fact. I am here to console... to befriend... to welcome. I will now show myself."

Instantly, a teenager-slim female figure appeared in the shadows and stepped forward, revealing a young woman with golden-blond hair flowing down below her shoulders, with a straight-cut bang over her forehead. She had pert little breasts, a perfect figure everywhere but especially at the hips, striking green eyes, a disarming half-smile (Ramón caught a very brief glimpse of two unusually-sharp-looking incisor-teeth), and she wore comfortable, Caribbean-style casual clothes.

For a second, Ramòn could do naught but to stop and stare. For a *white* girl... this one sure *was*, surpassingly pretty.

A wave of lecherous thoughts beset his mind. He suppressed them only with some difficulty.

"Who is you... where you come from?" he demanded. "*Mis compañeros* got this place locked down, tight! *Nobody* could get past our snipers –"

"Oh... I just 'dropped in'," smoothly responded the girl. "I have some special arts, so to do. May I sit beside you, brother? You can just go back up on the front-part of yonder car. There is room for us both."

Wary – but at a loss for something better to do – he could only say, "*Ciertamente, mujer* – but no funny business! I got *lots* of guys with guns 'round here – you make one move, an' –"

"Do not worry," she countered. "We have much to discuss."

"*Bueno...*" he responded, taking up a position on the car-hood.

Faster than he could have anticipated, the new girl sat down on the right, beside him; and again, it was all he could do, to avoid forcing himself on her, right then and there. But his animal-urges were quickly pre-empted by an anguished remark from her mouth,

"Sebastiàn is *dead*, my brother... oh, Sebastiàn is *dead!*"

Unexpectedly, her head came to rest on his right shoulder. She wiped away a tear, before it could touch any part of his body.

Her presence was so *desirable...* so... *vulnerable*. The urge to jump her was simply overwhelming. He had no idea how he was keeping control of himself.

"*Creo que tiene razón*," Ramòn managed. "I don' know *how* I know... but I *know*. An' honestly... I don' know what I'm gonna do now. Look at all these people out there, *mujer* – they *dependin'* on me! Sebastiàn... *he'd* know *que hacer*... but I don' know *shit* 'bout bein' *el jéfé!*"

"You will do just *fine*, brave Ramòn... just, *fine*," reassured the new girl. "For the Fates and the Gods have brought you to this point... that is, to take up with the Fire of *Amaiish*, where our fallen brother Sebastiàn has left off. I do not know how that this has occurred – I had believed that only *I* could pass the Holy *Fire* to a human, but evidently –"

She was interrupted by the arrival of a group of Latina gang-hangers-on, who had noticed the appearance of the new girl and who had approached the car and the sidewalk.

One of them – a fetching, buxom young thing with a Jackie Kennedy hairdo and torn jeans for clothing – stared in disbelief. The three others of the group also bore wide-eyed countenances.

"R... R... *Ramòn!*" she stammered.

"*¿Que tal?*" he responded. "What you want, Mireya? I'm kind of busy, *chica*... I got *business* to discuss with this, uhh, lady, who jus' show up."

"Ramòn," she persisted with a half-suppressed gasp, "Don' you *know*, who that is, sittin' beside you?"

The new girl's face showed a pleasant smile, although she shot a quick wink at the Latina gang-follower.

"No... she's jus' some *mujer* who show up from I don' know where," said a perplexed Ramòn. "After I done with her I'm gonna find out how she get past our snipers. *Eso no debería suceder... ¿sabes?*"

"I... uhh... don' think *usted* should be surprised that she do that," offered Mireya. "Listen, lady... I think you should tell him who you is. *Por favor.*"

The new girl turned her head slightly, so as to look Ramòn in the face.

"My name on this world is, 'Karéin-Mayréij'," she said. "Though some call me, 'Storied Watcher'. I have other names as well... though these are in languages that you likely would not recognize."

"Oh... well, that's nice to know, lady," clumsily responded the gangster. "*Yo me llama* 'Ramòn'... but I guess you know that already. How you *know* that, anyway?"

"It is one of my arts," answered the new girl. "Akin to the Ways of Venom – and the Ways of Majesty, that now live and burn in your own heart... the final gift of our fallen brother Sebastiàn. And I have come to validate that these indeed *are* yours to use wisely, my brother; and to lend you whatever advice that you would have from me."

"Ramòn... you's el jéfe ahora... but with all due respect... you *still* don' get it, *hombre*?" persisted Mireya. "Don' you know who 'Karéin-Mayréij' is?"

"No," he said with a shrug and a faked smile. "What's a 'Karéin-Mayréij', anyways? 'Zat like some fancy *coche* or somethin'?"

He felt something moving on his left shoulder, and, suppressing an urge to swat, he caught a quick glance of the little bug, dancing up and down in an agitated manner and doing something reminiscent of rolling its tiny eyes.

"Ramòn," exclaimed one of the other Latina girls (a portly one with long black hair and a huge bust), "She's the fuckin' *alien*! You know... the one that put the top half of the Washington Monument, in the White House lawn, 'few weeks ago!"

He turned to stare at the new girl in disbelief.

"*Es esto cierto?*" he warily demanded of the Storied Watcher.

"Your sister Juanita exaggerates," cheerily remarked the alien-girl. "I only deposited the top *third* of that obelisk, into the President's fine flower-garden. I will admit that I was tempted to do the whole thing – that is, all the way to its base – but I was worried that it might tip over, and thus, ahh, squash the President and his fine palace, all together. It *does* weigh around ninety thousand of your 'tons', you know."

Ramòn shot a long glance at the Storied Watcher.

"*Ella?*" he taunted, with a contemptuous finger-point. "*¡No me digas basura!*"

With an insouciant, wan smile, the alien-girl extended her right hand, moved her fingers and hand upward as if motioning for someone to get up.

"Going up?" she teased.

Then she, Ramòn and the defunct car upon which they were sitting, began to levitate into the air. They were about six feet up when the panicking gangster began to shout, "*¡Bueno... bueno! ¡Suficiente! ¡Déjame no caer!*"

With an equally-puckish gesture, the Storied Watcher gradually lowered the car and its riders, back down to street-level.

Ramòn quickly jumped off the car-hood and danced off into the street. He turned to address the alien-girl.

"*¡Esto no puede ser cierto! ¿Quién esta usted?*" he exclaimed.

"I am Karéin-Mayréij, the Storied Watcher, the Guardian of Planet Earth," she replied, with a Stentorian, half-godly voice, albeit with an earnest, humble look on her face. "More than that... I hope to be your friend – and I would tutor you in the Ways of the Holy *Fire*... if you will have me."

The gangster just stood there, totally at a loss; although in a bizarre display, the shimmering-carapace little insect on his shoulder seemed to stand to attention on its hind legs, as if it actually understood what was being said. Finally he said,

"What you got to 'tutor' me, *mujer*... that I don't already know?"

"Well," calmly stated Karéin-Mayréij, "First – and foremost – I have a short pledge, that I would you like to repeat, after me."

Tell... And, Show

It was now four and a half days after the events in Los Angeles.

The cathedral-sized, semi-ornate House Judiciary Committee Meeting Room in the Sam Rayburn Building, in the now-mostly-cleaned-up environs of downtown Washington, D.C., was – of course – packed to overflowing, with government-types, media-representatives and elite spectators.

They had been waiting overlong, and the brutally-bright TV-lights positioned everywhere – in addition to making the room as well-lit as noontime on a cloudless day – were quickly overcoming even the best of underarm-deodorants and makeup-jobs.

Probably a full five to ten per cent of those inside, however they outwardly appeared to be otherwise, were – in fact – discreetly-positioned guardians of the U.S. state, answering either to the FBI, or the Secret Service, or the Congressional Police, or, to one of the less-well-known state intelligence agencies. But as far as could be determined, there were none from either GrayWar Corporation, or from the now-disgraced Central Intelligence Agency.

The President, and Jerry Kaysten, had made sure of *that*, at least; and ingress-screening for everyone within the room, had been carried to levels unusual even for D.C.'s paranoid traditions.

In addition to the standard metal-detectors, every person entering the building had been given a rather intrusive body-search (this had caused numerous "scenes" as prospective visitors objected) and personal implements such as mobile-communicators, makeup-kits, cuff-links and concealed-carry-guns, were impounded.

The over-sized, tastefully-decorated walls and improbably-high ceiling of this place, had seen many important government hearings, over the years; but *this* one... *this* one was special – *unprecedented*, even – and the atmosphere within, was electric.

The entire spectacle had even pre-empted the nightly schedule of fake-reality shows, celebrity-gossip revelations, fake-news infomercials and computer-generated "mud-gladiator"-contests.

The portly, late-fifties figure of an American politician – a Caucasian guy with a squat nose, a clean-shaven, jowly face and a stretched-tight business-suit, arose from his seat in the center of the rear echelon of raised seats, behind the continuous desks reserved for the political class.

He banged a small wooden mallet on the surface of his own desk.

"This joint meeting of the House and Senate Select Committees on Homeland Security, will come to order," announced the man. "I'm Senator Chambers – I'll be managing the proceedings today. Staff... you may show in our first guest."

A murmur of anticipation rustled through the audience as the large doors at the far end of the meeting-room opened. A second later, through the opening, strode the slim, poised figure of Minnie Chu. She wore an overall-black women's professional business-suit, with pressed slacks, a formal jacket kept closed at the front with a single button and a black dress-blouse underneath the jacket. She wore no tie.

A very perceptive observer would have noticed a gold-linked chain around her neck, leading down to *something* evidently suspended underneath the open part of her shirt, in between her breasts. This item – whatever it was – was not visible, though.

The *nouvelle* FBI-director – escorted by two hulking, dark-suited Congressional policemen – walked at a dignified pace between the right and left sides of public seating, until she had reached the witness-table positioned about thirty feet in front of the rows of politician-desks at the near-end of the meeting-room.

Staring directly forward at her interlocutors, Chu said,

"Good morning, Mr. Chairman... members of the Committee. My name is Minnie Chu, and – as you know – I have been nominated by the President to be the Director of the Federal Bureau of Investigation, in view of the former Director Cesar Ochoa's injuries recently sustained and his subsequent inability to resume his former duties. I'm sure that all of you join me in thanking Cesar for his years of service to our country, and in praying for his speedy recovery. Thank you for allowing me to attend this hearing, and, hopefully, to provide complete answers to any questions that you may have."

"We'll certainly have lots of those... *that's* for sure, Ms. Chu," evenly replied the Senator. "Will the staff please swear the witness in?"

Chu – still staring deliberately forward – raised her right hand, while her left one came to rest on a well-worn Bible.

The hearing had now been going on for a little more than an hour, with Minnie Chu patiently explaining, and re-explaining (and, re-re-explaining), her account of the events of the last few weeks.

"The chair recognizes the honorable gentleman from the State of Missouri," spoke Chambers.

"So, ma'am," demanded a taller, bushy-white-haired male Senator to the right of the Chairman, "Can we please go back to this party of your story, where you claim that one minute, you're on the President's Airborne Command-Post... and the next, you're sittin' on a beach outside Atlantic City?"

"Oh... *certainly*, Senator," amicably responded the nouvelle-Director.

"Now, Ms. Chu," cajoled the man, "That's a long way down... and I didn't hear *anythin'* about a 'parachute', anywhere. And even if you *did* use one – there's no *way* that you'd have gotten far enough away from the airplane, before the bomb went off. I guess what I'm sayin', ma'am, is... 'your story isn't even *remotely* credible'. I'd remind you that you're under oath, in this hearing. Are you *sure* you don't want to – ahem – *correct* anything that you've said, so far, today?"

"Not at *all*, sir," deflected the former team-leader. "I didn't use a parachute because I didn't *need* one."

There was a laugh from the audience as the Senator persisted with, "Oh... I see, ma'am... I *see*. So... what *did* you do? Just flap your wings... or somethin' like that?"

"Not exactly, sir," countered Chu. "I don't need to 'flap', *anything*, to be able to fly. Which is what I did, Senator. I simply *flew*, down and away from the aircraft, as fast as I could. My understanding is that this capability is actually enabled by 'bending gravity-waves' with the powers of my mind, although this assumption has yet to be validated by formal scientific analysis. By the way, in flying away from the aircraft, I was shortly thereafter joined by a close friend – she's also someone who came to know the Storied Watcher quite well – who happens to be in the audience, here today."

The public-access ranks broke out in stares and whispered-questions going back and forth, while Sylvia Abruzzio – who was parked in the front row of seats behind the witness-table – just serenely smiled.

"Is that right?" asked the bemused man. "Well... if that's the case... why don't you give us a demonstration, right here and now?"

"Senator," replied the ex-team-leader, "I don't think this is an appropriate venue for spectacle; furthermore, the President has asked me not to engage in unnecessary public performances of this type... and if it's of any interest, so has Karéin-Mayréij. Apparently, she feels that doing so is 'boastful'; what she told us is, 'you should only use the Holy *Fire*' – by the way, that's the energy-source that empowers abilities such as flying – 'if she is needed, to do something important'. So I would respectfully ask to decline this request."

"Well," chuckled the Senator, "I think this committee can thus infer how much weight to give your testimony today, Ms. Chu."

"That's your choice, sir," countered the *nouvelle* FBI-director. "But for the record – and not just because I'm under oath – I can assure you that everything that I will tell yourself, and other members of the committee, today, will be one hundred per cent true – to the extent that I understand it."

"Well, now, Ms. Chu," remarked the Senator, "What's *that* supposed to mean? The 'to the extent' part of it, I mean."

"What I mean, Senator," explained Chu, "Is that there are many aspects of recent events – including some of those involving me personally – that are as yet, poorly-understood... or not understood at all. Some of these, you will appreciate, I will not be able to speak about in a public session like this one, for reasons of not interfering with ongoing law enforcement or national-security procedures. Others – for example 'how does Minnie Chu manage to fly' – are things that we will only, hopefully, come to understand later, with the aid of science. Finally there are issues for which currently-available evidence is scarce or inadequate. For example, 'where, precisely, did the Storied Watcher come from – what was her pre-history – before she was awoken on Mars, by Commander Jacobson and his crew'. I say all this simply because I want to be honest with the committee about what kinds of questions that I can, and cannot, answer."

Chambers broke in, saying, "I would remind everyone here today, that the mandate of this committee – and therefore what is in scope for this discussion – is limited, purely and simply, to the following subject : 'who in Tarnation has been settin' off nuclear bombs over the United States... and how can we be sure, that there aren't any more of them on the way'."

"What I can tell you on *that* subject, sir," offered Chu, "Is that according to the best information currently available to both the Bureau and to the government's other sources of intelligence... we believe that there are no more bombs on the way. All outstanding weapons within our own arsenal are now accounted-for, and we have implemented further measures at the border – and beyond – to warn us, in the extremely unlikely event that there might be another attempt to smuggle a stolen, foreign-manufactured weapon into the country –"

"Just a *minute*, Madam Director," interrupted Chambers. "According to the Administration's own testimony, one such bomb *already* got through our defenses... and it just went off, next to Los Angeles. What makes you so sure that there isn't another one – or two, or three – on their way here, right now? How do you know that you're catchin' 'em all?"

"The ex-Pakistani weapon that was somehow smuggled in to the United States, Senator, had this done under unusual circumstances... namely, the military and our intelligence-agencies, were, at the time, still recovering from the after-effects of the 'Lucifer' comet," explained Chu. "Furthermore, the government was also engaged in an intensive search for Karéin-Mayréij, who – at the time, as I can personally attest, from being on Project 'Red Rover' – was considered to be at *least* as much a threat as was the bomb. This was a unique set of circumstances, which we believe are very unlikely to re-occur. We are therefore quite confident that we're safe from future attacks of this kind."

The other Senator (the white-haired guy) spoke up.

"So is that all you – and the President – got, to reassure the country with, Ms. Chu?" he challenged. "Not very 'reassurin', if you ask me. I'd say your chances of bein' right, are about the same as me callin' which fine new race-horse is gonna win the Triple Crown, next time. You got any cash you want to put up, on that? Or maybe you aren't so 'sure', after all?"

There was a wave of nervous laughter, including the other committee-members and some of the crowd, upon hearing this *bon mot*.

The former team-leader looked distressed for a half-second, but then she regained her composure and replied,

"Senator... there *is* one *other* thing, as well."

"And what would *that* be?" pressed the other Senator.

"I had hoped not to have to refer to this," disclosed Chu, "Because... well, what I'm about to say will be a little, uhh, *unusual*... and it will likely be difficult for you, and for others who are hearing this testimony, to understand or appreciate. None the less, in the interest of reassuring the people that the threat of further nuclear terrorism now *is* truly over with – at least, in the short to medium-term – I suppose I'll have to let everyone know about it, now."

"*Do* enlighten us, Madam Director," cajoled Chambers. "This had better be *good*."

"Oh-kay," answered Chu, in a hesitating voice. "You see... one of the special powers granted to me by the Storied Watcher, is a kind of 'precognition'... it warns me of danger, when it's imminent. Apparently it's based on metaphysical powers that not even Karéin-Mayréij herself fully understands or can control – but she has assured me that it has never failed her, over many centuries of use. Prior to the events of the past few weeks, this sense was going off *constantly*, to the point where it was almost driving me crazy. But now – when I call upon it – I see, and feel... *nothing*. It feels almost like a calm sea, like, 'you can relax now'. Of course, I won't – but I want everyone hearing this today, that the power of an angel is saying, 'don't worry... the threat has passed'. That's what I was referring to, Senator. For what it's worth."

"So... some voices in your head are tellin' you, 'everything's fine, just *fine*'... and *that's* what we should use as reassurance, that New York, Atlanta or Seattle won't get nuked, tomorrow, or next week... do I have that right, Ms. Chu?" taunted Chambers.

A frustrated Chu answered back, "It's because of this power – among other things – that I'm even alive to *speak* with you here today, Senator. It's what warned me that former Chief Spiritual Adviser, Harold Crowford, had smuggled another bomb, aboard the Airborne Command Post aircraft. And there's one more thing, as well."

"I'd like to get back to worthwhile testimony, based on halfway-credible evidence," complained Chambers, "But just for the sake of completeness... go ahead, Ms. Chu."

"The 'other thing', sir," stated the *nouvelle* director, "Is that Karéin obviously also has the same ability. I asked her to turn it on, to validate my own results... which she did. I know it may not be very convincing for you, Senator – but consider that this is just one extraordinary ability among *dozens* of others that the Storied Watcher has bestowed upon her friends, including of course myself. You have television-footage of the alien-powers of, for example, Commander Jacobson and his 'Mars Gang' – there's no reasonable doubt that these are very real... and very potent. Why should this one be thought of, differently?"

"I'd say that 'meltin' an army-tank in front of the cameras' – an act that's a felony, by the way, but that's another subject – is a mite different than impossible-to-verify claims of 'seein' the future'," observed the committee chairman. "And we obviously can't ask the alien to corroborate your testimony here today –"

His words were interrupted by a light, melodious (but loud and clear) voice that seemed to come from everywhere and nowhere, at the same time.

"But, sir– indeed you *can*... if only you would invite her!" it announced.

"Did *you* say that, Ms. Chu?" asked a perplexed Chambers.

A beaming Abruzzio stood up from her vantage-point in the audience.

Her smile was matched by an equivalent one appearing on Chu's face.

"No, Senator," she said.

Come To The Mountain; Fly From The Mountain

The President had expected Karéin-Mayréij to visit the White House immediately after her sensational, surprise appearance in front of the Congressional committee; but in fact, her second East Coast destination – after politely bowing to the hordes of reporters and other rapt onlookers in the Rayburn Building, and then simply disappearing, as if into thin air – was to the hideout on top of Cass Mountain.

She did not bother to suppress her war-song upon nearing the redoubt, and – after being met in mid-air by her adopted son – she landed in the middle of the throng, in the waning hours of daylight.

After explaining why she was so late in arriving, and after advising that Devon and Saquina White had elected to stay in Los Angeles for the time being, the Storied Watcher then turned her attentions to becoming acquainted – or re-acquainted – with friends and lovers, new and old.

The alien-girl was overjoyed to discover that her paramour, Donny Wade, was among those awaiting (Billings tried, but failed, to disguise his jealousy); and Karéin-Mayréij also provided warm welcomes and embraces to all the other newcomers, among these "Sammie", the mountain-man and members of the extended Boyd, Jacobson and Wade families. She made penance to the Texas farm family as well, apologizing profusely for the wrongs that they had suffered and vowing to bring justice for them.

To the Cassie Young's disbelief, the alien-girl's tears had fallen on the farm-woman's shoes. The gesture was gratefully accepted.

Most of these humans (particularly Marie and Callum Wade and the Youngs from the Texas farm, all of whom at first just stood and stared, until given unrequited hugs by an alien demi-goddess), and not a few of the post-humans, could hardly believe that they actually were in the intimidating presence of a being such as this. But after only a few hours of friendly interacting with the Storied Watcher – who tactfully lost at most of the board-games to which she was invited to play, and who volunteered to hand-wash a pile of dirty dishes – it was as if she were a long-lost, beloved family-member.

"It's like she doesn't care that I'm a hooker... go *figure*, for an 'angel'," Sammie breathed to Donny, who grinned broadly and replied, "Well, hon... let's just say, you ain't the *first* to make a few bucks by doin' what you're good at."

A thought, from "completely out of the blue", then invaded Sammie's mind.

As I reckon these things, new sister, it registered,
Between "hookers" and "angels", there is little difference... except for how many gold coins, each may demand for the use of their gentle arts.
Then she perceived,

And who knows... perhaps you will have something to teach me!
I am always ready and willing to learn, you know.
It took a lot to make Sammie blush... but this was, evidently, enough.

Finally it was bedtime for the younger ones, though getting them to settle down proved difficult, under the circumstances (it took a personal "kiss goodnight" and a hauntingly-beautiful lullaby by an alien demi-goddess – with a certain 'pledge' artfully worked into its lyrics – to get Boyd's excited son and youngest daughter, to close their eyes).

The Storied Watcher wiped away a tear.

"I have spent *far* too long away from Sayuri and Elissha," she quietly sighed, while looking down. "Each minute is one less that I will have, to feel the joy of their love. Soon... I must return to them... I *will*, return to them!"

After the challenging child-rearing task had been accomplished, Karéin-Mayréij ushered her adult followers (minus Wolf, who had insisted on staying with his fire-dogs in the lower-area, "just to avoid smokin' anybody out") into the upper-shack containing the kitchen and said to them,

"You told me that Cherie had induced this 'television' to function properly... correct?"

"Yeah," responded Hendricks. "Life-saver. Weren't national league games, but at least we got *some* football and basketball on it, while you were off doing your stuff, all over the place."

"Well... just think of all these 'sports' that you can watch, on the many tee-vee screens in the President's nice palace, when I invite you thither," answered the Storied Watcher.

"He *better*," joked the third agent, "We're running out of munchies here."

"Anyway," continued the alien-girl, "I would propose that we turn it on and see if we can, ahh, 'pick up the news for today'. I was able to grab only a few bits and pieces, as I flew back here from the western ocean coast; to really lock on to a good signal, I would have had to fly lower... and doing so degrades my speed. It is the air-friction, you know. I mean, the kind that occurs when one travels above three or four times the speed of sound. Much easier in the strat-oh-speare, or higher. You know?"

"Oh... for *sure*," offered Donny, with a bemused smile on his face. "I ain't no stranger to flyin' high... but I guess what with the 'booze and drugs are poison' thing, those days are over. *Damn!*"

"Personally... I try not to fly faster than about Mach 0.8," deadpanned Brent Boyd. "Going transonic, all that noise – pisses off the neighbors, every *time.*"

"That is good to know, Brent," patiently remarked Karéin-Mayréij, as she took a seat in the middle of the half-sized couch facing the television. "You *can*, however, go much faster – when time permits, I will teach you, Cherie and some of the others, how to do this safely."

"So far... I'm just levitating," Hendricks interjected.

"You too, brother Will," answered the Storied Watcher to her elated acolyte, "But one learns to walk, ere one learns to run. Is that not right?"

"I can't *believe* we're having this conversation," noted the third agent with a rueful head-shake. "A few months ago, I thought my job was 'filling out investigation forms for the Bureau'."

"Well now, son," chided Boatman, "You all certainly *can* go back to doin' that... should you so choose."

"Given events lately concerning dear Minn-ee's career," observed the Storied Watcher, "I would not be making too many plans about your own, if I were you."

Hendricks obtained the remote-control unit and powered up the television. After switching away from the peewee baseball-game that came up first, he was able to locate the local news-channel.

A neatly-dressed, male Caucasian reporter with dark hair, standing as near to the White House as the media were now allowed to get, announced, "Hello folks... I'm Bill Marco-Haig of WHSV-TV Disney News Harrisonburg, reporting to you about today's news in the United States and beyond."

"*This* should be interesting," remarked Sam Jacobson.

"Well, first of all, Fred," stated the reporter, "I think our viewers should know that events have been unfolding so quickly that many of us in the news business, have been having a hard time keeping up with it. What everyone's talking about today, of course, is the sensational testimony given yesterday to the Congressional Homeland Security Committee, not only by the President's nominee for the post of Director of the Federal Bureau of Investigation – that would be Ms. Minnie Chu –"

Hendricks and Boatman did a high-five. They would have done more of a war-whoop, but for being "shushed" by several others in the room.

"But," continued the reporter, "Also by the alien, 'Karéin-Mayréij', herself, who somehow managed to appear at Chu's side, as if out of thin air. This, of course, sent the entire hearing into immediate upheaval. Fred... can we roll footage, here? Wait... okay... we've got it. Here it is."

The screen now showed the slim, demure figure of the Storied Watcher, dressed in stylish, semi-formal clothing (although, still less than the professional standard bedecking Chu), standing beside her ex-human acolyte.

The alien-girl was holding up her left hand, as she said to Senator Chambers,

"Sir – I pledge fealty to no single God, lest in so doing, I slight the others; but if you will accept it... I will solemnly swear to tell the truth today, binding myself on the power and honor of my ancestors. Will that be enough, sir?"

"I guess it will *have* to be," grumbled Chambers, just before the scene shifted back to Marco-Haig in front of the camera.

Guffaws erupted throughout the moonshiners' cabin.

"After testifying for about two hours, with numerous impasses with the committee-members, who – as one of them later told us – felt that many of her answers were incomplete or evasive," said the reporter, "The alien announced that she had, in her own words, 'spent enough time accounting for my recent activities'; and then – as unexpectedly as she had appeared – Karéin-Mayréij again vanished into thin air. The committee has announced its intention to subpoena the alien for a follow-on appearance... but, of course, there seems to be no way to compel her to actually testify."

"Well... *duh*," commented Hendricks, while the reporter droned on.

"You going back there, honey?" inquired Billings, who was sitting next to his alien girlfriend, on the mini-couch.

"Not in the short term," she answered. "They were not very polite; they behaved as if I were some – uhh – 'fraudling', who had no choice but to abase herself in front of these high-and-mighty minor-nobles of the American empire –"

"But you do *not* have to do that," noted the Russian. "Nor do I. Of course, the leadership of this country, is notorious for refusing to acknowledge inconvenient facts such as this."

"You speak the truth, my brother," affirmed Karéin-Mayréij, with an affectionate glance in his direction. "But anyway, Bob... you and I need to return to the island, as soon as is practical. Much work there will be to do, when we arrive. We have stayed here over-long."

The ex-salesman stared forward and nodded.

"That's a *long* flight," he observed. "By the way... it's 'fraudster', not, 'fraudling'."

"Will you keep me company, my love?" she asked, with a friendly smile. "And thank you for the kind Eng-lish lesson."

"Sure... just don't *drop* me," requested Billings.

"You can fly on your own, you know," she teased.

"To *where*?" he prodded.

"South Africa?" cheerfully proposed one of the older Jacobson daughters. "They got lions down there. You could go see them, Mister Billings."

"Oh... *sure*, kid," complained the ex-salesman. "Either I get eaten right away... or I use Sari's hokey-pokey on them, and then get arrested for 'cruelty to animals'. And I never really liked cats, anyway. No thanks! I think I'll just wear my seat-belt, thank you."

"What is a 'ho-kee-po-kee'... oh, never mind... I believe that I understand," spoke the Storied Watcher. "Hold on... they now speak of other matters. Let us listen."

The scene on the television had returned to the TV-studio, revealing a table, around which were arranged four guests (all conservatively-dressed Caucasians, two middle-aged males and a post-fifties woman), plus 'Fred' the news-reader.

"So now, ladies and gentlemen, as promised, WHSV-TV Disney News brings you our Nightly Round Table, in which we give you the 'News Behind And Beyond The News'. I'm pleased to welcome our 'regulars', from your left to your right, Dale Manners of our Business Desk, Ellen Singleton of our Richmond State House Beat, and Jared Kotelniko of our National Bureau, to help us explain what's going on to all you folks out there, tonight. Welcome to you all."

There were perfunctory acknowledgments from the three others, and then the discussion began, with back-and-forth, woefully-under-informed opinions being sent back and forth about recent events.

As near as those in the moonshine-shack could determine, the U.S. Army had now re-taken effective control of most of central Los Angeles, and damage to that city's most important infrastructure – though still extensive – was now slowly being repaired.

Though she was trying to pay attention to the newscast, a puzzled look showed up on the Storied Watcher's face.

She said, out loud, "Do any of you have a mobile com-moon-ee-kaytor? For I hear one making its 'someone is calling', sound."

"No," claimed Sam Jacobson. "After some near-disasters with us being tracked down by the government, using the signals given off by these devices, I asked our group to throw ours away."

"Well... I am still hearing a ringing-tone," countered the alien-girl.

"I don't hear nothin'," commented Dorsie.

"Me neither," added Yvonne Jacobson.

"Her ears are – uhh – a bit better than yours, dear," mentioned her husband. "Listen, you guys... now that Karéin has clued me in to it... I think I hear it too... far-off... maybe downstairs? Dorsie – all of you – any of you have a mobile? If so, we had better –"

"After what these two city-slickers put me through, few day back," said the mountain-man, "I done lost my one. But maybe Ezra or Cooter got one stashed away somewhere –"

Tommy – dressed only in his pants, with no shirt – appeared in the passageway to the underground-levels. He was holding a small mobile communicator with a fold-out video-screen, which was repeatedly playing a ringing-tone consisting of the first few chords of some country-ballad.

"Mister Billings," said the boy, "Is this for you?"

"No," answered the ex-salesman. "I think it must be for Mister 'Deliverance' over here." He pointed at Dorsie.

Warily, the mountain-man advanced towards the boy, saying as he went, "Y'all must know... ain't no good thing to be takin' 'nother man's call on his 'phone... 'specially when whoever's on t'other end, 'spectin' to hear Ezra or Cooter talkin'... I'll do the best I can."

"Do not worry," reassured the alien-girl.

The moonshiner took the communicator and activated its "pick-up" function. He held the device close to his left ear.

He said, "Dorsie here... I'm kin to Cooter 'n Ezra. Who's this... what y'all want?"

A puzzled look appeared on Dorsie's face.

"Who the hell's *that?*" he challenged. "What business y'all got with my folk, city-boy? This-here's a *private* line! Well – I don't think they need no more guns – they got enough already –"

"Boy's talkin' *shit*," grumbled Dorsie. "I'm gonna hang up –"

"Don't you *dare!*" exclaimed Brent Boyd. "Commander, it must be one of those 'NRA' hackers! Dorsie – hand the phone over to Commander Jacobson, please!"

"Who? Y'all mean them folks who's always runnin' the gun-shows?" asked the perplexed moonshiner; although, he complied with the request.

Bob, sent the Storied Watcher, *I am confused... I thought the "NRA", were people who were enthusiastic about guns – like you told me in the hardware-store, way back in Tucson... are they not?*

Yeah, honey, he communicated, they were.

Not sure what's going on, here...

"I'm putting you on speaker," said the former Mars mission-leader, as he hit a button on the communicator's control-array.

Boyd sent to his alien mentor and her boyfriend,

The "NRA" being referred to here, Karéin, isn't the one that you're familiar with.

It's a group of hackers – that is, computer experts who break the laws, as an act of defiance against the government.

The information that they gave Commander Jacobson and the rest of us, as we traveled across the country after you dropped us off in Florida, was absolutely critical *to our survival.*

For example it allowed Cherie and Wolf to prevent the Commander's family from being kidnapped and tortured by the Agency... like they did to Bob, Tommy and Elissha.

They're a bunch of unkempt punks... but their hearts are in the right place.

In that case, came back a loud and clear psychic message,

Honor to them... they will belong with me and my family!

The sound came through loud and clear, but the video-display on the communicator, showed nothing but static.

"This is Commander Sam Jacobson of the Mars Gang, here," he announced. "Who am I speaking with? What is the reason for this call?"

"My handle's 'Tri-State Sore Loser', man," came a distorted-sounding voice, from the other end. "We got another data-dump to do for you dudes... but we gotta be quick about it, 'cause we had to demon-dial a lot of mobiles to lock into the one that's where we need it to be, the Man might read the pattern... we got maybe fifteen or twenty minutes, *max*. Ready?"

"Yeah," said Jacobson. "But this is a standard communicator – it doesn't have the modifications that you guys added to the ones that we were using, earlier. The signal will be wide open for the Feds... is that okay?"

"We got our best software-only crypto on this circuit, man," the hacker pointed out. "Downloaded before call set-up. Should be able to fox the backdoor-chips on the handset... but only for a short time. Which we're wasting as we speak. Can I go ahead?"

"Please do," assented the former Mars mission-leader.

An intensely-interested Storied Watcher had now arisen. She stood at Jacobson's side.

"Okay... so here it is," spoke the remote voice. "First of all... we'd like to say a big 'thank-you', to all you folks, for what you did, over the past few days. We tapped in to a lot of the comms-channels going on at the time, and we *know* how you, like, saved all our asses. Two – and then *three* – *H-bombs*, man! We're all just in *awe*... 'specially 'bout the alien... how she dragged that fucker offshore – we monitored DoD's trackers, and they couldn't *believe* how she –"

"Thank you, new friend," interrupted Karéin-Mayréij. "I have just heard of your own noble exploits in loyal support of Commander Sam and his company. I have duties to which I must attend... but when these are over, you and your fellow, uhh, 'hackers', are invited to the next family-meeting that we will all attend. I should like to meet you and give you a hug."

"Uhh... Jacobson, man... who *was* that?" stammered the hacker.

"I think you can guess her name," responded the ex-astronaut, with a smile.

"Was that... who I *think* it was?" the remote voice asked.

"I discern your title to be 'Sore Loser'," offered the alien-girl. "A fine name, and one that oft-times, I would have had applied to myself! But my title is, 'Storied Watcher, the Guardian of Earth', should you be in doubt. Please accept my love in the interim, until we shall meet as friends. In the meantime... I would not divert this conversation from what you had intended to tell Commander Jacobson."

"Holy... *wow*," gasped the hacker. "Uhh... okay, I guess, and it's great to talk with you, lady."

"Thank you," she said. "You can call me, 'Karéin', as friends do. But if our time is limited, then I would beg you to please continue, 'Sore Loser'."

"Yeah... right," he responded. "Okay... well... so here's the update. Since we last got in touch with Jacobson and his team, we were trying to keep track of what was goin' on, we had cashed in all our cookies for gettin' inside circuits inside the Executive Branch and the Pentagon... but it was *hard*, man – stuff was goin' down, like, too fast... and it was impossible to figure out what was what... you know? 'Specially just before the two bombs went off, over the East Coast –"

"That is not a surprise," interjected the Storied Watcher. "These events all occurred over a very short period of time... there was not much time for decision-making. Tell me, though – I am intrigued – you say that you had 'inside circuits', during this period? Does that mean you were listening to what transpired between me, my family and the President, in yonder white palace?"

"What?" the confused hacker replied. "Oh, no, lady... I mean, 'Karéin'... nothin' quite that, uhh, 'privileged'... they got all of that on private, segregated channels, you need physical access to tap 'em, and that's a good way to get shot at the best of times – not to mention what we saw goin' down at the White House, recently – so we just do logical access stuff. Closest we got were some circuits goin' up to that plane that, who was it, uhh, that Chinese lady –"

"She is '*Vìrya* Minnie Chu'... a mighty hero of the Holy *Fire*, and a dear friend of mine," mentioned Karéin-Mayréij.

"What kind of information were you able to capture, from that plane?" inquired Brent Boyd.

He muttered to his former Mars mission commander,

"Hackers inside the network of the Airborne Command Post... wait till Mr. President gets a whiff of *this*."

Jacobson chuckled maliciously.

"We got mostly voice-recordings, goin' back a couple of days, from all over that crate," said the hacker. "Not much use, of course, since we got no idea who's speakin', most of the time. Oh... and we got a few still pictures from some of the internal security-cameras... that's about all of it."

"Hey... do me a *favor*, would you?" demanded Hendricks. "Whatever you do... don't lose those tapes. Of what went on in the 'plane, I mean."

"Who's that talkin'?" asked 'Tri-State Sore Loser'.

"Just a normal FBI dweeb who works for Minnie Chu, now and then," smartly replied the third agent.

"Jacobson – what the hell's goin' *on* down there, man?" exclaimed the alarmed hacker's voice. "You brought LEA along with you? You want to get me fuckin' *killed* –"

"Relax!" cajoled the former Mars mission commander, "Will Hendricks – the guy who just addressed you – absolutely *is* with the Bureau, as is his fellow-agent, Otis Boatman, and both of them are here listening to you now; but they aren't going to turn you in; and even if they, or Minnie – who, by the way, is now the Director of the FBI – tried to do that... well, I'm sure that there would be quite a lively discussion down here about it. Am I right, Karéin?"

"Definitely so," confirmed the alien-girl. "'Sore Loser', you have to understand that my company includes many who are from very different walks of life. But we defend each other against perils of all kinds. If Minn-ee were to prosecute you as part of her job... I would keep you safe. I doubt that it would ever come to that, however. Have no fear of us... of any of us!"

"Yeah," added Hendricks, "And if a guarantee from the most powerful being on the *planet* isn't enough for you – let me explain why I want those tapes : specifically, because Otis and I got our asses thrown off that plane at thirty thousand feet, 'parachutes not included'. Don't ask me *how* we survived, but we did. *Somebody* ordered that, and we'd love to find out who... so, if they're still alive – which frankly I doubt, but anyway – we can track them down and fuck 'em over. And I can tell you, Otis 'n me, we aren't the *only* ones out of Angel Lady's little entourage, who got a score to settle with people in the government... even though, technically, I guess we're part of it. This makin' any sense to you?"

"Think so, man," said the remote voice. "Listen, Karéin... if what he's sayin's true... what you gonna do about us 'NRA' folk? A whole *lot* of us have ended up in the Man's jails... or worse. Where's 'justice', for *us*?"

All in the shack – and, in fact, even, somehow, the hacker – heard the subtle, but portentous, chords of the Storied Watcher's war-song; though only those local to her, could see the determined light, burning suddenly in her eyes.

"Where is 'justice', my friend?" she answered. "I will *tell* you. Justice is coming, "Sore Loser'... it is *coming!* For you, for your fellow techno-warriors, and for all those who languish undeserving in these dungeons, that the American President claims to be 'ignorant' of. Very soon, he will have no choice, but to confront and acknowledge what is going on, below his very nose. I began this process when last we met him, in his fine white abode; but it is not finished, by any means. I can only ask you and your comrades to wait just a little longer... and to make common cause with me and those who call me, 'friend'. Will you do this?"

"Lady... those are the best words I've heard in the last fifteen years," said the hacker. "That's a 'yes', by the way."

"This is all great stuff," noted Jacobson, "But we're burning through our available air-time... we had better get back on track, if we're to get any 'net new' information."

"Yeah," acknowledged the hacker. "Listen... I got an idea. That handset of yours, has it got one of those 'receive file directly' buttons?"

The former Mars mission commander quickly reviewed the hand-set's controls, and replied, "Yes... I see it. Go ahead."

"Okay... hold on, just a sec... here goes," said the remote voice. "I'm sendin' an encrypted archive – password's 'MarsGang456AndKarein8910', by the way, no accent on the 'e' dudes – and there's another key on it, that's your voice Jacobson, so only you can unlock it... it's got a summary of what we've intercepted over the past week or so. Do us a favor and transcribe what's on the file to paper or something, then smash the phone so it can't be put back together... can't be too careful, you know."

"I see an indicator... hitting the 'receive' button... yeah, it seems to be coming down the pipe, we're about at ten per cent so far," observed Jacobson. "We'll follow your instructions. While this is being transmitted, is there anything very significant, that we should know about, first?"

"Well... where do I *start*, man," answered the hacker. "Okay... so here's the 'Top Three'. First, we intercepted some strange-looking command-sequences to, like, some Air Force plane, just before the second nuke got fired at Karéin. We couldn't fully decrypt the stream, but there was stuff in it that looked *scary*, like 'enable warhead' kind of shit, I mean. And what was even more weird, was it wasn't coming from anywhere in the Pentagon – when we compared the triangulation for it with GPS, it was coming from a part of the Rocky Mountains that's, like, fifty *miles* from the nearest road or airport. We looked at the overheads for that area and there's nothing except a big-ass mountain and trees 'n such. Can't figure that one out at *all*, man."

"Is the data related to this in the archive?" inquired Brent Boyd.

"Yes, it is," confirmed 'Tri-State Sore Loser'.

"That will be interesting, indeed," offered the Russian.

"Go on," requested Sam Jacobson.

"So Number Two would be," continued the hacker, "For you guys from the Bureau... did you hear there was a big terrorist bombing there, the other day?"

"We've been, uhh, kind of busy," grunted Boatman. "What *happened?*"

"Oh, well, sorry to have to break it to you like this," said the remote voice, "But the FBI HQ in Chicago, it, like, got *totaled* – ugly scene, man, like, half the building just *gone*, if you know what I mean... but anyway, what we thought interesting about the voice- and video-traffic goin' down right afterwards was, there was a shooting-incident outside what was left of the building, and, well, at first we thought it was the 'Mars Gang' that must have been behind the whole thing, 'cause –"

"That's completely *impossible!*" argued Jacobson. "We never got anywhere *near* Chicago. The furthest north we ever went was Missouri, or, I suppose, Kentucky, when we – ahem – visited Fort Knox. Whoever was responsible for the attack on the FBI buildings that you describe... it wasn't, 'us'."

"Well then how you explain the transcripts we got about 'a female terrorist, and her two male accomplices, firin' a death-ray at our security-guards, dude?" countered the hacker. "There's a pretty vivid description of what went down there, and it sure *looks* like one of you 'super-people' was involved, you know."

"Listen, Angel Lady," asked Boatman in the direction of the Storied Watcher, "*Please* tell me, 'that wasn't you'. I knew a lot of the people in that building. Most of 'em are decent Bureau staff, just tryin' to keep the gang-bangers and other low-lifes from runnin' the country into the ground. *Please tell me, 'it ain't so'."*

His gaze was sad and accusatory.

"Brother," spoke the alien-girl, "I *did* hear a brief account of this event, from Minn-ee, when we were all back in the House of White... but will you accept my word, that neither I – nor any of those who have lately returned with me, to this empire – were in any way involved with the tragedy that our friend 'Sore Loser', has told us of? I testify that I never visited this 'Chicago' city; my travels through the United States were all to destinations far away from this. And I was far too, ahh, 'busy', to make side-trips. I, too, lament the loss of life among your friends. But it was not me, or my fellow-travelers, who were responsible for this."

"Well then, Karéin," challenged Hendricks, "If it wasn't you – and it wasn't any of us – and it wasn't Sam's merry gang of thieves... then, who the hell *was* it? Or do we have, like, 'super-human terrorists' just showing up out of the woodwork, for no reason at all?"

"I honestly do not know, brother," pleaded Karéin-Mayréij. "We should set ourselves to finding out the truth of this. I have my suspicions... but I would prefer to keep this to myself, until there is more evidence. I would ask our 'Sore Loser' friend – brother, did your spy-information say where these 'super-humans' from the attack, went, afterwards?"

"Sorry," came the remote voice, "What we got, says that they got away in the confusion; after they zapped a bunch of guards, nobody wanted to chase 'em, I guess. That's all we got."

"I... *see*," reflectively answered the Storied Watcher. "Well, thank you."

"No problemo," said the hacker. "Listen... we're almost at the end of our window, so here's Number Three – and it ain't too good, I'm afraid. Remember that location in the Rockies, where we got the stream goin' to the bomber-plane, from?"

"Yeah, we got that down... I've been taking notes," said Brent Boyd.

"Well," mentioned 'Tri-State Sore Loser', "We also got some other signals from that originating-point, and they were easier to decrypt... probably, a weaker key, or something. Anyway, there's a couple of fairly long transmissions that contain some bad, *bad* stuff, man. Details are in the file, but there's language like, 'have you disposed of the body of the Mars Gang hostage yet' and 'no copies to be made of video of last session with her, it will stay in my personal possession'. There's a lot of bitchin' in the records, stuff like 'the subject was *known* to be elderly and infirm, there'll be consequences for coercive interrogation pushing her over the limit', and so on. There's also shit suggestin' that the Man is still doin' the full-court press for other relatives, for them to grab as bargainin'-chips. If I were you folks... I'd keep a low profile, you know?"

Quietly, Jacobson asked, "Do you have anything that... *identifies*, who – what victim, that is – that they were talking about? Or, who was responsible for what was being said?"

"'Fraid not, man," disclosed the hacker, "'Cept that there's auth-codes in the stream that look 'military' to us... or maybe it could be someone else, like the Agency, or maybe one of those 'black' spook-shops. They sort of look familiar, but we're not finished with our forensics on 'em. I hate to ask this of you all, but... you missin' any family-members, down there, man?"

A pall of dread descended over the atmosphere in the shack.

"No," responded the former Mars mission commander, his voice sounding hollow and anguished, "Not among us, here... but it wasn't for lack of *trying*, on the part of the government. It came down to *minutes*, between my family – and Major Boyd's – being safe, or being subjected to the same bestial treatment we witnessed up on Amchitka. Thank you again for the tip-off that allowed us to rescue them."

"'Least we could *do*, man," said 'Tri-State Sore Loser'. "Folks... I'd love to chat more, but we're runnin' the real risk of the Man tappin' our link. I got to bail... that okay?"

"Of course," said the Storied Watcher. "Thank you for giving us these insights, friend. We will not forget the bravery that you and your associates have showed, in all of this. You are now within the Company of the New People. It is a position of honor... be proud of that."

"Sure will, lady – been *amazin'*, talkin' with you," said the hacker. "Hope to do it again, soon. Tri-State Sore Loser, out."

The signal dropped.

"Commander," postulated Boyd, "You *do* know – I'd assume – who the most likely victim is, that this data refers to... do you not?"

"God help me... I sure *do*," confirmed Jacobson, his voice breaking. "The question is... what do we do, now? Do we tell her, without knowing for sure?"

"You refer to the mother of 'First-Of-The-Fire'... do you not?" quietly asked the Storied Watcher. "For Cherie warned of this, in our recent visit to the President's palace. Is there any chance that this terrible counsel, is mistaken?"

"Your assumption is correct, Karéin," stiffly replied Jacobson. "And, given what we've so far heard... I'd think that the chances of us being wrong about this, are remote."

"Yeah," said a stone-faced Hendricks, "And – I mean – suppose you *are* wrong. It still means the Agency – or whoever – tortured some other poor old lady, to death – same diff... they deserve to *die* for that. *Fuck* 'em, anyway!"

Karéin-Mayréij hung her head.

Tears were in her eyes as she softly cried,

"Yet *again*, do I fail in my duty! How shall I *explain* this, to our noble sister?"

Billings gave her a warm embrace.

"Don't blame yourself, Sari," he comforted. "You did what you thought you had to do, with the information you had, at the time; and you saved *millions* of people, by doing it. That's all that any of us can do."

He looked up at Jacobson.

"When Tanaka tracks down whoever's responsible for this," hissed the ex-salesman, "I want to be there. I don't care what the fucking President – or Minnie – says... this one's gonna get done, nice and *slow* – you understand?"

"I doubt you'll get the chance, Bob," evenly interjected Brent Boyd. "Unless you think you can send nightmares into a smoking pile of ash."

"Yeah, well," growled Billings, "Just let me watch... I'll count it as a 'win'."

Tommy – who had also joined the Storied Watcher's side – showed a familiar scowl and red-eyed demeanor of incandescent, grinding hatred.

"Mom," he demanded of the alien-girl, "Does this mean that the same people who did all that stuff to us down in the deep hole... they *killed* Miz Cherie's *mother*?"

"My soul weeps to say this, dear son," answered Karéin-Mayréij, "But I fear that your apprehensions are correct."

"*This* time – when we find who did it – I'm *not* holding back!" spat the boy. "I didn't fire again at the President, because I was afraid of hurting *you*, Mom. Will you stand back when we catch the bad guy who's behind this?"

With a sad, deflated look on her face, the Storied Watcher replied, "Tommy... I will not restrain you, nor Bob... nor *Vîrya* Cherie. The basest of wrongs, can only be avenged, in a certain, terrible manner. But before the miscreant responsible for this suffers the miserable death that he or she truly deserves... let us question him, or her. Else we will be wondering about the background of this cruel conspiracy, for years to come. Before we put an end to it – we must know the *extent* of it. Do any of you disagree?"

"No," answered several in the room.

"But no mercy, *this* time!" demanded a visibly-angry Brent Boyd. "Even if it turns out to be the *President*, who was behind it. I'll fucking *do* him in front of his wife and kids, if necessary! If that means I take my chances with Jerry, Minnie or Sylvia... so *be* it. I *owe* it to Cherie!"

By now, Wolf had returned from the lower levels.

"I *heard* that, pardner," he remarked, "'Spose you won't mind, if I tag along for the ride? I might even let Miz Thunder-Thighs get the first shot in, before I whip up that lil' ol' 'smokin' hole in the ground', thing."

"You'll get no push-back from *this* side," agreed Boyd. "Assuming, of course, that it really *was* the President."

"Nor from me," ominously added Sam Jacobson. "I never *trusted* that son of a bitch, anyway. Nor his weak excuses of, 'oh, poor little old me, I had no idea what they were doing in my name'. He had better hope that the trail doesn't lead to *his* doorstep!"

The former Mars mission leader turned to address Hendricks and Boatman.

"Any objections, gentlemen?" he asked.

"One condition," countered the third agent.

"What?" replied Jacobson.

"You help us do the same, to whoever threw us out of that plane," requested Hendricks. "My loyalty is to the Bureau and the Constitution... but I've seen enough. Need to do some *house-cleaning*, man. If that means I have to hand over my badge... I'm good with it."

"Deal," said Jacobson.

"Deal," echoed Boatman. "Commander – the only other thing is, take us with you, if you're gonna run up against Minnie. We'll run interference with her... okay?"

"Agreed," confirmed Jacobson.

"So now there's a big issue – namely, 'how do we communicate all of this, to Cherie'", observed Brent Boyd. "It would be *highly* inadvisable for us to do this over any communications-network... the government would certainly have all inbound transmissions to Cherie or the others who stayed back in the White House, tapped –"

"If they didn't *already* do that, to your hacker-friend there," noted Billings.

"Chance we'll have to take," opined Jacobson. "But Brent's *right* – we don't want to disclose that we have these 'NRA' guys working on our side, if we don't absolutely have to. Unless any of you can think of a better idea, I guess that means we should just call her up and ask her to fly back here, ASAP."

"The only other practical way would be to fly back ourselves," proposed Misha, "With yourself – and anyone else who wished to accompany you – in the *Express*, Commander. But that might itself cause problems, especially if the, ahh, 'welcome' were to be similar to the one that you first encountered."

"Or maybe just one of you could – uhh, I can't believe I'm hearing myself *say* this, but anyway – *fly* there, to deliver the bad news, in person," advocated the heretofore-silent, Laura Boyd. "God – what they did to her mother... that could have been *me* – or one of our *kids!* It's *sickening!*"

"Yeah... you know, that makes sense," agreed Brent Boyd as he embraced his wife. "We couldn't deliver the news in the White House, of course – that place is bugged fifteen ways to Sunday, and even anywhere in downtown D.C. might still not be safe – but the messenger could take Cherie somewhere more private, say some park in Waldorf or Manassas, or just out in the countryside somewhere... and let her know what we've found out, there."

"Any volunteers?" spoke Jacobson. "I could do it... but I think 'jumping all the way from here, to D.C.', might not be a great idea. As much as it's my duty, considering that Cherie reported to me, when all this started."

"That leaves me, Misha, Wolf and Karéin," commented Brent Boyd. "Plus – theoretically – Bob and Tommy –"

"Count me out," interrupted Billings. "I *hate* flying... or, at least, 'looking down, when I'm flying'. And I'm not very good at it, anyway. So, 'sorry'."

"Understood," acknowledged the former Mars mission pilot.

"Tommy," said Sam Jacobson, "I hope you won't mind, if we drop you from the list? I don't think this is the kind of thing for a boy – no slight meant, son."

Tommy crossed his arms and pouted, *sotto voce,* "*Why?* I can fly just as well as *they* can – and if the President gets in my way –"

"Son... do you remember what I told you, many days and nights ago, when we were all in Bob's automobile?" cajoled the Storied Watcher. "About how killing, leaves an indelible stain on one's soul?"

"Yeah," grudgingly admitted the boy.

"Sit this one out, kid," recommended Billings. "Something tells me, you'll get another chance... another shot. The bastard promised to play nice, from now on. What makes me think that 'old habits die hard'? He'll try this 'Gestapo' BS again. And when he *does*..."

"I hope you're wrong," opined Boatman. "But I wouldn't bet against it."

"Karéin," said Sam Jacobson, "Considering everything that's happened so far... I suppose we should give you right of first refusal. Do you want to fly to D.C. and inform Cherie?"

"Ordinarily I would do so," responded the alien-girl, "But with each hour that I further delay, the situation on yonder southern-ocean island redoubt, likely grows more strained... perhaps, more desperate. Ere the night is out, I simply *must* away, with the *Mailànkh Express* under tow; and mark you, we may then have many more to protect in these parts, since those who are now in the fortress, will probably have had their fill of residing there. We should make plans for this. I will ask those on the southern island where they want me to take them – but if there will be no agreement, we will come back to this mountain-top; and please tell the President to refrain from any military-tricks in the vicinity... or *else!* Can whomever travels to this empire's capital, so inform him?"

"Sure... but do you have any idea when you'll be back?" asked the former Mars mission commander.

"I honestly do not know, because that depends on what our brothers under the frozen island will decide," evaded the Storied Watcher, "But... if I were to guess... one week, perhaps less. I will do more of the trip this time, in the upper strat-oh-speare than beforehand, to preserve speed, although I will still maneuver to avoid tracking and interception. Thus it will be faster to travel there and back. It could be as little as two days. Brother Dorsie – would you mind remaining here and informing your kin, 'Ezra' and 'Cooter' I believe their names to be, correct? – that more of our friends may soon be coming hither? I would not want to, ahh, 'drop in', uninvited."

The mountain-man – at a loss about how to address as powerful a being as Karéin-Mayréij – managed, "Might take some fast-talkin', ma'am... but I reckon I can convince 'em. 'Long as they's shore y'all ain't no LEA or nothin' like that. An' by the way... what's in it fer *them*? If'n y'all don't mind me askin'?"

"Well... in our team, we *do* have people who can make gold, out of common stones," offered the alien-girl, with a insouciant expression and a shrug. "I *could* put in a good word with them, on behalf of your kinfolk."

"There's that... and the fact that she and some of the rest of 'em, almost *vaporized* the White House, last time they visited it," noted Brent Boyd. "That count enough as 'not LEA', for you?"

"Hallelujah!" wearily interjected Hendricks, rolling his eyes as he spoke. "Neither am I... 'cept my boss is now the Director of the Bureau, and I'm hangin' fine with a bunch of guys whose last trip to D.C. was meant to off the *President*. Not that 'bein' LEA' should color my judgment about the whole thing... right?"

Tommy, among others, found these comments to be most amusing.

"'Spose so," grunted Dorsie in Boyd's direction.

"Okay," stepped in Jacobson, "Now we've got *that* figured out... we should decide who's going to D.C.. Bob and Tommy are 'out', so that leaves Brent, Misha and Wolf. Any volunteers?"

"Why don't we *all* go?" proposed the bounty-hunter. "I mean... in different ways, most of us owe Cherie. At least, we all been ridin' *with* her. This *is* shitty news we're deliverin', after all. Might help to have more than one person as support for her."

"Brother Wolf," observed the Storied Watcher, with a smile, "Surely do you reveal that you have a gentle side. As always, I knew that was within you."

"Shh! Don't *tell* nobody... ruin my style," quipped the fire-master.

There was momentary silence, and then Boyd said,

"I'm up for it... on the one condition that we deliver the news, comfort Cherie as much as we can on-site, and then head back here. Until we're completely sure of the President's intentions and there's a track-record attesting to them, I'm not comfortable leaving my family for extended periods of time."

"I think they'll be adequately-protected," claimed Sam Jacobson. "Between myself, Will, Otis, Bob and, yes, Tommy – I have little doubt that anyone who tries anything funny against this hideout, will find out why *not* to."

"*Yeaahhh!*" growled the boy, in characteristic, menacing fashion.

"You're not going back to Bouvet, Bob?" asked Brent Boyd.

"Hadn't *planned* to," stated the ex-salesman. "Hugo's probably already royally pissed. I want him to unload on *her*... not me. Sorry, honey."

"I love *you* too, brave companion," sarcastically responded the alien-girl.

"So *that's* figured out... but what if Cherie wants to go off and disintegrate whoever's behind this shit, Mister Space Man?" mentioned Wolf. "I can *tell* you... she'll have yours truly, taggin' on behind. If she misses anything that'll burn... well, *you* know."

They caught a glimpse of an ominous red glow in his eyes.

"I doubt that she will know precisely where those responsible are located," countered Misha. "I will go along – if only to remind her of this. As much as I would like to see Professor Tanaka and my big friend here put a swift end to whomever killed her mother... indiscriminate attacks on targets that may or may not be involved, will make a bad situation much worse. As I recall, Karéin, that Wolf and I mentioned to someone else, some time back."

The alien-girl nodded affirmatively, but silently.

She stood up and turned to face the rest of the crowd.

"Much has now been decided, and we should prepare for these portentous voyages," declared Karéin-Mayréij. "I will check the *Mailànkh Express* to validate that she is still fit for the long trip that awaits us... I will make any necessary repairs. If any of you wish to come along, just to see what our southern redoubt looks like, just come up to me and ask... although, there is only space for one or two, given how many may want to step aboard for the return from Bouvet."

"Got it," said Jacobson. "I'd really like to see what you did down there... but I'll have to pass this time, unfortunately."

"It's a nice place to visit... like, a cozy little cave, if your name is 'Godzilla'," joked Billings. "However, it's a bit off the beaten track... you aren't going to get a pizza delivered there."

"I can stop off in that 'Rio' city, and acquire some more building-materials," half-seriously suggested the Storied Watcher. "A nice little, ahh, how does one say it... 'home-ren-oh'."

"Maybe next time, honey," deflected the ex-salesman. "You'd need every wall-fixture and carpet in Brazil... maybe, in South America."

"In the meantime," continued Karéin-Mayréij, "I would recommend that the three who will speak with our sister Cherie, should agree upon language to comfort, as well as to inform. Please tell her that my heart cries along with her own... and that we will be back soon. And if you have the chance, please tell the President that this is a *test*, of whether he will be on the side of justice... or if he will retrench into his old, disreputable ways. In the latter case, he will rue the day when will I return. Will you tell him this?"

"You can be *sure* of it," pledged Brent Boyd. "I'll deliver it in no uncertain terms!"

"But do not harm his children," warned the Storied Watcher. "They are of *us*, now; and they are not bound to the cruelty of his regime. They need to choose the Light over the Darkness... but they must make this choice, of their own free will. Do you understand?"

"Definitely," responded the Russian.

"Whatever Cherie wants to do... I'll do," said a stone-faced Wolf.

"I hear and honor your loyalty to your sister, my brother," said Karéin-Mayréij, "But of tests and quests there are lately many... and not all, to heads of state. Let us all consider what we may do, as future history-writers would record it. Let us not fail in the light of hindsight."

Wisely, none argued with her.

The Storied Watcher clasped her hands in front of her, did a slight bow and walked toward the shack-door leading to the outside, where the air-ship had come to rest.

"Wolf... Misha... you want to join me over at the table?" asked Brent Boyd. "You too, Commander... Donny, Otis and Will, if you want to participate. Grab a notepad and pen and we'll try to agree on what to say to Cherie."

"'Long as it has, 'the fucker *dies'* in it... I'm good with almost *anything*," remarked the former bounty-hunter, as he proceeded across the room.

"Problem is," noted Hendricks, as he pulled up a chair, "We don't know *who* the fucker is... or *where* he's at."

"You think Minnie does?" inquired Sam Jacobson.

"Well, if she doesn't," mentioned Boatman, "I'd bet you good money that she's lookin' pretty hard."

"She said as much in the first press-conference," Brent Boyd pointed out. "What we *don't* know, is if she has made any progress."

"Miz FBI had better," growled Wolf. "Because I reckon when she gets the news, Lady Thunder-Thighs gonna start with meltin' that mountain them 'NRA' guys were talkin' about... and work out from there. And she'll have some *help!*"

"From all of us, Wolf," argued Sam Jacobson. "Let's get this figured out. What do you think we should put first?"

Cassie Young from the ill-fated Texas farm, called out to all of them.

"You might start, Mister Rocket Man," she said, "With... 'sorry'."

Dropped In For A Quick Chat With Cherie

The three – with Boyd in the lead, and Misha and Wolf covering the flanks to former Mars mission pilot's left and right respectively – were now nearing the White House. They flew to the north-east at a speed in the low hundreds of miles per hour through the darkening East Coast skies, which were lit up by the ex-bounty-hunter's flame-trail and by Boyd's own, repressed brilliance, on top of three intertwined, background-theme war-songs.

The low-altitude trip had not been a long one, even allowing for careful maneuvering and brief altitude-climbing to avoid terrain-obstacles – such as high-tension wires and smokestacks – along the way.

All three of the travelers said inward "thanks" to the Storied Watcher, for having bestowed enhanced visual acuity, particularly the heat-seeing and the star-seeing senses.

This terrain-following would *be nerve-wracking, without the infra-red sight... and the ability to notice energy-signatures,* Boyd reminded himself.

Not quite like broad daylight – but the next best thing. Takes a bit of practice to train oneself to judge the real size and distance of something that looks "bright" because it's hot... but easy to do, once you get the hang of it.

What the Air Force wouldn't give, to have IR-goggles like these eyes she's put in my head!

Which is damn good... since otherwise, I'd have an excellent chance of flying into a power-line, a water-tower, a building... or just the side of a hill.

By the time that they flew over the Arlington Memorial Bridge (Boyd looked to his left and saluted as he passed by the Vietnam Veteran's Wall) and the Lincoln Memorial, the local air-defense alarms were in full hue-and-cry.

However – as they approached the White House itself, coming in for a smooth landing on the South Lawn Road, just to the east of the Eisenhower Building – this time, the three "more-than-humans" were met neither by a barrage of missiles, nor by machine-gun-fire. Instead, all that occurred was the appearance, as if from nowhere, of about five stone-faced, black-business-suited Secret Service agents, with the obligatory guns drawn.

"You're *trespassing!*" shouted one of the agents. "Hands up!"

Boyd allowed his glow to increase just enough to clearly illuminate everyone and everything within about thirty feet, but not so much as to dazzle or provoke the guards.

He did not, however, raise his arms.

"Hi fellows," he tried to start off with. "You probably don't need much of an introduction, if you've been reading your briefings. My name's Brent Boyd, of the 'Mars Gang', and my two friends here are 'Wolf', and Mikhail Grishin. We assume you know that you can't hurt us with those guns, but that any *one* of us can vaporize *all* of you, with just a hand-gesture. But look – we don't want any trouble, anyway... we're just here to deliver a message, and then be on our way. You understand?"

"Don't move a *muscle,* unless you want to get *shot!*" warned the in-charge, leading Service agent.

"Oh... by all means," amicably replied Boyd. "Guys... you heard what the man said. Let's give him some time, okay?"

"Fine by me," grunted a crimson-eyed Wolf, "Hope they know... they ain't the *only* ones with an itchy trigger-finger."

"Ah, but my friend," mused the Russian with a wry smile, "I cannot help but reflect that we are a long way from that jail-cell, back in Tucson. To abuse an American saying... the shoe of power, is now on the other foot... is it not?"

The grin proved infectious; it reappeared on the bounty-hunter's face.

"Yeah... s'pose you're right about that, pardner," ruefully allowed Wolf. "It's almost as good to have the gun in your hand and decide not to pull the trigger... *almost*."

The leading Secret Service agent was still muttering commands into his wrist-communicator when – in the blink of an eye – Jerry Kaysten's familiar figure appeared by his side.

"Service guys... you can stand down," he directed. "Hi there, Major Boyd... Misha... Wolf. What brings the three of you here, today? The Old Man's already turned in for the night. A bit early, I know... but he's had kind of a stressful week, if you know what I mean."

"Good to see you, Jerry," replied Boyd, who was mildly gratified to notice the Secret Service agents holstering their side-arms. "Actually, no... we don't want to bother the President. We're here to talk privately with Cherie Tanaka. Could you ask her to come out here, please?"

"No funny-business?" guardedly inquired the Chief of Staff. "You've got an *arrangement* with the government – the President, I mean – remember?"

"Oh... nothing like that," answered the former Mars mission pilot, "We just want to talk with her, off-site, for a few minutes. After that she'll either come back with us to that mountain that our families are parked on, or she'll come back to the White House. We're just giving her an update... that's all."

"Anything you can't tell me?" pressed Kaysten.

"We'd prefer just to tell Cherie," said Boyd, "And let her decide what she does with the information, past this point."

"Come on, Jerry... don't be an ass!" unhelpfully interjected Wolf. "There ain't nothin' fancy in all this... we just gotta *tell* her something. Then we're off. That's it."

Kaysten's brow furrowed, and it was obvious that he suspected something, but all he said was, "Okay, then". They caught a half-second's worth of his war-song, and then he rocketed back inside the White House.

For the next two minutes, apart from lame attempts to strike up a little light conversation with the very taciturn Secret Service agents, the three more-than-human men and their law enforcement minders, just stood in place.

Then Cherie Tanaka – dressed in an attractive, expensive-looking exercise-suit with matching canvas leisure-shoes – came walking at a measured pace towards them.

Kaysten appeared immediately behind her, but he rapidly caught up to come alongside.

"Hey, Brent... Wolf... Misha," she greeted, upon approaching within about ten feet. "Come to cash in those chits for an exciting overnight stay in this fine hotel? I have to admit... I'm kind of getting used to it. The food's really good."

"I fear we will have to, how does one say, 'take a pass on that', Madam," spoke Misha. "We have actually come to invite you to a quick conference – at a location of your choice, away from the White House."

Tanaka stared directly at Boyd.

What's going on here, Brent? she silently communicated.

We have news that you need to hear, he responded.

The less that Jerry and the President know about this... the better.

"Okay," evenly replied the poker-faced former Mars mission science officer. "You lead?"

"I'll lead," agreed Boyd.

The Secret Service agents – and, if truth be told, secretly, even Jerry Kaysten – were amazed and more than a little awed, at what happened next : three – and then four – potency-evoking war-songs, flashes of *Amaiish*-energy and a sudden, near-vertical departure from the South Lawn Road, heading to the south-west, a little thereafter.

They had flown over the Potomac, going almost due east; then Boyd indicated a turn to the south-east, with a hand-signal. They still flew low enough to read the highway-signs for Interstate 66, which they followed to Centreville (luckily, traffic on the highway was relatively light tonight, so not too many civilians on the road got a clear look at the four strange airborne "UFOs").

Then Boyd indicated "continue straight" and in about another thirty seconds, he brought them in for a landing in front of a Civil War-attired general-on-horseback, in the middle of a large field, quite far away from any other signs of human habitation.

The statue was dimly-illuminated by lights recessed into the surrounding concrete-pad, which extended perhaps ten feet outward in all directions. Other than for the sounds of crickets and that of far-off traffic, all was quiet. The four were obviously alone, in this place.

"Welcome to the Stonewall Jackson Monument, in the Manassas National Battlefield Park," announced the former Mars mission pilot. "I thought this location would give us a bit of privacy... the park's closed this time of night."

"Good choice, I reckon," offered Wolf. "More than one way. Yeah, we're away from prying eyes... but also, a lot of folks died here, I guess."

"Yeah," acknowledged Boyd.

"Guys," asked Tanaka, "Kidding aside... why all the skulduggery? What's so important, that you didn't want it to be said at the White House? Please don't tell me you're planning another attack on the President! You know I don't like him... but he has honestly been trying to reach out to us, recently. He's a politician, of course – but I really do think he's watching his step. It's an opportunity that we shouldn't waste."

An awkward, "you go first" impasse – lasting a couple of seconds – enveloped the three men. At length, the Russian spoke,

"We should read the Professor, the statement that we prepared back on the mountain. Shall I?"

"Yeah... sure... oh, the *hell* with it!" Boyd peevishly muttered. "I'm not *doing* that – this is something that a friend tells a friend, straight-up. Listen, Cherie... it breaks my heart to say this to you, so I'll just get it over with. We've come here to tell you, *we believe your mother to be dead*. It looks like – God forgive me for having to speak these words – she died under torment, probably at the hand of the Agency, or at least of *someone* in the government – the same sons of bitches, that almost got Sam's family... and mine. I'm *so* sorry, Cherie."

Tanaka – stepping reflexively backward as if she had taken a hard punch to the stomach – managed to stay on her legs, by propping herself up against the monument.

Boyd rushed over to comfort her, and held her as she doubled over and began to cry uncontrollably.

"*H... how?*" she gasped, through pouring tears. "*Where?* How do you *know?*"

The other two men had now closed in on her. Wolf stood in front while the Russian was on Tanaka's other side from Boyd.

"The 'NRA' people – the computer hackers – intercepted confidential messages, apparently emanating from a location deep in the Rocky Mountains," disclosed Misha. "The nature of the data, unfortunately, *does* seem quite specific and definitive; we looked it over closely and while the U.S. government is known for its use of 'disinformation', based on what I have seen, it seems very unlikely that it is faked or that it refers to someone else. I have it on a micro-chip that I am now carrying, in case you need to see the evidence for yourself. Professor, when we all heard of this – Karéin too, she was there at the time – we all were *sickened* by this terrible news. Please accept my most sincere condolences."

Wolf also gave the more-than-a-woman, a firm hug.

"Cherie," he said in a low, sympathetic voice, "I wish I could say 'they're shittin' ya' on this one... but I can't. They're probably right. I want you to know... whatever you decide from here on in... I'm with you all the way."

"Thanks," she weakly replied, looking up with welling eyes and a quivering chin.

"That goes for all of us," added Boyd. "*Whatever* the President does or doesn't want. The government's crossed a *line* here, and it needs to pay the *consequences!*"

"Indeed," stated the Russian. "You know, Professor... in my occupation, I have seen a lot of death. But this is not the kind of death one expects in a war, or even in the game of spy-craft – it is an outrage – an *abomination!* I am with you, as well. This needs to be put right."

Slightly regaining her composure, Tanaka struggled to right herself. After breaking from the hugs, she asked,

"Do we know... if the President had anything to do, with authorizing this? Do we know who's responsible for it? Who gave the order? I need to know, 'who gave the fucking *order!*'"

The other three could *feel* the rising anger coursing through her mind and body.

"Not precisely," explained Misha. "The hackers sent a data-dump which may throw further light, on this question. Furthermore, I think it is reasonable to believe that the same information, must now be in the government's hands, at some level – whether that is with Madam Chu, or with others, I cannot say. It is up to you to decide if you want to disclose what we know, to the President, or to Minnie. I could make a case both for and against, frankly."

Tanaka stared out into space.

"Give me a minute... will you?" she requested.

"Of course," agreed Boyd. "I'll go for a walk."

Which he did. After a couple of minutes of standing off at a distance of perhaps thirty feet, while the former Mars mission science officer pondered her options – and the fates of many others – she called out,

"Guys... I've made up my mind. Will you come here?"

The three men advanced to encircle her.

"I'll go back to the mountain, with all of you, except one – your choice who that is," explained Tanaka. "I'd like that one other person to deliver a message personally to both Minnie and the President."

"And what's that, pardner?" asked Wolf, with a malicious look on his face.

"Tell them... they have three days, from the moment they hear the message, to find who's behind this, and bring him, her or them, to the White House lawn, in chains and handcuffs," spat Tanaka, the fury rising in her voice, with each syllable. "Meanwhile, I – and anyone who cares to accompany me – will go out looking myself... and heaven help anyone or anything, that gets in my way! You *understand?*"

"We certainly do," responded the former SVR-agent, "But... how are you going to know that whomever the government brings, is actually the responsible party? The President could just bring *anyone* from America's jail-system – a, uhh, 'patsy' as it were – and then have that possibly-innocent prisoner, suffer in the place of those who are really guilty. How will you be sure that you have the right person, or persons?"

"I'll know," countered Tanaka, "And if not... I'll ask Karéin to pick his brain apart, on my behalf –"

"She's taking the *Express* back to Bouvet," interrupted Boyd. "She may not be available."

"I'll know," repeated the more-than-a-woman. "I'll just... *know!*"

"Can't speak for you two... but that's good enough for *me*," remarked Wolf. "Just better hope that when she fries whoever's in that cage, she don't miss and 'accidentally' hit the President."

"I doubt that Sylvia and Minnie would let him get away with a cruel trick like that, anyway," opined the former Mars mission pilot. "But neither would they likely camp on to the idea of a summary public execution. Cherie – as much as I'm on your side – we need to do a little more thinking through of what we're going to do."

"Did I ever tell you," she replied, "No – despite all the time we had together on the *Eagle* and *Infinity* – about my childhood?"

"No," he quietly confirmed. "I guess there was too much else going on. To keep us busy, I mean."

"I was an only child," explained Tanaka. "My Dad was white, he was an airline-pilot – after I was born, he shacked up with my mother for a short while... but it didn't work out. He left us all alone... never paid a cent to Mom. I heard he got remarried sometime later, maybe even had kids... I don't know. Mom raised me... worked two jobs to put me through school. She was the only person I had, in the whole *world*."

"Yeah," bleakly repeated Boyd.

"You know what she said to me, just before we set off for Mars, Brent?" whimpered Tanaka, her chin again quivering as she spoke, through returning tears.

"Don't remember," he croaked.

"She said... 'bring me back a star'," wailed the former Mars science officer. "Instead – what I've brought back to her, are Karéin's poisoned, accursed alien-powers, that have now killed my *mother! Damn* her! *Damn* her! Damn it *all!* Oh God – why can't I go back to the way things *were!* What good are these fucking 'powers', if all they lead to, is the cruel death of people who you *love!*"

Again, they moved in to embrace and comfort her.

The Russian softly commented, "I surely understand what you are saying... but the Storied Watcher did not cause this – at least, not directly. When she heard the news, she was distraught – she blames herself for not having stopped this outrage, before it happened. Do not be so hard on her. She regrets a great deal of what her appearance on Earth, has resulted in."

"Yeah, well, pardner," offered Wolf, "Them's easy words for Little Miss Flying H-Bomb to say – not so easy for folks like Cherie, or the Youngs from that farm back Texas way, to hear. Karéin's next to indestructible – we've seen her demonstrate that, lots of times – but her hangers-on and acquaintances... not so much. So that's where them motherfuckers in the government targeted, first. She's s'posed to be a *goddess* – right? It's a fair thing to ask, 'why didn't you see this comin', and do something about it?' –"

"What would you have had her *do?*" countered Boyd.

"Well, for starters," lazily replied the big man, "I'd have stuck around here in North America, after she set the whole 'race' thing in motion. The minute I caught wind of what was happenin', both to Cherie's mom, and your family – I'd have been there at the White House, or at Air Force One – wherever – tearin' a strip off the President – whichever one, either'll do – I'd just tell him, 'you call back them sumbitches you got goin' after our families, or I'll do you, right here and now'. Instead, she heads off to we know not where, and starts hollowin' out islands or whatever. She should have known this was gonna *happen*, Boyd! She fucked up, *big-time*... and the results are right there in front of you."

"If you're so *sure* of that," argued the ex-astronaut, "Why don't you just fly back there and tell her, to her face?"

"Might just *do* that," evaded Wolf, "After I help Cherie settle the score."

"This is not about Karéin, in any event," remarked the Russian. "It is about the Professor. Cherie – I will volunteer to fly back to the White House and deliver your ultimatum. Just one other question, however... how closely – if at all – do you want to work with Madam Chu? She already knew how volatile this situation was, and she undoubtedly had her Bureau intensively investigating it. They may have information that we currently lack. What should I say to her?"

"Tell Minnie," directed the former science officer, "That it's up to *her*. I'll start my own search now but I am willing to work with her. She can choose whatever method of communications that she thinks is most appropriate, as long as it isn't used as a method for tracking and potentially targeting me. If she – or the government – does that, then they should consider themselves my enemies, with all that entails. If she identifies and locates who did it, I'll owe her forever. And one other thing."

"Yes?" said Misha.

"When I find whoever did this," vowed Tanaka, "I'm going to *kill* him! I don't want to hear about 'trials', or 'due process', or 'presumption of innocence', or *any* of that bullshit. Whoever did this to my mother – my totally-innocent, loving, caring, helpless *mother*, who suffered and died on account of *me* –"

She could not continue, and again doubled-up, howling in undisguised grief.

Finally – after about thirty seconds of anguished weeping – Tanaka raised her head, to face the others.

"Whoever it is... he's going to *die*," she managed. "If it takes the rest of my life to find him... *he dies!*"

Boyd echoed, "He dies."

Wolf repeated, "He *dies!*"

With a nod and a quick touch of the amulet at the end of his neck-chain, Misha said, "I swear to the spirit of Saint Alexander Nevskiy... this criminal, will *die!*"

"I will deliver your message, Professor," he added, as he energized his war-song and rocketed into the night sky, on a curving trajectory leading to Washington, D.C.

Minnie To The Mountain

When Boyd, Tanaka and Wolf returned to the top of Cass Mountain – the latter's flame-trail carefully blanked out from public view by the former's counter-theme darkness-shroud – they discovered that the Storied Watcher had already decamped, with the *Mailànkh Express* in tow.

She had taken a foot-dragging Bob Billings, her adopted son Tommy, the two elder Jacobson daughters (who had to work on their parents for almost ten minutes of tearful pleading, before Sam and Yvonne finally relented) and Chris Young of the bereaved Texas farm-family (who had an equally-hard job of convincing his mother), along with her on the trip back to Bouvet Island.

"Far too much undeserved duress and heartbreak, has plagued you in my wake," the alien-girl had addressed them with. "Here... come with me on a short 'working vay-cay-shun'... and I will show you that good and great accomplishments, can *also* be our legacy."

And with that, Karéin-Mayréij, and the air-ship, had disappeared into the night, heading into the stratosphere at near-hypersonic speeds.

"I wish I had gotten more of a chance to talk to her," complained Cherie Tanaka, after undergoing about a half-hour of the expected welcomes and offers of condolence, from others in the moonshine-shack. "I wanted to ask her, if there's anyone *else* in her little band of post-human men and women, who can read minds."

Cautiously, Boatman put his hand up.

"*You*, Otis?" incredulously asked the former Mars science officer. "How come you never told us *before*?

"Well... not *exactly*, Professor," backtracked the former FBI agent. "She only told me about it in passin', while we were all down on the streets in L.A.. She said somethin' about 'noble Otis, when you see a scene where something is not right... you shall know this, and shall be guided to clues telling its secrets'... or some-such language. I honestly haven't had much of a chance to use it, not that I really know how to turn it on. Minnie's s'posed to have something similar, I think. Remember how she even *said* so, in front of Congress, the other day?"

"Yeah," acknowledged Tanaka. "And Tommy claimed that he could sort of read minds, too... just before he killed that son of a bitch – the guy who had been torturing kids – in the room under Amchitka. Oh well... I have to find some suspects, before we can interrogate them, anyway. If I do – will you help?"

"Of *course* I will, Cherie," sympathetically replied Boatman. "As I believe young Will made clear to everybody else here, before Brent and the rest of 'em went off and gave you the bad news 'bout your mother... *we're* gunnin' for someone, too : specifically, the jackass who ordered us thrown out of that 'plane, without a parachute. There's a lot of accountin' to be done. You help us... we'll help you."

"You have my word," pledged the former science officer.

"Listen – as much as doing it is going to make me sick to my stomach, I need to see what the hackers provided you with... about my mother, that is," demanded Tanaka. "Misha said that he had it on him – do you have a copy?"

"Yeah," confirmed Hendricks, "Actually the image that he took is the copy. The original's on this communicator over here – apparently it belongs to Dorsie's cousins... so don't break it or anything, or they'll be pissed."

"'Pissed', Will?" incredulously replied the more-than-a-woman. "'*Pissed*'? *Such* an inadequate word, to describe how I'm feeling now!"

"Yeah," he repeated, trying to avoid her incendiary glare. He tossed the phone over to her.

"You got a computer somewhere here? One that we could hook this up to?" asked Tanaka.

"Ezra 'n Cooter got an old one, downstairs somewhere," responded Dorsie. "Ain't been used in I don't know *how* long... but y'all welcome to try gettin' it goin' if'n y'all want to."

"Thanks, Dorsie," said Tanaka.

She went for the stairs.

An hour or so later, the atmosphere in the moonshine-shack was funeral-like, as almost all of those in the room just stood, or sat, mutely listening to Tanaka's dirge-like wailing, coming from parts below.

"I can't *take* much more of this," whispered Laura Boyd to her husband. "I'm worried it's going to traumatize the kids."

"I know," he quietly answered, "But we have to let her grieve, in her own way. Remember... Cherie has nobody left in this world – that I *know* of, anyway – to comfort her... other than us. As hard as it is, I'd prefer to let it run its course –"

He stopped, stared off into space for a second or two and then said, out loud, "War-songs!"

Hendricks, Boatman, Sam Jacobson and Donny Wade all looked up.

"Brent... I don't hear *anything!*" complained Laura Boyd.

"Yeah... you're right," spoke the former Mars mission commander.

After a second more of listening, he added,

"I hear Misha's music... but also..."

"That sounds like Minnie!" exclaimed the third agent.

"What's *she* doin' here?" queried Boatman. "Last I heard, she got herself a pretty important day job with the Bureau, back in D.C... right?"

The war-songs became louder, to the point where even the humans within the audience could hear and appreciate the half-psychic, half-audible melodies.

After a few seconds, the tunes abated. There was a knock on the door. Misha's voice was heard.

"Is it alright for us to enter?" he asked.

"Ain't nobody in here 'cept us chickens," quipped Hendricks. "Sure... come on in."

The door opened, revealing the Russian, accompanied by none other than Minnie Chu, dressed in impeccable – and very expensive-looking – women's professional dress-clothes, complete with equally-costly shoes.

"Guys? *Guys!*" she squealed with joy.

In a half-second, she was locked in a tight embrace with her two former field-agents.

"*Oh God,*" breathed Chu, "I heard back at the White House... but I didn't really *believe* you were, until –"

"I'll tell you, Minnie," answered Boatman with a broad, happy smile, "After we got up off the ground in one piece... I didn't believe it myself, 'till it sank in, 'bout a day later."

"Hey... and 'congratulations on the promotion'," added Hendricks. "You don't want a personal valet... do you? Like, 'shine your shoes and get you a latté twice a day', kind of thing?"

As she stepped away from the hug and straightened her clothes, the nouvelle FBI-director said, "I've got *much* bigger and better things planned for the two of you. Requisitions are already in."

The other two exchanged uneasy glances. Eventually Boatman offered,

"That's... uhh... *great*, Minnie... except..."

"'Except'... what?" she demanded.

"We... uhh... had to *defend* ourselves, after we landed back down in these-here mountains," disclosed the big black ex-agent. "It turned into a bad scene."

"A *really* bad one, if you know what I mean," said a grimacing Hendricks.

"I... *see,*" spoke Chu. "Well... it wouldn't be the *first* time that I've had to pull some strings to smooth things over, as Sam over there can attest. We can talk about the details later, when we get a free minute or two."

"Speaking of that," interjected Sam Jacobson, "To those of you around here who may not already have met her... this is Minnie Chu, Director of the Federal Bureau of Investigation – or, in other words, 'America's Top Cop'. Minnie's one of Karéin's original friends and she's helped the rest of us immensely, over the past few weeks. And in case any of you were wondering... yes, she *does* have some very formidable alien-powers, at least equivalent to our own. I'd advise all of you to stay on her good side!"

"Oh, don't be *silly*, Commander," demurely deflected Chu. "*Everybody* who I see around here, is on my 'good side'!"

"Well, I don't like that 'Top Cop' stuff, too much," snorted Dorsie, "An' I bet y'all... Ezra 'n Cooter prolly won't, neither."

The mountain-man was caught in Chu's stare, which – fortunately for him on this occasion – was merely mischievous, as opposed to lethal.

"What's your name, sir?" she asked, with a polite half-smile.

"Dorsie," he said. "Like my kin Cooter 'n Ezra – who built this place where we's all standin' – we... well, we make a livin' *brewin'* stuff and sellin' it, if'n y'all understand. They built this shack 'n what's underneath it, to keep away from the Law... all nice and discreet. They ain't gonna be happy 'bout all these 'alien-folks' hangin' here, in th' first place... and they ain't gonna truck with no 'Top Cop' –"

"Well, Dorsie," replied the former team-leader in a poised, professional manner, "I don't think you or your cousins have much to worry about. It's absolutely true that I *do* have to try to enforce the law, just like Otis and Will here have to... to do otherwise would be not to do my job. However, we *do* have considerable discretion about how and when we act, and we *do* take into account things like 'being one of Karéin's friends'... which I presume you are?"

"'B'lieve so, ma'am," said the mountain-man. "Although I only met the lady a few hours ago. Shore was an 'experience', I can tell y'all *that*."

"The first time with Karéin always is," offered Chu. "Speaking of her... where *is* she? I don't see Bob or Tommy, either...?"

"She and they headed off to, uhh, off *south*," evaded Brent Boyd. "She has duties to attend to. Said she'd be back later."

"If you don't want to say exactly, that's okay," allowed the *nouvelle* FBI-director. "I'll just ask her when she gets back."

"Probably better that way," observed Sam Jacobson. "It should be her decision as to how much she discloses to the government. Not that we don't trust *you*, Minnie; it's just your *boss* who we have reservations about."

The former team-leader stopped talking and looked as if she was trying to listen intently.

"Who's *that?*" she inquired. "Sounds like someone crying, far away..."

"Cherie," indicated Brent Boyd. "She's downstairs... reviewing the evidence that we came across."

"You can go down the stairs, over there... third room on the left, it's the one with the computer that she fixed up to review the files with," indicated Hendricks. "But I'd be *careful*, Minnie... the whole shitty thing's hit her hard. Can't blame her for not being in a good mood."

"I have some additional information," mentioned Chu. "I'm not looking forward to it... but I suppose I had better get down there and work with her. *If* that's possible, of course. Wish me luck..."

"Good luck," offered Boatman.

As Chu disappeared down the stairs, Wolf remarked, "Well... as I understand it from current events... if *anybody's* force-field will hold up when Cherie lets loose... it'll be Miss FBI's."

A Multiple-Murder Mystery

After about another half-hour, Chu's face reappeared in the entrance-way to the staircase. The former team-leader was followed by Tanaka, a few steps behind.

"So how'd it go?" asked Boatman. "You all's still both in one piece, which is nice to see."

"That was never an issue," deflected Chu. "I'd say that we *understand* each other now."

"Yeah," agreed Tanaka, through tear-stained eyes. "We do indeed. And *Vîrya Sài'ymë* has gotten to know 'Warden'. So there's *that*, too."

"I don't want to pry, especially about what happened to your mother," asked Sam Jacobson, "But I think it's only fair that the rest of us know if the two of you have made any progress in identifying the party – or parties – responsible."

Chu nodded and walked over to the moonshine-shack kitchen table. To the amazement of many of the humans (especially Dorsie), her telekinetic powers caused several of the chairs around the table to move away from it.

"Take a seat," she requested. "We need to talk."

Brent Boyd, Sam Jacobson, Chu, Tanaka and the Russian sat down, while the rest clustered around, still standing.

"We've compared notes," explained the *nouvelle* FBI-director, "And here's what we've come up with. It's been very difficult to get really good signals intelligence on these transmissions, because the President and the Bureau are still in the middle of purging NSA of possibly-disloyal elements... and *that* process is nowhere near complete. But we *have* been able to cross-reference the data-stream that, we think, activated the second nuke – the one that Karéin saved us from – and the transmissions that reference the appalling mistreatment of Cherie's mother. At least two of them appear to be coming from the same place and although we haven't been able to break the crypto, there are data-artifacts in each stream that look identical –"

"You mind puttin' that in English for the rest of us, Minnie?" grunted Wolf.

"No problem, Wolf," answered Chu with a mild smile. "What it means – we think – is, the *same* person, or persons, who somehow over-rode the military's normal safeguards and who ordered the second nuke fired, is the one who authorized – God help me for saying this – the cruel torture and murder of Cherie's mother."

"That's fine," interjected Brent Boyd, "But does it give us any further insight as to who exactly it might be?"

"We have theories... all unverified as we stand now," disclosed the former team-leader. "The leading candidates are, in this order, 'the conspiracy led by the late Harold Crowford and his Klan of Jesus Christ', 'senior officials in the Central Intelligence Agency', 'someone high up in the GrayWar Corporation', possibly Mr. Duke himself – he's gone into hiding, incidentally – or, maybe, 'someone totally new, as yet unknown to us'. As in, 'possibly whatever conspiracy was responsible for the Los Angeles attack'. There are many possible suspects, unfortunately."

"Well then, I'd submit to you... the path forward is pretty clear," proposed Brent Boyd.

"How's that?" asked Chu.

"Arrest everyone who you just described, bring 'em to some convenient location, wait for Karéin to get back to find out who really did it and who's lying... turn the latter over to Cherie. Case closed," coldly suggested the former Mars mission pilot.

"It doesn't *work* that way – which you know perfectly well, Major Boyd," argued Chu. "For starters – as I mentioned – we can't even *locate* Duke, and by the way the CIA Director and most of the late Reverend Crowford's organization also seem to have vanished into the woodwork. We're trying to locate them, of course, but doing that could take quite a bit of time, or it might not work at all. And then – even if we *do* find these suspects – it's a legal process. We can and will arrest them... but they get their Constitutional rights, there has to be a fair trial –"

"Oh... *really?*" challenged Sam Jacobson. "You mean like the 'due process' my family – or Brent's – or the Wades, or Mrs. Young's family over there – got?"

"Yeah... that's *bullshit* – and you *know* it, Minnie!" complained Wolf.

"She's not responsible for everything that the government did, beforehand," defended Boatman. "She can only try to apply the rules, from here on forward."

"I had heard about Donny's family, and Mr. and Mrs. Wade, I want you to know – I've already asked the President about the government making restitution to you about the farm," mentioned the *nouvelle* FBI-director. "He's agreeable but the paperwork will take a few weeks. This is uhh, the first I've heard of the Youngs – if you don't mind my asking, what happened...?"

Cassie Young spoke up.

"Air Force dropped bombs on our ranch... they was after Cherie Tanaka and Wolf, there. Killed my husband Jimmy. We buried him next to our house, that is, if it's there... they was still blowin' things up, when we left," she said.

"Damn near got *me*, too," added the bounty-hunter. "That was some *heavy* firepower they let loose with. Could easily have killed Cassie and her kids. I'm proud to say that I took down a few fighter-planes after that. Wished I'd had gotten *all* of 'em, before they let fly against these folk, though."

"I've done my share of that too," interjected Brent Boyd, "But I've never lost sight of the fact that those pilots have families... kids... too. They were ordered to execute completely criminal, immoral orders. But for accidents of history, one of them might have been me... or Devon. We've been over this many times before, you know."

"I'm very sorry for your loss, ma'am," carefully responded the ex-team-leader. "The government – under its previous leadership, that is, the former Vice-President – did many cruel and illegal things to perfectly innocent people, and it was probably on *his* orders that the attack you speak of, was carried out. If it *means* anything... the Vice-President ordered *me* to be murdered, as well, while I was on the Airborne Command Post. I could and *should* have killed him right then and there; but as it turned out, I believe he died when the first East Coast nuclear explosion vaporized that plane. He was on it, as far as I know. I hope you can count that as 'justice', of a sort."

"That may be," coolly replied the Texas farm-wife, "But it won't bring my Jimmy back... *will* it?"

"No ma'am... it won't," acknowledged Chu.

"Nor my mother," unhelpfully noted Tanaka.

"Nor my fiancée, Kai Lee, who's still missing," said the new FBI-director. "He appears to have been abducted in the same campaign as was directed at all the rest of you. So you see, Ms. Young... I have a *personal* stake in this, above and beyond wanting to get justice for Cherie, yourself and the Wades."

"So... where does this leave us?" asked Sam Jacobson.

"And," interjected Laura Boyd, "If we aren't completely sure that the creeps who tried to kidnap my kids and I, aren't still out there... what are we supposed to *do* – just sit up here on top of this mountain, for the next twenty *years* or something?"

"She's right," added Yvonne Jacobson. "I was *so* scared when they grabbed us. I don't want to experience anything like that ever again!"

"I don't blame you, ma'am – at times on the plane, *I* felt like that... and I had all of these 'alien-powers' to call upon," offered Chu. "The best I can come up with now is, the invitation to take you all to Camp David is still open. We've validated that it's completely secure. You'll be safe there, and – no slight meant to Dorsie and his cousins – it's a lot more comfortable than what you've got here."

A lively discussion broke out among the mountain-top refugees. Eventually, Sam Jacobson stated, "Minnie, given your new position, we understand why you had to remind us of this. But as you know, many of us are still suspicious of the President's real motives and intentions – and in any event, Karéin is expecting us to be up here on Cass Mountain, when she returns. We have to wait at least until then to make a final decision."

"I understand," responded the former team-leader. "For the record – I'm not one hundred per cent sure that he's completely trustworthy, either... but in politics, I suppose *no-one* ever is. All I can tell you is, so far he's been true to his word, at least as far as I've seen."

"Well then," grunted Wolf, "If we're stuck up here for the duration... 'sthere any way we can fix things up a bit? I mean... there's only three cots for sleepin' on, we hardly got any food left in the fridge, and Mr. Mars over there's been tellin' us we can't even go down the road to the ski-resort to pick up supplies, 'case the Army, or LEA, try to arrest us – don't have to tell you how them doin' that, might end up in a *scene*, Minnie. I'm gettin' cabin fever... and unlike a lot of these folks I can just up and fly to D.C. if I want to. Oh... and I need some of them plastic bags to pick up dogshit with, by the way."

This brought a roar of laughter from the crowd.

"I'll see what I can do –" she started to say; but she was interrupted by a barrage of loud, drum-beat knocking coming from the door to the outside.

"*Whoever* y'all is – y'all got ten seconds to git out of our place – or we's gonna come in there and carry y'all out by the *feet!*" shouted an angry-sounding male voice.

"Shit!" exclaimed Dorsie. "That's *Cooter!* Y'all git out of the way, right now!"

He raced over to the door and opened it, revealing two shotgun-toting Caucasian mountain-men – one lanky, taller, clean-cut guy with greasy blond hair and beady, staring eyes and another shorter, heavier-set man with dark hair and a full beard – standing directly outside.

"Hey, boys!" called out Dorsie. "Good to see y'all!"

"Dorsie," spoke the taller guy, "I *knows* we telled y'all got the right to hang here... but y'all s'posed to tell us beforehand, and –"

The man leaned over to look past Dorsie. He saw the crowd inside and complained,

"What in Jaysus Fuckin' Tarnation's goin' *on* in there? Y'all havin' a block-party or somethin', in our 'still?"

To Dorsie's dismay, he had been joined by Minnie Chu, standing right at his side.

"I can *explain!*" stammered the nonplussed mountain-man. "Ezra... Cooter... lot's been goin' down, since last I seen y'all. These-here folk... they's mah friends, after a fashion, 'leastaways. See –"

He was interrupted by the *nouvelle* FBI-director, who leaned forward and extended a hand to the taller man.

"Hi... your name's 'Ezra'... is that right?" she inquired.

"How you know, lady?" answered the man, with a tone of suspicion.

He was obviously taken aback by her poised, professional manner... and by a supernaturally *arousing* aura that Chu had somehow developed, about her.

"Lucky guess," she deflected, with a pleasant smile.

"What y'all *doin'* here, lady?" demanded the other, dark-haired guy. "We don't invite *nobody* up to these parts!"

"Oh, well, you *see*," airily remarked the more-than-a-woman, "My name's 'Minnie Chu', and I'm the Director of the Federal Bureau of Investigation... that is, 'America's Top Cop'. And you know what, Cooter?"

"What?" grunted the stone-faced, shorter mountain-man.

"Come on in... because today's the luckiest day of your life," replied Chu.

Don't Make It Four Or Five

From her vantage-point in the obviously-expensive, well-decorated seventieth-floor apartment-suite, Abruzzio looked out over the early-morning downtown Pittsburgh skyscape – including the former Agency building, now closed and cordoned-off for "official Federal government business" (as the yellow tape sealing all entrances, so announced).

The burgeoning glare of the early-summer sun reflected off the plate-glass windows of the surrounding skyscrapers, while, down below, the ant-like figures of office-workers hastening to make it in to work on time, came and went.

It was a fine, brisk Pennsylvania morning.

"Had to take a break?" asked Tanaka, from behind the former JPL scientist.

"Yeah... too much even for me and Rainbow," admitted Abruzzio. "Since the Bureau had that place seized, I've had hundreds of thousands of documents to go over, you know... I was able to access some new ones last night, by using that network-trickery I told you about, yesterday. But I get brain-fatigue. I *needed* a few minutes off."

"Don't worry about it... I really appreciate the help," reassured the former Mars mission science officer. "Forgive my impatience, but we've been going over this for the better part of two *days* now – I just can't *stand* the idea of whomever did that to my mother, still going scot-free!"

"You get any updates on Karéin?" inquired Abruzzio.

"Still off at that godforsaken island, apparently," disclosed Tanaka. "At least, according to what Minnie's saying, she hasn't showed up at Cass Mountain yet. Minnie's claiming that the Air Force was able to track her – Karéin I mean – up to a few hundred miles offshore, when she flew off south... then she just *disappeared;* but because of that, the military thinks we'll get a few minutes advance warning when she returns. Better than *nothing*, I suppose."

"Ha!" responded the bemused Mission Control staffer. "You know... she promised to teach me some more of the 'stealth' stuff – also how to fly a lot faster. When she gets back, that is."

"Same here," offered Tanaka. "God, you know, Sylvia – I can't tell you how proud and amazed I am, to be able to discuss things like this with you. We really *are* 'super-beings'... aren't we? But I'd trade it all in, in a half-second, to have Mom back."

"Yeah," quietly agreed Abruzzio. "Despite all these 'alien-powers', we can't predict the twists and turns of fate... be those wonderful or terrible. All we can do is to cope with them, as best we can."

Her puppy – now halfway into being a full-grown mutt – yipped a friendly confirmation, bringing a smile to both post-human faces.

"I hate to press you," persisted the former Mars science officer, "But... any nuggets of wisdom coming from the latest batch of papers? You know – the ones you were poring over, up to two a.m.?"

The ex-JPL ground controller leaned back on the desk overlooking the cityscape, facing outward.

"Honestly... just bits and pieces," she sighed. "I can't even review ninety per cent of it – the crypto on the data-streams and the documents is just too hard to crack. Minnie's telling me it might take the Bureau another six months to do it, if they can do it at all. Meanwhile... all I've got from the less-carefully-protected stuff are references to some guy named 'Top Dog', who seems to be off-site all the time. Whoever that is, he seems to have been tracking what went down on the ACP – you know, the plane that Minnie had to bail from, before it blew up – very closely."

"Well... why don't we cross-reference a search for that person's real identity and then have Minnie haul him in?" challenged Tanaka.

"Come *on*, Cherie!" protested the other more-than-a-woman. "This is the *Agency* we're talking about, for Pete's sake! They don't *keep* records like that! Everything's 'need-to-know', only. And remember... we don't even know that the Agency was behind what happened to your mother. Did you look at those records of what happened to the family that Karéin met up in the – what was it called – 'Santa Esmerelda' restaurant? They think it might have been the religious nuts who were behind that... or it might have been the Agency, or it might have been someone else. *Any* of them might have been the ones who murdered your mother. *Nothing's* certain, at this point."

"Karéin and Minnie both told me that you have a special power, when investigating stuff like this –" persisted Tanaka.

"It doesn't work like that, Cherie," the other more-than-a-woman tried to explain. "It requires a certain basic amount of evidence... of data that I can be sure is true and complete. Right now, I just don't *have* that. The moment I *do*,

I'll tell you. All I've got currently is a bunch of leads that all go in different directions; it's mind-numbing... alien-powers or no alien-powers."

"Oh-kay... *fine*," relented the former Mars mission science officer. "Look... if you need to clear your head... why don't we all pop down to that nice little sidewalk café that we passed by when Minnie first put us up here – the one a few doors down on the street from here? We can grab a coffee and a Danish or something."

"Sure," answered Abruzzio, "But you *know*... it all might as well be decaf, as far as we're concerned."

"Yeah... the 'no booze, no drugs, no poisons shall affect you', thing," grumbled Tanaka. "You know... as much as I appreciate Karéin's wonderful alien-powers... I really *do* think it should stop with coffee. Some super-powers just aren't worth it."

"My treat," said the other more-than-a-woman with a wry grin, as she grabbed her purse and – like Tanaka – reflexively reached for a pair of sunglasses.

Abruzzio and Tanaka – both wearing dark glasses and dressed like a couple of well-heeled tourists from "somewhere" (perhaps, New York) – were now down in the outdoor seating-area of the "Sunny Side Bistro".

"Rainbow" had been left in the suite with a doggie-biscuit and the promise of another one, based on a "no messes" policy.

The outdoor part of the café wasn't very crowded; other than for two other random customers at different tables, they were alone.

The two more-than-people had taken a table at the north-east end of the outdoor-area, with Tanaka facing south and Abruzzio looking outward. Their table faced east-by-north on to Liberty Avenue, with the not-fondly-remembered blue-glass-clad Agency building in view, to the right.

The former science officer had purchased a large coffee with latté frosting, while Abruzzio sipped on a double-strength espresso; both also ordered light pastry-snacks.

"How's the hazelnut croissant?" idly asked Tanaka.

Abruzzio wiped her mouth, swallowed and replied, "Quite nice, actually... tastier than I remember it being. Karéin's elevated senses, I suppose. 'The angel taketh away... the angel giveth', to abuse a saying."

"Yeah," acknowledged Tanaka.

She reached to an empty, nearby table, and retrieved a relatively fresh-looking, rolled-up newspaper.

Unfolding it, Tanaka began to read.

"Hmm," she murmured, "I thought these had gone out of style, like, twenty *years* ago..."

A young, trim-looking Caucasian waiter was passing by.

"Oh, no, ma'am," he informed, "The Post-Gazette's one of the few that refused to go all-digital. Manager here *hates* the computer versions, so he bought a lifetime subscription to the paper version. We always have a few lying around... feel free to take it with you, if you want. Refill?"

"Please," requested the former science officer, with a tap of her finger on the rim of her coffee-cup.

The waiter complied and then progressed to service the next table.

"So let's see... what they got to say," remarked Tanaka. "Yeah... the usual stupid, depressing stuff –"

"What?" demanded a mildly-interested Abruzzio.

"Well," continued Tanaka, "It's full of conspiracy-theories about Karéin... like, 'how can we be sure, she hasn't replaced the President, with a space zombie', kind of thing –"

"Oh, for God's *sake*," interrupted the frustrated ex-JPL staffer. "Didn't they listen to a *thing* that she said, in that first press conference in the White House?"

"Yeah, well... what did you *expect?*" countered Tanaka, while her eyes scanned the newsprint. "It sells papers, I suppose. "But there's a lot of other stuff as well. For example, 'where has the Mars Gang gone' – ha ha, now *there's* one close to my heart. U.S. dollar seems to have dropped to about half value compared to the Chinese, Brazilian and European currencies – remind me just to take some of Hector's gold chits with me, next time I take a foreign vacation – and inflation's jumped to an annual rate of twenty per cent, as a result. They're saying that 'the rule of law has now returned to the streets of Los Angeles, thanks to the help of two super-human followers of the Storied Watcher' – hooray for Devon and Saquina – oh... and there's supposed to be another 'Blaine Maine' movie in the works. Want more?"

"Nah," deflected Abruzzio. "It'll just distract me from concentrating on... well, *you* know, what I should be concentrating on."

"You're probably right," remarked the former Mars science officer, as she moved slightly to to the left in her chair, and began to fold the newspaper, "It's just bafflegab –"

A shocked expression appeared on her face, as the next few seconds passed simultaneously quickly as events are measured in Earth-time, while slowly as they are so done in alien-time.

There were staccato, rapid-fire "crack-crack-crack" sounds issuing from somewhere to the north-east (and high-up) on Liberty Avenue. One edge of Tanaka's newspaper was shredded by an incoming high-powered rifle-round, which hit and embedded itself into the pavement on the sidewalk further south; another shot destroyed a flower-pot at the edge of the café seating-area, while still another hit the low metal fence between the seating-area and the sidewalk, ricocheting and then shattering the glass in the café's outside window.

Two more rifle-rounds found their target – which was, apparently, Sylvia Abruzzio. The first hit her just below the neck, sending the more-than-a-woman careening backwards on to the concrete of the converted sidewalk, while another – impacting a split-second later, while Abruzzio was already off-balance – crashed into her midriff, almost in the middle of her lower torso.

And in various places around the United States and elsewhere – even as far as a certain, ice-bound island in the South Atlantic – a sharp burst of physical discomfort, plagued the Storied Watcher and her new-found followers.

Two jagged-, burnt-edged holes appeared in Abruzzio's clothes, as she fell. In the same instant, sparks and micro-fragments of shredded metal sprayed outwards from the wound-marks on her body. Upon coming down hard upon the floor, her sunglasses went flying and she rolled over to face downward, trying to crawl out of danger while spitting up blood and gasping for air.

"*Sylvia*!" shrieked a horrified Tanaka, while she shook off a sympathetic ache in her upper torso.

There was some kind of explosion – followed by a rain of broken glass – coming from far up in the apartment-building where they had been residing. The glass-shards fell to the sidewalk, about fifty feet from the café. A second later, passers-by (those who had not already hidden under cover) were astonished to see a small dog, literally *flying* through the air, on a course aimed directly at the shooting-scene.

Tanaka's war-song was already ramping up as – through glowing eyes, with charges of the *Fire* racing through her body – she crouched low over her stricken friend, so as to protect Abruzzio from more rifle-shots.

"Sylvia… *Sylvia!*" shouted the former Mars science officer. "You've been *shot!* Can you *hear* me!"

"Rainbow" had now landed next to her adoptive mother and began licking Abruzzio's face.

"Oh-kay… I *think*," barely managed the former JPL scientist. A dim, multi-colored aura enveloped her body, as she sputtered, "Wind knocked out… God it *hurts*, might be a broken collarbone… need some time… go *find* them, Cherie!"

A look of savage fury appeared on the face of the other super-woman, while her war-song echoed throughout the concrete jungle of downtown Pittsburgh.

"*Vìrya Sài'ymë*," she cried while throwing off her dark glasses, "*We hunt!*"

To the amazement of the onlookers – who were already uploading video of the "super-dog" to various sites on NeoNet – they caught a fleeting glimpse of what they had taken to be a New York tourist, rocketing north-east along Liberty Avenue, climbing at a steep angle.

Cherie Teruko Tanaka soared skyward, but – a second or two after she realized that her velocity would soon take her past the skyline – she applied the *Amaiish* equivalent of "braking-thrust", and slowed to a speed of perhaps fifty miles per hour or so.

Vîrya Sài'ymë, she sent,

These gun-shots must *have come from somewhere in this direction.*

Can thou find from whence they issued... a breach in a window, a puff of smoke from a building-top... some other thing that looks "out of place"?

Or can thou triangulate? That is – compare the angle that these hateful things approached at, and calculate that back to the point of origin?

This in no I training have, answered the living-breastplate,

Am blessed but mother trying I.

For a couple of seconds, Tanaka's festering anger was weighed against despair; but then, *Vîrya* Sài'ymë responded with,

Red building walled the points triangle of near corner to big... "K&L Gates" the says one that it on.

A is what "K&L Gates" mother blessed? King the that is name of a?

Not... exactly, little one, replied Tanaka.

But thank thee! Let us hasten thence!

In no more than a couple more seconds, the more-than-a-woman and her weirding "child" had arrived over the nearest corner of the K&L Gates building – a large skyscraper clad in dull reddish-colored outside-walls, one with an excellent field of view and line of sight to the unfortunate café's outside seating-section.

Far below, she took note of sirens – three police-cars followed by an ambulance – racing down Liberty Avenue, in the direction of the café.

There were no signs of an active shooter anywhere on the building's roof – which was bedecked with a complicated array of air-conditioning equipment, water-tanks, metal-tubing and other facilities-gear – but, directly below her, Tanaka's enhanced sight quickly took note of brass shell-casings strewn about, right at the corner of the skyscraper.

Damn, but those are big *casings... can't be a regular-bore rifle... has to be military-grade, large-caliber probably...*

Fuck! she inwardly cursed,

I've lost him – wait a minute –

Just past a row of three water-tanks near to a raised area in the center of the building-roof, the former Mars mission science officer took note of an entrance-door, one that probably led from the roof to parts below.

It was open, but just by a crack. The locking-mechanism was disengaged.

In another second-and-a-half, she was at the door, now standing on the K&L Gates building roof-top. She stepped inside, switching her senses to "indoor mode" while devoting power to her personal force-field.

Just in case the son of a bitch is waiting for me, mused Tanaka, as she surveyed the scene. She was in the topmost parts of a set of metal service-stairs leading to a landing about fifty feet below. There was another door there, and it bore faint infra-red marks as if it had recently been opened by human hands.

Her war-song was still playing, but subliminally… not, audibly.

She flew down to the landing and pushed through the doorway, into a well-appointed modern office-building interior corridor, with expensive-looking floor-carpets, tasteful wall-decorations and – unhelpfully – two or three business-suited office-workers, walking about.

One of these stepped into an open elevator, which was about three-quarters of the way down the corridor towards its far end, which had a prominently-marked "EXIT" sign leading to a staircase. The other two office-staff stopped and stared in a mixture of alarm and fascination at Tanaka's imposing presence – particularly, her dim-glowing eyes, and the not-completely-suppressed aura of *Vîrya Sài'ymë*, under the more-than-a-woman's outer clothes.

I don't see – wait, of course! quickly reasoned Tanaka.

Either he took the elevator – I should just blow the door off and pull the damn thing back up here, but I might hurt anybody else who's in there – or he took the stairs – but if I charge down there, I can easily beat him to street-level.

Okay, mother-fucker – jig's up!

She flew down the corridor until she was at the stairway-door, causing severe alarm to the office-workers in the corridor along the way. The door was forced open by a burst of telekinetic force and in the next seconds Tanaka was racing by flight down the staircase, again nonplussing the few workers who had decided to eschew the elevator in favor of exercise on the stairs.

Within perhaps ten seconds more, she had reached ground-level. The former science officer threw the door to the building's very large, chrome-and-leather-decorated front lobby, open. She charged forward – keeping her feet more or less on the ground – stopping in front of the front-desk, which was populated by well-dressed guards, one a tallish Caucasian man, the other a shorter woman with Eurasian features vaguely similar to Tanaka's own.

The two reflexively stepped backwards in surprise and worry at the sight of Tanaka's intimidating, war-song-reinforced, glowing-eyed presence.

"Lock down the *building!*" she shouted. "There's a sniper who shot people down the street, somewhere *in* here!"

"Who *are* you – you have no right to just barge in here and –" started the white guy.

"I'm someone who can kill you with the wave of my *hand!*" angrily retorted Tanaka. "And I'm chasing the bastard who just shot one of my best *friends!* Out of my fucking *way!*"

She did not get an opportunity to make good on her threats, however; because in the next instant, the elevator (or, rather, the one that she had been tracking, as it was actually only one of three which had an entrance in the ground-floor lobby) opened up.

In a half-second, Tanaka was in front of the elevator's open door. Before anyone could step out, her outstretched hands fired a warning shot of low-powered lightening-bolts at the floor less than a foot from the edge of the elevator-entrance. This was followed immediately by a more powerful shot that hit and destroyed the device's outside control-panel, which was on a part of the wall between the open elevator and the one next to it.

Screams of fear issued from the now-stopped-dead elevator, which appeared to contain two female office-workers and three male ones, all of whom warily backed off in a futile attempt to deny Tanaka a clear shot at them.

"Who... who *are* you?" wailed one of the women. "What do you *want?*"

The more-than-a-woman carefully looked them over.

"Oh-kay, asshole," she snarled, "Where'd you *hide* it? Step forward right now, and I *might* spare your life... or, at least, I might kill you quickly – which is one hell of a lot more than you *deserve!*"

"What you *talkin'* about, lady?" challenged one of the male office-staff. "Nobody here's 'hiding' *anything!*"

"One of you has *got* to be hiding a gun – a rifle – on you... if you didn't ditch it, already," pressed Tanaka. "I *know* so, because you just used it to shoot my *friend*, down the street, at the Sunny Side Bistro!"

Perplexed stares were cast back and forth within the elevator. After a second or two, one of the women said,

"A... *rifle?* Nobody here's got anything like that... hey, *wait* a minute..."

"What?" asked another one of the men.

"What about that guy who got off on the third floor?" proposed the woman. "You see that thing he was carrying?"

"Yeah," replied the man. "A golf-bag... so *what?*"

Instantly, Tanaka's *Fire*-powered fury became yet more overt and intimidating.

"Quickly – *quickly!*" she commanded. "What's he *look* like? Where was he going?"

"Don't *know*, really," offered the other woman in the elevator. "He was just a guy with dark glasses... that's all. Okay – I thought it *was* strange that he was wearing them inside the building, but I figured he was on his way to the golf-course or something, because he was dressed real casual. I think he turned to the left when he got off at the third floor... isn't that right, Jeff?"

One of the men in the elevator nodded and said, "Yeah... come to think about it, that *was* kinda weird... I mean, that side of the third's all BGP Legal, and Old Man Parivano doesn't like his guys dressed in anything that doesn't cost a few thousand, *minimum*. He'd get *shit* if he walked in the office dressed like that –"

Blessed mother, came a warning from a little internal voice,

Door-stair the! Eyes-glasses man a wearing!

Out of the corner of her eye, Tanaka descried a Caucasian guy, dressed in a Polo sports-shirt, casual slacks, a baseball-cap and smart-looking loafers. He wore expensive-looking dark eye-shades as well, but was not carrying anything. He had just exited the staircase and was heading at a brisk walking pace toward the outside door.

"Stay here!" she demanded of the elevator-dwellers.

In an instant, she was in front of the man from the staircase.

"Stop right there – or I'll *kill* you!" she bellowed.

He complied with the order, standing in place, with arms hanging limply at his sides.

There was an odd look on the guy's face, as if he were deep in thought. Then he collapsed to the floor, as if his legs had just given out from underneath.

As Tanaka approached closer, she could see froth coming from his mouth. The man's face was gradually turning blue.

"No... *no!*" she shrieked, "Not like *this!*"

Grabbing his shoulders, she shook him mightily, "You *fucker!*"

Mother blessed back him bring to can you try, came the voice of *Vîrya Sài'ymë.*

Force-life up give?

No, little one, countered Tanaka,

That is reserved for people who do not deserve *to die.*

He, surely... does.

But he has cheated us of the chance to interrogate him!

From behind her, in the direction of the building's street-level entrance, she heard sirens and the sounds of marching feet.

She turned – letting the man's limp body fall to the marble-tiled floor – to stare into the faces of five officers of the Pittsburgh Police Department, each with guns drawn directly at her.

"Hands *up!*" one of them shouted. "You're under *arrest*, on suspicion of first-degree *murder!*"

For a second or two, the former Mars mission science officer just sat there, dumbfounded at the incongruity of the situation. But then, rationality overcame her urges to blow these intruders to Kingdom Come, and she slowly complied, raising her hands – though neither stopping her war-song, nor tamping down the sinister glow in her eyes.

"This man," said Tanaka with a nod over her shoulder in the direction of the dead guy, "Is the assassin who you're looking for – his weapon, which I assume is a high-powered sniper-rifle, is probably secreted somewhere in this building. You should seal the building and lock all the entrances, then conduct a top-to-bottom search."

"We'll decide how to conduct our procedures, lady," gruffly retorted one of the cops, a big, heavy-set, older Caucasian guy. Turn around – we're going to handcuff you, and any resistance can and will be met with lethal force. You have the right to remain silent – anything you say, can and will be used against you –"

"*Stow it!*" complained Tanaka, although she did what the cop said and turned to face the lobby-desk, who stared at her still-glowing eyes. "I'm complying with you only so you can get going with the investigation... my name is Cherie Tanaka of the Mars Gang, and I can disintegrate all of you – the whole building, in fact – with the wave of my *hand*, if I want to. Except... I was told that we're now on the same side... or some such bullshit."

"That sounds like a *threat*, ma'am," remarked one of the cops, as Tanaka felt a pair of composite-manufacture handcuffs being forced over her wrists. "Not good!"

I can melt these in a half-second, she mused,
As well as just tearing them apart with the whim of my mind.
Didn't your jackass briefing-files tell you about that, you jerks?

"But I won't do that... at least not right now," committed the more-than-a-woman, "Provided you'll do just one other thing, for me."

By now, there was only one police officer – a younger, tall, dark-haired man – behind her, holding her wrists. Two had gone over to examine the corpse, while the others, including the big, older guy, had positioned themselves in front of her.

"I don't know *who* the fuck you are," he snarled, "But you're goin' *downtown* with us, lady. What'd you *do* to that poor bugger, over there?"

"Nothing," she parried, "Though *believe* me – I wish it *had* been by my hand, that he died. He must have poisoned himself, the moment he knew he wasn't getting away."

"She's right," called out one of the officers who had crouched by the dead man. "Cyanosis. Must have chewed on a capsule."

"Yeah... well... you can tell us all about it, at the station," persisted the senior cop.

"*Wait* a minute," demanded Tanaka. "I get one phone call... isn't that right?"

"Yeah," repeated the cop. "You got a lawyer? You'll *need* one."

"I don't *think* so," she countered. "I have someone completely different in mind... and when you talk to her, you'll find out what deep shit you're in, my friend. You can even make the call *for* me, if you like. Got a communicator?"

"*Sure* I do, but I'm not following you," he said. "You give up the right to be represented – that's *your* decision... even if it's a stupid one."

He retrieved a mobile communicator from his equipment-belt.

"What's the number?" he asked.

"I don't even remember it, exactly," she replied, "But you can just look her up, then send her a message – specifically, 'Cherie says, get your ass down here, ASAP'."

"Who am I supposed to send this *to*, lady? Maybe your weirdo cult-leader or something?" the cop grumbled, with increasing irritation.

With smug satisfaction, Tanaka said, "Just look up Minnie Chu, Director of the Federal Bureau of Investigation... I hear she's staying at the White House, these days; and if you don't get her on the first try, just ask the President to relay my message."

The look on the policeman's face was worth the proverbial million bucks, as the former Mars mission science officer added,

"But don't tell them, that you've got me in handcuffs... you're down by three ranks already... no need to make it four or five."

Boob's Nice Little Present

The morning sun illuminated the West Virginia mountainscape in a glorious way, resulting in a broad vista of tree-tops over rolling, ancient-mountain peaks. Far below and away, the more perceptive of the "Cass Mountain Crew" – as the refugees had come to self-describe – could see the occasional car traveling on the few alpine roads which gave access to the hide-out.

Even though the day was young, there was enough daylight to have enticed those inside, to come out and enjoy the fresh air.

By now, the Boyd, Young and Jacobson families had become familiar enough to regard each other as close friends, and the younger of them had – despite numerous warnings from their elders – worked out elaborate protocols about "how to play 'hide and seek', without Mom and Dad knowing about it".

One such escapade was ongoing – with Wendy Boyd and Brent Junior Boyd, against Kerri Young and Riley Jacobson, all in the game – when Sam Jacobson, who had, along with his wife been assigned the job of looking after the young 'uns, suddenly wore a look of alarm.

His gaze had a far-off quality to it.

"Yvonne," he demanded, "Get the kids inside!"

"What *is* it?" replied the worried woman.

"Car coming up the road... and it's got a siren," explained the more-than-a-man. "Might be the police. Damn it! I thought Minnie said, we wouldn't be bothered up here –"

"*Children!*" she called out, in an unmistakable, "no-nonsense" tone. "You all get right back here – *now!*"

Four reluctant faces (though Wendy Boyd hid again, immediately afterward), popped out from various hiding-places.

"What will you do?" asked Yvonne Jacobson.

"I'm going to jump right in front of them, and tell them to get their butts out of here," responded the former Mars mission commander. "Get the kids inside, and warn Brent and the others... okay?"

"Okay," confirmed the wife, as she motioned to the children.

A wary, diamond-energy-encased Sam Jacobson – all too experienced at combat with various entities of the U.S. government, and equally ready for yet another such encounter – launched himself off the ground and far up into the blue West Virginia sky.

By now, he had figured out how to (in a limited manner), maneuver while in mid-leap; furthermore – to his immense satisfaction – he had developed the ability to loiter at the apex of his trajectory, delaying his fall back to Earth by thirty seconds to almost a minute.

Not nearly as good as Brent's and Cherie's fancy-ass flying into the Wild Blue Yonder, he ruminated, while surveying the mountainside below,

But half a loaf... I'll take it.

This particular leap had been on a relatively short and low trajectory, and it did not take him very long to notice what his wife had alerted him to; he saw a West Virginia State Police cruiser with its rooftop prominently illuminated by brilliant flashing lights and its sirens loudly wailing, below him and about twelve seconds' driving-time away from the mountain-top chalet.

So there *you are, assholes*, he mused.

Let's see how well your brakes work.

For your sake – they'd better be good*!*

He invoked his powers and set himself to a change of course. In a half-second more, Jacobson was dropping out of the sky, aiming at a spot about one hundred feet in front of the squad-car's current location.

Thud!

The former Mars mission commander tried – and to his mild annoyance, failed – to land completely upright; instead, the weight of his upper-body forced him to momentarily bow slightly forward. It was an involuntary gesture that was quickly remediated, as he planted his feet firmly on top of the mountain-road's gravel surface.

Jacobson then folded his diamond-encased arms in front of him and waited, with the dense forests of Cass Mountain blocking practical movement or escape, in every direction except via the road.

In the next couple of seconds, the police-car wound around a corner. For a second, the ex-astronaut was consumed with worry that whomever was driving the vehicle, hadn't seen him, and that there would shortly be a catastrophic collision... which the car would, without a doubt, have come out the loser of.

However – with no more than about ten feet to spare – the police-car screeched to an abrupt stop, sending a billowing cloud of dust and debris forward. This, of course, impacted harmlessly off of the ex-astronaut's personal force-shield.

Two side-doors flung open, providing egress to the two tough- and determined- state police officers – both fit-looking young Caucasian males – who stepped out with guns drawn, pointing directly at Jacobson.

"Who *are* you!" shouted the officer on Jacobson's left. "Stand aside... we're on official business!"

"So am I – and you're *trespassing* here!" countered the former Mars mission commander.

The left-hand cop – clearly unnerved by Jacobson's prismatic shielding, by his sinister-glowing eyes, by his background war-song and by his aura of power and majesty – hesitated for a second.

Then he said,

"You... you're that 'Mars' guy... right?"

"You *got* it, buster!" defiantly replied Jacobson. "Fort Knox, multiple Army tanks ripped to shreds... the works. You try to arrest me, or try to get by and bother my team up there at the top of this mountain, and after I turn your guns and your cruiser into scrap metal, I'll ask my new friend – the President of the United States, that is – to get you a nice little job washing the cop shop latrine. If I were you, I'd turn that car around... okay, you can't really *do* that here, so just back up all the way down – and call it a 'win'. Any questions?"

"We can't *do* that!" argued the cop on the right-hand side. "We've got to deliver a *message*."

"What 'message'?" challenged the former Mars mission commander.

"It's from the Director of the FBI," explained the right-hand cop. "Basically, we've been asked to warn the folks up there on Cass Mountain, that their *lives* may be in danger. Apparently the Bureau believes there's some kind of plot against the President, and the alien's friends, or whatever – they don't know a lot of details, only that there have already been at least two assassination attempts, carried out by snipers with high-powered rifles, and –"

"Did you say, 'lives are in danger'?" interrupted an instantly-worried Jacobson.

"Bureau thinks so," confirmed the cop. "They wanted us to tell you, that everyone should remain indoors and away from windows, until –"

"*Shit!*" inveighed Jacobson. "Stay here until I return with instructions!"

A second later, he was sailing off into the sky, on a retrograde course aimed at the top of Cass Mountain.

The ex-lead-astronaut's wife stood just to one side of the doorway leading to the mountain-top shack's interior. Anxiously, she scanned in the direction of where the road disappeared into the tree-line, checking to see if an unwelcome police-car showed up in that spot.

Yvonne also waited for the last of the "hide-and-seek'ers" to scurry back to safety. Unfortunately, there was foot-dragging involved, as a young girl dawdled behind one of the boulders that littered the landscape.

"Wendy! Wendy *Boyd!*" shouted Yvonne Jacobson. "You git back here right *now,* or I'll sic your mother and father on you!"

As if on cue, the figure of Brent Boyd showed up in the doorway. He walked out on to the demi-porch that extended almost the width of the shack, in front of the door.

"Where *is* she?" he inquired, with an exasperated father's tone. "Why are you calling them all back in?"

"Sam heard a police-car coming up the road," explained Yvonne Jacobson. "He – uhh – he 'jumped' down the mountain, to cut them off. He's been gone for almost a minute, though – Wendy's still out there, and –"

Brent Boyd's eyes started glowing, as his war-song began to issue from the earth, the stones, the walls of the shack... in fact, from just about everywhere.

"*Damn* the President, anyway!" he growled, "This could be the start of an attack – might be a diversion, while LEA closes in from the other side, or maybe the Air Force plasters us from above or something – I'd better –"

There was a loud sound – sort of like a car backfiring – coming from somewhere in the trees, far away.

All of a sudden, a shower of sparks issued from a point squarely in the middle of Brent Boyd's chest. Whatever hit him had such impact-force that it knocked him about a foot backward into the shack and knocked him to the ground.

But – though grimacing in obvious pain – the ex-astronaut was far from out of the fight, and as he sprang back into action with every inch of his body starting to glow like the lamp in a lighthouse, he yelled, "*Yvonne! Wendy! Get down!*"

It wasn't necessary, in the case of Jacobson's wife, who was cowering on the porch with her hands above her head.

The ex-astronaut's warning was, unfortunately, prescient. From seemingly every direction of the compass, a fusillade of rifle-shots – possibly well-aimed, more likely not – crashed into the windows and the sides of the shack. Shrieks of alarm were heard from inside as the bullets shattered glass and wrecked various household-implements, ranging from the refrigerator to the TV-screen.

Mercifully, as near as Boyd could tell, there were no screams that sounded like the results of bullet-wounds.

His alien-powers were now rapidly ramping up, as was his war-song.

"Everybody in there – hit the deck!" he bellowed. *"New People – topside, now!"*

Multiple alien melodies were heard from inside and below, as Brent Boyd hurtled into the sky, flying at a low angle in the direction of where he had last seen his daughter.

With consummate luck, it turned out that there were only the three games-playing children – Riley Jacobson, Kerri Young and Brent Boyd Jr. – inside the shack, when the shooting started. They were accompanied by four others, specifically, Donny Wade, his aunt and "Sammie" the prostitute, as well as the mountain-man who went by the name of "Cooter".

The rest of the refugees were in the underground-sections of the moonshine-shack-complex, variously sleeping, attending to restless hell-hounds or poring over the records left by the Chu visit about Tanaka's unfortunate mother.

Only two of those inside – Marie and Donny – happened to be standing when the bullets came flying in, and all heeded Brent Boyd's abrupt warning, falling to the floor almost immediately. The children and the working-girl had clustered around the TV, and were about to turn it on when they had to hit the deck. Cooter was in front of the refrigerator and he dropped down, swearing a blue streak about "fuck Dorsie for lettin' them city-folk – ", or words to that effect.

Three terrified children – as well as the street-walker and Marie Wade – wailed at the top of their lungs, with shock and fear. But despite their fright, geometry worked to the advantage of those inside the besieged shack. It was almost at the apex of Cass Mountain, and whomever was firing at them could not have had a superior elevation, since most of the bullets seemed to come in at oblique angles, or even horizontally.

Donny Wade was the only person to be initially hit, having a coffee-cup shot right out of his hands and then being struck in his left upper thigh by a bullet that missed the bone by at least an inch. The projectile seemed to slow down in an odd manner upon impacting against the former trucker's jeans, and it ended up being stuck in his flesh, with one end clearly visible.

Wade immediately grabbed it and – though spitting in pain and on one knee – pulled the bullet right out, throwing it in disgust to the floor of the shack while cursing and covering the bleeding gash with his left hand.

He briefly removed his hand to steady himself against the floor, and the amazed others could *see* the deep and ugly wound, shrinking and self-healing with each passing second.

The trucker's back-country-beat war-song began to echo within the shack, as his eyes and trunk glowed with a cold fury. His fists clenched.

"No – you all stay *down* there!" came Boatman's booming voice, from the stairwell.

His head appeared just above the threshold, but he involuntarily ducked upon seeing another barrage of rifle-shots blasting through the shack's thin walls. The angle of the gunfire was far too shallow to seriously endanger those who were cowering on the floor, but it could easily hit any adult who stood upright.

From far down below, the war-songs of the bounty-hunter and the Russian, could now be heard. Wolf's fire-dogs – or, perhaps, Wolf himself – let loose a weirding, baying howl. Everyone within earshot immediately felt comforted, empowered and more confident, in some obscure way.

"What's goin' *on*, man?" came Hendricks' alarmed shout, also from the uppermost reaches of the underground-complex.

"Somebody's *shootin'* at the shack!" exclaimed the voice of the black ex-agent.

Another fusillade of gunfire, which wrecked yet more of what was inside the shack, attested to the veracity of Boatman's observation.

"Anybody *hit* up there?" shouted the worried third agent.

"Just me!" came the growling voice of Donny Wade, "And I'm *pissed* about it – I'm gonna *get* them motherfuckers!"

Two more war-songs sent adrenaline-chills into the psyches of the Cass Mountain refugees.

"*With* you, man!" barked Hendricks. "*Fuck* 'em, anyway! Playin' for keeps – more Mr. Nice Guy!"

"Heads-down... *gangway!*" shouted Boatman.

Three glowing-eyed, grimly-determined more-than-humans, bending over to avoid the rifle-shots that were still plaguing the increasingly-damaged mountain-shack, charged to and out of the door.

Sam Jacobson was at the apogee of his leap when he heard – and saw – the gunfire erupting. Reflexively slowing himself down to slightly above "loiter" velocity, he mentally fumbled to enable the Storied Watcher's exotic vision-modes, wasting a precious second before his eyes had re-adjusted.

He scanned below him in all directions save directly behind.

Far off – almost on the other side of the mountain, in fact – and to the right just inside the tree-line, his heat-seeing detected the tell-tale signature of a rifle-blast. The shot hit the boulder that Wendy Boyd had taken cover behind, spalling a cloud of rock-fragments in every direction. A half-second

later, the gun that must have been responsible for the short heat-increment –
not to mention its unlucky user, and everything else within perhaps six to
eight feet in the immediate vicinity – was vaporized by Brent Boyd's
scintillating, dazzling sun-beam attack.

There was literally *nothing* left intact or alive, where the former Mars
mission pilot had let loose. The metal in what must have been the gun, was
just an elongated pile of smoking, molten slag.

Holy Supernova, he mused,

How the hell did Cherie survive being hit by that*?*

Remind me not to try the same experiment...

While grimacing and squinting his overloaded eyes, Jacobson silently
prayed that the resulting forest-fire would quickly burn itself out. He found
himself also reflexively saying a prayer for whomever had just been
disintegrated – but immediately abandoned *that* nonsense.

Save it for people like Cherie's mother, he decided.

Now Jacobson detected (first) Boatman, (then) Donny Wade, followed
by Hendricks, powering up their war-songs and pouring out of the
moonshine-shack.

To his initial dismay the former Mars mission commander noticed the
black ex-agent being hit by at least two rifle-shots... which, though they
momentarily impeded Boatman's forward progress, seemed to simply bounce
off him.

Well... look at that, realized Jacobson,

Guess I'm not the only "tank" around here, any more.

*He's drawing the shooting away from Yvonne – she's almost back in the
shack, out of the line of fire. I won't have to land there and block it.*

Thank God for small blessings...

The hunting-team from the moonshine-shack fanned out in all directions.
Evidently they, too, were tracking the originating-points of the gunfire –
which was continuing, albeit at a somewhat reduced tempo.

The military-trained former Mars astronaut looked around for a sector of
operations that, as yet, did not have "friendly forces" assigned to it.

The search did not take long. Below him – almost directly to the left – he
detected repeated gunshots being fired straight at the shack's doorway,
alarmingly close to where his wife had just secreted herself.

Okay, asshole, he furiously resolved,

This one's for Yvonne... and Cherie!

Aiming for slightly behind where the muzzle-flash had been seen, an
angry Sam Jacobson plummeted from the sky.

"Damn – that *hurt!*" exclaimed Boatman, as he began to recover his
pace, after being hit, dead-on, by two successive rifle-shots.

It was one of the rare occasions in which the others had heard the normally-polite former FBI agent, say a swear-word. But despite the cursing, the gunshots – which would have been instantly fatal to any normal human being – just bounced off Boatman (although, they left prominent holes in his clothes), and he charged steadfastly forward, toward the spot in the tree-line that his senses had detected the gunfire originating from.

"Boyd greased that guy over there!" shouted a now-levitating, partially-flaming, bright-eyed Hendricks. "I'm seein' 'em with Mars eyes – you too?"

"For sure," confirmed Boatman. "Every time they pull the trigger... looks like they settin' off a firecracker at midnight!"

The others noticed that Hendricks' hands were encased in some kind of sparking, bright-white electrical-discharge.

"I'll get the one nearer the road, on the same side!" committed the third agent. He flew outward in the direction of the forest, weaving back and forth to avoid the multiple gunshots that were unleashed against him.

Donny Wade, meanwhile, had been second out the door, despite having been appreciably wounded only a few seconds before. He seemed none the worse for wear for this mishap, however; and so he bounded across the Cass Mountain-top fields, much faster than an ordinary man could possibly run, shrieking in the direction of yet another hidden sniper,

"You a *dead* man, motherfucker!"

Somehow, the words of spite seemed to echo within, and seemed to be amplified by, the former trucker's war-song.

Jacobson's aim was, if anything, too accurate; crashing through the tree-tops in a shower of pine-needles and broken branches, he landed his feet less than ten inches from the face of his surprised, balaclava-hidden-faced opponent.

Despite the blur of close mortal combat, Jacobson's mind still somehow had time to do a lightening-quick assessment of the sniper.

Camo-suited, noted the former Mars mission commander,

But where he should have insignia of rank on the collar – like the bars, or even an oak-leaf – just a tiny Christian cross?

Well-armed – but the gun doesn't look "military-grade", somehow – looks like civilian-market gear – and wouldn't the Agency also be using better stuff as well?

Anyway – back to business –

Jacobson's feet straddled the assailant's high-caliber sniper-rifle on each side of the gun. Fumbling for his side-arm, the man instantly jumped up in the first moves of an attempt to bolt the scene, only to be met by a diamond-hard, brutally-powerful punch to the side of his jaw (actually, the more-than-human had held back, as had he employed full force, he would likely have decapitated his victim altogether).

The sniper was knocked backward and to one side, falling apparently unconscious against a nearby fallen log. Blood trickled out from underneath his face-mask.

"Don't *go* anywhere, jackass!" spat Jacobson, as he bent down and snapped the gun into two pieces.

Again, he launched himself into the air, curving in the direction of the moonshine-shack.

As Jacobson loitered in mid-leap, he had a ring-side seat on the second phase of the battle. As Brent Boyd rocketed up and away from the scene, protectively cradling his young daughter in his arms, the Russian appeared at the door of the shack; but although he took to the air, Misha just hovered above the building, evidently acting as a backup-defense-line against any assailants who might somehow have sneaked up past the other more-than-human defenders.

Wolf, on the other hand, charged outward to cover the shack's rear-areas. Atypically for him, the bounty-hunter stayed only a few feet above the ground; this might have been to keep closer control over his two hell-hounds, which were striding, with flame and smoke issuing from their drooling, snarling mouths, toward a point in the woods.

Hendricks – now as much flying, as levitating – seemed to reach his opponent first. Jacobson saw a number of small-caliber gunshots fired skyward in an erratic manner – a couple hit, but just bounced off the third agent, who retaliated with a frightening-looking devil's-brew of lightening-bolts (obviously much weaker than Tanaka's variety... but still more than lethal enough to slay a single human target) and flamethrower-like jets of fire.

The one who I hit got off easy, mused the former Mars commander, as he saw the ugly, instantly-carbonized black smear in the forest, where Hendricks' hapless victim had been cremated.

When that guy camps off a few more alien-powers, Jacobson realized,
He's going to be near-unstoppable. Something for everyone, that is.
I wonder if he's been "studying"... me?
Remind me not to make that any easier for him.

Much the same unfortunate fate met Boatman's quarry, who was evidently square in the middle of the former FBI agent's "wave of disintegration", which was unleashed as Boatman – who suffered at least three more direct hits from rifle-shots, all to no apparent effect – got within a distance of perhaps fifteen to twenty feet from the hidden sniper.

Jacobson saw a large section of forest – at least thirty feet wide and almost fifty in length – simply *vanish* in a billowing cloud of black-and-gray dust.

My God, realized the ex-astronaut,
A human being was in there.

At least it was over, before he had any idea what hit him...

Karéin, he silently prayed,

I sure hope my force-field can stop that.

Otherwise... if Otis and I end up coming to blows... I guess it comes down to, "who fires first".

Damn good reason not to pick a fight... wouldn't you say, Sam?

Possibly because of his previously-inflected wound, Donny Wade took a bit longer to close the distance to his own selected enemy, but this mattered little to the ultimate outcome. Jacobson saw the trucker – weaving in and out to anticipate and evade rifle-shots – disappear into the tree-line, and thereafter could only get fleeting glimpses of the resulting hand-to-hand battle by using the Storied Watcher's *Um'nàhr'é*-ability.

But what the ex-astronaut *could* observe, was easy enough to deconstruct. Jacobson saw an impossibly-rapid series of martial-arts punches and kicks impact the sniper, whose body was then somehow propelled upward – at least as far as the lower branches of the surrounding trees – and when the opponent fell back to earth, he was motionless.

Jacobson's "Mars ears" heard a barrage of choice Midwestern swear-words. He also observed Wade relieving his now-unconscious (or possibly, worse) fallen enemy, of his side-arm. The trucker reversed course and headed out of the woods, into the open-area.

By now, Jacobson's loiter-allowance was almost depleted, and he induced himself to drop out of the sky, coming to land just short of the moonshine-shack's front-porch.

Thankfully, the incoming gunfire had now ceased, as the war-songs waned in volume and intensity.

"*Yvonne!*" exclaimed the ex-astronaut. "Yvonne – are you okay?"

"Sam... *Sam!*" came back a terrified-sounding voice. "We're *so* scared in here!"

In about another second, he was inside, crouching over his mortified wife, who had taken shelter near the floor-boards, by the now-wrecked television and several other panicked refugees.

The inside of the shack was a mess; only one window was still intact, the walls (especially those facing the driveway going down the mountain) were full of bullet-holes, and almost everything else above waist-height in the building had been either damaged or destroyed.

"Is anybody here hurt?" shouted Sam Jacobson.

"Scared shitless," came the voice of the working-girl. "But I ain't shot... I *think*. Donny got hit, though! Then he ran out, and so did the rest of them –"

"Yeah... I saw that," confirmed the ex-astronaut. "I'll say it again – if anybody in here needs medical assistance – Riley, where are you?"

"I'm okay, Dad," came the voice of the boy. "Kerri and Little Brent and me, we all hid out together. Dad – where are the bad guys? Are they coming?"

"No, son," replied Sam Jacobson, "I think they're dealt with. Come over here with me and Mom – bring your friends too – but stay down."

"Okay," said the boy, as he frog-walked across the shack.

The elder Brent Boyd now appeared in the doorway. Advancing inside to approach his own children, he let his daughter down from her position of having been cradled in his arms.

"That was *fun*, Dad," remarked Wendy Boyd, "Except for being *shot* at, that is. And what you did – to that bad guy with the gun, I mean..."

With a guilty look, she hung her head.

Her father crouched down and looked his daughter straight in the eyes.

"Wendy," he counseled in a soft but determined voice, "I did what I *had* to – to protect you and all the rest of us. When your lives are at risk, I strike back as hard as I can... and this time, someone *died* as a result. I'm sickened by what happened, but I'd do it again, if I had to, because he would have killed both me and you, if he had the chance. Let it be a lesson... it *isn't* a game, or a joke. Do you understand?"

"Yes, Daddy... I *do*," she responded, her expression equally serious.

"Make that two more, at least," added Hendricks, as he and Boatman came back inside. "You got nothing to apologize for, Brent. Fuckers were shooting to kill... we're just payin' 'em back in like coin."

"That may be," reflectively mentioned the black ex-agent, "But it doesn't make it *right*. I've been runnin' up my own score – and it sure isn't something I'm proud of, may God forgive me."

"I saw what you two guys did... impressive and frightening at the same time," observed Sam Jacobson. "Are we sure we got all of them?"

"Seems so," said the third agent. "Shooting's stopped, anyway."

Donny Wade joined them, just inside the doorway.

"Second *that* idea," he offered. "I ran all around the shack, lookin' for more of them fuckers with the guns... ain't seein' any. I took out one of 'em myself – *he* ain't goin' nowhere now. Rooskie's still hangin' above, just in case."

A deep, growling howl was heard coming from outside.

Alarmed glances were exchanged back and forth, and then those inside the shack heard Wolf's voice advising,

"Don't wet your britches, kids... me 'n the pups are just back from havin' some *fun*. Damn – but it was over *way* too fast, if you ask me. I didn't even get a chance to let loose on the son of a bitch. Pups beat me *to* it!"

They cleared out of the doorway to make way for the bounty-hunter, who, accompanied by his two hell-hounds, walked inside.

The female dog had something in its mouth.

"Boob – give 'em a nice little present... will ya?" cruelly quipped Wolf.

The dog barked and released a camouflage-clad human left arm – torn off and burned at the elbow-joint – which fell to the floor-boards, eliciting cries of horror and disgust among many of the nearby civilians.

Sam Jacobson arose.

"For God's *sake*, Wolf," he complained, "We have people in here who are already traumatized enough! Can you *please* get that thing out of here!"

A bemused Wolf shrugged, and with the wink of an eye, instructed,

"Come on, doggies… these folks ain't got no sense of humor, I s'pose. I'll take you out and you can play with it outside."

"Shouldn't we – uhh – put it somewhere?" suggested Boatman. "I mean… you could consider it to be 'evidence'."

"Plenty more of that out there," noted Sam Jacobson. "At least with the one who I, uhh, neutralized –"

They heard the sounds of sirens, followed by the Russian's war-song being energized.

"Shit," cursed the former Mars mission leader, "There's something that Misha doesn't know – Brent, can you please look after Yvonne and my family? I've got to get out there before something really *bad* happens!"

"Of course," agreed Brent Boyd, "But what –"

Before he could finish, his former commander was out the door and into the sky.

A Conspiracy So Massive As To...

Sam Jacobson had acted just in time, as it turned out; the Russian's two lethal war-daggers were building up *Fire*-energy in preparation for a strike against the police-cruiser, when the ex-astronaut cruised by Misha at an altitude of about a hundred feet off the ground, shouting (and psychically-communicating) one simple message : "*Stop!*"

Fortunately, Misha heeded the instructions and aborted the attack. After a short airborne discussion, he and Jacobson landed beside the State Police car and – much to the dismay of the three mountain-men inside the building – escorted the cruiser to the moonshine-shack.

"Sir… is anyone inside there, or elsewhere, hurt?" demanded one of the police officers, as the car arrived in front of the shack. "We can call a medevac chopper, if necessary –"

"Unbelievable as it may sound… we don't think so," answered Sam Jacobson. "There were only a few people in the building and they quickly hit the floor when the gunfire started. It has a basement, and luckily, most of our party were down there at the time."

"Speak for *yourself*, Mr. Space Man," grumbled Donny Wade. "Took one in the leg… but I got better. Good as new now – and don't ask me how."

The ex-trucker, Brent Boyd and Dorsie the mountain-man clustered around the vehicle, while Wolf and his war-dogs frolicked in the nearby meadow, entertaining themselves by playing "catch" with a now-badly-chewed, ex-human arm. Boatman and Hendricks stood far back, as much out of eyeshot as they could safely manner.

"That boy's got about as much tact as a prize hog in a mud-bath," sarcastically commented the former Mars mission pilot.

"I *heard* that," called back the bounty-hunter, though he was a hundred feet away. "Who *gives* a shit? Former owner sure don't need it no more."

"Officer," demanded Sam Jacobson. "Given what's just happened here, I need to speak to Minnie Chu, Director of the FBI... right *now*, please!"

"Anything you *say*, mister," warily replied one of the state troopers while he manipulated the controls of the car's radio-equipment, "But it don't *work* like that – we gotta go through the chain of command –"

"Unless you want two or three of us flying back to D.C. with blood in our eyes," warned Brent Boyd, "You'll throw your chain of command, out the window."

"Okay, *okay* – we *get* it," complained the trooper. "I'll use the special channel and the priority-code. Give me a minute."

After about two minutes more, involving three calls and quite a bit of pleading, it appeared that the link was up.

"Go ahead," said the trooper, as he delivered a hand-held, audio-only microphone to Sam Jacobson. "Just be aware – it's a secured circuit, but it's not military-grade. Could be tapped with the right gear, or so we're told."

"Chance I'll have to take," remarked the former Mars mission commander.

He spoke into the mike.

"This is Sam Jacobson here. Can you please get Director Chu on the line?"

"Speaking, Commander," came back a familiar voice. "Sam... what's going *on* there? I'm getting reports of gunfire –"

"'What's going on', you ask?" peevishly retorted the ex-astronaut. "Oh, well... nothing except a little old assault by what seemed like a platoon or more of guys equipped with high-powered sniper-rifles. They opened fire on us by surprise –"

"Anybody... *hurt?*" interrupted Chu.

"It's a miracle that I can say this, but – 'no'... at least not on *our* side," answered Jacobson. "But it sure as hell wasn't for lack of *trying*, on their part – we fought back effectively, of course... we believe that we've, ahh, *liquidated*, all of them. Minnie – who the hell's *responsible* for this bullshit? If it was the government, I *assure* you –"

"Will you wait just a *minute!*" again interjected the remote voice. "Commander, I can assure you it's no such *thing!* Want to know how I know?"

"*Do* update me!" challenged the ex-astronaut.

"Because – I'm guessing – whoever ordered and organized this attack, may be the same criminals who just tried to kill Sylvia and Cherie in Pittsburgh," explained Chu.

"Sylvia – Cherie –" gasped Jacobson.

It was an expression that was mimicked by many of those within earshot.

"Sylvia got hit and is in the hospital, even though it looks like they might have been aiming for Cherie," disclosed the *nouvelle* FBI-director. "That's what we know currently. Commander... I think this is a series of coordinated 'hits'. We have too many similar attacks in a short time, for it to be just a coincidence."

Jacobson stared out into space.

Eventually he said, "Acknowledged. I have to tell you... despite our powers, we're feeling pretty, uhh, *exposed*, out here. We were able to protect our families – and other civilians – *this* time, largely, I think, because they attacked from long range, in the daylight. What if next time, it's a close-range ambush, at night? What if they use anti-tank missiles next time? Or if they attack when we go out to pick up groceries? Or... 'whatever'. It's just a matter of *time* until they – whoever 'they' is – get 'lucky'. If you have a plan, Minnie... now's the time to inform us of it."

"We're obviously pulling out all the stops to locate whoever's behind this, and to bring him – or them – to justice," informed Chu. "In the meantime, Commander, can you please cooperate with local law-enforcement – I'm sending a Bureau field-team up there by helicopter to retrieve evidence... so for God's sake don't shoot them down when you see or hear them. Also, I'd suggest you keep your people as well-hidden as you can, until we've apprehended those responsible for these attacks. Are you *sure* you still don't want to go to Camp David?"

"I'm not going to pronounce on that myself," replied Jacobson.

He turned to the others.

"What do *you* think?" he asked. "It might be safer there, but on the other hand, Karéin might get back here with the *Express* and find nobody home. We could leave her a message saying where we want, I guess."

An unconvinced Brent Boyd moved to be close to the microphone.

He commented, "Minnie... if we were at Camp David – or any government facility, for that matter – wouldn't we have to rely on the 'protection' of the Secret Service, or of the police... or, of some other similar LEA group? What I'm saying is... 'we'd be asked to keep our powers in abeyance, and let someone else defend ourselves and our families... is that right?"

"Not... *exactly*," deflected Chu. "I'd ask you to exercise restraint and let the Service and other law enforcement staff, do their jobs. But we both know that neither they – nor I – could stop you, Major Boyd or the others, if you felt the need to take matters into your own hands. Which, for the record, I'm hoping that you don't have to do. And by the way, Will – Otis – if you can hear me, please take that as direction, unless there's no other option. We've got enough issues with the use of lethal force, as it is."

"Two cheers for *us*," complained the third agent. "And Minnie... we *hear* you, but I'm afraid it's a bit late. Whoever those fuckers that attacked us were – well, let's just say, for the ones that Otis and I dealt with... there isn't enough left of 'em to bury. You *gettin'* me here?"

"Unfortunately... yes," confirmed the nouvelle-Director. "*Try* not to kill anybody else, if you don't mind?"

"Only the ones that try to smoke *us*, first, Minnie," countered Boatman.

"Understood," she said. "What about Camp David? If you want to go there, I need to know now so I can arrange transportation."

The Cass Mountain team of more-than-humans broke out in a lively debate, with opinions both for and against a move to the presumably better-defended government facility being offered up.

Hendricks and Boatman disappeared into the moonshine-shack and, after a delay of about five minutes evidently spent underground, showed up again.

The third agent said, "We talked to everybody... half of 'em want to pay the President's little chalet a visit; the other half are saying, 'you'll have to drag me there by my feet'. That's where we're at."

Upon being so informed, Sam Jacobson stated,

"Honestly, Minnie... we can't get a clear consensus, here. Which I think means we're staying put, at least until Karéin returns and we can decide jointly what to do. We're running very short of supplies up here... is there any way you can arrange to have some delivered?"

"You mean stuff like groceries and so on?" inquired Chu.

"That, and everything else from toilet-paper to toothbrushes to cooking-plates," explained the ex-astronaut. "Imagine a group of twenty or so people stuck camping up on the top of a mountain, having brought nothing along with them... that's the situation."

"And a TV," interjected Hendricks. "Buggers shot out the one they had up here. In fact we need a new fridge and a new stove as well. Pretty much *everything* that Cooter, Ezra and Dorsie had put in the shack, got hit. We don't know if any of it works any more."

With an exasperated tone, the nouvelle-Director replied, "I'll see what I can do... but all of this, and much more, is already there at Camp David, you know."

While the open conversation continued, a nervous Boatman took Hendricks aside and whispered,

"Listen, Will... you think it's a good idea, showin' our faces this much? I mean... you *remember* what happened back there on the highway? These boys here in the car... they might know the ones who we... well, *you* know?"

The third agent replied, *sotto voce*, "I gotta believe that Minnie will get us out of all this – I say we act as if nothing happened. It was dark, it went down fast... they probably don't have a good ID on us, anyway, unless they put the squeeze on Dorsie. Which we should make sure, doesn't happen."

Boatman silently nodded affirmatively.

"It's not what we know you've got over there, that we'd like to enjoy," observed Sam Jacobson, "Rather, it's what you *might* have over there, that we're scared of. If *that* makes any sense."

"Coming from a guy and a team that defeats entire Army brigades and that has just turned back a coordinated assault by professional assassins, not particularly," sniffed Chu, "But that's only my opinion, I suppose. Expect to see a few more helicopters coming your way, laden with whatever we can glean from the Executive Office logistics-department. Can I speak to the state troopers who made their communications-equipment available, please?"

"Of course," obliged Jacobson. "We disabled the only mobile communicator that we had around here, some time ago, which is probably why we didn't answer if you called in a warning. Officers... over to you."

He handed over the microphone.

"This is Officer Jack Morrow speaking, ma'am," said the first policeman, who had disembarked from the car's passenger-side. "What can I do for you?"

"First," directed Chu, "Please establish a perimeter at the base of Cass Mountain, covering all roads, trails and other convenient avenues of access. *Nobody* is to get past your checkpoints until and unless I *personally* approve it. The only exception's the Bureau staff who are now on their way – we've dispatched two helicopters and two cars, with sixteen agents and forensics-specialists. They all have Bureau biometric ID... make sure you challenge them for it. Second, leave your cruiser up at the moonshine-shack, so we can use the radio for communications with Commander Jacobson and his team –"

"Excuse me, ma'am," protested Morrow, "But if we do that – how are we supposed to get back down to the station? It's several *miles* by foot!"

"Don't worry about *that*," offered Brent Boyd. "We have 'airlift' capability in spades, up here."

"Yeah... but don't forget your seat-belt," impishly added Hendricks. "Oh... and you might not want to look down."

"You mean, a 'copter, ma'am?" he pressed.

"That's up to you," said the nouvelle-Director. "You can get a ride back with the Bureau when their work is done, but that might be a day or more... it will depend on what they find. Or, you can take your chances with the 'Mars Gang', who can airlift you all on their own, if you need to get home sooner –"

"We *promise* not to drop him," unhelpfully quipped Brent Boyd. "Pinky-swear."

A look of alarm appeared on the face of the trooper, but he said nothing. However, his partner remarked, "We're stuck up here for awhile, then. Listen... as it's now a crime scene, Jack, I guess we got to inspect the premises –"

Cooter appeared in the doorway. He said, "Y'all do whatever y'all want to – but ain't *no* po-lice, gettin' inside this-here shack! I ain't havin' *nobody* meddlin' with mah operation... nor samplin' mah *product!*"

The mountain-man was met with six or seven bemused gazes.

"Hey, man... you sure got a sense of *humor* there," insouciantly mentioned Hendricks.

"Why'd *that* be, city-boy?" challenged Cooter.

"Well, for *starters*," explained the former FBI agent, "This place is now surrounded by some of the most powerful super-beings on the planet – me and Otis included – and there's jack *shit* you can do to keep us out, if we wanted to let these cops in – not that that's on the agenda... you know? And even if we stand by, Cass Mountain's now on the radar-screen of the entire FBI, not to mention just about every other LEA in the country and probably the whole U.S. Army, Navy and Air Force. Oh... and about your 'product'..."

"What *'bout* mah product?" countered the mountain-man.

"Short while ago, Dorsie met up with Little Miss Nuclear Angel... right?" observed Hendricks.

"Yeah... so *what*?" said Cooter.

"She *nice* to you?" asked the third agent of Dorsie, with a wry smile.

"Reckon so," confirmed the mountain-man. "Even gave me a hug, right out of the blue... said somethin' bout 'y'all an' Ezra an' Cooter now *mah* b'loved kin, be proud of that'... didn't really understand what she was sayin', but figured it weren't a good idea to be pressin' her on the issue. So what?"

"How'd you *feel*, after getting that hug?" maliciously asked Hendricks.

"Well, I don' know... okay... come to think of it, I *did* feel kind of nice... busted mah left arm few years ago, always had to favor it since then, but all of a sudden, it don't hurt no more when I lift stuff with it," replied Dorsie. "Who *cares*, anyways?"

"Bit of advice for all of you 'shiners up here," proposed the third agent.

"What would *that* be, city-boy?" grumbled Cooter.

"Go ahead and serve up whatever 'product' you've got up here," concluded Hendricks, "While it's still worth doing so."

Big-League Hitter

Much unlike himself, "Top Dog" hadn't been shaving; there was thin stubble on his normally military-clean cheeks, chin and throat. He hadn't changed his white business-shirt recently, and he had even dispensed with the red power-tie that – no more than a few weeks ago – he had worn consistently, like a talisman of leadership and success.

Still, this wasn't much of a disadvantage. There was absolutely *nobody* else (unless you counted the disheartening images on the TV-screens in a couple of communications-rooms, or the few robotic servitors attending to his every need) in this forlorn, underground, concrete-walled place, to interact with him.

I hate *being so unkempt,* he mused,

But a change of appearance... well, that *can't be avoided, given the project.*

He had been walking the miles of silent corridors – still near-immaculate, if you didn't count a bit of dust, here and there – for *days*, now.

Another man, might have been unnerved by the quiet, by the isolation, by the loneliness, by the solitude.

Another man, might even have gone mad. But not *this* man.

His mind was made up; his cause – and what he knew he must do, to fulfill it – was clear.

I wish we hadn't lost almost all our real "professionals" up on Amchitka, when the bomb went off, he inwardly complained.

If that asshole MacGammon had just followed orders, *and had got them into adequate shelter, before...*

And then, the two of our last four, on that plane... I mean, they were told *to off both Chu and Crowford... they had clear orders... what the hell* happened?

Bottom of the barrel afterwards, and the outcome was predictable... I should have known *the whole thing would fuck up, big-time... now it's up to me to set things right.*

Never send a bunch of boys out, to do a man's job, he resolved, while reaching into the weapons-locker in his smallish personal-room.

Out came the custom-throated-and-ramped, perfectly-personally-balanced, folding-up .50 caliber semi-auto sniper-rifle that had served him so well, in his early days. Constructed as it was out of the latest, specially-engineered composite-materials, the weapon was far smaller and lighter than it should have been, given what it was set up to fire.

Let's see... where's the... oh, yeah... there it is.

Hope the Agent D-1811 toxin's still good... should be, after all, it's been sealed inside the DU discarding-sabot rounds, for all these years, and it was supposed to be guaranteed for at least thirty... so what if it's $20K per round – I'm worth it, don't you think?

That, and the special, high-grade plastique *detonator that's the other half of each bullet... never failed me before... good memories – like my third-to-last hit, before I graduated to a desk-job – didn't that Brazilian state governor, just 'go to pieces'?*

Call the guys with the green garbage-bags and the water-hose, 'clean-up on Aisle One'...

After retrieving these tools of the trade, Top Dog carefully secreted them in his special, X-ray- and emissions-sniffing-proof duffel-bag. He slung this over his shoulder and then strode purposefully out of the sleeping-quarters, turning to the right down the long, noiseless corridor. After a trip of around three minutes, he reached a steel door – expertly recessed into the surrounding concrete, to the point of being almost impossible to detect – at the end of the walkway.

"Identification value is Spiderweb 052," he spoke. "Validate."

A thin red light coming from somewhere above the top of the portal momentarily illuminated his eyes.

"Validated," came a metallic, computer-speech-type voice.

"Ingress," said the man.

Soundlessly, the door moved away from him by about an inch. Then it disappeared to the right, into what must have been a holding-slot in the wall. Beyond this, was a darkened room.

"Lights," he ordered.

Now the chamber before him was partly illuminated, with deep shadows kept only partly at bay by soft lighting, issuing from luminescent panels on the ceiling and the floor.

The room had multiple, relatively narrow walls on every side, arranged almost like a half an octagon (or some equally-multilateral shape). On each wall were translucent panels of some glass-like substance, labeled "A" at the left to "D" on the right. Behind the three left-most panels, one could see a vaguely-humanoid shape standing – or, perhaps, hanging suspended. There was a stainless-steel platform about the size and shape of a dinner-table, in the middle of the room.

Top Dog advanced within.

"Equipment Bay 'C'," he directed. "Authorization value is Flat-Out, 7222."

The third panel from the left opened with a very slight "whoosh" sound, as well as the issuance of something akin to steam, or maybe dry-ice-fumes.

He walked over to the equipment-bay. Within it was something that looked sort of like the shotgun-marriage of a diving wet-suit, a SWAT outfit and a suit of Kevlar armor. The suit included a tight-fitting head-covering similar to what the Apollo astronauts wore underneath their space-helmets, as well as unobtrusive enhanced-vision-goggles and a pair of close-fitting, silicone-coated foot-coverings.

All in all, despite its obvious protective-value, the suit was a marvel of miniaturized technological achievement.

Okay... so you've got these "alien-powers", he reflected, with satisfaction.

Did you think we'd throw ordinary Wet-Ops people at you, this time?

Meet "Hitman 2.0", bitch!

"Activate. Diagnostic. Validate combat-readiness," said the man.

Instantly, dim, mostly green-colored lighting showed up at various locations upon the suit.

There was a delay of a couple of seconds, and then the same computer-voice as had been heard outside repeated, "Diagnostic complete. Validation complete. Full capability available."

"Lock to my identity," he demanded. "Auto self-destruct on prohibited use case and on cessation of life-functions."

"Locked," came back the impassive reply. "Auto self-destruct parameters acknowledged."

Without further ado, Top Dog reached into the mini-chamber and lifted the suit out. He laid it on the stainless-steel table, carefully examining its every nook and cranny.

The best we could do, based on what we got out of that house in Tucson, he mused.

That alien-metal used as economically as we could... just scraps left after using most of it, up on the island.

If only we had more time to figure out how to reverse-engineer it!

Maybe a futile exercise anyway... composition had the scientists stumped – "molecules we've never seen before, got no idea how to make them"...

Anyway... what I've now got here is a testament to how fast our engineers can work... with the right motivation.

This little baby will get the team and I, where we need to be.

Up to us, to do the rest.

A thin smile showed on his face as he retrieved a carrying-case, about the size of a small suitcase, out of the wall-recess that had also accommodated the battle-suit.

He placed it at the head of the table and opened it, revealing an interior lined with some kind of shielding as well as foam impressions exactly corresponding to the dimensions of the suit.

"Unlock 'A' and 'B'," commanded the man.

The first two protective panels opened up, providing access to what was behind them.

As he had done for his own battle-suit, Top Dog retrieved the two other suits – plus associated carrying-cases – from the leftmost and next holding-chambers.

"Activate. Diagnostic. Lock to pre-identified bio-signatures and configure for auto-destruct, same parameters. Validate combat-readiness, for Instances 'A' and 'B'," he spoke out loud.

After a second or two, the reply came back : "Diagnostic complete. Validation complete. Bio-signature-lock and auto-destruct functions activated. Full capability available for Engagement Suits 'A' and 'B'."

He briefly examined the gear.

Let's not count on these guys, even though they're the two best ones left in the Agency, he ruminated.

None of the "alien" shit here... just the best we could do with what we already had.

Still... at the very least, there's two more targets to distract our adversaries...

Top Dog lifted the pieces of the suits, one-by-one, into their intended resting-places inside their respective carrying-cases. Though these were bulky when carried all together, there were enough belts and straps to make the job practical, even for one man.

You've met the Pewee team, you little alien whore, he thought.

Get ready to play in the big *leagues, with the 'pro's', bitch... sudden-death!*

With his gear now fully accounted-for in his baggage and a stern, determined look, loaded himself for bear, wheeled in place and headed for the single exit out of this place.

Strike Four

It wasn't a particularly busy day at the The Shoppes At Gateway mall in Springfield, Oregon; but even so, hundreds of people were present when the shooting started.

It was all over in about three minutes – substantially before the first elements of the local Rapid Reaction team showed up on-scene – but in that time, thirty-eight shoppers lay dead, with nearly fifty more crippled or clinging feebly to life, after the onslaught.

When the police finally arrived in force and executed their "active shooter" routine, to their consternation, they found... nobody. The forensics teams combed the crime scene, as they always do, and at first they found next to no useful evidence.

All they got were accounts from a few traumatized eye-witnesses, about "some guy dressed in a SWAT suit, except you'd blink once or twice and he was just... gone".

Then, an astute local cop, looked underneath one of the blood-smeared corpses.

"Hey, Manny! Get a load of *this!*" he called out, to one of his fellow-officers.

With the help of his friend, the first cop rolled a body on to its side.

"See that deck of cards?" he exclaimed. "It was under this poor guy, all the time!"

"Yeah," observed the second cop. "What the hell you think it *means?*"

"Dunno," replied the policeman. "I mean... a hand of deuces... *anything* beats *that!*"

The students crowded into the cavernous St. John's Lecture Hall at Idaho State University in Pocatello, on this day, weren't expecting anything other than a boring exposition of trade theory, on the part of the doddering, past-retirement-age Professor Benjamin Wildrom.

It was almost lunchtime, and many in the audience were thinking more of what would be on the menu in the cafeteria, than they were of the intricacies of trans-border commerce.

"And so," the old man started to explain, "We can see that the Heckscher–Ohlin theory of international trade, applies even to today's unsettled times, because –"

There was a sharp *"crack!"* sound, and to the horror of the onlookers, Wildrom had spoken his last words, as his head exploded in a spray of blood and cerebral tissue. Those in the first row who were contaminated by this grisly shower, however, had little time to revile it, as in quick succession, at least six of them met an equally-appalling fate.

The panicking students rushed toward the exits; but the latter were somehow closed and locked from the outside. A small number of the more resourceful ones, tried to hide while activating personal mobile communicators, to record the carnage (and to say last messages to parents and family).

Nobody could tell where the gunfire was coming from, however; it seemed to be issuing from every direction. Once or twice, those inside caught a glimpse of a black-suited figure, which was visible only for a second or two; then it again vanished.

More gunshots rang out. Finally, it stopped, as the last standing student was cut down.

Aside from those mortally wounded, one terrified, blood-splattered young woman had been "lucky" enough only to take a bullet to the upper-thigh. She crouched behind a pile of bodies and an upturned table, on one side of the lecture-hall's stage, at the lowest-level of the chamber.

Silently, her communicator's video-recorder scanned the surroundings. There appeared to be nothing except for the cruelly-abused corpses of her fellow students – scores of them – strewn like blood-stained rag-dolls, in various grotesque poses, throughout the lecture-hall.

Suddenly – to the woman's dismay – a voice sounded from the communicator.

"Chelsea! Why aren't you picking up, honey?" it said.

It was her mother.

Reflexively, the student hit the "Mute" button on the device.

But it was too late. From seemingly nowhere, there appeared in front of her, a black-battle-suited assailant, his face obscured by some kind of helmet and night-vision goggles.

"Of Number Two," spoke this man, "You're the last."

"What do you m –" the student tried to ask, as she stared into the muzzle-flash.

When her body was found, four cards – all "threes" – were found along with it.

The Emergency Waiting Room of the Greater Denver Health Center was crowded, almost to the point where the security guards – who were used to dealing with druggies, alcoholics and the occasional rowdy gang-member – were about to turn people away, at the front doors.

The room's benches were chock-a-block with those suffering from various maladies ranging from "the sniffles" to serious internal injuries, resulting from car accidents and the like. Regardless of severity... they waited, waited again, and waited yet more.

It had been thus for a very long time; in *this* America, there was no "socialist government healthcare", and for those without access to very expensive, private-sector health insurance, the wait to see a doctor – or even a nurse at the reception-desk of the Denver Health Center – could amount to a day, or a week, or more.

That was... if the erstwhile patient, didn't expire, while in the queue. Happily, the Health Center had only seen two such cases in the last week and a half. Local management counted *that*, as a "win".

Just after sundown, there was a commotion outside, quite a distance away, probably at the far edges of the surrounding parking-lot, followed by the unhappily-familiar sounds of low-caliber gunfire. Instinctively, two of the Emergency Waiting Room's guards, with their guns unholstered, headed outside towards the source of the disturbance, while the third – per standard protocol – stayed back at the nurses' station.

The ominous, barking sounds of weapons-fire were heard from outside, again. Many of those who were still ambulatory, rushed to the large, sliding-glass doors to see what was happening. They could just see a fire-fight going down, at least a hundred feet away, in the parking-lot.

Suddenly, the guard in the nurses' station doubled over, with blood gushing all over the desk and floor where he fell. Though he had been wearing a Kevlar-II breastplate, his neck was unprotected from the gunshot – coming from a direction that seemingly contained, "nobody" – that nearly took his head off. A second later, two nurses standing nearby, met the same grisly fate, as quick pistol-shots shredded both of the hapless women's bodies. A burly male paramedic, charging toward where he thought the gunfire to have been originating, took a shot to the forehead and died instantly.

Screams reverberated through the Waiting Room.

"There's someone *shooting!*" shouted a terrified civilian, who had been waiting alongside her significant other, a guy hobbling around on crutches with an obviously-broken right leg. A half-second later, her warning proved accurate, as she was shot – this time, by something much more powerful than a pistol – right through the heart. As her distraught mate wheeled to tend to the dying woman, he, too, was hit : the first high-powered round took off his left arm, while several more shots killed him outright.

Strangely, however – though the area was brightly-lit – only the briefest of glances were gained, of those responsible for the ongoing massacre. The few who escaped, by running further into the hospital, saw what looked like a man in a SWAT suit – but the image was indistinct, as if glimpsed only for a fleeting second, in the reflection of a mirror.

The same terrible fate met dozens more in the Waiting Room; and though the more on-the-ball of those in the room dashed out the doors, this availed them little, as someone outside was waiting with a gun. A hail of auto-rifle shots put paid to the idea of escaping, along with it, to the lives of at least ten civilians, who were cut down while stepping outside the building.

By now, the two other guards were also dead, having been shot in the back, while trying to engage what they thought were urban gangsters, somewhere further out into the parking-lot.

As suddenly as it had started, the shooting stopped, and a ghastly silence – broken only by the far-off sounds of police-sirens – fell over the bullet-scarred, blood-splattered Greater Denver Health Center Emergency Waiting Room.

One of the only two genuine survivors of the atrocity – a guy who had been shot in three places, and who had fallen behind a gurney, over which was draped the lifeless body of a paramedic – wondered,

Who would shoot up a hospital?

Eventually, the SWAT team did show up. But they seemed to neglect the wounded, for a moment or two; instead, they concentrated on something that had apparently been found, at the bloodied, shot-to-hell nurses'-station.

Over the static of one of the gendarmes' mobile radios, the guy under the gurney could just make out, "Roger that – call Special Forensics – I see a hand of "fours" set up here, on the counter".

As temples to the gridiron gods of the National Football League went, Arrowhead Stadium in Kansas City, Missouri, wasn't the most impressive of the species; in fact, the place had seen better days since its last renovation in the mid-'20s, and the rebar in its concrete walls was actually showing a little rust.

None the less – even though the formal pro football season wouldn't officially start until a few months from now – the stadium was still packed with spectators.

Yes, it *was* only an exhibition-game, between the Chiefs' "B-Team" of wannabe pro-bowlers who had fallen just short of making the cut for the real team, and an equivalent Montana Mavericks farm-team; but after all... it was still football.

That, was all that counted.

The hundreds of hatch-backs and station-wagons parked in the lot, each one hosting its own little tailgate-get-together, had been partying hard for about three hours now, under the calm, clear, Midwest evening skies.

Those attending the *ersatz* celebrations – the partakers of beer, frankfurters and extra-thick pretzels – noted a loud, satisfied war-whoop coming from inside the stadium, as the multiple portable TV-screens located in the backs of cars confirmed that the home team had eked out a narrow – but gratifying – 21 to 20 victory over the "Horsemeat Boys of Montana" (as the hated away-team, were universally known).

With reluctant admission that the partying was soon to be over for the night, the tailgaters began to slowly pack up the beer-coolers and *hibachi-*grills, as a flood of satisfied ticket-holders issued from Gate C of the stadium.

The first echelons of those coming from inside the building started to cross Red Coat Lane, when it was observed that two large, black SUVs had been parked about two hundred feet apart on this street, facing each other, and preventing vehicular traffic in either direction. The rear passenger-side doors opened on both SUVs, but it did not appear – as far as anyone could tell in the limited illumination provided by overhead lights – that anyone had disembarked.

All of a sudden, the terribly-familiar "crack-crack-crack" sound of automatic-rifle fire began to be heard, somewhere in the vicinity of the two dark vehicles. Carnage erupted among the football-fans exiting the stadium, as high-velocity rifle-bullets shredded and mangled arms, legs, heads, and torsos, throughout the crowd.

A second or so later, it was the tailgaters' turn; but instead of gunfire to plague them, the car-partiers fell victim to explosive devices – grenades, perhaps, though nobody could really tell where they were coming from, or who was throwing them – that completely disintegrated those unfortunate enough to be nearby to where they landed, while still doing crippling and often fatal damage to victims only slightly further away.

The onslaught lasted only about thirty seconds, during which time, nearly a hundred and twenty football-fans were mowed down, with at least twice that many left moaning on the concrete, with crippling, savage injuries. A few of the wounded or dying, thought they saw two – or was it three – mysterious, battle-armor-wearing assailants; those who lived to tell the tale, swore that "those monsters... it was like they was blinkin' in and out of view, right in front of ya".

The doors on the two SUVs closed and the vehicles did an about-face, roaring down Red Coat Lane in the direction of I-70, leaving a sea of unjustly-spilled blood to stain the hallowed entrance-way to the home of the Kansas City Chiefs.

And in one of the pools of now-extinguished human life-essence, the local police found four playing-cards... one a spade, one a diamond, one a club and one a heart... all with a denomination of, "five".

What We Pay You For

The mood in the Oval Office was the definition of "grim", as Minnie Chu stood – both literally and figuratively – "on the carpet", in front of the President.

Kaysten, as always, stood behind his boss, on the left. Uncharacteristically, he seemed rather taciturn today.

The view to outside was obscured, compared to only a few days ago; the thick, bullet-proof glass recently installed in the Oval Office windows, had seen to *that*.

There were also Secret Service agents stationed at every entrance, both inside and outside. The presumption was that they'd be the first to take the next sniper-bullet, or bullets; what each individual agent thought of the strategy, was not recorded.

"You *know*, Ms. Chu," mordantly observed the President, "I had honestly thought that having two H-bombs aimed at me and a third about to go off, out West – not to mention a pissed-off alien with blood in her eye – I thought *that*, was about 'as bad is it can get'. I guess I was wrong... wasn't I?"

Ever-poised – though inwardly frustrated – the *nouvelle* FBI director replied, "Well sir... I'd have to acknowledge that what we're now dealing with, is certainly a *different* challenge, compared to the huge risks that we recently overcame. It's obviously a serious situation; we're doing our best to find those responsible. Did you hear the latest news? After the briefing about the attack on the Jacobson party, up on Cass Mountain."

"You'll have to be more specific," peevishly remarked the U.S. leader. "There are so many of these incidents going around these days, that I've lost track of them."

"I just got a call from Cherie Tanaka, down in Pittsburgh," explained Chu. "She's under arrest for murder – a misunderstanding, I'll deal with it of course – but what occasioned it was, she chased down a sniper who had just shot Sylvia Abruzzio. The guy committed suicide... chewed on a cyanide capsule, apparently. Cherie and Sylvia were sitting in an outdoor café and all of a sudden they were hit by a barrage of gunfire – Sylvia was hit in the neck –"

"My *God*," spoke a shocked Kaysten. "Is she still alive?"

"Yes... Ms. Abruzzio's one of the *good* ones," added the President. How *is* she?"

"In the hospital, sir," said the former team-leader. "She's hurt, but we don't know exactly how badly. I've instructed the Pittsburgh Police Service to put her under 24-hour guard, in case there's another attempt on her life, and I'll ask them to station Cherie with her, as well."

"What's the status of the investigation?" demanded the President.

"We *are* making progress, sir," hopefully advanced Chu. "Especially since we've got the upper echelons of the Agency purged and replaced by loyal Bureau personnel... same's true of the Secret Service. Some of the systems have taken a while to come back on-line, and there are others that for some reason we still don't seem to have access to, but the results have been encouraging. There's a *lot* of good evidence coming in –"

"Let's get right to the point," countered the U.S. leader. "When are we going to catch the sons of bitches who *did* these killings, out West? Where was the latest one?"

"Kansas City, sir... outside the football-stadium," informed Chu. "An *awful* scene – no doubt about that. We've got local forensics-teams on-site, but we haven't been able to send any of our best people – they're all committed to trying to find whoever killed Cherie Tanaka's mother, also who shot at her and Sylvia Abruzzio – and then, the assault on Sam's team on top of the mountain. The plain facts *are,* sir... we're encountering a shortage of trained personnel; that's all there is *to* it."

There was a dark, sullen look on the President's face, as he fell silent for a few seconds, considering his options.

"Are we one hundred per cent sure that neither Jacobson – nor any of his friends, like for example that big jerk with the long hair and the bad flaming attitude – had anything to do with this, directly or indirectly?" he demanded. "For that matter... what about the alien herself?"

"'One hundred per cent', sir? I'm afraid that's something that I can't honestly claim," replied Tanaka. "But I'd remind you – Sam's own family and friends appear *also* to have been attacked. Unless we're going to get into conspiracy-theories that he staged this himself just to throw us off, the chances of him having plotted crimes like this, are *remote*. After all... why would us 'super-humans' even *need* to hire assassins, in the first place? Commander Jacobson could just hop all the way here and then destroy everything – and everyone – in sight, all by himself. As for Karéin... rumor has it that she's flown off to 'somewhere'. She's apparently not even *in* the United States, currently."

"I *still* don't trust Jacobson," mentioned the President.

"Can't blame you for that, sir," offered Kaysten. "Showing up here with a mission-statement to *kill* you... that's an excellent way to get off on the wrong foot with someone. I'm just glad we were eventually able to smooth it over."

"Yeah – no *kidding*," conceded the U.S. leader. "But in any event... I'll have to do another press-conference very soon. I'll need something *positive* in the way of hard accomplishments, to tell the people. Just, 'we're still looking', is going to be a hard sell."

"I fully understand, sir," evaded Chu, "The Bureau's pulling out all the stops, following up on the leads that we *do* have – for example, the real identity of the assassin who committed suicide, back in Pittsburgh – I can *assure* you –"

A small light on the U.S. leader's phone handset on the Resolution Desk, began to flash on and off.

"That's the 'important' beacon," the U.S. leader observed. "Just a minute."

He picked up the phone and began to listen to whomever was at the other end of the connection.

Then he looked up at his erstwhile FBI-Director.

"There has been a mass shooting in Indianapolis," he said.

Get Me Some Of That Blood

They had gathered in a tidy-swept – though almost devoid of normal dining-tables, chairs, living-room couches, televisions and just about everything else you'd expect to find – one-room farm-house, at the end of a long, dirt-surfaced driveway.

Top Dog – now dressed in his trademark, utterly-conventional dark business-suit, with a pressed white shirt and red tie, plus black, lace-up shoes – had been the first to have arrived.

He had first visited the dilapidated barn nearby, to ensure that no "hostiles" had preceded them to the location. Thankfully, none were found to be hiding.

Reflexively, at first, he stood in the shadows. One of his subordinate team-leaders – another trim and spare, dark-haired white guy, much in the Director's own image – had shown up a few minutes later. This man stood at the other end of the farmhouse floor, surveying the territory for signs of intrusion or assault.

But, of course... none came.

Unusually – considering everything else that was going on – both the Director, and the others of his team, had abandoned the trademark black SUVs, in favor of a collection of nondescript, beat-up, superannuated Patriotics and other, similar cars of the *hoi polloi*.

Top Dog waited.

He elected to stare outside through one of the three windows in the place, looking over the almost-treeless, brightly-sunlit Great Plains landscape, taking note of a hawk drifting lazily on the air-currents far overhead.

A metaphor, he mused.

The predator and his prey.

The last car was just pulling up to the house, but there were no signs of anyone other than the invitees.

Good.

We can get going.

Keep this short... no idea if the bitch has compromised the core systems yet.

Probably not... the self-destructs should do their stuff... but not something to take a chance about.

There was a knock at the front door; it was done in characteristic Agency-code : first, a quick rap and a longer one; then a pause, followed by two quick raps, then a final pause, then a long hit, a short rap, another long hit and a short hit to conclude the sequence.

"You may enter," he stated, in his typical, expressionless monotone.

The door opened, revealing the second of his understudies. This guy had a slightly more ruddy complexion, and he had reddish-brown hair; but otherwise he could have been mistaken for the Director himself, unless the two of them happened to be standing side by side.

Funny how that works out, reflected Top Dog.

Not planned... but I'll take it.

"You're a bit late," he chided, in the direction of the man who had just opened the front door.

"Apologies, sir," conceded the man. "There was a police checkpoint on State Road 32. I don't think it had anything to do with us, but I took a detour, just to be on the safe side."

"Acknowledged," mentioned the Director. "Then let's get down to business... shall we?"

There were mute nods from the other two men, who just stood at ease, while the door closed and the Director began the briefing.

"You and your teams have done pretty well," he observed. "Our intercepts are telling us that the Bureau and their associated ass-kissers haven't yet been able to glean any forensics that would significantly blow our cover... and the card-decks are adding the intended air of intrigue. As I had predicted they'd do, they're pulling resources from other fronts – especially those associated with the alien, and also local protection in D.C.. In other words... 'so far... so good'."

"Thanks," said the dark-haired agent, in a flat tone that might have come from his boss.

"So," continued Top Dog, "We've executed the preliminaries with acceptable efficiency... but our window of opportunity won't last forever, so we need to click into high-gear, starting now. Time-synchronization still working for both of you?"

"Understood, sir," said the red-haired agent. "And yes... cross-confirmed, down to the millisecond. Heartbeat working on all the devices."

"Time-sync working nominally over here," added the first agent.

"We need to do a few other preparedness-checks," spoke the Director. "How are the suits holding up? Any failures to report... fixes that you need?"

"Five by five, sir," said the dark-haired agent. "The stealth-mode – that is, the light-bending stuff – it's great for the few seconds that it's on. Timing my actions to account for the charge-up and cool-down intervals took a lot of practice, at first – you got to calculate exactly where you'll be when the ten seconds are over with. It kind of sucks that it throws off the accuracy of our shooting so much; we found that we had to wait until we came out of the effect, to have a good chance of hitting anything. But the rest of it – like, the built-in sensors and close-combat weapons – those have been, well, like Christmas, frankly. Of course we've only had a chance to use the weapons against relatively 'soft' targets. We'll see how we do, when we encounter a skilled opponent. *Sir.*"

"You'll be getting the chance to do that, very soon," observed the Director.

He turned to address the other man.

"Any comments from your side?" he asked.

The red-haired guy responded,

"Pretty much the same," he disclosed. "I found that I had to be a lot more careful about flexing my muscles – I had a jam in one of my guns and tried to clear it by forcing the bolt open, and I broke the damn thing clean in half! I couldn't *believe* how well the strength-enhancement subsystems worked... I mean, in a suit that looks so, uhh, *lightweight.* All I *can* tell you, sir, is that any *normal* man will last two seconds *max*, when up against yours truly, wearing this thing. I'm one hundred per cent confident about that."

"Hmm," phlegmatically commented Top Dog, "But you *won't* be up against 'normal men' – you'll be fighting something much, *much* more dangerous... you're aware of that?"

"Yes," echoed both other men, in unison.

"Alright, then," continued the Director. "Now... as to your teams. As you know, each of you were assigned two of the best wet-ops guys that we could find, after recent events. How have they been holding up?"

"Well, sir," mentioned the darker-haired man, "Honestly... there's been a little grumbling – all professionally-stated, of course, nothing that goes against regulations – about 'wasting our time on such soft targets'. I'm hearing comments like 'expending expensive ammo on bodies that we could do just as easily with a .45'... you know? At least on *my* side, they're chomping at the bit, to get out there and do some real work."

"Yeah... same here," repeated the other guy. "Also, two of my team were real envious, they wanted to try on my suit – a request that I had to deny, of course."

"They've got the best standard-issue gear that we could find," responded Top Dog. "They'll have to make do with that. You've briefed them on the final orders for the mission?"

"Down to the last word, sir," said the first Agency guy. "They know what they've got to do."

"So do mine," added the red-haired agent. "They're locked and loaded – as am I – and we'll execute the mission, right to the end, come what may. *Sir.*"

"That's good," replied the Director, "I want each of you to tell the members of your team, how much both I personally – and your country – appreciate what they're about to do. And that brings me to what I wanted to conclude with. Please pay careful attention, since I'll want you to repeat what I'm saying, to your teams."

He paused for a second, and then declared,

"Frankly... it's now a very simple decision : either we succeed, or our American way of life will be extinguished, once and for all. If the former, the work won't be over with, by a longshot... but we'll still have a path to normalcy. If the latter... well, everything the Agency has done in the last fifty years, will be used to persecute us with. They won't care that we did it all, to keep this country *safe*. We'll be sacrificed to appease a bunch of weak-kneed 'human rights' crusaders, who don't know the first *thing* about America's enemies... and who care even less. They might as well just give the deed to the White House, to the Muslims and the liberals – I don't want to live in *that* kind of world! So we've got nothing to lose, by pulling out the stops and taking chances that we otherwise wouldn't ever take... including wet-ops against the man currently posing as Commander-In-Chief. Do you understand?"

"We *do!*" gravely indicated both other men, in near-unison.

Again Top Dog paused, as if he were pondering what to say.

Eventually he went on,

"I'm not going to pretend that this is going to be *easy*. It's obviously a heavily-fortified position, and we'll be operating without much of the intel that we're used to having – our assets in NSA are going dark, one by one. You'll have to exploit all your tactical force-multipliers; for example the suits can auto-disengage most of the internal door-locks within the target-area. Also, use your stealth-mode to achieve surprise whenever you can. The Marines and the Service are ready for a shoot-out; don't play their game – use your exotics to maximum advantage and keep moving. The moment they have you cornered, you're as good as dead. But remember – even if there isn't a door handy, you may still be able to simply smash through some of the interior walls. They won't be expecting something like *that!*"

"Roger that," replied the men.

The ex-Director continued, "We'll need to set up properly – because once we strike, there's *no* going back. And as you know from the briefings about the nuke on the airplane – it's obvious that we're dealing with at least one other player – Crowford's boys – who also seem to be in this game. They're much less experienced than we are... but they're problematic, just by getting in our way."

"*Then*," he said, speaking slowly and carefully, "We've got the alien and her little gang of brainwashed half-human groupies. I *know* they seem intimidating – but remember that old Agency saying : *if it lives... it can die.* We can thank our unknown, amateur friends for reminding us of that – we've already seen how even a shot by someone equipped just with a regular rifle, can put one of the monsters into a hospital. That means, this particular target got hurt... *badly.* It means in turn, that it *can* be killed, with better aim and a little more firepower! Always keep that in the back of your mind."

"But, sir," nervously commented the first agent, "Even if we succeed in all that... there's still the alien, itself. We've all *seen* what it can do – the damn thing's near-*indestructible!* We can't *possibly* –"

"Negative thinking – I won't *hear* of it!" snapped Top Dog. "Besides... as both of you know – or should know – *everything's* got a weak-point! We *know* what at least one of these is, for the bitch – it suffers when its offspring, or its slaves, get hurt or killed. We've got intel that – for reasons that we can only guess at – it *can* be vulnerable to small arms, despite what we've seen over the Atlantic recently. Not only *that*... but I have something to reveal to you now about the project – this is 'eyes only', and it's not to be repeated to *anyone…* is that *understood?*"

The other men nodded in acknowledgment and said, "Yes, sir… for *sure.*"

"I've had the Agency's best scientists working on this up to now; they've used advanced data-mining to predict what substance the alien is most vulnerable to – our version of 'Kryptonite', if you like," explained Top Dog. "We call it, 'Special Number 106-299'".

"So we got a magic bullet?" asked an instantly-elated Agency guy.

"We're hoping so," confirmed the director. "While obviously I can't get into the details, I *can* disclose that it's a very rare, synthetic radioactive isotope. Our exotic-weapons folks had to work very hard to get it stable enough so as not to decay and become useless; but even with that, our window of opportunity with this 'magic bullet' is *very* limited. The scientists have been able to get me only one dose of it, for use in the upcoming project. When I get close enough to the alien, I'll press home the attack at all costs."

"Best news we've heard in about six weeks, sir!" agreed the other man.

"So," stated the Director, "The bottom line is : we *do* have a chance, here! It may not be 70, 60 or even 50 per cent… but whatever it is, we've got to exploit it *ruthlessly!*"

"Now," he continued, "We have incomplete intel about exactly *who*, within the target-areas, count as 'the monster's friends'; although, it's clear from that disgraceful press-conference, that the President is now *completely* under the creature's control. However improbable it might seem, I believe that this is actually our best opportunity to finish off the alien. We've modeled the facts with the Agency's best A.I. systems, and seven out of the ten outcomes that the computers generated, indicated that next only to its so-called 'family' – who we'll just have to hope are hanging around the target-site, when we strike – the more powerful and influential the slave, the more likely it is that liquidating that particular zombie, will mortally wound this 'Karéin' creature."

"So just to be absolutely clear about the objective," inquired one of the other assassins, "The President's 'Target Number One'?"

"Unless we're lucky enough to stumble across Billings, the boy or the girl... yes," coldly confirmed Top Dog. "At the very least, dealing with Clark will prevent the alien from taking complete control over the Executive Branch, at least temporarily. As you know, we've been coordinating with GrayWar to get a replacement for him in there, the moment that the deed is done, but – considering the many variable factors that are out of our control – there are no guarantees. The country might go into chaos, which might or might not work to our advantage. We'll just have to stick to our plan and hope for the best."

"So, apart from our so-called 'President'," he continued, "You'll have to seek out the half-humans; you've been given all the data we have on the ones who we've previously confirmed – photos, voice-signatures, *et cetera* – and your suits should auto-ID and auto-target them. The suits are also pre-programmed to resist each of the half-aliens' known abilities – like lightening-bolts, death-rays, whatever – to the extent that they can... although I'd still advise you not to get hit, if you can avoid it. This is a once-in-a-*lifetime* opportunity to grease a large number of these zombies, all at once; I believe that will push 'Karéin' over the edge – or, at least, weaken it to a point where we can easily finish it off."

"Sure hope you're right, sir," offered one of the agents.

"You *better*," vowed Top Dog, "Because if I'm *not*... well, *you* know. In the past, we'd been assuming that just stressing or eliminating one of its hangers-on, from long range, would do the trick. We saw the effects but they just weren't enough. *This* time – we do it at close range, when the creature's as weak as we can make it... *then*, we press home our attack – no matter *what* the risks... no matter *what* the cost!"

"But," interjected the second agent, "How do we know that the alien will even *be* there? When we want to land the final blow, that is? And what happens after we liquidate it?"

"Leave that to *me*," claimed the Director. "My guess is that it can only control Clark by being physically close-by him; it's almost certainly somewhere on the White House grounds. And anyway... once a few of its little sycophants – particularly the President – are breathing their last... I have a feeling that it'll show. After that's all done, the second phase of our plans will follow naturally. I've been in contact with Mr. Duke of GrayWar, and we have a working agreement about running the country, after Clark has been dealt with. He has a candidate to assume the office of President, as well as a convincing narrative to use when the time comes. Of course, the person involved is fully aware of the debt that he'll have to the Agency; so if this all comes off properly, we'll be fully back in business. *Order* will have been restored!"

He fell silent for a few long seconds. Then he said,

"So... that's it. It's 'do or die'! I can't say it more clearly. The fate of the Republic is in our hands; your *country* calls you, to great things. How will you answer?"

"I'll do my *duty*, sir!" declared the first agent. "To the end. I'm not a fan of the pills, you know; so I'll always keep one in the chamber... just in case."

The second agent pledged, "You know, sir... the Japanese put it best : 'when given a mission by his lord, the *Samurai never* fails; he either succeeds or dies, because death is not failure'. That's what I believe... what I intend to do."

The Director was the epitome of the "unsentimental man"; but on this occasion, he caught himself wiping a tear.

"Gentlemen," he offered, *"Never* has a Director of our Agency, had a finer team, to put his trust in! I *know* the hour is dark; but I want you and your men to *believe* in yourselves – you're the deadliest wet-ops professionals on this *planet*. You *can* pull off this mission; if I wasn't one hundred per cent sure of that, I'd never have asked you to go. When you head out that door, you'll be doing a great service to the Republic. I'm *so* proud of you!"

"With you to the end," committed the first agent. "It's in the blood."

"Is that right?" said the Director, with his trademark half-smile.

"Then," he directed, "Go out... and *get me some of that blood!*"

The Shepherd's Dilemma

With a lot of intense discussion among the Cass Mountain refugees beforehand, Sam Jacobson had entrusted the safety of his family to the other "more-than-humans" and had boarded a FBI helicopter bound for downtown Pittsburgh, Pennsylvania.

The Bureau agents alongside him had all been briefed on the activities of the "Mars Gang", so there were many suspicious side-glances and little in the way of light conversation during the hour-long trip.

These guys probably consider me a murderer, he mused.

One who got away with it, because nobody can bring him to account.

What did Voltaire say – yeah – "killing a man is murder... unless you do it to the sound of the trumpets..."

After arriving at a local heliport, the former Mars mission commander was whisked away in one of those black limousines that had, at other times, been a harbinger of fear.

They're at least trying *to be civil,* he noted,

Look on the bright side – at least they got me a good-looking business-suit, a silk tie, a white dress-shirt and a pair of leather shoes that fit nicely.

Only took five minutes in the men's washroom at the helicopter-building to put it on.

If they had just remembered to get a new pair of underwear... oh well.

But this ride, too, was uneventful, and at length, Jacobson found himself getting off an elevator, at the 12th floor of the Pittsburgh UPMC Mercy Hospital. Two FBI agents – both taciturn, well-built males – stepped off immediately behind him.

A male, Caucasian doctor – accompanied by a couple of interns, one female, the other an Asian male – greeted the former astronaut.

"Commander Jacobson," he offered, "Great that you could make it up here. I'm Chief Resident Mark Burgess. My two assistants are Mr. Shih and Ms. Savitz."

The interns spoke some bland pleasantries.

"Well," Jacobson responded, "I wish I had a different reason to make the trip. How is she?"

"You want the good news or the bad news?" reparteed the doctor.

"Straight out, if you don't mind," requested the former Mars commander.

"Well," said Burgess, "She's alive, stable, and recovering more quickly than I've ever seen anyone do. That's the *good* news. The *bad* news is, the police showed us examples of other items in the area that got hit by the same bullets, as hit Ms. Abruzzio. She should have been cut in *half* by that shot! I can't fathom how she survived at all, frankly."

"Is she comfortable? Is she conscious?" asked Jacobson.

"Yes, to both questions," confirmed the doctor, "Although it's worrisome... she doesn't seem to be responding to our treatments. For example we tried to give her a sedative, but it had no effect whatsoever. We tried asking Ms. Tanaka, but she didn't want to tell us –"

"You won't get *me* to, either," interrupted Jacobson. "Nothing personal, I assure you... but despite the presence of my fine Bureau handlers here, there are still quite a few unresolved issues between my team and I – that includes Cherie Tanaka but not Sylvia, by the way – and the government. So we aren't really in a position to do a lot of explaining. May I see them, now?"

"Of course," agreed Burgess. "They're together, in a private room at the other side of this floor... under Pittsburgh Police Department, round-the-clock protective guard. Ms. Tanaka hasn't left Abruzzio's side since this all went down. This way."

"Thanks," said Jacobson, as they started walking.

The group – including the doctor, the interns, the former Mars mission leader and the two Bureau agents – proceeded in the appropriate direction, leading to "oohs" and "aahs" as Jacobson passed by the nurses' station and was recognized for who he was. After a short walk they arrived at a closed door, outside of which were two uniformed PPD constables.

"This area is access-restricted," announced one of the policemen.

"As it *should* be," remarked Jacobson.

"Thank you gentlemen," spoke Burgess. "You already know me, as I've been attending to Professor Abruzzio; but I'd like to introduce Commander Jacobson, of the Mars mission and also, more recently, of the so-called 'Mars Gang'. We're accompanied by agents of the FBI. We need to see the patient and Ms. Tanaka, if you don't mind."

"Alright... I guess," answered the cop. "Strange times... you know, as little as two weeks ago, the 'Mars Gang' were 'Public Enemy Number One' – now we're all just one big happy family... right?"

"Oh... let's not get *ahead* of ourselves," stiffly corrected Jacobson. "I'd say we're more like the Hatfields and the McCoys, who've agreed to put the guns away for a nice week-end at the State Fair."

"I... *see*," carefully observed the policeman.

He nodded to the other cop, who entered a keypad combination that unlocked the door to Abruzzio's room.

In they all went (except for the two PPD guards), with the doctor leading the way, followed closely by Jacobson, the interns and the FBI agents.

The room was brightly-illuminated, but in an odd way : it had normal indoor-lighting, but also, daylight leaked in. This apparently issued from a window that was partly-blocked-off with a large steel panel, bolted to the floor in front of the window so as to deny a clear shot to anyone outside.

The place was also clearly too large for a single occupant; it had probably been converted from a double-room. In its middle was a hospital-bed with a raised head-end, containing an upright Sylvia Abruzzio. She was dressed in a typical hospital patient-smock, with a large bandaged-area just below her neck.

Sitting on a chair beside Abruzzio and the bed was Cherie Tanaka, who was dressed in attractive, high-class, flexible sports-clothes. And beside Tanaka, was the puppy, "Rainbow".

"Well... hello there," greeted Abruzzio. "We just heard about what went on, up on the mountain. Did everybody get through it safely?"

"Yes – but it was a miracle that they *did*," answered Jacobson. "Like it evidently was with yourself."

He leaned over the bed, briefly embracing the former JPL scientist and receiving a kiss on the cheek from her. The gesture was repeated with Tanaka, who whispered a few encouraging words into his ear.

He hears a "yip" by his feet, and in an instant, the dog had propelled itself into the air, flown around Jacobson three times, and then landed a sloppy puppy-kiss on the side of the former Mars mission commander's face.

"Wait a minute... when did she learn to fly?" asked a bewildered Jacobson.

"Just before I got shot," answered Abruzzio. "*Impressive*, don't you think?"

"For sure," agreed Jacobson. "More than some of the rest of us have learned to do. So listen... what *happened* to you, Sylvia? Who the hell *shot* you?"

"Sam," interrupted Tanaka, pointing at the FBI agents, "Do these guys *have* to be here?"

"Oh... no *problem*, ma'am," courteously replied one of the agents. "We'll wait outside."

The two agents wheeled in place and went out the door, closing it as they exited.

"Do you mind if we stay?" asked Dr. Burgess.

"Can you promise not to reveal anything that we discuss, that we declare to be a secret?" demanded Tanaka.

"Sure... 'doctor-patient privilege' and all that," said Burgess.

"Good enough for me," agreed Abruzzio.

Jacobson used his telekinetic powers to pull a chair near to the bed – a gesture that duly impressed the humans within the room – and he sat on it in reversed-position, with his arms resting on the back of the chair as he addressed his two more-than-human compatriots.

"So how much do you know?" he asked, in their general direction.

Abruzzio spoke first.

"Don't ask *me*... I just got shot," she deflected. "I've been watching the news, though. All those massacres – Sam, something *has* to be going on –"

"We have a lot of mass shootings, all the time," countered Jacobson, "Do we have any idea who was *behind* any of these attacks? Not just the one against the two of you... but did you hear what happened to the rest of us?"

"No," echoed the two others.

"It's been concealed from the press, so far," offered Jacobson, "And as everything went down on top of the mountain, there weren't any witnesses except us and a few police. Which is a *good* thing, I'd say. The fewer 'visitors' we have up there, the better."

"What exactly happened?" asked Tanaka.

"*We* got attacked, too, just after Karéin left for parts unknown," explained the former Mars mission commander. "From all sides – it was a well-coordinated ambush by at least six or seven assailants, each armed with sniper-rifles. Ezra and Cooter's shack was shredded by rifle-bullets and it was a *miracle* that nobody – except for Donny, that is, and of course he just shrugged it off – got hit. We were also lucky that they opened up at an oblique angle, so most of the shots went high, as opposed to down to the cabin-floor, where my family and others were hiding. Needless to say, Will, Brent, Otis, Donny, Wolf and I responded... *forcefully* to the attack, and after a few minutes, none of the enemy remained combat-effective."

"I can just *imagine*," ruefully commented Tanaka. "Pity I wasn't there to add my two lightening-bolts' worth. What intelligence were you able to get from examining whatever was left of them?"

"Frankly… not a lot, although the Bureau's still up there," responded Jacobson. "The guy who I beat the shit out of is apparently still – barely – alive and in a hospital somewhere; all I was able to observe about him, in the very short chance that I had, was that he was using civilian – not military – grade weaponry… and in place of normal military rank all he had was a small insignia of a cross. As for the ones who Brent, Wolf and Otis opened up on, well… you *know* what they're capable of, and let's just say, the forensics teams can't even tell where the bodies were supposed to have been. But the Bureau agents have had enough time by now to do a preliminary report… have either of you heard any more from Minnie about this?"

"Got a call from her, saying basically 'get well soon'," noted Abruzzio. "I asked her, but she just gave me the 'ongoing law enforcement investigation' evasion routine. She also wanted to know all about the unfortunate little incident that Cherie and I just experienced… especially about how I got so badly hurt by a couple of rifle-bullets. It was a short call… she's *very* busy, as you can appreciate."

"Speaking of that," inquired Jacobson, "The 'bullet' thing, I mean – I was wondering about that, as well. I mean… we've all been under far more powerful assaults by various forces, up to and including fighter-planes and even nuclear weapons. No disrespect meant, but Sylvia – how the H did they hurt you so badly, with just a rifle?"

"I'm honestly not sure, Sam," she answered, "But – and you weren't there to hear it, at the time – when we were down on the streets of L.A., when Karéin 'revealed' our alien-powers, that is – she said something about, 'the Holy *Fire* is sometimes fickle'… she also mentioned that if you're caught off-guard, sometimes it can take a second or two for your natural defenses to kick in. Maybe it was just a lucky shot? Your guess is as good as mine."

"If it's of any interest," stated the doctor, "A normal human being hit by a high-energy round like that, would *certainly* have been killed. Almost decapitated, in fact. I used to work in a downtown ER – we'd get gang-bangers who took a shot to the neck, and you could never do anything for them, they were always D.O.A… it was ugly – I can personally attest to that. So whatever 'defenses' that you've got, you can thank them for the fact that you're here talking to us."

Tanaka shot a determined stare at Burgess and his acolytes.

"This subject is strictly off-limits, outside this room!" she ordered. "It's not to be discussed with *anyone* else, under *any* circumstances – do you understand?"

"Sure," replied the doctor, "But why?"

"Because if you tell anyone – especially the government – about it, *I'll kill you! That* a good enough reason?" hissed the more-than-a-woman.

"Yes ma'am," uneasily spoke Intern Shih.

"That's not very nice of you," complained Intern Savitz.

"I just had my mother cruelly tortured and murdered, in addition to being targeted for murder myself, along with Sylvia," countered the former science officer. "I'm not in a particularly good mood."

"What I think Cherie *means*, Doctor," tactfully remarked Abruzzio, "Is that the country seems to be *crawling* with people who want to kill us – and some of them might still be in the government. We've reached a working relationship with the President, but the next administration might not abide by it... so we have ample reason to be cautious. Any vulnerability that our enemies can exploit, might be the end of us."

"Minnie and Jerry were there with you, when the Storied Watcher disclosed this... isn't that right?" asked Jacobson.

"Yes," confirmed Abruzzio.

"So they'd know about this potential weakness... right?" he added.

"I'd assume so," said the former JPL scientist. "But even given Jerry's loyalties... there's a good chance that even *he* wouldn't have discussed it with his boss, or with the government. He, Hector and Minnie are kind of in the same boat as we are, on this front. At least that's *my* guess."

"*Maybe*," offered Jacobson. "So... what do we do now? There's clearly someone out there gunning for us; our opponents seem to have come up short on their first try, but there's no guarantee that there won't be a second, or a third... or a 'n'th. Sooner or later, they're going to do some irreparable damage. My family and the others are still up there on Cass Mountain, and I don't like them sitting there as a static target – what if the next 'try' is a missile or something, and we happen to be asleep at the time? Militarily speaking, we need to stop 'defending', we need to regain our mobility and start carrying the battle to the enemy –"

"Whoever *that* is," unhelpfully interjected Tanaka.

"That's what 'reconnaissance' is all about," persisted Jacobson. "Cherie – any more information on the search for your mother's murderers?"

"Just bits and pieces from my end," replied the former science officer. "Sylvia?"

Abruzzio's countenance now took on a godly, "above-all-of-them" look.

"I've been going over it in my head, since I – *ahem* – had the opportunity to rest and relax a little," explained the former JPL scientist. "I was 'over-concentrating' before... I remembered something Karéin told me, about 'you must clear your mind of all mundane worries and tensions, Sister Sylvia, to empower the blessing of divine insight'... so that's what I've been doing. I've gone all the way back to the shoot-out at the Hotel Tucson, in fact – and the truth has been revealed! It *has* to be the *Fire* talking – the enlightenment is *miraculous*... it's like an avalanche of connections that were right in plain sight before, but that I had somehow missed. It's something that the human side of me can't fathom, and never could have figured out by myself. And Rainbow was right there, helping me along... right, little lady?"

The dog sat on its hindquarters, looked Abruzzio right in the eye and let out a strange sound that several amazed humans in the room, could have sworn sounded like the word "yes", in English.

Again, Tanaka warned the doctors and interns, "This is also *strictly* off the record... is that understood?"

The three gravely nodded acknowledgment, although Rainbow let out one of her cheery "yips", which did serve to lessen the tension.

Under intense scrutiny from her two more-than-human friends, Abruzzio related, "If you remember what happened all the way back at the hotel, something hasn't been adding up, right from the start. I talked to Minnie, Jerry, Misha and Wolf about it, and even though the President's motives in calling Hector, myself and Karéin herself to that event, were anything *but* lily-white... it's clear that neither he, nor the Bureau, nor the Service, nor even the Agency – at least not at *that* time – had intended for lethal force to be used against the Storied Watcher. In fact, the President had given strict orders to the contrary – and there's no evidence that anybody in the government disobeyed him. So... *someone* in that room – someone answering to a completely *different* chain of command – *has* to have been the one who fired the first shots."

"Go on," requested Jacobson.

"Then," she continued, "We have the fact that several people trying to race out of the building were shot dead by a sniper somewhere in downtown Tucson. Jerry stated that the President was as bewildered as *he* was, about who was behind that. Then, we have Minnie's account of how that preacher, what was his name again – oh yeah, 'Crowford', *that* was it, wasn't it – went apeshit-crazy and set off the nuke that he had somehow smuggled aboard, trying to kill Minnie and Karéin all together at once – that *certainly* wasn't something that could plausibly have been cooked up by the government – the former Vice-President was himself aboard and the President obviously had no foreknowledge of it."

"Then," concluded Abruzzio, "There's the fact that *someone* – and that *can't* have been either the Vice-President or the President – ordered the release of the *second* nuke, the one on the missile, the one that Karéin dealt with – against the airplane. Doing that would have required a complete compromise of normal military channels of command... something that's *way* beyond anyone except a tiny handful of senior military or intelligence-agency personnel. Finally, we have the recent spate of attacks, all carried out by conventional sniper-fire, against the folks up on the mountain and against Cherie and myself."

"So what's the conclusion?" pressed the former Mars mission leader.

"First," proposed the ex-JPL-scientist, "I think we're dealing with two *different* conspiracies. I'd bet you that one of them is associated with Crowford's religious-cult. As to the other, I'm betting it's the Agency, given what happened to Cherie's mother, and given what we saw them doing up on

Amchitka – not to mention what the President disclosed to Jerry and me back at his house-arrest-place by the lake. Both groups are murderous creeps who want to see all of us *dead*, but at least one of them – who I'd assume are the religious nuts – don't seem as efficient or well-armed as the other group. Furthermore... the two conspiracies may be working at cross-purposes. They're getting in each other's way, in other words. Possibly we could exploit that."

"Yeah," pondered Jacobson, "Now that you put it *that* way, it sure starts to make sense... but assuming you're right – how do we track these sons of bitches down, and do to them what needs to be done?"

"Let's say you were a shepherd... how would you catch a wolf that's eating your sheep, one by one?" replied Abruzzio.

"Well... I'd stand watch over the whole flock, and when the thing raises its ugly head... I'd plug it with my trusty shotgun," said the former Mars commander, with a wan smile. "Not that I have anything against wolves, you know – make sure you tell our flaming friend I said that."

"I'll make a note of it," pleasantly answered Abruzzio, "But suppose that you've got a really *big* flock to protect – too many sheep to keep an eye on each one, all the time. And suppose there are at least *two* wolves – one really big, mean, dangerous one... and another that just takes the easy pickins'. What would you do then?"

"Hmm," temporized Jacobson, "I think I know where you're going with this... but I can't say I'm happy about it."

"Sylvia," interjected Tanaka, "*Please* don't tell me that your plan involves setting up the humans within Karéin's entourage, as 'sacrificial lambs'! *Surely* that isn't –"

"It *is*," countered Abruzzio, "I don't want any of them to get killed or crippled, of course; but it's a risk that we have to take. Think it *through* – we've got to make these miscreants believe that they'll get an easy 'kill'... something that they think will grievously wound us, possibly Karéin too, in the way that they hurt *you*, by murdering your mother."

"That outcome is the *last* thing that I would wish on anyone," slowly remarked Tanaka. "I'm not enthusiastic about this idea, Sylvia; but anyway, please tell us how you intend to make it work."

The former JPL scientist – her eyes now with a faintly-glowing kaleidoscope-effect, to the astonishment of the nearby doctor and interns – elaborated,

"Our persecutors have to think that we left some of these human family-members temporarily-unguarded... an oversight, a screw-up, on our part. Correction – *two* groups of family-members, done so at the same time, in different locations, with bread-crumbs to the target spread differently to each conspiracy. Then, we hope that they go for the bait, *and*, we should make it *look* like they got away with it. We should use our powers to surveil the situation and shadow the assassins back to their home bases... by doing that, we've got at least a *chance* of identifying whoever's in charge of each conspiracy. It'll take a great deal of careful planning, and good luck – but the insight tells me that it's the only way."

"How do we even know they'll find us and take the bait?" demanded Tanaka. "We could be sitting around waiting, for days – weeks – *months* – while these bastards murder other, helpless victims. They might not even get to us at all! How can we be sure of getting their attention?"

"We *can't*," deflected Abruzzio. "We'll have to be patient – I won't mislead you. But I have some ideas about how we can make them an offer they can't refuse. I'll fill you in on the details later."

"Sylvia," observed Jacobson, "A mission like this could be *suicidal*, for an ordinary human being! You just experienced – yourself – what it's like to be on the receiving end of a bullet... and that was *with* your personal force-field to protect you. Now imagine that you had to repeat the experience, with, say, only a thin piece of body-armor under your clothes, and nothing at all to protect your head or extremities. You understand what I'm saying?"

"I sure *do*," she acknowledged. "But we have to assume that our opponents have done enough reconnaissance to know which of us can likely withstand a conventional attack – after all, all they'd have had to have done would have been to have watched that press-conference that the President held, right after the nuke-incidents. If we just trot one of, uhh, '*us*' – Karéin's 'chosen ones' – out there, the enemy won't take the bait. Sorry... as little as I like to say it, the logic's *inevitable*."

"For God's *sake*, Sylvia!" complained Tanaka. "The chances of getting a helpless, completely vulnerable spouse, or a child, or a relative, *murdered* – while we just sit around impotently watching it happen – are probably *much* higher than the odds of us positively identifying the killer, or killers, and then tracking them all the way back to 'wherever'... and that's assuming that the assassins don't just chew on a cyanide-capsule afterwards. Which, I'd remind you... one of them has already done! If the slightest thing goes *wrong*, we lose family-members, forever; but everything has to go *right*, for it to work at all. I love and respect you, sister... but this is just a *crazy* idea!"

"Sam... didn't you say," inquired Abruzzio, "That the Storied Watcher had visited everybody up on Cass Mountain, before the shooting started there?"

"Yeah," confirmed the former Mars mission commander.

"Did she get along with all of them?" pressed the ex-JPL scientist.

"Of *course* she did," said Jacobson. "*You* know her. Even had Donny and Bob palling up with each other, which I thought was quite an accomplishment, considering... well, *you* know the story. So what?"

"Well, Sam," advanced Abruzzio, "How do you know that there even *are* any 'purely human' beings up there, any more?"

"Oh, wait a minute... *now* I see what you're getting at," interjected Tanaka, with a slight smile. "But Sylvia – she's more in control of it now. At one point she said, 'I believe that the blessing of *Amaiish*, falls only on those to whom I wish to bestow'. Did she make any of the Cass Mountaineers, take the pledge?"

"Not that *I* heard or saw," he replied. "Then again... I wasn't with her all the time she was up there."

"The point is," continued Abruzzio, "Your families – at least, some among them – may already have gotten a little spark of the Holy *Fire*. It may help them survive, if – God forbid – they actually get hit. But our opponents can't possibly know about it, if in fact the supposition's true. They'll think that these people are just normal humans – as vulnerable as any human being would be."

"Would you bet the *life* of your wife or child on an untested theory like that?" asked Jacobson. "We obviously can't test it out ourselves, by trying to shoot one of our loved-ones and then hoping that 'Sylvia was right'."

"I don't know how to answer that," evaded the former JPL scientist. "Other than for Moira – and yes, I *will* ask her – I don't have any close family-members involved here... at least not yet."

Abruzzio looked down at the small Catholic crucifix on the neck-chain between her breasts, and crossed herself, while momentarily closing her eyes.

Holy Mary, Mother of God, she silently prayed,

May Thou bless our plan...

And may Thou protect all Thy servants who risk their lives in the service of Thy Angel.

The room fell silent, for a couple of seconds.

Then Jacobson offered,

"Whose loved-ones, will be asked to take a chance like this?"

"I'd put it another way, Sam," said Tanaka.

"What's that?" he asked.

"I'd say," she explained, "'Who will volunteer?'"

Time For Plan "B"

An out-of-sorts Sam Jacobson – accompanied by the bounty-hunter and an equally-frustrated Tanaka – sat in the driver's seat of a high-end, rented SUV, parked by special (and very expensive) permit on the early-evening streets of downtown New York City, about a half-block from the theater within which a lame, quickly-contrived play entitled "Alien-Girl – A Spaced-Out-Of-The-World-Musical" was being staged.

Given the day's-worth of strategically-placed "teaser" advertising in the *New Yorker* magazine, it was a kind of miracle that anyone at all had come to the event; but even so, only a third of the hundred and twenty seats in the theater were – in fact – occupied, and then only, by a variety of bored and profoundly-unimpressed patrons.

There had been a solicitation over social media for a playwright and a musical score; this had deliberately been done in the open, and the results had been rendered in less than a day and a half. This was undoubtedly due to the advertised, up-front payment of ten thousand dollars, payable in gold coins.

However, the quality of the work reflected the schedule; it quickly became evident that the play-material had been mostly created by random computer-algorithms, with no editing or proof-reading; and much of the music seemed to have been pirated more or less directly from last year's hit parade.

Jacobson's wife, as well as the others, had complained that "I hardly *know* these songs... how do you expect me to sing them in front of an audience, even with these *karaoke*-earbuds?"; to which, the response had come, "well, dear... at least you were on Earth to *hear* them – which is more than Cherie and I can say for ourselves".

However true the commentary of the former Mars mission commander, it did not make up for Yvonne's mediocre talents; although, this was somewhat offset by Boatman's recently-improved ability, and by Cassie Young's natural voice. Both of the latter had spent considerable time in church-choirs, which helped to rescue the performance from utter disaster.

Even Laura Boyd – who had claimed that she had never been able to carry a tune – now seemed to have somehow found a passable singing-voice.

"We're wasting our *time* on this, Sam," complained Tanaka, from the back seat. "Second day... and not so much as a *purse-snatching* going down, within blocks of here. On top of trotting the folks out into the shopping-malls in Pittsburgh and Reston, the day before last. Not even a nibble there, if you recall."

"That was only for two hours in each case, and your *alternative* is...?" chided Jacobson.

"All *I* know is," she pouted, "That I'm losing credibility with the President, and with Minnie... I warned them that I'd be flying all over the place, blowing up buildings, until I flushed the rats out of their hiding-places. And here I am."

She threw up her hands and stared sullenly out of a dark-tinted window.

The streets accommodated a few people going back and forth on foot, but otherwise there was no sign of anything in the least way, "interesting".

"What *I* want to know is, 'where the fuck's Little Miss Nuclear Goddess'?" demanded the bounty-hunter, who was in the front passenger seat. "We got all this unfinished business... and she just takes off to Antarctica or wherever. What the hell's there to *do* down there, that would tie her up this long? You'd think that just for Cherie, she'd put in a little *effort*."

"Dunno," answered Jacobson. "It's been several days now... not sure why she'd be taking so long. I can only hope that everything's still alright."

"Even if she shows," observed the former Mars science officer, "I doubt that she'd be able to add a lot of value – after all, consider how she came up blank herself, in her original search for Bob, Tommy, Whitney and the rest of them. Ironic, isn't it – both Karéin and the three of us here, we've can crush Army tanks and blast fighter-planes out of the air... but we can't deal with a bunch of scumbag hit-men who are hiding their sorry asses out there... *somewhere*. Pretty pathetic, if you ask *me*."

The portable, modified, digital-to-network radio-set that they had located on the seat next to Tanaka, lit up, with a soft "beep".

She grabbed its old-school microphone, hit the "talk" button and said, "Tanaka here... go ahead, Sylvia."

"Secured at your end?" came Abruzzio's familiar, slightly-distorted voice.

She was not whispering, but did seem to be speaking at low volume.

"Yes," confirmed Tanaka. "The 'Software Crypto' light's showing green... I plugged in the algorithm like the hackers instructed me to do, and by the fact that I'm getting you, it must be working. They told me that we've only got a safe fifteen minutes to talk, per session, though. Go ahead."

"Any luck?" asked Abruzzio.

"Nothing," replied Tanaka. "Three performances so far... not so much as a nibble. This is the last one for today, thank God – I'm getting cabin-fever, sitting all day in this damn car. Oh well, look at the bright side..."

"What would *that* be?" idly asked the former JPL scientist.

"Theater-critics haven't laughed us off the stage, yet," explained Tanaka. "Which is amazing, if you think about it. Apparently Amina had some acting-classes, back in high-school... I heard she's a 'natural' up there. 'A star is born', in other words. Funny, eh?"

"Yeah," allowed Abruzzio. "We may not catch any murderers... but maybe we're in the running for a Tony?"

"Manage those expectations," cautioned the former Mars mission scientist. "On both fronts. Anything happening at your end?"

"They've been sitting in and around the Air and Space Museum lobby for six hours, after the second reading from the mission-notes I supplied them with. Got a little hassle from Building-Security, and I thought that might work to our advantage," described Abruzzio. "But *nada*, if you know what I mean. They've been doing multiple postings on social media about 'wow, what a great place this is, and why don't all the rest of our best buddies come right on down and chill with us' kind of thing... but I guess it just isn't having the impact that we thought it might have. Shouldn't have been a surprise, really; either it's being drowned out by all the gazillions of other stuff up there on Neo, or our quarry haven't had time to react, or both, or something else. Disappointing... that's for sure."

"Yeah," agreed Tanaka. "Listen – how are you holding up? After... well, *you* know."

"Just fine," replied Abruzzio. "It's just a bruise now... aches when I touch it or flex it... but no biggie. Actually, the only issue that I've run into today, is when a guy flicked the end of his cigarette on the top of my head –"

"Say again?" interrupted the former science officer. "He... *what?*"

"Oh," wryly explained Abruzzio, "I'm sitting here in the shadows on one side of the Museum, along with Brent Boyd... we're a concrete bollard with a sand ashtray on top, you see."

"You're a – oh, *I* get it," answered Tanaka. "I envy you that gift... just don't teach it to Hendricks, oh-kay?"

"If I do... it'll be for a very good reason," parried the former JPL scientist.

"Good thing it's you and not me down there," grumbled Wolf. "If it'd been me, I'd have lit up more than his stogie."

"That's why we're *here*... and you're *there*," pleasantly replied Abruzzio.

"Anyway, Sylvia," broke in Jacobson, leaning backward over the driver's-side seat, "I think we're just spinning our wheels here... you know? I'm about ready to pack up for today."

"Agreed," came the remote voice. "Either these contrived 'public events' aren't viable at all, or there's something we're doing wrong... or we just need a *lot* more time."

"Yeah," sighed the former Mars mission commander. "Time that we may not *have*."

There were a few seconds of silence, and then Abruzzio echoed, "Time that we may not have... for sure. We move on to Plan 'B', then?"

"I *hate* that idea!" protested Jacobson. "Far more dangerous than even *this* risky-business!"

"The definition of 'insanity' is 'doing something that isn't working... and thinking that doing more of it, is going to work any better'... isn't it?" mentioned Tanaka.

"That's 'assuming' that *anything's* going to work," countered Jacobson. "And to quote another definition... you know what we do when we 'assume' things, right?"

"I sure *do*," conceded the former Mars science officer. "As in, 'assuming' that Minnie isn't listening in to everything that we're saying, right now."

"Well, then, folks," proposed Abruzzio's faint voice, "Let's give her something *worthwhile*, to hear. I say, 'Plan 'B''."

After another short pause, Jacobson mumbled,

"'Plan 'B', then. Brent?"

Boyd's heretofore-silent voice – speaking at a subdued volume – broke in with, "You're right, Commander... it's a *huge* risk. But given what we've seen – or actually, *not* seen – so far... it may be the only way. Yes... I'll go for it... reluctantly. Talk about 'wearing out our welcome with the Old Man', if you know what I mean. God help us if they catch us napping, though."

"No *kidding*," agreed Jacobson.

"'Plan 'B'," stated Abruzzio. "I'll get it going, from my end. Check in tomorrow... 9 a.m.?"

"Confirmed," said the former Mars mission commander.

"New York, over and out," concluded Tanaka, as she dropped the connection.

Dasher Out At Aquia

"Dasher here... and I don't *understand* it, Sam," complained Abruzzio, over the short-range, encrypted radio. "I had expected my credit-card to be totally tapped out after renting all these extra SUVs and laying out for these nice new clothes that we've all got on... but even with buying food for all of us on the way, it still seems to be fine. I'm worried – could it mean that someone's been tampering with the account? Which in turn, means that our cover may already be blown? Dasher out."

From his vantage-point in the second black-colored, tinted-windows SUV in the multi-car convoy heading north on I-95, Jacobson hit the "talk" button on his microphone and replied, "Blitzen here. I hear you, Sylvia – but wasn't that the whole *idea?* Blitzen out."

Before she could reply, the sound of Boatman's voice, coming from the fourth SUV in the line, interjected, "Donner here – bet you two to one, that's Minnie havin' sported you some easy cash. She told me she *owes* you, after all that stuff with the airplane... you know? Donner out."

"Dasher here, and yeah," obliquely acknowledged the former JPL scientist. "But it's not *her* that we're trying to attract. Speaking of that... where are we now, folks? Dasher out."

"Blitzen here," came Jacobson's voice. "Just passing Stafford, Virginia. Should be only about another half-hour, or maybe a bit more if the traffic keeps getting worse as we near D.C.. We're on schedule, in other words. Blitzen out."

"Donner here," again sounded Boatman. "We're getting pretty close now... so I want to do one last check. Specifically – it's us who's goin' on the tour... and the rest of you poor 'civilians', you're just gonna cool your heels on Pennsylvania Avenue... right? Donner out."

"Dasher here," said Abruzzio. "That's the plan, all right... everybody knows what to do? At least the ones outside can admire the North Portico. We've *got* to be on time, though. We blasted the itineraries for the 'civilians' all over social media, public profiles, and remember we got our hacker-friends to seed that info even further afield – if the bad guys are going to show, it will be here... I *hope*. And remember – we're trying for capture – not kill – here. Dasher out."

"Yeah," came the voice of Sammie, "'Sit around and get shot', by guys who can fire at us, but we can't shoot back. Oh, sorry... Comet on... or off... or whatever."

Another voice – that of Brent Boyd – now sounded on the radio-link.

"Rudolph here," it announced. "Listen, everybody... kids need a pee-break. My maps are showing a rest-area just up the highway, around Aquia. Can we pull off there for ten minutes or so? Rudolph out."

"Dasher here... roger that," confirmed Abruzzio. "We'll pull off at the Aquia Mall exit. Blitzen, Donner, Rudolph, Comet, and Cupid... do you copy? Dasher out."

One by one, acknowledgments came in from the other vehicles in the convoy.

"Let's not make it too long," concluded the former JPL scientist. "After all... we don't want to keep the President waiting... *do* we? Dasher out."

Started Out As A Sunny Day

"Nice day today, man," idly observed Hendricks, as, through his mirror sunglasses (a fashion-item mimicked by Boyd and – with minor variations – several other members of their expedition), he set his gaze to scan over the north side of the White House, from his vantage-point on Pennsylvania Avenue with Lafayette Square behind him.

The SUVs had to be parked several blocks away, as vehicles were not allowed this close to the White House; the second bait-group had to proceed to this place, entirely on foot.

They were pleasantly surprised to discover that the street had been re-opened to public pedestrian-traffic after the recent "incidents" affecting the U.S. Presidential palace, as well as all of D.C.; this was, as they were informed by a bored Park Police officer, "because the Old Man wants to prove that everything's back to 'business as usual'".

Sammie had a sudden fit of the giggles upon hearing this, although the others quickly forced her to suppress it.

"You know... I like it more when it's really sunny," quipped Boyd. "Just *suits* me some way, I guess. And by the way... their facial-recognition systems have probably got a positive ID on me by now – maybe you as well... right?"

"Yeppers," agreed the third agent, with a vague positive nod.

"You got the beacon for the helo?" asked the former Mars mission pilot, *sotto voce*.

"Sure *do*," confirmed Hendricks, "Got the 'no-fly-zone' IFF transponder set up on it, but we'll still have to sprint ten city blocks to get on board the damn thing – unless of course you want to try your hand against all those nice White House air-defense missiles and such."

"Oh, *no*, you don't!" countered Boyd. "Had more than enough of *that* already, in the *Express*. On the same topic... you handed out the trackers?"

"Roger that," stated Hendricks. "One to everybody, 'civilians' included. Stick to anything once you pull the tab – should be good for fifty miles coarse, twenty high-precision, at least ten days uptime. You got yours, and the mini fold-out console?"

"Wish I had more time to test it," grumbled the former Mars mission pilot. "Heard that from the Commander and a few others as well."

"Not much to learn, really – just turn it on and the magic of GPS-2 does the rest," remarked Hendricks. "Funny, you know... when we were in the Bureau I thought this was 'restricted-access' stuff; but now you can just buy 'em off Neo, you don't even have to go to the dark networks. Everybody's a spy, in other words. Go *figure*."

"Least unusual thing that's gone down, lately," observed Boyd.

"Yeah," agreed the third agent.

They just stared around for a few seconds, studying the surroundings. There was a moderately-large crowd milling around the fencing that separated the north side of the White House grounds, from Pennsylvania Avenue.

"We all ready... all here?" mentioned Hendricks.

"I see Callum, Marie, Sammie and Donny, all wandering around," observed Boyd. "Oh... and Misha way over there. Hope he isn't going to wander any further... holy crow, can he *ever* dress the 'tourist', eh? Where's Sylvia, though?"

"Told me she was going to be a bush... see her over there?" chided Hendricks, pointing to a very normal-looking piece of shrubbery in the shadow of a tree, beside a trash-bin.

The former Mars mission pilot did a double-take.

"Oh... yeah... I can just make her out, in *Um'b'as'ài*," he commented. "She seems to be masking the IR-bands... good girl. Ha, ha – I see the dog in there, too. Hope she doesn't decide to find a bush to 'go' on. Break our cover."

"Wish *I* could do that," remarked Hendricks. "The hidey-tricks, I mean. I got the star-sight down cold, you know."

"Maybe you *will*, someday," replied Boyd.

"Yeah," said the third agent, as he stared outward and continued to carefully survey the surroundings and the situation.

Nothing seemed to be out of the ordinary; there were tourists here and there, along with a couple of concession-stands that were selling frankfurters, ice cream and various other delicacies.

Also – as Hendricks noted with mild interest – a white panel-van had pulled up at the south-west corner of 15th Street N.W. and Pennsylvania Avenue; it seemed to be disembarking a team of three black-suited LEA-types, who were obviously "authorized" as they presented their credentials – which were apparently accepted – to the checkpoint maintained by the

Capitol Region Police, at the entrance to the pedestrian-only sections of Pennsylvania Avenue.

From behind the building came the sounds of a band playing.

The two Missouri farm-owners approached.

"What's *that?*" asked Marie Wade.

"President's got some kind of diplomatic thing going on," explained Hendricks. "On the South Lawn. That's on the other side."

"Oh," said the farm-wife.

The third agent noted that the Russian was paying close attention to the recently-arrived LEA team, each member of whom was carrying a large duffel-bag over his back. The black-uniformed, dark-visored men were walking, very slowly and nonchalantly, towards the crowd in which Hendricks, Boyd and the rest of the bait-group, had parked themselves.

"It was in the briefings that we got before we headed out... remember?" added Boyd.

"Well, there was a *lot* of stuff that you super-duper folks wanted the missus and me to learn up on... but you all know about 'teachin' and old dog new tricks'... right?" offered Callum Wade.

They stopped and listened for a few seconds more. There was a brief introductory speech, from a voice that – even at this distance – sounded recognizably like that of the President. After a couple of minutes, the discourse changed.

"Hey... whatever that is, it ain't in English," noted the Missouri farmer. "Can't tell what they're *sayin'*."

"German," informed Boyd. "I had to learn a few words of it, back at NASA... interface with the European systems, in the early stages of our flight. Always wanted to get over there and see that country... wonder if I got enough juice in me to fly the Atlantic... hmm... I think I heard 'friendship' in there, somewhere."

"Must be easier than Angel-Girl's crazy-ass lingo," mentioned Donny. "Didn't she say you were the only one who knows it? I guess it must have been hard have learned or to speak, considerin' it's, like, *alien –*"

"Z*'ec'h mò't 'tsch'd'd'éi'm*," cheerily replied Boyd.

"What the hell's *that* mean?" inquired Callum Wade.

The LEA team had now reached the crowd at the midpoint of Pennsylvania Avenue, with a direct line of sight to the North Portico of the White House. Whatever they had been carrying had been laid on the ground.

At first, the men seemed to be talking privately amongst themselves. Then they split up, with one going to the left, one to the right, and the third standing guard over the collection of baggage on the pavement.

"I said, 'you got *that* right'... more or less," responded the former Mars mission pilot. "A lot of it doesn't translate well into English, or *any* human language; like, there are twenty or more words each for 'you', 'me' and 'us', depending on who 'you', 'me' and 'we', are in relation to each other. And there's a lot of words that refer to stuff that I've never seen, for example people with four legs, 'the Sun that comes out at night', alien religions, magic spells... *et cetera*. On the other hand, it has no words for things like 'telephone' or 'computer'. By the way, technically, I didn't have to 'learn' *anything* – she kind of mind-melded with me, then I woke up with the mother of all headaches... and there it was."

By now, the Russian – who had been roaming all over the courseway, in all directions – had rejoined Hendricks and Boyd.

"This is fascinating, and I do not want to seem unnecessarily restrictive," he spoke in Boyd's direction, "But should we be openly discussing such matters? The American government has listening-devices everywhere, after all."

"*Relax*, Misha," reassured the former Mars mission pilot. "If Minnie and Jerry have got the systems in there, working... they already know we're here."

"Well then... why ain't they *arrested* us, or whatever?" asked Donny.

"Maybe they *will*, in their own sweet time," answered Boyd, while the dialogue in German continued from the opposite side of the White House. "Which would be okay, I suppose, I just hope they do it to Laura too – damn lame idea, sticking her and the rest of them out there as sitting ducks..."

The two LEA-agents who had been roaming, had now returned to the baggage-pile directly in front of the lawn leading to the North Portico.

"I suppose that I am just not used to a, uhh, 'mission', in which the objective is partly to be discovered," grumbled the ex-SVR agent. "I have surveyed the area... not much has changed since my – *ahem* – original training, back at 'headquarters'. However... I *am* concerned about a few things."

This remark brought immediate attention from Hendricks, Boyd and Donny, although the third agent continued to scan the area as he maintained the discussion.

"Specifically...?" asked the former Mars mission pilot.

"First of all," opined Misha, "We are wide open here – there is nowhere for the 'civilians' to hide. Secondly, there seem to be very few local police or other guards up here; perhaps that is because they have been re-allocated to protect the event on the other side of the White House. This means that if we are attacked, we will be on our own to deal with it. Although – we *do* have this group of police-agents who have just set up, over there."

He discreetly pointed to the LEA-types who were standing together, near the fence separating Pennsylvania Avenue from the White House North Lawn.

"I cannot exactly put my finger on it," cautioned the Russian, "But something about them, *worries* me."

"Not following you, man," commented Hendricks. "A second ago, you were saying that you wanted to see *more* cops up here –"

"I know," said Misha. "It is just a *feeling*... that is all. Probably nothing more."

"Look like a SWAT team," offered Donny. "Never liked them guys... but I s'pose you gotta expect to see 'em here, 'specially considerin' what went down with you 'space gangstas' a few days ago."

"I really *must* protest," complained the Russian, "Even if what Major Boyd says is true, we should not –"

His missive was interrupted by something sounding like firecrackers exploding, issuing from the other side of the White House.

A shocked look came over Misha's face. It was quickly matched by similar expressions for Boyd and Hendricks.

"Shots *fired!*" exclaimed the third agent.

That Little Voice In My Head

"Wow... never in my *life* did I think I'd get *in* here!" gushed Yvonne Jacobson, as the group waited in the White House East Wing Colonnade corridor marshaling-area, along with four or five other, eager families. "Even when Sam got selected as an astronaut, all we got were some parties in Florida. But now we're at the *White House!*"

"Yeah," remarked Cassie Young, "Impressive... *that's* for sure. Just wish my Jimmy could have seen it."

This got her a hug from two of the others, accompanied by some words of comfort.

"You see where them astronauts ended up?" she whispered discreetly to Boatman, who was impeccably-dressed in a new business-suit, complete with authentic silver cuff-links, red power-tie and lace-up black dress-shoes.

His attire was not atypical; Abruzzio's credit-account had provided for smart new, two-steps-below-Fifth Avenue-grade clothing for everyone in the troupe.

"Commander 'n the Professor are hangin' at the back of the line," mentioned the big ex-agent. "I think it's as much to keep Wolf honest, as anythin' else."

"*Could* have been worse," snorted Cassie Young. "He *could* have brought them two dogs of his. Carpets'd go in the first ten seconds."

"They don't let pets in here," observed Boatman. "And there you *go*, for 'why'."

"Well," complained Amina, "I'm still let down that they closed off the biggest rooms for – what was it – oh yeah... that 'state meeting' or whatever it was. I mean... we had to stand in the security line for an *hour*, and all we get to do is look in at, like, half of what we're supposed to see."

"I guess we're lucky to be let in here at all," deflected Boatman. "They don't usually do it if there's anythin' *official* goin' on. President's probably tryin' to show that everythin's back to normal after... well, *you* know."

The remark got him a lot of smirks from the others, evident of some mixture of pride and guilt.

"I know what you mean, Amina," offered Laura Boyd, "I would have liked to see at least the whole East Wing, myself. But do you *hear?* That 'meeting' seems to be starting. I can hear music playing outside... sounds like it's coming from the other side of the building."

"I don't... can't hear *anything*," countered Cassie Young. "You *sure?*"

"*Sure* I'm sure," answered Laura Boyd. "Faint... but clear as a bell."

"Yeah," added the teenager. "I sort of hear it too. Weird. Sounds really far-away..."

Boatman raised an eyebrow.

"Guess I need to get my ears checked," grumbled the Texas farm-wife. "Maybe they got whacked-up, with what went down at our farm back west."

"Don't know how you can *miss* it," said the Mars mission pilot's wife. "They're speaking in some foreign language."

"Can we go see?" asked Amina.

"Don't think we're allowed in that part of the White House," cautioned Boatman. "That's gonna be either West Wing or the south side, and they're *always* closed off. You can even be in the government and they won't let you down there – "

He was interrupted by an amplified human voice coming from the far end of the corridor, to the west.

"Ladies and gentlemen," it announced, "You may now proceed to the parts of the White House that are designated by the signs, as 'open to the public'. Please do not go anywhere that you don't see such a sign. The next area that you will be entering is the East Garden Room. So named for its proximity to the gardens re-done by former First Lady Jacqueline Kennedy, this room is..."

While the orientation droned on, Laura Boyd whispered to Boatman, "Otis... I'm *scared*. About all this. I just wish Brent were here."

"Why'd *that* be?" inquired the former FBI agent. "Any more than usual, I mean?"

"I've got this voice in the back of my head," explained the astronaut's-wife. "Every time I try to ignore it... it keeps on coming back, like a song you can't stop hearing... but much worse. I've never felt anything *like* this, before."

His expression now even more serious than normal, Boatman asked, "What's it tellin' you, Mrs. Boyd?"

"It's saying, 'something *big's* about to happen'," warned the woman.

South Lawn Siege

The cherry-blossoms were resplendent along the Potomac on this beautiful, spring-to-summer-transition day; but though the display was impressive enough, the *real* action today was in the South Lawn of the White House, just below where the South Lawn road curved to meet the Truman Balcony, overlooking the expanse of grass going a football-field's-length or more, to the south.

A huge, dark-green tarpaulin (actually, four of these, carefully stitched-together and duly-decorated with imaginative artwork) had been discreetly draped over the Storied Watcher's little lawn-ornament, which lay slightly to the east, between two stands of trees. The area containing it had also been cordoned off to protect it from souvenir-seekers, or from the merely curious.

"We ready?" inquired the President, dressed in his immaculate Sunday best, as he – along with an extensive entourage heavy with State Department diplomats – waited just inside the White House South Portico.

"Think so," confirmed Kaysten. "Chancellor Gebirgen and his folks are already there – they're waiting on the South Lawn. Press is set up, too."

"You ready?" asked the President, in the direction of a short bald-headed, elderly Caucasian man with a bow-tie and a pair of *pince-nez* spectacles.

"Yes, sir... I am," replied the man. "It's been an... *interesting* few weeks – I can certainly say that – but it's good to be back at work."

"No kidding," offered the U.S. leader. "Good to have you back, Jacob."

"Thank you, sir," said the Secretary of State.

Minnie Chu's trim figure – wearing professional-looking dress-clothes on the outside, but, in fact, with a tight-fitting, black Spandex-like suit underneath – walked forward to address Kaysten and his boss.

"Mr. President," she implored, "I have to ask you again – please, *please* postpone this event! Or, at least... why can't you meet the Chancellor in here? How much of an imposition can *that* be? Wait a minute –"

Answering an alert from her mobile communicator, the former team-leader seemed momentarily preoccupied with information coming in via her earphone.

"This event's been on the schedule for *months* – long before our alien-friend decided to drop in on us all," countered the President. "The tradition's that I meet foreign dignitaries on the South Lawn, for the beginning of a diplomatic visit – isn't that right, Jacob?"

"Very definitely so," echoed the Secretary of State. "Madam Chu... while we all take your concerns very seriously, this is one of those situations were, bluntly put... appearances *matter.*"

"We've got to show the country that we're back to normalcy," added the President. "And anyway – we've got all our defenses set up... right, Curt?"

"What the... well what are *they* doing here, for God's sake? They were supposed to tell me –" Chu was heard to complain. "Look... I'll deal with them later, but just keep them away from everything, until –"

Kortish's stolid, bull-necked, dark-suited body approached.

He answered, "That's right, Mr. President – Service is up to full strength, they're deployed along with the Park Police, and we've got plain-clothes agents scattered within the crowds. Given that all of the alien's, uhh, 'hangers-on' are accounted-for, and that none of them appear to be hostile right now, we believe the risk to be acceptable."

"Yeah... *you* know, Minnie," interjected Kaysten, "He can't hide in here, *forever*. We'll be alright."

"But the voices... the *voices!*" complained the *nouvelle* FBI-director. "And I saw you grimace a minute or two below, at the same time when I got that aching feeling in my gut. Something's going *on*, Jerry! And –"

"We were over this, earlier today, back in the Oval Office," interrupted the U.S. leader. "Jerry's right, Ms. Chu – I simply *can't* put the affairs of the government, on hold permanently. Come on... let's get out there, get the introductions and the speeches over with and enjoy a nice state lunch with the Chancellor. We've got a lot of business to discuss with him."

"Indeed we do," reinforced the Secretary of State. "We *need* those currency-support loans!"

"I'm doing this under protest, sir," countered Chu. "I'll be standing by, looking out for trouble."

"Thanks – and you *do* that, Ms. Chu," said the President. "I very much do appreciate it. Never hurts to have a super-being – excuse me, *two* super-beings – playing bodyguard. And thanks for flying back here from that mountain so you could be here for the occasion. Makes me feel, well... a bit more *secure.* "

"I wish I could say so of myself, sir," grumbled Chu.

"Look at the *bright* side, Minnie," quipped Kaysten. "At least you don't have to give a speech."

"Yeah," she sourly acknowledged. "Because if I *did*... it'd start with, 'everybody go home, right away'. Starting with our unanticipated guests, who want a tour of the White House."

"Who do you mean?" asked the Chief of Staff, as the President straightened his tie and led his entourage out into the sunshine, descending confidently down the stairs of the South Portico.

The formalities had now gone on for about a half-hour, with the President's podium, prominently so identified by the seal of the United States, to the left of that of the Chancellor of the Federal Republic of Germany. Both podiums were on a platform about two feet off the ground.

Before them were arrayed crowds of onlookers numbering into the low hundreds, including dignitaries of various sorts, members of the press, Washington society-guests and numerous government civil servants.

The bands had played the national anthems of both countries, and the two leaders had delivered short, anodyne, pre-prepared speeches extolling the virtues of "trans-Atlantic partnerships" and "restoring relations to their postwar levels".

"And so," came the translated concluding words of the German leader – a good-looking, tall, well-tanned, blue-eyed man with bushy white hair – "As we resolutely move forward from the alarming and tragic events of the past weeks, the Federal Republic and the European Union look forward to a new era of coöperation with the United States, based on mutual –"

Like a rocket, the figure of Minnie Chu – her eyes glowing and her war-song starting to play – streaked across the scene before of the shocked crowd. In much less than a half-second she was flying seven feet off the ground in front of Gebirgen…

Just in time to take a rifle-round that had been aimed directly for his head.

The shot hit Chu in the middle of her chest, resulting in a shower of sparks while she continued forward, coming to an unceremonious crash-landing in the South Lawn.

The Chancellor, meanwhile, was instantly surrounded by three German security-guards, one of whom took a bullet in the back and collapsed in a spray of blood, while the other two ushered him toward the South Portico.

Pandemonium broke out instantly, within the crowd, with people running in terror, in every direction.

In the next seconds, Kaysten mimicked the *nouvelle* FBI-director's heroism by interposing his own body between the source of the gunfire and the President, who reflexively crouched at the first sound of gunfire.

He, too, was hit, but less directly; a shot struck his shoulder at an oblique angle and ricocheted off. The Chief of Staff grimaced but was able to carry on protecting the President.

Kortish, however, was not to be so lucky. He threw himself at the U.S. leader, covering the President from almost every angle not already blocked by Kaysten.

Along with two other Secret Service agents, Kortish had almost convoyed the President into the White House, when the senior agent was hit by two more rifle-rounds. One – which was partly-stopped by a Kevlar-II flak-jacket – hit him in the upper back, while the other struck the back of his neck, nearly decapitating him.

The shot to Kortish's back would certainly have hit the President, had it not impacted against his loyal bodyguard. The Service agent fell face-down, with blood from his lifeless body gushing out over the South Portico pavement just short of the entrance to the White House, like some macabre *tsunami*.

Then – after perhaps eighteen or more shots had been fired – the fusillade seemed to abate.

Dazed and moaning in pain, Chu spat out grass and dirt while supporting herself on one knee.

She surveyed the scene.

Warden, she silently implored,

Where did the shots come from?

Tell Mother cannot dear I, he replied.

Least from directions at three.

Away from far... to us of south all.

Thanks, she mused.

We should chase them down... but we have to protect the President!

Airborne, she raced across the South Lawn, forcing herself to ignore the pleas of the several badly-wounded attendees who were strewn all over the blood-splattered scenery. Chu reached the rightmost ground-floor entrance to the South Portico in a second or two, stepping inside and looking around desperately until her eyes fixed on the U.S. leader, still buried in a pile of Secret Service agents.

Kaysten was between the *nouvelle* FBI-director and his shaken, horrified boss.

"What the... what the *fuck!*" he cursed. "Who –"

"I don't know – neither does Warden," spoke the former team-leader. "Is he alright?"

"Guys... *guys!*" shouted the Chief of Staff, while holding his right hand over his left shoulder and grimacing all the while. "We're inside, and Minnie and I are both here – let him *up*, please!"

Reluctantly, the human-shield made up by the Service agents, decomposed itself, revealing the ashen-faced figure of the President, underneath.

He stood up, on wobbly legs.

"Jerry – Minnie – you're... thank *God!*" exclaimed the U.S. leader.

"Are you oh-kay, sir?" demanded Chu.

"Physically, 'yes'," offered the President. "Jacob – Gebirgen – what about them?"

"Lost track of the Secretary," answered Kaysten, "But the Chancellor got away, I think – thanks to Minnie stopping a shot that was meant for him – hell of a good job, Minnie! I think Gebirgen's on the other side of the Portico... like, in the Map Room."

"Thank you *ever* so much, Ms. Chu," demanded the President.

Grimacing as she ran one hand over a burn-hole almost in the middle of her dress-suit, the former team-leader replied, "Now I sure know how Sylvia felt."

The U.S. leader's eyes searched the surroundings. He addressed the Secret Service agents.

"Where's Curt?" he pressed.

"He didn't *make* it, sir," evenly responded one of the agents, a muscular, crew-cut Caucasian guy. "Took a round to the neck. If it's any consolation... it had to be pretty much instant, sir."

Chu's mobile communicator appeared in her hand, next to her ear. She stepped away, evidently in intensive discussions with others in the Bureau.

Tears came to the President's eyes.

"No... *no!*" he choked. "Not *Curt*... not *him!* Where *is* he? We need to –"

"Outside, sir," answered the agent, "But we can't let you go out there, sir – *far* too dangerous! The shooting's stopped but we haven't located those responsible for it. We'll recover Agent Kortish's body as soon as we've cleared the perimeter."

As if to reinforce the point, one of the few undamaged windows in this part of the White House, was again perforated by an incoming bullet. Luckily, this round's trajectory was much too high to have actually hit anyone in the Diplomatic Reception Room.

"Mr. President," implored the newly-in-charge Service agent, "It's *far* too dangerous even in here! We've got to get you to somewhere safer!"

"I agree," supported Chu. "We should try the West Wing."

She moved to position herself between the President and whatever was outside.

"They'll hit *me* first," she explained. "I've already taken one... I guess two or three more gets me the hat-trick."

"Thanks," said the President, as he moved further inside the room, towards the Center Hall. "I know now that I made the right choice, about the Bureau."

They heard shouting just to the west.

"*Was zur Hölle ist gerade passiert?*" angrily exclaimed a Teutonic-sounding voice.

"*Zumindest der Kanzler ist in Ordnung – hast du gesehen, wie diese Frau ihn gerettet hat?*" came back a breathless reply.

"*Und der Präsident?*" called out another voice.

"*Ich denke dass er in Sicherheit ist... aber einer seiner Wächter wurde erschossen,*" answered the second voice.

"Oh-kay," they heard Chu say.

She turned to address Kaysten and the President.

"Secret Service and the Bureau are now engaged in an intensive search for the shooters – and – given the many directions that the gunfire came from – there may have been multiple assailants," she said. "Until we've secured downtown D.C., sir – and that may take *days* – it would be extremely inadvisable for you to show up in public –"

"I need to do a quick press-conference, Ms. Chu," countered the U.S. leader. "The people need to see that I'm alive, and – relatively – unharmed."

The familiar figures of the First Lady and her two offspring, appeared in a doorway to the west. She rushed over to the President.

"Clark – *Clark* – oh thank God, you're *alive!*" wailed the distraught woman.

As he held his wife close to his heart, the President answered, "Yes... I am... but Curt didn't make it."

"*Curt?* From the Service, you mean?" asked the First Lady.

"He died protecting *me*, Kathy," quietly stated the President. "He died doing his duty. We'll attend his funeral, of course."

"Oh man... that *sucks!*" remarked Matt, while his sister sobbed and wiped tears.

"It sure *does*, son... it sure *does*," reinforced the U.S. leader.

"Mr. President – about you appearing in public," interjected Chu, "There may be more snipers out there. Until this is all resolved, we need to be *very* cautious! You should just go on TV."

"Absolutely agreed, sir," spoke up the Secret Service agent who had informed about Kortish. "If you want to do a conference, that's your decision, sir... but we'll need to close the curtains and confiscate *everything* from anyone who enters the Press Briefing Room. That is, 'notepads and pencils only'."

"Understood," acknowledged the President, with a nod of his head.

"Thank you, sir," said Chu.

She stepped away and again began to work her communicator. Then the *nouvelle* FBI-director, looked up at the President.

Her face wore an exasperated expression.

"Sir," she announced, "I forgot to mention that apparently we have members of the Jacobson team – family-members, Sam's wife and others – on the White House premises –"

"For God's *sake!*" exclaimed an angry U.S. leader. "What the hell are *they* doing here? Jacobson was supposed to *tell* us if – *wait* a minute... could *he* have had something to do with –"

Although seemingly distracted by information coming in to her earpiece, Chu countered with, "I doubt it, sir; they were in the line-up for a tour of the White House's public-access areas, once the Gebirgen thing was over –"

"How did these people get on the grounds, in the first place?" protested a frustrated President. "We normally close things up when there's a state visit –"

"He got a special pass... remember, sir?" reminded Kaysten.

Chu turned to the bodyguards and requested, "Can we please have the Service send someone to take them aside and keep them out of harm's way?"

"Yes ma'am," complied one of the Secret Service agents, who stepped back and began to utter commands into his own communicator.

The President turned to Kaysten.

"So, Jerry," asked the President, with a weary sigh, "What alien-magic you got today, for us to tell the people?"

The Chief of Staff replied, with a frustrated wince, "Well, sir... 'alien-magic', I got *that* in spades – but somehow, I don't think now's the right time for us to be telling jokes on live T.V.."

"Then what should I start with?" asked the U.S. leader.

Kaysten shrugged and said, "How about... 'what can possibly be *next*'?"

Perhaps, on that day, the Chief of Staff was displaying a latent alien-power of precognition; because in the next few seconds, the sounds of gunfire again erupted.

"Where's *that* coming from?" exclaimed a panicked First Lady.

"Sounds like the East Wing," commented one of the Secret Service agents. "No – wait – not just from there – on the other side of the White House, or maybe –"

There were more sharp "crack-crack-crack" sounds – and then the percussive 'thuds' of explosions, somewhere on the north side of the building, as the alarm-lights began to flash a brilliant, on-and-off red.

A couple of seconds later, they heard a warning-broadcast coming over the White House public-address system, demanding that visitors stay in place.

"Let's *go!*" called the leading Secret Service agent. "I'll over-ride any doors that auto-locked!"

"We need to go now!" echoed Chu.

With the guards, the *nouvelle* Bureau-chief and Kaysten forming a protective-shroud, the group began to move warily into the Map Room, heading for the West Wing.

"Isn't the guest assembly-area in the East Wing?" inquired Chu.

"Damn right!" confirmed Kaysten. "Which is exactly where Jacobson's folks will be!"

"Sir," forcefully shouted the Service agent, "We've *got* to get yourself and the First Family to the bunker – we're under *siege!*"

Bullets At The Fence

The enhanced hearing of Brent Boyd, Will Hendricks and the other "more-than-humans" standing on Pennsylvania Avenue detected what was going on south of the White House, a split-second before the rest of the tourists in the area realized what was happening.

For a second or two, there was just stunned silence; then some random person in the crowd (not one of the Boyd / Jacobson party) shouted "there's *shootin'* goin' on – let's get *out* of here!"

A few people – probably less than four – did exactly that; they began to sprint for parts to the east, west and north. However, many more – including the third agent and the rest of his entourage – just froze in place, crouching down in the open, as if this would afford any real protection.

The LEA-agents, oddly, didn't attempt to hide. Instead, they just stood there, apparently stunned, for a couple of seconds. Then they started arguing amongst themselves, though the conversation seemed strangely garbled; not even Boyd or Hendricks could tell exactly what was being said.

"What the hell we do *now?*" shouted Donny. "You think they're shootin' at them folks on the tour?"

Sounds of utter mayhem, including rapid-fire gun-discharges, screams and sirens, were now issuing from somewhere on the other side of the White House.

"Doesn't *sound* like it," offered Hendricks. "Too far-off – like gunshots out in the open, not muffled by being behind walls or anything –"

"Well if there's a gunfight going on, and we were here for, *you* know what – shouldn't we go *to* it?" persisted the trucker.

The LEA-agents bent over the carry-bags and began to quickly unzip them.

"Just what you want to *do* – jump the fence and run through the White House lawn?" asked Boyd, trying to keep his voice as low as possible, while still allowing it to carry over the din.

"*Somethin'* like that... yeah," admitted Donny.

"The fuckin' place has land-mines – not to mention hidden Marine guards and a dozen other defenses to blow your ass into next week," warned Hendricks. "Step on the wrong patch of grass, and – **shit – look** *out!*"

He did a dive to the pavement, rolling with superhuman agility to avoid a barrage of bullets, fired from newly-retrieved guns wielded by the LEA-agents. Boyd did the same, though he dodged in the opposite direction, while the Russian – some distance away, closer to where Abruzzio sat cloaked under her protective mirage – also hit the deck.

None of them – nor the ex-trucker, who found the inadequate protection of a small bollard – were at first, hit; seveal rounds directed at Misha seemed to hit an invisible barrier about a meter or so away from him, and were thereby deflected away at random angles.

The Russian disappeared entirely, only to reappear behind a tree-trunk, about a second later. His two lethal living-daggers appeared momentarily – on either side of his midriff – but then the weapons vanished again; it seemed as if they were being held in reserve.

To Donny's shock, he saw his uncle – who had fallen to his knees – throw his hands up in the air, shouting in a loud voice, "Officers! Don't shoot – we *surrender!*"

One of the LEA-agents stopped, stared at Callum Wade for a half-second, then raised an unusual-looking pistol, and fired. One round struck the Missouri farmer in just below his right rib-cage, sending the unfortunate man flying backwards, as his horrified and terrified wife crawled to his side.

Blood seeped out from a wide, smoking hole in the farmer's dress-shirt.

Marie Wade – and an ashen-faced Sammie, who dashed over to the scene of the crime, crouching all the way – fully expected to be shot dead for their efforts. Indeed, the apprehension was well-considered, as shots struck the pavement all around, thence ricocheting upward and outward.

But in fact, the "civilians" were not targeted, only because the LEA-agents started to fire randomly into the crowd, mowing down helpless tourists and others in sickening fashion. There did not seem to be much method to the madness; the agents simply shot anyone who they took notice of.

One of these psychopathic police-officers pulled a box about the size of a large mobile-communicator, out of a holding-pocket in his SWAT-suit. He pressed a button, and almost in unison, four powerful explosions erupted from the North Lawn of the White House.

Fortunately, these were far enough away that the shrapnel issuing from them – which rained down on some of the beleaguered tourists on the parkade a second or two later – did not immediately injure any of the bystanders.

"S*hoot my **uncle**, mother**fucker!**" shrieked Donny, as – to the consternation of the still-cowering Hendricks, Boyd and others – the enraged ex-trucker, his body lit from inside with flickers of the *Fire*, charged at impossible speed headlong at the nearest of the LEA-agents – the one who had unloaded against Callum Wade.

The dark-garbed man instantly retrieved his spring-tracked pistol and began frantically firing at Donny; but a couple of the bullets, which at first looked well-aimed, somehow were deflected away, while one solid shot hit the ex-trucker in the thigh. This in no way stopped a snarling, furious Donny, whose right hook crashed into the LEA-agent squarely in the chest, propelling him backwards by ten feet or more, as if he had been launched from an ejection-seat.

The murderer landed with his back up against the fence, and, amazingly – considering how much kinetic energy had struck him – struggled to regain his footing. Onlookers could see large cracks in the breastplate of his body-armor.

Donny raced to again close the distance.

The other two LEA-agents – to the astonishment of all around – took a short run at the fence separating the North Lawn of the White House from Pennsylvania Avenue and – despite being obviously-laden with war-gear – easily cleared the top of the fence in a single bound. They landed inside the North Lawn and began rushing towards the White House.

Two previously-hidden gun-turrets popped up from different locations within the North Lawn. They pointed their machine-guns at the agents but for some incomprehensible reason, refrained from firing.

"They might be going for the *President!*" shouted a crouching Hendricks.

"We gotta *follow* 'em!" retorted Boyd. "If they get *in* there –"

"You do that, you're gonna get shot *yourself!*" warned the third agent. "Secret Service will –"

As Boyd arose and began to head for the fence, seemingly in defiance of Hendricks' warnings, in the next half-second, Donny reached brawling-range of his own quarry.

The ex-trucker unleashed a flurry of *Amaiish*-fueled punches of bone-shattering potency against the black-suited man; but incredibly, the guy stayed on his feet and – wielding a previously-hidden, machete-like combat-knife – lunged repeatedly at Donny, inflicting a couple of ugly-looking, bloody wounds on the ex-trucker's rib-cage and left arm, including one stab that certainly would have killed or incapacitated a normal human being.

This did nothing to dissuade Donny, however, and he pressed home his attack with even more-crazed ferocity, landing a spread of crushing fist-blows – any of which would *surely* have knocked a normal opponent unconscious, or worse – but which in fact seemed just to crack the man's body-armor and to rip off parts of it.

Not just Donny but all who could see the ongoing struggle, were astonished to see how his opponent somehow survived a haymaker to the head – one that shattered the agent's dark-tinted helmet-visor, while opening a long fissure in the helmet itself.

Jesus... he can punch right through an oak door, mused Hendricks, *And he hit that fucker in the head, straight-on!*

How come the son of a bitch isn't dead?

"Fuckin' *die!*" screamed the ex-trucker, a split-second before the LEA-agent was propelled at least ten feet to the east, after being tackled side-wise, by a charging Misha.

The black-suited man rolled another few feet on the ground, inexplicably regained his feet and then stumbled off, apparently in the direction of 15th Street.

"*Get* him!" bellowed Donny.

"*Leave* him!" countered the Russian.

Boyd tried to get a telekinetic-lock on the fugitive; but somehow, it wasn't working; the man escaped his grasp as effortlessly as a minnow slipping through one's fingers.

Though he did not realize it, the same failure affected Abruzzio.

What the... she reflected,

My mind-grab stuck me to the side of an airliner flying at hundreds of miles per hour – how can it "miss" against an ordinary human?

"But he'll –" raged Donny.

"I affixed a tracker!" explained Misha. "Let him *go!*"

Apparently without being noticed, a horrified Sylvia Abruzzio emerged from the shadows and rushed over to the stricken Callum Wade.

Boyd had a decision to make. He did so.

Trying as hard as he could to avoid the outward manifestations of the *Fire* becoming visible, and also attempting to suppress his war-song – the former Mars mission pilot took a long-jump and cleared the top of the fence dividing Pennsylvania Avenue from the North Lawn of the White House.

He hurtled forward in hot pursuit, noting with alarm the two black-suited figures that had, by now, almost reached the North Portico – shooting three hapless Secret Service agents dead with little apparent effort, along the way.

Not Boring Anymore

"This is borr-ing... *borr-ing!*" complained Amina, as she rolled her eyes and – against the written rules – leaned up against one of the walls of the Center Hall of the White House Ground Floor.

"How you figure *that?*" asked Boatman.

"All we get to do is to stand around here in the corridor, and stare in at these stupid rooms," answered the teenager. "For example... this 'Vermeil Room' here. It's, like, *totally* cordoned-off – we can't even go *in* there! Why don't they at least let us, like, maybe sit on one of the chairs, or on the sofa, and take a selfie... or something?"

"Those are all *antiques* in there, dear," cajoled Laura Boyd. "This place gets *thousands* of visitors, every year. If even a few of them got to use the furniture, it would fall apart. The White House is partly a museum, you know."

"I *still* think it sucks!" pouted Amina. "And I wish Jen was here. At least *then* I'd have somebody to hang out with."

"Honey," commented Yvonne Jacobson, "I don't blame you for feeling that way – and both Sam and I wanted our kids to see the White House, get the private tour, West Wing and all – but I'm glad that Riley, Jen and Jeannie took off to go... well, *you* know where. Remember why we're all here?"

"Yeah... I *get* it," answered the teenager. "But nothing's gonna happen anyway –"

"*Wait* a minute!" interrupted an alarmed Laura Boyd. "Do you hear – oh my *goodness* –"

"What you h – *uh-oh!*" repeated Boatman. "Listen, folks – sounds like somethin' *bad's* goin' down – south side I mean –"

A heretofore-unnoticed, recessed red light located in the ceiling, started to flash on and off in brilliant fashion. Others like it also lit up, further down the Center Hall corridor and inside the Vermeil Room.

A whiff of fear was palpable in the air, as Cassie Young demanded, "What we do *now?*"

As if to answer, a command came over the White House internal public address system.

"**Emergency – emergency –** *emergency!*" it broadcast at high volume. "This facility is now in lock-down – all entrances and exits are secured! Sit on the floor, remain in place and obey law-enforcement personnel – lethal force can and *will* be used against anyone who does not cöoperate!"

By now the staccato noise of automatic-gunfire could be easily heard even by the human members of the expedition; but in perplexing fashion, the mayhem didn't seem to be only to the south; there were also gunshots somewhere to the north, although initially these sounded further-off than what was happening on or near to the South Lawn.

"I... I guess we'd better do what they're saying," proposed Yvonne Jacobson, as she prepared to sit down in a spot close to where Amina had been reclining. The gesture was matched by many of the other civilians who were on the tour, further down the corridor.

"Well now... just *wait* a minute," argued Laura Boyd, "If the bad guys are coming our way, should we be just sitting down, all lined up to be shot?"

"Damn straight," supported Cassie Young. "Anywhere to *hide* around here?"

"Door to that movie-theater back there's locked," observed Amina. "There's nowhere except these museum-rooms – the ones they said not to go into."

Now – while the sounds of chaos continued to the south, with the reverberations of bullet-impacts on the south side of the mansion testifying to what was going on – they could hear gunshots issuing from the north side, unnervingly-near them.

In the next second, the welcome figures of Cherie Tanaka and Sam Jacobson, who had – in defiance of the previously-announced demands – charged forward from the back of the queue, appeared just to the east. They were followed by the bounty-hunter, who had somehow been convinced to wear semi-formal clothing for the visit. (Wolf's two hell-hounds were nowhere to be seen.)

The former Mars mission science officer clasped her hands together and pressed them against her chest, just above the waist.

"*Vîrya Sài'ymë*," intoned Tanaka, "What peril is there here? Tell me so that I may warn our kin!"

For a second, the more-than-a-woman stared vacantly forward, and then she spoke aloud, "She says that men with guns are coming, from the north; and there are more to the south, who are shooting from long range. Sam – we've got to –"

Wolf's eyes started glowing in typically-ominous, bright-red fashion.

"You *know* the plan!" countered Jacobson. "Wolf! *Stow* it! Everybody – get down – hide, as best you can! If they show up... we'll try to take them alive!"

"All fuckin' dressed up and nowhere to go," complained the bounty-hunter.

Ignoring the access-warning-signs, Amina led the dash into the White House Historic Library, where – accompanied by Laura Boyd, Wolf, Cassie Young and Cherie Tanaka – she crouched behind one side of the doorway. Sam Jacobson joined his wife and Otis Boatman on the other side, while some of the civilians in the line-up moved an antique sitting-couch away from one Vermeil Room wall and then attempted to hide behind the displaced furniture-piece. A few more scattered into the China Room and other areas.

Bullets whizzed down the Center Hall, as Secret Service agents, apparently down the hall to the west, engaged the intruders in a furious fire-fight. Screams issued seemingly from everywhere, but especially to the west and east.

"*Shut the door!*" they heard someone yell, from across the Center Hall.

A furtive glance revealed a horrifying sight : those who had hidden in the Vermeil Room had been trying to close the wooden door leading into that room, but the portal had been propped open by a door-stop to facilitate visitor-viewing, and the extra time needed to remove the latter proved fatal.

As two tourists tried to force the door shut, a black-suited assailant – Jacobson and Tanaka got but a fleeting look at the guy – opened fire through the doorway, splattering the civilians' bodies backwards into the room in an orgy of blood and gore.

Sam, frantically sent Tanaka, *we can't just stand around and watch this all happen!*

But the plan – oh, the hell *with it, anyway – Otis, Cherie, Wolf… protect everyone!* came back the response.

She nodded affirmatively. A "soap-bubble" effect expanded from her figure, enveloping Laura Boyd. Meanwhile, on the other side, Boatman moved to place his body between the wall, the carnage outside and Yvonne Jacobson.

"Them rounds go right through the *walls,*" he whispered to the astronaut's-wife. "I guess I take 'em first... thick hide on me – I *hope!*"

The eyes of Sam Jacobson began to dimly-glow, but he did not seem to be enshrouded in his well-known diamond-like protective-covering. A thrilling, pounding war-song started to murmur from the walls and floor-boards.

"Back you up –" started the bounty-hunter.

"Be ready to," countermanded the former Mars mission commander, "But *please* – protect the civilians first – and remember, no war-whoops or ranged powers – you'll give us away... not to mention *wrecking* the place!"

Wolf was literally fuming, as he replied, "Well, wasn't that the fuckin' *idea*, a day or so ago?"

However, the bounty-hunter grudgingly mimicked Boatman's maneuver. He interposed himself between the wall and Cassie Young, muttering to the woman, "If you feel it gettin' hot, lady… stand back a bit."

Jacobson charged out of the White House Library doorway, toward two men in black SWAT-suits, who were trying to machine-gun a small, pinned-down section of Secret Service agents in the Ground Floor Center Hall.

Dead Men Never Learn

The faked credentials had worked perfectly; posing as a "temporary-assignment GrayWar facilities-engineer", Top Dog had cleared the perimeter guard-post, and had been issued an access-card for the entirety of the Eisenhower Building.

With focused determination, and now in full battle-gear (having donned it in the same, secret chamber that the Agency records had attested to being in the bottom-level of the building), he headed down the basement-corridor.

Upon entering one of the "restricted" areas, Top Dog was almost immediately challenged by a Marine guard, who made the unforgivable mistake of not shooting the moment that the former Agency-chief came into sight. One perfectly-aimed, silenced pistol-round that hit the unfortunate guard in his left eye, exiting what was left of his head in an ugly splatter of cranial-matter all over the floor, prevented an inconvenient alarm.

Okay, then, he mused.

Not off to the best of starts.

Got to get topside, then off to business... somebody might notice that useless little fucker not checking in for roster.

He strode down the corridor, whispering "Eisenhower Office floor-plan" into his throat-mike. An image of his route out instantly appeared on the interior of his helmet-visor; but instead of picking up the pace even more, instead, he came to a full stop, marveling at what showed up to his left.

Slightly off the floor and down from the ceiling and expanding to a width of about five feet, it looked as if there was a hastily-covered hole of some sort; it had been sealed off by an amateurishly-constructed layer of shingles and nails that could easily be dislodged by just a boot-kick.

Standing in front of the breach, Top Dog used his helmet-sensors to look behind, and to his astonishment, there was a tunnel leading due east.

I don't believe this! he inwardly gasped.

It's not on any of the Agency maps... but if my IR-, low-light and sonar-readings are right... the damn thing must go all the way to the basement-levels of the White House!

And I'm not detecting any traps – no Claymores, no poison-darts, none of the shit that we normally use to deter intrusions.

So it can't be a honey-pot...

What the hell? Who the fuck made this... and why isn't it sealed up, yet? Is another hit-team ahead of me?

Well... opportunity knocks, I guess... but when I get out the other side, I'd better be ready for a warm reception.

So much the better!

Top Dog used a combination of boot-kicks and strikes with the butt of his combat-rifle, to shatter the shingles and thus clear enough of a space for him to enter the tunnel.

He checked his battle-suit's cloaking-gear and found it to be operational.

Only five charges, though, he noted.

One for ingress, three for combat... one for egress.

Let's never lose sight of that...

Moving carefully by experience and reflex, he stepped deliberately forward to the east, traveling a hundred feet or more.

He came to what appeared to be the end of the passageway, which was – again – incompetently-sealed-shut, albeit this time by a somewhat more durable barrier, apparently made out of plywood and metal brackets. This was not completely solid, however; there were openings between some of the planks.

Carefully, the former Agency-director moved up close to the second barrier and looked through one of the spaces within it.

At first, all he saw was a large, dimly-lit, rectangular meeting-room; but a quick switch to infra-red-mode revealed the outline of a human – a fairly big one, probably a male – reclining in a chair by the doorway leading from the room to parts elsewhere. The heat-vision-mode, though imprecise, revealed a medium-sized plastic-and-metal, gun-shaped object, near the man's belt.

Whoever this guy was, he wasn't moving; as a matter of fact, he was snoring loudly.

They never learn... do *they?* smugly reflected Top Dog, as he positioned the muzzle of his silenced, custom-throated, high-velocity assassin's-pistol, right up to one of the gaps in the slat-wall. It was pointed at the somnolent man's head.

The former Agency-director pressed the trigger. The gesture obtained its intended effect, and – after a short pause to ensure that no aid would immediately come to the just-dead Secret Service-agent, Top Dog kicked in the second barrier and jumped down into the chamber behind it.

It's the fucking Situation Room! he exultantly realized.

I didn't even set off any of the perimeter-integrity sensors – whoever dug this tunnel, must have done that, back, "whenever".

Hat's off to you – whoever you are.

And... know what?

I'm... in!

Not The Safe Route

Three Secret Service agents, one German BND agent and Jerry Kaysten formed the vanguard of the phalanx, with another German and Minnie Chu – her side-arm drawn, facing backwards – as the protective-team traveled rapidly down the ground-floor corridors of the White House.

In the center of the team were the President, the First Lady and their two offspring, along with Susan Feldner and the Secretary of State. The latter, elderly man had suffered a gunshot-wound to the leg, and had to be supported by Matt and Clairie as he hobbled along as best he could.

Chu had inquired after Melissa Claremont, Hector Ramirez, Moira Sullivan and the two GrayWar guys; but wherever they were within the White House, they weren't answering the hail, and there was no time to go looking for them.

There had been only one stop along the way, in which a bloodied and half-dazed Federal Republic Chancellor had been invited into the protected middle of the group. He was assured by the President that "this is the first time that a foreigner, has ever been invited into the White House Bunker"; but somehow, the German leader did not seem impressed by this singular honor.

None the less, he accepted the invitation, and now accompanied the President and his entourage.

Avoiding the outside patio of the West Colonnade for obvious reasons, the group passed through the Palm Room, then the Press Corps offices, then through the Press Briefing Room. They reached the top of the stairs leading to the West Wing roof and to areas below, just to the north of the Cabinet-Room.

"Hey... *whoa*," cautioned Kaysten, as he advanced slightly to the top of the stairwell, and looked downwards. "I remember the lighting changing when the emergency-stuff gets triggered – saw that in the tests – but it's quite dim down there, more than it should be... Agent Chance, Agent Chiarelli and you there, sorry I forgot your name – you guys want to check this out?"

"Bill Jackson, sir," spoke the third Service agent, a younger guy.

"Of course, sir," complied one of the Service agents, a brush-cut, Caucasian person apparently of Italian-American ancestry.

He advanced to the top of the landing.

"I think I see – he started to say, an instant before being pushed roughly aside by a charging, yelling Jerry Kaysten, who – in the next half-second – was struck by a spray of gunfire originating from further down the staircase.

The unfortunate Chief of Staff dodged with super-human speed, but he still took at least two bullets to the right side of his body, producing a shower of sparks that momentarily spewed outward and upward.

He fell, moaning and cursing, backward into the protective-crowd, reflexively moving his hands over where he had been hit.

Oddly, however, there didn't seem to be any blood yet spilled in the engagement.

"*Mr. President– get* **down!**" ordered the other Service agent, while a similar order was shouted out in German, causing Chancellor Gebirgen to emulate the defensive-crouch immediately adopted by the U.S. leader and the rest of the civilians within the group.

As quickly as it had appeared, the gunfire abated. The stairwell was quiet.

Chu – still warily covering the rearward-flank of the team – called backward to the vanguard.

"What's going *on?*" she demanded. "I heard – I *felt* – bullet-impacts –"

"Enemy down the stairs, in the basement-level, ma'am," shouted one of the front-flank Service agents. "Kaysten's *hit!*"

"*Shit!*" cursed the former team-leader. "Jerry – *Jerry! Speak* to me!"

"Uhhh," moaned the Chief of Staff. "Damn... that *hurts!*"

"I *know* it does!" acknowledged Chu. "But feel for it – you should have a bruise, not a hole –"

After a second or two, Kaysten muttered, "Roger that. What the H... I guess that's Her Angelic Craziness' force-thing, doing its job... but *man* does it ache – I can hardly stand up. Oww..."

"You'll *live*," cajoled the *nouvelle* FBI-director.

"I'll go down there, chase that son of a bitch – so fast he'll never see me coming –" growled an angry Kaysten.

"Jerry... *no*," countered the President. "We'll catch the bastard – but you've *got* to protect the Chancellor and myself!"

The Chief of Staff glowered, but grudgingly nodded his head in agreement.

"Sir," asked Agent Chiarelli, "Did you see where the gunshots were coming from?"

"Uhh... no... not really," admitted Kaysten. "Think it was from below... but might have been from up above, too. Honestly not sure."

"They might have both egress-routes – like, both to the lower levels and the roof – covered," warned the other Service agent.

"Now listen," continued Chu, "We've *got* to get the President, his family, and the Chancellor to somewhere *safe!* We obviously can't go *this* way. Sir – is there another route?"

"*Sure* there is," interrupted the first Service agent, who had now cautiously retreated from the top of the stairwell. "And if we could just get to the lower-levels, we could get to the tunnels, maybe to the PEOC or just out of the grounds entirely. There's another set of stairs by the Vice-President's office – but we have to assume that the intruders have *those* covered, as well. *Far* too risky to lead you down that way, unfortunately."

"If we can't get to the bunker... can we get everybody to a helicopter?" asked Kaysten.

"We'd have to call for one – and it's too dangerous to go outside, anyway, sir," countered the Service agent. "There may still be assassins out there with clear lines of sight to both the lawns. If they've got a MANPAD, they could shoot us out of the sky. Or they could just shoot down the 'copter on its way in."

"Agent Chance," demanded the President, "Please call for at least two helicopters; send the first one in ahead of the second, but tell them to watch out for possible attacks. If they both make it, we'll put me on one 'copter and the Chancellor in the other. I hate using these folks to draw fire that's meant for me... but I don't see a better alternative right now."

"On it, sir," responded the other Service agent, a hulking, bald-headed Caucasian guy. "Should be no more than about five minutes or so. And for the record, sir... don't feel guilty about issuing the order. In the Protective Detail, we all know that this kind of stuff, goes with the job."

"Thank you," said the U.S. leader, with a solemn head-nod.

The Service agent began to work the keypad on a specialized, larger-than-normal mobile communicator. He whispered into it, although Chu and Kaysten – as well as the two Presidential children – could still hear a command to "hover in place until egress route validated".

"Minnie," queried the Chief of Staff, "We could go first to scout it out, then protect him with our bodies, get him into a limo –"

"What if they hit the President with a 'lucky shot' or something?" argued the *nouvelle* FBI-director. "And we have *two* heads of state to protect, anyway – this would be different if we had, say, Sylvia, Cherie or Hector to lend a hand – "

She stopped in mid-sentence.

"*What?*" interrogated Kaysten. "Oh... wait..."

"You *hear* it?" she asked.

"Yeah," he confirmed, with a wary tone of voice. "*Damn* it, anyway! Where the hell are all these assholes *coming* from?"

"What are you *talking* about, Ms. Chu?" demanded the President.

"Gunfire to the east of us, sir!" she disclosed. "And if I'm hearing right... it's coming our way!"

Mars-Lungs, Between Boyd And Eternity

Brent Boyd – trying as hard as he could to muzzle his war-song and the other tell-tale signs of the *Fire* – saw the two black-suited murderers disappear into the North Portico of the White House.

They were moving at amazing speed for ordinary humans sprinting on foot, and in fact the former Mars mission pilot struggled to keep up with them (he dared not fly, considering the need for minimum conspicuity). Luckily, the gun-turrets that had somehow ignored the intruders, did so for him too.

Assholes must have some kind of built-in ECM, he reasoned.

He tried to slow the LEA-agents down with a telekinetic grasp, but the range was too long – and the black-suits' movements too erratic, or was it something else entirely – for him to get a reliable lock on either one.

This is going to be fucking great! he noted with frustration.

They're geared-up like some comic-book bad-guy... and Superhero Yours Truly, gets to fight with both hands behind his back.

Lovely!

Okay... can't blast them from range, that would show up on the cameras – but if I can get into grapple-range and I let fly... who'd know?

Immediately after the murderers' entrance into the building, there were the sounds of a furious fire-fight. Bullets smashed through the White House windows, flying outwards toward the North Lawn at an alarming rate; the shots only narrowly missed Boyd himself, whose progress was retarded both by the need to bob and weave, and by the need to avoid land-mines hidden – to "human-eyes" but not to "Mars-eyes" – in several belts across ingress-routes within the North Lawn.

How did those fuckers miss stepping on one... or several? he reflected while reflexively ducking and crouching.

They've got to have some kind of enhanced-vision-gear, in those helmets; and they cleared the top of the fence with a leap that no human being could do.

Who knows what other tricks they've got up their sleeves?

Whoever they are, they're not ordinary terrorists... that's *for sure.*

He had now reached the columnar array that separated the North Portico proper, from the driveway that came right up to the entrance to the White House. The ornate doors had bullet-holes in them, and it looked as if the locking-mechanism had been shot off. The portal was open to the outside.

Out of an abundance of caution, Boyd stopped his forward-movement and used a column as ground-cover.

There was a peculiar "popping"-sound coming from inside the North Portico; it was different and more subdued, compared with what one would have expected from gunfire.

Taking a chance, Boyd peered out from the right-hand side of the column that he was hiding behind. He saw wisps of something looking like smoke – or mist – appearing inside the building and seeping out the doorway.

Hmm... thick enough to obscure normal vision in places, but I can see through it with Mars eyes – might be a chance to get in there without being shot as I step through the door –

He charged forward into the peculiar "mist", but came to a dead stop about a foot inside the White House North Entrance Hall.

Immediately, the former Mars mission pilot felt light-headed, almost nauseous; he had only a couple of seconds to take note of the carnage that surrounded him.

There were five dead government staff – two uniformed guards and three in plain-clothes – collapsed in various grotesque positions within the Entrance Hall; but only two of these appeared to have been shot. The prone faces of two of the other three looked upwards in contortions of agony, with traces of froth on their lips, with congealed blood having issued from their eyes, ears and nostrils.

Boyd felt like puking, and he honestly couldn't tell if it was from the scene, or from the strange gas that his instincts told him, was close to overwhelming even the Storied Watcher's protective body-tricks.

Shit, he realized,

That stuff would be certain death for a human... they'd have only seconds!

What a way to die... you cruel mother-fuckers!

He stumbled out of the White House and took a deep intake of relatively clean air outside, then braced himself and held his breath.

Fire... *fortify me*, prayed Brent Boyd, as he raced inside.

He knew that his eyes were now glowing. He didn't care.

Upon again coming into contact with the slowly-abating traces of the infernal gas, the same symptoms started to affect him, but – possibly due to refraining from inhaling – they were minimally-manageable, and he had time enough to strip a pistol, complete with belt, holster and several extra clips, from one of the fallen police-officers.

I'll avenge *you!* he silently vowed, as the ex-astronaut stepped forward, catching the briefest of glimpses of his quarry, who were receding further into the White House, disappearing down the stairs to his left.

Upward, The Rough Way

Damn, he thought, *I wish we had this thing two years ago.*

I'd even have settled for one *year ago – all things considered.*

If we just had something like this, back at the Hotel Tucson...

Using the suit's direct mind-wave interface, Top Dog switched it into "stationary defensive mode", with sensors at nearly full-power, while he paused for a few seconds to consider his options.

It was nearly pitch-black down here – he had knocked out all the lights in this part of the West Wing's lower-level – but this didn't impact his situational awareness one bit; the suit's helmet and visor instantly displayed the surroundings with a combination of computer-controlled light-enhancement and infra-red, that might as well have been noon outside on a cloudy day.

IFF tagged that target as a half-alien, he mused.

Good hits... but no confirmation of a kill.

That *sucks...*

Strange, considering the mushroom-rounds should go right through standard-issue Service lightweight body-armor.

Couldn't *have been Little Miss Primary Target...*

Fucking acoustics, resonance sensors and imaging didn't get a good look.

Oh well.

Maybe it was that bitch FBI-dame who's been hanging around here, lately?

Auditory-boosters caught a mention of "Mr. President" – stroke of good luck, there – if he's really nearby, it'll be my singular pleasure to grease Clark, his snob society wife and those two little spoiled teenagers, just before I smoke his little alien puppeteer.

Country will be better off without weakling appeasers like him!

Anyway... even with all my combat power-ups, not a good idea to give up the element of surprise... Service might have something "special" up there at the top of the stairs, like maybe a portable AT-round, or a Claymore or two.

Something that the suit might not be able to handle, in other words.

Got to assume that they've got the other conventional egress-routes covered in the same way – they ain't stupid... I'll have to give them that. Let's hope our strike-teams closed off access to the PEOC and knocked out the elevator, per the plan.

And too far to the west, takes me right back by the Service barracks. Had to tippy-toe past 'em with the stealth-stuff on my way here, and I've been lucky that they're not on my ass already – not sure why they didn't respond to the shooting around here – maybe there are none of them in there?

Anyway... let's not get into a gunfight with them just yet.

I'd win – but too much of a distraction.

Let's take a detour...

Using the low-light vision-modes, he looked around. There were doors all around, leading to various rooms in the White House West Wing basement.

Auto-map... on... latest layout from Agency archives... check... okay.

That one to the west, three doors down – old section, the ceiling wasn't reinforced to the same five-pounds-per-square-inch overpressure-standard that the core areas got layered on – there's where I outflank 'em!

I can even zip outside and take them from the north if necessary.

Bit of a risk... but I should be safe with the stealth-thing going, even if that's just for a short time.

Okay... now for our latest little techno-trick... let's keep it quiet for the moment...

Following the directions and moving in front of the fourth corridor-door, he pointed one of his gauntlets at the portal's locking-mechanism and activated yet another of the suit's functions.

Supposed to be ninety per cent chance... at least that's what they told me...

Top Dog allowed himself a thin smile, as the lock disengaged, leaving the door wide-open.

Service really shouldn't have let the Agency tap into the White House's internal networks – including the physical access control one, he smirked.

Oh... but it would have been the Puzzle Palace that they'd have to have used, to clear the bugs.

Yeah... bit of a challenge there, boys.

Tough luck!

Cautiously, he ventured inside. The first room was evidently just a store-house, as it contained nothing but shelves containing paper records and various other supplies. He moved to the door on the room's opposite side and again engaged his suit's unlocking-trick. Again, the lock auto-disengaged.

Top Dog peered inside the next area. It, too, was uninhabited, but it was evidently some kind of personal office, complete with a large desk, several chairs and a white-board on the far wall.

Where's the weak-point... yeah, there... get ready...

He pointed up at a part of the ceiling just above the desk. A half-second later, something looking a lot like a child's toy sticky-dart, fired up at the targeted-spot.

It hit precisely where he had aimed, and firmly affixed itself to the ceiling.

Crouching in the far corner of the room, he counted,

Three... two... one...

There was a percussive blast, and no doubt it would have been a bad idea to have been right underneath the chosen spot; but in fact almost all of the shaped-charge's explosive force was directed upward. It punched a hole in the ceiling at least eighteen inches in diameter, shredding not only the expected structural-materials but also ventilation-conduits and a spider's-nest of computer-cables.

As the debris and gypsum-dust began to settle, Top Dog could just see all the way into the next floor above.

Let's get up there, before whoever might be in that room, gets their wits about them...

Activating the suit's "high-power" mode, he jumped first on top of the desk; then he crouched down, tensing his hip- and thigh-muscles.

Then – rocketing upwards with impossible speed and kinetic-force – he smashed through the ceiling, heading for the first floor of the White House West Wing.

To The West, Then

After waiting a second or two to be sure he hadn't been noticed and wasn't about to be ambushed, Brent Boyd – pistol in hand – escaped the last vestiges of the gas-cloud, dashed to his left and reached the top of the stairs leading downward from the North Portico Entrance Hall.

There they are, he noted, as he peered downward, reflexively tensing his body to dodge possible gunfire.

But in fact the assassins seemed not to engage him; nor, in fact, did they pay any attention to him. Instead, they raced further down the stairs, and though Boyd did not have a clear line of sight, it seemed that the two murderers were heading for the ground floor staircase-exit.

Shit! silently inveighed the former Mars mission pilot,

If they turn left – they'll run right into Sam, Cherie, Otis, Wolf and my wife –

No, you don't, fuckers!

You so much as lay a scratch *on Laura, and – 'rules of engagement' or no – I'll fucking* vaporize *you!*

Boyd's apprehension appeared to be justified; there were sounds of gunfire, followed immediately by shouts of alarm and anguished screaming, issuing from the Ground Floor of the White House.

Oddly, he also heard – perhaps in or around the West Wing – fainter and further-off sounds of gunfire or of muffled explosions.

Whole damn place *is under siege!* his military mind told him.

We could be and likely will be attacked from multiple directions at once… got to keep that in mind, tactically.

Where the hell's the Service… the Marines?

Unless, of course… they're already dead.

Throwing caution halfway to the wind, Boyd got a running start and – using the guard-rail surrounding the stairwell as a fulcrum – propelled himself over the edge. It was a long drop, one that would certainly have crippled or killed a normal man falling the same distance.

He plummeted downward, but – all the while, having to concentrate diligently to avoid the *Fire* from blossoming to its full splendor – was still able to slow himself in mid-fall. He landed squarely and without injury on his feet on the stair-landing going upward to the First Floor.

A dismaying scene of carnage awaited the former Mars pilot. The two black-suited guys were in the Center Hall; one of them faced to the west and was shooting an assault-rifle at unseen enemies, whose repeated bullet-strikes seemed to be having little effect, due to the SWAT-suit's impressively-robust body-armor; the other assassin was firing his own rifle indiscriminately into one of the White House's museum-rooms, on the far side of the hall.

From within the targeted area, a sickened Boyd could hear terrified screams accompanied by shouts of "stop shooting – we *surrender!*"

Jesus, he reflected while trying to force the Storied Watcher's "fast-thinking" trick to activate,

What if it's Laura – or one of the other civilians – in there?

Even if I break the rules and fire all I've got against the bastards, the photon-beams might go right through the walls and hit whoever's in that room... including possibly my own wife!

Same bullshit if I use this pistol... I don't know if the civilians are directly in the line of sight behind him, through those walls –

Fine, you sons of bitches – let's dance!

Using a quick and hopefully invisible burst of gravity-bending power, Boyd rocketed off the stairwell, propelling himself straight at the assassin who was slaughtering the beleaguered civilians in the Vermeil Room.

In the briefest of half-seconds, Boyd thought he heard a note or two of Jacobson's unmistakable war-song; and in the next clock-tick – as the former Mars mission pilot collided with his quarry, intending to tackle the SWAT-suited-guy in classic Green Bay Packers style – the hapless man was simultaneously subjected to the brutal impact of a hard-charging Sam Jacobson, coming at full speed from a half-visible door behind and to the east.

Unbelievably, the assassin still managed to trigger some kind of close-in defense system – akin to a Taser but with enough output to cripple or kill an ordinary human – and the thousands of volts hit both Boyd and Jacobson, stunning them momentarily, albeit doing little real damage.

The combined kinetic and electrical energy-discharges threw all three combatants off-balance, and each ended up sprawling on the White House Center Hall floor, while Boyd's pistol went flying out of his hand as well.

For somewhat less than a full second, the assassin – along with his two more-than-human attackers – tried to come to their wits.

Jacobson was the first to react; with his hands clenched into fists, he again tried to close the distance with the black-suited-guy.

A nonplussed Brent Boyd got up to a low crouch a half-second later. This proved a wise move, as a hail of gun-shots – apparently issuing from a group of pinned-down Secret Service agents down the Center Hall to the west – whizzed dangerously close-by.

While trying not to lose his focus on the knocked-over assassin, the junior ex-astronaut did a double-take at the other gunman, just as the second SWAT-suited man just... *disappeared.*

What the hell? wondered an astonished Boyd.

Karéin – Bob – can do that… Sylvia too, after a fashion, not to mention that dog of hers…

But a normal human?

The man who they had just tackled now disappeared as well, although – when Boyd did the inevitable double-take, he thought he caught a vague "shimmer" in the air, where the assailant had been, a split-second earlier.

The former Mars pilot heard Jacobson's equally-perplexed mental broadcast.

Maybe whoever this is, figured out how to copy the "light-wave-bending trick"?

Set those Mars-eyes to the high and low bands – maybe it only works with visible light… but be ready for an attack at any time, coming from any –

Right on cue, one of the SWAT-suited guys appeared as if out of nowhere. His auto-rifle was already pointed straight at Jacobson, who was no more than two steps away.

The former Mars mission commander – despite supernaturally-elevated reflexes – had no time to dodge; he was hit in quick succession by five or six high-velocity rounds at point-blank range.

A worried Boyd saw at least two of these shots draw blood, as the stricken and momentarily-stunned Jacobson was knocked backwards and then prone, by the impact of the bullets.

For Christ's sake, *Commander*, mentally complained Boyd,

Turn on that diamond-armor of yours!

Trying… not to… give us… away… came back the pained reply.

Any… more… like… that… I'll… say… 'the… hell… with… it'…

A second later Boyd's infra-red and ultra-violet vision-modes became fully active and he saw the other assailant charging down the Center Hall to the west, evidently planning a second attack against the Secret Service agents hiding, albeit with badly-inadequate cover, near the Palm Room.

The junior ex-astronaut could no longer restrain his rage-induced *Fire*; his war-song began to echo throughout the hall, as – for a second time – he propelled himself against the assassin who had just shot Jacobson.

Again, Boyd tackled the SWAT-suited guy, whose assault-rifle was knocked out of his grasp. The assassin reacted quickly, retrieving an evil-looking combat-dirk and attacking with this weapon. His strength was unbelievable; it was all that the former Mars mission pilot could do, just to avoid being overwhelmed and stabbed in quick succession.

Trying to regain the upper hand, Boyd unleashed his photon-beam attack (though, with somewhat reduced potency; he didn't want to slice the man in half, after all) from both hands, as he grappled with his quarry.

Though he tried to use telekinesis, it proved very difficult for the ex-astronaut to get a good lock on his opponent; this might have been due to the frantic, close-in nature of the battle, or possibly, something else was interfering.

And Boyd was shocked to see that the attack hadn't immediately incapacitated or killed the assassin; instead, he had merely burned two fist-sized holes in opposite sides of his opponent's body-armor. None the less, the force of his assault did seem to have stunned the man, who toppled over backwards with the ex-astronaut's knees pinning down the murderer's arms.

Jacobson – though still slowly bleeding from two places in his chest – had now staggered to his feet.

There were sounds of mayhem from far down the hall to the west, and both of the former Mars mission crew feared for the fate of the Service agents there.

Boyd summoned up his alien-enhanced strength and – after a couple of hard cuffs to the supine man's head – roughly tore off his antagonist's battle-helmet.

The former Mars mission pilot caught a brief glimpse of a glowering, male Caucasian face, a second before – to Boyd's astonishment – he was thrown clear by a display of upper-body-strength far in excess of anything possible for a normal human being.

Damn, thought the former space-pilot,

This guy's stronger than any body-builder… maybe even stronger than me!

Falling head over heels and landing with his back against the south wall of the Center Hall, Boyd was immediately struck by three more bullets, evidently fired from the amazingly-durable SWAT-guy's pistol.

The ex-astronaut's hidden, Kevlar-II breastplate stopped the two rounds that hit his chest, but one bullet hit his left shoulder; this ricocheted off in a spray of sparks. The impact hurt like hell.

Grimacing and covering the site of the injury with his right hand, Boyd – to the dismay of the assassin, who had clearly thought his opponent to be *hors de combat* – forced himself immediately back to his feet with a well-practiced martial-arts forward-flip maneuver.

He prepared to attack, but the former Mars mission pilot was at first worried that the murderer would get off another fusillade of pistol-rounds. Boyd's concern was curtly alleviated by Jacobson's out-of-left-field assault, which delivered a crushingly-powerful fist-punch to the SWAT-guy's midriff. This not only split his power-suit's armor clean in half and knocked it from his body, but also propelled the unfortunate man so hard against the south Center Hall wall that – without the protection of his combat-helmet – he was knocked unconscious, with blood issuing from his nose, ears and mouth.

"Brent – you see the other –" started Jacobson.

"Fucker went down there… *that* way," interrupted Boyd, while motioning to the west.

"*Shit!*" swore the former Mars mission commander, "He could be going for the Oval Office –"

"Yeah, but before we deal with that," remarked Boyd, "We can't let *this* asshole get back into the fight. *And*, we've now got a prisoner."

"He's out," commented Jacobson, pointing in the direction of the defeated assassin, "Let's not take any chances… we should strip and immobilize him."

"What are we going to use as… wait a minute, *I* got it," offered the junior ex-astronaut.

Boyd crouched and stepped forward at a smart pace, while a thin but intensely-hot photon-beam issued from his remaining good right hand, burning through the red-with-gold-trim Center Hall carpet all the way to the marble floor below. Using his alien propulsive-abilities to accelerate the process, he repeated the maneuver five more times, resulting in the creation of three narrow segments of carpet, each about ten feet long, to serve as *ersatz* body-restraints.

"Okay – good job there – let's get him trussed –" said Jacobson.

He and Boyd saw the familiar figures of Tanaka and Wolf, venturing slowly and cautiously from the door leading to the White House Museum Library Room.

"Has the shooting stopped?" asked the former Mars mission science officer.

More percussive sounds, mostly coming from the west but with some seemingly further away to the north and south, answered the question.

"Around *here*… yes," responded Boyd. "Laura with you? She okay?"

"Yeah… the civilians who were with us – including Laura and Yvonne – are fine, though they're badly shaken up," reassured Tanaka. "Otis is protecting them. But we and they saw what happened to the people in the Vermeil Room – it's *horrendous!* They need our *help!*"

A cacophony of desperate wails coming from the referenced location, grimly supported Tanaka's claim.

"Help us with this bastard first," demanded Boyd. "Lift him up so we can strip him of his gear and put the straps on him. He's out… shouldn't be able to resist our telekinesis."

Tanaka complied; in short order, the defeated assassin was securely bound with Boyd's *ad hoc* restraints.

"I'll get the people in the room over to the Library so Otis and I can protect them, if there are more of these assholes hanging around," stated Tanaka. "I'll try to heal anybody who's been hit, as best as I can."

"Okay," answered Jacobson, nodding his head.

"Listen, guys," advised Tanaka, "*Vîrya Sài'ymë* has been warning me, that these are no ordinary bunch of terrorists – she's detected some *very* advanced technology on them, including defenses that she thinks can partly negate our elemental-attacks. And, she believes that we haven't yet encountered all of the intruders. We shouldn't take *anything* for granted."

"Well... no *shit*, about the technology," grumbled Boyd. "I'll try to stick to the plan as much as I can, but if it looks like we're completely outgunned – down comes the façade and I'll hit 'em with everything I've *got*. Commander?"

"Agreed," confirmed Jacobson.

"Agreed," echoed Tanaka.

"Well... say these suits they got, can handle ten thousand degrees... we'll just see about a *hundred* thousand," snarled the bounty-hunter.

The former Mars science officer proceeded rapidly into the Vermeil Room. In only a second or two, all her more-than-human compatriots could feel her mental distress (and that of her symbiotic *alter-ego*), as she beheld the carnage that had been worked in that place.

"You want *me* to do somethin'?" inquired Wolf.

"Yeah," directed Boyd, while he located and retrieved the pistol that he had found upstairs, "*Watch* this son of a bitch... if it looks like he's trying to slip loose, give him a swift kick in the head. He's damn strong, but that might just have been from the suit we just took off him. If he doesn't get the message, by all means make a bonfire out of him – just don't wreck any more of this fine carpeting, than I already have."

"Fuckin' best advice I've had all day... all *week*, actually," savagely growled the bounty-hunter, with a malicious red glow in his eyes.

"We *do* need him alive, you know," cautioned Jacobson.

Wolf took two long strides and put one triumphant boot on the prone assassin's chest.

"That'll depend on if he's a good boy," he smirked.

"Well," added a wincing Jacobson, as he felt around the bullet-strikes on his chest (which were healing, though slowly), "I'm not inclined to argue his case... but maybe just start with a hot-foot – okay?"

Wolf responded with a gruff affirmative nod.

"He loses a foot or two – well, as long as his mouth's still workin' when you get around to talkin' to him, who *gives* a shit?" he added.

"Certainly not *me*," coldly offered Boyd.

"You, Cherie and Otis should be on the lookout for any more of 'em," requested Jacobson. "Place seems to be *crawling* with them, as far as I can tell."

"Yeah," interjected Boyd, "And listen... can you help Cherie to get Laura and the rest of the civilians – including those poor folks who got shot up – into one room, so it's easier to guard them? I know it's going to be hard for them to see what those bastards did, but maybe that's a *good* thing – drive home that this isn't a *game*... you know?"

"Gotcha," agreed Wolf. "Wish this was all goin' on in a parkin'-garage or whatnot... least there I wouldn't have to worry about burnin' down a museum."

He grabbed the unconscious SWAT-guy's feet and began to roughly man-handle him towards the Vermeil Room, even though the bounty-hunter could have just done so with his telekinetic-abilities.

At this moment, more sounds of utter mayhem, began to be heard; the echoes of gunfire and explosions seemed to be coming from somewhere in the west, past the far end of the Center Hall.

"That's *got* to be in the West Wing," observed Boyd. "Bet you dollars to donuts, that they're going for the President! What you want to do?"

"Not a couple of weeks ago," reminded Jacobson, "We were on our way here, with plans to possibly *kill* him."

"No *kidding*," answered the former Mars mission pilot. "We don't owe him jack *shit*, frankly... I'd rather protect Laura and whatever happens to the asshole... it *happens*."

"But we're here *now*," noted Jacobson. "He gets greased – there's a fair to middlin' chance that it'll get blamed on *us* – *whatever* the facts."

"You got a point," acknowledged Boyd. "How the hell'd we get *into* this, anyway?"

"We *wanted* to get attacked," said the former Mars mission commander. "We just didn't count on our tormentors, assaulting on such a broad front. Nor did we – or the Secret Service – count on them being decked out in these super-duper bio-mechanical battle-suits."

A frustrated, pained silence persisted between the two more-than-human ex-astronauts, for perhaps two seconds.

"Well," suggested Boyd, "If the bugger's gonna get smoked – it should be *us* doing the smokin'... nobody else. At least *that* way, we'll actually be doing what we're being accused of."

"Keeping our powers under check is looking like an increasingly impractical idea," stated Jacobson, "But all the same... we should get some ordinary weapons, if only to start off with."

With Boyd's assistance, he grabbed the defeated assassin's combat-knife and assault-rifle along with several clips of ammunition, while giving the man's sidearm, holster and pistol-ammo-clips to the former Mars mission pilot.

"Just like old times, down Amchitka way," sighed Jacobson. "I don't want the grenades... we need precision-weapons – not ones that can take out entire rooms or buildings."

"'Double your gun – double your fun'," quipped Boyd. "*Heard* that, somewhere."

"To the west, then?" pronounced Jacobson, with a wan half-smile.

"To the west," echoed Boyd.

Side by side and with their guard very much "up", the two ex-astronauts marched down opposite sides of the White House Center Hall corridor, heading towards the Palm Room.

Minnie Stares A Jigsaw

Everyone in the West Wing room at the top of the stairs, could easily hear the gunfire raging, just to the east, in the direction of the Center Hall.

"I hear what you're saying, Lieutenant," argued Minnie Chu, perhaps rather louder than would have been advisable, "But we can't stay pinned-down like this, forever! There's still shooting going on over to the east – main part of the building, I mean – and it sounds like it's getting closer."

"I agree," chimed in Kaysten. "We've got to get our butts *out* of here... we're just sitting *ducks!*"

The Italian-American Service agent responded, "Ma'am, our tactical-rules for situations like this are clear – if the President isn't coming under fire right now, in *this* location... then by definition, it's 'safer' than somewhere else where he *could* get attacked. We're supposed to wait here for reinforcements."

Gebirgen muttered something in German; one his bodyguards offered a translation of it as, "The Chancellor says that as far as he can tell, these 'reinforcements' are just as likely to *kill* us, as to rescue as."

"Tell him that I'm *terribly* sorry about all this," apologized the President. "I've no idea how it could have happened. This is supposed to be the most secure building in the United States, you know."

"I understand," came Gebirgen's voice, in accented – but good – English. "Still... it is not the 'welcome' that I had expected."

"You can say *that* again," ruefully admitted the U.S. leader.

Somewhere to the west, there was a sharp explosion that momentarily shook the inside White House walls.

"That was *too* damn close!" remarked Kaysten. "Can't be more than two or three rooms away, far as I can tell. Minnie – sound right to you?"

Chu paused and concentrated for a second, and then responded, "Yeah. I tried to get a vision, but all it's telling me is, 'don't go out on the lawn' – as if I needed *that* advice, ha ha."

The Presidential daughter spoke up.

"Daddy," she implored, "If they're coming at us from the east – and there's explosions going on to the west – and we can't go downstairs, or upstairs, or outside, to the lawn... they're closing in on us! Where are we *supposed* to go?"

The urgency of the situation became yet more clear, when a loud explosion – sounding as if it were very near, perhaps in the Palm Room or even in the Press Corps Offices, from which they had only recently egressed – echoed through the building.

Mercifully, there was another sound – the steady "thump-thump-thump" of helicopter-turbines and -blades.

"They're almost *here*," announced Agent Chance, as he stared forward and held an earphone into his right ear. "Got a track on the beacon in my communicator and a direct channel to Walt Beck at the controls... above us, with another one standing by... no incoming yet, but – oh *crap* – wait a sec –"

He started talking directly to the pilot.

"Reading you five by five," spoke the Service agent, "What the *hell*? Well, why haven't they been suppressed? Oh... I *see*. Yeah – okay – armor holding up? Good – gotta be rifle-caliber and maybe the odd fifty, only... do the evasive if you got to, just keep up high enough so they've only got LoS to your undercarriage, so they can't put one through the windshield or the rotor-head... listen – you see any hostiles in the stairs leading down from the roof?"

He waited, listening, for about ten seconds and then said, "Well, *that's* just great... who made *that* decision? I'll tell them – be back to you in a minute. Hold *on* there, Walt – we're *counting* on you! Chance out."

He turned to address the President.

"Copter's hovering at about fifty feet above and away from the White House and he's still getting shot at – but his lower-quarters armor is handling the impacts so far, sir," explained Agent Chance. "Walt's also seeing random rifle-shots landing all over the ground floor outside, and now it's coming both from the north *and* the south – makes no *sense*, they don't seem to be shooting at anything in particular, although they do seem to be targeting the windows, maybe looking for a lucky hit – the bullet-proof glass is stopping most of these rounds and our guys are engaging the enemy. We've taken some casualties, unfortunately. Anyway, it's *way* too dangerous for him to land on the lawn. There must be *dozens* of hostile snipers out there, as near as the pilot and observer can tell."

"Can't they just land on the roof?" asked Matt.

"It's not stressed for the weight of an aircraft of that size," countermanded the third Service agent. "Might go right *through* the roof or might foul his undercarriage so he can't take off again... he *could* hover just above, but either way, the angle and the fact that he isn't maneuvering, might give the enemy a good shot at the interior of the 'copter, or its rotor-mechanism."

"And, the egress-route to the upper deck is closed off – steel doors, locked, and Walt's seeing some kind of device that he doesn't recognize attached to the latch... might be a bomb," interjected Agent Chance. "We don't *dare* risk it, until we can get a disposal team up here to examine it."

"Nuts," complained the President. "We're *still* pinned!"

There was more gunfire to the east. Ominously, it sounded as if the battle was ongoing no further away than the eastern parts of the Press Corps offices, or perhaps even the west side of the Press Briefing Room.

"Yeah," echoed Clairie, "So near and yet so far. If we could just get up to the roof and then, like, go up a ladder that they dropped from the helicopter while he's still high up there... wouldn't *that* work?"

"I *suppose*," allowed Agent Chiarelli, "Except that you'd still be very exposed while being hoisted aboard – and it wouldn't be easy to hold on, if the 'copter was doing evasive maneuvers in the meantime. With all due respect, miss... this is a waste of *time*. We've no way to get up to the roof, anyway!"

An odd-looking smile now showed on the *nouvelle* FBI-director's face, as she addressed the Presidential daughter.

"Little new sister," pronounced Chu, "Surely do your words speak prophetically! 'No way out', you say, Agent? Let me *show* you one!"

"What you *mean*, Minnie?" started Kaysten; but then, in the next breath, he changed to, "Oh – *I* get it! Hot damn – the bastards won't be counting on anything like *that!*"

"That's right," confirmed Chu. "They'll think we're going for the helicopters... we'll sneak by while they're concentrating on those."

"Mr. Kaysten, forgive me," asked the Secretary of State, "But what the Dickens are you and the Director, *talking* about?"

"Just reading her *mind*, sir," evenly replied the Chief of Staff. "We *do* that, you know."

"Ah," uneasily responded the elderly man, feigning comprehension.

"For the non-psychic ones among you," explained Chu, "Here's the plan. Agent Chance, please tell both helicopter-pilots to lower their rope-ladders, as if they're planning to pick up evacuees, and ask them to prepare to descend to their minimum safe hovering-altitude – but make sure they don't *do* that, until they get the go-code from yourself. Under *no* circumstances are they to go lower, beforehand – keep them at *least* a hundred feet up in the air and not directly over the White House, please. And – can you radio the our personnel up there, to vacate the middle of the roof and hide behind the railings at the edges?"

"Sure... I'll do it now," he answered, "Most of our guys are already hunkered-down anyway, because they're under continuous fire... they'd get smoked if they emerged from cover. But – why?"

"Just *do* it!" she demanded.

"Fine," deflected the perplexed Service agent.

He whispered a set of partly-coded orders into his mobile communicator.

"So what's the rest of the plan?" inquired the President.

"Sir – I need you and the Chancellor to stand clear of the rest of the group... as you two will be the first ones out," requested the former team-leader. "I'll also need Matt, Clairie and Jerry to join you over there. I presume you have a safe place, away from the White House, where you can be deposited?"

"Yes ma'am," interjected Agent Chiarelli, "Blair House and the Secondary Immediate Refuge – the President knows where that is – are both clear and the Marines have them fully-secured; I've had confirmation as of about ten minutes ago. But how are you going to get the President and the Chancellor up to the roof, in the first place?"

The same smile showed on Chu's face as she disclosed, "I'm going to open a hole in the ceiling, and then I'll lift the President and the Chancellor out of here. Any more questions?"

The battle to the east was still raging, with gunshots that sounded as if they couldn't have been more than fifty feet away.

"Ma'am," uneasily noted the Service agent, "That's… *impossible!* We've no bursting-charges, and the interior ceiling bulkhead is reinforced steel – it's meant to withstand bombs, up to seventy pounds of TNT!"

"Just *watch* me… *you'll* see!" she countered. "But I'm not going to pretend it's going to be a walk in the park. You, Mr. President, and the Chancellor, will be on the inside, with me; then Jerry, Clairie and Matt will be on the outside, as 'human shields' –"

"*What?*" exclaimed the First Lady. "Over my dead *body* will you use my *children* to –"

"It's oh-kay, Mom," quickly reassured the Presidential daughter. "*Now* I get it! Karéin *told* us about this… she said something like, 'and your bodies will be proof against most perils and fast shall you recover, though pain shall still you feel'… or whatever. I'm willing to take the chance, to protect Dad. Matt?"

"As if you had to *ask*," supported the Presidential son. "I'm 'in'. Mom, Clairie's right. Better *us* to take the first shot, than *him*. It's a risk – but I'm willing to take it."

There were tears of gratitude in the eyes of the U.S. leader.

"I'm *so* proud of both of you!" he managed, addressing the teenagers.

"But please – can't you take Kathy, too?" he implored.

"Why not *everybody*, all at once?" asked Feldner.

"I need a light load, so I can accelerate as quickly as is safe, considering that I have human passengers, Susan," enigmatically explained Chu. "I guess I *could* take the First Lady, too, if necessary… no more than that, at least not for the first trip. We need to expose ourselves to gunfire as little as possible –"

She was interrupted by the sounds of a battle, happening in the next room to the east.

They all heard someone – it sounded like a White House guard, or a Service agent – shouting, "Hold the line no matter *what* he does, no matter what he uses against us – we can't retreat any further – you *know* why!"

"Sir – you want to talk it out here, and quite possibly get shot… or you want to *fly?*" pressed Chu, in the direction of the President.

"Mr. Chancellor, sir – *can* you, please?" asked the desperate U.S. leader, of his German counterpart.

"I have been listening," said Gebirgen. "I will instruct my staff."

He moved to be next to the President and Kaysten, while issuing a series of orders in his native language to his personal BND guards.

There seemed to be a lively discussion for a few seconds; but eventually, the Chancellor's desires seemed to have prevailed over those of his understudies, and the German agents reluctantly moved to protect Feldner and the Secretary of State.

"All of you," commanded Chu, with the majesty in her voice waxing in each syllable as her eyes began to dimly glow, "Stand back, while I show you how I'm going to get us out of this place. Agent – send the signal to the 'copters and the people on the roof."

"Already done, ma'am," he stated. "Confirmed that they're in position."

All in the room – and not a few more in and around the White House – heard the humming, exciting cascades of the more-than-a-woman's war-song.

She stopped for a moment, and then – speaking in a Stentorian tone, much more loudly than anyone would have expected, and to no visible person – Chu warned,

"And to *you* – whoever you are – who *dares* to violate this place and threaten the lives of innocent people... here's a taste of what awaits, if you're stupid enough to still be here, five minutes from now!"

The thrilling song and power of *Amaiish* surged not only through the body of Minnie Chu, but – in some measure – it touched the entire group, as, with extended arms and clenched fists, she stared deliberately up at the ceiling, and...

Fired!

It was the first time that those in the room, save the Chief of Staff, had seen the *Gaze of the Khùl-Algrenàthi'i* up close, as the lethal, warbling, red-and-orange rays (Kaysten noticed that their color was rather different from what he had observed on the streets of Los Angeles; they were both brighter and more yellow-tinted, and he also noted that Chu was trying to keep the beams lower-powered and relatively narrow) blazed from the eyes of the former team-leader.

The death-gaze blasted clear through the White House's vaunted ceiling-armor, as well as through everything else in the way, exiting through the building's roof to the shock and alarm of the Marine and Secret Service guards positioned thereupon.

Wielding this fearsome power like some kind of other-worldly jigsaw, Chu started to drew a wide oval – about six feet wide and more than eight from long end to end – in the ceiling.

"My *God*," gasped the President, "What would happen if you *hit* a living being with that –"

"Nothing *good*, sir," she calmly replied. "If it's any consolation... it would be over, very fast."

"Doesn't it... uhh... *hurt* your eyes?" he pressed. "And how can you even *see*, through all that?"

"Yes... it *does* hurt," she admitted, while continuing to trace out the pattern on the ceiling. "At first, so much that I could hardly open my eyes after using it. But now... I'm *handling* it. And I can see just *fine*, although what I'm looking at, appears *different* – better-illuminated – kind of hard to describe, really. Amazing what one can get used to... don't you think?"

Chu's face showed a wry, but intensely-proud, smile.

"For God's sake, don't turn your head and look at anything except the ceiling," uneasily demanded the U.S. leader.

"I don't blame you for being concerned – I asked Karéin the same thing – but you don't have to worry about errant death-rays, sir," she reassured. "It only works if I deliberately force its use against a specific target... it turns off automatically if I break my concentration. Sort of a built-in safety-feature, which, for the record, I'm sure glad was part of her little alien-power package."

The President shook his head in disbelief.

As the current position of her *Gaze* began to approach the point at which it had first struck home, the former team-leader called out.

"Jerry – Matt – Clairie – I need your help, now... use your telekinesis on the section that I'm cutting out... it's going to be messy enough as it is – don't want it crashing to the floor and covering us with dust."

"I'm no good at this," reminded Kaysten, "But hey... the old college try..."

"How are we supposed to...?" whispered the male teenager to his sister.

"Just focus on it and imagine that you're grabbing it with your hands," counseled Clairie. "And don't ask me how or why – I don't know *squat* about how it works."

"Sure... anything you *say*, sis," reluctantly replied Matt. "Here goes nothing."

"Three – two – one... *now!*" directed Chu, as she cut away the last intact part of the ceiling-section and then extinguished her deadly *Gaze*.

Immediately, a huge chunk of the White House's interior and exterior structure came crashing down, only to be first slowed, and then stopped altogether at a height of about six feet off the floor, by the combined telekinetic abilities of the four more-than-humans.

"You three are doing really well," remarked the *nouvelle* FBI-director. "You're all a lot stronger than I had anticipated. I can *feel* you off-loading me."

"Thanks... I guess," muttered the Presidential son, "As if I knew what I was doing!"

"You can ease off your mind-grasps now," requested Chu. "I'll let it down."

So she did; the excised section of the West Wing roof came to rest on the floor with a slight "thud", spraying gypsum-dust about a foot in all directions.

They heard someone in the next room to the east yelling, "Come on out, you cowardly sons of bitches – *show* yourself!"

This invective was, of course, followed by the sounds of yet more rapid-fire gunshots.

The President and his entourage looked upward – through the hole that had just been opened – and saw sky. They also heard the helicopter turbine-engines, considerably louder than before; and the gun-battle was now close-by, just into the next room to the east.

"Okay everyone… *quickly!*" shouted Chu over the engine-sounds, "Mr. President, Madam First Lady, Mr. Chancellor – gather as close to me as you can – embrace me with your arms and try to lock your hands together. Jerry, Matt, Clairie – same idea, but you're outboard of the others. We won't be going far, but we'll be going upward fast – be *ready* for it!"

"At least with Ms. Abruzzio, I had a *boat* to sit down in," grumbled the President, *sotto voce*.

"Well, sir," phlegmatically offered Kaysten, "That's true… but for creature-comforts, it still beats the first time *I* got taken for a ride, by Her Angelic Highness. *Believe* me on this one, okay?"

Chu sighed and rolled her eyes.

Half-comprehending stares went back and forth, as the evacuees-to-be attempted to follow the instructions. It became immediately evident that the former team-leader was much shorter than the male humans clustered around her; she compensated for this by slightly levitating, so at least her head and shoulders were level with theirs.

After a few seconds of awkward groping and forced invasions of personal space, the President stared into the face of his acting FBI director.

"You know, Minnie," he commented, "Not a minute ago, I saw those eyes of yours, blast right through a *wall*. But up close, they look perfectly normal… except for that weird back-light…"

Chu allowed the red-and-gold glow of the *Fire* to illuminate her pupils more brightly, a move that caused both the President and his thoroughly-uncomfortable wife to reflexively duck and wince.

"*These* days, sir," she opined, "I'm not sure that 'normal' is a relevant concept. A week ago I wouldn't have thought that flying like a bird, would be 'normal' for me. But… here we are."

She then shouted out a last request to the remaining coterie of Secret Service and BND agents.

"Hold on and protect the Secretary and Ms. Feldner!" implored the former team-leader. "We'll be back, once the President and the Chancellor are safe!"

"Roger that!" exclaimed Agent Chiarelli. "Glad you're on *our* side, ma'am!"

Turning to address the more-than-humans, as her war-song again began to was, Chu demanded, "New People – your Holy *Fire* and your defenses, to full *power* – let's *fly!*"

And so she – and they – did, while the ordinary humans left behind in the West Wing of the White House stared upward, scarcely believing what their eyes beheld.

But the travails of the refugees in this place, were far from over; for, a half-second later, the wall to the west… *exploded*.

Back Home, We All Hate D.C.

"Uncle Callum – stay *with* me!" shouted a distraught Donny Wade, as he tended to his fallen relative.

Sammie and Abruzzio – along with the former JPL scientist's little dog – had joined the trucker and his aunt, by Callum Wade's side, while the Russian and Hendricks each crouched down, hidden pistols at the ready, about twenty paces distant to the east and the west.

"*Doctor* – we need a *doctor!*" shrieked Marie Wade, in all directions.

But the entreaties went for naught; even if medical help had been in the vicinity, the terrible fact was that there were many other victims lying about, in much worse shape than the Missouri farmer.

Callum Wade was lying prone. His eyes were half-glazed, and he was breathing faintly.

"I have medical training, and Karéin taught me a few things," disclosed Abruzzio. "You guys support his head and shoulders – I'll check the wound."

Gingerly, the more-than-a-woman unbuttoned the farmer's dress-shirt, revealing the lightweight armor-plate behind it. The others also detected a faint, violet-colored glow issuing from her finger-tips.

To the dismay of the onlookers, near the bottom of the protective-covering, there was a round, still-slightly-smoking hole about the size of a quarter in Callum Wade's chest. From this issued a steady stream of ichorous, bubbling, dark blood.

"Shit!" inveighed an angry Donny, "That thing was supposed to stop any pistol-round… fuckers *got* to be using dum-dums!"

"If it's any consolation," observed Abruzzio as she carefully examined the bullet-hole and what was below it, "Although his chest-wall – and possibly his lung – has been perforated… were it not for the armor, the shot might have cut him almost in half. You're right – for *sure*, that was no ordinary bullet. We've got to get him to a hospital, ASAP!"

"Can't we, like, call for one of those helicopters we got standin' by?" demanded Sammie.

"Anywhere around the White House is restricted airspace – doubly so now that gunfire has broken out," observed Hendricks. "Any 'copter that doesn't have a military transponder will get shot down long before it gets *near* here. Pilots *know* that, by the way."

"What are we *supposed* to do, then?" complained Sammie. "Just sit here and watch him *die?*"

"I'll have no talk like – *wait* a minute –" interrupted Abruzzio.

She shot a glance at "Rainbow", whose body was tensed in classic "wary-dog" fashion; the puppy's face was pointing – English Setter-style – to the north, with a deliberate, kaleidoscopic stare in its eyes.

"What *is* it, little lady?" asked the former JPL scientist.

An angry growl came back as the answer.

"Uh-oh," warned Abruzzio, "*Attack* on the way, from that direction! Everybody, *down!*"

All of a sudden, an odd effect met the eyes of humans and their more-than-human brethren; it was as if a scene-distorting, funny-house mirror, reflecting images of the pavement around them, had instantly appeared in front of them, making it extremely difficult to tell what was happening in that direction; although, their vision still seemed to be normal, to the left and the right.

A half-second later, the now-all-too-familiar sounds of gunfire erupted from somewhere to the north.

"Who the hell *is* that, who's shootin' at us?" demanded a frustrated Donny. "I can take it, but my folks is sittin' *ducks –*"

"Just a sec," instructed Abruzzio, as – with multi-colored eyes – she stared forward, at and in fact through, the mirage-barrier. "You see *that?*"

"Indeed," came the voice of the Russian, from one side. "Whoever it is – and I can clearly see the firing-flashes from buildings at the far side of Lafayette Square – they do not appear to be shooting at us."

"Well then, who *are* they –" asked Marie Wade.

The sounds of rifle-bullets striking the North Façade of the White House made the question moot. Most of the shots did little except to chip the plaster on the outside of the building; but about every fifth or sixth one, did more significant damage, including perforating the mansion's supposedly "bullet-proof" windows. There were also apparently many shots targeted at the roof-level of the White House, in classic "sniper-versus-sniper" fashion.

"They're targeting the Marines and the Service guys up on top, plus the entrances and the windows," remarked the third agent. "Anybody who tries to get out of there is gonna get capped as soon as they step through an exterior doorway. And those aren't just standard-caliber... at least some of 'em gotta be using .50s."

"*Rainbow!*" commanded Abruzzio, "Remember what Mommy told you to do, if this ever happened! *Sic 'em!*"

The dog's head moved in such a way that the others could have sworn it was nodding affirmatively.

They had never seen the animal's demeanor being such as this; it let out a frightening-sounding, guttural growl, baring its fangs; then Rainbow rocketed off its feet into the air. A couple of gunshots appeared to have been aimed at it; these missed badly.

The humans of the group were able to track the little dog over a distance of about twenty feet; then it simply disappeared, as if it had vanished into a hole in the sky.

"Sylvia – what's it going to *do?*" demanded Hendricks.

"*She*, is going to protect her master, as well as her master's pack," informed the former JPL scientist. "I've asked her not to kill... but I also told her, not to be too careful about it."

"Let us hope so," advised Misha. "If your dog just irradiates – but does not kill or immobilize – one or more of the snipers – we can track them that way."

Suddenly, Rainbow reappeared; it circled over Pennsylvania Avenue – dodging gunfire, this time from concealed U.S. military and Secret Service snipers on and around the White House – as if searching for something.

Finally, the dog flew over G Street NW and then disappeared inside an open car-entrance at the north side of the building between G Street and the north-west branch of Pennsylvania Avenue.

"What's it *doin'?*" asked Sammie. "I thought it was s'posed to –"

A peculiar noise now came from the building that Rainbow had entered; it sounded like synthesizer-enhanced bellowing of a big dog or perhaps of a wolf, but there was also a stirring, musical back-beat element to it.

In the next second, Rainbow reappeared, flying a retrograde course out of the street-level entrance. The dog was now accompanied by Wolf's two flame-and-smoke-encased hell-hounds, who – though they could not exactly fly in the manner that Rainbow had learned to do – still managed to leap many-score feet vertically and hundreds of feet horizontally.

The alien-powered wolf-pack, with Rainbow in the lead (though, she had adopted the tactic of "popping" in and out of visibility, Misha-style), followed by "Boob" and "Tube" behind and to opposite sides of Abruzzio's pet, advanced rapidly to the north up 17th Street NW.

"Damn *nasty* little mutts," cracked Donny, upon observing the break-out of Rainbow and her two canine friends. "Sure wouldn't want to be the mailman deliverin' to *your* place, or to the big dude's. Listen, Sylvia – while the pups is goin' after them fuckers up there past the park... can you fly Uncle Callum to a hospital?"

"It isn't good idea to go airborne, this close to the White House," demurred Abruzzio. "Not to mention, the minute we popped up, we'd be a very attractive target for the snipers at the far end of the park. But tell you what – we *can* still sneak out of here on foot. I'll keep the mirage up to our north, but stay down as we move, because it may flicker and give us away – it's hard to keep it working if it isn't stationary, and remember, it just stops light – not bullets. Let's head to 15th Street – we'll be out of the line of fire, and maybe we can find an ambulance. Will – Misha – Donny – can you cover us? I can handle Callum."

All three nodded affirmatively. Abruzzio's telekinetic abilities then gently lifted the stricken ex-farmer by about two feet off the bullet-scarred Pennsylvania Avenue pavement and began to float him to the east. Hendricks, the trucker and the Russian – both alert to the real possibility of yet more attacks – took up flanking positions.

A glance backward over shoulders revealed the images and sounds of two military helicopters – as yet, somewhat less than a mile away – approaching the White House.

"Bet they're planning an evacuation," observed the third agent, "But with the sniping unsuppressed – remember it's coming from both directions – their chances won't be good. One of those heavy rounds could easily take out a rotor-head or the tail-stabilizer."

"Indeed," confirmed Misha. "And that assumes that the enemy does not have a portable surface-to-air missile-launcher. If fired from such a close range, it could hardly *miss*."

"Can't you make this – what the hell you call it, oh yeah, 'mirage' – to cover the whole White House?" inquired Donny.

"I can't make it that big… at least not so far," deflected Abruzzio. "And to *do* that, I'd have to drop the one that's now protecting *us*."

"No shit?" commented Sammie. "Fuckin' *bad* idea, then… President can save his *own* ass!"

"Amen to *that*," remarked Marie Wade.

"Sylvia… I'll help you get the civilians out of here," said Hendricks, "But after that – I got to follow the dogs and chase down whoever's sniping at the White House, from the other end of the park."

"Thought you were retired from bein' a cop?" commented Donny. "After what they did to you up there in the 'plane… I'd have thought you didn't owe the government nothin' more."

"Yeah, well, man," grudgingly acknowledged the third agent, "We got a saying : 'the Bureau may leave *you*… but you never leave the Bureau'. Just wish Minnie and Otis were here to lend a hand."

"I have no doubt," offered the Russian, "That they have their own challenges to deal with, currently. However, if you and Madam Abruzzio will permit it, I will accompany you."

"Donny and I should be able to protect the others, for the time being," allowed the former JPL scientist. "But… I don't think Misha has the authority to place anybody under arrest?"

"I doubt that will be a practical consideration," obliquely responded the Russian, "Given the likely tactical situation."

"Yeah… just forgive us, if we forget to read 'em their fuckin' Miranda rights," added Hendricks.

The others – Sammie and Marie Wade (all the while, holding on tight to her husband's hand) – walked in a crouch, beside the levitated, half-conscious Callum Wade.

"You folks remember," complained the streetwalker, "How I told yas all, 'back home, we all hate Washington, D.C.'?"

Some Pop Culture For You

I want to just charge in there and kick some traitors' ass, mused Top Dog,

But let's remember the battle-plan – and let's stick to it!

Time for some recce…

He advanced through the half-wrecked interior of the West Wing First Floor office-room into which he had just erupted, moving almost all the way up to its eastern wall – evidently, this had, at one time, been the quarters of someone fairly high-up in the hierarchy, given the decorations and furniture – and enabled his spy-gear, pointing its field-of-detection ahead and to the north.

Way *too much idle chit-chat, and more shooting… sounds like it's over there in the middle of the building…*

Good as far as it goes, as long as our guys keep 'em guessing and keep 'em tied up – wish I had voice-comms with the strike-teams, but too risky in here, Service might still have the RF-emission-locators on-line...

Got to concentrate… hope the auto-sensors will pick up any threats on my rear-flank…

Need a precise location-fix – "Press-Secretary's Office"… makes sense.

According to the map, that means I have to move eastward, into the corridor… damn, that's an exposed position.

Let's use the motion-sensor to scan for hostiles…

The former Agency-chief enabled "wide-field-mode" on his battle-suit, sweeping his forward field of view in all directions, in a clockwise motion.

Good… nobody by the Oval Office or Cabinet Room… negative for the Roosevelt Room, too… hmm… a few faint positives far off to the south-west and north-east… probably staffers trapped by the lock-down…

I'll come back and smoke them too, if I have time... every little cut laid on the bitch counts, after all...

Gingerly, he ventured into the corridor between the Press Secretary's Office and the Cabinet Room. Luckily, there seemed to be no opposition in the area, although he noted a furious gunfight breaking out in or around the Palm Room. This was accompanied by a sudden, intense flash of light, as if someone had set off a double-strength thermite-grenade somewhere in the western side of Center Hall.

Keep track of that engagement... could get in our way...

Moving slowly and deliberately, he turned north-east – briefly facing the West Colonnade to check for opponents – and then edged up to the north wall of this area.

Strong signals from in here... let's see who it is...

Top Dog listened intently for thirty seconds or more, with the voice-enhancement filters turned up almost as far as they would go.

Bingo! he exulted,

References to "the Chancellor" and "Mr. President"... better still, that little faggot Kaysten and the Chink whore that the idiot made Bureau director – should have had her 'disappeared' back in Steeltown, just goes to show what happens when you try to play the 'nice-guy' – but still, we got a target-rich environment!

Let's plan it out, though... what's the intel saying...

"Kaysten : accelerated movement and some kind of hypnotic power; Chu : may be able to levitate or even to fly, also possibly can use a close-range weapon detected from events on the plane, exact characteristics unknown"...

Okay... enable the mitigation-features... I'll forego stealth-mode for the time being, I need situational-awareness more than I need non-conspicuity...

The Service will have that door covered – I'll need a better way in...

Clark, you'd better have said your prayers – because you're living out your last minutes!

He activated the narrow-field communications-link on his battle-suit, and spoke softly into his throat-mike.

"Top Dog to team, with voice-print authentication, on one-time pad channel," he whispered, "To avoid future compromise of our operations, this will be my first and last message to you all. Primary objective identified and located. Proceed per plan. Liquidate all available targets, retain minimal ammunition and egress to pre-determined *rendez-vous*. Your country is *depending* on you... good luck! Top Dog, over and out."

Though there were none here to see it, suddenly, a deep frown appeared on his face.

No – no – no! he furiously pondered,

You're not going to fucking get away from me – not now – not when I'm so close!

Time to smash through this wall and finish the j – wait *a minute – what the hell's she* saying?

"A taste of what awaits, if you're stupid enough to still be here"…

Well, honey – I've got a little taste of something for you, *too!*

Let's see – three bursting-charges, one down, two left – don't need to fire this one, I can just stick it to the wall and then 'boom', there we go – hold on – is that music?

Who the hell would be playing synthesizer-rock, at a time like this?

There was a subconscious melody playing in the back of his mind; it was unfamiliar, but still catchy and exciting, in an ominous kind of way.

A report showed up on the HUD-display of his combat-visor. It reminded him of field-reports, to the effect of "when one of the alien's slaves is about to use a special ability, this may manifest by the presence of unusual sounds, including but not limited to something similar to music".

The music – still ongoing – was followed by a weird, trilling, warbling sound, akin to that made by the zap-guns on any number of old science-fiction movies and TV shows.

Well… we knew there are at least two of the half-human monsters in there, he silently acknowledged.

A 'two-for-one sale' – a real killing! he grimly resolved, while affixing the bursting-charge to the eastern wall.

The Agency director retreated until his back was up against the opposite wall. His bionic suit could still detect some kind of discourse going on, just to the east, but the exact nature of it was difficult to make out.

The unusual sounds quickly abated; then there was a perceptible shudder within the White House's interior structure, as if something fairly heavy had just been dropped on the floor.

What's this the real-time IFF's saying? he pondered.

Four alien-signatures? *Two strong ones and two faint ones… maybe false-positives… a long-range echo?*

This isn't an exact science, I suppose…

Now they're all fading away – in the vertical *axis? What the* fuck?

Top Dog tensed up, preparing himself for the heat of battle.

Ready or not, traitors… here I come… and there, you die!

He detonated the demo-charge on the northern wall, and – with his auto-rifle at the ready – smashed through the breach, sending shards of wood, gyp-rock and metal, flying in all directions.

For a second or two, his combat-visor auto-switched to low-light mode, due to the billowing cloud of debris and dust that accompanied his entrance into what was revealed as the western end of the West Wing's press-corps area.

The former director had expected to be shot at; and, indeed, in the next seconds, he saw at least three initially-stunned plain-clothes agents pulling out pistols and firing at him, while two civilians quailed and scrambled for cover (of which there was precious little).

The battle-suit shrugged off the bullets, albeit with some physical discomfort as well as minor damage to some of the suit's systems.

Reflexively, he shot one of the guards dead with the assault-rifle, blowing the unfortunate man's head off in an ugly spray of blood and brain-tissue against the northern wall of the new room. He then took one of the others out of the battle with a couple of shots to the chest – this guy was evidently wearing a flak-jacket, but it availed him not against Top Dog's high-velocity rounds – and blew the right leg of a third Service-agent clean off at the knee. The man screamed and thrashed about on the West Wing floor, as his blood gushed in several directions.

The master-assassin was about to finish off the rest of his prey – consisting of two terrified civilians who he recognized as the Secretary of State and the White House Communications Director, plus one guard who somehow looked slightly different from what he would have expected of a Secret Service agent – when, as the dust-cloud started to settle, he happened to glance upward.

Dumbfounded, he did a double-take. There was a huge hole in the West Wing ceiling, showing blue sky beyond. The suit's audio-sensors picked up the very clear sounds of helicopter-turbines and blades, along with the receding timbre of the same alien-music that he'd heard earlier.

The only remaining combat-capable agent brandished a pistol, and – with exemplary bravery, considering the tactical circumstances – interposed himself between the former Agency-chief and the two cowering civilians.

The guard shouted, in somewhat European-accented English, "You are under provisional arrest – surrender or I will *shoot!*"

Top Dog marveled at the man's fool-hardy, suicidal temerity, so instead of blasting him immediately to Kingdom Come, the former Agency-director decided to channel ancient pop culture.

Growling through an amplified exterior-facing speaker, he warned,

"I'll be *back!*"

Then – with a HUD-lock on the undersides of a helicopter hovering overhead and just within line-of-sight, to one side – Top Dog enabled "maximum jump-mode".

Skyward he streaked.

Off Come The Gloves

Boyd and Jacobson – alien-senses and pistols very much at the ready – advanced at a brisk pace down either side of the Center Hall, in the direction of the Palm Room.

To their mutual disgust, they tallied a terrible body-count of more than a dozen civilians and White House staff, who had been summarily murdered by the assassins. The victims' bullet-riddled bodies littered the floors, seemingly all around. A few weren't just shot; they seemed to have been mutilated by some kind of bladed weapon, either before or after they died. One or two had what appeared to only be superficial stab-wounds; yet, they were still stone cold dead.

Shit, mentally communicated Boyd to his former boss,

If we got fourteen civilian casualties just here in the main hall – what about the rest of the White House?

I'm trying not to think about that, came back the reply.

Except to keep it in the back of my mind, when I deal with the next bastard.

Though they did not initially come under fire, except indirectly by misdirected shots from the beleaguered Service agents and Marine guards at the west end of the corridor, the two ex-astronauts took no chances; they dodged in and out of the vaultings on the north and the south, as they moved.

It did not take them long to find the area of engagement. They saw the back of a battle-suited bad-guy – identifiable with high confidence as the one who they had briefly encountered, at the east end of the Center Hall – about twenty feet ahead of them. The assassin was also using the architecture of this part of the White House as cover; he was shooting methodically at a group of guards just outside the doors leading westward into the Palm Room.

To the paradoxical dismay of both Boyd and Jacobson, the battle did not seem to be going well for the Secret Service and Marines. Just as they crept near, the two ex-astronauts observed one uniformed defender being dropped by a well-aimed rifle-shot, fired by the fugitive assassin; and a quick glance around revealed three more dead Service-agents and two more fallen Marines.

Shit, sent Boyd to his former commander,

I know that a while ago, we might have had to fight these guys... but seeing this, still makes me sick – not to mention, "pissed off".

I hear you, came back the mental reply,

And take note of the damage inflicted by whatever kinds of bullets these sons of bitches are using – some of the guards are wearing body-armor... and it's being shot right through.

Yeah, ruefully responded Boyd,

Remind me not to get hit!

You get his attention, while I – look out!

His message was interrupted by the alarming appearance of a small, egg-shaped metal object, followed less than a half-second later, by the shock of a powerful explosion, just behind them and in the middle of the corridor.

Boyd felt the impact of shrapnel over many parts of his body (he was barely able to get his arms up to protect his eyes), as the blast-wave knocked both him – and Jacobson – forward by six feet or more. Tumbling head over heels, the two ex-astronauts ended up in awkward positions, resting respectively against the north and south vaultings within the Center Hall. Their guns went flying off in various directions.

Almost immediately, a hail of rifle-shots were directed at them – and – ominously – not just from the front-flank, but in fact, also from somewhere to their rear.

What the fuck! managed Boyd,

Must have walked right past an ambush – but how – senses are supposed to –

Got hit, but most of it bounced off, interrupted the senior ex-astronaut.

Not so lucky, Boyd sent back.

Feels like twenty bee-stings all over me – damn lucky none in my eyes – No time to worry about it right now –

Lesser beings would have been quickly exterminated by multiple hits, right then and there – but Boyd and Jacobson called their elevated reflexes into action and dodged frantically.

None the less, the assassins' aim was good; the former Mars mission commander took one round almost in the center of his chest and Boyd's already-aching left arm was hit squarely in his upper bicep.

While Jacobson's concealed breast-plate – plus his innate physical resistance – reduced the bullet-impact to merely "agonizing" as opposed to "fatal", the shot that hit the former Mars mission pilot struck home in a place not protected by armor.

Boyd swore the proverbial blue-streak as he slapped his right hand over a deep, bloody gash on his right arm, while simultaneously trying to activate the Storied Watcher's "self-healing" tricks.

No point retreating! sent back Jacobson,

I'll attack forward!

Roger that – gloves are off! came the reply.

Watch your eyes!

Acknowledged, answered the former Mars mission commander,

But no death-rays – see if you can dazzle 'em –

About a second later – to the half-muted sound of Boyd's war-song – the former Mars mission pilot unleashed his flash-attack. A super-brilliant light, akin to staring directly at an arc-welding-torch, illuminated the west end of Center Hall and, in fact, all the way to at least the middle of the main White House building.

Good thing I was facing away, came the rueful message from Jacobson.

A half-elated, wholly-enraged Boyd saw a combat-suited figure – very similar to the guy who they had been chasing, but subtly different in minor details – appear, as if from nowhere, beside one of the Center Hall vaultings, about ten feet to the former Mars mission pilot's east.

The new-found opponent, who had been wholly-invisible a second ago, seemed dazed – or stunned. He just stood there for a second, with an auto-rifle plainly at the ready, but not pointed at any of the obvious targets.

With his combined military, alien and innate war-skills all very much active (despite the continuous pain of the war-wounds), Boyd didn't hesitate to exploit the opportunity.

Using his telekinesis to lock on to his own, discarded pistol from behind, in a half-second he had the weapon in his grasp (doing this required removing one hand from the arm-wound, which hurt plenty). He then drew a bead on the momentarily-vulnerable assassin and fired, unloading at least four shots – all of which hit dead-on – against his target, following up the fusillade with an alien-powered body-slam that knocked the black-suited guy back by eight feet.

For the second time, Boyd went *mano-a-mano* with one of the battle-gear-wearing enemies; and again, he was nonplussed by the guy's impossible strength, being barely able to force an arm with a combat-knife, to one side.

However, this time, the former Mars mission pilot was better-prepared. He forced a shroud of inky blackness to envelop both combatants and then – using a greatly-weakened photon-beam as well as a burst of telekinesis, impossible to resist at this point-blank range – struck precisely at the relatively-weak locking-joint between his opponent's combat-helmet and the man's war-suit.

For a split-second, Boyd allowed himself to speculate,

How did I know – or guess – that that was the weakest spot on his suit?

But he had no time to contemplate this further, as the maneuver was effective; it knocked the helmet clear, allowing Boyd to get in a vicious punch to the side of the now-blinded enemy's head. The ex-astronaut followed up this attack with the grip of his pistol used as a bludgeon; he hit the assassin's head so hard that it might well have crushed his skull.

The guy started bleeding from his nose, ears and mouth and then collapsed, apparently unconscious. A couple of blood-stained teeth fell from his lips.

Maybe I killed him… maybe I didn't, mused Boyd, as he quickly stripped the man of weapons, retrieving the knife, a fully-loaded pistol and an extra clip for it, at the same time.

Not that I give a shit, either way… next time I'll shove those grenades up his ass!

There was neither the time nor the equipment available to restrain the disabled assassin, although it was clear he wouldn't be waking up anytime soon.

The former Mars mission pilot allowed himself a short time-out, and noticed – with a combination of fascination, disbelief and gratitude – that small pieces of grenade-shrapnel were being forced out of the wounds that they had inflicted on him. The process was exhausting, and Boyd felt momentarily fatigued and dizzy; but after only a few more seconds, he was almost back in shape for battle.

Meanwhile, Jacobson had taken advantage of his former pilot's dazzle-attack to close the distance on the assassins at the far west end of Center Hall.

Trusting his compatriot to handle threats from the east, the ex-astronaut had expected a warm reception; but instead, he reached the threshold of the Palm Room, only to discover that the scene of the battle had shifted yet further west, into the West Wing Press Kitchen or even into the Press Room. He noted, to his dismay, the bodies of two Marine guards as well as one plain-clothes victim who had likely been a Secret Service agent.

All three fallen men had apparently been trying to hold the door leading to the Center Hall, perhaps to cover a retreat by fellow-warriors. The two Marines had clearly been shot dead, but the other man seemed physically intact, except for a grayish pallor over his skin and a small knife-wound just below his neck.

The subconscious stench of poison offended Jacobson's senses.

I wonder if that's what someone who Karéin kills with her own venomous bite, looks like... he thought.

A week ago, I might have killed you, unhappily ruminated Jacobson, as he looked with sad eyes upon the corpses,

But today... I might just die for you.

Don't ask me how that makes any sense...

The former Mars mission commander was snapped out of his reverie by renewed sounds of mayhem, coming from the rooms just to the west. He heard impassioned yelling to the effect of, "where the hell are they all *coming* from?", "they're shooting right through the windows!" and "Marines – no more *retreating!*".

As if to reinforce the point, a stray rifle-round – apparently fired from the south – perforated one of the Palm Room's windows, near the top.

Aren't those things supposed to be "bullet-proof?" he wondered.

Quickly retrieving a new pistol and some spare clips from two of the dead White House guards, out of respect, Jacobson paused momentarily to whisper a few words of prayer over the bodies. Then he cast his gaze back to the Center Hall, noting – to his immense relief – that Boyd's figure was still standing, about twenty feet to the east.

"Brent!" softly called the former Mars mission-leader, as he stepped back into the hall, out of the line of fire from points further west. "You okay?"

"*Think* so," came back the reply, "Took him down good... but sure got the wounds to show for it. Thank God for Karéin's self-healing-tricks – I'd be next to *dead*, without them. How about you?"

"Pretty much bounced off," said Jacobson with a wry grin, "But no doubt I'll be feeling it for the next few hours."

"What *I* don't understand, you know," offered the junior ex-astronaut, "Is... weren't you shrugging off HEAT-rounds, back at that airport? How the H is just a *grenade* hitting you that hard?"

"I got no idea," answered the senior ex-astronaut. "But didn't she say something about 'the Holy *Fire* will aid you as circumstances demand, but perhaps not always as you would like'? I just wish the damn thing would make up its *mind*."

"Shh... she – or it – or whatever – might hear, and get mad," quipped Boyd. "By the way," he added, "The weak-point for those assholes is the junction between the helmet and the body-armor – hit it hard and it disrupts their control over the rest of the suit... at least for a while."

"Good to know – I'll aim for there, if I can," pledged the senior ex-astronaut, while distributing the available clips of ammunition evenly between himself and Boyd. "Ready to chase the bastards? I can hear them – they're *definitely* trying for the West Wing."

"Yeah," agreed the former Mars mission pilot, "Sounds like a big-time shoot-out going down, ahead of us... I'd have suggested a flanking-maneuver, but we got incoming both from the north and the south – not that much safer outside than in here, in other words. Watch out for another ambush – one grenade was *more* than enough, thank you."

"You can say *that* again," echoed Jacobson. "And –"

His next sentence was cut short by a now-familiar, eerie, buzzing, warbling sound, coming from the west.

"That's *got* to be Minnie!" observed Boyd, "And she's using the big guns!"

"She wouldn't do that unless she or the President was really in trouble," remarked Jacobson, as his diamond-like force-field encased his body. "Let's go... gloves are *off!*"

The figure of Brent Boyd, for his part, began to glow with an almost-intolerable incandescence.

"About *time!*" he growled, as, stone-faced, he raced forward to join his former boss, charging towards the White House Press Room.

Three, Two, One... Geronimo!

For a few seconds, the upward-flying Minnie Chu – and her thoroughly-frightened collection of VIP passengers, who were hanging on to her body (and to each other) for dear life – believed that their gambit was going to pay off; although they did, indeed, take note of multiple sniper-shots inbound against both themselves and the nearby-hovering helicopters, none of this gunfire came particularly close.

Don't want to climb too fast or too far, reasoned the former team-leader, as she approached an altitude of a couple hundred feet off the ground.

These folks probably can't handle rarefied air...

"Warden" warned of a vicious gunfight breaking out down in the West Wing below, exactly where his owner and the President had been, not five seconds earlier.

"Where's Blair House?" she shouted in the President's direction, while slowing her rate of ascent, after putting some distance between the evacuees and the whirling rotor-blades below.

"It's that building over there – just north-west of Jackson and Pennsylvania," interjected Kaysten.

The *nouvelle* FBI director shot a glance towards the block to the north of the Eisenhower Building, and commented, "That's *awfully* close to the White House itself – how do we know it's safe – isn't there *anywhere* else in D.C. that we could –"

She was unable to complete the question, because at that precise moment, Chu and her airborne group were sent careening, head over heels, by the blast-wave of a powerful explosion detonating no more than twelve feet below them.

Instantly – despite desperate telekinetic efforts by both Chu and Kaysten to keep everyone together – the First Lady, clinging to her son in mortal terror, flew off into space; she was joined in her plight by Chancellor Gebirgen, who was also thrown clear, albeit all on his own.

Meanwhile, Kaysten himself – though not completely dislodged by the blast – ended up hanging for dear life, onto one of Chu's legs. The President and his daughter somehow managed to hold on.

To make matters worse, a volley of rifle-shots – coming from points *below*, as opposed to from the snipers known to be hiding to the north and south – besieged the former team-leader. It was impossible to determine whether any of the civilian passengers had been injured by these attacks; Chu hoped against hope that any incoming shrapnel would be deflected by her personal force-field, and perhaps those of Clairie and Kaysten.

She tried frantically to stabilize herself and to re-establish a mind-grasp-lock on the errant White House refugees, but apart from having to maneuver in mid-air to avoid a continuous barrage from her unidentified assailants, the ballistic-trajectories of the hapless First Lady and Chancellor were diverging; it was impossible to concentrate on both at the same time.

While still dodging renewed – and worryingly accurate – rifle-fire from below, the *nouvelle* FBI director reversed her direction of flight (because of the involved centrifugal-force, a blanching Kaysten almost went flying upward and away).

Engaging the Storied Watcher's fast-thinking ability, she tried to survey the scene.

What she saw and otherwise perceived was – to say the least – alarming.

The First Lady and Matt were plummeting downward, heading toward the hole that Chu had just opened in the West Wing roof; distressingly, the German Chancellor was on a trajectory to collide with the rotor-blades of the first helicopter. On the second 'copter, some guy in a weird-looking *uber-*SWAT-battle-suit was simultaneously clinging to the aircraft's open side-door, struggling with someone inside while still directing rifle-shots upward at Chu and the President.

Who the hell is *this guy?* she wondered.

For a split-second, the image of a bland, nondescript, half-familiar male Caucasian face – that of a senior government official, who she had met on at least two occasions – appeared in her mind.

And how does he fight off a bunch of Marines with one hand, while he's pointing a rifle up at me and damn near plugging me with each round?

No time to ponder – if I don't rescue Gebirgen, he'll be killed!

Jerry – try to lock on to the First Lady – we're going for the Chancellor –

So with the aghast President clinging to her body and Kaysten still grasping the *nouvelle* Director's leg, the former team-leader flew downward at the highest speed that she could muster. Almost immediately, however, she was beset by a spray of rifle-fire, as well as at least two shots of a visibly heavier caliber.

Chu dodged energetically and was able to evade the latter attacks – which flew several hundred feet further into the air behind her and then exploded noisily – but she was hit twice, once in the left shoulder and then in a glancing shot off the upper-part of her forehead.

The Presidential daughter cried out in pain as she, too, was hit in turn; a rifle-bullet tore a deep, bloody gash halfway down her right arm, although it then ricocheted away without penetrating any deeper. Another shot, oddly, bounced off completely, even though it was aimed squarely against the junction of Clairie's neck and clavicle.

"*Oww – oww –* Daddy, it *hurts* – it hurts *so* bad!" she moaned.

The President's eyes were filled with tears, not only from the onrushing air-pressure, but because the bullet that had injured his daughter's arm, would certainly have hit him. He could not understand how he had escaped a number of other shots that seemed to be aimed right *for* him.

Completely at a loss as to how the round to her head hadn't instantly killed her, the former team-leader none the less was badly-affected; dazed by the bullet-impact while trying to regain her wits, Chu – along with her three passengers – spiraled back toward the White House. She was barely able to take note of a vicious fire-fight, breaking out in the West Wing, apparently near to where she had breached the building's ceiling.

Falling. Mother are we! exclaimed Warden.

Deflected I bullets man elderly at some not but this I all can!

To her dismay, Chu felt the telekinetic lock that she had by now almost established on Gebirgen, dissipate into nothingness.

Oh my god – he's going to go right into the rotors – she thought, with horror welling in her gut.

But the Chancellor's demise – though clearly imminent – was not to be.

A window on the third floor of the central White House residence exploded outward, showering reinforced glass all over what remained of the West Wing roof; then – a split-second afterward – some of those around caught a glimpse of something moving *fast*, streaking at a steep incline from the smashed portal. It was followed by another indistinct figure, traveling too fast for even more-than-human senses to easily identify.

Two war-songs – familiar to the ears of Kaysten and Chu, though not to those of many others – serenaded the former team-leader's ears, as Gebirgen – by now no more than ten feet above the lethal 'copter-blades, and falling fast – was struck, side-on, by the first of the flying things.

The dazed, shocked German leader was propelled far to the north-west, well out of danger. He was then again contacted by the flying-creature, which seemed to take firm hold of him as the Chancellor and his strange rescuer disappeared far up into the sky.

The other flying-figure – encased in a swirling, translucent cloud of air-currents – chased the First Lady and her son, as the two of them plummeted back into the West Wing. In doing so, the second airborne creature was hit repeatedly by gunfire originating from the SWAT-suited man, who by now seemed to have taken control of the first helicopter.

Though in fact, the bullets thus fired seemed to all be deflected harmlessly by the second flying being's hurricane-shroud, he still stopped in mid-air, as if either trying to recover from the effects of this gunfire or just trying to make sense of what was going on.

The First Lady, with her son underneath her, disappeared into the hole that Chu had opened; but for some unknown reason, the rate of their descent seemed to slow appreciably just before they reached the height of the roof.

The *nouvelle*-Director was beginning to come back to her senses and was able to slow her descent, while re-scanning the scene. But though Gebirgen now seemed out of immediate danger, another incipient disaster loomed.

The assassin in the first helicopter seemed (thankfully) to have temporarily stopped his shooting-spree; but the respite soon proved illusory, as the craft's nose suddenly pointed straight down, in the direction of the West Wing. It began to crash-dive as the SWAT-guy jumped clear of it; he executed a leap that would have been completely impossible for a normal human being. He came to rest on the rooftop of the central part of the White House, brandishing a futuristic-looking auto-rifle, pointing it right at Chu and her passengers.

There are still people down there in the West Wing... including the First Lady and Matt! she realized,

If it hits and then explodes – lock on, lock on, come on –

Try as she might, the former team-leader could gain only a weak telekinetic hold on the 'copter's tail. She could feel it slowing – albeit not nearly enough – but she was evidently too far away, not to mention that the helicopter undoubtedly weighed several tons and had built up substantial kinetic-energy in its dive. And again, her concentration was disrupted by a new barrage of gunshots from the malevolent opponent on the White House rooftop. The assassin was, in turn, shot at from multiple directions, but though hit, he seemed largely undeterred.

The nose of the crashing helicopter was almost at the West Wing roof, as its rotor-blades impacted with the building, flying off in all directions and instantly killing at least one of the Marine guards who had been hiding there. It looked as if it would fall through the breach, undoubtedly killing those remaining in that part of the West Wing.

With disgust and rage building in her veins, Chu – along with the President, his daughter and Kaysten – braced for the worst.

But then, against all odds, the seemingly-unstoppable downward-motion of the crippled helicopter inexplicably halted.

A half-second later – to the tune of Jacobson's pounding, back-beat-replete war-song, all around saw the former Mars mission commander – clad in his trademark diamond-shrouded force-field – explode right through the roof of the West Wing Press Briefing Room. Holding the helicopter by its nose with both of his big, heavily-muscled arms, he leaped far clear of the White House with the craft still in his grasp, landing on the North Lawn and then depositing the helicopter upright on the grass. In doing this, he was immediately engaged by far-off snipers and black-suited intruders close up against the White House, although the incoming gunfire merely bounced harmlessly from Jacoboson's protective shielding.

While the senior ex-astronaut was preoccupied with this task, Brent Boyd's war-song – counterpoised against the sounds of rapid-fire gunshots – echoed below.

An eye-blinding light illuminated the inside of the West Wing, while the battle, marked by explosions that shook the building's structure, seemed to be raging on. This was followed by another high-intensity confrontation – complete with two more war-songs – further to the east, perhaps in the Palm Room or in the western reaches of the Center Hall.

One of the windows facing from the West Wing (perhaps in one of the Press Rooms), to the North Lawn, exploded outward. A brilliant, multi-colored lightening-bolt shot through this; the discharge was followed by another one that seemed to go right through the building's outside walls.

Luckily, both attacks dissipated before they hit anyone in the North Lawn or in areas further afield, but they were succeeded by yet *another* explosive blast. After this, a black-suited intruder – covered head to toe in flame – flew out of the North Portico's main doorway, landing on the driveway just beyond. A column of smoke wafted upward from his charred and apparently-lifeless body.

More assailants – apparently less comprehensively-geared than those so far identified – were seen, either executing flanking-maneuvers just outside the building (thus themselves coming under sniper-fire, from the hidden gunmen far off to the north and south), or, as near as anyone could determine, probing the interior defenses of the White House.

*"You're a **dead** man, Clark… **traitor!**"* came an electronically-boosted threat, from the SWAT-assassin on the White House residence roof. By the time this threat was heard, he was already airborne, after executing another impossible jump.

As he flew through the air, the assassin directed what must have been a grenade-launcher at the front windscreen of the one remaining helicopter. The projectile pierced clean through and exploded inside, killing everyone aboard and sending the now-flaming 'copter crashing downward.

It was on a collision-course for the second floor of the main White House residence; but just before reaching that point, the second of the original two emergent super-humans, still surrounded by his hurricane-shroud, managed to interpose himself between the disintegrating aircraft and the building's roof. Onlookers felt the air-pressure in the area increase greatly – several of them experienced instant ear-aches – and noticed that the man's whirling, tornado-like air-shield was now rotating much faster, as well as incorporating dark, cumulus-like clouds within it.

There was also a subtle, rapid, melodic beat playing, somewhere in the man's vicinity.

The plunging helicopter hit the air-powered protective-shield square on; but it simply bounced off like a ping-pong-ball from a paddle, coming to rest on the South Lawn.

Chu's new ally was far from finished with the encounter.

From one of the deep-gray cloud-structures within his air-shield, issued a yellowish-white lightening-bolt, similar to (though apparently less powerful than) what some of the more-than-humans had seen fired by Cherie Tanaka, oft-times before. This attack – which hit the SWAT-suited assailant with devastating effect, setting the front-facing part of his equipment afire and propelling him backward, into the air – was accompanied by a thunder-clap that reverberated throughout the area.

Way to go, Hector – you've got him! exulted Chu; but her enthusiasm was premature. As the master-assassin was about to land on top of the West Wing, near the Oval Office, he simply… *disappeared*.

What the – marveled the former team-leader.

I had him in clear sight, a second ago… where'd he go?

Anyway – no time to worry about the fucker –

She stopped her downward motion and again began to ascend, slower than she would have preferred to have done, given that the battle was still raging below and that inaccurate, random sniper-fire was now incoming from the south.

"Mr. President," said the *nouvelle* FBI-director, pushing her voice to be heard above the din of war, "Are you and Clairie oh-kay? I'm going to fly out of here – need to get you to safety –"

"I'm *fine*," prevaricated the President, "But Clairie's been hit – she took bullets that were meant for *me*... sweetheart, can you hold on?"

"Yeah," confirmed the daughter, "I'll live, but I don't know how – it hurts like hell – sorry Daddy – like I've, uhh, been *shot* – but, like, there's no hole there anymore – just a big bruise – but I was bleeding real bad, a minute ago... if *that* makes any sense."

"Welcome to the New People," cajoled Chu. "Oh-kay, folks, we're out of here –"

"*Wait!*" countermanded the U.S. leader. "Not without my wife and Matt!"

"Mr. *President*," pleaded the former team-leader, "Be *reasonable!* There's a *war* raging down there... you've got to trust the Service and the Marines to –"

"Sir," proposed Kaysten, from his perspective of hanging on Chu's foot, "Minnie's right – your safety has to be our Number One priority. Let *me* find the First Lady and your son. Minnie – can you fly over to the hole you opened up, so I can drop back down there?"

A nonplussed Chu stammered, "Jerry... it's got to be more than a hundred feet to ground-level – are you *sure*?"

The Chief of Staff's eyes were glowing now, brighter than anyone had yet seen; and his body was lit up from inside, by the glowing tendrils of the *Fire*. His staccato-beat, adrenaline-stimulating war-song surged through human and more-than-human psyches, alike.

"I'll be alright," he vowed, "And I'll get them out... not sure *how*, but I *will!* Mr. President... do you trust me?"

"Yes... I do," answered the President. "May the Lord be with you!"

"Very well," echoed the former team-leader, "And may the power of an *angel*, also fortify you for battle, my brother!"

"Let's *do* it!" demanded Kaysten.

Chu – dodging rifle-fire inbound not only from the south, but now also from the north and below – slightly adjusted her flight-path so as to position herself, and the hangers-on, over the breach latterly opened in the West Wing roof.

"Three... two... one... *Geronimo!*" counted Kaysten.

He released his grasp, and thereby immediately began hurtling earthward; but unlike before, there was no fear on his face – only a look of steely determination.

"*Beware*, murderers!" loudly exclaimed Chu, "A warrior-prince of the Holy *Fire*, descends upon you!"

She turned to address the evacuees.

"We're done here," declared the *nouvelle* FBI-director, as she guided the group upward and away.

Not To Worry About Walls

Reasoning that glowing like the lamp in a lighthouse wasn't the best way to hide, Boyd had temporarily suppressed his *Fire*-abilities. Despite having to keep constant watch to the west due to the ongoing gunfire coming from that direction, he still managed to shout backward over his shoulder.

"*Cherie!*" called the ex-astronaut, into the Center Hall. "Thinking-range yet?"

"No," came back the reply. "Some kind of interference, and they're all *over* the place – I'm worried about Otis and the –"

The discussion was interrupted by another burst of automatic weapons-fire.

He heard Tanaka's familiar war-song, followed by the ominously well-known sound of her lightening-attack, going off. Then there was a loud, percussive explosion that shook the walls.

"*Wolf!*" shouted the former Mars mission science officer, "Be careful – a few more like that could bring the whole *building* down on us!"

"You'll *live*, so will I – them bitches *won't*," growled the bounty-hunter, from a hidden position back in the hall somewhere.

He then spoke towards the Palm Room, taking care to keep the volume low.

"Listen, spacemen," warned Wolf, "Ms. Thunder-Thighs ain't kiddin'… fuckers are *everywhere*… gotta be *dozens* of 'em! Where the fuck they *comin'* from?"

"*You* tell *me*," responded Boyd. "Got a bunch of 'em up ahead, just inside the West Wing. Are the civilians okay?"

"Boatman's got 'em all hidin' in one room… handed a couple of guns off to 'em as well," explained Wolf. "Also sealed the door so they can't gas it. Won't shit ya – ain't very safe – but then *nowhere* in here is, these days. At least these fuckers don't have all the gear that the one who you fought, had on him."

Silently, the ex-astronaut said a prayer for the safety of his spouse. He then addressed his former boss.

"Commander," said Boyd, "Yvonne, Laura and the others are safe right now… but who knows how long *that* will last? Whatever we're doing – we had better get it over with, ASAP! I'm for using all the firepower at our disposal."

"Acknowledged," answered Jacobson.

"Listen, Sam… Brent," interjected Tanaka, "*Vîrya Sài'ymë* is detecting a battle going on, outside – *above* us, just to the west. She thinks Minnie's involved, and there are, in her words, 'bad-guys with better-than-human abilities', as well. It doesn't make *sense*… Karéin's followers are all accounted-for, so how could we be fighting someone with alien-powers? Anyway, be careful – remember, Minnie doesn't know we're here."

"Well… she – and they, whoever they are – are about to find out, I suppose," grunted Jacobson. "The nice way for *her*… the hard way for *them*."

A few bullets whizzed by, followed by two more that respectively shredded the Palm Room's woodwork and shattered one of its still-intact clay flower-pots.

The former Mars mission commander seemed not to take much account of this relatively light gunfire, however. Instead, he was staring off into space, as if concentrating.

"Commander?" pressed the former Mars mission pilot.

"They're only offering *token* suppressive fire, in our direction," observed Jacobson. "I'm hearing a knock-down battle going on further west, though. That's our chance to attack – and I *don't* mean through that way to the right, where they're hiding… I'm not worrying about walls. *With* me?"

"Sure," committed Boyd. "Bust through and I'll degrade their visual abilities. I just wish we could use our main offensive powers... but without knowing who or what's beyond, we can't risk collateral damage. We'll have to count on Cherie and Wolf to cover our rear-flank."

"Yeah… mine's even less precise than yours," admitted the senior ex-astronaut. "I might take down half the West Wing, by using it at full strength. But none the less, we need to hit them *hard*, and *fast*. Shoot to *kill!* Ready?"

"*Damn* ready!" confirmed a determined-looking Boyd, with pistol in hand.

"Three… two… one… *go!*" counted a glowing-eyed Jacobson, as an encasing of pseudo-diamonds appeared all around his figure. His bass-beat war-song began to rattle and hum, as the former Mars mission commander, after backing up by perhaps ten feet, wheeled and hurled himself right at the Palm Room's western wall, shaking the building all the way down to its foundations as he contacted the barrier.

Like the proverbial juggernaut, Jacobson smashed clean through the wall despite its hidden interior reinforcements, sending a spray of twisted metal, splintered wood and crushed gypsum-dust flying ahead of him. He barged into what had been the White House Press Corps Office. Boyd followed, less than a half-second behind.

Immediately, the instinctive alien-danger-senses of the two more-than-human men alerted them to the presence of enemies.

There appeared to be two groups of intruders within the room. The first – consisting entirely of assassins clad in relatively conventional combat-gear and lacking combat-headgear – was encamped within or just outside the Press

Kitchen to the right, covering an outside portal to the North Lawn. A larger group – mostly the same type, but this time including one guy in the same kind of SWAT-suit and -helmet that Boyd and Jacobson had tangled with earlier – were clustered at the far north-western end of the Press Corps Office.

Both groups seemed understandably nonplussed at the manner in which the two ex-astronauts had made their unexpected appearance.

The second enemy formation seemed preoccupied by a battle with unknown parties further within the West Wing, perhaps in or around the Press Briefing Room; they seemed to have been caught unawares, but the first group was not, and after the surprise wore off, its members challenged the two ex-astronauts with a barrage of rifle-fire. This stopped abruptly, when Boyd's off-theme darkness-field suddenly enveloped the north-eastern quarter of the room, leaving the first group of enemies effectively blind.

Forgot to ask you… how long does it last? communicated Jacobson.

Scary stuff – looks like they all disappeared into a big black hole – I can just imagine what it must be like, being inside that thing…

It fades a second or two after I stop concentrating on it, responded Boyd.

Far as I know – only had a couple of chances to test it –

Then… forward, to the west! directed Jacobson.

I'll take out their leader –

Calling on his alien-powered "zero to five hundred in one second" ability, the former Mars mission commander charged forward, aiming directly at the guy in the advanced combat-armor-suit. He struck home with tremendous force, sending the SWAT-suited enemy flying into the Press Briefing Room to the west, while scattering five other, conventionally-equipped enemies in the immediate area, to the left and right.

Despite the impact, the assassin foot-soldiers reacted with surprising vigor; they quickly righted themselves, aiming auto-rifles at Jacobson's back and at the front-flank of his former Mars spacecraft pilot, who was following about twelve feet behind. However, this was to no avail, as the intruders were, in the next second, dazzled by a new trick on the part of Brent Boyd.

Though refraining from his familiar, area-effect flash-attack, the ex-astronaut was still able to illuminate his body with such a brilliant, pulsating glow, that looking directly at it was impossible for ordinary human eyes.

The onset of his exciting, electric-rock-beat war-song did not help his enemies to understand what was going on, as Boyd set himself to the savage business of war.

Seeing that Jacobson was tied up dealing with the leading, power-suited enemy, Boyd did not hesitate. Still glowing like an arc-torch and using a deadly mixture of U.S. military and alien-powered close-combat training, he took full advantage of his opponents' temporary disorientation. While alternatively dodging a couple of poorly-aimed rifle-shots, Boyd emptied his pistol against the heads, necks and groin-areas of three assassins, dropping them instantly.

Realizing that he was out of accessible ammunition and observing that the two remaining intruders were about to spray rifle-fire indiscriminately in his direction, the former Air Force pilot dropped his pistol and used telekinetic powers to quickly position his combat-blade at the ready. He executed a martial-arts rolling-dive, taking the legs out from one of the assassins, then cutting his throat with the knife.

Boyd unleashed another pulsating glow, momentarily disorienting the other enemy. This maneuver gave the ex-astronaut enough time to close the distance and knock the man's auto-rifle from his grasp.

The two now fought hand-to-hand, and though Boyd's opponent was clearly well-trained in manual combat – landing a couple of painful kicks and fist-blows – he was no match for the former Mars pilot's alien-empowered tactics.

He's using some type of Taekwondo, and he's got a bit of body-armor, realized Boyd.

What style of Vrùn-Ch'é *did Karéin recommend against that?*

Oh – right – the "Snapping-Turtle"… but I didn't have time to really learn it that well…

So I'll just use the one she did *teach me, a.k.a. the "Long-Clawed Lion"… punch the* shit *out of you, fucker – that works for* me*!*

With his hands formed into a talon-mimicking shape, Boyd bellowed out the guttural growl that his alien mentor had recommended, as a starting-move for this style of martial-arts combat.

He narrowly missed another couple of dangerous kicks – one in particular would likely have crippled any human opponent, had it landed home – and then went fully on the offensive, using the "Long-Clawed Lion"'s high-powered, combination punching-, chopping- and slapping-attacks to land devastating blows to his opponent's torso (using the Storied Watcher's techniques, this hit went right through the armor) and head.

The hapless assassin went down, with blood pouring from his ears and nose. This earned him a vicious kick to the skull as Boyd's finishing-move.

The former Mars mission pilot allowed himself a second or two to catch his breath, retrieve his gun and survey the situation. To his alarm, he noticed that – probably due to being preoccupied by close combat – his dark-trick had abated. A few of the opponents from the first group, originally in the Press Kitchen, had now advanced into the Press Corps Offices, giving them a clear line of sight to Boyd's and Jacobson's rear flanks. Their guns were at the ready, and they raised them, targeting the ex-astronauts.

Boyd set about to preparing another shroud of darkness, and was ready to project it on top of the emergent enemies; but then – to shouts of alarm, issuing from the eastern part of the Press Corps Offices – instead, the assassins turned backward and to the left, firing rapidly in that direction.

A half-second later, to the ex-pilot's grim satisfaction, he saw three of the intruders instantly rendered *hors de combat* – or worse – by a barrage of Tanaka's multi-colored lightening-bolts. Luckily, these were aimed at an oblique angle toward the outside walls of the White House, and thus had no chance of hitting either Boyd or Jacobson.

Ouch! reflected Boyd, while the battle between the former Mars science officer and the assassins, raged on.

I've been on the receiving end of that little light-show of yours, Cherie – no desire to repeat the experience!

While his former under-study was fighting with the subordinate assassins, the diamond-clad Sam Jacobson struggled with the guy outfitted with a powered combat-suit.

The man *should* have been killed outright by the brutal kinetic-force of Jacobson's initial, charging assault; but, amazingly, he not only survived this, but in fact appeared to quickly regain his composure, jumping back to his feet while unloading some well-aimed rifle-shots at his more-than-human tormentor. This maneuver was all the more impressive, considering that the assassin was also being fired at by a beleaguered group of worse-for-wear Secret Service agents and Marine guards, who were in defensive positions at the far western end of the Press Briefing Room (these rounds only narrowly missed Jacobson himself, as he was more or less within the line of fire; but they shredded the chairs arrayed in the room, facing the Presidential podium).

Two of the assassin's bullets struck home, and though the ex-astronaut knew they would have blown even a Kevlar-armored victim in half, they caused him only slight discomfort, bouncing harmlessly off his force-field.

Observing the futility of using gunfire, the SWAT-suited guy dropped his auto-rifle and started reaching with both hands for grenades suspended from his belt. One of the bombs looked like a conventional blast-fragmentation unit; the other – different in both shape and color – had a "skull-and-crossbones" logo.

Oh, no, you don't! raged Jacobson.

Hands off that damn nerve-gas!

He lunged at his opponent.

The leading-assassin immediately disappeared from sight, in much the same manner as had the guy that Jacobson and Boyd had engaged back in the Center Hall, a few minutes earlier.

However, the former Mars mission commander had anticipated the move and had partially activated his *"Um'nàhr'é"* vision-mode. Though he could see only a faint outline of the assassin – based on heat-leakage coming from the combat-suit – it was more than enough for Jacobson to target his attack.

Eschewing Boyd's martial-arts moves in favor of brute force and traveling faster than any human being could possibly have done, Jacobson closed the distance, bounded off a press-seat and landed an alien-powered haymaker right to the man's gut. This was followed up by a kick that knocked the hapless assassin far backward, this time up against the northern, outside wall of the Press Briefing Room.

The ex-astronaut noticed an immediate increase in infra-red emissions coming from various joints and fissures in the combat-suit; he again advanced and aimed punches at these apparent weak-spots, while pinning the now-prone opponent's arms so as to preclude access to the grenades.

Suddenly, Jacobson felt a surge of electricity assaulting the outside of his diamond-shroud. It reminded him of the trap that almost electrocuted him in the Amchitka dungeon; but for yet another time, his force-field largely negated an attack that would likely have been fatal to a human being.

Two more vicious, super-powered punches cracked the guy's helmet. A third hit knocked it clear of the man's head, exposing the latter to a final, devastating punch that – as far as Jacobson could tell, not that he cared – probably crushed the assassin's skull.

Seeing that his own opponent had been rendered "combat-ineffective", Jacobson crouched down, planning to retrieve whatever weaponry that he could (minus the gas grenades) from the fallen assassin. This plan was interrupted by a number of off-target gunshots coming from the western half of the Press Briefing Room.

At first, the former Mars mission commander assumed that these were exclusively fired by the White House guards at the far end of the room, and, indeed, some of them were; but then Jacobson noticed that someone *outside* was firing through the windows (or what was left of them; several had been shattered by high-powered rounds, particularly incoming from the south).

The ex-astronaut reflexively raised one arm to protect his head, even though he knew that his diamond-shroud made him effectively invulnerable to this type of attack. He then shouted toward the Service agents and Marine guards,

"I'm Sam Jacobson of the Mars Gang – and I'm here with my team to protect the *President!* Cease your fire!"

A voice from a hidden guard replied, "We *know* who you are… *terrorist!* Drop your weapons and *surrender!*"

There was a commotion, somewhere further to the west.

"For Christ's *sake,*" started Jacobson, "I don't have *time* to –"

He was cut off by a combined, top-volume, top-priority, verbal and mental alarm, on the part of Tanaka.

"Thunderchild to Diamondback – *Vîrya Sài'ymë* says, 'emergency'! Above us, outside! Sam – *go!*" came the plea.

He didn't know how he knew what his former science officer was referring to; nor did the former Mars mission commander know, *how* he knew what he had to do.

Yet... without the slightest hesitation... he *acted*.

No worries about walls – nor ceilings, was Sam Jacobson's parting thought, as – with big, muscled legs tensing and then propelling him – he rocketed upward and slightly to the west, smashing through the West Wing roof as if it were made of tissue-paper, into the troubled skies beyond.

Jerry The Renovator

Albeit with some difficulty, Kaysten had managed to stay upright on his trip down, and his legs were already moving far too rapidly for human eyes to make out, by the time he descended through the breach in the West Wing roof.

Holding his arms out horizontally as he landed, none the worse for wear – and bedecked in the *Fire's* energy-bursts, complete with glowing eyes and rapid-fire war-song – he looked every bit the part of an avenging hero.

The guise was not just impressive but opportune, as the Chief of Staff had fallen right into the heat of a heated battle. He had only a second or so, in which to take measure of the situation.

To his dismay, Kaysten saw an obviously-badly-hurt, terrified, dust-covered First Lady glued to the West Wing floor, just next to the immobile body of her son. The Secret Service agents that had – only a few moments ago – been assigned to protecting the President, now lay either dead or crippled. Only one guard – the youngest of the three – seemed in any way functional, and he was suffering from several serious wounds.

Meanwhile, at the far western end of the room, near a set of stairs going upward and downward, were clustered the rest of the President's former party : an aghast but apparently-unharmed Susan Feldner, a wounded Secretary of State and a wary German BND guard, crouching in ambush-position by the other two.

To the far east, in the passageway to the Press Briefing Room, he could just make out the figures of one or two Service-agents; but these were evidently tied up in a fire-fight with enemies further to the east.

There was also another unexpected sight; the south wall had been blown wide open, as if someone had fired a bazooka at it, or through it.

What the hell... mused Kaysten.

Who – or what – could do something like that?

But he had no time to ponder the issue, as – almost immediately – he had to dodge gunfire, directed into the room from unseen assailants outside on the North Lawn. Some of this was inaccurately aimed at the small coterie of

White House guards at the eastern end of the room, but most of it seemed to merely be suppressive. Kaysten quickly found out why – a black-suited assassin was trying to climb through one of the broken windows facing to the North Lawn, while some undefined alien-sense warned him of hostile movement to the south, near to the strange rupture in the room's southern wall.

"Speed is armor"... "speed is armor"... isn't that how the saying goes? he thought, while hurtling himself toward the invading north window assassin, with both arms in front, ending in clenched fists.

Seem to remember from the history-books, that's what they said – before all those British warships got blown up...

Moving at least a few hundred miles per hour, the Chief of Staff made hard contact with the intruder, knocking his quarry backward into the North Lawn.

Using tricks patiently taught to him by the Storied Watcher some time ago, Kaysten was barely able to stop his forward motion. In fact, for a brief moment, his head and shoulders protruded out the window, and he could see what was going on outside.

He noticed a group of five or six well-armed assassins (including the guy with whom he had just collided, who was knocked out cold, on the North Lawn driveway just outside the walls of the White House) creeping forward. Some of the newly-identified enemies had been firing into the building, but upon Kaysten's appearance, they backed off and assumed a more defensive stance. Oddly, however, two more of the enemy-group lay dead in bloody-mess-guise, as if they had been shot by someone firing from the north.

This theory seemed much more plausible when – in the next half-second – Kaysten realized that the snipers responsible for this carnage, were targeting him, too. Two rifle-bullets hit the West Wing's northern wall, perilously close to where the Chief of Staff had stuck out his head.

Sensibly deciding that discretion would be the better part of valor, Kaysten reversed course and charged back to the south at high speed. He arrived at the breach in the southern wall just in time, as three assassins were approaching the area from the West Colonnade, with another four some distance further behind them. Though their progress was halting – they were coming under rifle-fire from afar to the south, and thus had to crouch and hide behind whatever cover they could find – the heavily-armed intruders were no more than eight to ten seconds away from entering the opening in the wall.

To add to the challenge, he could plainly hear a vicious gun-battle raging in the Press Offices, just to the east.

Hooboy, thought Kaysten,

Those thugs get in here, the First Lady and the rest of the civilians – including but not limited to Yours Truly – we're toast!

There are a couple pistols lying around – but I never was very handy with guns... how am I supposed to deal with this?

Yeah... she did teach me quite a bit of that funky alien Kung-Fu of hers – but even at high speed – against a whole damn squad *of combat-trained goons, each with a rifle?*

Pretty risky, I'd say... and I doubt they're in much of a mood to hear a joke...

Desperately, he looked around for something – anything – to use, to provide a modicum of protection.

Hey, noticed the Chief of Staff,

That big-ass piece that Minnie sliced out of the ceiling... that would sure block the hole in the south wall... but the damn thing's huge – it would take six or seven strong guys to even budge *it –*

What if... oh, come on, Jerry – you got to be dreaming!

But didn't she also *say, "When the time comes, Jerr-ee, believe in yourself, and place your trust in the Holy Fire... she shall not let you down"?*

What have I got to lose?

Oh... yeah... my life... that's what.

Remind me to think up a routine about that – bet it'll be a real killer *–*

Trying to ignore the burgeoning threat that was now no more than five or six seconds away, he wheeled in place and – with the other-worldly energy called *"Amaiish"*, illuminating both his eyes and body – Jerry Kaysten, much to his own surprise, locked a powerful telekinetic hold onto the section of the West Wing roof that Chu had excised, not five minutes before.

The Secretary of State and Feldner, along with the BND agent, gasped in astonishment as the roof-chunk – which must have weighed more than a half-ton – lifted off the floor, rotated so as to have its long end in the vertical and began to slowly move, without any obvious physical support.

A thrill of might and accomplishment raced through Kaysten's veins, as he reflected,

So this is what it's like, to get your mind working like a ten-ton crane... holy shit, *doesn't it make you feel like a god – like Sylvia probably felt, back at the Old Man's prison-house – maybe I lift this whole* mansion, *for an encore?*

Careful, careful... crazy stuff, I can sense *the stresses within it, where it might crack... extend my virtual hand to support it right there... move it gently – uhh, whoops, out of time – okay then, just drop the fucker anywhere near the hole –*

Releasing his cargo at a height of about a half-foot off the White House floor, in front of the opening in the south wall, Kaysten was initially worried that the roof-fragment would tip back over and possibly injure one or more of the civilians in the room. But the fear proved unwarranted; there was a satisfying "thud" – causing, in turn, a shudder that raced through the building's structure – and part of the relocated section slumped into the breach, filling it nearly completely and making ingress by human-sized beings out of the question.

With the outward signs of the *Fire* within him abating, the Chief of Staff turned to address the civilians and their one remaining operational guard.

"Wow, Jerry," commented an obviously-impressed Feldner. "That was *amazing!* How'd you *do* it, anyway?"

"Just some improvised home renovating," he quipped. "If Angel Lady ever drops in here again, you can learn the 'ins' and 'outs' of it, right from the horse's mouth. But listen – my little wall-job won't keep them out forever. Mrs. First Lady – what's your status? You and Matt don't look so good..."

"I… I think something's broken… my arm," whimpered the Presidential spouse. "I landed right on top of Matt – he broke my fall – I'd surely have been killed, otherwise. He's unconscious, but he *is* breathing, as far as I can see. Oh Jerry… you really *are*, one of, uhh… *them*, now… aren't you?"

"'Fraid so, Ma'am," politely responded Kaysten. "And if I *wasn't* – you wouldn't be happy dealing with who's behind that wall. We've got to get you *out* of here, as quickly as possible."

Looks of despair went from one person to another and back again.

"To exactly… *where?*" complained Feldner. "Can you fly us out of here, like Minnie did?"

"Uhh… not really," answered the Chief of Staff, with a sheepish cringe. "I kind of, uhh, haven't learned that one yet... that is, if I ever do."

"The terrorists are all *around* us – what can we *do!*" wailed the frightened Secretary of State.

The BND agent spoke up. He said,

"And the helicopters are obviously no longer an option."

"Thinking… thinking out loud," stammered Kaysten. "I can't fly you out – but, uhh, I bet I could at least lift you up to the roof, or what's left of it? Not safe – but maybe saf*er* than here –"

"Didn't Mr. Chance – God rest his soul – didn't he say that there are people *shooting* at the roof?" argued Feldner.

"Yeah... he *did*," admitted Kaysten, "And I saw more of it on the way down. Okay – that's one's off the list."

Think, *Jerry… think* fast – he mused.

He heard shouts from the far end of the room, to the east. These were followed by weird-sounding noises that reminded him of alien-powered war-songs, although he couldn't exactly place who owned which song.

"Let's get everybody over there, by the remaining guards," he directed. "At least that way, we'll have some firepower on *our* side."

Wary, despondent stares were exchanges among the civilians; but as they were all at a total loss to propose a better plan of action, the Secretary of State (supported by Susan Feldner and the BND agent) limped eastward, while Kaysten assisted the blanching First Lady; the Chief of Staff also levitated her unconscious son in tow behind. "Jackson", the Secret Service agent, tried to provide cover for them, although he was so badly-wounded himself that he could barely stand up.

As quickly as they could manage, they traveled to the southwestern edge of the Press Briefing Room, whereupon they were briefly greeted by a group of Secret Service Agents and Marine guards. These were themselves preoccupied by a gunfight against outside opponents to the north and south, along with a heated conversation with someone in the next room, who Kaysten couldn't see. The Chief of Staff did, however, notice a ragged hole in the roof of the room, similar to – but considerably smaller than – the one that Chu had opened up, some time before.

Kaysten attempted to strike up a conversation with the guards, but was brusquely told to "get *down*, sir… can't you see it's *dangerous* here, sir?"

The Chief of Staff had two or three sarcastic responses at the ready. He didn't get to use them, because two of the windows in the western room facing the North Lawn, now burst inward. Through the breaches thus caused, leaped two intruders, followed almost immediately by two more close behind.

They hesitated momentarily as they surveilled the chaotic, battle-damaged surroundings; then, casting a malevolent glance to the east and seeing the cowering Executive Office refugees (and the backs of the White House guards), began to raise their automatic rifles.

There appeared to be nowhere to run or hide; a massacre was no more than a second or two away.

Shit, he reflected,

Didn't want to fight these guys… well… here we are…

Hmm… she said this "Verun Shay" thing wouldn't work too well against another New Person – bounce right off our personal force-fields, and anyway, the rest of 'em got trained in how to counter-punch against it –

Maybe I should have tried it on that jerk Billings, none the less…

But these jerks are just humans, even if they are trained killers…

Fire *of the Angel,* silently requested a grimly-serious Kaysten,

I need you – err – I need "thee" – now!

Pour it on, Karéin!

And for the second time today, the blessing of the Storied Watcher fell in large measure upon the shoulders of the Chief of Staff. His war-song echoed throughout, as his eyes and body began to shine. He felt utterly confident in his abilities, and he ignited them at full power.

Streaking forward at the intruders at an impossible speed, Kaysten relied upon what he had learned of the alien martial-arts taught him, by Karéin-Mayréij. Oddly – though he had feared having forgotten the maneuvers of the technique – he had no trouble at all, in recalling how to attack and defend.

What did she call this style, again –

Oh, yeah… "The Giggler" – well, what do you know –

Joke's on you, *bitches!*

The more-than-human man was now moving so fast that it seemed as if he were fighting a collection of statues; his arms lashed out repeatedly in lightening-fast strikes against his victims' knees, heads, necks, ears and, especially, eyes. Two enemies immediately fell to the floor, crippled and screaming in pain, holding hands over the bloody remnants of pulped, shattered eyeballs – the signature effect of this sinister, other-worldly fighting-style. A third collapsed with the arteries in his neck crushed by a brutal hand-chop.

Once or twice, the Chief of Staff made the mistake of landing a blow against an opponent's torso, resulting in badly-bruised fingers as the strike was turned back by Kevlar-II body-armor; but even at this, the sheer velocity of his assault caused severe damage to his victims.

Despite all this, the last of the assassins – who had entered the room through the furthest-west window – was too far away for the Chief of Staff to immediately engage. This intruder was hit at least once by pistol-fire from Agent Jackson, but the damage seemed to be negated by the assassin's breastplate. To Kaysten's dismay, the intruder stayed on his feet and was still able to get off two retaliatory rifle-shots.

One of these went wildly astray, but the other – either by aim or by fluke – hit the Presidential adviser on his left side, just below the ribs. It put a ragged hole in his jacket, hurt terribly and caused an ugly, slowly-bleeding wound; but somehow, the Kaysten realized not only that the bullet had been deflected away, but that it would have blown away half his torso, had he been a normal man.

Groaning in pain, the Chief of Staff lost his balance and stumbled, but he was charging forward at his opponent so fast that there was no chance of a course-correction; the two collided at high speed, with Kaysten's elbow connecting hard, with the assassin's chin.

Both combatants tumbled, head-over-heels, colliding with the room's western and southwestern walls at high velocity; and both were stunned by the impact, but the Presidential adviser recovered more quickly.

He saw the assassin reaching for a belt-grenade.

Keep your fucking hands off *that!* mentally snarled Kaysten.

Moving with impossible speed, he put the boot to the side of his opponent's head, resulting in a spray of blood and dislodged teeth from the man's mouth. More blood oozed from his right ear as he collapsed. A second later, half the assassin's head was blown off by a well-aimed pistol-round, fired by the one remaining, partially-functional Secret Service agent.

The exhausted, brutalized Chief of Staff ached all over, as he allowed himself a moment of respite, in which to take account of the situation.

He reached to cover the wound on his left torso, grimacing as he saw his hand smeared with blood; yet – to his surprise and gratitude – he couldn't detect a bullet-hole.

"Jerry! That was *awesome!*" called the rapt voice of Susan Feldner, from her cowering vantage-point at the eastern end of the room. "I never *knew* you were, like, a Kung-Fu expert! Are you hurt?"

"No... and yes," he managed, while walking over to where the civilian refugees were hiding. "Asshole plugged me in the chest, but somehow – don't ask me how – I'm, uhh, *dealing* with it."

"Are you... wearing... a... vest, sir?" gasped the crippled Service agent.

"Nope... just what Little Miss Nuclear Angel blessed me with, some time back," replied the Chief of Staff. "Thanks for the backup, man. I'll live – but we need to get you to a doctor."

"Just doing my job... and avenging Chance and Chiarelli," managed the Service agent. "They were brave men."

"Yeah," acknowledged Kaysten. He addressed the others.

"You folks over there, okay?" he asked. "They took some shots in your direction –"

It might have been his imagination, but Kaysten thought that he heard a dull "thud" sound, coming from the part of the room that he had just vacated.

"We seem to be undamaged," interjected the voice of the Secretary of State. "Ms. Feldner's observations are indeed apt. My God, Jerry – where did you learn to *fight* like that? We never *suspected* –"

"The answer is, 'at a campground, up in Canada'," explained Kaysten. "From a certain little alien-girl, who claimed she'd used those slick martial-arts moves to, uhh, 'crush demons', or whatever. Listen – there might be more of those bastards around here, and, frankly, I'm zonked from the last battle... I doubt I can even use harsh language against the next ones we run into. Can you get the attention of those Service guys over there?"

"I'll try," said the Secretary of State, "But they seem to be arguing with someone in the next room – can't see him... wait – can hardly move on my bad leg, but I'll just – hey, isn't that guy one of the 'Mars' –"

"Who?" exclaimed the Chief of Staff. "What the hell are *they* doing here? I thought that Jacobson was –"

"*Jerry – look out –* behind *you!*" interrupted Feldner.

Faster than any human being could have done, Kaysten wheeled in place, to surveil the western half of this battle-damaged, blood-splattered room.

He saw a *new* intruder, bedecked in some kind of futuristic, black-and-dark-gray-colored combat-gear, complete with a sealed helmet and visor, plus auto-rifle and various other, sinister-looking weaponry.

The combat-suit looked a little the worse for wear – parts of it were charred and pitted, as if they had been hit by some high-intensity thermal-attack – but it was still unlike anything that Kaysten had ever seen, being used by the U.S. military.

"Clark seems to have fled – like the traitorous coward he *is*," snarled the newcomer's electronically-boosted-and-modified voice, as he pointed at the

First Lady and her son. "But that's okay… I'm sure he'll be back, when he finds out what I'm going to do to *you!*"

Your Side… My Side… No Side

There was a set of stairs between the West Wing Press Briefing Room and the Press Corps offices; it was the only suitable hiding-place for Brent Boyd, as he tried to reason with the White House guards at the far western end of the Briefing Room, while crouching low to avoid pot-shots being directed inside the building by assassins to the north and south.

He thought he heard a war-song, and then felt the south wall of the West Wing, shudder momentarily, as if something heavy had struck it.

"Look, for God's sake," shouted the former Mars mission pilot, "Sure, Commander Jacobson and I *are* from the Mars Gang – but we're on *your* side!"

"Make a move out into the open, and we'll shoot you *dead!*" warned one of the besieged Secret Service agents, who were hunkered down in the short corridor between the Press Briefing Room and the room just to the west of it.

Boyd looked over his shoulder and saw the welcome figures of Tanaka and Wolf, joining him from their previous positions back in the Press Corps offices. Both of the more-than-humans were also reflexively keeping their heads down.

"What about those pricks back in the Palm Room and the Press Kitchen?" he whispered.

"Smoked a lot of 'em… rest fucked off," grunted the bounty-hunter.

"Yeah – but they might try to circle back," advised the former science officer. "We'll try to cover your rear flank, in case they do."

"Where'd Mr. Diamond-Nuts go?" inquired Wolf.

Boyd pointed to the jagged hole that Jacobson had smashed in the ceiling.

"Through there," he indicated. "Just took off, all of a sudden."

"He's missin' all the *fun*, then," offered the bounty-hunter. "Listen… don't know if Little Miss Unguided Nuke told you, but she gave me this hidin'-trick where I can fuck with people's eyes – I'm there, but they just can't see me, or some-such shit. It worked on me back down L.A. way… want me to try it, to sneak forward?"

"Can you make it just work on the terrorists, or the White House guards?" asked Boyd.

"Uhh… don't know," admitted Wolf. "I think she said it works on everybody within a certain distance. How far that is, I can't say."

"Nix on *that* idea, then," requested the former Mars mission pilot. "If it works on us too – and we can't see you when and if we open up with our own attacks – we might hit you by mistake."

"*Knew* there had to be a catch to it," grumbled the bounty-hunter.

"By the way, Sam was acting on an alert from *Vîrya Sài'ymë*," explained Tanaka. "She was warning that 'a big air-bird was about to crash into here'… Sam stopped it. Or, at least… I *hope* he did."

"You are not authorized to be on these premises, and the building's in lock-down," came another directive, from one of the White House guards. "Lay down your weapons *immediately*, and –"

His voice stopped abruptly.

Though it was difficult to make out given the persistent sounds of combat all around, Boyd's alien-enhanced ears detected some kind of commotion happening further to the west, behind the stubborn White House defenders.

He then heard, "Shit! Get some guys back there to – what the hell's he *doing*?"

A worried Boyd discerned the tell-tale noises of gunshots, and other mayhem, coming from the room to the west of the Press Briefing Office. A couple more random rifle-rounds came in through the windows, scoring the surrounding walls.

Then – after no more than twenty to thirty seconds of tense waiting – everything again fell relatively quiet, from that direction.

The former Mars mission pilot thought he heard words to the effect of, "He did *what* – *four* of 'em – all by *himself*?"

"What's going *on* over there?" he called out, to the defenders. "Do you require assistance?"

"Listen, asshole," retorted the partly-hidden White House guard, "If you really *are* from this 'Mars Gang', that makes you a terrorist by our standards – and a very *dangerous* one, at that –"

More rifle-rounds flew in from outside. They were far off the mark.

"You got no fuckin' *idea*, just *how* dangerous!" undiplomatically interrupted Wolf, loud enough to be heard at the other end of the room. "You wanna find out… check out what's left of them fuckers, back behind us!"

"Jesus H. *Christ*, man – *stow* it!" complained an irritated Boyd, in the direction of the bounty-hunter, "Our families and us are already being shot at by dozens of *real* 'terrorists' – the *last* thing we need, is to add the Service and the military to the enemy-list!"

"This is Cherie Tanaka of the Mars Gang speaking," called out Tanaka. "We're aware that you guys are doing your duty, trying to protect the President… but surely you remember that he gave all of us the right of free access to this building? We're *not* the ones that you worry about – the White House is under terrorist attack, and they're right outside, right now – let us help you *defend*!"

"You can tell all that to the President, when we locate him," countered the White House guard. "Until then, you had better –"

For a second time, Boyd (and now, the other two) intercepted the sounds of something peculiar going on, some distance behind the group of entrenched guards in the west end of the Press Briefing Room. Then they all heard,

"Marines – look out – intruders, behind *us!"*

Call It A "High-Level Meeting"

In what had to be the most unusual meeting between heads of state in recent history, the President had encountered Chancellor Gebirgen, in the possession of an African-American teenager from Detroit, at an altitude of several thousand feet over downtown Washington, D.C..

"Jus' don' look down… y'all be *fine*," advised Melissa Claremont, as she approached Minnie Chu, herself carrying the U.S. leader, plus his wounded daughter. "That's what ah had to do, when ah first learned to fly. 'Sides… wid them clouds up here, y'all can hardly tell how far up we is."

"I will try to remember this advice," answered Gebirgen. "And thank you very much, for rescuing me, Ms. Claremont. When this is all over, I will invite you to see my country as my guest – hopefully, under better circumstances than what we have encountered, today."

"Don' let it get y'all down bajiggity," counseled the teenager, with a cheery smile. "Y'all hook up wid Angel Lady – like ah did, back Idaho' way – an' *strange* shit got a way of catchin' up wid y'all. Jus' don' let it trip y'all none… that's what ah do."

"Uhh… undoubtedly," politely responded the Chancellor.

They were now within hailing-range of Chu and her coterie of hangers-on.

"Mr. *Chancellor!*" called the President. "Are you hurt?"

"No – but I owe my *life* to this young lady," relied Gebirgen. "Another second or so, and I would have been… well, I am sure that you are aware of the situation down there. What about yourself, sir?"

"Pretty much the same," remarked the U.S. leader. "Obviously, I'm shaken-up – and I'm worried for Clairie, who got hit protecting me –"

"I'll *live*, Daddy," interjected the daughter, "Just don't ask me *how*. Where they shot me, it feels – uhh, *hot* – like, I can hardly touch it with my fingers – but the swelling's going down. And the bruises are *way* smaller. It's no fun, but better than getting killed, I guess."

"Welcome to the New People, little sister," beamed a gratified Minnie Chu.

"Thank God for *that*," said the President, "But about Kathy and Matt… they *fell* – I can only hope…"

"I'm sure they'll be alright, sir," deflected Chu. "Someone would have, uhh, *caught* them –"

"They might be lying down there, badly-injured, or..." argued the President. "We've got to go back to get them out!"

"Sir – with all due respect – that'd be *madness!*" protested Chu. "A few minutes ago when we were above the White House, we were attacked by assailants whose numbers, equipment and motivation, we can only guess at. At least one of them – the guy with the power-suit – may even have the ability to go invisible, so he'd have an excellent chance of getting the first shot at us. I will *not* return you to that unsafe situation and thus put your life at great risk! What we need to do is to get you to somewhere out of harm's way. Didn't somebody say something about a 'Secondary Refuge', where you could direct operations, from a secured facility?"

"Yes, but it's in Fort Belvoir, ten miles from here," explained the U.S. leader. "It will take too long to get there and get set up. Blair House is secured, it has a strong bunker and it's almost right below us. Take me down there, *immediately!*"

"But Mr. *President* – that's right *across* from the White House – what if –" pleaded the *nouvelle* FBI-director.

"That's an *order!*" he insisted.

"For the record, sir," stated Chu, "I think this is a *very* bad idea… but, you're the boss. I'll have to fly us off to the west a bit, then drop down to as low an altitude as we can manage, without risking running into overhead power-lines or whatever. The fewer 'hostiles' who see us arriving at Blair House, the better."

"Agreed," confirmed the President. "One more thing."

He turned to address Gebirgen.

"Mr. Chancellor – we can have you flown over to Fort Belvoir… or to Andrews, if you'd prefer – uhh, young lady over there – am I correct in assuming you can do that?"

"Fly y'all to th' South Pole an' back, if'n y'all fwuntoo," bluffed Melissa. "But ah ain't shore it a good idea, goin' to no Army base. Last time ah did somethin' like that – over th' White House – they done shot me up good. Try that 'gain, an' ah promise y'all, it gonna turn out *different* – ah gonna make it some hot! Y'all jus' aks them Air Force fighter-pilots, all 'bout that!"

"If I am correctly understanding my airborne friend's jargon," offered Gebirgen, "She does not believe it advisable to approach a U.S. military installation without pre-clearance and without some way of identifying herself. In the short term, acquiring all that appears to be impractical… so if you will allow me to accompany you to Blair House – which is where my family is staying for this visit to America, in any event – that would be my preference. Is this permissible?"

"Of course," answered the President, "But Minnie's right – there *is* a risk, in us going there. We might be going right back into a shooting-gallery. I'm only doing it to save my wife and son. Do you understand?"

"Perfectly," said the Chancellor. "My wife and daughter are also down there. I hope that they are already in your bunker... but I would like to know for sure."

The President shot a stern glance at his FBI understudy.

"Let's *go!*" he demanded.

The eyes of the former team-leader were glowing, as she called out to Melissa Claremont.

"Sister," said Chu, "*Follow me, with* Amaiish *at full-bore – and be ready!*"

A serious-looking nod from Melissa provided confirmation, and downward they plunged.

All He Wants, Is A Little Company

The wary Chief of Staff had whispered to the nearby Agent Jackson, the other Service agents and Marine guards, "Let *me* try handling this asshole... but be ready to fire at the drop of a hat, if things go south."

Now, an angry and frustrated Kaysten shot a hostile stare at the combat-suited, Johnny-Come-Lately assassin standing in the western half of the room.

"I don't know who the hell you *think* you are," challenged the Presidential adviser, "But you'd better get *out*, while the getting's good!"

"Oh, *really* – Mr. Jerry Kaysten... isn't it?" sneered the man in the SWAT-suit. "And just *who* is going to stand in my way, now?"

"That'd be *me*," riposted Kaysten. "Want an idea of what I'll do to protect the First Lady and her son? Look all around! I've got four to my credit – want to be the fifth? And how you know my name?"

I can't see jack shit past that helmet and visor, reflected the Chief of Staff,

But somehow, I know that I know this guy... just got to figure him out...

"Let's just say, 'I've made your acquaintance before, in happier times'," answered the electronically-distorted and -amplified voice. "As for these bodies on the floor, well... when you're fighting a necessary war, a few casualties are inevitable. Now... I see you've got a few bum-buddies backing you up, over there. Let's even things up a bit... shall we?"

There was no apparent movement from the leading-assassin; but the moment he stopped speaking, there was an sharp explosion behind him, just to the west of where Kaysten had sealed the breach in the south wall. Yet another hole was opened in that wall, and through it poured five intruders of the sort that the Chief of Staff had just defeated.

Worse was to come, because at the same moment, another four more jumped in through the smashed windows facing the North Lawn; although, oddly, Kaysten could hear that at least one more prospective intruder had been shot dead while climbing up the side of the building, outside.

Doesn't make sense, he mused,

Service and Marines would all be deployed in here... and they certainly wouldn't be firing random shots at the White House without authorization... which the Old Man can't have granted.

Why the hell are they shooting their own guys?

The reinforcement-assassins had their auto-rifles deployed and pointed squarely at Kaysten, the Secretary of State, Susan Feldner, Jackson, the First Lady and her son (Matt seemed to be slowly coming to, although he was clearly still unable to move or fight); and had they opened fire, the other Service agents and Marine guards in the corridor between this room and the Press Briefing room, would undoubtedly also have been easy targets.

Yet – despite the fact that they clearly could have done so – the intruders refrained from unleashing an immediate massacre. Instead, they merely remained at the ready, while the guy in the combat-suit kept talking.

"*You* over there!" he called out, pointing at the First Lady, "Make a *move*, and I'll order my friends here," – he motioned to the right and to the left – "To open fire. We can end your lives in a *second*... which would be a shame, considering that I want that privilege all to myself –"

"Maybe they *can*," coldly remarked the Chief of Staff, "But if they *do*... you'll be the next to die, by my own hands. One hundred per cent guarantee, jackass!"

"To do that... you'd have to outrun a *bullet*," taunted the SWAT-suited man. "A few *dozen* of them, in fact."

"Guess *what*, asshole?" countered Kaysten. "You're looking at the only person on the *planet*, who can *do* that. Okay – one of the only two. Go ahead – *try* me!"

The other guy fell silent for a second or two, as if he was thinking something through. Eventually, however, he said,

"Well, Mr. Kaysten – as much as I'd like to liquidate both you and Clark's smug little society-girl over there, right here and now... I'm a patient man, and given that you all over there are now my prisoners – and that I can kill you all with just a gesture to my soldiers – I have only four modest demands to make of you today."

"I have no authority to commit the government to do *anything*," argued the Presidential adviser, "But just out of idle interest... what's on the old bucket-list for today?"

"Don't *push* me!" warned the leading assassin. "But because I know you're lying about what orders you can issue – given that you're the most senior Administration official present, and that the Vice-President seems to no longer be with us – here's what I want."

Sullenly, Kaysten – and the others – listened, as the man counted out his demands.

"One," said the guy in the combat-suit, "Those guards you have over there must disarm – they're to throw all their weapons over to this side of the room. Two, you need to get Clark here, by himself – no tricks, especially, I don't want to see that 'Chu' woman anywhere in the vicinity – in front of me within thirty minutes, and I'll let dear Kathy there, go her merry way. Three, once he's here, get the alien's so-called 'family' – that is, Bob Billings, the little girl and the Indian-boy – in here, no more than a half-hour later. Last but certainly not least, tell that bitch named 'Karéin-Mayréij' to show up, but to wait outside the room, in no less than thirty minutes after that. Do all of the above and I'll let the rest of them – including yourself – vacate the premises. Fail on *any* demand – or try *any* funny-business – and I'll shoot these people, one by one, every ten minutes, until Clark smartens up. *Got* it?"

"This is *insane!*" protested Kaysten. "The President will *never* agree to anything like that! And besides – we've got no idea where the Storied Watcher and the rest of them, even *are*... she flew off with them some time ago, saying she had 'business elsewhere', or words to that effect. She *might* come back... but we've got no idea when or where – nor do we have any way of communicating with her. She hasn't been on the best of terms with the government lately, you know. We have *zero* control over her."

"Oh... *please*," complained the leading assassin, "You expect me to *believe* that horse-shit? I *know* better, from my own sources!"

"Look," persisted the Chief of Staff, "Suppose that the President plays along with you, and then Karéin miraculously drops in to use the bathroom, or whatever. Do you *seriously* think you'll be able to order her around, just because you're totin' that gun? Use your *brains*, man! This is a creature that shatters comets for breakfast and that eats H-bombs for lunch, and no, I *don't* want to know what's on her dinner-menu. The best outcome you'll get, is for her to shred that funky combat-suit you're wearing into confetti, and then pick your mind apart, neuron by neuron. The worst one is, well... you *don't* want to know. What I'm saying is... you can't possibly *succeed* here!"

"Leave that challenge to *me*," calmly responded the masked man. "But be assured – when the time comes... everything will be nice and ready."

There was a smug confidence about the manner in which this was said, that unnerved not only Kaysten, but indeed all the others who he was trying to protect.

The stone-faced Chief of Staff fell silent for a couple of seconds, as he silently pondered his options.

I want to tear this fucker limb from limb, he considered,

But something tells me he has a plan... and he's already stage-managed a successful assault on one of the most heavily-guarded buildings on the face of the Earth. So I have to assume he knows what he's doing.

And about outrunning bullets – well, yeah, maybe that's a bit of a stretch... but if I pull the Fire up to full-speed and move there, and there, and then there –

Yeah, I'll dodge them, and then I'll get the drop on Mr. Loudmouth... but if I do that, the rest of them can't miss the First Lady, her son, Susan and the Secretary of State.

She said something about "you cannot let the luxury of your powers, blind you to the vulnerability of those under your protection"... didn't she?

Why does she have to be so bloody right, all the time?

"As I said," interrupted the man in the SWAT-suit, "I'm a patient man... but my patience has *limits*. You'll communicate my demands to the President in the next minute – and I have a clock running to keep precise time – or my men will start shooting. Starting, with that boy over there. You now have sixty seconds."

I can't take chances here, realized Kaysten.

Not with Matt's life, and not with us as outnumbered as we are, with the civilians in jeopardy.

I've got to wait for an opening...

"For God's *sake*," protested Kaysten, "Give us a little *time!* Most of the White House's telecom-systems are off-line, thanks to your private army turning this place into a shooting-gallery! There's nothing in here that we could use, anyway –"

The SWAT-suited guy looked around the room, but he didn't reply for a second, as if he were checking a reference-source not visible to everyone else. Eventually he said,

"I'll have to concede, that much is true... we'll have to move to somewhere with working communications. I happen to know there's one such set-up, just outside the Oval Office. Now I need the guards to hand over their guns, and the hostages to line up, single-file, as we travel back through the West Wing. Remember – the first one who fails to fully cooperate, will be the first one to get a bullet through his head. *Got* it?"

Never taking his eyes off of his interlocutor, Kaysten spoke, loud and clear, "This is an order from the Chief of Staff, acting on behalf of the President, to the Secret Service and the Marines. Guys, I feel the way that all of you probably do about this, but we're outnumbered and in an exposed position here... we can't risk the lives of the First Lady, her son, the Secretary of State and Ms. Feldner. Do as he says – disarm. Toss your weapons over to him."

There was angry dissension immediately evident among the guards.

"Mr. Kaysten," one of them was heard to say, "If we do that, we'll be at this guy's *mercy!*"

"I *know*," grudgingly acknowledged the Presidential adviser. "But better to live and fight another day."

"By the way," unhelpfully added the lead-assassin, "I have a second strike-force outflanking you all, to the east... not to mention many more just outside these walls. You're completely surrounded! Should you little Service and Marine boys try to resist, not only will dear Kathy here die in the next second, but you'll all follow her shortly after that. You had better *listen* to what your Chief of Staff is saying. *He* knows when he's outgunned!"

"Unfortunately, sir," whispered one of the Marine guards to Kaysten, "He's right about that... we've got terrorists behind us, in the Press Briefing Room. My guys have them stopped – but – uhh – there's something you should know –"

"Shit... okay... understood," answered the Chief of Staff, *sotto voce*. "Tell me the details later, if you don't mind."

"But *sir* –" persisted the guard.

"Not *now!*" snapped Kaysten. "We yank this jerk's chain, and a lot of innocent people are going to *die!* We've got to wait at least until Minnie gets back here."

"*Do it!*" he ordered, out loud.

"I'll give you ten seconds," said the assassin. "Hands on heads when we move; they come down – you'll be shot dead, with no further warning! My men all have grenades – which they'll drop instantly, if anyone tries to intervene!"

After a couple of seconds of delay, one by one, the remaining White House guards unhappily removed pistol-holsters and handed over a couple auto-rifles.

The SWAT-suited guy addressed his followers.

"Bind their hands behind their backs and march them to the corridor behind the Oval Office," he directed. "Stay away from the windows."

As the hostages were arrayed, Kaysten walked over to the lead-assassin, just out of arm's-length, and remarked,

"You'll never get *away* with this, you know. When Karéin shows up –"

"Why... Mr. *Kaysten*," interrupted the combat-suited guy, "Whoever said anything *about*, 'getting away'?"

It's "Us"... Reluctantly

A perplexed and deeply-worried Brent Boyd turned to Tanaka and whispered, "You figure out what's going *on*, over there?"

She shook her head.

"Mars ears got *pieces* of it," she explained, "*Vîrya Sài'ymë* has a bit more. She thinks one of those talking is Jerry Kaysten, and there's another

one whose voice-print closely matches her records of the Agency-director...
although it's being electronically-distorted, somehow –"

"Any voices of people who we know... like Minnie, Hector, or
whoever?" inquired the former Mars mission pilot. "What about the
President, or that German guy?"

"Just Jerry, as far as we can tell," stated Tanaka. "I'm not hearing either
the President or the Chancellor, but there's another voice... no, two... first
one sounds like the First Lady... second one might be Feldner... remember,
she's the Press Secretary. Hold on – more coming in..."

To their mutual alarm, the three more-than-humans (plus the bio-
mechanical breastplate) heard the noise of an explosion somewhere to the
west; but contrary to expectations, this was not immediately followed up with
sounds of a fire-fight, although one or two more random rifle-shots from
outside, did enter the next room.

The former Mars mission science officer cast her gaze downward, as if
concentrating. She stayed silent for quite a long time.

"An argument's going on," she finally spoke. "Somebody's talking about
'demands'... yeah, that's Jerry's voice, for sure... *uh-oh...*"

"'Uh-oh', *what?*" asked Wolf.

"Kaysten just ordered the Marines and the Service guys to hand over
their weapons," mentioned Tanaka. "Whoever he's dealing with, must have a
lot of firepower... sounds like he's got guns trained on Jerry and whoever
he's with. *Vîrya Sài'ymë* thinks she heard a demand like, 'surrender the
President, or I'll kill'... or words to that effect. How can he *do* that, if the guy
isn't even *there*? Wait a minute... what's *that?* Huh? We're – *what?* Oh,
yeah... oh-kay, I suppose *that* makes sense, from their point of view..."

"Cherie," queried Boyd, "Give us a little more *detail*... remember, we
can't 'hear' your – uhh – 'child', there –"

"Oh... of course," she apologized. "The two of us were just able to
overhear one of the Marine guards warning Jerry, that there are a bunch of
'terrorists' to the east of them... that'd be *us*, I guess."

"Say *whaat?*" responded a surprised Boyd. "Oh... right... yeah – I see
your point. But he's got it all wrong! Unless Commander Jacobson jumped in
there and threatened to kill whomever Jerry's guarding – which I highly
doubt – they've got us confused with the *real* terrorists. What a goddamn
mess!"

"Well," proposed Wolf, "If that's the case... why don't we play the part?
Catch 'em by surprise, and blast 'em to Kingdom Come –"

"Oh, *sure*," sarcastically countered the former Mars mission pilot,
"That's just a fuckin' *great* idea! Any one of us, not to mention the
Commander, could level the entire West Wing, if we used our powers to the
fullest – and we'd *certainly* kill everybody in the line of fire, possibly
including Jerry himself. Truth is... we may be the only ones capable of

rescuing whoever's with him, and that appears to include members of the First Family."

"Why do we even want to *do* that?" complained the bounty-hunter. "What's in it for *us?* Or have you forgotten what that fucker was *doin'* to us, not two weeks ago?"

Boyd hung his head.

"I honestly don't have a good answer for you on that," he admitted. "Speaking only for myself... a sense of *duty*, maybe? I don't expect you to understand."

"You're right... I *don't!*" grunted Wolf. "And anyway – where the fuck's Minnie? Isn't it *her* job to protect the President?"

"Given that the President doesn't appear to be there, she's probably doing exactly that," commented Tanaka. "Just a sec... *Vîrya Sài'ymë* is saying that the hostages are being herded out of there... it sounds like the destination is the Oval Office, or somewhere in that area. She's also noticed that some of the terrorists are carrying 'bombs'. Which means, if we don't neutralize every last one of them, before they set them off..."

"Figures," offered the bounty-hunter. "Wouldn't bother *me* too much, and I'd wager that both of you have shrugged off bigger shit... but not too great for all them civilians."

"Yeah," bleakly agreed Tanaka.

"Whoever the hell it is, who's stage-managing this siege," observed Boyd, "God only knows what he's got planned... but I'd bet you good money that it ain't gonna to be too pleasant. Listen, folks – I'm going in. It's fine by me if you two want to just hang here and cover the rear-flank, maybe wait for the Commander to drop back in, and so on –"

The former Mars science officer – her face wearing a broad, knowing smile – tapped Boyd on the shoulder.

She said, with a half-suppressed giggle, "Now, *now*, Brent... you expect me – uhh, sorry, Little One, 'us' – to just sit here and get *bored* to death? I didn't even bring a good book to read!"

After a second or two of hesitation, the bounty-hunter spoke up.

"Fine, *fine*... fuck it anyway!" he grumbled. "Keep you two out of trouble. Or make it double, when and if you get into it. But I got no idea how you're gonna sneak up on the fuckers, considerin' that the place is *crawlin'* with 'em."

"Neither do I," disclosed the ex-astro-pilot. "What I wouldn't give to have Karéin – or Sylvia – or I'd even take Billings – here with us. Well... when the time comes, we'll at least have cover of darkness."

"Until it gets lit up, 'bright red'," ominously mentioned Wolf.

"If it has to get lit up," replied Boyd, "You can be sure you'll see a lot more than, 'just red'."

The bounty-hunter nodded in acknowledgment.

"Works for *me*," he agreed.

"They're leaving that corridor," announced Tanaka. "We can tail them… but we'll have to stay low going across the room, to avoid getting hit by gunfire from outside. I'll keep my force-field as wide as possible… stay close. No war-songs, if you can possibly manage it. Ready?"

"Told Little Miss Hotfoot to can it," remarked Wolf. "And she's the only girl who ever really listens to anything I say. I'm ready."

The former Mars science officer rolled her eyes.

"Ready," echoed Boyd.

An almost-invisible, spherical, soap-bubble-like *something*, appeared over the three more-than-humans, as Tanaka said,

"Let's go."

Two For An Abrupt Introduction

"Damn good to be working with you again, Hector," whispered Jacobson, as the two followers of the Storied Watcher – crouching low upon what was left of the roof of the White House West Wing – surreptitiously observed the goings-on, below.

The two were observed with astonished, half-suspicious stares by the few remaining White House guards who were taking cover in this place, although none of the latter saw fit to actually fire at either of the more-than-human men. The government-employees were more interested in developments elsewhere; there were signs of some kind of high-intensity battle – resulting in several large fires, apparently on the verge of going out of control – in and around the buildings just north of Lafayette Square.

"Happy to oblige," responded the former JPL scientist, speaking as quietly as he could do, considering the gunfire that was still incoming from both the north and south. "Thank goodness you grabbed that second helicopter, just in time… I tried telekinesis to slow it down, but I didn't get a clean lock, and I *had* to stop the first one. I didn't see where Melissa went, but hopefully she'll be back soon. I *did* see Minnie fly off somewhere – she had a number of people hanging on her. Are there any other members of your team, nearby?"

"Otis is protecting our families back in the East Wing, and bunch of others, led by Sylvia, Will and Misha, were supposed to be over by the North Lawn – I'm not sure what's going on with them. Brent, Cherie and Wolf are down there in the White House, in the next room to the east," disclosed Jacobson. "But the White House guards had them under fire, supposing they're 'terrorists'."

"I can sort of understand why," remarked Ramirez, with a wry smile. "Listen, Commander… who *is* that guy – the one in the combat-suit, I mean?

I hit him dead-on with a lightening-discharge that should have *killed* a normal man! How can he possibly still be operational?"

"I don't know," said Jacobson, "But that's some very advanced, mil-spec gear that he's wearing… I doubt you could just order it off Neo-Net. Brent and I also ran into another one who looked the same, a short while ago – let me tell you, it was anything *but* easy fighting that guy… took all of our tricks to finally overcome him. All this probably means, there's part of the government that's trying to *kill* its Commander-In-Chief. Not a good situation… don't you think?"

"No *kidding*," answered Ramirez. "What you – *whoa!* You see *that?*"

Reflexively dodging to avoid a random rifle-bullet, the former Mars mission commander did a double-take. He noticed that most of the sniper-fire now seemed to be coming from the south; it had almost ceased, from the north.

"Shit… yeah," he confirmed. "Maybe Jerry *could* have taken him on – especially if we dropped in to help," he observed, "But I'm counting eight – no, nine – more of the bastards, who just came in through those windows… they shot at me when I dropped off the 'copter. If Jerry's protecting civilians and there's a fire-fight, there's a good chance they'll be killed in the cross-fire. Can you hear what's going on down there, any better than I can?"

The ex-scientist concentrated for a few seconds and then mentioned, "Something about 'get the President', I think… hard to make out, with all this noise. Oh, wow – now the White House guards are surrendering their weapons, and they're lining up. Commander – we can't just stand around here, watching this happen! What you want to do?"

"I'm *thinking*," said Jacobson. "We're dealing with a hostage situation – see that woman? That's the First Lady, and I think it's her son – what's his name, 'Matt' – by her side. We could try to get the jump on the guy in the combat-suit… could you knock the rest of 'em off-stride with that hurricane of yours?"

"Sure," answered Ramirez, "But I'd hit the hostages, too. If I ran it at high enough power to incapacitate a terrorist, it might injure or kill an ordinary civilian. I was also thinking of transmuting their grenades into something inert, but that ability requires touch. If I missed one or two of them…"

"Yeah," glumly acknowledged the ex-astronaut. "It burns me to just watch them get herded out of there, but at least until we can catch that guy in the combat-suit off-guard – maybe, separate him from his foot-soldiers – we've got to tread very carefully. However… I was thinking…"

The former JPL scientist turned his head to look right at Jacobson, saying, "What?"

"Well," answered Jacobson, "As we saw, around nine of the buggers went into that room, to reinforce the guy in the suit… but that still leaves quite a few more of them outside. Did you see how they're slowly moving west, too? But they're keeping their heads well down, to avoid being shot by whoever-the-hell-it-is. We may not be able to safely engage the terrorists *inside* the White House... but as to the ones forming the defensive-perimeter *outside*..."

There was an evil-looking smile on his face. It was accompanied by a dim glow in the back of his eyes.

"Want to have a little fun, kickin' some big-time ass?" proposed the former Mars mission leader.

Ramirez' own eyes were also starting to shine, as he insouciantly replied, "I guess they already meet you on the north side... so why don't I get to know them a little better? You can introduce yourself to the ones in the south."

Jacobson nodded and started counting,

"Three... two..."

A breeze – ramping up fast, to a gale – started blowing, from nowhere.

Going Over Their Heads

A frustrated Sylvia Abruzzio – accompanied by Hendricks – stood in front of the three-deep detail of Marine, Army, Secret Service and Park Police guards. The latter were reinforced by a large number of armored personnel carriers, armored cars and even a couple of tanks, arrayed all around Blair House.

The two more-than-humans hadn't been able to get any closer on foot than the junction of 17th Street NW and Pennsylvania Avenue, and getting even this far had taken all available guile.

The Wades, plus Sammie and two other civilian victims of the shoot-out that had wounded Callum Wade, had decamped in the back a blood-soaked, crowded ambulance.

It was cold comfort that the other evacuees were far worse off than was the ex-farmer; one victim expired *en route,* and the other was missing two fingers and an entire leg, in addition to having been shot in the thigh.

Meanwhile, the Russian – reasonably concerned that his presence would do nothing to advance Abruzzio's cause – had been left in the outside patio of a coffee-shop further up the avenue, with instructions to await the return of the Wades. Wary of a repeat of what had befallen Tanaka and Abruzzio back in Pittsburgh, he sat with his back against the building's outside-wall, while constantly scanning the surroundings for signs of danger.

He had also initially balked at being left (nominally) in charge of the three alien-powered, blood-splattered dogs; however, "Rainbow" seemed to have Wolf's two hell-hounds relatively settled down, and Misha had finally relented with the comment, "of course… if they fly off and set another few buildings on fire, do not expect *me* to show up with a water-bucket".

When queried by inquisitive bystanders about "is that *smoke*, comin' from that-there dog's nose?", the ex-SVR-agent showed a sly smile and deflected with, "It is a special, genetically-modified breed that we only have in Israel… do not tell me, that you do not have them here? And I thought that everything was so much more – ahh – *advanced*, here in America!"

"*Listen*, man," pleaded the third agent, "I'm Will Hendricks of the FBI – okay, I *was* from the Bureau, long story there – and I've got some very important information about the terrorists for Director Chu, to whom I directly report! You've *got* to let me in!"

"That goes equally for myself," supported the former JPL scientist. "My name is Sylvia Abruzzio and I'm a personal friend of Minnie Chu, not to mention of the President himself. We *saw* her and him fly in to Blair House, along with a number of others – so we *know* they're in there, somewhere. We have *vital* intelligence information for the President! You need to put us in touch with them, *immediately!*"

"Ma'am," stolidly responded one of the Marine guards, "*Surely* you must understand, that even if the President or Director Chu *were* here, we couldn't confirm that even under *normal* circumstances – and we have an ongoing terrorist attack at the White House. You should go home – this entire area is *dangerous*, not to mention, off-limits! Haven't you been watching the *news* lately?"

"No," riposted Abruzzio, "Actually… Will and I have been too busy *making* the news. For example, one of the members of our party jumped the fence and went inside the White House, a few minutes ago. The only reason that Will and I didn't do the same, is that we had *civilians* to protect."

"What's *that* supposed to mean?" asked the guard. "Forgive me, Ma'am," he offered, "But you don't look much like a terrorist, to *me*."

Considering her attire – looking every bit like the modestly-dressed librarian visiting D.C. – the observation could easily have been believed.

"*Don't* I?" countered the former JPL scientist, with a contemptuous tone. "Did I mention that both Will here and I are also close confidantes of the Storied Watcher, and that we both have extra-human abilities – like those of Director Chu?"

The Marine rolled his eyes.

With a sigh, he quipped, "*Sure* you do, Ma'am… like I'm Mighty-Man, and my buddy Bobby here's Santa Claus."

He looked over his left shoulder and called out, "That *right*, Bobby?"

"You *bet*," played along another Marine. "And y'all better be a good boy – no more knockin' back that Tennessee moonshine all week-end – or no more presents under the tree for *you!*"

Both guards cracked up laughing, at this *bon mot.*

Abruzzio turned to address Hendricks.

"Will," she remarked loudly enough to be heard for ten feet in any direction, "Do you think these nice army guys would try to shoot at us, if we, say, dropped in on Blair House, directly from above?"

At equal volume, the third agent replied, "I don't know if they're stupid enough to try something like that against two super-human people like us, who can blast them into next week, with just an idle thought. Be such a *shame* if you had to, like, radiate them into an overdone TV-dinner. If I were them, I'd take the *easy* way out – I'd hope for Agent Hendricks makin' it gnarly quick with a few fireballs or lightening-bolts."

"Want me to carry you, as we fly right over our friends' heads, and show up on the roof over there?" she continued.

"No *way!*" he demurred. "Did I mention that I've graduated from just levitating? I may not be able to fly as well as you or Minnie... but I'm more than good enough to do the few hundred feet over to that rooftop. Even throw in a bit of evasive, as a matter of fact."

Initially, these comments garnered nothing more than bemused smiles on the part of the military guards; but the smirks quickly turned to looks of consternation and alarm, as the eyes of the two more-than-humans began to glow and as their war-songs intertwined in some indescribable way.

Just before she lifted off, Abruzzio again directly addressed the guards.

"Will's got a great sense of humor, you know," she warned, "But raise those guns against us, and what will happen... that won't be the least *bit* funny."

As the shocked soldiers looked warily on, two flew over their heads.

Mirages and Dogs

"Not now... *please!* I'm trying to deal with a *crisis* here!" complained the President, as he considered his options. He did not take his eyes off a large computer-generated, 3-D map of the White House, here in the middle of the bunker deep underneath Blair House.

Every route in to or outside of this refuge – especially the ones leading to tunnels connecting to the White House – was heavily-guarded, with blast-proof, corridor-blocking steel doors ready to drop, at the push of a button.

"Understood, sir," acknowledged the Secret Service agent, who had just appeared in the doorway leading to upper levels of the secondary residence. "We'll place the two intruders that I referred to, in custody... we'll interrogate them as soon as things calm down."

"If you don't mind my asking," interjected Chu, who – having abandoned business-wear altogether, in favor of a tight-fitting, black stretch-suit with multiple pockets and a belt – was also tied up in observing the virtual model of the White House.

"Just how did these 'intruders', *get* here, in the first place?" she complained. "That shouldn't have *happened*, you know – I'm concerned about the integrity of your defensive-perimeter."

"They... uhh... *flew* in, Ma'am," disclosed the agent in the doorway. "Landed on the roof, about two minutes ago."

"What do you *mean*, 'they flew in'?" incredulously demanded the *nouvelle* FBI-director. "Now the terrorists are *parachuting* in, or something? Why didn't you shoot them out of the sky?"

"Minnie," cautioned the President, "We need to concentrate on the matter at hand... my wife and son are in mortal *danger* over there!"

"Sorry, sir," apologized Chu. "But you remember how I was concerned about your personal safety, being this close to the scene of the battle –"

"Actually, Ma'am," said the Service agent, "They just... *flew*, all by themselves... from the street below. Kind of like you and that other lady did, carrying the President and the Chancellor, a few minutes back. There was this weird 'music', and –"

"*What?*" shot back a surprised Chu, as she stared at the guard. "Who – *names*, please!"

"Uhh... one of them's calling himself 'Hendricks'... the other's apparently 'Abruzzio' – said they had to talk to you –" mentioned the Service agent.

"Get them down here... *immediately!*" ordered the former team-leader.

Under any other circumstances, it would have been a serious breach of protocol for a subordinate government employee, to have greeted his superior with a tight hug; but in at least this case, Hendricks threw caution to the wind, upon being ushered in to the Blair House bunker.

"*So* good to see you again!" breathed Chu, as she slowly broke the embrace. "Where's Otis?"

"In the East Wing of the White House, last *I* remember," answered the third agent.

"He's *in* there?" stammered the *nouvelle* FBI-director. "But the place is under *siege!*"

"Forgive the French, Minnie, but... 'no *shit*'!" offered Hendricks. "I was outside with Brent, Sylvia, Misha, Sammie and the Wades, and then all of a sudden a bunch of snipers off to the north, past Lafayette Square, opened up hard on us. Callum Wade took a round to the chest – we managed to get him into an ambulance, but he's hurt *bad*. Listen – there's a lot more to tell you, but Sylvia and I have some important intel that you and the President need to hear."

The U.S. leader managed to tear himself away from consultations with his military and Secret Service advisers long enough to consult with the two.

"Ms. Abruzzio – nice to see you again," he greeted. "Minnie… I assume this is Mr. Hendricks, who you have told me about, previously?"

"Yes, sir, it is… I mean, I *am*," interrupted the third agent, as he extended a hand, which gesture was accepted by the President. "It's, uhh, an *honor*, sir."

"Skip the formalities," directed the U.S. leader. "If you've got information that we can use, please provide it immediately – we have a *crisis* ongoing in the White House, and we're running out of time to deal with it."

"What he means, Will," explained Chu, "Is that the West Wing – and maybe the rest of the building, too, we're not sure – has been taken over by a large group of very well-armed terrorists. Some of them are equipped with techno-combat-gear that we've never seen before. They've already murdered dozens of innocent people and they're holding the Chief of Staff, the First Lady and her son Matt, along with a number of other civilians, hostage. Their leader has issued an ultimatum –"

"Who the H *are* these guys?" asked the third agent. "Muslims… eco-freaks… Democrats… what? Who's their leader? What we got on him?"

"We're *very* short of good intel here," offered the *nouvelle* FBI-director. "The terrorists' leader hasn't identified himself and his demands were delivered privately, over an internal government channel; so far, the public only knows that there's shooting going on at the White House. But what he's asking for, is plenty bad – he's requiring that the President surrender himself in the next twenty minutes, or he'll start *killing* the captives."

"*Jesus*," gasped Hendricks. "Hold on – Kaysten's one of 'us', you know. Didn't he try to put up a *fight?*"

"Don't know," parried the acting Bureau director. "But judging from the lack of mental stress on the rest of us, he must be healthy, as far as I can tell."

"Minnie," asked Abruzzio, "Do we know where these terrorists – and the hostages – are located?"

"We're pretty sure they're somewhere inside the West Wing," answered the former team-leader. "But we don't know precisely where. We *do* know they're not in the Presidential Emergency Operations Center, which is under the East Wing… we still have video from there, and the entrances to it were sealed when the shooting started. Unfortunately, the terrorists may now be in control of the rest of the White House's systems, including alarms, sensors and safety-barriers; the underground passage-ways seem all to be blocked off. They also might have booby-trapped the doors and the elevators, and so on."

"*Wonderful*," muttered the third agent.

"Mr. *President*," remarked Abruzzio, "Of course you can't be considering giving in to these demands – right?"

"Of course I *can!*" countered the President. "The lives of my wife and *son* are at stake! We need a *plan*… and fast!"

"Will," asked Chu, "You said that Otis is already inside the White House… assuming he's okay, do you have any way of getting in touch with him, or with anybody else who we know?"

"'Fraid not," answered the third agent. "We all had mini walkie-talkie units, but there's something jamming the signals anywhere within a block of the place, in any direction. That also goes for Brent Boyd, who chased a bunch of the terrorists in there when the shooting started… and also for Tanaka, Wolf and Commander Jacobson, all of whom were with Otis in the East Wing. A lot of the family-members – like Jacobson's and Boyd's, for example – were in there with them. Which means, *they're* potentially in danger, as well."

"Wait a minute… what in God's name are all these people *doing* there?" queried an exasperated Chu. "I thought Sam and I had an *agreement!*"

"Long story," deflected Hendricks, "I'll fill you in on the details later, but what both you and the President need to know is, we had *nothing* to do with these 'terrorists' – it's just a coincidence that they showed up on the same day as we lined up for a White House tour. Anyway, Minnie – bottom line is, far as I know, we've got most of the 'Mars Gang', plus Otis, in there, *somewhere*. You've also got yourself, myself and Sylvia here, as assets."

"Add my little friend Warden, and Melissa Claremont to that," mentioned Chu. "She's been assigned to guard Chancellor Gebirgen, who's also here at Blair House. Although she's on strict orders to stay with him and fly him out of here, at the first sign of danger."

"Add *me*," chimed in the Presidential daughter, who had been sitting, with her legs up, on one of the leather-upholstered chairs in the bunker.

"Clairie… you were *shot*," cautioned the U.S. leader. "I let you stay down here and didn't force you to the hospital, over my better judgment, but –"

The teenager stood up straight to face her father.

There was a dim, but clearly-perceptible glow in her eyes, as she defiantly vowed, "I'm *fine* now, Daddy… and I'm going in to rescue Mom and Matt!"

"Honey," pleaded the President, "You *know* I can't risk –"

"He – they – can't *hurt* me," interrupted Clairie. "If that terrorist tries to kill Mom, or Matt… I'll kill *him*, *first!*"

A few of the more perceptive beings in this place, began to hear a new war-song – a bright yet somehow ominous one – playing in the background.

Abruzzio cast a long stare at the Presidential daughter.

Little sister, silently cautioned the former JPL scientist,

Karéin warned us all about this – Amaiish *is going to your head!*

I know that you feel *invincible, but you aren't* – at *least, not yet.*

I'll speak on your behalf so you can assist with whatever plan we agree on – but you have to trust me.

Do you trust me, Clairie?

The stare was met by an equally serious-looking one on the daughter's part, as her mind reached out and answered,

I trust you, Ms. Abruzzio.

Clairie then said out loud, "Did I do that right?"

"You sure *did*," replied the former JPL scientist, with a kindly chuckle. "You will be a mighty sister of the Holy *Fire* someday, Clairie; use your powers wisely. Oh... and call me 'Sylvia', whether verbally, or mind-talking."

"Can we discuss this later?" requested the President.

"Of course, sir," answered Abruzzio. "To round out the list of assets, we can also call on Rainbow and Wolf's two dogs. They – along with Will and Misha – took out a large number of other terrorists, north of H Street. We think that we got all of them... of course we can't be one hundred per cent certain. There's more to say about that, but we can leave it for later."

"I appreciate that, Ms. Abruzzio," said the U.S. leader. "The clock's ticking. I've asked the Service and the Marines for a plan, and they can certainly storm the building – but that's out of the question, given the circumstances. If we don't have an alternate approach in the next five minutes, I'm afraid my only option will be to surrender myself."

"I'm *thinking*, sir," quickly responded Chu, as she pondered furiously. But the outlook appeared bleak, based on the inadequate information she had on what was going on, in the West Wing.

"I heard that you, uhh, *flew* in here, Mr. Hendricks," commented the President. "I'm already familiar with most of Minnie's abilities, and those of Ms. Abruzzio and Miss Claremont. Do you have any other of these 'alien-powers', that might be useful in a hostage-rescue situation?"

"Sort of, sir," answered the third agent. "My personal *shtick* is to copy other peoples' powers... but they have to agree to let me camp on to 'em, first. So far I'm doing a decent – weaker – imitation of Tanaka's lightening-bolts and Wolf's flamethrower, and I'm working on Boyd's light-show. Also I have some telekinetic powers, and I seem to be bullet-resistant. Finally, I'm pretty good at hand-to-hand combat, so I'm sure I can take on a terrorist or two."

"Well," grunted the President, "That will certainly help... if we can get you a clean shot at them, without endangering their hostages."

"You *bet*, sir," replied Hendricks. "And I have no doubt that goes for Otis too... wherever he is."

"What are *his* abilities?" pressed the U.S. leader.

"I'll let him fill you in, himself," parried the third agent, "But, in general – he's a juggernaut, kind of like Commander Jacobson. He also has a ranged attack that's just – well – *lethal*, to anything in front of him, out to twenty feet or more. I'm sure he wouldn't use it in the White House, though... too much of a chance of hitting innocent people, and a few shots of it could bring down the whole *building*."

"I… *see*," said the President, with a grim expression on his face.

"Sir," interjected Abruzzio, "As little as I like proposing something so dangerous… I have an idea."

"Let's *hear* it!" demanded the President.

"Before I get started, sir," continued the former JPL scientist, "I need to be honest; what I have in mind may sound a little – ahem – *ambitious*."

"As long as it gets Matt and Kathy out of there, alive," said the President, "I don't care *how* crazy it sounds."

"Even if," pressed Abruzzio, "It all depends on a mirage… and a dog?"

Four Furry Spy-Paws

Though she had been growing up rapidly – as dogs do – this one wasn't particularly big; indeed, she could have been, and often was, mistaken for being just a puppy. Her almost-comical, calico coloring certainly didn't make her any the more imposing.

However she had been regarded by the strange-looking big dogs who walked on two legs, now, Rainbow crept cautiously on to the South Lawn of the White House, having been off-loaded from a well-armored limousine about a block away, after repeated instructions and a tearful hug by her master-cum-companion. The Russian was also present, as he had been alerted to the task-at-hand by a friendly visit on the part of two stern-looking Secret Service agents.

After a couple of doggie-steps, the animal seemed to disappear altogether; where she had been visible to human eyes, scant seconds previously, there was now only a faint distortion, as if someone had placed a virtual magnifying-glass over first the pavement of the South Lawn ring road, and then over the White House lawn-grass.

Gingerly, Rainbow moved forward; her innate senses detected the hidden land-mines and motion-sensors, and she contrived tactics to evade all of these.

To the west, there were two bad, black-suited men, huddled down behind trees on either side of the entrance to the South Portico. They seemed to be very apprehensive about something-or-other, as if worried that they would immediately be attacked.

One of these gendarmes stood up, brandishing his bang-stick, when the *ersatz*-puppy approached the entrance to the building. Rainbow instantly froze in place; but – after doing an apparent double-take and seeing nothing – at length, the terrorist shrugged and just returned to where he had camped out.

Still under her camouflage-shroud (now mimicking the appearance of polished marble floor-tiles and luxurious red carpet-coverings), the dog cautiously poked her black button-of-a-nose inside the building, taking note of the signs of recent mortal combat – and of the numerous dead human bodies, lying in grotesque final poses, everywhere.

The combined stench of gun-cordite, of poison-gas-remnants and of death in general, assaulted her senses, almost to the point of overwhelming her sensitive nose; but – mission ever in mind – she pressed on.

In big house... find nice Big Dogs... find bad Big Dogs... tell Mommy, reasoned the more-than-a-canine.

She was about to head for the Center Hall in the interior of the building – and had, in fact, almost reached the far end of the Diplomatic Reception Room – when, suddenly, she stopped and looked from side to side.

Rainbow saw the fire-scarred corpse of a black-suited terrorist, his upward-staring eyes and face frozen in a strange rictus of death, as if he had been killed by some fearsome weapon that had done its lethal work almost instantaneously.

The little dog casually paced over to the other side of the doorway leading to the Center Hall, until she was next to the dead intruder's face.

Need mark way back, came a thought, to the animal's enhanced mind.

She lifted her leg.

A Nice Kind Of Tomb

None of the publicly-available maps – indeed, not even those known to most of the U.S. government – showed the location of this bunker, deep underneath the West Wing of the White House, but Top Dog – accompanied by four of his subordinate gunmen – was not deterred.

Instead, he confidently ushered the First Lady and her son, accompanied by Jerry Kaysten and the crippled Secret Service agent, downward through a long set of spiral stairs, used his combat-suit's tricks to unlock all the barriers and then led the way to the erstwhile refuge.

The Secretary of State and Susan Feldner – along with several, tightly-bound-and-handcuffed Marine-guards and Service-agents, had been sent off, under guard, to the Situation Room.

Always have a spare set of hostages handy, mused the Agency-leader.

If you have to off them, the sounds of the gunshots won't lead to where you're hiding the crown jewels.

The trip had gone almost completely to plan, except for a couple of odd readings on the motion-sensors in two of the lower corridors, which had indicated the presence of a living object, supposedly the size of a small child. Top Dog's combat-helmet spectral-analyzers and radiation-detectors also threw a couple of alerts; yet – upon closer examination, and careful inspection of the affected areas – there was nothing to be found, stopped or killed. The only beings in these wide, fully-stocked hallways (piled floor to ceiling with survival-supplies, in places) were the Agency-director, his gendarmes and the hostages; this was plain for all to see.

Well, he reasoned,

I guess a few glitches are to be expected... given that we had to hack these intrusion-detection systems to grab control over them, in the first place.

After the hostages had been forced into the steel-and-concrete-reinforced, bank-vault-like chamber, Top Dog temporarily removed his combat-helmet and turned to address his captives.

Immediately, Kaysten's face wore a look of angry recognition.

"So it's *you!*" he snarled. "Fucking *figures!* The President *told* us – and the Storied Watcher, by the way – about your little scheme to off Karéin, by torturing and murdering her friends and family. That *almost* got the Old Man vaporized by Little Miss Nuclear Angel – but they've reached an understanding about it. She, he and we are *on* to you, asshole... and 'seeing *is* believing'."

Top Dog's face, for his part, just had a broad, cruel smile on it.

"Ooh... such *spunk*," he taunted. "Especially for somebody whose life I can snuff out, at the drop of a hat. But anyway... time's-a-wastin', and there are some things you need to know, about the pickle you now seem to be in."

Kaysten just stared forward for a second or two, as if he was straining to see something.

Out of the corner of my eye, down the corridor, by that big steel door...

The shadow of a dog?

Must have been my imagination... now it's gone...

All I see is a bunch of storage-boxes piled up on the side of the hall... thought I had counted all of 'em – but I guess I missed one?

After regaining his concentration, he said,

"You know... there *is* something I don't understand."

"And what would *that* be?" responded Top Dog, with mock pleasantness.

"Why'd you blow up the Airborne Command-Post?" inquired the Chief of Staff. "The President and I thought that George was your main man. What would you have to *gain* by smoking him, along with Blanchard, Warnock and the rest of them?"

"Oh... that was all *Crowford's* doing," explained the Agency-director. "I *do* give him credit for having had the right idea as far as the alien's concerned; but his execution – pardon the pun – was crude, at best... so I can't take any of the blame for the fiasco with the airplane. Messy, *messy* – no doubt about it!"

"You can say *that* again," ruefully agreed Kaysten. "As in, 'just about messed up the entire eastern half of the country.'"

"Well," offered Top Dog, "Play with dynamite without knowing what you're doing – that usually ends badly. But truth be told... I've had to pick up the pieces left over by Mr. Crowford's amateur-hour-show, for *weeks* on end. For example... all those snipers at either end of the White House lawn – I can *assure* you, they don't answer to *me* – so I'd have to assume that they're kind of Harold's parting-shot, from the great beyond. But it's all good... once I'm finished with my business *here*, I'll get around to dealing with *them*. A little tough love, you might say – after all, can't have people with *guns*, not following orders from legitimate authority... don't you *think?*"

The irony of Top Dog's point was not lost on Kaysten, as he answered, "Can't have *that*... but what's the point of sticking us down here?"

"So... the Agency's pretty much the only part of the government, other than for the Service, the Joint Chiefs and the Commander-In-Chief himself, who know about this place," mentioned the director. "The PEOC's just there for office-parties and to distract idiot civilians into thinking that they know where the President goes, when the shit hits the fan. Oops! Sorry for my colloquial there. Always happens when I get *excited*, you know."

A glowering Kaysten was about to step forward, but was deterred by the sight of four assault-rifles pointing directly at himself, the First Lady and Matt.

"For the record... *I* knew about the Secondary Bunker, too," he snapped. "And you'll never get *away* with this! When Karéin shows up, she'll –"

"My, *my*, Mr. Kaysten," chided Top Dog, with undisguised condescension, "Still crying out for 'Mommy' to come rescue us, are we? Well... leaving aside the fact that the alien has no way at all of locating you – and without giving away too much of the game – let me fill you in on a little secret about how I'm going to handle this 'Storied Watcher'... shall I?"

"What?" riposted the Chief of Staff. "Maybe you ate six cloves of garlic this morning, and you're going use bad breath or something, on her?"

The Agency director smiled and replied, "Oh... something a little more – ahh – 'potent' than *that*, I'm afraid. You've heard about 'Kryptonite'? I mean... I'm sure you've read your share of comic-books."

"What's he *talking* about?" whispered Matt, who had lately come around enough to stand – albeit, shakily – on two legs. "She ate an *H-bomb* –"

"No fucking *idea*," said Kaysten, *sotto voce*.

"See... ever since the fiasco back at that hotel in Tucson, I've had the Agency's best minds working on an 'antidote to the alien problem'," expounded Top Dog. "While of course you'll understand why I can't get into the details, let's just say that we have a high level of confidence, that when she's – excuse me, 'it's' – exposed to this nice little substance in the proper dose... this planet will be rid of the creature, once and for all."

"Is that even *possible?*" the Presidential son again whispered to the Chief of Staff.

"Theoretically... *anything's* possible," evaded Kaysten, below his breath. "That doesn't mean it's likely."

"*Look*, jackass," he challenged, "To say this is 'insane', would be the understatement of the *century*. Karéin has a personal force-field – if your intel's as good as you claim it to be, you surely know that already – that can shrug off a nuke, at close range. Fire a bullet or a rocket at her, shoot her with an arrow, it's all the same. Unless you plan to somehow get her to *eat* this 'substance', I don't know how your stupid idea gets past Square One. And all of this assumes that she'll even *show* – by no means a safe assumption, as I've told you before. So go ahead… do your worst, for all *I* care. My money's on Miss Nuclear Angel, all the way."

The Agency-director raised one hand, and immediately, the assault-rifles – with safety-locks clearly disengaged – were again pointed ominously in the direction of the hostages.

The First Lady quailed and crossed herself, although a stone-faced Kaysten, accompanied by Matt, just stood impassively in front of the Presidential spouse.

"If I were *you*, Mr. Kaysten," growled Top Dog, "I'd watch that motor-mouth of yours. Bound to get you in *trouble*, sooner rather than later."

The Chief of Staff did not reply.

"Now here are the facts," continued the Agency-director, "One, your lives depend on the Old Man, coming through, promptly and fully. If he *doesn't*… you won't get any further warning, when the time comes. Two, there's no way out of the bunker you're now standing in, except through the doorway between you and I… and *that's* built to resist overpressure from a few hundred kilotons, a quarter-mile away. Three, the outside of the doorway will be rigged with some nice little 'surprises', just in case somebody figures out some slick trick to open it without my personal authorization. Those are only the measures that I care to disclose… I'm sure you'll appreciate, there are more. And by the time I next see you – that is, if you're still alive – you can be sure that the alien will be *dead*."

"As *if*," volunteered Matt. "I *met* her, you know. So did Dad and Mr. Kaysten. You may think you're scary with all those guns, man… but you don't know the meaning of the *word*, until you've met Karéin up close. She can fucking *kill* people just by *looking* at them! It almost *happened* to Dad! You think you're gonna fight *that?*"

"Leave serious business to the adults," spat back Top Dog. "We're playing for *keeps* here, boy! Did you think I'd have tried something like this, without being completely sure of the outcome? And I know all about how the monster has taken complete mental control over your poor, incompetent father. If you have any respect for him… you'll *welcome* it, when I put a quick and merciful end to his life and free him from the nightmare he's now trapped in!"

"Matt," cautioned the First Lady, "Don't *provoke* him further!"

"Dad's *fine* – and you're fucking *nuts!*" defiantly responded the Presidential son, in Top Dog's direction. "The only thing I wonder about, is which one of the million ways that Karéin has to kill someone, that she'll use on *you*."

"You'd do well to remember my advice to dear Jerry here, regarding insolent tongues," hissed the Agency-director. "But anyway... I've got to go, so some parting observations. At least you'll be comfortable in there; the bunker's equipped with a microwave, a fridge, lots of food and drink, nice comfy furniture, and a bathroom, complete with a shower and towels. I hear there are even some board-games! Try to keep yourselves occupied – it'll help pass the time... and who knows how much time you have left?"

I might be able to do the ol' hundred-yard-dash out of here – maybe even off some of these goons he's got accompanying him, mused Kaysten.

But probably not a good idea to take him on, what with that combat-suit he's porting...

I'd have to scram, and that would leave the First Lady, Matt and the Service guy, all by themselves.

I damn well hate being so passive – but looks like there's no good alternative...

"I'll match mine against yours, any day of the week," he commented. "The minute you meet Little Miss Nuclear Angel, you'll be measuring it in *micro-seconds.*"

Top Dog turned to the four gendarmes who were accompanying him.

"You have your orders," he directed out loud, while re-positioning his combat-helmet. "They won't get out... but if somehow they do – or if some wannabe hero tries to rescue them – *kill* them, immediately! Is that *understood?*"

"Yes, *sir!*" bellowed the four, almost in unison.

He looked over his shoulder, while walking away.

"It makes a nice bunker, you know," he called back, to the hostages, "But it makes an even better tomb."

The door swung shut with a solid "thud".

They were trapped.

False Gods For Weak Men

"This is the Executive Office convoy speaking," came the amplified, highly-directional loudspeaker voice, from the armored limousine, as it slowly approached the North Portico of the White House. "Per agreement, the President will disembark as soon as we are next to the building. Do *not* engage... repeat, *do not engage* – or the deal is *off!*"

A grim-faced President stared out of the bullet-proof windows and observed that the two camouflage-suited terrorists who were guarding the entrance to the North Portico – though they had assault-rifles trained on the car in which he was riding – did not immediately open fire.

"Well," he spoke absent-mindedly, to no obvious addressee, "At least, their leader – whoever the hell that is – seems to have gotten the message."

"We'll be oh-kay, Daddy," supported the daughter, who was next to her father, in the back seat of the limo.

"I'm either stupid or insane – or both – to have let you come along, you know," he said. "All it's likely to accomplish, is for you to die along with your mother, your brother and I."

"*Nobody's* going to die, Daddy," countered Clairie. "I *promise!*"

"This is *real*, Clairie!" he tried to argue. "Real people get hurt... and worse. I have no doubt that he's planning to *kill* me, and if that's what it takes to save your mother and Matt, then so be it... but I can't handle losing *you*, too. Just stay in the car – *please!*"

"I will *protect* you," came back an unnervingly-confident-sounding reply.

The U.S. leader would have carried on his protests, but the vehicle had now reached the threshold of the North Portico. The rear, passenger-side door opened to provide access to the entrance-way, while the rest of the limousine provided a modicum of protection against sniper-fire from the north; although, in fact, no shots from that direction had been observed, for several minutes.

The President turned to the limousine's chauffeur.

"Tell the appropriate parties that we're here," he requested. "They know what to do."

"Be careful, sir," answered the Secret Service agent who was driving the vehicle. "Just got an update – we're still detecting gunfire in parts of the West Wing. Whatever's going on there... it isn't over yet. Could be some of our guys are still holding out, somewhere."

"Acknowledged," answered the U.S. leader. "Let's hope you're right... and may God protect them, if so."

He stepped gingerly out.

The President tried to immediately shut the car-door – hoping to pre-empt his daughter's next move – but the maneuver was to no avail; though Clairie had been too far over on the driver-hand-side of the limousine to have reached the door-handle, somehow, *something* very strong seemed to be preventing the car-door from closing.

In the next two seconds, the frustrated U.S. leader was joined by his offspring.

"You aren't going to obey me, if I order you back into the car," he complained.

"Sure aren't, Daddy!" she sweetly chirped back, taking hold of his hand.

"I love you," he responded.

They were almost in the doorway to the Entrance Hall, now. They were both horrified by what they beheld.

The room was scarred by numerous bullet-holes, had almost all of its windows either broken or shot out entirely, and was strewn with bloodied, mutilated corpses, including some dead intruders but more Secret Service agents and Marine-guards. There were also other, less-easily-understandable types of damage; small sections of walls and columns seemed to have been hit by thermal-attacks; the structures were charred and, in some cases, blown apart.

Clairie's face went white, as the magnitude of what she was getting herself into, hit her like the proverbial ton of bricks. Only a few days before, the impact of such a scene would have made her puke or faint; but now, something that she couldn't quite pinpoint, put steel in her spine.

Two heretofore-unseen terrorists – each brandishing pistols, pointed directly at the President and his daughter – stepped into the entrance-way.

"Our commander was expecting only one person – yourself," they challenged.

"This is my daughter, Clairie," answered the President. "She has asked to accompany me, and to escort my son and wife back, when I surrender myself to your leader. Clairie's no threat to anyone... like me, she's completely unarmed."

The two gendarmes hesitated for a moment; then one of them spoke up.

"Well, she's potentially another hostage, I suppose... you understand that there are no guarantees about what our commander will do with this young woman?" he ominously remarked. "And, of course... like yourself, she'll be thoroughly searched, before being allowed ingress to the interior of the building. If either of you attempts to resist or escape, we have orders to use lethal force. In that case, we will not *hesitate* to shoot!"

"My expectation is that she'll be allowed to, along with Matt and Kathy, per our agreement," declared the President. "It's only *me* that your leader wanted. The only thing that we have on us, is body-armor. If you have to remove it... go ahead."

"No guarantees!" repeated the terrorist.

The President did not respond. He sent a glance to his daughter.

"Well," he unhappily whispered, "Here we go."

After being subjected to a humiliating search – in which their Kevlar body-armor was fairly ripped off their bodies, along with every other thing that could have possibly functioned as a tracking-device – the President and his daughter were allowed to proceed onward. However, the trip to wherever the terrorist leader was been encamped, proved to be a circuitous one. Even just within the North Portico, the two gendarmes who were escorting the President and his daughter, forced their hostages to detour away from large areas of the room, for no apparent reason.

While this was ongoing, Clairie had tried to say, "Daddy… something smells really *wrong*, here,"; but she had been confronted by a glowering demand to cease talking.

Oddly, the terrorists did not direct the President and his daughter, in the manner that he had anticipated. Instead of just proceeding down the stairs to the Center Hall and the lower floor of the main White House building – thence, to the West Wing – they did a quick turn and were put in an elevator that – upon the discreet entry of a series of special codes – descended far below the publicly-known parts of the mansion.

They emerged into an well-lit, spotlessly-clean underground corridor wide enough to accommodate at least five persons, from side to side; the area was guarded by two more, gun-toting terrorists. The President recognized where he was, although the area was completely new to his daughter.

The sons of bitches have somehow got control over everything in the building, he silently realized.

The Service told me that the systems are all locked down with special computer-codes – only a select few – like poor Kortish, God rest his soul – are supposed to have access to them.

Whoever these guys are… they aren't a bunch of illiterate Muslim Salvation League savages – they must *have inside info, to have pulled this off.*

Who the hell's in charge *of all this?*

"This way!" ordered one of the men who had taken control over the two hostages, topside. The gendarme pointed to the west.

"This place gives me the *creeps*, Daddy," whispered Clairie.

"I don't blame you, dear," he answered, *sotto voce.* "They built it so I could get out of the White House, in case of nuclear attack."

"No – what I *mean* is… it weirds me out, in a funny way… like, how she *told* me it would," she said.

Clairie looked up at her father, right into his eyes.

His visage was one of wary surprise, as he saw the dim glow in her gaze; but he was relieved that none of the guards seemed to have noticed what was going on.

"Honey," he tried to caution, "You shouldn't let that –"

"No *talking!*" curtly reminded one of the terrorists.

Mutely, the daughter nodded her head. Her eyes were normal, now.

Holding Clairie's hand, the President walked forward, toward what he knew to be the catacombs underneath the West Wing of the White House.

At the end of a long walk to the west, the President and Clairie were ushered into a second elevator, which this time went upward, until it opened into more familiar surroundings; the U.S. leader recognized entrances to the

Vice-President's office to the left and to the office of the Chief of Staff, to the right.

The uncomfortable poke of a gun-barrel in the square of his back, signaled that movement was required, so the President, with his daughter by his side, turned south and then east, walking down Executive Mansion hallways that he had trod in much less stressful circumstances, many times in the past.

He thought that he heard the occasional rifle-shot, coming from somewhere to the south and impacting possibly near the Press Briefing Room, or thereabouts; but he couldn't see outside and thus couldn't really be sure.

I thought that being here with a couple of H-bombs about to be dropped on my head, was about as bad as it could get, he ruefully mused.

Or was it, perhaps, being stuck here trying to deal with an angry, godlike alien, who could disintegrate me just because she's having a bad day?

I was wrong... what's next?

Lord – I don't want to know!

"Neither do I, Daddy," whispered Clairie, without turning to address him. Luckily, none of the gendarmes appeared to have overheard her.

The two hostages did a half-turn to the left and north, and were now in the mini-corridor just to the west of the Oval Office. Therein, they saw six more terrorists of the type who were behind them. But there was another guy wearing the kind of combat-suit, complete with enhanced-technology motorcycle-helmet, that the President had seen very briefly in his recent trip upward, while hanging on to the body of a flying FBI-director.

An electronically-distorted, partially-amplified male voice accosted him.

"Ahh, Clark... so *nice* to see you back where you belong!" it taunted. "We had them do the DNA-tests back there, just to preclude the ol' 'stunt-double' trick. You passed with flying colors, so I'm sure that you, are 'you'. Welcome!"

"I don't believe we're on a first-name basis," evenly responded the President. "You're in charge here, I assume?"

"Very much so," answered the man in the combat-suit. "And who's *this*... your daughter? *Splendid!* Excuse the vernacular... but, 'my cup runneth over'."

"I'm just here for, like, 'moral support'... *sir*," Clairie tried to say, without allowing the anger she was feeling, to leak out into her words. "Dad's kept his side of the bargain – where's Mom and Matt?"

"Just like your brat brother – punching way above your weight," unctuously observed the combat-suited guy. "Well... you'll find out quickly enough, who calls the shots around here, I suppose."

"Is it too much to ask, for me to at least know who's behind all this?" requested the President.

"Kaysten feigned surprise," offered the man in the combat-suit, "So I'll expect nothing less from yourself."

His prediction was prescient, although the President did a good job of suppressing the reaction, upon seeing the face of the Agency-director, when the combat-helmet came off.

"Don't tell me – let me guess," managed the U.S. leader, through pursed lips. "*You* and Crowford were behind the little *putsch* to replace me with George... *weren't* you?"

"You give me too much *credit*, Clark!" deflected Top Dog. "Actually, that was originally *George's* idea... albeit enthusiastically supported by Bezomorton and a couple of others. I only camped on when it became clear that you were going to chimp out, on the whole business of dealing with the alien. We had an *agreement* about how to rid the planet of it, once and for all, and you reneged on it, *big*-time – remember? When you started to go easy on the monster, I had no choice but to act."

"I bailed on your damnable plan to torture and kill Karéin, when it became clear that – in addition to being morally disgraceful – it couldn't possibly *work!*" growled the President. "Unlike you, I've met her up close... and I can *assure* you – you're certifiably *insane*, if you think you can overcome her! If I hadn't changed course and tried to reason with her – oh, and with Jacobson too – we'd be standing in a pile of smoking rubble, right now. You don't understand what you're *up* against! I *do*."

"Oh... *please!*" sneered the Agency-director, "Did you think I didn't know about the cute arrangement that you had with Jacobson, that bitch 'Chu', and the alien itself? The Agency and the Palace were listening in to all of the conversations between the lot of you – we know *everything* there is to know, about your little conspiracy to hand the whole country over to them! You basically *admitted* as much – on national TV, none the less – in that press-conference you held with the Mars Gang and the alien all standing around as your chaperones, a while ago! For God's *sake*, Clark... you seem to be the only person on the *planet*, who doesn't realize how completely the alien has got you under its control –"

"You're fucking *crazy!*" incautiously interjected Clairie. "Dad's right about Karéin... she's not so bad when you get to know her – but trying to *kill* her is a really, *really* bad idea. And what's this shit about 'Dad's conspiring with Karéin, Minnie and Jacobson?' The Commander was 'this' far from trying to kill Dad himself – I was *there* – I *saw* it! You've got it all *wrong*, man!"

"So... you've met the alien too... would I be correct in assuming that, young lady?" inquired Top Dog.

"Damn straight," came back the sharp-tongued reply. "It didn't go very well at first, that I'll have to admit – Angel Lady was royally pissed when she first laid it out for Dad... but we all eventually made up. So *what?*"

"Oh... just that the monster's obviously got *another* little mindless drone under its control," claimed the Agency-guy. "Whoops! Correction : '*two* more drones', counting your brother, too. Oh well."

Clairie groaned and rolled her eyes.

"I give *up*," she sighed in the direction of her father. "This guy's drinking the Kool-Aid... big-time."

"One more thing, before you take me wherever you're planning to take me... just for the sake of completeness," requested the President.

"Now that we're in 'confessional-mode'," quipped Top Dog, "What?"

"Were *you* responsible for the second nuclear weapon – the one on the cruise-missile, that is – that was launched against Washington?" pressed the U.S. leader. "I don't see what you *possibly* could have had to gain, by slaughtering millions of innocent Americans. Or, for that matter, in trying to blow up the Command-Post, with George, Harold and the rest of them on it."

"Well, Clark," offered the director, in his usual, aggravating monotone, "You'll appreciate that neither are you in a position to demand that kind of intel... nor am I in one to disclose it. But let's just say that decisive actions had to be taken at the right time, to stop the criminal conspiracy between the alien, yourself, the Mars Gang and the alien's various other hangers-on. If things had gone according to the original plan, a lot of the collateral-damage would have been avoided... but, as they say – 'the best-laid plans of mice and men', right?"

While the President glowered, Top Dog elaborated,

"Oh, and as far as Crowford's concerned...I'm afraid that he and those Bible-thumpers of his, were kind of acting on their own; for example, they beat us to Billings' place in Tucson by mere *minutes*, and everything went south after that – if they had just kept their amateur noses out of our *business*, everything would have been kept under *control*! Later on, the Agency thought Mr. Crowford to be in on the conspiracy between you and the alien, but after he went on that shooting-spree on the airplane... well, we had to kind of adjust our evaluations. Considering how it all turned out, I guess we'll never know what dear old Harold had in mind... pity!"

The President maintained a reflective silence for a couple of seconds, and then he said,

"The only 'conspiracy' around here, my friend, is the one that you've organized. And I'll say to you, the same thing that I said to Jacobson, when he barged in here with blood in his eye and a chip on his shoulder... how do you plan to run the *country*, after all's said and done here in the White House?"

"I'm afraid, Clark," ominously purred Top Dog, "That you'll just have to take it on faith that I've got a comprehensive plan – again, can't go into details, but suffice it to say that we can *always* find someone who wants to play 'President'. The arrangements have already been made, in fact; and my understanding is that the nominee is already on his way over here. Just a quick show in front of the press to demonstrate he's in charge, 'go home and everything will be back to normal tomorrow', and Bob's your uncle –"

"Karéin will *never* let you get away with something like that!" argued Clairie. "It's true that she has her differences with Dad– but when she finds out what *you're* up to – your ass is grass!"

"You're assuming that there will even *be* an alien, after everything's been taken care of," countered the director. "Over here on the Agency side, we've been – ahh – 'perfecting our tool-kit', you might say. When the time comes – and that time is much nearer than anyone thinks – we'll rid this planet of the monster, once and for all. Considering that you're under its control, I don't expect you to appreciate how important a mission this is... but maybe, once it's dead, you'll wake up and realize what a debt you owe to those of us who stood up and fought back."

"My money's on Karéin," riposted the daughter. "And on Dad."

"We'll *see* about that," smoothly replied Top Dog. "And as a matter of fact... so will *you*."

He turned to his gendarmes.

"Take them down to where we're keeping the others," he ordered.

Four gun-toting terrorists advanced, but the President held out an upstretched palm to stop them, as he angrily accosted the Agency-director.

"What's the *meaning* of this?" he exclaimed. "The deal was for me – and *only* me – to surrender myself, and for you to free Kathy and Matt, in return! I'm the one you wanted, and I've kept *my* side of the bargain – now keep *yours!*"

"Why, Clark," remarked Top Dog, "How is it I remember – oh, yeah, it was a NSA intercept, from when the alien had invited itself on to that plane with the laser-gun – that when you're holding a hand of twos, you're in no position to bargain? Be a real nice, quiet, compliant hostage, and when all's said and done, I *might* let a couple of your family-members go... just 'pour encourager les autres', you know? But no promises! You're in no position to ask for them... and I'm in no mind to grant them."

"*Damn you!*" spat the President. "I've no special love for the alien, regardless of what you may think – but when she gets here, I hope she does to you, what she almost did to me. God *help* you when she does!"

"There are no 'Gods', Clark," sniffed Top Dog, "Only false ones like this so-called 'Storied Watcher', who are worshiped by naive and weak men."

Again, he turned to address his subordinates.

"I want him kept alive," he demanded. "But that doesn't necessarily mean, 'in good health'. As for the loud-mouthed teenager... she tries to run, you have my permission to shoot her. Otherwise – throw her in there with 'Daddy', and report back here when it's done."

"Yes, sir!" came the reflexive acknowledgment.

One of the gendarmes shouted at the President,

"*Move!*"

The U.S. leader grimly whispered to his daughter, "What did I *tell* you? I'll regret letting you come along for the rest of my life... however long *that* is."

He tried to keep walking straight forward, even though he was completely astonished by the thought that came next into his head.

Real soon now, so will he, Daddy, it declared.

Off They Go... And Yet, We Suspect

Despite the accomplishment of having successfully double-crossed the President of the United States, Top Dog was anything *but* elated, as he spoke into the microphone, from his vantage-point in the underground West Wing meeting-room.

"I'm not interested in hearing your fucking *excuses!*" he shouted, with uncharacteristic fury. "You either call off the attack, in the next five *minutes*... or I'll liquidate Clark – along with his whole family – right here and now!"

The clearly-appalled voice of Minnie Chu, from her vantage-point underneath Blair House, responded, "For God's sake, please, *please*, I *implore* you – don't *talk* like that! We've sent out orders to every branch of the military, as well as to the Service, the Park Police and anybody else around D.C. who could *possibly* be carrying a gun, to stay at least three hundred feet away from the White House! Whoever's doing this – they don't answer to me, or to the President!"

"I *told* you," persisted the combat-suited spook-*cum*-terrorist, "I'm *done* with your clumsy lies! My men are being attacked both on the north and south sides of the building – they've suffered significant casualties already, and I'm not putting up with any more! You press this bullshit any more, and I'll have nothing to lose – I might as well smoke the hostages and be done with it!"

"Look," pleaded the *nouvelle* FBI-director, "Can you at least tell me what these guys – the ones who you believe to be from the LEA or the military, I mean – what they look like? How would I tell them from your, uhh, 'soldiers' –"

"Five *minutes!*" came back the curt interjection. "Any longer, and I'll kick Clark's severed head, out on to the South Lawn! It'll be followed by those of his bitch wife and his two snot-nosed brat kids! Oh... and just for old times' sake, I'll do Kaysten and Feldner, right after that!"

He cut the connection.

"What are we going to *do*?" asked Hendricks. "You can't call off an attack that the government didn't even *arrange!*"

"If that's even true," reminded Abruzzio. "Ever since Karéin dropped down here, it's been one fiasco after another, with the government's right hand not knowing what its left is doing. He could be *right*, Minnie – it could be some branch of the military, the intelligence-agencies or just local cops, acting completely on their own."

"There's only one way to find out," vowed Chu, with a familiar glow building in the backs of her eyes. "I'm going *in!*"

She turned to the senior military officers, also in the Blair House bunker.

"General," demanded the former team-leader, "You're in charge here, until I return. In the meantime, there's to be *no* attempt – I repeat, *no* attempt, under *any* circumstances – to send troops or police-forces in to the White House! Is that *understood?*"

A late-middle-aged, tough-looking Caucasian guy in Marine fatigues replied,

"I can confirm our compliance to that order only because it conforms to the last directives given to us, by the President himself, ma'am… but do I have it, that you're planning to approach the White House, all by *yourself*? The place is *crawling* with armed terrorists! Surely you know… that would be *suicide!* "

"No, she isn't, yes it is, and no it won't be," interjected Hendricks. "She'll have *me*, going in with her."

"Will –" started Chu; but she was again interrupted, this time by Abruzzio, who said, "And Minnie will have *me*, as well. The plan was always for me to get in there, as soon as Rainbow returned with the info we asked her to find out. God willing, she's probably on the way back, right now. This just means that we'll have to accelerate the schedule."

"*Listen*, you two," argued the *nouvelle* FBI-director, "This is *my* job, not –"

"You want to talk it out, and give him an excuse to off Jerry and the President – or you want to fuckin' get *going*, Minnie?" defiantly parried the third agent.

Two more pairs of eyes – and two more bodies – were now showing the foreboding signs of the *Fire*, building within them.

Again, Minnie Chu addressed the Marine general.

"Be ready to take the First Family and the other hostages to safety, when we deliver them here," she directed. "In the meantime – hands off the White House. We'll try to stop whoever's now attacking the terrorists without casualties, of course; but if my brother and sister here – or I – have to open up with the full gamut of our alien-powers, it will quickly become a lethal environment for human beings. The *last* thing we want, is 'collateral damage'."

"Acknowledged," said the military man, observing the changes in the three more-than-humans standing close by him. "I hope you don't take this the wrong way, but... you *scare* me, ma'am."

"That's good," wryly offered Chu. "I just hope I scare *them*, too."

Turning to Abruzzio and Hendricks, she proposed, "I'll do the north; Will, you and Sylvia do the south, and get her as close as you can to the Oval Office... you and I meet up with her, when we've dealt with this issue. Agreed?

Both of the others nodded affirmatively. Their faces wore grim determination.

"Force-fields... *on!*" declared Chu, as they hurried to the door. "Let's *fly!*"

After the three followers of the Storied Watcher had left the underground Blair House bunker, one of the mid-rank military-men – a younger tough-guy, wearing the insignia of a Major on his uniform – in the facility, approached the Marine general who had been talking with Minnie Chu.

"Glad they're on *our* side, sir," he commented.

"*Are* they?" bruited the general.

"She's the Director of the FBI, after all," observed the major. "The President wouldn't have given her that position, if he didn't have confidence in her... wouldn't you say, sir?"

"That's *possible*," responded the general, "But from time to time, I find myself asking, 'what if that jackass in there – the terrorist guy, I mean – what if he's even *partially* right about the President not being in control of his own mind?' Who knows what these 'half-aliens' are really *up* to? We don't have any decent intel about what's really going *on*, in there! Maybe they want to kill the President and have him replaced by a zombie or whatever... or maybe the alien's got such complete control over him, that she'll just make him kill *himself.* Remember – as little as a couple of weeks ago, she was a sworn enemy of the United States – she was threatening to set the whole *country* on fire!"

"You *do* have a point, sir," remarked the major. "Just between you and I, sir... I think it was foolish for the President to have put his trust in the alien. Although, I guess he had little real choice about doing so."

"Well, that's kind of the whole *point*... isn't it, Major?" noted the general. "What does it matter, whether this 'Karéin' being is directly controlling the President's mind, or if she's just blackmailing him, the old-fashioned way? Or what if that damn 'Mars Gang' – or any of the alien's other half-human offspring – was doing the same? The result would be the same."

"Yeah," agreed the other man. "And for that matter... how do we even know that you and I are really thinking what we *want* to think, right now?

How do we know that Director Chu – or the alien, wherever she is – isn't, like, making it all up for us?"

"We… *don't*," evenly responded the general. "But – based on what we know to have been the Director's demands – we *do* have a way to test it out. If we really *are* under her mind-control, we could not do what I'm about to order."

"Sir?" asked the other soldier.

"Major," said the general, "Please activate the standing Joint Marines / Rangers / SEALS strike-force, per standard FPCON DELTA PLUS hard-target infiltration-procedures. Report back here in ten minutes, and be ready to move, on my go-ahead."

"Yes, *sir!*" enthusiastically replied the major, as he saluted, turned smartly in place, and strode quickly in the direction of his command-console.

A Goddess Outside… And A Deck Of Cards

The skies to the east were already darkening slightly, though this was only dimly-visible through the few and small pressure-resistant windows on the *Mailànkh Express*.

Indeed, the three-airship formation – with the *Express* in the lead and the other two latterly-constructed ones (thus built from materials scrounged on the way south) joined to it, both by conventional multi-strand steel-wire cables and by the Storied Watcher's mighty telekinetic grasp – were flying so high that the surroundings were a deep stratospheric blue, in any event.

"I don't know what Sari thinks she's *doing*," groused Billings to no-one in particular, as he peered outside, through a porthole. "This trip is taking *way* longer than she let on earlier, and –"

"Well, Bob," said Whitney Claremont, exercising her newly-regenerated tongue, "She *did* say it a wicked long way, back from that damn rock she stuck us all on, 'till yesterday. Ah'm jus' happy to be goin' home in th' first place. What y'all *'spect*, anyways – one of them new super-sonic business-jets wid th' wet bar an' them nice-lookin' stewardesses, maybe?"

"As a matter of fact…yes!" said the former floor-tile salesman. "After all I've been through, a little eye-candy – cover those ears, kid, and yes I know your Mom ain't too bad-lookin' herself – and a good stiff drink, even if it won't knock me back into my seat anymore… *that* can't be too much to ask for. And she *told* me that she can fly at however many thousand miles per hour, 'even in this nasty, confining atmosphere'. I don't understand what's *taking* us!"

One of the Compton refugees spoke up.

"I think Señor Billings *tiene razón*," he offered. "At least 'bout how she's flyin'. We're *circlin'*… not goin' straight forward."

Several of the others nodded affirmatively.

"You feel it too," mentioned Billings. "I thought it was just my imagination. I'd better ask her... uhh, whoops – disengaging that lock and opening the hatch at this altitude... that'd be a *bad* idea, wouldn't it?"

"Well, no *shit*, Bob," complained Claremont, "Didn't y'all 'member what happen to Melissa, when she went so far up that there ain't no air? Y'all want us all to pass out, or worse?"

He shot a glance at Tommy.

"Kid," requested the ex-salesman, "You've got him there... don't you?"

"Sure *do*, Mr. Billings," cheerily responded the boy. "I'll just ask him to talk to Mom, once he's out of the air-lock."

"Well," groused Billings, "I don't understand why she doesn't just mind-talk, right at me... like she did before. Why do we have to have *Vayran* – uhh, *Voyran* – uhh – *whatever* his name is – as the go-between, anyway?"

"Mom didn't say, exactly," deflected Tommy, "Except I think it's got something to do about, 'helping him and his brothers and sisters, to learn English'."

"Swell," said the ex-salesman. "I would have just bought him a dictionary... but, fine by me."

"*Væran* Ss'éth'ch' says, 'what's a 'dictionary'", Mr. Billings," answered the boy. "Oh... and he's saying he doesn't have eyes, or a mouth, either."

"Tell him... oh, *forget* it," grumbled Billings, as Tommy pulled out the animated-dagger – its self giving off waves of frightful cold, although this had strangely little effect on those within the airship – and deposited it into a small compartment on the side of the *Express*.

"Thou understand what we want Mom to tell us?" asked the boy, of the weapon.

Tommy looked up at the rest of the passengers.

"*Væran* Ss'éth'ch' is ready," he announced.

The boy entered a short combination on a key-pad near the airship's forward control-cabin, and the dagger was sealed into a compartment behind a folding, locked hatch.

There was a slight "whoosh" sound, as the Storied Watcher's weird offspring, flew outward to consult with its erstwhile mother.

Billings had expected the cold-dagger to have returned after a short confab with the Storied Watcher; but whatever the two alien beings had been discussed took considerably longer – about a half-hour, in fact.

At length – quite without any forewarning – the airlock-compartment re-opened. Out of it flew hibernal *Væran* Ss'éth'ch'. He immediately positioned himself in Tommy's outstretched hand, and began to rapidly vibrate.

Billings and the others had seen this before; it was some inscrutable form of communication, which his girlfriend had – for some reason he couldn't quite fathom – decided to teach to her adoptive son, first.

"Okay, kid," ventured the ex-salesman, "What's it – err, 'him', *my* bad – saying? She give any reason why we're in a holding-pattern, a few thousand miles from the nearest airport?"

"Wow, Mr. Billings... lots to tell you," excitedly replied Tommy. "Mom had *Væran* Ss'éth'ch', *Væran* Ksé'l'ch' and *Vìrya* I'ëä'b' too, form, like, kind of a big computer-network – or maybe an antenna – going nearly all the way up way into space, so they could get close enough to one of those satellites to read its TV-signals and then send them back to *Vìrya* Ahn'jë. That was so Mom could, like, watch the broadcasts on her sunglasses – *you* know, the ones that became part of –"

"*Sure*, I know all *about* how they got integrated with *Vìrya* Ahn'jë – okay, actually I don't know *squat* about that and probably never will," interrupted Billings, "But, uhh... you mean Sari's brought the whole flight to a creaking stop, just so she can watch *TV?* Back in Tucson, she told me she found it dead boring –"

"No – *no*, Mr. Billings," said Tommy. "It's not that at *all!* Mom said she's watching news-reports of something really, uhh, 'serious', going on at the White House – there's, like, a terrorist incident, and –"

"Whoa!" gasped the ex-salesman. "Who? What? Don't *tell* me – it's Jacobson and his crew... *isn't* it?"

"Well, she *did* say that the news-guys were talking about the 'Mars Gang'," commented the boy. "But –"

"Can't say I blame ol' Captain Sam, after what that jerk President tried to do to them –" mentioned Billings.

"But Bob... didn't Angel Lady an' y'all say that th' Commander an' th' President, they done made up?" asked Claremont.

"Yeah – that's what they *said*," offered Billings, "But what it looked like to me was that they just papered things over, to avoid pissing off Sari; not a surprise, considering that's what the young man over there and I did, too. I guess the gloves have come off now... oh well, say 'goodbye' to the White House and 'hello' to 'smoking hole in the ground'. No skin off *my* ass, frankly –"

"Mr. Billings... I don't think it's exactly like that," Tommy tried to correct.

"What you *mean*, kid?" inquired the former salesman.

"Mom wanted you to know, it looks like the White House came under attack by a bunch of 'terrorists'... and they're *not* Commander Jacobson or Professor Tanaka – or any of them – as far as she can tell. It's still going on, right now, and it's all very mixed-up down there, and Mom doesn't want us to show up there, until it's all, uhh, 'dealt with'."

"Well... what the H does she expect us to *do*?" complained Billings. "Just float around up here doing Lazy Eights until Kingdom Come? It's going to get awfully stuffy in here as it is, and yes I *do* know that our alien sides will keep us alive, but it still won't be very enjoyable. Can you have Mr. Freeze there – sorry Prince whoever-you-are – go out again and ask her to at least let us land somewhere, like, say, Bermuda, so we can –"

"Uhh... there's something *else*, Mr. Billings," spoke Tommy. "Mom says it's really, *really* important."

"What?" asked the ex-salesman. "Maybe she's getting tired of dragging a few hundred tons of metal endlessly back and forth, at umpteen thousand feet and God knows how many thousand miles per hour? You can tell her, '*I'd* be getting zonked too, if I were doing that'... all the better reason to get a move on, and get over with it."

"Why... ah would too, Bob," laconically quipped Claremont, "'Cept ah ain't never dragged nothin' bigger than a toboggan 'hind mah ass... an' ah ain't never done it nowhere 'cept the ground. Day y'all figure out how to get this ship we on, goin' like *she* do... come back an' bitch all y'all wants to."

A few of the others in this confined space, laughed out loud.

"I'll – uhh – make sure she hears that," answered the boy, as politely as he could do. "But what I wanted to tell you was, Mom said that we can't go down there – or show up anywhere that we'd be seen or where we might get, you know, *involved* – until 'your brothers and sisters have passed the final test'. Those were her own words."

For a second, Billings appeared as if he were at a loss; but then, a knowing look came over his face.

"Ah – so *that's* what's going on," he observed. "Makes sense, I suppose... in a 'Sari' way, that is. You know, kid – she's my girlfriend, and she's your mother, and speaking just for myself I love her dearly, but... times like *this*, I have to admit, I can only guess at what she's got in mind, or what weirdo powers she's using to accomplish it. You know?"

Tommy – his own visage suddenly and uncharacteristically serious – remarked, "I sure *do*, Mr. Billings. *Half* of Mom is just a nice, kind lady who wants someone to love, not to be alone... but the *other* half is... well... sometimes, especially when I turn on the *Fire* myself, I *think* I get it... but really, I don't. I don't think *anyone* does, and that includes *Væran* Ss'éth'ch' and his brothers and sisters, even though she brought them to life. Maybe, uhh, 'Venerable One' *sort* of does, I guess... but only because she's known Mom for like, a million years, or something."

"Y'all got *that* down right, boy," commented Claremont, "An' th' other half – that's in all of *us* by now, ah reckon. Lawd forgive us!"

The cold-dagger again started vibrating, and somehow – in some bizarre way – the rest of the living entities in the airship knew that *Væran* Ss'éth'ch' was confirming Tommy's commentary.

A few seconds of uncomfortable silence ensued, and then Billings offered,

"Well... *that* bridge was crossed a long time ago, and we all know that there ain't no goin' back. Thank God she thought ahead enough to outfit this rig with a Port-A-Potty. Did anybody remember to bring a deck of cards?"

All In An Effin' Day's Work

The three more-than-humans, sticking closely together, had flown to the roof of the West Wing (at least, to what was left of it) without incident, thanks to Abruzzio's mirage-tricks.

She had worried that an experienced observer could have detected the distortion in the sky caused by her light-bending tricks – and possibly this might have happened – but the trip was short and direct enough to give any likely assailant, inadequate time to react, aim and fire.

There had almost been an unfortunate incident with the few, beleaguered Secret Service agents and Marine guards remaining on the roof, as Hendricks, Abruzzio and Chu "popped" into visibility, as if from nowhere; but impassioned "don't *shoot* – we're here to rescue the hostages!" entreaties temporarily prevented a premature engagement.

"You see any hostiles left, to the south?" asked Chu, of her compatriots.

"Nope," responded the third agent. "Just crippled and dead bodies – and whatever hit 'em, sure as hell's something that *I* don't want to tangle with! Some of 'em are, like... *missing* parts, if you know what I mean."

"Yeah," murmured the *nouvelle* FBI-director. "Pretty much the same to the north. I don't know if any of them got out in enough time to report back to their leader – and I'm very worried about how he'll react, either way. Either of you see who or what *did* this?"

"Negative," said Abruzzio. "Whoever it was, they aren't here now –"

One of the Marine guards, who had obviously overheard the conversation, spoke up.

"Hey... lady!" he called out, while crouching down even further, to avoid one of the increasingly-rare sniper-rounds being directed at the White House, from the south. "*We* saw them!"

"Oh... oh-kay," replied the former JPL scientist. "You get a good look at them? Can you ID them?"

"It was them two, uhh, 'Mars Gang' guys – one with this shiny shit all over him, and the other who, like, made this big wind-storm come up all over the place," explained the soldier. "They were up here with us, all of a sudden this crazy music started playin' and then they just, uhh, *flew* down there and lit into the terrorists. Flew down... just like *you* flew up here, 'matter of fact."

Uneasy glances were exchanged between Hendricks, Chu and Abruzzio. Eventually, the former team-leader said to the guards,

"If you're accurately describing them, you probably saw Commander Sam Jacobson and Space Scientist Hector Ramirez – and for the record, only the Commander technically belongs to the Mars Gang."

"Hector is my best friend," interjected Abruzzio. "We both worked at JPL in Houston. You have nothing to fear from him... or from me."

"They *answer* to you, lady?" demanded another of the guards, this time, a Secret Service agent wearing a ragged, combat-scarred business-suit.

"That's... *complicated*," deflected Chu. "In theory they *should*... but anyway – if you see them, stay out of their way, and make sure that the rest of the White House's guards do so too –"

"Who are *you* to order us to do *anything*?" challenged the agent. "For all *we* know, you're just some weirdo alien terrorist –"

"I'm FBI Director Minnie Chu, if you didn't already know," countered Chu. "My two friends and I are here on direct orders from the President, who we believe is being held hostage, along with the rest of the First Family and some others, by the *real* terrorists. I have all the authority I need to order you around but I don't want to do that – I need your *help*, because if we don't work together, the President and his family may shortly be *murdered!* Neither you nor I need *that* on our records!"

There was a slight pause, as the enhanced hearing of the three more-than-humans picked up an argument going on between the remaining guards. Finally, one of them – a Marine – said,

"Yeah... I recognize you from that press-conference... damn, ma'am – you really *are* a super-hero... aren't you?"

Chu allowed her eyes to glow momentarily as she shot a proud glance at the guard and replied, "Sure am – as are Agent Hendricks and Professor Abruzzio, beside me. Any *one* of us could kick the terrorists into next week – but we've got to be very careful that we don't hurt any of the hostages, in the process. You understand?"

"Yes ma'am," continued the guard, "But what you want us to *do*?"

"For starters," requested the former team-leader, "Which way did Jacobson and Ramirez go?"

"We had our heads well down for most of it," disclosed the guard, "But I think I saw one of 'em goin' back in the building... busted right through a window like it was tissue-paper."

"Damn," observed Hendricks, "We should just yell at the top of our lungs, 'Diamondback come out'... but if the terrorists hear that..."

"Agreed," supported Abruzzio. "Sam may have gone back to check up on his family – or he may have gone further into the West Wing, chasing the terrorists. If the latter, we had better catch him before he attacks again, and –"

"Listen, Director," interrupted one of the Service agents, "We've got five guys down up here from them fuckin' snipers and the battle with the helicopters... two are already KIA, and the other three won't last much longer if we don't get them to medical help. Anything you can do?"

"He's *right*, Minnie," mentioned Hendricks, *sotto voce*. "Mars eyes – or maybe Mars soul – is seeing it... life-force's bleeding out of 'em. *Shit*."

"We came up here to rescue the President... and that's exactly what I plan to do," steadfastly pledged Chu.

"We can't just leave 'em up here to *die*," argued the third agent.

"Can you get them down off the roof, while Sylvia and I go hide down by the Oval Office and wait for Rainbow?" asked the *nouvelle* FBI-director.

"More load than I've ever telekinesed – if that's even a *word*," answered Hendricks, "But yeah... I *think* so. There's no rounds incoming from the north, so I can float 'em down on that side, get 'em far enough away from the White House for an ambulance. Might take a couple of trips, and if anybody takes a pot-shot at me, expect to see a few finest Tanaka-imitation lightening-bolts flyin' back at 'em. Then I'll join the two of you outside the building... okay?"

She extended a hand; the gesture was warmly reciprocated.

"You ever think we'd end up doing something like this?" ventured Chu, with a wry smile.

"No... and I didn't think I'd get thrown out of a 'plane without a 'chute, at ten thousand feet, and live to tell about it, either," he grumbled.

"Add 'with an H-bomb about to go off in said 'plane', and that's what Sylvia and I had to deal with," pleasantly replied the former team-leader. "All in a day's work."

"All in a fuckin' day's work... *right*," muttered Hendricks, as he rolled his eyes.

"*Go!*" she directed.

The third agent nodded his head, and – crouching all the way – moved rapidly over to where the remaining White House guards were protecting their fallen comrades.

While Hendricks was attending to his medevac duties, Chu and Abruzzio – flying slowly all the while under the former JPL scientist's mirage-field, to deter gunfire from snipers far to the south – drifted down to a position deep inside the shadowed interior of the bushes just south of the Rose Garden.

It was a tight fit inside the foliage and both more-than-women were plagued with scrapes and insect-annoyances; but both also understood why self-secretion was absolutely necessary. By moving some of the branches discreetly aside, Abruzzio and Chu found that they had line of sight to the damaged windows of the Oval Office.

They noticed that there were no terrorists still functional outside the West Wing; all of those that had latterly being standing guard, had been brutally dealt with, apparently by Jacobson and Ramirez.

Almost immediately, Abruzzio did a double-take.

"She's *here*," she whispered. "Over there, by the other side of the bushes."

"I'm looking with my Mars eyes," quietly answered Chu, "But I don't see –"

She stopped in mid-sentence and then said, with a smile, "Oh... *there* you are! Holy samoley, honey – are you ever hard to see, even for one of us!"

She was rewarded by a subdued "yip" and a friendly puppy-lick.

"Can you give us a second, please?" requested Abruzzio.

"Of course," said the *nouvelle* FBI director.

For about thirty seconds, the former JPL scientist and her alien-powered puppy just stared at each other, although Chu could somehow tell that the dog and the master were engaging in some kind of interactive communications. Eventually, Abruzzio spoke up.

"She saw us up on the roof, which is how she traveled to meet up with us here," she disclosed. "And there's much more... not all of it very good, unfortunately."

"Did she locate the President?" asked Chu. "Or Clairie?"

"Not exactly," deflected Abruzzio, "But she *did* track the two of them as far as an elevator by the Vice-President's office – she couldn't get into it without being detected because it was so crowded; that almost happened the first time she did it, which was when she was tailing the First Lady, her son and Jerry... they're in a holding-cell deep underneath the West Wing. There's no way out of that and the entrance to it has been rigged with booby-traps and so on... there may be more inside the bunker. My guess is that the President and his daughter were taken down there as well."

"Did she get a good look at the terrorist leader?" asked the other more-than-a-woman. "Or how many soldiers that he's got working for him? What's their disposition? What's his end-game?"

"Dozens," said the former space-scientist, "Although Rainbow never saw more than five or six alongside him at any one time... it looks like the rest may be dispersed inside the building. She couldn't understand the dialog that occurred between the terrorist leader and his captives – like the President or Kaysten for example – so she can't tell me exactly what he's out to accomplish, but you're going to love *this* –"

"What?" stuttered the former team-leader.

"She's saying that both Jerry and the President immediately recognized the boss terrorist, when he took off his helmet," mentioned Abruzzio. "They both got into arguments with him. Rainbow says he's a 'really bad man', whose picture she remembers seeing back in that big building back in Pittsburgh. That's all she knows."

"Hmm," murmured Chu. "*That's* interesting… that was where you and Rainbow had that, uhh, encounter, with the Agency guy, in your room… right?"

That encounter on the top floor, she reflected.

If I had just zapped the fucker – how much of this would have been avoided?

"Correct," confirmed Abruzzio. "Whoever the terrorist leader is, he's obviously somebody pretty high-up… and he certainly has a lot of firepower and a well-thought-out plan. Our problem is, we don't know exactly what it *is*. Given what he's demanded, I'm pretty sure it involves Karéin."

"Yeah," said the *nouvelle* FBI director. "Oh-kay, then. What about the Mars Gang, Hector or the rest of them? She see any of *them?*"

"No," said the former JPL scientist, "But she didn't go looking, anywhere other than the West Wing, and she was 'hiding' all the while… maybe they just missed her as she went by them, or something."

"Perhaps," mentioned Chu, "But as long as they're hanging around, outside our control… they could *easily* mess everything up. *Damn* Sam Jacobson, anyway! That guy is the proverbial loose cannon!"

"You have a point," observed Abruzzio. "But it's a chance we'll have to take."

At this moment, they saw Hendricks' lanky figure landing just to the north of them, with his back flat against the bullet-scarred West Wing wall. He looked around for a couple of seconds – as if searching for hostiles – and then, crouching low all the way, dashed under cover, to where Abruzzio and Chu were hiding.

"Done," he whispered. "I waved down an ambulance, and boy were they surprised to see me, like, *flying*... but a couple of those poor bastards who I transported, probably won't make it. There's still a few snipers way down to the south – they took pot-shots at me, but missed by a mile. I don't think anybody saw me coming in. How are you holding out here?"

"We're set up, and I think we're still undetected," stated Abruzzio, "We had better get going with our plan, or we'll time out on the asshole's demands. You ready?"

Chu nodded affirmatively but responded, "Are *you? You're* the one who has to do all the heavy-lifting here, after all."

"As I'll *ever* be," said the former space-scientist. "You bring that mini-flashlight? Ha ha… if we only had Mr. Boyd here with us."

"Oops," answered Chu, as she fumbled around and came to the realization that the item had been mislaid in the confusion.

"You got the next-best thing," offered Hendricks.

He held up his right index finger, which promptly started glowing, in a very believable imitation of what the former Mars mission pilot would have been able to do, with his own digit.

"He teach you that?" marveled the *nouvelle* FBI-director.

"Nah," quipped the third agent. "Just gave some folks we met, 'the finger'. I kind of took it to heart, you know?"

Chu regarded Abruzzio and said, with an arched eyebrow, "You know, Sylvia... I thought we could decide whether or not to give away our powers to him – but what happens when he starts learning all by himself?"

"Ahh... I'm just a pale imitation," interjected Hendricks, with a wry smile, while his finger glowed ever the brighter.

A duly-impressed Chu continued, "Sylvia – you got the photo?"

"Right here," echoed the ex-JPL scientist.

She held out a family-portrait of Bob Billings, Tommy, Elissha and a pretty, young-looking, blond woman.

With dimly-glowing, kaleidoscope eyes, Abruzzio studied the photo intensely, while the third agent – guarding against giving their position away by cradling his finger with his other hand – illuminated the picture.

Too Many Cooks With Guns

The bunker underneath Blair House was now transformed into a full-scale military command-post, as the general approached the major.

"Sir," greeted the subordinate officer.

His face foretold of a problem, well-anticipated.

"I'm hoping you have a good *explanation*, Major," growled the general. "I was expecting our conversation to be about sending in the Joint Strike Force... instead – *this!*"

"I'm sorry sir... but we don't – at least, not yet," abashedly responded the major. "Frankly... it took us completely by surprise."

"It shouldn't have!" complained the general. "I mean... downtown D.C.'s locked down, all the way to a five-mile radius in any direction from the White House. How the *hell* do we now have reports of hundreds of 'troops of unknown command', marching in the direction of that building? I'd say, 'what am I supposed to tell the President'... except that he's stuck in there at the mercy of a terrorist, right now. The *mother* of all fuck-ups – wouldn't you say?"

"Can't blame you for being frustrated, sir," evaded the understudy, as he pressed a micro-speaker into his right ear and stared forward, while trying to comprehend what was being broadcast.

"Uhh... hold on, sir... something's coming in, over the regular networks – looks like we've got a positive ID on at least one of these formations... say *what?* What the *f* –"

"What's the intel?" pressed the general.

The major looked up, half in disbelief.

"We've got real-time, via Disney News, on at least four columns of them, approaching the White House from north, south, east and west," he disclosed. "They're GrayWar Legion."

"*What?*" gasped the exasperated general. "What the hell are *they* doing here?"

"There's more, sir," spoke the major. "Apparently Secretary DeWitt, the Secret Service and the Bureau – also the D.C. police – just got a private communiqué from Mr. Duke. The news media don't seem to have it yet. It's pretty short… you want me to read it?"

"What have I got to *lose*," sighed the general.

"He's saying, 'as the conventional military has proved unable to resolve the situation at the White House, GrayWar is assuming control of operations, in downtown D.C.' – and he's ordering us to stand down our forces."

"*That* will be the day!" angrily exclaimed the general. "Those amateur soldiers of his, try a frontal assault on the White House and that terrorist asshole will kill the President, for *sure!*"

"Your orders, sir?" asked the major.

"Contact Mr. Duke and tell him to call back his mercs – or they'll be met with lethal force, the moment they try to enter the grounds of the White House," directed the general. "Then, contact the Joint Strike Force."

"Sir?" repeated the major.

"Ready or not – we're going *in!*" ordered the general.

Savior Of The Republic

"This is the Secretary of Defense, acting on behalf of the President, under the rules pertaining to chain of command," sounded the voice of Arthur DeWitt, over the highly-encrypted, point-to-point channel between the Pentagon and the White House communications-shack. "I *urgently* need to speak with the individual calling himself leader of the group now in physical control over the White House."

"This is he," responded Top Dog, from his vantage-point just outside the Oval Office.

"Do you care to either identify yourself, or to state the goals of your group? Do you have a manifesto?" asked the Secretary. "As of now – other than for the President – we have no idea what you're trying to *accomplish*, here. Hence, we don't know how to defuse the situation, without further conflict or loss of life."

"You can call me, 'Savior Of The Republic'," mentioned the Agency-director. "And as for my goals… well, they'll become clear quite soon; but you can tell the public that we're here to restore legitimate authority to the

Executive Branch – and in so doing free it from the malicious influence of the alien. That enough to get you going?"

"I believe so," offered DeWitt.

"So... what's there to discuss?" challenged Top Dog.

"Sir," stated the Secretary, "I have confirmation that the President was delivered to you, about twenty minutes ago. We're awaiting the return of the First Lady and her son, along with her daughter, who as you know accompanied the President on his trip in. When can we expect to see these people delivered in good health, to the North Portico?"

"When you deliver on the *other* demand I made of the government!" retorted the Agency-man. "And I'd remind you : time's running out – *fast* – on that. If you want any of the hostages set back in anything other than a box, you had better –"

"*Sir*," interrupted DeWitt, as politely as he could manage, "As we've already said, while we *have* reached out to Karéin-Mayréij over the public airwaves – asking her to immediately drop whatever she's doing and hurry over to the White House – she hasn't yet responded to us. We don't even know where she is – and we have no control over what she'll do, if and when she hears the message. You'll *have* to give us more *time* –"

"You've got until the top of the hour!" warned Top Dog. "If she doesn't show by then, Kathy's head will be the first to roll; I've been tolerant way past a fault already, considering the number your boys have been doing on mine, outside the building. And – 'scuse me –"

The circuit appeared to be dead, and DeWitt frantically ordered his subordinates to do whatever it took, to get it back on-line. But before they could act, the "Receive" indicator-light again became active.

"Yes?" said the Secretary of Defense. "As I was saying, sir –"

"It looks like your little exercise in begging, may have hit pay-dirt," taunted the Agency-man.

"Sir?" inquired DeWitt. "What do you *mean?*"

"I've got to go," shot back Top Dog. "I'm told... she's *here*."

Them Or Us

"Sorry, Mr. President," argued the Chief of Staff, "But I don't think there's any other way out of here... and I've searched every *inch*, Mars eyes and all."

He had rarely seen his boss so upset – except perhaps in that unfortunate encounter with the Storied Watcher, scant time ago.

"Think, Jerry... think!" pressed the U.S. leader, as he paced all over the bunker, checking the walls for the slightest sign of any hidden artifice. "There has to be something we can *do!* You can see how badly hurt Kathy is – we can't just sit around here and wait for her to get worse, nor for that son of a bitch to show up and *murder* us! We've got to get *out* of here!"

"Yeah… and poor Jackson over there ain't doing too well, either," observed Kaysten, as he glanced at the wounded Service agent, who was slumped up against one wall. He had stopped bleeding, but was clearly still in distress. The First Lady had taken to recline on a couch on one of the far walls. She was half-asleep, though still obviously in pain.

After moving to the part of the bunker furthest from its doorway – the bathroom – the President motioned to Kaysten, his daughter and his son, who walked over to be alongside.

It was a tight fit, but they all managed to enter the vestibule, whose entrance was directly in the line of sight with the main doorway to the outside corridor.

"Listen," whispered the U.S. leader after closing the door, "All three of you have… *powers*… right?"

"Sure," confirmed the Chief of Staff, "But I don't think any of the ones I've got, are much use for getting us out of here. Unless we can get those assholes outside, to start listening to my jokes. Too bad we don't have Minnie in here – she'd cut through that door in a couple of seconds."

"As I've seen," agreed the President, *sotto voce*. "I'd even settle for Jacobson or that loud-mouthed bounty-hunter, at this point. Matt… what about *you*, son?" he asked. "Thank the Lord that you've recovered from the fall, so quickly."

"Yeah," commented the teenager, "If getting hurt and getting better fast is a 'power', then I'm your guy, I guess. But – this is *weird*, Dad, and you'll just have to believe me – I don't, uhh, feel like I've got *anything* in me that could knock a hole in that door. If you want me to rush those pricks with the guns, when and if they open the door… just say so. Happy to try."

The U.S. leader gave his son an earnest, parental arm-shake and replied, "Let's pray it doesn't come to that… but if the time comes – be *ready*."

"Absolutely," gravely nodded Matt.

"Clairie," whispered the President in the direction of his daughter, "You said, 'I'll protect you', when both of us were gullible enough to believe that terrorist. If so… now's the time. What you *got* for us?"

The daughter looked quite uncomfortable as she admitted, "Uhh, Daddy… not really a lot, to be honest. I've already tried my telekinesis against the door and I couldn't even feel it budge."

"For the record," added Kaysten, "So did I. I think I stressed it a bit but not enough to bust it… and trying much more, in addition to tiring me out big-time, would make it vibrate – the guards would detect that for sure. Probably not a good idea unless we can be sure to deal with 'em when they come looking."

"Right," said Clairie. "Daddy… this 'alien-powers' stuff is – uhh – like Matt said, it's weird-ass – one minute you feel like a god, and the next minute, it's, like, 'back to business as usual'. But, listen – Karéin told us a story like, 'when you need her the most, Holy *Amaiish* will come through for you'… *et cetera*. I sure hope she wasn't kidding us."

"So do I," muttered the President.

"Listen, kids… I mean, 'brother and sister'," proposed Kaysten, "If it looks like we're backed into a corner and the terrorists are planning to shoot, we can't let them pick us off, one by one. Tell you what – I'll clap my hands once, and that will be the signal to rush 'em… pour it on with everything you've *got*, and hit them as hard as you can, even if that means 'killing'… it sucks, but it's 'them or us'… you *know?*"

"Yeah," quietly agreed the daughter, "I know."

Her eyes started glowing, but she suppressed the manifestation.

"Roger that," confirmed Matt.

"Oh… and before any of this happens," continued the Chief of Staff, "If – God help us – we've got to fight for our lives, just before it goes down, reach deep down and ask Angel Lady for all the *Fire* you can get. *I* did, up there, just before taking on a few of 'em – and it probably saved my butt."

Matt nodded, and Clairie said, "Oh-kay."

"Hey, kid," offered Kaysten, with a smile, "Did you know… you sound a lot like her –"

There was a knock on the bathroom door. It was Jackson, who – though still barely able to move – had some how made it across the room.

"They're outside," he advised. "I just heard, 'you are to egress immediately, five seconds warning – we'll shoot anyone directly in front of the door, when we open it.'"

"Shit!" cursed Matt. "Let's get *out* of here!"

"You're right," echoed Kaysten, as the four rapidly clambered out of the vestibule. "Let's get out."

Morte Perpetua Ad Daemoniorum

With every molecule in and of his body radiating alertness, Top Dog cautiously opened the semi-hidden door leading from the outside corridor, to the Oval Office, by just a crack.

During the single second that he allowed himself to peer through the opening and thence through the windows in the Presidential room, he caught a glimpse of four human-sized figures, standing near the Rose Garden just outside the Oval Office.

There was a bored-looking, slightly-out-of-shape man in cheapish used-car-salesman garb, a cherubic little girl about four years of age and a slightly-older Amerindian boy with black hair and an intense-looking stare.

Finally – to his suppressed elation – Top Dog saw a very pretty, young-looking woman with green eyes and blond hair cut into a bang. She was wearing stylish, semi-formal evening-wear and seemed to be talking to the man, though the Agency-man couldn't quite hear what was being said.

The young-looking woman's complexion was rather more pale than that of her compatriots, although Top Dog put this down to the fact that the man had a tan and the boy's skin was normally darker than what would be expected of a Caucasian.

The woman – moving slowly and deliberately, like she had already been wounded – or as if the mobility of her arms and legs was somehow impeded – stumbled slightly but then sat down on a park-bench, next to the bullet-shredded flowers of the Rose Garden.

There appeared not to be a line of sight for the few remaining snipers at or near the far end of the South Lawn; none the less, a couple of rifle-rounds still hit the White House, further to the east.

Oddly, the fact that they were evidently under fire did not seem to perturb the group of newcomers, who just continued their conversation; the man, for example, didn't even crouch or try to make himself a less conspicuous target.

Damn, he mused... the monster is here *– right* now!

Now or never! Either it dies in the next five minutes – or I do!

Wait a minute... it can't *be* that *easy... can* it?

Why isn't the bitch rushing in to save Clark's sorry ass?

Something ain't right *here!*

Repositioning his combat-helmet on to the top of his battle-suit, he engaged its visual-enhancement-technology and again risked a quick glance through the narrow opening in the doorway.

A orange-red-colored message appeared on the interior heads-up-display.

"PRIORITY TARGET IDENTIFIED", it indicated.

"Confidence-level," he whispered.

"TARGET FACIAL MATCH CONFIDENCE 91.65%."

"RANGE-LIMIT FOR VOICE-PRINT MATCH EXCEEDED",

Came back the imagery on the HUD.

Fuck it! he mused,

If it wasn't standing outside those windows, the voice-ID thing would be able to tell me for sure... still, ninety-one per cent... that's got *to be it!*

And fucking Clark's late getting up here – I wanted to smoke him first, right in front of her...

On the other hand, the teams have wasted a lot of targets of opportunity in this building, earlier on, and some of those have got to have been its followers...

Maybe it's weak enough already!

"Sir," said one of his black-suited, pistol-wielding fellow-warriors, from behind, while the ever-watchful Top Dog peered cautiously through the doorway-opening.

The four outside visitors – including the alien-girl – were still talking. The man had now joined her on the bench, and his hand was very near to her own, although they were not touching.

"Not *now* – and keep it *down*, for God's sake," he implored, with a vehement whisper and a hand-gesture. "The monster's right *out* there!"

"Oh… understood, sir," came back the equally-low-volume reply. "It's just that we have the traitor-President and his family, along with the Chief of Staff and the others, under guard in the hall. What are your orders?"

"Marvelous!" he responded. "*Perfect* timing! I have five minutes, fifty-two seconds to the hour. Do you confirm?"

"Confirmed, sir," answered the black-suited soldier.

"When the second-count hits 'zero' – *shoot* the captives – *all* of them! Leave none alive! You've now got thirty seconds – *do* it!"

"It *will* be done, sir!" said the other man, as quietly as possible.

He turned and ran out of the room, as Top Dog – working frantically but effectively – retrieved an unusual-looking, red-and-yellow-striped bullet, with the marking *Special Seaborgium-299* emblazoned on it.

He chambered the round and then looked through the scope of his rifle, which imagery the HUD machine-interface put directly into his combat-visor (along with a running count of the time, now showing ten seconds to go).

With the muzzle of the gun barely showing through the door-opening, he aimed directly for the center of the alien-girl's chest.

We get only one shot, knew the former director of the Central Intelligence Agency.

A thought entered his mind, from long-lost boyhood days as an altar-boy in the Deep South.

Morte perpetua ad daemoniorum! it cried.

Clap For A Fight To The Death

There was a look of cold hatred on Kaysten's face, as he had been forced to allow his arms and feet to be bound with law-enforcement-style plastic restraints. It was matched by the same sullen expression on the part of all the others, even though – perhaps as a quaint nod to the dignity of his office – the President and his two children only had their hands bound behind their backs. Meanwhile the First Lady was allowed to hobble forward, unconstrained other than for her injury.

Six heavily-armed gendarmes – three behind, three in front – were there to prevent attempts at escape, as the President and his associates and family were frog-marched, first through the underground tunnels, then upward via the elevators and finally through the West Wing – to a position halfway down the hall to the west of the Oval Office.

Two of the three soldiers behind them, retreated further west, eventually disappearing around a bend in the corridor next to the Chief of Staff's office. The other one moved ahead of them. He was joined by two more gendarmes who had evidently come from further east within the building.

"Where are Feldner and the Secretary of State?" demanded the President. For this, he was given the privilege of a rifle-butt, thrust squarely in the middle of his back.

"Wait *here!*" one of the terrorists brusquely bellowed. He then exited the corridor, going into the set of small rooms behind and just to the west of the Oval Office.

The hostages were now standing in the middle of West Wing, east-to-west corridor, about twelve feet from a group of six stone-faced terrorists with rifles prominently at the ready.

"Daddy," whispered Clairie, "I have a really *bad* feeling about this."

"Me too," confirmed Matt. "I think it's show-time."

"Stand ready," said Kaysten, under his breath. "I can hardly move my hands – Mr. President, you do the clapping. If and when."

"*When,*" hissed Matt. "Damn – I can *feel* it, flooding into me – sis, do you –"

Clairie's eyes were closed, but they could tell that she was starting to breathe deeply. She nodded affirmatively.

There was the smell of smoke, and a quick glance at the back of the teenager revealed that her arm-restraints were starting to spark, char and melt.

A second later, the same started happening to the tie-clamps that confined Matt's arms. Neither Presidential child seemed in the least troubled by the flames and molten plastic that encircled their wrists.

Two war-songs – both as-yet-unheard, both portentous yet different in their own ways, began to be heard just at the limit of human audibility.

The same gendarme who had just left, stepped out of the doorway leading to the Oval Office.

"On your *knees!*" he shouted, pointing at the blanching President and the rest of his coterie. The firing-squad raised their auto-rifles, disengaging the safeties as they aimed.

The U.S. leader – though silently saying a prayer and supporting his fainting wife, as her legs gave out – forcefully clapped his hands.

They heard an unusually-loud rifle-shot being fired from somewhere near to the Oval Office, as – in the next second, without any other warning – at least six terrorist assault-rifles set to full-automatic, barked out their lethal projectiles, firing down the West Wing hall to massacre the First Family.

But both Clairie and Matt had already reacted, as the guns opened up and as Kaysten – his body reverberating like a tuning-fork – fell to the carpeted floor, rolling toward the assailants like a bowling-ball.

Sounds of gunfire and other mayhem – accompanied by a veritable symphony of alien war-songs – issued forth, from the direction of the Oval Office; but those in the corridor had no time in which to pay attention to anything other than their own life-or-death struggle.

The daughter was first to step forward; with her buzzing, post-punk electric-rock war-song ramping up rapidly, with flashes of the *Fire* in her chest and with bright-glowing eyes, she thrust her arms forward with outstretched palms, in the classic "Stop!" hand-motion. Her father – though resigned to his own fate – was horrified at the expectation of Clairie being cut apart; but in fact, her gesture was anything *but* futile, and her demise was not to be on this day.

Faster than the human (or meta-human) eye could discern, at a distance of about four feet in front of the daughter, there appeared a shimmering, faintly-gold-colored, translucent barrier, akin to a mirage caused by a pocket of hot air.

Immediately, this strange thing was hit by the fusillade of terrorist rifle-bullets – more than sixty rounds. Of these, perhaps half seemed to simply disappear, as if instantly-vaporized; but the rest – reduced, in the process, to molten darts of fused metal – somehow reversed course, hurtling backward at murderous speed.

The results were grimly predictable : four terrorists dropped at once, with their body-armor shot clean through by the hellish, transformed bullets that they had themselves unleashed. The reflected-projectiles also severed arms, legs and other body-appendages; one gendarme had the top half of his head blown off, spraying the West Wing carpets and walls with an ugly splash of blood and brain-tissue. Another was literally torn to pieces, with little recognizable as a human being, left of him.

The remaining two terrorists had scant more time in which to react, because – a half-second later – they were struck by the President's bright-eyed, war-song-playing son, who had been rocketing forward straight at them (he seemed to pass through his sister's force-barrier with no ill effects, and might have been hit by a few bullets, but these seemed to deflect away from him) much too quickly for the terrorists to re-aim or even squeeze their triggers again.

As his clenched fists made contact with his adversaries, Matt's other alien-powers began to manifest : each kinetic strike was accompanied with a shower of sparks and a percussive "boom" that hit with tremendous force, throwing his quarry backward like the proverbial rag-doll shot from a cannon.

Nobody who was hit by this fearsome attack, was seen to get up afterward; the points of impact where Matt had struck home, were consistently marked with ugly, radial burn-marks in a shallow indentation, as if they had touched a high-voltage power-cable.

The battle lasted only a couple of seconds, after which every terrorist in the firing-squad had either been incapacitated, slain or completely dismembered. Kaysten was now unencumbered; he had used the confusion to shred his arm- and leg-restraints.

A white-faced Clairie stared at the carnage that her new-found ability had inflicted on the terrorist squad.

"Oh my *God,*" wailed the distraught daughter, "Did *I* do *that?*"

She fell to her knees as if about to puke.

"*Fuck* them!" angrily cursed Matt, standing defiantly astride the broken body of one of his own victims, with his hands clenched into smoking fists. "They *deserved –*"

Both war-songs started to abate, but the invective of the Presidential son was cut off by the figure of a man in a mechanized combat-suit – partly on fire from the weapons of some unknown enemy – crashing through the doors leading to the Oval Office.

This badly-damaged – but still, apparently, combat-effective – enemy, impacted against the opposite wall of the corridor ahead and to the left of them, righted himself, turned and – through an electronically-boosted helmet-loudspeaker – declared,

"The monster's *dead,* Clark – and you're *next!*"

To The Aid Of A Mirage

Lost in concentration as if she were in a trance, Abruzzio stared straight at the images that she had created just outside the Oval Office. Her determined, single-minded stance was exactly mimicked by that of her pet, who was also frozen in place, looking at the scene through multi-colored eyes.

"Fuckin' *amazing,*" observed Hendricks, *sotto voce,* upon observing the holographic images of Karéin-Mayréij, Billings, Tommy and Elissha, as they seemingly interacted with each other. "She's even got them *talking…* and if I didn't know better, I'd *swear* those were their own voices –"

"Shh," cautioned Chu, "You'll *distract* her."

"Fucker hasn't showed," noted the third agent, now whispering more narrowly in the direction of his former boss. "How long she can keep this *up?*"

"Ten to fifteen minutes, for sure," spoke Abruzzio, without breaking her forward concentration. "It's tiring just for one… try animating four. Like playing a piano concerto for four people, all at once."

"Shit... no *kidding*," acknowledged an impressed Hendricks. "I can't imagine what doing that, must be like."

"Maybe, someday, brother... you *will*," offered the former JPL scientist, with the slightest hint of a smile showing on her face.

"Yeah," he murmured.

Chu turned to look at Hendricks.

"Will," she warned, "I just had a vision of something *terrible* going on, in there – alarm-bells going off all over the place – that door there, on the other side of the room –"

They saw a muzzle-flash, considerably larger than what they had observed from mundane rifle-shots, coming from a spot about shoulder-height, where the semi-hidden door on the far north-west side of the Oval Office opened outward.

For a split-second, all three more-than-humans, and the dog, reflexively ducked; but then they realized that they were not the target. Instead, the single gunshot had been aimed at the holographic image of the Storied Watcher.

There was a loud, agonized shriek, and the *faux*-alien-girl-image – now, splattered with apparently-ichorous blood and complete with all the trappings of a fatal injury – fell over backward, behind the park-bench on which it had been projected.

For a second, both this hologram and the other ones flickered, but then they returned to full composition.

"Ha!" quipped Hendricks, "I gotta *hand* it to you, Sylvia... you left nothing to the imagination – Sylvia – *Sylvia!*"

But as if having been sucker-punched by some invisible opponent, Abruzzio herself was now lying prone, staring upward through kaleidoscope-eyes, with her hand pressed hard against her heart. Moaning and writhing in pain, sweat broke out on her brow, as she tried to cope with a wound that none of those present either anticipated or understood.

"What the *hell* –" cursed the third agent, as he hurried over to assist the former space-scientist.

"She's somehow still keeping the images up, but –" spoke Chu.

There were the sounds of gunfire and muffled explosions – also, just at the limit of audibility, those of previously-unknown war-songs – from somewhere further inside the West Wing building.

The *nouvelle* FBI-director did a double-take, as the situation went rapidly out of control.

Five familiar war-songs were playing. The diamond-covered figure of Sam Jacobson – appearing as if from nowhere – hit the ground just in front of the Oval Office, and then smashed through the door separating the office from the South Lawn, as if the former was made of tissue-paper. Jacobson – followed by Hector Ramirez, a half-second later – charged into the Oval Office; but once halfway inside, as Wolf, Cherie Tanaka and Brent Boyd appeared near Abruzzio's holograms – the ex-Mars mission commander and his former JPL assistant, stopped for a second, as if unsure of where his enemies were hiding.

"Karéin's hurt *bad!*" yelled Boyd, as – with the bounty-hunter by his side – he reached toward the image of the stricken Storied Watcher.

He angrily shouted at the hologram of Bob Billings, "For Christ's *sake*, Bob… why are you just *standing* there – do something!"

"You're bein' *played*, pardner!" remarked Wolf. "I'm headin' inside!"

A second later, Boyd's accusations came to an abrupt halt, as – with a surprised look on his face – he seemed to realize the deception that was afoot. But he and Wolf had to dodge a barrage of high-velocity rifle-shots that had actually been aimed at Jacobson and Ramirez, by someone further inside the White House, shooting into the Oval Office.

Tanaka – who was just outside, looking through one of the garden-side windows – had a clear line of sight to the fracas inside. She unleashed one of her lethal lightening-bolts right through the window, aiming the discharge squarely at where the gunfire had been issuing from. Both the Oval Office window and the semi-hidden interior door were instantly blown to pieces by this attack, which was supplemented – a half-second later – by a less-potent (but still very lethal) lightening-shot fired by Ramirez, directed at the same location.

A fusillade of rifle-bullets – as if fired by an unseen assailant who had lost his balance – sprayed all around, impacting the ceiling and interior walls of the Oval Office, shattering many of the remaining windows from the inside out. But the onslaught stopped relatively quickly, momentarily pausing the action.

Jacobson turned to address the bounty-hunter, who was running at high speed to enter the building.

"*Wolf!*" he shouted, "I'll chase him! Hector – get the other door!"

The bounty-hunter replied by unleashing a fireball – clearly, with restrained-energy-investment, though it was still more than powerful enough to kill a normal man – at the main door leading from the Oval Office to the set of small rooms just to the west. The portal-barrier was blown to smoking bits, with small fires breaking out all around it; fortunately, Wolf had enough presence of mind to re-absorb these into his body, as he ran through the entrance, hunting for enemies further beyond.

He let out an ululating, eerie howl as he went, yelling, "I'm *comin'* for ya, fuckers!"

Meanwhile, Ramirez went for the door on the northeast leading to the President's Secretary Office, using telekinesis to defeat its door-handle lock. He disappeared off to the north.

Jacobson, for his part, barged through what little was left of the semi-hidden door, located more to the north-to-west side of the Oval Office. Moving at great speed, he entered the interior of the building, being presented with a wide corridor going diagonally from north-east to south-west.

In the far south-western end of this hallway, the former Mars mission commander could just see the backside of a man in a damaged – but, evidently, still functional – mechanical-techno-combat-suit.

The terrorist had a rifle in his hand and was aiming it at unseen opponents, or victims, further to the west, just out of sight.

He shrieked, through some kind of voice-amplification,

"The monster's *dead*, Clark – and you're *next!*"

Should Have Been A Nice, Easy Slaughter

With the aid of bio-mechanical precision and with his auto-rifle loaded with explosive-tipped rounds, Top Dog – purposely ignoring everything else (in particular, the appearance of a guy in a weird-looking, crystalline armor-suit, behind him and to his left; also, the bloody corpses of many of his soldiers) that was going on, around him – aimed squarely for the President of the United States.

"*Death to traitors!*" he inveighed, while squeezing the trigger.

At first, the ex-Agency leader was elated at merely being able to get an attack of *any* kind off, given the multi-front engagement that he had somehow gotten himself into. But though fifteen or more rapid-fire shots instantly rattled out the barrel of his gun, he observed – to his dismay – that none of these actually hit their intended target.

Instead, the President's forward-charging son was struck repeatedly, being at first knocked back on his feet and then sent flying by the detonating rounds – any one of which should not only have killed a normal man, but which in fact should have torn him in half.

Fuck! silently thought Top Dog,

Why doesn't the little shit just die!

However, Matt was very definitely knocked out of the battle, as – with smoke issuing from multiple bullet-hits, and blood pouring out of numerous ugly wounds – he lay prostate on the floor, cringing while trying to cover his head with his forearms.

Fine, mused the ex-assassin,

Now I'll finally get the little fucker's old man –

Again, he depressed the trigger, sending forth a spray of explosive bullet-fire that should have reduced every living thing within a thirty degree cone in front of him, to a bloody pulp.

He exulted in advance, at the carnage he felt sure was about to ensue.

But instead, what Top Dog saw was some kind of strange, subtly-yellow-tinged, near-transparent distortion-field, spanning most of the center-parts of the West Wing hall, appearing between himself and the President, the First

Lady and their daughter. Clairie's eyes were glowing and there was a look of undisguised hatred on her otherwise-soft-featured teenage face.

There were several loud explosions as his bullets hit this strange barrier, and then suddenly, the former Agency-leader was thrown backward by the brutally-forceful impact of what he instinctively knew had to be high-caliber gunshots, or something much more potent than a normal rifle-bullet.

Instantly, his combat-suit registered multiple system-failures and burn-outs, but there was no time to review the warnings on his HUD, since one round – or part of it – hit and fractured his helmet's supposedly shatter-proof visor. Wisps of smoke, undoubtedly from damaged circuitry, began to offend his nostrils; it was becoming difficult to breathe.

Thinking fast as he rolled and then activated the suit's auto-recovery function, Top Dog jettisoned the now-useless headgear, steadied himself and re-readied his rifle.

"*Jacobson!* He's *mine!*" he heard the voice of Kaysten shout, from down the corridor to the west.

He had practiced well for this eventuality.

As he hit the belt-catch that released two grenades – one fragmentation, the other, nerve-gas – Top Dog whispered, "stealth".

Instantly, everything around him went to black, as he turned to the right and – though effectively blind – ran as fast as he could, to the north-east.

More frantic yelling, coming from somewhere behind him, met his ears.

Sam Jacobson's Belly-Flop

Jacobson wasted a full half-second checking his left flank, as he scanned the north-east for signs of opponents; in fact, the gesture was not completely wasted, as his Mars senses warned of two terrorists, approaching from far-off in that direction. But the delay cost him dearly, because it gave the combat-suited enemy enough time to yell some kind of curse at whoever his targets were, out of sight to the south-west – and to open fire on these unfortunates.

The former Mars mission commander was about to charge, when he heard the haunting melodies of two distinct – yet heretofore-unknown – war-songs, coming from the corridor beyond the combat-suited-terrorist. A fraction of a second later, he observed – to his grim satisfaction – how the guy with the gun had himself become the target of someone with a *lot* of firepower; the assailant was struck by multiple, high-velocity bullet-impacts.

The man *should* have been killed instantly, but instead was simply sent flying backward. He righted himself with incredible speed, although it did appear as if his battle-suit had been severely compromised, since his helmet – whose dark-mirror-tinted visor had been cracked by one of the bullet-impacts – was quickly jettisoned.

Jacobson got only the briefest of glimpses at the man's face; it was clean-shaven, dark-haired, middle-aged and otherwise nondescript. Yet *something* about it, was alarming, revealing and enraging, all at once.

The ex-astronaut heard a voice – it sounded like Kaysten – yelling, "He's mine!". But Jacobson had no time to ponder his irritation at being denied the chance, to take down the combat-suited terrorist. The latter man dropped two fist-sized, almost-round objects from his belt, and then just… *disappeared*, as Jacobson had seen happen with other, similarly-geared enemies, back in the White House Center Hall.

"*Look* out – *grenades!*" yelled the former Mars mission commander, as he executed a flying belly-flop on top of the two hand-bombs, just before they both exploded.

Money On The Mutt

"What the hell do they think they're *doing?*" spat a frustrated Minnie Chu, as she observed the onslaught of the Mars Gang and its hangers-on, against the terrorists inside the West Wing. "They're going to ruin *everything!* What if that sonofabitch terrorist offs the President, because he thinks we've reneged on our part of the deal?"

"Dunno," offered Hendricks. "I sure hope Mr. Jacobson knows something we don't, otherwise it's all on *him* – although I doubt he – much less Wolf – really *give* a shit if the President gets smoked. What you want to do, Minnie?"

"How's Sylvia?" she asked.

"Out of it," replied the third agent, as he bent over to examine the prone Abruzzio. "But alive and well as far as I can tell. How in God's name is she keeping those illusions going, while she's in *this* state?"

"Karéin's voodoo magic," said the *nouvelle* FBI-director, with a shake of her head.

"They've entered the building," observed Hendricks, as he did his best to surveil the movements of Jacobson, the bounty-hunter, Ramirez and Tanaka, after their invasion of the seat of Presidential authority.

There were the sounds of muffled explosions and rapid-fire gunfire – and the hint of previously-unheard war-songs – coming from further within the West Wing, past the Oval Office. A short pause ensued.

"We have to decide what we're going to do," directed Chu. "Our first priority has to be the President – but we can't leave Sylvia here all by herself. One of us will have to stay here and watch her, until she comes to."

"Yeah… okay… *whatever*, boss," grumbled the third agent. "Please forgive me if I just wanted to get some licks in, you know?"

"*Ohhhh,*" they heard Abruzzio moan. Her eyelashes fluttered and she licked her lips – a gesture that was immediately added-to by the dog, which brought an immediate smile to the more-than-a-woman's face – as she unsteadily attempted to sit up.

"Sylvia... *Sylvia?*" quietly implored the former team-leader. "Take it easy... looked like you got hit – but you didn't – what's going *on?*"

"I was concentrating on the image of Karéin, trying to make her speak convincingly," explained the scientist, "And then... whammo! That shot hit the mirage, but it felt like something had torn out *my* heart... feedback of some type that I hadn't guessed was possible, I guess. Damn – did that ever *hurt!*"

"Nice of her to warn you about that kind of thing happening," sniffed Chu.

"How are you keeping those mirages up, anyway?" inquired a fascinated Hendricks. "I mean... you were out cold."

"*I'm,* not," replied Abruzzio, with a wry smile, as she shot a loving glance at the puppy.

"You mean *she...* holy *cow,*" commented the third agent.

Rainbow's tongue hung out in classic "cute-dog" fashion. Her eyes mimicked the multi-colored glow in those of her master.

"Sylvia," asked Chu, "While you were out, our friends Jacobson and Company charged in there... God help the President. Are you feeling strong enough to wait here, while Will and I go inside the building?"

"Sure... I'll be back to normal in a minute or so," confirmed the ex-JPL scientist.

"Rainbow," said Chu, "You can drop the holograms now – the bad people are all gone –"

Her instructions were cut short by the sound of an explosion coming from the West Wing, around the Cabinet Room. Numerous shards of what appeared to be shattered structural-materials were thrown skyward, and – about a second later – the figure of a man, wearing a bio-mechanical combat-suit – albeit without the expected helmet – appeared, as if he had jumped upward through a hole in the roof.

His leap carried him perhaps five feet above the roof, to which he fell back, coming to rest on his feet. After rotating in place to survey the surroundings in all directions, he crouched down and seemed to be working a key-pad on one arm of his combat-suit.

All the human-sized beings – Abruzzio, somewhat less steadily – now stood up, so as to clear the top of the bushes and to thus have a clear line of sight to what had transpired. The dog levitated in place, turning its gaze to the West Wing roof; a second or two later, the mirage-replicas of the Storied Watcher and her family, flickered and then slowly faded from view.

"*Shit!*" complained Chu, "Except for the lack of a helmet, that looks like the guy I tangled with, while air-lifting the President out of here, the first time. Wish we could kick his ass – but we've got to go inside and deal with –"

Rainbow shook her head, growled and barked. Then – mimicking an English Setter's best pointing-act – she straightened herself out, and, all the while floating in mid-air, stared straight at the man on the roof.

"She's saying that we have to *get* this guy," declared Abruzzio.

"Works for *me*," remarked Hendricks. "Minnie, *you* can go in there and –"

"*No!*" contradicted the former JPL scientist, "All three – err, *four* – of us."

"But the *President!*" argued Chu.

"This is more *important*, Minnie!" countered Abruzzio.

"How do you know that?" exclaimed the former team-leader.

"Because Rainbow's *never* wrong about things like this!" came the reply.

The scientist's eyes were glowing and hints of her war-song began to be heard, as she started to levitate. The puppy flew at her side.

"My money's with the mutt," quipped Hendricks, as he, too, summoned the *Fire* and lifted off the ground. "Never really *liked* the President, anyway."

"Fine – there goes the *country*... not to mention, my career," sourly mentioned the *nouvelle* FBI-director, as – with bright-glowing eyes and an unsuppressed war-song – she rocketed into the Washington, D.C. skies.

All She Wants To Do, Is Talk

Refusing to believe his luck at having successfully dodged the half-alien beast in the crystal-suit, Top Dog had sprinted – near-blind – out of the eastern end of the corridor to the north-west of the Oval Office. It was a near-miracle that he didn't run right into a wall... or, for that matter, into an enemy.

The suit's stealth-mode light-bending gear timed out, just to the west of the Cabinet Room, and he could again see his surroundings. There were two of his fellow-warriors right there, when he appeared. They did not appear especially surprised to see him.

He pointed to the south-west.

"Hostiles over there," he commanded. "Call for reinforcements – then go *kill* the enemy! And be ready – they have substantial firepower. Permission is granted to use your grenades and gas, as necessary."

"Sir!" answered the two, as they readied their rifles and began to advance to the south-west.

Every chess-player has to sacrifice a pawn, now and then, he mused, as he raced into the Cabinet Room.

Don't like making more noise than necessary, reflected Top Dog.

Easiest thing to do would be to just hop up through that nice big hole that the bitch zapped into the ceiling, above the Press Room...

But that's exactly where they'll expect *me to go.*

Could try one of the windows... but likely hostiles surrounding the building, spoiling for the ol' ambush...

We'll have to hope that Duke's boys come through – but in the meantime, I need to get out of here.

Primary mission has been accomplished...

Even if he somehow dodges the remaining assets we've got down there, and even if GrayWar draws a complete blank... we can deal with Clark at our leisure, now that I've pulled the teeth of his little alien nanny!

He threw the last of his bursting-charges up at the ceiling, and – after verifying that its vacuum-cups had affixed it securely – stood back as he enabled the "detonate" command.

Boom!

The hole thus produced in the White House ceiling was rather small – the structure was obviously reinforced to resist exactly this kind of attack – but it was (barely) large enough to accommodate him, albeit with his auto-rifle held close to his chest.

So – after taking note of an audible warning about "fuel-cell level nearing critical depletion" in his ear-piece – Top Dog moved under the breach, tensed his legs, and rocketed skyward. He overshot the roof-top slightly, but was easily able to right himself and land on two feet.

Damn, he mused, *I wish they hadn't knocked out my helmet – I'm back to Eyeball Mark One to recce the situation...*

As quickly as possible, he looked in every direction, searching for enemies. There were apparently a few government agents left on the roof, to the east; but they seemed completely hunkered-down, and – oddly – neither engaged him, nor even moved in his direction. The sniper-fire from the south was still going on, but it was down to the occasional, wildly-off-the-target rifle-round.

Maybe they know what's good for them, he exulted.

How many have I got to my credit, by now?

But anyway... back to business – out of power for more bunny-hops... better call for egress help... just gotta get them to land somewhere on to the lawn...

Quietly, he uttered,

"Keypad".

Instantly, a metal case – affixed to his lower left arm – popped open, revealing a recessed array of color- and symbol-coded push-buttons.

Rapidly, Top Dog started to enter in the code that would summon the means of his escape. He was almost finished, when his senses alerted him to the presence of something – well, something strange.

Who's playing music, at a time like this? he thought.

Oh shit! he realized, upon seeing what appeared to be an Asian-American dressed in tight-fitting black Spandex, another female looking like a mousy librarian, and a more worrisome, tall, red-haired man brandishing a pistol, literally *flying* through the air, in his direction.

He did a double-take.

Is that a dog? wondered the perplexed Agency torpedo.

Surround him! came the mental command from Minnie Chu; and the other three flying more-than-humans, implemented almost perfectly.

Chu herself maneuvered so as to drop from the sky to the north of the man in the incomplete combat-suit; Abruzzio landed on the roof to his south-west, while Hendricks did the same to the south-east. Rainbow, meanwhile, hovered by the former JPL scientist's side.

Instantly, the man's auto-rifle came to his grasp. He pointed it at Chu.

"Back *off!*" he yelled. "I'm done here... all I need to do is leave. Make one hostile move and I'll blow you *apart* – and be aware, the bullets in this gun can put a nice big hole in a *tank!*"

The *nouvelle* FBI-director stared at the man in the suit; her gaze lingered overlong. Eventually she said,

"You!"

"What's *that* supposed to mean?" he challenged, while still drawing a bead on the former team-leader.

"Remember *me?*" she taunted. "Pittsburgh? The top floor? You know... where you threatened my *life* – and those of my friends – one of whom, stands here today."

"Damn *right!*" spat Hendricks. "You squeeze that trigger, asshole – and your head goes in the next *second!*"

"I'll *kill* her!" warned the man in the combat-suit.

"No... you *won't*," answered Chu.

There was a strange, sinister look in her eyes, and on her face. She was staring directly into the assassin's eyes.

"Don't *try* me!" growled the man. "I'm going to jump down to the lawn, now... stay *back!*"

"Hey there," she called, with an odd tone in her voice.

"I think we got off on the wrong foot – why not be friends? You don't want to shoot me... *do* you?" purred the *nouvelle* FBI-director, as her buzzing, entrancing war-song hummed from the very air-molecules. "What you want to do is just to lower that gun... you don't have to throw it away. We just need to *talk.*"

"What are you... *talking* about..." he stammered, with wide eyes.

They noticed that his grasp on the weapon – and his otherwise-taut, combat-ready stance – seemed to be loosening.

"Stay *back!*" he repeated.

"Look... I'm unarmed," claimed Chu. "I just want to talk. Don't *shoot!*"

The man was clearly struggling to react – to flee or to fight – but *something* seemed to be impairing his ability to do so.

More than one "Evil Eye" on Ms. Minnie Chu, silently sent Hendricks to Abruzzio.

She fuckin' got to teach me a bit of that witchcraft... think of the deal I can get, buying my next car.

I know, responded Abruzzio.

That's a scary gift... I couldn't lift a finger against her, if I tried.

Rainbow is saying the same to me!

The former team-leader took a series of slow, carefully-planned steps in his direction. The others held their breath as she approached closer, until she was about an arm's-length from the terrorist.

"Oh-kay," she offered, with a smile hiding thinly-disguised contempt. "Let's talk."

"Bb... bb...aa... kk..." said the man, as if in a trance.

Chu's war-song began to wax mightily. Her eyes were glowing as she stared directly into those of her combat-suited victim.

"You look *awfully* tired," she commented. "Don't you want to take a short break?"

The man gasped and drooled. His eyelids fluttered, and for a second it looked like he was about to fall asleep.

But then – suddenly – he seemed to come to.

"What the fuck are you *doing* to me?" he hissed. "I'll –"

However, he never got to do whatever he had been planning. This was primarily due to Hendricks, who had stalked the man from behind, while Chu had the assassin's attention. Using the butt of his pistol, the third agent struck a vicious blow to the back of the terrorist's head, apparently knocking him unconscious while leaving a bloody wound in his scalp. The assault was followed up with a brutal right hook, propelled by much more force than could have been mustered by any normal man.

In fact, the dazed assassin could not have used his gun anyway, due to Abruzzio's vice-like telekinesis, which had locked on to the weapon while he was distracted. The gun fell from his hands but was caught in mid-air, then was deposited on the rooftop.

"He... *dead*?" exclaimed Chu, upon seeing the punishment that had just been inflicted on the man in the combat-suit. "Not good, if so – I *recognize* this prick – he's with the Agency. We need him *alive!*"

"Much to my regret," observed Hendricks, "I can tell that he's still breathing. Sorry... I *tried* to take his head off. Guess I'll need some time off, to work on my boxing."

"You'll have to use up your quota of vacation-days," quipped the third agent's former boss. "I'll try to keep him out of it... but he might have a suicide-pill – check his mouth!"

"I suppose that falls to *me*... what with the scientific training," groused the ex-JPL-leader, as she felt the somnolent man's teeth and gums. "I'll use a low-level rad-scan, should heat the materials differentially... *nada*. If he's got one... it's somewhere else on him. Yuck! Blood all over my hands!"

A quick burst of high-energy microwaves – powerful enough to be uncomfortably felt by both Hendricks and Chu – burned the offending bodily-fluids off of Abruzzio's fingers, sending the assassin's blood and saliva skyward in wisps of oxidized smoke.

"Sister," directed the former team-leader, "I see a lot of metal-scrap around here – I'm betting it'll make a pretty good set of restraints. You want to help me bend it around him?"

Abruzzio nodded and raised her arms. Her own war-song sounded in the background, as she and Chu, working together, lifted twisted-and-torn girders, stringers and random pieces of sheet-metal, forming these into elongated, wire-like structures, as if the two women were children manipulating play-putty.

The dog – ever on cue – fetched a clump of disconnected computer-cables, depositing these at Abruzzio's feet with a happy "yip!". The ex-JPL-scientist gratefully accepted these, using them to further bind the still-unconscious terrorist.

Slowly-congealing blood dripped from his nose and mouth, as the tightly-restrained assassin was laid on the ground in prone position.

"What you want to do with him, Minnie?" inquired Hendricks.

"We should get him downstairs... somewhere we can keep an eye on him, when he comes to," proposed Chu. "God knows whatever other tricks he's got hidden away in that combat-suit. Until we can get him out of it, we can't be one hundred per cent certain that he won't trigger one or more of them and then run amok all over again."

"Agreed," said Abruzzio. "But what do you want to do, if he comes to, before we can do that? How far can we go, in trying to subdue him?"

"Would I be right in assuming that those microwaves of yours, could short out the circuits in his battle-suit?" countered the *nouvelle* FBI-director.

"I think so... at this close range, even if it's EMP-hardened," commented the former JPL scientist. "But to be sure of completely knocking it out, I'd have to use a dangerously-powerful burst. It might *kill* him – not to mention, any ordinary human in the vicinity."

"If it comes to that – *do* it!" ordered Chu. "I think this guy is the ring-leader, and we can't afford to have him get loose. The only caveat is the President... under no circumstances is he to be put at risk. Understood?"

"Definitely," confirmed Abruzzio.

"Yeah," echoed the third agent.

"He's out… shouldn't be able to actively resist," noted Chu. "Let's all lock on to him, then lift him down to the Oval Office. Be on the lookout for snipers."

They stood around the fallen Top Dog, gently lofting him upward with combined telekinetic forces; to her amusement and gratification, Abruzzio noticed that even little Rainbow was lending a paw.

Then – as her own feet had just left the West Wing roof – Chu's expression turned to one of alarm, as she stared off to the north and then to the south.

"What is it… oh," asked an equally-nonplussed Hendricks. "What the *hell* –"

"Didn't you tell the Army not to assault this place?" remarked Abruzzio.

"Sure *did*," replied the *nouvelle* FBI-director.

"Then who are all those soldiers, marching down the streets, toward us?" asked the third agent. "I got a decent look at 'em with Mars eyes – somehow I don't think they're either U.S. Army or Marines. Fatigues look different."

"Just when you think it's under *control...*" muttered a frustrated Chu.

She looked at the others.

"Let's get this asshole down there," she said. "Then… I guess we've got another battle to fight."

Now, Honey, You Know Why

Jerry Kaysten had temporarily left his boss and the rest of the First Family behind, in his single-minded task to chase down the murderous assassin who had shot Matt; but after seeing Jacobson's diamond-encrusted figure falling on a bunch of grenades (the former Mars mission commander was literally bounced off the ceiling by the blast, but seemed otherwise unhurt), the Chief of Staff reluctantly decided that protecting the rest of the civilians was the higher priority.

He reversed course and in a half-second was tending to the President and his son.

"How *is* he?" gingerly asked Kaysten, while the prone Matt moaned. Smoke was still coming from the six or seven open, bloody bullet-wounds on his upper torso and arms. His mother was crying and cradling him, but his sister – notwithstanding the expected distraught expression – was bright-eyed, *Fire*-supplied and warily standing guard, to one side.

"He should be *dead*," answered the gravely-worried U.S. leader, "Given how many of those shots he took – did you see where the stray ones hit the walls? They made holes the size of a damn tennis-ball!"

"Yeah," agreed the Chief of Staff, "Those sure weren't ordinary rifle-bullets that the asshole was firing –"

"Look *out!*" yelled Clairie, as the door on the south wall, leading to the Oval Office's supporting-rooms, exploded outward in a hurricane of smoke and fire. Within the conflagration, spilling out on to the West Wing corridor-floor beyond, were the grim remains of what must have been a terrorist foot-soldier; the corpse was so badly-charred as to be almost unrecognizable.

"Whoever you are – step forward and I'll *kill* you!" shrieked the alien-powered teenager.

Her bright-but-portentous war-song seemed to be contesting another one; the latter was also enervatingly-exciting to human ears, but it was more sinister – a crackling, hissing electro-rock dirge.

"I don't know *who* you are," warned a gruff male voice from the south, beyond the carbonized doorway, "But I'm huntin' them terrorist fuckers, and *nobody's* gettin' in my way! Here's a little taste of what's in *store* for you, if you don't get your ass *out* of here!"

Clairie was standing about two feet outside the doorway, with her force-shield fully powered-up; suddenly, the barrier was hit by a roaring jet of flame, the terrible heat of which could be felt even at a distance of ten or twelve feet, wherein were located the other members of the First Family.

The teenager screamed as if in agony, though – to the relief of her aghast father and mother – she did not seem to be physically harmed. However, the battle was now seriously joined, as her gold-tinged weirding-barrier reflected a substantial amount of the unseen assailant's attack, back upon him.

There was another howl of pain and confusion, coming from the rooms leading to the Oval Office, while the Presidential daughter – the front-side of her clothing fuming and slightly-blackened, though she herself did not appear to be burned – staggered backward, out of line of sight to the portal.

"Shit – shit – *shit!*" she cursed, "That felt like sticking my head into a fuckin' *furnace! Owwww!*"

"Why you *bitch!*" angrily yelled the attacker, "No human being could *do* that – and it *hurt!* Fire *never* hurts me! You got five *seconds* to clear out, before I burn down this whole fuckin' *place*, with you *in* it!"

There was a surge of heat – instantly painful even to Kaysten and the cowering First Family, though they were relatively far away – coming from the doorway. The opposite side of the corridor-wall started to discolor and smoke.

The Chief of Staff was about to charge into an almost-certainly futile battle, but he was beaten to it by the unexpected, diamond-enshrouded figure of Sam Jacobson, who bounded right over the heads of the civilians in the middle of the corridor.

Despite the murderous heat, the ex-astronaut stood just outside the doorway and shouted,

"*Wolf!* These aren't terrorists – they're *civilians!* Turn it *off*… or you'll feel my shock-wave! *You* know – the one that pulverizes concrete and that knocks tanks flying!"

After a couple of seconds, the intense heat subsided, although it did not end completely.

They heard coming from somewhere in the rooms to the south,

"Jesus H. Christ, Jacobson… who the fuck *is* that, back there? It's like I got hit by fifty lit cigars, all over!"

"So did *I*," muttered Clairie, as she gamely (and – fortunately – successfully) tried to extinguish the nascent fires that were starting to combust within her clothing. "Who *is* that dude, anyway? If it hadn't been for my, like, alien-powers… I'd look like a used-up match-stick, by now."

The former Mars mission commander – still encased in his adamantine fortress – did not directly address the question. Instead, he just said,

"Did Karéin mention to you," he asked, while staring with glowing eyes, in the Presidential daughter's direction, "That it wouldn't be a good idea, to fight your 'brothers' and 'sisters' of the Holy *Fire?*"

"As a matter of fact… yeah, she *did* say something like that, to Matt and me," admitted Clairie.

"Well, then, honey," patiently offered the ex-astronaut, "Now you know why."

One Better – With A Sandwich-Bag

The first of the other "more-than-humans" encountered by the Chu-Hendricks-Abruzzio trifecta – upon carrying their unconscious prize down to the Oval Office – was Hector Ramirez, just back from parts to the north and east.

The former JPL scientist hadn't much to report – except, perhaps, how the White House Cabinet Room "could use a little fixing-up", after it had been hit by the proverbial hurricane, in the course of dealing with two more garden-variety terrorists encountered in that place.

There were two other egress-points – one on the western Oval Office wall, with charring clearly evident all over it, while the other – to the north-west – was simply smashed wide open. Chu and Hendricks followed the western path while Abruzzio, her dog, Ramirez and the tightly-bound, telekinetically-levitated terrorist advanced into the other portal.

The latter three came upon a battle-scarred corridor running diagonally from the south-west to the north-east; this also contained a large number of dead intruders, their bodies cruelly-abused by some fearsome attack.

The Abruzzio group looked to the south-west and saw a small crowd of people, including the First Family (one member of whom was lying on his back, obviously in distress), Wolf (who was in a shouting match with the diamond-encased Sam Jacobson), Jerry Kaysten, Minnie Chu, Brent Boyd and Cherie Tanaka. Multiple war-songs hummed along in the background, just above the level of human audibility.

Tanaka was bending down over the President's son. A barely-visible, violet-colored light extended from her forearms, washing over the teenage boy's wounded body.

"*Hey* there!" accosted Abruzzio. "Are you under attack? Can we help?"

"Not right now… unless you count this guy's big mouth," came a response from a young woman, who the ex-JPL scientist recognized as the President's daughter. She was pointing at Wolf.

"Yeah, well, you smart-ass little –" started the bounty-hunter. He was interrupted by Jacobson.

"Can you two give the rest of us just a *minute*, before you take it outside and annihilate each other?" complained the former Mars mission commander. "Sylvia… who *is* that you've got with you?"

The Abruzzio group advanced until it was within a few feet of the President and his crippled son.

"Oh my *Lord*, Ms. Abruzzio," gasped the U.S. leader. "You *got* him!"

"Uhh… who's 'him', sir?" responded the scientist. "You mean *this* guy?"

"He's the head of the Agency," explained the President. "Didn't Ms. Chu tell you?"

"Yeah… in passing," disclosed Abruzzio. "We've got him nicely trussed-up, and we've verified that he doesn't have a chewable suicide-pill in his mouth, but until we get him completely out of that suit we can't be one hundred per cent sure that he doesn't have some other way to prematurely end his sorry life."

"'Agency', you say?" growled Boyd. "Just leave him with *me* for thirty seconds, and I'll be happy to do that for you… I guarantee you'll be able to fit what's left of him, into a freezer-bag."

"No – you won't," challenged Tanaka, as she glowered at the helpless Top Dog. "Because I'll do you one better… sandwich-bag!"

"That's a chance that we'll have to take, and, Major Boyd, Professor Tanaka, as little as any of us – myself certainly included – like it, I suppose he's entitled to due process," advanced Chu. "But Mr. President, the number one priority *has* to be to get you and your family to safety – we've been very lucky so far, that you weren't hurt while trying to escape –"

"You can thank my *children* for that," interjected the President. "Clairie and Matt used their – uhh – 'alien-powers', to defeat those bastards who you see over there," – he pointed to the mangled bodies of the terrorists at the bend in the corridor, to the east – "They had already pulled the trigger on us. Unfortunately Matt got hit… we've got to get him to a doctor!"

"It's… *okay*… Dad," mumbled the wounded Presidential son. "Hurts like hell… I'll *live*… don't ask me how."

"Ms. Abruzzio," ventured Clairie, "You remember how, like, back in the car, I told you how cool it must be, to have these 'powers'?"

"Sure *do!*" answered the smiling ex-JPL scientist.

"It… *is*," gushed the daughter. "Except for the part where, like, if they don't start working at the exact right time, you get fuckin' blown to *bits* – sorry about the French, Daddy – and you're scared *shitless* five seconds before, because, like, you've got no *idea* how you're gonna make it out alive. You know?"

"You mean Angel Lady didn't mention that there's a *catch* to all this 'alien god' shit she dropped on us?" quipped Hendricks. "Aww… shucks!"

"And no take-backs, either," added Ramirez. "Like it or not… you are now a super-hero, young lady. You will have to play the part."

"Welcome to the *team*, sister-warrior," congratulated Abruzzio. "You too, Matt."

Clairie beamed while her brother – still lying on the floor with his forebody propped up against the West Wing wall – gave a weak "thumbs-up" gesture.

"What's *that*, little one?" spoke Tanaka, out loud.

The former Mars science officer had her hands pressed against her chest; she was staring forward, as if addressing someone unseen.

"What are you hearing from 'Sister-Many-Guises', son?" echoed Chu, while touching the locket suspended and secreted under her neckline. "What does she speak of?"

She, too, looked absorbed in a conversation with a ghost.

"*Vìrya* Sài'ymë is saying that there are men with guns approaching," warned Tanaka. "*Hundreds* of them – and some are almost *here!*"

"Damn! More terrorists?" asked Hendricks. "Wait a minute… that doesn't make any *sense* – reference the prick we got in leg-irons, why wouldn't he bring all of his soldiers along with him, when he first invaded the White House? If he's got so many troops, what does he *gain* by having 'em sit outside and wait, while all the fun's going on, in here? Does your, uhh, 'daughter' have an explanation for *that?*"

"No," disclaimed Tanaka. "But – and this doesn't add up, either – she thinks they're coming from all directions… including *below?*"

"She must mean the underground tunnels," said Kaysten. "Well… now it's *us* holding the key hostage – that is, 'Mr. CIA Asshole' there. Listen – if Wolf didn't burn out everything in the communications-room –"

"*Should* have… but didn't… guess I missed," interjected the bounty-hunter.

"Hat's off to *you*, then," continued the Chief of Staff. "We can broadcast a warning to his underlings that we'll smoke him, if they don't back off. Mr. President… what do you *say?*"

"We can't countenance *murder*," countered the U.S. leader, "But that doesn't mean that we can't leave them guessing about –"

There was a look of alarm on Boyd's face. He turned to address Jacobson.

"Commander," said the former Mars mission pilot, "We left our families over there in the East Wing – Boatman's guarding them, but even with *his* powers, what if –"

"Yeah," acknowledged Jacobson. "We had better get over there... shepherd them out of danger."

"I'll go with you, when you're ready," vowed Hendricks.

"Me too," added Abruzzio.

"Good," said the former Mars mission commander.

Rainbow turned to face the door on the south wall, from which Wolf had come. She pointed her nose at the portal and growled.

"Sir," interrupted an alarmed Tanaka in the President's direction, "*Vìrya* Sài'ymë is saying that some of them are now in the Oval Office!"

"Cherie – watch the corridor to the west, please!" shouted the former Mars mission commander, as he ran to the east. "Brent – you and I should cover those two doorways."

A veritable symphony of electrifying, exciting war-songs began to wax in volume.

"*On* it!" pledged the former Mars mission science officer. "*Vìrya* Sài'ymë – gird thee for *war!*"

Hendricks and Wolf moved rapidly to join her. In a half-second, the bounty-hunter was enshrouded in fire; though next to Tanaka on the left, his infernal aura did not seem to bother her.

The third agent was on Tanaka's right-hand side. Elfin charges of energy danced over his fore-arms, as he said to the other two,

"Been studying both of you... fuckers fire at *me*, and they'll get a nice taste of that ol' smoke-stack lightening."

"Suits *me*, pardner," returned Wolf, while Tanaka just smiled.

"Affirmative," said Boyd, as he moved into position to have a clear shot through the southern-wall doorway that Wolf had come from.

"Clairie – Jerry – with me – protect the President, Matt and the First Lady!" ordered Chu, whose eyes were glowing with the now-familiar *Fire*.

Amazingly – considering the now-shrinking wounds that he had suffered only a few minutes before – the Presidential son came right to his feet. Energetic charges of *Amaiish* lit up his body and fists, as his eyes stared forward with a deliberate, ominous shine.

"Fuckin' bring it *on!*" he shouted, as his sister – herself staring forward in the direction that the last attack had come from – grabbed one of Matt's biceps, stole a quick glance and a smile in his direction, and then powered up her force-field. Kaysten and some of the others noticed that it was now larger and deeper than it had been before. The reflective-shield was raised behind where Jacobson and Boyd were standing.

Ramirez, Abruzzio, the dog and Kaysten moved to join Chu and the First Family. A whirling wall of air-currents, centered on the Tex-Mex scientist, began to manifest itself, just outside of Clairie's force-field, behind the backs of Wolf and Tanaka; it knocked down the few wall-paintings that were not already shredded by gunfire and threw up a haze of dust and dirt.

Thus the odd company of U.S. elite citizens and more-than-humans waited, for perhaps ten seconds more, collectively holding their breath.

Finally, the figure of a helmeted man in fatigues and army-boots, carrying a rifle, appeared in the angled corridor, to the north-east of where Jacobson was standing guard. The man's combat-gear looked substantially different from what had been observed on the terrorists, thus far encountered. The insignia on his collar marked him as someone of at least lieutenant-rank, or possibly higher.

"Drop that weapon and get down on the ground," shouted the former Mars mission commander, "Or suffer the *consequences!*"

Instantly, the soldier was illuminated by a beam of light from Brent Boyd's left hand; the right was still trained on the southern door.

"Raise the gun and I'll *vaporize* you!" he spat.

The newcomer was either extremely brave – or, perhaps – he was just stupid, because instead of heeding the warnings, he stayed in place and began to talk back.

"I'm here to inform you, that you're under *arrest!*" he announced.

"Oh… is that *so?*" challenged Jacobson. "On whose authority, if you don't mind me asking?"

"Sam!" called Tanaka. "Wolf, Will and I can see some more of these guys… they're at the far end of the corridor. They're taking up firing-positions! I'm raising my screen – we'll attack on your orders!"

As she had indicated, another force-field – akin to, but subtly different from, the one belonging to the Presidential daughter – appeared in the corridor to the west of where the former Mars mission science officer, and the bounty-hunter, were tensely waiting.

Slightly back of it – closer to the three more-than-humans – yet another translucent barrier came into view. It was smaller and less substantial-looking than Tanaka's own.

She turned her head momentarily to look at the third agent.

"You've been hitting those 'alien-tricks' training-books hard, young man," she observed.

Proudly, Hendricks winked at her.

"Bunch of grunts with rifles and pistols," observed Wolf, *sotto voce.* "Don't them dumb shits ever *learn*?"

"Too bad their next lesson's gonna have to be their last," whispered the third agent, in reply.

Meanwhile, Jacobson continued his contretemps with the newly-appearing soldier.

"I'm here from GrayWar Legion on express orders of Mr. Duke," announced the warrior. "We're protecting the new President-Designate of the

United States – Grady Wyckheiser. He'll be making an announcement to the country from the Oval Office, in a few minutes."

"Unbelievable" Seems Blasé

A nonplussed, diamond-enshrouded Sam Jacobson stood, mutely unbelieving, for two or three seconds; then he responded,

"Uhh… 'Grady Wyckheiser? Who the hell's *that*… and who's he, to me?"

Kaysten – who, along with everyone in or around the First Family, had been carefully following the conversation, called out to the former Mars mission leader, "Commander – he used to be a Republican Senator from Alabama… but he's been retired for four or five years, now."

An exasperated Boyd interjected, "This is *bullshit!* The *real* President is right *behind* me! What gives you amateur soldier-boys the *right* to –"

"It's the position of President Wyckheiser – and of the new Administration – that the tragic death of the previous President, plus the recent demise of his natural successor – the Vice-President – has forced Mr. Wyckheiser to reluctantly assume control of the –"

"I'm very much alive, as you can plainly see!" shouted the President, as he arose from his previous crouch.

"What nonsense is *this*, now?" he muttered to Kaysten and his wife.

"*Got* to be Duke," observed the Chief of Staff. "He's making his big play for all the marbles, now – hitting us while we're down. The only question in *my* mind is, 'who else is *in* with him'. I'd say Bezomorton… but the bugger's probably dead."

Ramirez powered down his hurricane-shield, although the other force-fields remained very much in effect. The war-songs abated somewhat, but did not subside altogether.

Abruzzio noted, with suppressed alarm, that the trussed-up, captive terrorist-leader seemed to be slowly returning to consciousness. She tried to get the attention of the others, but they were preoccupied with the unfolding situation near the Oval Office.

"Look," Jacobson tried to argue, "This 'Wyckheiser' guy is simply an ordinary citizen… he has no Constitutional right to show up to the White House, as anything other than a *tourist!* When the Secret Service finds out about this, they'll escort him out of here, *pronto!*"

"That's pretty rich… coming from a guy who *himself* was about to overthrow me, less than a week ago," whispered the President.

Kaysten had a look of acknowledgment on his face as he nodded affirmatively.

"Well, sir," quietly offered Chu (even though she knew full well that Jacobson could probably still hear), "Whatever we think of the Commander's recent conduct... given the circumstances, we had better keep him on our side."

"The President-Designate has a well-thought-out Constitutional rationale, for all this," sniffed the soldier in the doorway. "Furthermore... the building is now being occupied by troops of the GrayWar Legion, who are fully in support of Mr. Wyckheiser. We have several hundred involved in this operation. Resistance is *futile!* Please lay down your weapons immediately and don't resist arrest, and we'll guarantee your right to a fair trial; if you can't afford an attorney, one will be provided for you –"

"Hold your fire... and your tongue," temporized Jacobson. "I need a few minutes to consult with my – uhh – Commander-In-Chief. You make one hostile move, and my friend Mr. Boyd over here, will reduce you to *atoms.*"

The soldier shrugged and said, "We're assembling the military police-contingent that will take you under arrest and escort you to confinement-premises, now. Do not leave the area you're now in, or you'll be subject to lethal force. We have you surrounded on all sides."

While Boyd shook his head in disbelief, Jacobson hurried back to where the President and the others in the middle of the party, were encamped.

The former Mars mission commander asked the President, "What you make of *that?*"

"I'd say, 'unbelievable'... but then again, considering what else has happened recently, the term seems rather over-used," answered the frustrated U.S. leader. "But to my mind, the most important question is, 'could he actually be telling the truth, about having all these soldiers in control of the building'. We don't know if he's bluffing about that."

"Unfortunately, sir," mentioned Chu, "I don't think he's bluffing; Sylvia, Will, Rainbow and I *did* see hundreds of these troops marching on the White House, a few minutes ago. Cherie's war-child, and Warden, confirmed it too."

"Yeah," added Kaysten, "And don't forget... GrayWar had access to the White House on a routine basis, anyway; they were already running half of the place's systems. They'd probably have little difficulty getting on premises. The only resistance they might get would be from the Marines or the Service... and *they've* been bled dry by the terrorists."

"So what do we do?" asked Abruzzio.

"First," stated the President, "We walk in on a broadcast."

Legalities Later

The GrayWar soldier was still standing in one of the two doorways leading to the Oval Office, as the conversation between the more-than-humans and the First Family, continued – albeit at as low a volume as possible.

"Sam," noted Tanaka, "The soldiers at the far end of the corridor are advancing on us... slowly, but steadily."

"Acknowledged," mentioned Jacobson. "Hold your fire for now, please."

"If that's what you want to do, sir," opined Chu, "We had better get underway, as soon as possible... he could start the broadcast at any time."

"And it's in his interest to do so," chimed in Kaysten. "As little as I like to admit it, Commander – you're absolutely correct; I can't figure out how he's going to explain his claim on the Presidency. All this is *wildly* unconstitutional!"

"Someday, Jerry," responded Jacobson, "You and I – your boss, too – will have an interesting little discussion about the 'legalities' of how the government's been acting, since before Karéin showed up on the scene. Right now, however, it looks like 'possession is nine-tenths of the law'. Listen, Mr. President – if we try to force our way in there, it could get ugly, *fast*. As you know, my team and I don't answer to you... but neither do we want to work at cross-purposes. If these GrayWar twirps start shooting... what level of force do you want us to use against them?"

"Very important question," added Chu. "Sir – you've seen my primary alien-power... so you know what would happen if I used it against those soldiers. Cherie's, Brent's, Wolf's, Sylvia's, Will's, Hector's – for that matter, Commander Jacobson's own attack – they're all equally-devastating, each in a different way. We could be looking at *scores* or maybe *hundreds* of lives lost."

The dog let out a short, sharp, bark.

"Oh... and Rainbow, too," said the *nouvelle* FBI-director. "Don't let that puppy-face mislead you. She can do most of what Sylvia can. Including the 'radiation' thing."

"But she wouldn't... *would* you, little lady?" chided Abruzzio.

Another, more friendly-sounding "yip" came from the animal's mouth, resulting in nervous chuckles all around.

"Ms. Chu's not *kidding*, Dad," remarked Clairie. "What I got hit by, from that big dude behind us – that wouldn't just have killed a normal person... it would have, like, burned them down to a *cinder*. It hurts just to *remember* how bitchin' *hot* it felt! It was, like, *way* hotter than any burn I've ever had before... but it *didn't* burn me... but it almost *did*. Don't ask me how this all works – I really don't have a clue."

"Love *you* too, honey-buns," came back the inevitable repartee from Wolf. "Put another year and an inch or two on you, and call me up for some *real* fun."

He got an elbow from Tanaka for this *bon mot*.

"Clairie speaks the truth," gravely supported Abruzzio, in the President's direction. "Remember how Karéin said, 'you will never know how it feels to leap into the unknown, with only the Holy *Fire* to protect you'... or something like that? Well... there you go."

The President hung his head for a second or two, as if he were pondering a number of unpalatable options. At length, he said,

"This 'telekinesis' that many of you seem to have – could we use it to immobilize the GrayWar guys?"

"It's much more difficult to use – to 'lock on', that is – against an intelligent being, who's actively trying to resist," explained Abruzzio. "The same amount of force that I could, for example, bend a steel girder with, might be totally ineffective against a strong-willed human opponent. Still… with all of us working together… Commander – what have we got to *lose?*"

"I'm good with that," answered Jacobson, "But if they start firing at me… well, that usually doesn't help me concentrate... you know?"

"*Tell* me!" interjected Matt.

"Sam," warned Tanaka, "*Vîrya* Sài'ymë says she has intercepted a radio-message going back and forth between the GrayWar forces to converge on here, and to take us into custody – lethal force authorized! There are five more of them down the corridor from us!"

"Wolf was right, a few minutes ago," muttered Jacobson. "These guys are on a *suicide*-mission! Mr. President – if they start shooting, we've got to – if only to protect yourself and the First Lady –"

"I'd like you and your team to use lethal force only as a last option," requested the President, "But I won't call you back if you feel you have no other choice."

"Understood," said the former Mars mission commander.

He called out in both directions.

"You all hear that?" directed Jacobson.

Various affirmative declarations came from the front and rear of the combined group, just as the GrayWar guy in the doorway lowered his gun and barked out,

"Hands *up!*"

West Wing Shooting-Gallery

A large force of GrayWar soldiers, with auto-rifles prominently pointed eastward toward the main group of First Family refugees and their more-than-human protectors, advanced from the western reaches of the West Wing corridor, until they were no more than fifteen feet from Tanaka, Wolf and Hendricks. Meanwhile, two soldiers joined the original one in the north-east doorway, while four more issued from the charred portal on the southern wall.

"This is the President – the legitimate one – who now addresses you," shouted the U.S. leader. "Lay down your weapons and obey my orders! I'm surrounded by super-human bodyguards who can disintegrate you *instantly!* Don't make a tragic mistake that will cost you, your *lives!*"

"He isn't bluffing!" supported the man in the softly-glowing diamond-suit. "I'm Sam Jacobson of the Mars Gang, and – for the time being at least – my team and I are executing the President's orders... you've *seen* what we can do, at Fort Knox and elsewhere! Open fire on us and *you will die*, in the next two seconds!"

"I'll give you the count of five, and then we'll start shooting!" warned the GrayWar lieutenant. "*Five!*"

At least ten more-than-human war-songs again began to be heard, just at the limit of human consciousness and audibility.

"Minnie," whispered the President, "Can you give him a demonstration – let him know what you're capable of – without doing permanent harm to him?"

"I believe so, sir," answered the former team-leader. "The gun. His hands might get burned... but he'll *live*."

"*Four!*" counted the GrayWar leader.

"*Do* it!" he demanded.

Chu turned to the Presidential daughter.

"Clairie," she requested, "When you hear my war-song playing... drop your screen... oh-kay? Wouldn't be a good thing if my *Gaze* bounced back off of it, in our direction."

"Sure, and 'no shit'," quietly replied the teenager, "But you better hope those dudes don't shoot straight, if they open up on us. My power was all that kept Dad from being hit – not to mention yours truly."

"*Three!*" came the ominous count.

To Sam, Brent, Cherie, Jerry, Clairie, Sylvia, Wolf, Will, Hector and Matt –

Oh, and you too, Rainbow... if you can hear me, broadcast Chu,

I'm going to fire a warning-shot, at much less than full-power.

This isn't the start of a war... at least I hope not!

Don't unleash your own attacks unless they fire at you – use your telekinesis to immobilize them, or at least slow them down!

Various permutations of "understood" or "acknowledged", were spoken out loud, by the others. There was also a subdued "yip" on the part of the dog.

"*Two!*" exclaimed the GrayWar lieutenant.

Clairie's gold-translucent reflective-screen suddenly disappeared.

"This is a precision warning-shot – don't return fire, or my next attack will cut you in *half!*" Chu shouted back, as – with her buzzing, warbling, enervating war-song waxing rapidly, she stood up, stared right down the muzzle of the lieutenant's rifle, and unleashed the infernal *Gaze of the Khùl-Algrenàthi'i.*

The death-ray hit home almost precisely at the intended mark; it split the auto-rifle's barrel down the middle, hit the weapon's receiver – melting at least a third of it into a flaming *mélange* of charred plastic and molten metal – and then detonating the round in the chamber, resulting in a localized explosion and the burning, wrecked gun being immediately dropped from the unfortunate soldier's badly-singed hands.

He was in no condition to count down to "one", as he stumbled backwards in pain, shock and confusion, leaving two junior soldiers to uneasily guard the doorway.

The GrayWar mercenaries located at other points – down the hall and at the doorways to the Oval Office – unlocked their safeties and pointed their guns directly at various members of the President's entourage.

"Lock *on!*" called Chu, as the invisible telekinetic powers of multiple more-than-humans reached out to envelop their opponents' weapons and bodies.

Some of these efforts – particularly those directed at the gendarmes who were more stalwart-of-mind, or who were physically-distant – failed or were only marginally-effective; but collectively, they achieved their purpose. Most of the dumbfounded and demoralized GrayWar soldiers – finding their arms, fingers and gun-triggers locked in place, or interfered with as if wrestling with a professional – began to step backward.

The enhanced hearing of some of the more-than-humans – particularly Tanaka, Hendricks, Jacobson, Boyd and Abruzzio – picked up messages of panic setting in, amongst the mercenaries.

Looks like you got their attention, sent a smug Jacobson.

The proverbial 'hard way', returned Chu.

Oh well – better than having yet another human casualty, to answer for. And you know what?

No... what? he responded, knowing that most of the others could hear what was being communicated, on the more-than-human party-line.

It doesn't hurt my eyes any more, disclosed the *nouvelle* FBI-director.

Matter of fact... the more I do it... the better it feels.

I'll take your word for it, came Jacobson's mental reply.

"They're backing off," observed a gratified President. "Now's our chance!"

"You're *fucked,* Clark!" came an unrequited comment. "Did you think we hadn't *planned* for this? You're just playing your part in the *script!*"

Multiple heads and eyes searched around for its origin. Matt was the first to identify it.

"It's that dude who you've got all trussed-up, down there," he pointed out.

And so it was; the heavily-restrained Top Dog had now recovered from his head-injuries, and he was in fine, truculent form.

"Warden's saying, that the 'vid-e-o things', are starting to power up, to our left, in the 'Oblong Office'" advised Chu.

"We had better get in there to shut it down, ASAP!" added Boyd.

Along with Jacobson, he started moving toward the southern wall door.

"Just a second," requested the President.

He addressed the Agency guy.

"What the Dickens do you mean by 'the script'?" demanded the U.S. leader. "As I see it... you're here at my mercy – trussed up better than a prize turkey on Thanksgiving Day – and I have a team of super-humans, working with me... if perhaps not, *for* me. How do you figure that I'm, uhh... 'effed'?"

"*Because*, Clark," spat out Top Dog, gasping slightly as he struggled against the metal straight-jacket that confined him, "GrayWar's head-count outnumbers the regular Army, by two and a half to one – you can't run the government, if they don't *want* you to! You've heard of Grady Wyckheiser, I presume?"

"Just now," admitted the President. "He's a has-been ex-Senator from Alabama... I think I campaigned for him once. I wasn't very impressed – he only won because the State Electoral Office threw away half the Democratic votes down there. So *what?*"

"*Figures*," muttered Tanaka to the other two who were, along with her, keeping a careful watch on the gendarmes threatening the group, from the west.

"You thought they was countin' them votes one for one?" replied Wolf. "You got a better chance of winnin' the lottery, than of winnin' a fair election, pardner."

"Yeah," whispered the former Mars mission science officer, "But wait until Karéin sees this bullshit happening, live and in Technicolor. Remember how she said, 'things have to change'?"

"I'll believe that when I *see* it," grunted the bounty-hunter. "Jackass President's just playin' nice because he needs us. The moment he don't... back to business as usual, I reckon."

Tanaka nodded affirmatively; then she spoke aloud, "Mr. President – Vîrya Sài'ymë tells me that the 'tee-vee boxes' are now sending out a signal."

The U.S. leader looked at Jacobson and his former Mars mission pilot. He also tapped Kaysten on the shoulder.

"Gentlemen," he requested, "Is there anything you can do, to – ahh – force a 'postponement' of the broadcast that's apparently about to go live, in the Oval Office?"

"Sure," responded Boyd, with an evil grin. "Commander... ever heard of a TV-show 'going dark'?"

"I'll get their attention, through the other door," proposed the senior ex-astronaut. "Jerry... can you zip past them, get in there and pull some plugs?"

The Chief of Staff's frame began to vibrate faster and faster, until his figure was blurred and impossible to focus-upon, even for more-than-human eyes.

"They won't *see* me – hey, I'll even mess his make-up!" quipped Kaysten. His voice was warbling weirdly; it sounded as if it was being processed by a computer reverb-filter.

Three war-songs began to play in the background.

"*Go!*" shouted the President.

The three – with Jacobson barreling forward to the north-east and with Kaysten, followed close behind by Boyd, rocketing through the charred, still-smoking southern-wall portal – acted immediately. A second later there were sounds of mayhem – including panicked yelling and isolated gunfire – coming from areas near to the Oval Office.

After a few more seconds, the sounds of rapid-fire gunshots and muffled explosions became more prominent. It seemed that they were no longer just coming from the area of the Presidential office; the noises of high-intensity battles resounded from the west end of the building and from somewhere to the north-east, down the corridor extending in that direction.

"What's going *on?*" speculated Abruzzio. "Sam, Brent and Jerry only went to the Oval Office… but now I'm hearing gunfire all *over* the place!"

"You're right," confirmed Hendricks. "There's shooting going on somewhere behind those GrayWar jerks who got their guns trained on us. What the *hell?*"

"'So what', Clark?" hissed Top Dog, in the direction of the President. "We've got you where we *want* you… *that's* what!"

The fracas in and around the Oval Office appeared to last only perhaps thirty seconds to a minute, during which time those in the hall – including the defiant Agency-leader – remained silent, for the most part, as they concentrated on trying to hear what was going on.

Presently, a previously-unseen person stumbled through the north-east doorway, as if something behind him had pushed him thence.

Vaguely reminiscent of what Bob Billings might have looked like – had the salesman aged another twenty years – this formally-attired, balding, clean-shaven Caucasian man was tall with rather too much around the waistline. He had a bland, unattractive (yet, not ugly), utterly-forgettable face, with bushy eyebrows and a slack jowl. There was also a small pin-emblem of the U.S. flag affixed to the front of his dark-gray, conservative business-suit.

The sounds of gunfire were still ongoing – if anything, they were more noticeable now – to the east, north-east and west.

"*Move it!*" came the voice of Sam Jacobson, from unseen parts to the east.

"Okay… *okay!*" protested the man in the suit. "There's no need to be *unpleasant*, you know!"

Kaysten and Boyd emerged from the southern-wall doorway. The Chief of Staff hurried over to re-join the First Family.

Jacobson – still clad in his diamond-covering – became visible. He was standing close behind the newcomer, pushing the latter forward.

The President stood up and walked forward until he was almost beside the barely-sitting-up Top Dog.

The U.S. leader addressed the newly-appearing man.

"Why, *Grady*," he offered with mock courtesy, "I hear you're gunning for *my* job, these days. Care to *explain?*"

"Mr. President," interrupted Boyd, "Before you get into all that – there's something you should know."

"Yes?" answered the President.

"We were able to shut off the broadcast and get *this* guy out of there so easily," explained the former Mars mission pilot, "Because his GrayWar guards all ran like scared rabbits... but not from *us*. There's a pitched battle going on outside the building, between dozens of mercs and some other bunch of intruders. I got close to one of the Oval Office windows and was able to catch a glance of them... they look like a SWAT team or something."

"More terrorists?" uneasily queried the U.S. leader.

"Hard to tell," answered Boyd. "They don't look exactly like the guys who we were fighting, before the Graywar twerps showed up. Anyway, GrayWar looks like it's on the losing side of the battle –"

"There's *shooting* going on down the hall!" shouted Tanaka. "Wolf, Will – get ready!"

Three war-songs re-initialized, as Chu took hold of the President and urged,

"Sir... stay *down! Sylvia* – Hector – Matt and Clairie – full *power!*"

Five more war-songs began to play.

"We're *flanked!*" they heard someone far down the West Wing corridor, shriek.

"What are we fuckin' going to *do!*" yelled another. "Them fuckers down the hall with the glowing eyes, are blockin' our only way out –"

Bullet-rounds began whizzing down the hall. It looked as if the shots were being fired from some unseen location at the far western end of the corridor, where it had a bend to the north.

"Shields *up!*" exclaimed Tanaka, as she and Hendricks re-powered their force-fields. This had the desired effect; the few stray bullets that came close to the President's group, were deflected harmlessly away.

But the mercenaries at the far end of the corridor were now in desperate straits. The rate and accuracy of the gunfire directed against them was becoming steadily more intensive. One GrayWar guy screamed as he was hit in the shoulder, resulting in a blood-spraying wound that took him out of the battle. He fell to the ground, moaning in pain. The rest of them were pinned down but were being slowly forced to the east, nearing where the three more-than-humans were standing guard.

"Holy *shit!*" remarked the third agent. "Those mercs sure *are* taking it heavy! Who the hell are they *up* against, anyway?"

"Don't matter none to *me*," sniffed Wolf. "They get their asses kicked... well – shit *happens*. Just saves me a little fire – both kinds, that is."

"Mr. President," Tanaka called out, "It's ugly to watch – we're seeing the GrayWar guys at the far end of the hall, being picked off, one by one. This could easily turn into a *massacre!*"

The President hesitated for a second or two, as the ferocity of the assault against the GrayWar forces midway down the corridor increased. Two more mercenaries fell; one of these died instantly to a rifle-shot in the head, while the other took a round in the lower abdomen, falling prostate in a pool of blood.

"Tell them to... uhh... surrender," asked the U.S. leader.

Meanwhile, Jacobson had ushered Senator Wyckheiser, to a position beside the President, the First Lady and those who were protecting them.

"Hey, *you* down there – yeah, *you* GrayWar jerks!" immediately shouted Hendricks, to the west. "Throw down your guns and crawl toward us! Keep your heads *down!* Make any hostile move and what you're dealing with now, will look like a fuckin' Sunday school picnic!"

After a short amount of panicked babbling, the mercenaries – at least, the few of them who were still mobile – began to comply. They were about ten feet from Tanaka, Hendricks and the bounty-hunter, when – propelled from a hand that momentarily appeared around the bend at the far end of the hallway – a small, metal object bounced toward the GrayWar soldiers and the more-than-human rear-guard.

It exploded with a deafening "bang", a powerful shock-wave and a brilliant flash of light. A half-second later – as the shock-wave hit and bounced off the double force-fields – a fusillade of machine-gun-fire was unleashed by a group of six or seven new, SWAT-suited and -masked assailants, who appeared in tactical-crouch-position at the far end of the corridor. This attack was also easily deflected by the force-fields, although a couple of the ricochets thus caused unfortunately hit the crawling, hapless mercenaries, causing yet more grievous wounds.

Wolf – now enveloped in his punishing flame-shroud – levitated so as to have a line of sight over the two protective-screens. Before anyone could call him back, he unleashed a multi-shot barrage of blazing, baseball-sized fire-bolts at the newly-arriving attackers. This was assisted, in the next second, by a brace of Tanaka's multi-chromatic lightening-bolts, accompanied by Hendricks' yellow-white-colored, weaker facsimiles thereof.

The retaliatory-strike had the expected, devastating effect; it not only immediately silenced whoever had been attacking from the far end of the corridor, but also blew away much of the hallway's western wall, revealing parts of the Chief of Staff's office immediately beyond it. Little more than dismembered, smoking lower-legs – still grotesquely-inserted into army-boots – was left of the intruders who had foolishly attacked the more-than-humans. Small fires burst out all over the area; some of them looked like they were slowly spreading.

"*Damn*," muttered Kaysten to the President. "Her Nuclear Highness already did quite a number on my office – any chance I can get a bump-up on the ol' reno-budget, sir?"

"Get me out of this in one piece, Jerry," the U.S. leader replied, "And you can fix it up with old teak, golden nails and a Vermeer or two."

Both of the President's offspring laughed out loud, upon hearing this. Abruzzio, Chu and Ramirez merely smiled, but the President's visage then turned grim.

"I sure hope that whoever those three opened up on, were the *bad* guys," he remarked, with a wary grimace.

"Remember what I said back at the reservoir, sir?" said Abruzzio. "The part about, 'you've got a half-second to either defend yourself, or get shot dead – and you make the best decision that you can, and you'll have to live with the consequences?'"

"Yeah," ruefully conceded the U.S. leader. "But it's a damn *mess*."

"That it *is*," added Ramirez. "For the record, sir... my approach has been simple : I only fire back at those who are trying to kill *me*... or to kill people who I know not to have hostile intent. But I don't hold back, 'when and if'."

"Amen," supported Chu.

The resounding noise and smoke of the more-than-humans' initial onslaught had partly cleared, but it was being supplemented by more coming from the burgeoning fires lit by the impact of (particularly) Wolf's attack and (to a lesser degree) those of Tanaka and Hendricks.

Gunfire to the north and east, away down the corridor in the opposite direction compared to where the battle had just transpired, was becoming nearer and louder. The conflict outside – probably on or around the South Lawn – also seemed to be picking up.

"Listen, folks," advised Chu, "We just witnessed a pitched battle down there – in another minute or two, we might be dealing with one coming from the east, or we might be attacked from the direction of the Oval Office. Be ready to fire, with zero notice... do you understand?"

"You got it," responded Boyd. "I'm hearing sounds of movement near there, right now –"

A number of terrified GrayWar mercenaries appeared in both doorways leading to the Oval Office. They had apparently dropped their rifles elsewhere, and their hands were held high, as they shouted, "Help... *help!* We *surrender!*"

Both Jacobson and Boyd stood to block the path of the demoralized soldiers-for-hire.

The former Mars mission commander asked, in a loud voice, "What the hell's going *on* here? What are you jerks running from?"

One of the mercenaries – a young, Hispanic-looking guy – replied, "We're getting our *asses* kicked out there, man! Dunno who they are... but they fuckin' *never* miss, when we get into a fire-fight with 'em! Listen, man... we *know* who you are – like, the 'Mars Gang' and such – just take us *prisoner!* Those fuckers out there are gonna *kill* us!"

The two dumbfounded ex-astronauts stared blankly at each other.

What you make of that*?* sent Jacobson.

You mean, "am I surprised that these GrayWar pricks, are a bunch of incompetent, yellow-bellied cowards?" silently answered Boyd.

The answer – if you needed *one – is, "no".*

No shit, answered Jacobson,

But what you want to do *with them?*

Well, sent the former Mars mission pilot,

*Better "inside the tent, pissing out", than "outside the tent, pissing in"…
I guess.*

Although – frankly – one part of me says, "send 'em back out there".

Gunfire's getting closer, observed Jacobson.

You may yet get your chance to fight somebody else, on the behalf of GrayWar.

Lucky fuckin' me, responded Boyd.

That's what Devon would say… right?

Right, answered Jacobson.

"Come over here by the President, and when you get close, unholster and drop your side-arms," called Chu. "Grasp the pistols by their barrels. You make one false move, and I'll cut you in *half* – is that *understood?*"

Her eyes were glowing brilliantly, as if to warn that the threat was not an idle one.

"And if she misses," added an ominously-glowing Boyd, "I… won't."

"Yes, *ma'am!*" said one of the other mercenaries, a clean-cut, even younger Caucasian man who might have still been in his teenage years.

Sheepishly, six or seven GrayWar types carefully stepped over to where the President and his entourage were standing.

"I'll have a word with Mr. Duke, about your willingness – or lack thereof – to do your jobs," complained Senator Wyckheiser.

"Yeah, well," shot back one of the now-disarmed mercenaries, "They told us that all we'd have to do, would be to show up here and take control… like, there wouldn't be anybody left who was *shootin'* at us. They said that by the time we got here, them Agency guys would –"

"That's privileged information – keep your mouth *shut!*" barked out Top Dog, from his restrained position lying on the floor, with his back up against the north wall of the hallway.

Immediately, Rainbow moved uncomfortably close to the former CIA director. She snarled and bared her fangs.

"It would seem," dryly noted Abruzzio, "That you aren't in a position to enforce demands of this type. I'm sure the President and the Acting FBI Director will want to hear all about the subject, in due time."

"You can *bet* on it!" confirmed Chu.

"Now, now, honey," cajoled the former JPL scientist, to the dog, "Leave the man alone... for the time being, at least."

Rainbow backed off somewhat, but still had the Agency-chief squarely in her determined, hostile stare.

There was more shooting, apparently coming from close-by, outside. The sounds of the battle were accompanied by wails of despair from other groups of beleaguered GrayWar soldiers.

"Sir," remarked Chu to the President, "I think it's clear that we can't rely on GrayWar to fend off whoever they're fighting against, for very much longer. You *saw* how I got you out of here, once before – I can do that again, only *this* time, I have much more backup... uhh, no offense Jerry –"

"Oh... none taken," responded Kaysten, with a sly smile. "Too bad you weren't here to see me trying out Angel Girl's little alien kung-fu moves, though."

"Jerry fought very bravely," spoke up the First Lady. "He saved our *lives!*"

"Anyway, sir," continued the *nouvelle* FBI-director, "The point is... there may be yet *another* group of terrorists besieging the building – we need to get you and the First Family to safety. You want me to open up the ceiling?"

"Just a second," temporized the President.

He turned to address Wyckheiser and Top Dog.

"What do you two know about what's going on, outside?" he demanded. "Don't tell me, let me guess – the Agency's assassins are fighting it out with GrayWar, to see who gets final control of the Oval Office... right?"

The trussed-up CIA chief remained sullenly silent, but the ex-Senator did respond. He said,

"For reasons I don't care to get into... that seems quite unlikely. Whoever's attacking the White House – and my so-called bodyguards on loan from Mr. Duke – they're somebody *else*, I'd wager."

"Whoever they are," observed Abruzzio, "Minnie's right – sir, although we can and will defend you... the middle of a pitched battle isn't a good place for you or your family. Rainbow and I can fly, too... if Minnie wants to, ahh, open up a new skylight in the ceiling above us, we can help escort you out of here."

The dog chimed in with one of its trademark "yip" sounds.

Two more panicked GrayWar soldiers barreled through the entrances to the White House. They stumbled forward, eventually falling to the floor in front of Top Dog and Wyckheiser. Immediately after the fugitive mercenaries, there appeared four of the masked, SWAT-garbed opponents (two at the north-east entrance, the other two at the southern wall) who Tanaka, Wolf and Hendricks had disintegrated, not five minutes earlier.

One of the intruders – evidently of higher rank – remained standing, while the other three crouched down with their rifles raised and pointed in classic precision-shooting style. Multiple war-songs began to wax quickly in volume and pace. Clairie's reflection-shield was already up; it protected her father, mother and others in their vicinity, from all angles except for due west.

"*Terrorists!*" came the electronically-boosted voice of the leading-attacker.

"Drop your weapons and move away from the President with your hands in the air – or we'll shoot you *dead!*"

New Orders For The Lieutenant

Jacobson and Boyd refrained from raising their arms; but – at least for the moment – neither did they, nor their more-than-human compatriots further to the west in the hallway, immediately attack the newly-emerging gunmen.

"You can't hurt me with just a rifle," offered the former Mars mission commander, "And that goes for Major Boyd over there, and for the other followers of the Storied Watcher, who you see behind me. Mind telling me who you are?"

"Step away from the President!" repeated the shouts of the leading-attacker. "Do it *now!*"

"Which *one?*" muttered Hendricks to Tanaka, while both of them continued to watch to the west, for signs of a flanking-maneuver.

"We seem to have more Presidents running around here, than a dog has fleas," observed the former Mars mission science officer.

Inevitably, Rainbow let out a sharp bark, upon hearing this.

"*Shh!*" chided Abruzzio, to the animal.

"I'm the President," called the U.S. leader, "I'm in no immediate danger. The people who surround me aren't 'terrorists', by any means – but Commander Jacobson isn't exaggerating… if you try to use force against him or his friends, I can't be responsible for what happens to you, thereafter.. Please identify yourself. Are you with the Agency or with GrayWar?"

There was a pronounced pause, after which the leading-intruder slowly replied,

"I'm Second Lieutenant Willard Hopeka, sir," came the response. "I'm in command of the Joint Strike Force team allocated to the Oval Office and this part of the West Wing. We're here to *rescue* you, sir!"

Dumbfounded stares were passed back and forth, among those standing in the vicinity of the First Family.

"So… you're with the *Army*, then, soldier?" inquired Chu.

"Yes ma'am," confirmed the SWAT-suited guy. "*Wait* a minute... I recognize you from the TACEVAL-data... you're the Director of the FBI, aren't you?"

"Uh-huh," sighed the former team-leader. "You know... I asked your superiors to hold off on any further assaults against this building, until I had another chance to consult with them."

"And you're a bit on the late side," added Kaysten. "I sure as H could have used you guys a few hours ago, when I had to deal with the *real* 'terrorists'!"

"I can't speak to that, ma'am and sir," answered Hopeka. "I can only say that we're acting on lawful orders from senior levels in the chain of command. And that we've encountered violent resistance from armed opponents, since we've entered the White House grounds. We're still trying to clear them from the South Lawn, for example."

He addressed his fellow-warriors.

"Ease up," he called. "Inform HQ that Objective Alpha has been located in good condition. Set teams for egress-config, per plan."

The crouching snipers slowly arose, but their weapons were still very much at the ready.

"*You*, there!" shouted Tanaka, from the opposite side of the main Presidential party group.

"Yes, ma'am?" responded the lieutenant.

"Were your men engaged against GrayWar mercenaries, further down this corridor, to the west of me, a few minutes ago?"

"Yes, ma'am," said Hopeka. "Based on prisoner-insignia and lack of effective resistance, we believe that most of the unauthorized armed staff on the premises, *are* GrayWar. We've also encountered a few who may be from some other group. Most of those ones, however, have been fighting to the death, and they've proved to be difficult opponents. As to our own west-flank group, we've had no word from those guys for a while, though. We're sending reinforcements to see what happened to them."

Oh... shit! sent the former Mars mission scientist.

You did what you had *to, Cherie,* came Abruzzio's reply.

I sure hope the courts think the same way, silently replied Tanaka.

"Fuckers *shot* at us," commented Wolf. "They got what you'd expect them to. I ain't makin' no apologies!"

"I *heard* that," angrily retorted the President. "I know that you, Mr. Hendricks and Ms. Tanaka were protecting my family and I... but that doesn't make it any less a tragedy!"

"Sir," guardedly interrupted the leading SWAT-suited guy, "What are you referring to?"

"Something *terrible*, son," evaded the U.S. leader. "We'll have to deal with it later –"

"Ha!" interjected a sneering Top Dog. "So poor old innocent little Clark, has a bit of the red stuff on his hands... what a *pity!* That always was your biggest weakness... you haven't got what it *takes*. Well – like I tried to tell you some time ago – 'if you can't stand the heat, get out of the kitchen' –"

His commentary was interrupted by a hard slap on the side of the face, inflicted by a furious President.

"When I unleash Karéin on you," he snarled, "I'll stand by, watching every second of what she does, and – may the Lord so forgive me – I won't shed so much as a crocodile tear! I've been told, she can lock your pathetic mind in a nightmare that never –"

"The monster's *dead*, Clark!" cackled the former Agency-director. "I shot it with a little 'something' that the boys in Wet Ops brewed up especially for the task... and I *saw* the bitch fall, with a big hole blown right through its heart! Or hadn't they *told* you?"

The horrified, shocked look on the President's face was matched by equal ones on the parts of his two children, and of Kaysten.

"Can it be *true?*" whispered a half-elated First Lady.

"You're *lying!*" angrily shouted the U.S. leader, with his face pushed very close to the Agency torpedo's own. "You can't kill someone like *her*, with just a *gun!*"

"Corpse should still be just outside the Oval Office," said Top Dog, with a confident shrug. "Go see for *yourself!*"

Things are not always as they seem to be, broadcasted Abruzzio, while the other more-than-humans maintained a stony silence.

"*Right*," quietly murmured Clairie.

Her brother nodded knowingly, out of Top Dog's field of vision.

The deflated, aghast, glowering President remained mute for a few seconds. Then – pointing to Top Dog and Wyckheiser – he said to Lieutenant Hopeka,

"Take these two men – ring-leaders of a terrorist conspiracy to overthrow the government of the United States – into custody; they're to have no contact with anyone, under any circumstances, until you get further direction coming from myself, personally –"

"We'll *see* about that, Clark!" taunted the ex-Agency-chief. "Now that you don't have your little alien chaperone to get your nuts out of the fire –"

"And shut *him* up – I don't care *how* you do it!" spat the President, as he cast a baleful glare at Top Dog. "Also, Hedrick Duke of GrayWar is to be considered an enemy of the state and is to be arrested at the first possible opportunity. Gather your forces and do a top-to-bottom search of the White House. Give GrayWar staff one warning before you shoot them, but any remaining armed individuals who violently resist are to be shot on *sight* –"

"Except for Otis Boatman, who's somewhere in the East Wing, protecting a group of civilians," interrupted Jacobson.

"And Moira Sullivan," insisted Abruzzio. "God willing, she's safe… hiding somewhere."

Reflexively, the former JPL scientist whispered a "Hail Mary" and touched her crucifix.

"Yes," agreed the President.

He again addressed the lieutenant.

"Report back to me in the Oval Office and inform your superiors when your operations are complete," he requested. "These are direct orders from your Commander-In-Chief. Do you acknowledge?"

"Yes, *sir!*" answered the Strike Force leader. "But, sir… our objective was – and is – to egress you and the First Family, from the building. What are your plans?"

The President turned to Kaysten.

"Jerry… do you think you can get the audio-visual stuff in the Oval Office, working again?" asked the U.S. leader.

"I *think* so," replied the Chief of Staff, "But it's not going to be pretty… the place is full of bullet-holes, scorch-marks and busted windows. Even the Resolute Desk has a few gouges taken out of it. Just the *sight* of it won't be a big confidence-builder, sir."

"Well… those are the least of the issues we'll have to talk about," noted the President.

While Kaysten disappeared through a doorway and started to get the audio-visual infrastructure up and running, the President turned to Jacobson.

"It's vital that the people see that I'm still alive, and still in the Oval Office," said the U.S. leader. "I'm planning on going live, in ten minutes; but apparently there's a battle going on outside, and the last thing we – or I – need, is to have me shot in the back while I'm in front of the camera –"

"Sir," interjected a frustrated Chu, "Surely you can't be *serious* about this! There's a clear line of sight to the Oval Office from many vantage-points outside the White House, and some of the windows have already been shot out! The entire *building* is the definition of an 'unsafe environment'… and the Oval Office is the first place that the terrorists will aim their guns at!"

"Sir," echoed Lieutenant Hopeka, "With all due respect to yourself and your office, the Bureau Director is one hundred per cent right about that – I'm under strict orders from my higher-ups to egress you to a safe location. My failure to do so will be considered 'dereliction of duty'. *Please*, sir… let my team get yourself and the First Family, to safety! We have an egress-route through the underground tunnels, set up, with substantial friendly forces at each checkpoint. We need to *leave*, right away, sir!"

"Mr. President," spoke Jacobson, "Exactly what are you asking the Mars Gang – and, I suppose, Karéin's other empowered-followers – to *do*, here?"

"Keep the snipers, the terrorists, GrayWar and whoever the hell else is trying to kill me, today, off my back… long enough for me to do a ten-minute broadcast to the nation – *that's* what," answered the U.S. leader. "After that, we'll all go off to Bl – I mean, to a safe location – together. Fair?"

"So we should risk our *lives*, so you can keep your job-approval ratings up… is *that* what you're saying?" prodded the former Mars mission commander.

The President looked thoroughly frustrated, but – ever the polished politician – he kept his cool and responded, "I wouldn't put it that way, Commander. Consider the circumstances : I have a pretender to the throne – Mr. Wyckheiser – standing right here, and by now, the people surely know that the White House has been under relentless terrorist attack, for many hours. Rumors about my demise are probably running wild. There already were elements of the government that weren't under my control, *before* all this – not to mention those little incidents with the three H-bombs – happened; now try to imagine putting Humpty Dumpty back together again, if the idea that I'm no longer around, gets traction within the public… and within the military. I'm just asking for a few minutes on TV, to set the record straight, and to reassure the public. If you don't want to assist, of course, that's your decision – I'm going ahead, regardless; I'm willing to accept the risk. Do you understand?"

"I'll help," pledged Chu.

"So will we," said Abruzzio, while the dog gave another of its goofy grins. "We've got you *this* far, sir… seems kind of pointless not to complete the job."

"My wind-screen can probably deflect any incoming bullets," remarked Ramirez, "Although the noise associated with it, might interfere with your broadcast."

"Just do whatever you can, Mr. Ramirez," requested the U.S. leader. "Any aid would be appreciated."

"We've got your back, Dad," added Matt.

"Yeah," echoed Clairie. "They shoot at you… I'll make sure they get a nasty surprise."

"Thank you all, *so* much," spoke the President.

An outmaneuvered Jacobson managed, "Tell you what, Mr. President – speaking only for myself, it looks like you already have a reasonably complete set of defenses; however, I'll agree to keep watch over the South Lawn and related areas for the duration of your address, as long as thereafter, I have your permission to go find Otis Boatman and verify that our families are out of harm's way. Brent – Cherie – Wolf – Will – and the rest of you… any objections among you?"

"Not from me," quickly responded Boyd. "When do we get going?"

"I'll fly top-cover," stated Tanaka. "If there's ground-fire to be had, they can direct it at me."

"Yeah... and I can just guess what happens if them fuckers let loose on you," grunted Wolf. "Wouldn't want you to have all the fun, by yourself. Reckon I'll tag along up there."

"Well," ruefully acknowledged the President, "I can see there will be some, ahh, 'visual distractions', around here, while I'm speaking."

"If it's okay, sir," asked Hendricks, "I'd like to stay in or around the Oval Office, in case anybody else shows up wanting your scalp. I think you saw what I'm capable of, a few minutes ago?"

"Try not to fire off any lightening-bolts while we're on air, if you don't mind," requested the U.S. leader.

"Pinky-swear," said the third agent, with a sly grin on his face.

"Sir," interjected Lieutenant Hopeka, "As I'm under command direction to get you out of here, I must execute it unless given a countermanding order, from higher authority – like the Commander-In-Chief. Other than what's to be done with the detainees... do you have new orders for the Joint Strike Force, sir?"

"Yes," quickly elaborated the President. "I need four of your men to provide local security for the Oval Office, during the broadcast. Please also muster a detachment to get Kathy – the First Lady, that is – to safety; she needs medical assistance. Continue with clearing the building, and be on the lookout for the Secretary of State and Susan Feldner, who were taken somewhere else when we were imprisoned... oh, and also look for any wounded Secret Service agents, particularly one guy named "Jackson", who was left behind when we were removed from where we were being kept. Make sure you keep track of where Commander Jacobson and Major Boyd are, so we don't have any more 'mistaken-identity' incidents. Help them to get their families out of here, if they so request. Inform your higher-ups, of these orders. Any questions?"

"Yes... I *do* have one, sir," replied the lieutenant. "My orders were to evac your entire *family*... not just the First Lady. With reference to your two children, didn't you mean for them to accompany the First Lady, out of here? They're in *danger* here, sir!""

"No... they aren't," obliquely responded the U.S. leader. "They're much safer than I am, in fact."

"With all due respect, sir... I don't see how that's *so*," argued Hopeka.

Clairie closed her eyelids and bowed her head.

Then she threw her head back, and – with bright-glowing eyes, a faintly-glowing aura outlining her trim figure and an air of power and majesty, to the accompaniment of multiple gasps from those around her – she self-levitated about a half-foot above the floor and drifted over to confront the soldier.

Several of those around, noted that the carpets underneath the teenager were fuming and discoloring, as she passed over them.

Holy shit! sent an impressed Boyd,

That kid sure is a fast learner!

"*This* is why!" she proclaimed, with outstretched-arms and a proud smile.

"Any *questions?*"

"No *ma'am!,*" uneasily replied the SWAT-suited man, as he stepped backwards to avoid Clairie's infernal presence.

The Presidential daughter gradually came to rest on her feet.

Matt clapped appreciatively.

Little sister, admonished Abruzzio,

Remember what I said, about 'giving in to the luxury of the Fire*'?*

It's a luxury you can't afford!

Sister Sylvia is right, came Tanaka's commentary.

Clairie – your powers are racing far ahead of your judgment.

Promise me that when the Storied Watcher returns… you'll ask her for advice about this?

You mean she isn't – like – dead? answered the teenager.

As far as we know… she's very much alive, disclosed the former Mars mission science officer.

We're just keeping up the charade to fuck with that asshole from the Agency… play along with us, oh-kay?

You bet! answered the elated teenager.

I knew the fucker was lyin' through his teeth… I mean, they couldn't smoke Karéin with a nuke… and he thinks he did it with a rifle?

Dream on, dude!

A formerly-unknown mind now remarked,

That's… damn… good… to… hear… thanks…

Who's that? broadcast Abruzzio.

Matt winked at the ex-JPL scientist and gave her a "thumbs-up" gesture.

Yo, bro, sent Clairie,

Can you believe this is really happening?

No, he responded.

Can we say, "out of my comfort-zone"?

Yeah, admitted the sister,

But it's bitchin' great! I can't get enough of it!

Every time I use it, I feel like a fuckin' god!

And yes, you two "aunties"… I'll have a sit-down with Angel Lady, if you want… but for the record –

She never told me it would, like, come to me, this fast!

I thought it was all about – like – "pushin' a pen across a desk"!

That make any sense?

Sure does, sent Tanaka.

You're a super-hero now, Clairie… and that comes with responsibility.

Didn't she tell you anything about that?

Yeah, acknowledged the teenager.

But, like… I sorta thought she was shittin' us!

Like the one she put over on Mom and Dad... about Matt and me being "sacrifices", I mean.

Practical jokes aren't Karéin's thing, observed Boyd.

Especially where death-rays or godlike-powers, are concerned.

Well then, argued Clairie,

How do you explain the top of the Monument, sitting there in Dad's lawn?

While the mental back-and-forth was ongoing, Hopeka stepped away, gave some hand-signals to his fellow-warriors and began whispering cryptic code-talk, into a hidden microphone within his combat-helmet. Three more camo-suited soldiers proceeded to the vicinity of the First Lady and supported her in walking upright.

The sounds of gunfire in the further reaches of the White House continued to reverberate.

Kaysten's face re-appeared in the north-eastern doorway.

"I think I've got it going," he announced. "I did a quick check – raced back and forth – and there's nobody right outside the Oval Office... but I can't guarantee that there aren't any hostiles still out there on the South Lawn. Oh – but what are we going to do about your speech, sir?"

"What do you mean?" answered the President.

"Well," said the Chief of Staff, "We haven't had a chance to write anything down... I mean, we usually take *hours* to go over it and get it right. You know – that ol' 'spin', thing... package it up for the folks back home."

"Jerry," wearily sighed the U.S. leader, "Today – written script or no script – I don't think I'll be short of things to talk about."

Who You Answer To

In truth, Boyd and Jacobson paid only lip service to the pledge they had made to the President; the two ex-astronauts – enhanced senses and reflexes very much at the ready – waved goodbye to their more-than-human friends, who were encamped just outside the Oval Office. The former Mars mission crewmembers then ventured out on to the South Lawn, looking for ongoing battles. However, although there were dead bodies aplenty, only sporadic shooting was going on, and it seemed far-off.

None the less, there indeed was some "excitement" experienced on the short trip to the East Wing, as, halfway across the Rose Garden, the two Mars Gang members were intercepted by a detachment of five of Lieutenant Hopeka's Joint Strike Force commandos.

There were a few tense moments, as the diamond-enshrouded more-than-human – and his brilliantly-glowing compatriot – engaged in an armed stand-off with the suspicious soldiers; but, fortunately, a radio-check with

Hopeka himself, quickly resolved the misunderstandings. After being reluctantly issued permission to "continue on your way… but stay out of trouble" (to which Boyd had smartly replied, "oh… so you want us to stay away from Earth, altogether?"), Jacobson and his former Mars mission pilot headed rapidly for the South Portico entranceway.

Once inside the building, the two encountered more Joint Strike Force squads, but these seemed to be busying themselves in disarming and processing much larger numbers of rather pathetic-looking GrayWar mercenaries. Boyd and Jacobson raced through the Diplomatic Reception Room, entering the Center Hall – and a Joint Strike Force roadblock – immediately thereafter. More calls to Hopeka were required to avoid yet another stand-off. Finally, they were allowed to proceed to the east.

The south sides of the parts of Center Hall where they had first encountered the terrorists, bore the gruesome signs of a secondary, intensive battle. There were bloodstains – and signs of even worse stuff – all over, as if someone standing next to the wall had been hit by a cluster-bomb, or some equally-lethal attack. The wall itself also had an oddly-pitted and -dented quality; it looked like someone had ripped parts of it apart with some kind of gigantic chain-saw. The gashes in the wood and plaster had blood and other forms of gore, deeply-embedded within.

With a mixture of hope and dread, Boyd knocked on the closed door to the White House Museum Library.

He knocked once… twice… thrice.

There was no answer.

"Otis? Laura?" he called out. "It's me – Brent Boyd! I'm with the Commander. You *in* there?"

After a delay of perhaps three seconds, a voice – instantly and thankfully recognizable as that of his wife – responded,

"Oh, thank *God!* Otis… it's Brent, and Sam Jacobson – come *on*, man, we can open the door, now!"

"Well, after all we… okay then, fine, ma'am – but you all had better hope that there's no more of *them* around… you know what I mean," sounded another familiar voice.

The door slowly opened, revealing Laura Boyd, who practically flew into her husband's waiting arms.

"Sam… *Sam!*" shouted Yvonne Jacobson. She mimicked the Boyd spouse's actions. "You're back… we were so *scared!*"

"We shouldn't have left you," admitted the former Mars mission commander, "But boy – do we *ever* have a story to tell. Is everybody okay?"

"Over here… yes," spoke Otis Boatman, who was now standing upright, having previously been in a crouched position behind an overturned table. "Lord help me – I can't say the same for some of the other folks who didn't make it in here, with us. Commander – what in Jehoshaphat has been goin' *on*, around here? Just when things looked like they was about to calm down, and we thought them terrorists was on the run… all of a sudden, a whole bunch of different ones show up at our door, and start shootin', not only at us, but at each other! I tried to get your folks out of here, two *times* I did – but each time, we ran into so many of these guys with the guns, that I had no choice but to retreat back here. Is it *over* now?"

"Far as I know, it *is*," offered the ex-astronaut, "But, never say 'never'. I take it you had to defend Yvonne and the others?"

Boatman looked awkwardly downward and mumbled, "Lord forgive me… yes – I did. There was four of 'em standin' in the doorway – we offered to surrender, they weren't havin' it, my Mars ears picked up somebody sayin', 'just shoot the civilians in that room, and move on, we need to reinforce the West Wing operations', they lifted up their guns, and… well, you *know* what happens next –"

"Yeah," confirmed Jacobson, "We sure do. Without getting into the details… pretty much the same thing has happened elsewhere, and the results have been just as unpleasant. Don't worry about it, man – we've got your back; neither the government, nor anybody else, is going to come after you about it."

"'Cept for the Lord," quietly offered the big, black ex-agent. "Ain't no evadin', answering to Him."

"Yeah," repeated the former Mars mission commander.

Just then, his eye caught a glimpse of a flicker on one of the few still-operational video-screens (most of which had been shattered by stray bullet-shots or other explosive impacts), in the Center Hall. A second later, the familiar Presidential emblem, appeared on the screen.

"Ladies and gentlemen," came the voice-over, "Here is an important message, from the President of the United States."

America, Meet My Kids

The scene unfolding on the TV-feed, in front of Sam Jacobson and a quickly-burgeoning crowd of onlookers within the Center Hall, was repeated millions of times, in front of various video-displays, all around the world.

It was also intercepted by the war-children of a certain alien-girl, as she hovered high above the Atlantic Ocean; and from thence – via some close-range wireless-networking trickery – it was simulcast to some of the video-screens within the air-ship, held in the Storied Watcher's invisible telekinetic grasp.

As the image of the eagle holding leaves in one claw and arrows in the other, faded from view, it revealed a haggard – but defiant- and still-well-dressed – President. Dimly visible behind him – on the opposite side of the bullet-riddled exterior Oval Office windows – were the indistinct figures of Abruzzio, Ramirez, Rainbow and also Minnie Chu.

The U.S. leader's son and daughter, along with Will Hendricks, a force of well-armed soldiers and Jerry Kaysten, were all in the Oval Office, maintaining careful watch on all the available ingress-routes.

The President started to speak, almost immediately.

"My fellow Americans," he intoned, "I'm speaking briefly with you tonight, to reassure you that – contrary to widespread rumors, as well as understandable concern on the part of ordinary citizens – both I, and the First Family, are very much alive and well. Furthermore – despite the series of brutally-violent, cruel, treasonous and despicable terrorist attacks that have lately been directed against the White House – and you can see some of the marks of that battle, right here in the Oval Office – I am still very much in charge of the Armed Forces and of the federal government in general. The White House is now being secured by elements of our armed forces, and any remaining terrorists in or around here, will soon be captured or eliminated."

The President leaned forward and stared deliberately into the camera, as he proclaimed, in an unusually-tough and -loud tone of voice,

"In other words… the terrorist attack *has been defeated* – despite the senseless deaths of many dozens of innocent people around here, *the attack has entirely failed!* I am *still* your President – I am *still* in charge – and I am *still* here in the Oval Office! The terrorists have accomplished *nothing*, except for *murder!*"

He paused for a second or two, and then said,

"Many of you will want to know exactly what has been going on here, and let me say… so do I. As matters stand, all I can do is to explain what I am currently aware of, either through personal experience or by first-hand account."

"To begin with," he explained, "Early this morning, snipers of unknown affiliation fired on the ceremony on the South Lawn, in which I was welcoming Chancellor Gebirgen of the Federal Republic of Germany, to the White House. Although the Chancellor and I survived – Mr. Gebirgen is in a secure location, by the way – we suffered many casualties, including a brave Secret Service agent who was a close personal friend; he gave his life without hesitation, to save my own. The terrorist attacks became more intensive, with the physical security of the White House itself becoming compromised."

"Following standard protocol," continued the President, "I was immediately evacuated from the building, but unfortunately, the terrorists were able to take two members of my family, hostage. I agreed to surrender myself so that the terrorists would let my loved ones go, and so I returned to the White House. But the terrorist leader reneged on the deal and tried to have me murdered, instead. This treachery *almost* succeeded – my family and I came within a couple seconds of being shot dead – but this was prevented by two incredibly brave and amazing people, who you'll be meeting shortly. All

I *can* say is, the Lord must have a reason for keeping Yours Truly around; because lately, He certainly *has* had many opportunities in which to do the opposite."

"Now," elaborated the U.S. leader, after sitting back a bit and drawing a deep breath, "The obvious issue is, 'who *are* these terrorists, and how did they so successfully execute an attack on one of the most well-defended buildings in the world'. I'll admit that currently, we don't have a good answer to this question, except to say that we believe – on the basis of strong evidence – that at least two and possibly three *different* groups were involved in the attack on the White House. We suspect that one these conspiracies includes renegade, treasonous ex-members of the Central Intelligence Agency. Another involves – at least to some extent – the GrayWar Corporation. As to the third, investigations are continuing, but we have no doubt that we'll get to the bottom of the plot, in due order."

"Therefore, as of right now," demanded the President, "I'm directing all GrayWar staff to immediately surrender their weapons to the nearest depots of the regular armed forces, to stand down from their current assignments – whatever these may be – and to refrain from implementing orders from superiors within the GrayWar organization. I'm also ordering Mr. Hedrick Duke – CEO of the GrayWar Corporation – to report to the nearest law enforcement location, where he'll be taken into custody, to await a fair trial on treasonous activity against the United States. Mr. Duke, if you're listening... the jig is *up!* There's nowhere you can hide, that we won't find you – make it easy on everyone, and just give up, before we have to come and *get* you. Your little plot to stage a *putsch* with Mr. Wyckheiser – who, incidentally, is now in my custody, along with one other key individual whom I'm sure you know – has utterly *failed!* Please avoid further bloodshed and tell your forces to surrender. Should you refuse to do so, I'll hold you *personally* responsible for the consequences!"

"There's much more that I could say about what my family and I – not to mention the many brave and selfless White House staff, some of whom have given their lives in furtherance of their duties – have been through today," expounded the President, "But apart from not wanting to interfere with ongoing law enforcement and intelligence operations, honestly, there's not a lot more that I'm one hundred per cent sure of – so I'll hold off on the speculation, for now. However... I *do* have two very important, heroic young people – of whom I'm *incredibly* proud – who I'd like to introduce to you, here and now."

He looked away from the camera.

"Clairie? Matt?" he called. "Could you come over here, please?"

There was a broad smile on Kaysten's face, as he nodded approvingly.

The two wide-eyed, blushing Presidential offspring stepped uneasily forward, towards the Resolution Desk. Though they were very familiar with the media, both were utterly unprepared for being the center of attention, in a context such as this.

The President stood up, pushed his chair back slightly and stretched out his arms to embrace Clairie on his right, and Matt on his left. Kaysten's deft camera-work kept the focus and the field of vision perfectly aligned.

"People of America," he spoke, in his well-known, fatherly tone, "What you are seeing today, is not just the love of a father, for his children; nor is it only the gratitude of a man whose life has just been saved, *by* his children; though, it's all of that. It's also the amazement of a father who has witnessed his children *becoming* something far beyond anything that he – or any human being – could possibly imagine achieving."

He looked first at his daughter, and then at his son.

"You can *show* them," he remarked. "Show the people, who you *are*, now."

Two war-songs began playing, as – to shocked gasps, literally around the world – the eyes of the two Presidential offspring showed a dull glow.

Clairie – enshrouded in a glowing aura of majesty – stared directly at the camera, and, in a Stentorian tone, warned,

"This is a message for the terrorists – and for anyone else who's thinking of stabbing Dad in the back. You'll have to get past *me*, first! *Understand?*"

Matt added, with a defiant growl, "And not just *her*, either. Go ahead – ask the last jerks who tried it, how well it turned out for them! Bring it *on!*"

The President again sat down and nodded in turn, to each teenager. Matt and Clairie – with their alien-powers diminishing in conspicuity – walked back into the Oval Office, outside the camera's field of vision.

The U.S. leader – sitting straight up – spoke into the camera.

"In an earlier address to the nation," he noted, "I stated that your government had recourse to super-human defenders; well, now you've seen two of them – the two closest to my heart. I've seen Matt and Clairie use their powers, first-hand, and let me just say… I sure wouldn't want to be the one standing in their way. To the enemies of the nation – including but not limited to the terrorists who attacked the White House – I say, 'you'd do well to heed my childrens' advice'. You *will* fail – and we *will* bring you swiftly to justice!"

"My fellow Americans," he concluded, "I know we have all been through some troubling times, lately; and I won't pretend that it hasn't been tough on everyone – including my own family – nor will I claim that no mistakes were ever made. What I *will* promise is that I will remain as your President, at least until we have gotten to the bottom of all this and have ensured that it will never happen again. As accurate information about the attacks – and who was behind them – becomes available, you have my personal assurance that I'll share it with everyone. In the meantime, please go about your business as you always have done, knowing that your President is still alive and in charge, and that your government continues to function. God bless each and every one of you... and God bless the United States of America!"

The "On-Air" light on the A/V indicator went off.

"Out of the *park*, as usual, sir!" enthusiastically congratulated Kaysten.

As the broadcast terminated and the Presidential seal replaced the scene of the President at his desk, Jacobson turned to his former Mars mission pilot and said, "What do you make of *that?*"

"I gotta hand it to the bugger," ruefully remarked Brent Boyd. "If bullshit was an alien-power... he'd be ten times better at it, than she'd be."

"Hmmph," grumbled Billings, as he observed the last moments of the broadcast, from inside the *Mailànkh Express*. "If she – oh, and 'they' – can pipe *that* idiocy in here... how come I can't get her to give us a baseball-game, or even just a movie from the back-catalogs?"

"I'm not sure, Mr. Billings," answered Tommy. "But *Væran* Ss'éth'ch' is saying that Mom has a message for us."

"Oh... yeah?" said the salesman. "What *is* it? Like, maybe, 'she hasn't heard that many lies told in that short a time, in the last ten thousand years'?"

The boy – holding the cold-dagger firmly in one hand, even though both it and most of his forearm, was now covered in hoarfrost, seemed momentarily to be in a trance.

He came out of a blank-looking forward stare and offered, "Mom says, 'hardee-har-har', and also, 'the President may think himself a convincing liar – but, in fact, he is naught but a rank amateur, in such things'. But anyway, Mr. Billings... that wasn't what Mom wanted to tell us."

"Fine... so what *did* she want to tell us?" asked Billings.

"It was, 'the test is over... thus can we now go hence'," disclosed Tommy. "Uhh... what's *that* supposed to mean, do you think? Hold on – something else she's saying –"

"Yeah?" prodded the salesman.

"Mom says," spoke Tommy, "Hold on to your seating-belts."

Fireworks After The Fireworks

The next three days around the White House – though, in fact, packed chock-a-block with important events – seemed almost anti-climatic, to those who had experienced, or suffered through, the bloody day before.

Those hurt in the siege had been sent for medical attention, which was – for the most part – timely and successful; for example, the First Lady, Callum

Wade, Jackson the Secret Service agent, the Secretary of State (Feldner and Moira Sullivan were located nearby to the Secretary and, though terrified, were found to be unhurt) and many others, managed to survive their wounds with due amounts of rest in bed and other care.

Others – among them Kaysten and the President's two children – seemed to recover all on their own, in rapid order.

As for the White House itself, the building had been tightly locked-down right from the termination of the President's speech, after which it was searched top to bottom by the soldiers of the Joint Strike Force; there were a few sporadic fire-fights during this process, which lasted over a full day.

Eventually, over three hundred sullen, dispirited GrayWar mercenaries were thus rounded up and marched off to impromptu prison-camps, set up elsewhere in the D.C. area.

However, the two most important detainees – Top Dog and Senator Wyckheiser – were, once stripped down to their underwear and issued orange prison-garb – thrown into separate makeshift jails, in the underground-levels of the West Wing.

The former store-rooms used for this purpose had only one way in (the bounty-hunter had been procured to weld together a set of steel bars for each *ersatz*-cell; he had grumbled about the task, complaining "why don't you just let me make a bonfire out of 'em, pardner – I'll even bring some wienies for you to roast"), and were in a dead-end corridor guarded by six full-time, heavily-armed, stone-faced soldiers. They had been given "shoot to kill" orders, in the event of an escape-attempt.

As the President stood in front of the room where the former Agency director was being confined, he heard a barrage of taunts and insults.

"It's *dead*, Clark!" shrieked a sweating, agitated Top Dog. "The witch is *dead*… and with it, your lib-tard hopes for a new, bleeding-heart tomorrow! It's only a matter of *time* until my guys find me, and deal with *you!* Get *ready*, Clark! 'Back to life… back to reality!'"

As he walked away from the scene, the President turned to one of the JSF guards and muttered, "I thought I *told* you to shut him up!"

"Very sorry, sir," responded the soldier. "He's been at it for *hours*, now. Some of my guys were wearing earplugs, but I told them to ditch 'em… might interfere with situational-awareness. If it's any consolation, sir… we're more than a hundred feet underground. You won't be able to hear him, topside."

They heard a loud voice coming from the improvised jail, two doors further down. It called out, "Tell him to put a sock into it! Your keeping me down here, listening to *that*, hour after hour, is an *outrage!* Where are my *rights?*"

The President turned, faced down the corridor and bellowed,

"Your 'rights', died along with Curt Kortish!"

He addressed the JSF sergeant in charge of the guard-detail.

"Give them enough food and water to keep them alive," directed the U.S. leader. "Not one *calorie* more! And give 'em a Bible… nothing else. With what they've got to *answer* for – it will be required reading for both of them."

"Acknowledged, sir," replied the Army Ranger. "We'll ensure that they'll have plenty of time to contemplate the future."

"If," carefully offered the President, "They *have* one."

Immediately after the building was declared "free of hostiles", the remaining White House staff were – under Kaysten's persuasive direction – assigned to clean-up duties, especially for the signs of battle that had scarred the Oval Office.

Though adequate supplies were locally available, some of the damage clearly would have to wait for dedicated crews to repair. For example, Tanaka's lightening-bolts – and Wolf's fireballs – had blown out the west-most wall of the West Wing entirely, just north of Kaysten's office; all that could be done in the interim, was to cover the breach with a tarpaulin.

The quarantine of the Presidential mansion led to a rather awkward confrontation between Jacobson and the U.S. leader, when the former requested permission from the latter, to egress the Jacobson and Boyd families (and other civilians), from the premises. At length – after considerable urging on the part of Abruzzio and Chu – the Mars Gang leader relented, but only at the price of being allowed to stay in the areas of the mansion normally reserved for the First Family itself.

Other than for those on official government business, there had been no visitors to the White House, with the double exceptions of Wolf's two hell-hounds. The two "more-than-dogs"– seemingly answering some ethereal call on the part of little Rainbow – had showed up at the front gate to the East Wing, with the Russian following frantically behind (Misha had thought Boob and Tube to have gone off on their own, and the three of them together caused a minor stir in downtown D.C., as they alternatively lept and flew through the air).

The Joint Strike Force guards almost caused a disaster when, with raised guns, they confronted the hell-hounds and the Russian; but none too soon, the bounty-hunter arrived on scene with the friendly comment, "you boys want to get roasted from the front by my two pups, be my guest – or you can be barbecued from the back, by yours truly… it's all good".

Hopeka's soldiers – no fools they – relented and allowed the dogs into the mansion, under Wolf's tutelage and Rainbow's leadership. Aside for a few more scorch-marks on the carpets and some of the furniture, they caused no more immediate commotion.

Misha was offered the opportunity to stay in the White House along with the others, but he politely declined, stating that "he had some things to catch up with, at my nation's embassy". When word of this reached the Mars Gang, it caused considerable apprehension; but a half-day later, the ex-SVR agent checked in with Donny, Sammie, Marie and the recovering Callum Wade at a local hospital, assuring the Wade clan and the Jacobson crew, that all was well.

The JSF force that had rescued the President had been augmented by regular Army, and there were at least two well-armed soldiers posted at ten-foot intervals in the building's main corridors. There were four more guarding the entrances to the Cabinet Room, the Oval Office and several other high-criticality rooms within the White House.

Both the North and South lawns had been garrisoned by almost a regiment's-worth of military equipment, including tanks, armored personnel carriers and dug-in infantry with machine-guns and missile-launchers. Helicopter-gunships were stationed on roof-tops no more than a half-mile distant; the latter measure had originally been meant for the top of the White House itself, but the damage to the West Wing's roof-structure (though now at least patched well enough to prevent rain from entering the building) had precluded the landing of anything above minimal weight.

On the morning of the fourth day after the siege, Jacobson, Tanaka, and Boyd – along with Abruzzio, Ramirez, Hendricks and Boatman, stood outside the White House Cabinet Room, just to the north of the Oval Office.

The two male ex-astronauts had been issued with military dress uniforms appropriate to their rank, while the former science officer and the other civilians had been provided with business-wear of the best type, including imported shirts, suits and leather shoes.

The bounty-hunter had been invited to the meeting, but had declined, saying, "there's a NFL-game on at the same time and them terrorists shot up the only DVR in the building… gotta *prioritize*, you know, pardner".

"Wow… I should fight more terrorists – I haven't had duds *this* good, in, like, *ever*," quipped the third agent, as he stood in the hall, straightening his exquisite silk tie. "I'm afraid to eat a salad or sip coffee, in case some of it gets on this spiffy outfit."

"And nothin' *ever* fit you all *that* good, young man," offered Boatman. "They had to re-take all my own measurements, after I – umm – lost a bit of weight, if I don't mind sayin'. Shoes pinch a bit, though. Sure hope they let us keep these clothes… no *way* I could have paid for 'em, on what the Bureau was payin' me."

"Hate to burst your bubble, man," said Hendricks, "But I don't think you and me are still on the payroll."

"Have to talk about Minnie about that," answered the black ex-agent.

"I miss Devon," remarked Tanaka. "He and Saquina should be here."

"Are they still in L.A.?" inquired Abruzzio.

"'Far as I know," said Boyd. "I think the President sent out the word that they should come here… don't know if they heard it, or paid attention to it."

"Speaking of that," advanced Ramirez, "Where's *Karein?*"

The comment was met by bewildered stares and shrugs, from the others. The door opened, revealing Feldner's familiar, pleasant smile.

"The President's about to call the meeting to order," she instructed. "Please take your seats."

The more-than-human troupe walked, single-file, into the White House Cabinet Room. The place did bear the scars of the recent battle – one bullet-pierced window was precariously held together with duct-tape, and there were a few other holes in the walls – but for the most part, the damage had been at least superficially papered-over.

The arrivees beheld a large group of mostly past-middle-age, white men – with perhaps two or three females and minorities – arrayed in tight order, sitting on thickly-padded, leather-bound business-chairs around the room's trademark, oblong, well-polished, mahogany-wood center table. Three-quarters of the available seats were already occupied by Cabinet-members and other high-level functionaries, but the southern end of the table was largely unoccupied. Paper note-pads, water-glasses and cups of fine china filled with coffee, were in front of each seat.

The President was in his special, slightly-higher chair, midway between each end of the table. He had Chu on one side and Kaysten on the other. There were armed guards standing discreetly at each of the room's four corners.

"Mr. President," spoke Jacobson.

"Mr. Jacobson," answered the U.S. leader. "Glad you and your friends could come."

"How's your family doing, sir?" politely inquired the Mars Gang leader. "I've heard the First Lady's out of danger."

"Very much so… she's resting comfortably," confirmed the President. "Matt and Clairie are, in their own words, 'better than fine'… they're tied up with answering fan-mail from young people, all over the country. And as you can see, Jacob's on the mend, too."

"Mr. Secretary of State," greeted Jacobson. "Good to see that you're none the worse for wear, from that unfortunate –"

The elderly man threw up his hands and offered, "Commander… at *my* age, just 'a *little* the worse for wear', is about all one can reasonably expect. If I still have two working legs and two working arms – not to mention a working head – I'll count that as a 'win'."

There was a wave of restrained laughter, upon hearing this.

"But I'll be fine, in due course," said the Secretary of State. "Chancellor Gebirgen is okay, as well, by the way… he and I had a short talk, this morning."

"May we take a seat?" asked Tanaka.

"Of course," said the President.

The more-than-humans did so, and were now arranged around the south end of the table.

"We'll get right down to business," commenced the President. "The reason why I've called this meeting – and invited our friends down there –"

I hope by "friends", he doesn't mean "us", Sam, sent Tanaka.

He can think of me – at best – as an "acquaintance", responded the ex-astronaut.

Yeah, added Boyd,

Just because we saved his ass… doesn't mean we have to vote *for him.*

" – Is because we need to take a step back and figure out, first, 'where are we now', and second, 'where do we go from here'," continued the U.S. leader. "A lot of this has to do with the business of running the government, which shouldn't be much of interest to Commander Jacobson and his team, although they're welcome to hang around and listen to the exciting stuff – like next quarter's labor participation forecast, or the upcoming Congressional schedule, for example."

Does that include the plans for how many kids he's going to torture, next month? maliciously broadcast Boyd.

Enough mind-talking in the peanut-gallery, silently complained Abruzzio.

I want to hear what he's saying…

And besides – Matt and Clairie might overhear us.

They could be right outside, for all we know.

"So, with that said," offered the President, "The first item on the agenda is the one of most interest – namely, 'what have we found out about the terrorists, who caused so much chaos, only a few days ago'. As you may know, Director Chu has been assigned primary responsibility for overseeing the investigations. I'll turn the floor over to her… Minnie?"

The former team-leader looked poised and polished, as she addressed the crowd, saying,

"Thank you, Mr. President. While obviously our efforts in this area are continuing, and will do so for some time into the future, we do have some results to share with yourself and – with your permission – Commander Jacobson and his team. May I, sir?"

"I have no objection," said the President, "As long as Mr. Jacobson and the Mars Gang understand that this is privileged information… we'd prefer it not to be disclosed to the media without our knowledge and consent."

"Speaking only for myself," responded the former Mars mission leader, "While it will depend on what Minnie has to say… I'm not planning to rush out and do any interviews in the next few hours, if you know what I mean."

"If it's evidence of more government crimes, sir," evenly stated Boyd, "I'm afraid I can't make any such commitment."

"Ditto," echoed Tanaka.

"I don't think you have to worry about that, Major Boyd," stepped in Chu. "It's the *opposite*, in fact."

This *ought to be good*, he mentally remarked.

It is, Chu sent back.

Navigate the shoals and thickets between "your job" and "nobility", sister, advised Abruzzio.

We know you're up to it.

The *nouvelle* FBI-director nodded her head slightly, and kept speaking.

"So... we've been interrogating the prisoners taken in the recent siege of the White House, as well as following up on the forensic evidence collected so far. There's much more remaining to analyze, but – based on what we've already got – we've come to some preliminary conclusions."

The others in the room stared intensively at Chu, as she related,

"First : we believe that the group of terrorists responsible for the initial attack – that is, the gunfire directed against the ceremony welcoming Chancellor Gebirgen – was the doing of the so-called "Klan of Jesus Christ", of which, you may recall, former Spiritual Adviser, Harold Crowford, was one of the leaders. This conclusion is based on correlation of evidence collected from sniper-positions in buildings facing on to 15th and 17th Streets, around or just south of the Ellipse – and also from around Lafayette Square, at the north end of the North Lawn – with very similar insignia, weapons and so on, identified in the attack against Commander Jacobson's encampment on Cass Mountain in West Virginia."

Crowford... he was the Bible-thumping nut, who set off the bomb on the plane you were on... wasn't he? mentally inquired Tanaka.

Even so, sister, responded Chu.

I don't think you ever met him.

Let me tell you... you weren't missing anything.

Though she was simultaneously using telepathy, the former team-leader didn't miss a beat as she explained,

"Law enforcement and military forces actually cornered several of the 'Klan' shooters; but they all either fought to the death, or committed suicide, to avoid capture. Thus, unfortunately we don't have any first-hand testimony, in this case. Also – significantly – we do *not* believe that this group of assassins, coordinated their attacks with those of the others, about whom I'll speak, in a moment. It seems to have been largely a coincidence that the two assaults happened to occur on the same day... although there may be an alternative explanation."

Uh-oh, Boyd directed to Jacobson.

Nothing to apologize for, deflected the ex-astronaut's former boss.

Chu paused momentarily, looked at the third agent and said, "And Mr. President... I'd also like to personally congratulate Agent Hendricks, for the help he provided in silencing the snipers who were responsible for this first attack. Also, Mr. Grishin of the SVR, and – last but not least – the three dogs owned by various members of the Mars Gang and others associated with it. All of these fought very bravely alongside local law enforcement and military forces, at significant personal risk. Thank you!"

"Well," commented the U.S. leader, "I think you just got a promotion, Mr. Hendricks."

"Thank you, sir," answered the third agent.

Does he know about your little 'encounter' with those cracker cops, back in the mountains? ventured Boyd.

No, silently responded Hendricks.

He doesn't have to, sent Chu.

At least not until I figure out how to explain it to him.

"I can't speak for Wolf, but as for me, I don't 'own', Rainbow," corrected Abruzzio. "I think of her more as a child... no, a sister. She may not technically be a 'person'... but she's far more than just a 'dog'."

"After what she did for us," quipped the President, "She can dine on aged T-bone steaks, now to the end of her life – I'll be happy to foot the bill!"

There was more polite laughter. Then Chu continued,

"Second : We have a high level of certainty that the second terrorist group – the one that actually physically invaded the White House grounds and that so cruelly murdered dozens of innocent people, encountered there – originated in the Central Intelligence Agency. Specifically, we believe that the former director of that agency – who's now in our custody, and who goes by the internal Agency code-name, 'Top Dog' – was responsible for organizing and implementing this attack."

"Also," elaborated the former team-leader, "We believe the former Agency director to have been conspiring with the CEO of GrayWar Corporation – Hedrick Duke – and with others, notably former Senator Grady Wyckheiser. Evidently their plan was to murder the legitimate President and then appoint Mr. Wyckheiser as 'acting President' in the ensuing confusion. We base these conclusions not only on extensive forensic evidence collected on the White House premises, but also on first-hand testimony by numerous individuals who were involved in battle with both 'Top Dog' and some of his lieutenants, all of whom seemed to possess unusually-advanced close-combat gear –"

"The Commander and I can both attest to *that*," interrupted Brent Boyd. "We hit those, uhh, 'jerks', with enough force to kill or cripple two or three normal men... they just took the lickin' and kept tickin'. Whatever those combat-suits were made of, I'll guarantee you can't buy it off of NeoNet. *Thankfully.*"

"So did I," added the normally-taciturn Ramirez. "I was reluctant to unleash such an attack, but I felt it necessary to do so, up on the rooftop. I was astonished to see my lightening-bolt hit home... yet, apparently, it failed to stop the man in the battle-suit. As Major Boyd says, the amount of energy expended here, *should* have been more than enough to have... uhh...

'eliminated' my opponent. I certainly hope we do not have any more encounters of this type."

Though none saw it, a couple members of the uniformed military represented at the table, scribbled notes to the effect of, "possibility : found counter-measure to alien-powers".

"Thank you for the information, and for your assistance in the battle, Major Boyd... Mr. Ramirez," smoothly mentioned the *nouvelle* FBI-director. "Both are greatly appreciated, as are the efforts of the Storied Watcher's other friends, for example Commander Jacobson, Professors Tanaka and Abruzzio, and many others."

She stopped, paused for a second, shot a long glance at Jacobson and said, "At this point, however, I *do* have to deviate slightly from the script. Commander – as I said, your assistance in resisting the terrorist attack was critically important in helping to get many people safely out of here; we were very lucky to have had you on the premises, when the siege began. But you have to admit... it *was* quite a coincidence, not only that the Klan of Jesus Christ happened to attack on the exact same day as the unrelated Agency plot was unleashed – but *also* on the same day that the Mars Gang, and those traveling with it, just 'happened' to be at the White House. If there's a good explanation for this... now's the time for you to tell us about it."

The former Mars mission commander didn't immediately respond; it seemed as if he was carefully considering what to say. Eventually, he replied,

"Well, first of all, Minnie... with all due respect, and as you well know, my team and I don't report to either yourself or the President – so if this is going to turn into a cross-examination, please tell me –"

She tried to feign a more friendly stance, and interjected, "Look, Sam – talking to you as a fellow 'New Person' – not as the Bureau-director – I just want to know what you were planning to *do*, at that time; and I'm obviously not the *only* one who's noticed the fact that all of you were here, on the same day as the two terrorist attacks were launched –"

"She *definitely* isn't," forcefully mentioned the President. "Anybody with half a *brain* can't fail to notice it!"

"Yeah," camped on Kaysten. "Haven't you jokers been watching the news shows, lately? Every second broadcast starts with 'Mars Gang plot to kill President, stopped only by Joint Strike Force rescue'! What are Susan and I supposed to *tell* them, anyway? You guys show up here just as the bullets start flying, when – last we had it – you were hiding out up on a mountain in West Virginia or something. What would you *expect* the media to conclude?"

"What, exactly, are you accusing us of?" icily remarked Tanaka. "Like, 'being part of the two conspiracies to murder yourself and then take over the government'?"

"We could have done that *weeks* ago," unhelpfully pointed out Boyd. "What the hell would we have to *gain*, by camping on to a plot to kill the German Chancellor, and then slaughtering half the people in the White

House… while our own *families* – who, by the way, are just as vulnerable to bullets as any other normal human being would be – were sitting right there in the middle of the battle?"

The President – having evidently forgotten about 'Mars Ears' – leaned over to whisper to Chu.

"Minnie," he asked, "Is that *true*? You mean their families were here – at the White House – all the way through the siege?"

The *nouvelle* FBI-director nodded affirmatively and the tried to take charge of the deteriorating conversation.

"No… *no!*" she argued. "Brent – Cherie – Sam – nobody's 'accusing' you, of *anything!* All of us who have inherited Karéin's powers know how things have a way of going sideways, no matter how carefully we try to do otherwise. I have no doubt that you have a good explanation… I just want to hear it."

Well then, sent Jacobson, not particularly caring if Chu could over-think, *Do we tell her… and him?*

He's going to be pissed, responded Boyd.

Sure *he is*, observed Tanaka,

But what can he do to us about it?

I guess there goes our nice luxury suite in the White House, quipped Boyd.

Maybe it's time, added Abruzzio.

Rainbow had a little 'oops' on one of the carpets in the Lincoln Bedroom.

"Very well, then," spoke Jacobson. "I'll tell you; but only on the condition that once you hear the full story, you – this means you, Mr. President – will try to defend us from the hatchet-job that, per Jerry's comments a minute ago, the media seems to be doing on us. Unfortunately the Mars Gang doesn't have a very well-developed PR infrastructure, of our own."

"That, Mr. Jacobson," replied the U.S. leader, "Will of course depend on what you have to say. The government will have no problem in supporting you, at least on this particular issue – as long as it's a tenable position."

"I guess you'll have to decide for yourself," deflected the ex-astronaut. "Sylvia… you had a hand in planning it… want to explain?"

"Sure," said the former JPL scientist. "Basically, after the sniper attack on our temporary refuge on Cass Mountain – and the second one that, recall, landed me in hospital and might have killed me – the Mars Gang, and its hangers-on, decided that we had to take the fight to the enemy, as opposed to just sitting around and letting *them* get the first shot at *us*. So we decided to lay a trap for them, by having some of us appear in public, after leaking the details of time, place, *et cetera*, to NeoNet. The idea was that they would attack the 'civilians' – the families, most of whom are just ordinary humans –

but that the 'New People' would step in at the last minute and potentially take some prisoners, who might lead us to the leadership of the conspiracies –"

"And you didn't try to coordinate this with myself or the Bureau?" incredulously demanded Chu. "*Sylvia...* where's that 'godly insight' that Karéin supposedly bestowed on you?"

"Even us genii have a bad day sometimes, I suppose," parried Abruzzio, as she explained, "First we tried the scheme in a location away from the White House... but despite a great deal of effort, nobody showed. We realized that we could keep doing the same, potentially indefinitely, with zero success – and the bastards who murdered Cherie's mother, were still out there. *Sooo...*"

"Yeah?" broke in Kaysten. "I can already tell where *this* is going."

"Well," carefully stated the former JPL scientist, "We figured that we'd have to go somewhere that was absolutely *irresistible*, to a murderous terrorist who hates all three of the Storied Watcher, her followers, and *you*, Mr. President. Actually, we were prepared to visit the White House continuously over several weeks, if necessary... but as it turned out, they took the bait, right on Day One. Our big mistake was assuming that we could keep the situation under control; but the terrorists attacked in far greater force than we had anticipated –"

"May He forgive me for taking His name in vain," interrupted a visibly angry President, "But for Christ's *sake*, Ms. Abruzzio – are you telling me that the Mars Gang, and yourself, deliberately made the White House into a *battleground*, causing the needless deaths of hundreds of innocent people, including Curt Kortish and, almost, my wife and myself – just to play amateur detective... when you had all the resources of the FBI, right at your disposal? I can't *believe* what I'm *hearing!*"

Kaysten's own indignation might have been feigned, but it seemed genuine enough, as he piled on,

"You know... you guys really *do* take the cake! I just about got *killed* in there – three or four times over! I had to fight a whole roomful of armed terrorists, all by *myself!* I *still* can't figure out how I got away with it, with my skin intact – but are you telling us, here and now, that it was all *your* doing, right from the *start?*"

"What would you have had us *do?*" contested Jacobson. "Just sit around, waiting for the terrorists to pick us – or members of our families – off, one by one? We cooked up the idea in Sylvia's hospital-room, after she had been hit by multiple shots that would have killed *you* in a half-second, Mr. President. What she says is true – we underestimated the magnitude of the attack that the conspirators were able to bring against us – but we have nothing to apologize for... *nothing!*"

"You could have hidden out in Camp David," reminded Kaysten.

"We *did* propose that, to our families, and to some of the others," noted Boyd. "We couldn't get a consensus, because, frankly... many of us, including but not limited to 'yours truly', don't trust the government. Which meant that we were on our own – and that we had to have it out with the pricks who were responsible for the Cass Mountain assault, once and for all."

"The Bureau was – and is – doing everything that it could, and can, to track down and apprehend the terrorists who were responsible both for the attack on Cass Mountain, and on Cherie and Sylvia in Pittsburgh, and on the White House," argued Chu. "I've been personally overseeing the investigations. Did any of you consider that by going off half-cocked on this scheme, you could have ruined any chance that we might have had, of *catching* anyone?"

"The scum who tortured and killed my mother are still out there!" shot back Tanaka. "I gave everyone a deadline – it's long past, by now. Should I just sit around, twiddling my thumbs, while you and your friends in the government take their own sweet time, in bringing me *justice*, Minnie?"

"And your 'alternative' was… *what*, Cherie?" countered the *nouvelle* FBI-director. "Just issue a public invite for every terrorist in North America to the grounds of the White House, and hope your lightening-bolts happen to vaporize the ones who did this to your mother? How would you even *know* that you got the right ones?"

"I figure that if I disintegrate every last member of the Agency, sooner or later… I'll hit pay-dirt," ominously replied the Mars mission science officer. "I'm about one inch away from doing exactly *that*… and I'm sure I'll have some help from a hot-headed big guy with two mean-looking hell-hounds, too."

An exasperated Chu threw up her hands, shook her head and rolled her eyes.

"Where the hell's Karéin when you need her?" she muttered.

The President's head was also shaking as he stated, "I can't express how profoundly disappointed I am in the lot of you so-called 'more-than-humans'. I thought we had an *agreement*, Mr. Jacobson – and you betrayed it in the most fundamental way. Out of your own impatience and vanity, you senselessly endangered everyone in and around the White House – and you very nearly engineered not only my own death, but that of my family too, not to mention, the violent overthrow of my administration, and its replacement by Wyckheiser's little Agency- and GrayWar-supported *putsch*. We only avoided a complete collapse of Constitutional government in this country, by the narrowest margins! You brought those sons of bitches right to our *doorstep* –"

"Mr. President," interrupted Abruzzio, "Don't you think you're being a little *unfair*, here? Neither Commander Jacobson nor I – and I'm just as 'guilty' as he is – had any idea of how this was all going to turn out! The prudent thing for him and Major Boyd to have done, would have been to escort their families out of the White House, the moment the shooting started – and to have then left you and everyone else, to sink or swim on your own. Instead, the two of them – along with the rest of us – risked our lives to save yours. Does that mean *nothing* to you?"

"I don't know, Ms. Abruzzio," coolly responded the U.S. leader. "If someone drives your car off a cliff and then gives you a parachute at the last minute, does that count as 'rescuing you'?"

"I think it's more like, 'a terrorist carjacked you and drives your car off the cliff, and a follower of the Storied Watcher flies you to safety'," countered Abruzzio.

"If it hadn't been for Sylvia's mirages," reminded Hendricks, "That 'Top Dog' prick from the Agency, probably would have had you *shot*, Mr. President. He *said* as much, if we didn't offer up Karéin on a silver platter, for him."

"And if it hadn't been for Minnie's 'beguilement'-trick," added Abruzzio, "We probably wouldn't have caught him. He'd still be out there, planning another attack. The point is… we all tried our darnedest to help, Mr. President, when we realized what was going on. Maybe you *can* question our original decision to make the White House the venue for our terrorist-trap – and we all mourn those who were slain during these atrocities – but it wasn't *us* who targeted the civilians in the building, sir! It *was* us who tried to *protect* them! We're the *good* guys… we're all on the same side, here – whether or not you want to acknowledge it."

"Tell that to Curt Kortish's widow," said an unimpressed President. "Anyway… in view of this information – with whatever authority I have, as well as whatever ability to enforce it – I'm going to say the following. Mr. Jacobson, whatever working relationship that I may have had with you and your little 'Mars Gang' clique, should be considered defunct as of right now; and you're no longer welcome on these premises. Of course, practically speaking, there's nothing I can do to physically eject you, should you decide to dig in your heels. I'll give you up to four hours to get your families and dependents somewhere else to stay, and if you're short of money, Jerry can make the necessary arrangements. After you leave, I'd request at least 72 hours advance notice, before any of you return here, for any business –"

"Mr. President," carefully stated Jacobson, "Speaking only for myself, I have no problem in assuring you that my family and I will abide by your wishes; we had only been staying here because of the quarantine, anyway. Brent, Cherie, Hector, Sylvia, Will, Otis, Wolf, Misha and the lot of them can make their own decisions –"

We should have let that CIA dude smoke his conniving ass, sent Tanaka.

Even if that would mean that 'Top Dog' and GrayWar would end up selecting the next President? responded Jacobson.

Out of the frying pan… into the fire…

Don't worry… I'll be paying the son of a bitch from the Agency, a nice little visit, answered the former Mars mission science officer.

Would just have meant that I'd have done him that much sooner.

"With that said, I'd note," continued the ex-astronaut, "That the fundamental issues that originally brought the Mars Gang to your doorstep – that is, the first time – remain largely unresolved. *I'm* very disappointed too, sir; I'm distressed at the lack of gratitude that I'm seeing, from your side of the table. You had better hope that you'll never again need help of the type that my team and I provided around here, recently – because when and if you call us… we won't be answering. Of *that*, I can assure you!"

"Sam is *so* right," echoed Tanaka. "Next meteor that drops on your head, you had better hope that Minnie isn't on vacation that day."

"I don't really *get* vacations," Chu tried to joke.

"You know what the sad thing is, sir?" complained Boyd. "Halfway through that firefight, we got into an argument about exactly this – namely, 'why the hell are we risking our asses, to save your own'. I pressed on simply because of a sense of duty. Well, sir… I guess you won't have Brent Boyd to kick around anymore. I sure hope you'll never need him."

"As a matter of fact," dispassionately offered the President, "As you may have heard lately, I *do* seem to have a couple of half-aliens – pretty powerful ones as I understand, if a little wet behind the ears – to protect me, here in the White House. I'm sure I'll be alright, without a 'Mars Gang' hanging around. Considering what you've accomplished over the past week… how could I do any *worse?*"

Kaysten unctuously laughed, at this.

He has a point, silently remarked Jacobson.

His daughter, in particular – from what I heard, she may eventually be a formidable opponent.

If it ever comes *to that… which of course I hope it won't.*

What on God's Green Earth was Karéin thinking *of, when she laid the Fire on those two?* speculated a frustrated Boyd.

Angels move in mysterious ways, answered Abruzzio.

Jacobson came slowly to his feet. He looked the President directly in the eye and said,

"If that's how you feel, sir… I believe you've got a cabinet-meeting to run; and if there ever was a sincere invitation for my team and I to remain here to attend it, clearly, that's no longer the case. Unless we have anything else to discuss, I'll head out and ask my family to start packing."

"I don't believe we do," answered the U.S. leader, with mock courtesy.

"*Sam –*" called a distraught Chu. "It doesn't have to end like this – can we talk later, *please –*"

Jacobson's face showed an equally-feigned, polite smile.

"Ah, Minnie… your boss has spoken," he chided. "Always gotta do what the boss says… *don't* we?"

The tension was deflected, if not broken, by the appearance of a young, blue-uniformed Air Force staffer, rushing into the room with a paper bulletin in his hand.

"Excuse me, sir," he exclaimed, to the President. "Very sorry to interrupt the meeting, but I have an emergency message!"

"Not another –" growled the frustrated U.S. leader. "When does it *end?* Okay... what *is* it?"

"Sir," said the orderly, "UFO inbound – tracking for the White House – ETA, six minutes, thirty seconds!"

Please Skip The Rest Of My Meeting

"Mr. President," warned one of the uniformed military brass at the Cabinet Room table, "You need to get to the bunker, *immediately!*"

Two of the JSF soldiers stepped forward, from the corners of the room.

"We're ready to escort you, sir," one of them said.

"I'll go with you too, sir," volunteered the young Air Force staffer.

"Relax," countered the U.S. leader. "After all that's happened around here, I'm not going *anywhere.* Jerry – where are Matt and Clairie?"

"I've got them on my speed-dial pager-app," answered Kaysten, as he retrieved and fiddled with his mobile communicator. "Just got to press this one button, and – okay, there we go; they should be here any moment."

"Sir," spoke one of the generals, "We *do* have anti-air defenses – surface-to-air missiles, anti-aircraft guns, ECM, *et cetera*, deployed locally. I'll need your authorization to fire on the incoming object."

"Wait a minute – *wait* a minute!" exclaimed Jacobson, from the other end of the room. "We don't even know what this thing *is* – nor do we know if it's hostile!"

He turned to address Boyd and Tanaka.

"Brent – Cherie – do you two think you could –"

"Already *on* it!" loudly replied Boyd. "Cherie – you want to lead? I'll cover your six!"

"You *got* it, brother!" confirmed Tanaka.

Boyd glanced at the President.

"This doesn't change *anything*," stipulated the former Mars mission pilot. "I'm not protecting *you*... I'm protecting everybody else in here, who never *did* anything!"

For some of those in the Cabinet Room, the dual display of glowing eyes, bursts of *Amaiish*-energy within bodies and exciting, haunting, adrenaline-pumping war-songs that ensued, was familiar; but for the many who had never yet seen it, the demonstration was little short of overwhelming (most of the humans witnessing the spectacle had to cover their eyes with hands, due to Boyd's scintillating presence).

Both of the ex-astronauts were now floating in mid-air, at a height of perhaps a foot above the room's central table.

"Sorry about the window, Mr. President," remarked Tanaka as she – followed a second later by Boyd – telekinetically burst one of the Cabinet Room's large, archway-style plate-glass windows looking out to the east, powered up her *Fire* and war-song to an impressive roar, and then rocketed out, executing a fast upward turn into the skies beyond.

"Let's hold off on the missiles and the gunfire for now," instructed the President. "You can use the jammers, however."

"Yes, sir," replied one of the uniformed brass. He got up from the table, went over to the inside wall and started to quietly issue commands into his communicator.

"Honestly… *those* two!" muttered Chu, as she started to move in the direction of the nearly-wrecked window.

"It *could* have been worse," mentioned Abruzzio.

"How's that?" inquired the Secretary of State.

"Easy… they *could* have had Wolf along with them," quipped the former JPL scientist. "You wouldn't just be missing a *window*."

Chu's own war-song began to play – albeit much more softly – as she levitated slightly so as to look downward on the debris-field extending out on the lawn. Her telekinesis reached out to the largest pieces of glass and metal-reinforcements littering the area, carried the shards back to be on a level plane with the window-jam and then arranged them into a rough approximation of a completed puzzle.

Then – to the continued astonishment of the humans in the room – Chu's fiery *Gaze* – at much less than full-power – welded the remnants in place, producing a very rough-looking and burn-marked, albeit mostly intact, facsimile of what had originally been a Cabinet Room window.

As she again landed on her feet and calmly walked back to her original place at the President's side, the *nouvelle* FBI-director cast a look of feigned diffidence and said, "Forgot to ask you, sir… did you want me to fly out after them? I think I'm good up to about forty thousand feet or so."

The U.S. leader's own visage was one of mordant humor as he observed, "For those of you who haven't been around here, over the past few weeks… *there's* what we've been dealing with. No, Ms. Chu… I'm sure that having two lethally-armed, potentially-hostile demigods flying around over D.C., will be quite enough. If you don't mind just sticking around here, until we –"

The door to the outside corridor burst open, revealing the figures of the two Presidential offspring. Their eyes were glowing dimly, although no war-songs were yet issuing from or around them.

"Dad!" called Matt. "Mr. Kaysten called us – are you in danger?"

"Not sure," replied the President. "We've got a UFO inbound. Major Boyd and Professor Tanaka have flown out a window, to intercept it. Would you two mind joining me – stand right back there, but keep an eye on the wall and windows behind me – for a few minutes, until we figure out what's going on?"

The teenagers complied, but as she found her assigned place, Clairie powered up her reflection-shield and – to the amazement of those in the room, particularly the ones between the force-field and the more-than-human girl – the translucent, amber-colored barrier appeared directly behind the President, protecting him from inbound projectiles.

"I bet I can keep it going for *hours*, if you need me to," mentioned the daughter.

She shot a glance at the barely-intact, jury-rigged, damaged window.

"Whoa," commented Clairie. "They sure must have been in a hurry!"

"Let's just hope that whatever it is… they stop it," evenly replied her father.

"They *will*, Mr. President," spoke Jacobson, "Just like we *always* do when there's an emergency – no matter *how* badly we get treated, by the government. 'We answer to a higher authority', is how I'd put it."

Yo, Commander, sent Clairie,

You don't sound too happy.

What's goin' on?

Your father is blaming us for the attacks on the White House, responded Jacobson.

After we risked our lives to save him and your mother.

Oh… and you and Matt too, before we knew that you could – uhh – look after yourselves.

Your father believes that we led the terrorists here… and therefore everything that happened subsequently, is our fault.

Well… did you? came the uncomfortable – but not hostile – query.

Sort of, broke in Abruzzio.

Minnie has been chasing these murderous swine for weeks, with little in the way of success… we wanted to set a trap for them – it worked only too well.

But you've got to believe us, Clairie… we did it so we could put an end to these plots, against ourselves, against our families, against your father… and against the country!

Should we have just sat around and waited for them to pick us off, one by one?

They shot me and almost killed me, a few days beforehand!

Dad's pissed, came a broadcast that had Matt's mind-signature upon it.

You know that look he gets?

Yeah, confirmed Clairie. *And you know what?*

What? responded the male teenager.

It's up to us to smooth things over.

Say… what? came back Matt's confused inquiry.

Why's that our job?

These guys went right across the country, leaving a path of destruction!

Because, answered Clairie, with a telepathic message that somehow exuded insight,

That's what Karéin would want *us to do, dude.*

How do you know? he pressed.

I just... do, she responded.

I'm as sure of it as I am that I'm standing here, powering this weird-ass energy-shield that's behind Dad's head, even though I don't know squat about how it works...

"Daddy?" she spoke out loud.

"Yes?" he replied.

"If you've got a bone to pick with Commander Jacobson and his folks, maybe Matt and I could help straighten it out... *you* know, 'neutral third-party' kind of thing?" said Clairie.

"Sweetheart," answered the President, using a firm tone that both of his offspring well knew signaled, "end of discussion", "I appreciate your wanting to help... but this is about affairs of state, and you know what the rules have always been within our family, about you getting involved in that. There's a lot about this that you didn't hear and don't understand –"

"Dad," interjected Matt, "We *do* understand. We've got the whole story."

"How *would* you?" challenged the U.S. leader.

"We just... *do,*" countered the teenager. "It's – uhh – 'alien-stuff', I guess."

"'Alien-stuff', huh," suspiciously muttered the President. "Is that *right?*"

"Yeah... it *is,*" admitted Clairie. "Look, Daddy... we're on your side, all the way – we won't let anybody mess with you... *you* know that. We're just sad that you and the Commander's posse are raggin' on each other. Isn't that exactly what the terrorists would *want* you to be doing?"

"Both of you are *way* out of line here!" growled the President. "I'll have no more of this; one more such outburst, you can exit this room and I'll take my chances with –"

His remonstration was cut short by sounds of mayhem from outside on the South Lawn, to the south of the Cabinet Room. A second later, another JSF soldier – a young, red-haired, Caucasian Marine who had, evidently, been guarding the Oval Office – appeared in the doorway leading to that place.

"Mr. President, sir," he shouted, "We have an unidentified object – accompanied by two flying beings, one of which is glowing brightly – landing on the South Lawn! We've tried to ID it, but it corresponds to no known aircraft configuration... it just looks like an oblong shape with no sharp edges, and no obvious means of propulsion. Permission to open fire, sir?"

The Blame... And The Plan

There was a weary look on the U.S. leader's face as he ordered, "Under *no* circumstances, are you to engage this, uhh, 'object'! Is that *clear?*"

"But sir," the soldier tried to argue, "It might be a terrorist trick – a diversion, or maybe even it's one huge bomb –"

"Believe me, son," offered the President, "My guess is, it contains something – excuse me, some*one* – who's *far* more dangerous than any 'bomb'. When she emerges... can you usher her in to the Oval Office, please?"

"Beg your *pardon*, sir?" stammered the young Marine. "Who do you –"

There was more commotion coming from the south. Those in the room overheard shouting and orders to the effect of, "stop where you are – or we'll shoot you *dead!*"

The President stood up rapidly and began moving towards the Oval Office. He turned to address the rest of those in the Cabinet Room.

"Stay here until I say otherwise," he ordered. "Clairie... Matt... Jerry... Minnie... can you come with me, please?"

"You *got* it!" enthusiastically answered the teenage son.

As the U.S. leader, with Kaysten, Chu and his two offspring in tow, reached the entrance-way between the Cabinet Room and the Oval Office, he noticed that Jacobson, Ramirez, Abruzzio and Hendricks were also getting up.

"I don't believe you folks were invited," sniffed the President.

"I don't believe we *needed* to be," countered the Mars Gang leader.

"Don't I get a chance to talk with her, first?" complained the President. "After all... it *is* my house, you know."

Let it go, Sam, advised Abruzzio.

Let's pick our battles.

This is getting ridiculous, *you know,* silently argued Jacobson.

We came to D.C. planning to trash the place – something we're still more than capable of doing – and now we're down to begging the bugger for an appointment!

I feel like Gulliver, bound by a thousand little strings...

We should give Matt and Clairie a chance to do their thing, came back the reply.

Y*o, Commander,* came another mental message,

He's just in a bad mood. He's very "old-school", you know.

We'll work it out. You trust us?

Yeah, Jacobson replied,

For the time being, anyway... don't let us down, kids.

I have a feeling that Her Angelic Highness wouldn't like seeing this place reduced to ruins, just as she shows up for, well... whatever she's here for.

Royally stewing, the former Mars mission commander again took a seat. He heard talking from the direction of the Oval Office going on for as much as a minute, while he stared at the faces of the bureaucrats, politicians, uniformed military and other hangers-on around the table.

He realized that he could have completely overheard the conversations going on, in the Presidential office; but somehow, Jacobson could not motivate himself to do so.

He tried to joke,

"Well, here's how it ends, folks… the 'demi-god' gets told to sit in his chair, and like a good little boy, he has no choice but to obey. If you find it pathetic… you're not alone."

"Now come *on*, Commander," gently chided the Secretary of State. "In my line of business, one frequently finds oneself in exactly the same position : you have enough power to crush someone who isn't cooperating – *they* know it, *you* know it, and *they* know that *you* know it – but using that power will just make a bad situation, that much worse. Knowing when to refrain from violence isn't a mark of weakness… it's a mark of maturity."

"Funny that you didn't mention that to your boss when he was going along with the Agency, as it tortured kids and tried to kill every member of my team, including myself," retorted Jacobson. "Before we got these wonderful 'alien-powers' that we're too bloody timid to actually *use*, when we should be knocking a few heads together, that is."

"Well, I had no knowledge of that," deflected the Secretary of State, "But if I did, I can assure you that I would have had no part of –"

The doorway to the Oval Office opened, all by itself.

Into it – to the gasps of all in the room, the 'more-than-humans' excepted – appeared the shapely figure of the Storied Watcher.

Unlike previous visits, she was this time apparently alone and was clad in her complete set of battle-gear, with the blue-flame-flickering armor of *Vîrya* Ahn'jë' on her head and frame (the war-child's burning essence had been commanded to stop at approximately ankle-height, so as not to further damage what was left of the White House's expensive carpets), with *Væran* Fàiagàryuu in his scabbard, *Vîrya* I'ëà'b' on her arm and the two elemental-daggers bound to her leggings.

Her eyes were glowing dimly, and – even to her followers – her shining, godly and immensely-desirable presence seemed even more majestic and intimidating, than it had ever been. Her war-song – or, at least, *a* war-song – was playing its haunting melody, just below the range of normal audibility. The humans in the room, meanwhile, were thoroughly unnerved, and several of them ducked and hid under the table. This understandable reaction was partly set at ease by one of the alien-girl's trademark, odd-looking half-curtsies and a friendly hand-wave.

Jacobson, Hendricks, Abruzzio and Ramirez all immediately arose and wheeled in place, to greet their alien mentor.

"I am told," spoke Karéin-Mayréij, "That lately, this fine palace has been the scene of much strife… but that – as humans would say – 'the good guys won'. Judging from the bullet-holes and broken windows everywhere, I would agree with at least the first claim. As to the second…"

"Welcome back, Karéin," advanced Ramirez. "You're sure right about the battles that have been waging here. Thankfully, we're all okay… but many others in and around the White House, weren't so lucky."

"That is indeed sad… but such are the terrible wages of war, from times immemorial," evenly observed the Storied Watcher. "The President claims that he has been besieged by legions of these 'terrorists'… but that they were beaten, and that now their forces are scattered hither and yon. A test worthily passed! I congratulate all of you!"

"More 'tests', Karéin?" complained Abruzzio. "Why didn't you *tell* us… why didn't you *warn* us? We sure could have used you around here, a few days ago!"

"There are good answers to all these questions, sister Sylvia," replied the alien-girl, "Though you may not at first wish to acknowledge the reasons behind them. I will explain what I know, when we have a little more, ahh, 'privacy'."

"There's a great deal that we should explain to you about what's been going on here, and yet more to discuss," mentioned Jacobson. "What are your plans?"

"Bermuda," she said. "Some of our new-found kin are now enjoying an 'all expenses paid vay-cay-shun' yonder, while the rest are here in our air-ship, parked outside. And as you know, in times recently passed, we had all agreed to meet there. It will be a parting of the ways in pride and love, with fond wishes for the future, I reckon."

She paused for a second, looked down at the floor, then looked up again, and announced,

"But first… the President speaks of a prisoner – an important one, whose cruel treachery has brought much grief to many, including myself – being held, in the dungeons below this palace. I would, ahh, 'consult' with this foul knave, and I have been given dispensation to do so. You should be there, when this transpires; though I caution… it will not be pleasant to behold."

"You *bet* we should attend!" growled the former Mars mission commander. "Brent, Cherie and Devon, as well. And everyone else who that bastard has wronged!"

"I contacted the Prince of Snows, already, by tel-o-phone," remarked the alien-girl. "He and his beloved still busy themselves in assisting the people of their big city, far out on the western reach of this continent, and though they could fly here, it would take them considerable time. Thus they declined the invitation, but they have requested that we, ahh, 'conference them in' with tel-e-vision things. Jerr-ee will make the necessary arrangements. Min-nie,

Jerr-ee, the President and his two princelings will also attend. Their father objected, but Matt and Clairie were *most* insistent."

"Oh, my dear *Lord!*" gasped Abruzzio, with a shudder, as she reflexively crossed herself. "Karéin – if this is what I *think* it is – I know the swine deserves no mercy, he repeatedly tried to kill *me* as well… but as I stand before God, still must I plead for his life! My faith teaches that only God can take a life… and what did you tell us, about 'blood brings only more blood'? He deserves a fair *trial*, at least!"

The countenance of the Storied Watcher was simultaneously sad, compassionate, vengeful, reflective and impartial as she replied, "For whatever that it is worth – I promise you, it will not be *my* hand, that he may die. I am Earth's protector – not her house-executioner. But those who the Gods Themselves have severely condemned… there is *no* escape, from such a doom! Still less for those whose own savage acts, never-regretted, spill the noble blood of the soul, day by day, until there is naught left but a sinister, shriveled, recondite core, with all paths from hence leading only to evil upon more evil. *I* may not snuff out the life of such a black-guard; but neither will I save them from a fate that they have chosen, for themselves!"

The room was silent for a short while; then Hendricks said,

"If it's alright with you, Karéin… even though Minnie and I were more responsible than anybody else was, for catching this 'mother', I'll take a pass on this one. Enough bad memories to do me for the next hundred years or so, already… you know?"

Gravely, Karéin-Mayréij nodded and replied, "If that is your wish, I will respect it, and never think the less of you. Especially because you and your sisters Min-nie and Sylvia – and yes, little Rainbow too – easily accomplished what I so tried to do... and yet could not. I am greatly in your debt, my brother!"

"I'll just stay around here, protecting the White House, I guess," offered Ramirez. I don't need to see this."

Abruzzio added, "Me neither. You want me to ask Otis?"

"Yes," requested the Storied Watcher. "But hasten to do so, and likewise for Wolf and Melissa. Tell her that Whitney will be alongside us, as will be Bob and Tommy. Elissha is too young for such hard business, and my other daughter – bless the Gods – knows nothing of it. So she will stay away."

"What about Donny and Misha?" asked Jacobson.

"I'll call them," pledged Ramirez. "But they might have a hard time getting on to the premises."

"If that should occur," warned the alien-girl, "Tell those who would bar their way, that my brothers are allowed hence under the approval of the Storied Watcher of the Many Worlds… and that should they refuse, why, they should – ahh – watch out for a comet or two, to be dropped on their heads."

She allowed herself a wan smile, which was matched by some of the others.

"What about your kin?" she then asked, of the ex-astronaut. "As far as is known, some of them were afflicted by this man's foul cruelties."

"I'll have a talk with Yvonne, as I assume Brent will have with Laura," said the former Mars mission commander. "But I doubt they'll want to see it, if it's going to be as ugly as you're making it out to be."

"Justice," carefully stated Karéin-Mayréij, "Is often proportionate to the wrongs that it seeks to set right; and if the latter be terrible, then so will be the just consequences. At least... this is how it has worked for me, in ages immemorial... when it *has* worked."

"Karéin," came the President's voice, from somewhere behind the alien-girl, "We might as well get this *over* with."

"I will need a few minutes, sir," she responded, speaking without turning around. "For I need to contact as many as possible, of those who this man's crimes, have touched. I will ask them to gather with us, before we go thence."

"Well... fine, I suppose," grumbled the U.S. leader. "I'm sure we'll find something else to talk about. Do you want to take a seat in the Cabinet Room?

"That would be agreeable," she affirmed, while entering the room and causing yet more trepidation among the cowering human attendees. "Except, I refrain from sitting in these fine chairs, lest the essence of *Vîrya* Ahn'jë', ahh, should set them on fire. I will just levitate, if it is alright by you."

As she pulled her legs and cape up from underneath her – leaving her hovering in mid-air, with no visible means of support – the Storied Watcher drew more gasps of disbelief.

"Yes... thou mayest," she whispered to her arm-shield. "These are the affairs of king-craft. Take note! For thou art not the only one who must thus be tutored, dear child!"

By now, the President – with Chu at his side (Kaysten had stayed behind in the Oval Office, to handle logistics for the dungeon-visit), and with his two children standing immediately behind him on the left and right respectively – had also regained his own seat. Tanaka and Boyd – both looking unusually self-assured – had re-entered the room.

Karéin-Mayréij looked straight at him and said, "I believe that you were already conducting a meeting, when I arrived here, sir? I am sorry to have interrupted it. Please, do pick up where you left off. I will just observe... the whole process of governing a 'bananas-republic', is *most* interesting."

At this, giggles erupted from Matt and Clairie.

"You're *too* funny, you know," offered the daughter.

The alien-girl feigned surprise and responded, "How is *that,* young princess of the American Empire?"

"You've got to be, like, the only person on this *planet,* who *likes* Cabinet-meetings," claimed Clairie. "Like, I've heard Dad say, multiple times, that he *hates* –"

The Storied Watcher arched an eyebrow at the President.

"I am also given to understand, that valiant Commander Jacobson and his noble team of space-heroes, are no longer welcome here, sir," she remarked. "Is this so... and if so, why? Can we not resolve these issues, in a friendly manner? For – as you know – 'common enemies, make strange friends'."

"Well," he started, "It's *complicated*... you see..."

Shaking his head in Jacobson's direction, the frustrated U.S. leader said,

"Touché, Commander. I have to compliment you on your timing... or is it, *her* timing. You can stay here, at least for the time being. All I ask is... *please* tell me, that the stupid little stunt that you pulled a few days ago – you *know* what I'm referring to – is the last one in your bag of tricks."

"Oh, for *sure* –" the former Mars mission commander tried to say; but he was cut off by his demi-godly alien-friend.

"Sir," asked Karéin-Mayréij of the President, "Do you refer to the gambit of 'attracting the terrorists to this palace', which Clairie and Matt briefly informed me of, when I stepped into the Oval Office, a few minutes ago?"

"Yes," confirmed the President, "But... how did you hear about all that? We didn't discuss it at *all*, when you first showed up here!"

Matt bent forward and did a gesture involving his index finger tapping the side of his head.

"Sorry, Dad," he awkwardly consoled. "It's kind of like an alien party-line. Pretty confusing sometimes, I can tell you. I just wish I could turn it off."

"Do not worry, young prince," reassured the Storied Watcher. "In time, you will learn to do so."

"Oh... I *see*," said the President, with a knowing grimace. "So, you know. So, fine. What's this got to do with *you*, Karéin?"

"Because, sir," evenly replied the alien-girl, "As much as it was the doing of my brother Sam, my sister Sylvia and the others... it was mine own."

"I'm not *following* you," he protested.

"What I am saying, sir, is," stated Karéin-Mayréij, "These attacks on your palace – as evil, savage and cruel as they were – they were all, part of the plan."

The Fact Of Not Understanding

The dumbfounded, suspicious President looked the alien-girl straight in the eye and accused, "You mean to tell me, that the idea of sending the terrorists to this building, was your *own*?"

"No, sir," replied the Storied Watcher.

"Oh... so somehow, you connived with Mr. Jacobson over there, to do it, then," proposed the U.S. leader.

"No, sir," repeated Karéin-Mayréij.

"Then how can it all be 'part of the plan'?" he challenged.

"Because it *is*, sir," she evenly responded.

"I don't appreciate you playing word-games with me, young lady!" he protested. "Why can't you be the least bit straight-forward with me and just tell me what's going on?"

"Because you would not *understand* it, sir," sniffed the Storied Watcher. "And by the way, I would remind you that I *am* your elder by a few hundred thousand of your 'years'. Not that seniority necessarily implies superiority."

Again, Clairie let out an inopportune giggle, while Jacobson, Boyd and Tanaka – from their vantage-point at the south end of the table – sat, cat-who-ate-the-canary-like, relishing every last second of the dialog.

"What do you *mean*, 'I wouldn't understand it'?" peevishly demanded the U.S. leader. "I can understand English just as well as anybody else in this room."

"I have no reason to doubt your fluency in your native language, sir... but that is not what is at issue here," she stated. "What, ahh, *enabled* – yes, I believe that this is the correct word in Eng-lish – these events – *not* what *caused* the events – is something that is simply beyond your ability to comprehend."

"So you're *not* going to tell me, then?" he complained.

"No," she said. "But I *will* tell, *them*."

The alien-girl pointed to the President's son and to his daughter.

"Why?" he pressed. "Why not just tell *me*?"

"Because," she dismissed, "*They, might* understand. Eventually. Sir – do you remember how I advised you, 'the Holy *Fire*, is forever with-held, from you, as punishment for your role in the torment of my family'? That was no idle sanction! You do not know or understand how severe the punishment that I have inflicted, really is. But so it *is*. This is but one of the many wondrous things that you *could* have enjoyed – that you *would* have enjoyed – had it not been, for what you did, and admitted to –"

"Look, Karéin," interjected Matt, "Sis and I appreciate you letting us in on your little secret and everything... but we've all, already been *over* this about Dad, what he did and didn't do, and so on, and so on. If you've still got a bee in your bonnet about all that, well okay fine, but what's the point in rubbing it *in*, all over again?"

"Yeah, Karéin," echoed Clairie, "Dad's just a human – and I guess that's all he'll ever be – but we love him!"

She hugged her father, looked up at her alien benefactor and added, "He's just trying to run the country and it hasn't been easy doing that, lately. Stop *raggin'* on him! We *all* make mistakes. I bet even *angels* do! Just tell bro' and me, and we'll try to pass it on to Dad. Or is *that* out of bounds, too?"

"As with so many other things that will come with the flowering of your own nobility and powers," answered the Storied Watcher, "That is a decision that you must make on your own. I will not prohibit you from disclosing the truth to your father... but neither will I counsel you as to how to explain it to him, in a way that he could understand. Is that oh-kay?"

"Guess it'll have to be," offered Clairie. "Dad... you good with that?"

"I don't know why this has to be such a mystery," he groused, "But as obviously I don't have any way to force you to be more forthcoming, Karéin... I'll wait until I hear what Matt and Clairie have to tell me. I *will* say, for the record, 'shame on you, if you had any direct role in bringing the siege to my doorstep'. We had dozens – no, *hundreds* – of innocent people, killed or wounded! You speak of blood on *my* hands... well, look in the mirror!"

"Dad," whispered the daughter into her father's ear, "Remember who you're *talking* to – she's the one person on the *planet*, who I can't protect you against –"

Still staring forward, he did a slight affirmative head-nod.

"Mr. President," solemnly replied Karéin-Mayréij, "I *do*, indeed, have some shameful, tragic misdeeds to answer for. They afflict my soul now, and that sadness will stay with me, for as long as I shall live. There is no escape for me, from this penance. But the events of the recent past are not what I am suffering for... nor *should* they be. No... *those* crimes were elsewhere... long ago, and very far away. You say, 'look in the mirror'? I will *not!* For indeed do I fear, what – *who* – may, some day, look back at me."

There was a murmur of concern, among the Presidential cabinet-members and advisers, most of whom had by now re-taken their seats.

"Another one that I just wouldn't understand, Karéin?" taunted the President.

"Aye," she pensively responded. "And I hope that none – save myself – ever *will* understand. For the *knowing* of it... ahh, let us not go there... oh-kay?"

"She's right," spoke up Jacobson, from the end of the table. "You should let it go, Mr. President."

"*Please*," echoed Tanaka.

An announcement came over the White House's internal public-address system.

"Attention... *attention!*" it blared out. "Those who are planning to accompany the President on the current matter, should gather in the Center Hall, at the junction of the North Hall, in ten minutes! Please bring photo ID and proof of U.S. citizenship, and leave all weapons in a secure place, as the military escort will not permit any to be taken on this expedition. Thank you."

"Hmm... 'photo eye-dee'... I do not believe that I have that," observed Karéin-Mayréij. "Shall your courtiers then deny me access?"

"Well… there's only *one* of you… right?" mentioned Clairie. "The 'ID' thing is just so they can tell you apart from everyone else. Hardly seems necessary in your case, Angel Lady."

With a pleasant smile, the alien-girl nodded to acknowledge the comment.

"I'll vouch for you… and for anybody else who's missing identification," obliged the President. "Given the circumstances, I doubt we'll have much of a problem with imposters."

Inevitably, a near-perfect mirage representing a smiling Abruzzio, appeared right alongside her.

"Most impressive!" congratulated a beaming Karéin-Mayréij. "Sister – your arts have burgeoned, in my absence!"

We used a trick very similar to this, to convince the bugger who you're going to 'see', that he had successfully managed to shoot you dead, sent the former JPL scientist.

By the way… he doesn't know that yet.

Maybe he never should.

Indeed, silently replied the alien-girl.

But his goal was to slay me… is that correct?

Yes, responded Abruzzio.

He hates you with a passion.

He believes that you are – uhh – an evil being, who's trying to run the United States as your personal fiefdom… enslaving everybody along the way.

He was one second away from killing the President, when Matt and Clairie used their new powers to save their father's life, and the lives of many others.

Another test worthily succeeded! happily communicated the Storied Watcher.

I will bow before your glory, princelings!

How does it feel, to be noble, mighty and heroic?

'Scuse my French, lady… but honestly… it's kind of a tie between 'fuckin' terrifying' and 'fuckin' awesome', responded Matt.

Hmm, answered the alien-girl, in a way that somehow denoted irony.

But I do not comprehend… why should I aim to become a tyrant-queen?

It seems that this fine little empire already has a king… who resents both my presence, and that of Commander Sam and his crew.

Oh, come on, Karéin, interjected Clairie's mind.

He just feels, like, out-gunned.

Can you blame him? interjected Chu.

"Okay," retreated the President, "Maybe we *will* have a problem."

The holographic image shimmered and dissolved, as the former JPL scientist said, "Don't worry, Mr. President… Rainbow and I won't be going."

The Storied Watcher's legs now extended downward to touch the floor, and she again stood upright.

"I would go with you now," she requested, "But perhaps being in the fortress of my war-children – as you see here and now – that would be, ahh, *distracting*. I have more human-looking clothing available in our air-ship, on yonder lawn. May I have a few minutes more, in which to effect this?"

"Karéin – you're roughly my height and frame, I bet," observed Chu. "I have several spare business-suits, complete with blouses, shoes and everything else, available, right around the corner from here. Mr. President... could I, uhh, 'loan' one to her, and then expense it?"

"I don't think there'll be a problem with that," answered the U.S. leader. "I do have one request about this, however."

"What's *that*, sir?" inquired the *nouvelle* FBI-director.

"It should be one of your darker-colored ones," he said.

Take It As A "F-Off", Clark

Downward, downward they trod; under close guard by heavily-armed soldiers at every turn, the troupe of odd bedfellows – human and post-human, plus three super-powerful canines – methodically descended stairs and elevators, having to pause at the latter and proceed in smaller groups, until the lot of them had arrived at each successive subterranean level.

Several of those invited had either not replied, or had not been able to navigate the thicket of White House defensive check-points, within the allowed time-limits.

Among the more unusual of the late-comers was the Russian, whose sudden appearance at the outermost barriers – more than a block away from the mansion – had almost resulted in a shooting-incident; but fortunately, the guards there had placed a phone-call to Minnie Chu, who provided Misha with appropriate clearance. Melissa, meanwhile – flying too fast and circuitously to be properly tracked by the local air-defenses – had landed right on top of the White House residence roof, and had been ushered down from there to meet up with both her mother and brother.

"This ain't gonna be no fun," advised Whitney Claremont, "But ah owes it to y'all to see th' wages of sin."

There was little chit-chat while on this macabre journey, except for a brief comment by the Storied Watcher to the effect of, "you know... many times have I stepped much further-down into the dark reaches of the Underworld, than to where we now travel; but somehow... this still seems almost as dank and dreary as any such dungeon".

Finally, the last of the group stepped off the last of the elevators. They were now hundreds of feet below the surface, and – given the narrowness of the corridor into which they were advancing, plus the number of people who were being accommodated by it – the icy tendrils of claustrophobia began to work their sinister magic, among some of the travelers.

The bounty-hunter – who had raced over to join the expedition, at the last minute – had to duck at several points along the way.

"Didn't I say that 'over my dead body, would I venture down into another one of the government's holes in the ground?'" grumbled Brent Boyd.

"Do not worry," reassured Karéin-Mayréij. "Should the need for rapid egress beset us, I will just have my war-children hew a way upward for us, as was done on yonder northern island, to which you refer."

She was now dressed only in Chu's well-tailored business-pant-suits, complete with expensive women's leather shoes (some alien-trickery had been necessary to make these fit properly).

The Storied Watcher looked every bit the part of a female executive – she had even consented to a bit of perfume and to have a brooch used to arrange her locks at the back – but she had steadfastly refused "that wax-stuff that you call 'lipstick'". However, her animate-shield, body-armor, sword and two daggers, were nowhere to be seen.

"I thought you left those – uhh – 'children' of yours, topside," stated the President.

"No... they are here, sir," contradicted the Storied Watcher. "You just cannot see them. Except for Tommy, of course."

"Is this the man who did all those bad things to us, Mom?" asked the boy.

"Thus we suspect," answered the alien-girl, "But we do not yet know. Never should we condemn someone, without the strongest of proof."

"Well... speaking just for myself," quipped Billings – who had even put on a dress-suit for the occasion – "I say, 'shoot 'em all, and let God sort it out later'."

"All fine to profess, my beloved," answered Karéin-Mayréij, "But what will you do, Bob, when the only 'god' in these parts... is, 'you'?"

"Yeah... there *is* that," ruefully admitted the ex-salesman.

"You don't really need your 'war-children' to protect you," followed up the President. "Not with what *you're* able to do... I mean, after lifting half the Monument over here... it couldn't be much of a challenge to throw off whatever's above us... right?"

"That may be so, sir," acknowledged the alien-girl, "But they *are* my children. They need to see the face of he who has caused so much evil."

"So does *Vîrya* Sài'ymë," observed Tanaka. "You can't see her either... but she's here, too."

Warden, dear little one... if thou has eyes, silently requested Chu as she touched the locket between her breasts,

Close them.

"The President of the United States!" they heard a military voice from the other end of the poorly-lit, narrow corridor, announce.

Immediately, the many soldiers whose backs were to the walls at about four-foot intervals, came to attention.

"At ease," spoke the U.S. leader. "Let's get this over with. Are the cameras working?"

"Yes, sir," confirmed the JSF lieutenant in charge of the guard-detail. "We've confirmed that Major White and his wife are connected in."

The President turned to whisper to the Storied Watcher.

"Can you please give me the first crack at this guy?" he requested.

"Of course, sir," she agreed. "Should I 'disappear'?"

"No," he asked, "Just stand back a bit, out of his field of vision."

She nodded her head, affirmatively.

The President – flanked by two big, tough-looking soldiers, and followed by his children, immediately behind – walked at a dignified pace, past the cell in which Wyckheiser was being held.

The pretender was curled up in a fetal-position in one corner of his confinement-room; he did not react to the advent of visitors.

It was different when the U.S. leader and his mini-entourage, reached the cell containing the former CIA-director. Instantly, the sweating man with staring, half-sane-looking eyes charged toward the barred doorway – an action that caused the guards to lower their guns and point them straight at the prisoner – but then Top Dog stopped, took a careful look at who he was being confronted with, and said, with an unctuous smirk,

"Why… *Clark!* So *nice* of you, to bring the family. Oops… but I don't see your dear wife. Something hasn't… *happened* to her... has it?"

"Are you finished?" stiffly responded the President.

"Am I finished… am I *finished?*" parroted the imprisoned ex-spook, throwing up his arms in mock indignation as he spoke. "I should think *not!* After all, Clark… down here, I've nothing *but* time, in which to think about what to say… and then to *say* it, loud and proud! What should we talk about today, Clark? How about, 'how's the weather up there'? Any meteor-showers on the forecast for today? Got a good umbrella?"

"It's just *fine*, mother-fucker," replied Matt, in a poorly-suppressed growl.

The stone-faced President raised his left hand in a "cease and desist" signal to his son.

"Now... *you* listen to *me!*" spat the U.S. leader. "You – more than almost anyone else in the government – should know what the penalties are, for crimes of the types that you've committed, or been responsible for… including but not limited to, 'aggravated murder', 'mass murder', 'torture', 'criminal conspiracy', 'terrorism', 'treason', 'insurrection', 'attempting to violently overthrow the legitimate government of the United States' –"

"Oh – *spare* me the laundry-list of slights, real or imagined!" interrupted Top Dog. "You know... they say that history is written by the victors, but they never anticipated an outcome like *this*. Sure – maybe you're holding the key now, and bully for *you* – but *I'm* the one who has changed history... and so shall it be written. Do anything you *want* to me! I'm satisfied with the outcome."

"I have discussed this matter with the Director of the FBI and the Attorney-General," continued the President, "And – in exchange for a full and complete confession, including a detailed, minute-by-minute, one hundred per cent truthful account of everything that you've done, going back to your first days with the Agency – I'm prepared to recommend a reduction in sentence, to 'life without parole, in a maximum-security facility'. I'm sure you know what the alternative is. Do you need a few minutes to consider your options?"

"Take a *hike*, Clark!" sneered the former Agency-director. "Surely you know, that I'd prefer to *die*, rather than to give up the most private information of the organization to which I've devoted my *life!*"

"I can assure you that whatever you say, will be considered 'government top-level secret', and it won't be revealed to –" started the U.S. leader; but he was interrupted by a loud voice calling from behind him.

"No... you *can't!*" it countered.

An irritated President turned his head and looked down the corridor.

"Who *said* that?" he exclaimed.

"That would be me... *sir*," insolently responded Brent Boyd. "This is exactly the kind of thing that you promised *not* to do, when first we showed up at the White House!"

"Yep," supported Tanaka, while Jacobson maintained a tactful silence.

"Major Boyd... who the hell's conducting the interrogation here – *me*, or *you*?" complained the President.

"The rules of the game have changed," claimed the former Mars mission pilot. "You *agreed* to it! I'm just reminding you of that. You can like it, you can hate it... but you can't ignore it!"

"Major Boyd," hissed the President, "Do you want me to have you escorted out of here?"

"Go ahead... *try*," defiantly riposted the ex-astronaut. "Did you bring your sunglasses?"

Brother, came a mental note,

I know as well as do you, that the President, postures as if he had powers, that he has not.

But please... forebear a confrontation, for the moment.

There will be plenty of time in which to ensure that he keeps his promises.

Come on, *Major Boyd,* added a teenage girl's mind-signature,

Cut Dad some slack!

He knows *he can't keep this shit, all covered up.*
He's just lying to a liar, to get the fucker to do what he wants him to.
I hear *you, honey,* responded Boyd,
But how about, instead of 'just more lies', he tries, 'the truth'?

"It doesn't matter, anyway, Clark," persisted Top Dog. "I'm not telling you jack *shit!* Okay… I *sort* of take that back. I *will* say – repeat for the crowd you've got out there – that everything the Agency or I did, going back to at least when that monster showed up on Mars – was to protect this *country*! I've taken some tough decisions – the ones that weak-kneed, so-called 'leaders' like yourself have been unwilling to face up to – just so the United States of 2041 and beyond, looks like the U.S. of 2040, and before. Yes… I'll admit we made some mistakes – in particular, Crowford's clumsy meddling really put us off-track, for a while – but ninety per cent of the messy-bits could have been avoided if you just hadn't chickened out, at the start! Did we liquidate a few more than we had to? Did we rough up some kids, to get through to their parents? Yeah – but when you're fighting for the survival of your *species* – your *race* – the gloves are off… they *have* to be!"

The President stood, impassive and poker-faced, through the tirade.

"But it's all good!" proudly claimed the former CIA torpedo. "It's *dead* now… and its poison, though maybe still there in a few sad cases – how are those ol' kids, eh? – will die out, with the passing of years. And the Agency will survive; you can purge it as much as you and your Chinese whore Bureau director want to, but the same challenges – traitors, liberals, do-gooders, Muslims, Commies, free-thinkers, foreigners, you name it – remain… and sooner or later, the same methods and tools will have to be used, to put 'em in their place. The Agency's a force of *nature*… you can't stop it. All you can do, is *pretend* to!"

"Should I take that as a 'no'?" patiently requested the U.S. leader.

"You should take that as a 'fuck off'," spat back Top Dog. "Go ahead, have me shot… I don't care, but I'm not talking. Truth be told… I was good to go, I'd have done the deed myself – the damn suit malfunctioned, and the backup was in the helmet, which your smart-ass daughter somehow shot off my head. Oh well – the rest of it worked well enough, you'll have to admit."

Ha, ha, came Clairie's mental invective.
Thanks for the compliment!
And fuck you, *too, jackass!*

"So that's it?" offered the President.

"Yeah," responded the former Agency director, "That's, it."

There was now a cruel, thin smile, on the face of the U.S leader.

"What's so funny, Clark?" prodded Top Dog. "Planning the length of the rope?"

"Not… *exactly*," evenly answered the President.

"What, then?" pressed the prisoner.

"I have someone who I'd like you to meet," said the President.

The Test Is Over

The Storied Watcher had overheard the President's conversation with Top Dog, but she had instructions of her own to issue.

"Brent... Cherie... Sam... Whitney... Bob... Tommy... Curtis... Melissa... would you come with me, please?" she called. "And could those others by this holding-cell stand aside, so that my kin can see in?"

As the others around the cell obliged, the alien-girl stepped, deliberately, down the center of the corridor. In a few seconds, she had reached the junction of the cell and the corridor. Those who she had invited, gathered to either side. She turned to the right, now facing inward toward the prisoner.

"I don't think you've ever had the... *experience*, of meeting my friend here, who goes variously by the title of 'Storied Watcher' or, to use her given name... 'Karéin-Mayréij'," said the President, as he reached behind the much shorter alien-girl, holding her with his arm around her slim shoulders.

He immediately regretted the gesture, because the touch of her – even through two layers of clothing – brought about a physical reaction that he thought would never again grace him, given his advanced years.

He concentrated diligently to suppress it and succeeded, with great difficulty.

Relax, sir, came an unrequited mental-message.

Do not be ashamed.

This is a thing of love and pleasure, which is far too often neglected in this society you have, with all its contrived 'decency-rules'.

If you both will allow it... I will tutor your spouse on these gentle matters, and, perhaps, re-kindle a spark that was always there.

Clairie looked at her brother and wiped a tear.

Now within the cell, at first, Top Dog's visage was one of stunned non-comprehension; but a second later, it changed to his usual, suspicious, sneering disposition.

"Oh... come *on*, Clark!" he taunted. "A stunt-double in a *business-suit*? Where's the fancy-ass 'Medieval Times' armor and weaponry? Is *that* the best you can do?"

Karéin-Mayréij shrugged off the embrace of the U.S. leader and stepped one pace forward.

There was a dim glow in the back of her eyes, and her saturnine face looked as if it were being illuminated from below; indeed, there was a faint, golden aura that outlined her entire frame.

And her four fangs were slightly extended, making her resemble a beautiful – yet, menacing – she-demon.

She raised her right arm, making a restrained hand-wave gesture. Instantly, the welded stainless-steel bars separating the confinement-room from the corridor, were torn into twisted, pretzel-like shards. These were ripped out of the concrete sides of the doorway into which they had earlier been set – an act that sent dust flying hither and yon – and were thus effortlessly tossed aside.

The President stepped gingerly back, as the Storied Watcher's presence began to give off a blistering heat-field (though her ordinary business-suit did not seem to be affected by this). She advanced into the room, forcing the shocked, un-nerved Top Dog further and further back into the cell.

"But I shot you *dead!*" he shrieked. "I *saw* you *die!* What *are* you… some kind of fucking immortal zombie? *Damn you!*"

The alien-girl stopped her forward movement, about halfway into the confinement-room. She stared at the captive.

"I am Karéin-Mayréij – the Storied Watcher of the Many Worlds… the Guardian of Planet Earth," she melodiously intoned. "And I am *not* 'immortal'… though it takes more to kill me, than it does so to do, with a craven knave such as yourself… does it not?"

Again, she slightly waved her hand, and Top Dog was sent careening backward, until he impacted the back-wall with enough force to knock the wind out of him. He fell to his knees, gasping and struggling to get back on his feet.

"Long have my kin and I labored – through many savage travails and near-encounters with our own demise – to look upon he who is most responsible for what has beset us, over the past months," she accused. "Frankly… I had expected to see someone far more – ahh – 'impressive'; but he who grovels before me now, is naught but a coward who corrupts kings and who torments the helpless – even young children, including mine own *son*, who is here with me today. As some have said – and I cannot put it better – 'pathetic'. *Pa-thetic!*"

She turned and looked over her shoulder, calling out to the throng behind her, in the corridor.

"I can *smell* the evil coming from him," she observed, with a puckered-up expression on her face. "What a foul stench!"

"*You're* the 'evil' one!" he tried to bluff. "Everything I've done, has been on behalf of my *country!* Specifically to save it from being enslaved, by *you!*"

"I say to the princelings, and – yea – to all of you," counseled the Storied Watcher, "I have advised that you should conduct yourselves with nobility, grace, wisdom and restraint, if you would be a god or goddess of the Holy *Fire*. Well… behold the opposite of all these things! It is not hard to be enlightened. Just look at this man… and do the reverse, of what he has done!"

By now, Top Dog had managed to again come to his feet.

"Just get it *over* with!" he wailed.

There was a whiff of fear in his voice.

"Oh no... not so soon... not so *fast!*" she ominously responded. "Sit down on yonder bench, so we can – ahh – have a nice little talk."

Never taking his eyes off his super-human inquisitor, the former Agency-head complied, sitting at one end of the metal bench that had been affixed to the far wall of the cell. Karéin-Mayréij advanced and sat down near to the other end.

"I presume that our mutual friend – the President over there – has explained to you, that I have certain... *abilities*, to reach inside that evil-besotted mind of yours, to reveal thoughts, facts or secrets, that you choose not to disclose, by more mundane means of communication?" she advised.

He did not answer.

"I will, ahh, take that as a 'yes'," she maliciously joked. "But the use of this art is distasteful to me, not least because my mind must perforce go wading the swamp of your own, black-diseased one. Therefore, I will make you a deal : just do what the President has requested of you – provide him with a full, honest history of your deeds and misdeeds, leaving nothing out and nothing glossed-over. I will review the output, and if any of it turns out to be less than the whole truth – as I know this already to be – woe betide you!"

"I've got nothing to tell you... or Clark," replied Top Dog. "Except to say – I've nothing to apologize for... *monster!*"

He rose to his feet, while the Storied Watcher remained seated. He turned in the direction of the President, and the crowd outside, and, with sweat running down his face, bellowed,

"Don't any of you sheep realize, what's *happening* here? Don't any of you, *care*? You let her kill me – or turn me into one of her nice, compliant zombies – and there goes our race's last *chance*! What's *wrong* with you idiots?"

"I *can* kill you – or, reduce your mind to the intellect of an insect – with nary but a thought," warned the alien-girl. "But – unlike you – it is not my way to cripple or kill, helpless opponents. Alright then. You will not divulge the details of your crimes, in the – ahh – 'easy way'. This I comprehend. But in exchange for my mercy, I would require just one little concession from yourself – that is, to win my refraining from doing *this* –"

Through glowing eyes, she stared deliberately at the former Agency chief. There was an irritating, high-pitched noise, somewhat like what an electronically-boosted mosquito would sound like.

Top Dog reeled backwards, as if struck hard by a sledgehammer in the middle of his stomach. Screaming in obvious agony, drooling from his mouth and then urinating within his convict-garb, he fell to the concrete floor of the cell, gasping and choking, while those outside who could see looked onward with a combination of grim satisfaction and horror.

Come on, honey, savagely thought Billings,
Why'd you let up?

Because, Bob, came a reply from Tanaka,
The 'monster' in the room, isn't named "Karéin".

Whatever this terrible attack was, it lasted only a couple of seconds, and then the countenance of Karéin-Mayréij returned to its previous, only-slightly-frightening self.

She got up, walked calmly over to where he was slowly recovering from her invisible assault, got down on one knee, uncomfortably close to where the stricken man had landed, and – speaking through fang-bedecked lips, loudly enough to be overheard back in the corridor – slowly snarled,

"Now... *you* listen to *me*, my friend! As I have heard from others – and indirectly experienced myself – you fancy yourself skilled in the cruel arts of 'torture'. Well... compared to *my* familiarity with that hellish subject – suffered, learned and practiced as a victim, as an on-looker and as an inquisitor – over many millennia of your time... you are but an, uhh, kin-der-garden student!"

The captive ex-Agency torpedo looked thoroughly frightened, in a way that nobody had ever seen him before, as the alien-girl went on,

"And do you know what? Your primitive, human-techno-limited skills in this art, all have one big drawback : namely, 'if one pushes the level of agony past a certain point... the victim will simply die, and thus find the surcease of oblivion'. I advise you now – *my* techniques, have no such limitation! Just *imagine*, if you dare! Endless life... accompanied by endless agony!"

Her voice lowered significantly, as if she was trying to limit the potential audience, and she quietly related,

"The Karéin-Mayréij who you see now before you, is *not* the 'monster' that you caricature her to be... but you *can* push her a very long way, in that direction. You have already pushed her much further than she ever had anticipated, or had wanted to have done. Deep within this body – within this soul – there is someone... *else*. Someone more terrible than your pathetic, limited little human mind, can possibly envisage. Someone who has committed ghastly crimes that make *your* crude misdeeds, look like child's-play! Refuse my next request, and you may *indeed* succeed in your misguided quest to show the people of this world, what a mortal peril was released, up yonder in the caves of *Mailànkh*. Doing so will avail you not; you will already be screaming away what is left of your sanity, in a private hell of your own making. Do you understand what I am *saying*? Do you understand the choice that is laid before you?"

Jaysus, silently communicated Boyd,
Are you guys getting *this?*
Sure am, responded Jacobson.
Nothing we didn't really suspect before... from back on the Eagle and Infinity.
Yeah, added Billings.
She kind of warned me about it, just after I first met her.

At the time, I thought it was just, like, bad drugs, or whatever.

Not so sure, these days...

Is Mom saying she's a bad person? timidly ventured Tommy.

No, sent Tanaka.

I think what she's saying, is that there are both good and evil, in all of us... including, inside her.

Give her some credit for acknowledging that, if you don't mind.

I sure as hell hope you're right, Professor, came Clairie's broadcast.

Because if it's something else... we're all fucked, *big-time!*

The by-now-utterly-terrified Top Dog merely nodded his head.

"Very well, then," remarked Karéin-Mayréij, as she rose to her feet.

"Get up," she ordered.

Slowly – upon rubber legs – the former Agency director complied.

The two were now standing, close-by each other.

"I am ever true to my bargains," she spoke. "And thus I have one question – only one question – to ask of you. Answer it fully, and truthfully."

"Yeah?" muttered Top Dog, still trying to recover from the Storied Watcher's most recent assault.

"What I want to know," interrogated the alien-girl, with a determined, icy stare, "And what I *will* know, one way or another, is... the President states that the idea of torturing me – and my loved ones – in order to weaken me, was yours; and, that he only assented to it when he discovered that the dastardly scheme was already underway. He further asserts that you refused to stop it, even when he insisted that you do so. *Are these claims true?*"

"*No!*" yelled the former assassin, at the top of his lungs. "Not on your *life!* You know... maybe I'm not so scared of your so-called mental-skills after all, if they're so useless that they can't even tell you when Clark's lying through his *teeth!* You want the *truth*, Ms. 'Storied Watcher'?"

"*Karéin!*" shouted the U.S. leader, "What do you think you're *doing,* here? Can't you *see* that the man is lying? He doesn't know *how* to truthfully communicate! You're *way* off-track! You weren't supposed to –"

"Dad," cautioned Matt, as he lightly touched his father's shoulder, "Don't *push* her!"

Team, warned Jacobson, not caring that the two Presidential offspring could overhear,

We should be prepared for anything.

The Storied Watcher listened to this, then shrugged her shoulders.

"Say what you have to say," she coolly demanded of Top Dog.

"The truth is," spat the ex-Agency chief, "Clark was in it up to his *neck*, right from Square One! *Surely* I don't have to remind you of how many times he lied to your face – for example, consider that little scene in the Tucson hotel-room, with the fake family he put up on the screen – that was entirely *his* doing! It's true that he turned to the Agency to actually *implement* the plan to, uhh, 'stress' yourself and your family... but that was because we were the only part of the government that had the necessary – uhh – 'skill-set'. What we were doing was simply 'Standard Operating Procedure', which he had *personally* authorized for any number of other detainees, going back years, beforehand. He was just doing to your 'family', what he was happily doing to liberals, Muslims, traitors, terrorists, protesters, abortionists, illegal immigrants and other enemies of the state… the record's there for all to see. Do you think the operation could have continued, without his informed consent? He's the fucking *President,* for God's sake! Everybody – including me – *answered* to him! Listen, my alien friend… he's been out to get you since you crashed down here, and *that* won't change – *whatever* happens to me!"

"Really?" evenly inquired the alien-girl. "If true, this would mean that the *President* is the most culpable, in the bestial plot to afflict my family – including helpless children – to bring me to mine knees. That would have… *consequences.*"

Karéin! came the alarmed, silent outcry, from Clairie.

The dude's a fuckin' liar – can't you, like, use your mental powers to tell?

He was lyin' to us, about you!

Top Dog looked elated as the sweating, unnerved President pleaded, "For God's *sake*, Karéin – use your *brains* here! There's *no* serious doubt that the man over there with you, ordered and oversaw the precise details of these crimes – and that he persisted, long after I had withdrawn any approval that I – foolishly – might have provided, earlier! For example… take the case of Cherie Tanaka's mother… what would I *possibly* have had to gain, by authorizing her cruel torture and murder! And that happened *long* after I was out of the chain of command!"

"Clark… you really have to *work* on the 'lying' thing – you're a fucking *amateur* at it," hissed Top Dog. "Yeah… of *course*, we did the old lady – a big f-up, actually, we didn't *mean* to off her, but it was a rush-job, and we didn't have access to the right facilities or tools at the time – but it was under the exact set of National Security Council directives that you had *yourself* issued, a couple of years ago! *Remember*, Clark? *You* know – the part that says, 'any and all coercive techniques are hereby authorized, when necessary to elicit information from enemies of the state'? Bezomorton, George and you all *signed* it!"

He turned to look at the alien-girl.

"Ask him to show you the Executive Office records about the document entitled, 'NSD-2038-81D'," proposed the former assassin. "You'll find it all there, with his personal siggy, registered in great penmanship. It's *his* policy… and he owns it!"

"'It was not of my doing'… so you *say*, sir," addressed Karéin-Mayréij, to the President. "Except that – during my initial travels with Bob, Whitney, Melissa, Curtis and Tommy, I personally witnessed many examples of the specific kinds of cruelty, of which this knave speaks – and there is no *question* that this all was authorized by yourself, because it was well before my beloved were taken hostage, in the attack on Bob's house in Tuc-son. For example, I saw several helpless American peasants being publicly executed on tee-vee, for transgressions of the many, stupid and oppressive laws, that your kingdom seems to have passed at every turn. Bob... do you remember that incident?"

"You're fuckin' *right* I do!" growled Billings, from somewhere in the crowd just outside the cell-entrance. "We were at my place... before it got blown to bits and then burned to the ground, that is."

"Do you remember what I said to you, at that time?" continued the Storied Watcher.

"Yeah," smirked the former salesman. "As I recall, you said something about, 'the tyrant who runs this place, by fear and cruelty... he had better watch out, in case somebody a lot more powerful shows up and turns the tables on him'... don't remember it exactly, but is that close enough?"

Couldn't have put it better, Bob, unhelpfully sent Brent Boyd.

What goes around, comes around, sneered the ex-salesman.

Gloat all you want, cautioned Jacobson,

But this could turn real ugly, real fast.

Let's try to protect the civilians, if we can.

You all know that I will protect the President... don't you? cautioned Chu.

Angel Lady, came Clairie's desperate-sounding broadcast,

Dad's no 'tyrant'! He didn't mean to hurt anybody... and he didn't invent all this shit! All he did was not to stop *it!*

Child, responded the alien-girl,

The test is now upon you : to neither betray your kin – your father – nor to make excuses for his crimes.

As a noble sister of the Holy Fire, you are called to a higher duty – your father has disgraced himself, by the facts not in reasonable dispute... and you must find a way to redeem him.

For God's sake! silently cried the daughter,

How am I supposed to do that?

Start thinking about how you will, came the reply.

Better still... you would already have been thinking.

This is an art of one of your station : to always be 'one step ahead'.

"Karéin," argued the U.S. leader, "We already talked that issue out! I committed to making changes – a commitment that I'm dead-serious about keeping. I can't undo the past... all I *can* do, is try to do better in the future. How can you *possibly* ignore all that, when I tell you the truth, and he just spouts lie after lie –"

"Ah, but *sir,*" interrupted the Storied Watcher, "*You* claim that *he* is lying, and *he* claims that *you* are lying, about the singular issue of, 'who was behind the torture and attempted murder of my family'; but there is a *third* possibility, that neither of you seems to want to address. Namely… what if *both* of you are lying? In other words… what if you are both equally-culpable?"

Karéin! Clairie sent, with the power of her frightened transmission over-riding all the other mental chit-chat in the vicinity,

You said that turning Matt and me into, like, 'alien-people', paid Dad up, for all this! How's it now you're dredging it up again!

Yeah, added the Presidential son,

What was the point of all that… if you're just gonna turn around and whack our father, anyway?

I'll have to fight you, even if you burn my –

Shut up and watch – and learn! came back the reply.

You know, the crushing power of the Holy Fire.

You have yet, to master the subtle power of guile!

"If *that's* what you're accusing me of," exclaimed the scowling Top Dog, while pointing an accusatory finger at the President, "Then I plead *guilty* – that is, 'guilty of obeying and implementing the orders that *he* gave me'! So… I'm one of his 'court executioners', as you like to call it. *Sure* I am! But whatever I'm guilty of doing – *he's* guilty of having ordered… and never forget, if I hadn't been willing to carry out his orders, I would have been next in line for the firing-squad! That's how a police-state *works*, after all! If – in view of this – you want to kill me, Ms. Alien Terrorist, I'm prepared to meet *my* fate… are *you*, Clark?"

The shaken, worried President walked slightly to the left and put his back up against the concrete wall.

He closed his eyes momentarily, re-opened them and offered,

"I can't *believe* we're having this conversation… I can't *believe* that you've put me on a level with… *him*. I'm a flawed man, who owns up to his transgressions and his failures – and they are legion – and who tells you the truth as best he understands it. He's a pathological liar and a psychotic killer, who lives, eats and breathes, only to hurt and kill people who can't fight back. But obviously, Karéin… you *could*, and you *did*. So now… here we are. Do with me, whatever you will. I don't care. Just get it over with, and more power to you, with whatever happens afterward."

"Here again," explained Karéin-Mayréij, "You think too much – ahh – 'inside the crate' –"

"It's, 'inside the *box*', dear," corrected a gloating Bob Billings.

"Thanks," said the alien-girl. "Please excuse my poor skills in Eng-lish. However, as I was saying… you imagine that there is only one outcome : namely, 'that I would consider both of you culpable, and therefore would mete out justice appropriate to the magnitude of these crimes, to each… it could be just a quick application of the *Visage of Destruction* – returning you to dust, in a half-second – or something much longer and more painful –"

Two war-songs started to be heard in the hallway. There was a commotion, as members of the Mars Gang tried to prevent Matt and Clairie from pushing their way forward.

"Let us *in* there!" shouted the male teenager. "It may be suicide – but I'm not going to let her off Dad, without a fight –"

"You're *right!*" loudly answered Brent Boyd. "*You* open up on *her – she* opens up on *you –* and *we're* standing right in the line of fire! That's on top of the fact that the two of you will cave the *ceiling* in on us! Ain't gonna *happen!*"

Tommy's ominous, flesh-crawling war-song could now be heard.

"You stay *away* from Mom!" he warned, from under glowing eyes.

Billings – with yellow-green *Amaiish*-energy pulsating through him, as well as in the backs of his eyes, stood beside his adoptive son and challenged,

"Did they tell you two little brats, that my *Fire,* cancels out your own? Don't make me show you how, the hard way!"

"*All* of you!" shouted Chu. "Hands off the President! If you've got issues to deal with him on… take them outside and deal with them later! Or *else!*"

Her eyes were glowing, too.

"*Everybody!*" shrieked Tanaka, "Back *off!* Let's hear what she has to *say!*"

"But there is another choice… another path," remarked the alien-girl, as the struggle outside the cell-entrance sounded as if it were about to deteriorate into open combat.

"And that is, simply to leave both of you guilty… but alive," she said. "To leave these matters to the Gods – and to their celestial plans, which unfold yet in front of our eyes, as here we stand – to deal with, as they will."

Instantly, the burgeoning battle in the corridor, had the fuel taken out of it. The war-songs abated in force and volume.

The President – still standing impassively with his back against the cell-wall, commented,

"Well… that's good to hear, from *my* point of view, at least. Always a good day, when you dodge being disintegrated, for one more day."

He turned to address Top Dog, and sarcastically observed,

"And by the way, you obsessive jackass – here's the 'alien mistress' who, according to the bullshit that you've been saying ever since 'Lucifer', has turned me into a nice, subservient little space-zombie. Congratulations on getting a front-row seat on how Karéin and I sometimes – uhh – don't quite see eye to eye. As in, 'a minute ago, I thought she was about to *kill* me'. It's far from the *first* time! You should *try* it, sometime… you'd quickly appreciate the challenge of trying to negotiate with an opponent who's got a permanent full house, and you have a hand of deuces and threes. The only reason that I still bother is to stop the country from falling apart, should I resign or… well, *you* know."

"For the record, sir," interjected Karéin-Mayréij, "In the analogy of this 'pokering-game' – not *now*, Bob, you can correct me later – at first you stupidly over-played your hand of 'deuces'… as I believe that I mentioned to you, when I was on the big airplane with the laser death-ray at its front. But subsequently, you have done exceptionally well, considering the actual balance of power between us. I hope that your children will learn from this. They need to."

"Well then, Clark," bravely ventured the former Agency director, "Perhaps now you see, why I – and Crowford, for that matter – was *right* about her, all along. But the whole thing's gone as far south, as south can go… and there's no way out, now. Along with the rest of our species on this planet… we're *fucked*, and that's that! I hope you're *happy* with how things have turned out!"

He pointed aggressively at the Storied Watcher – who sighed and feigned a thoroughly-bored look – and expounded,

"Sooner or later, she's going to *kill* you, Clark – my guess is 'sooner' – like, when she and you disagree on, say, 'who's the better hop-jump rapper… Bad Daddy A-hole or Junior Smart-Lips'. I'll likely be dead by then anyway, which I guess is a *good* thing, because I won't have to watch the whole sorry mess going down. Oh well… I *tried*. Came up a bit short… but I *tried*. Do I at least get a merit-badge to put on my tombstone?"

"That is not for *me* to decide," sniffed the alien-girl. "Nor for your master, the President. And for the record, knave… you know *so* little of the stain that taking the life of a sentient being, leaves on one's soul. Your own natural life is a brief one – my arts descry that it will mercifully be shorter yet – but for the likes of *me*, causing the death of a thinking person plagues me for ages untold. Let this be heard – and let it be taken to heart – by all those who now live with the Holy *Fire*. *You* will never know the import of this… but *they* will. And they must govern their actions accordingly."

"If we're on the record now, Karéin," mentioned the U.S. leader, "He's no friend of *mine*. I wish I had never *met* him!"

"Perhaps," observed the Storied Watcher, "But please forgive me for observing, sir, that with the important exception of your princelings – upon whose growth in maturity, wisdom and judgment, so much depends – you *do* seem to be rather short of 'friends', these days."

"I thought of *you*, as one, you know," said the deflated man.

"I will repeat : 'the blessing of the *Fire* is with-held, as punishment for your misdeeds'," she countered. "Still… I will not use the word, 'forever', this day. For who among us, knows the secrets of the future… either five minutes, or five hundred years, hence?"

A hush fell over the crowd. It lasted a few seconds; then the President said,

"Are we done here?"

"I've nothing more to say," growled Top Dog.

He walked over to the wall-bench and sat down, with his legs extended and arms crossed.

"I have one thing," stated Karéin-Mayréij. "A 'farewell', if you like it, which I have sought to deliver, for many weeks now."

"What?" he sullenly demanded.

"May the pitiful, dying screams of Elissha's brother Korey," spat the glowing-eyed alien-girl at Top Dog, through savagely-extended fangs, "As his helpless, innocent body was rent asunder by your bestial torturers – may his wail serenade you, on your journey to the Abyss of the Unending Dark! For from where *you* shall go, blackguard – there is no egress... until the Wheel of Time shall spin no more, and this world shall come to its final end!"

"Who – or what – the hell's all *that*?" he demanded. "You're talking gibberish... I don't know those names!"

But – other than for a smile that was half-saturnine, half-cruel – the Storied Watcher did not reply.

Instead, she merely cast a long glance at the human man who had been the author of so many of her travails, wheeled on her heels and stepped slowly and deliberately out of the cell.

She turned again upon reaching the corridor, and headed away from the area, toward the elevators. Silently, most of the expedition proceeded behind her.

The President – who, along with his two emotionally-drained offspring, had elected to follow at a discreet distance – was about halfway down the corridor, when he glanced over one shoulder and noticed that several members of the Mars Gang had tarried at the entrance to Top Dog's cell.

Multiple war-songs began to sound, although in the next seconds, only Jacobson's figure was visible at the far end of the corridor.

"Sir," exclaimed an alarmed JSF guard, to the President, "They're not supposed to be *in* there! Should my men go back there and get them out?"

"Mr. *President*," interjected a worried Minnie Chu, "I *know* how everyone feels – but this man has important information, and we can't just throw due process out the window!"

The U.S. leader's right hand signaled negatively.

"Some things," he gravely instructed, "However terrible – can't be changed... nor *should* they be."

"Aye," solemnly supported Karéin-Mayréij. "A doom that one has brought on oneself – that is the worst kind... and it cannot long be evaded."

Those in the corridor heard Tanaka's voice.

It dripped with cold hatred.

"My helpless, innocent mother was a *mistake*... a fucking *mistake*, you say?" the former Mars mission science officer, was heard to shout.

"How'd you like *another* little 'mistake' – fucking *swine!*"

"*Smert' ubiytsam!*" growled the voice of the Russian.

"Fuck *you*, mother-*fucker!*" cursed the voice of the bounty-hunter.

"This is for Cherie – and Tommy – and everybody else who you've abused and murdered, you evil son of a *bitch!*" angrily exclaimed Brent Boyd.

The next events all occurred almost at the same time.

There was a bright glow from inside the room, accompanied by the crashing sounds of thunder.

A wave of suffocating heat came shooting out of the cell, afflicting everyone in the corridor, even though they were many feet away.

The cell – and half the corridor – was bathed in incandescent light, so powerful that it caused those within (except for the Storied Watcher), to squint and cover their eyes.

Finally, there was a brief flash of some kind of green-tinted light, resulting – a couple of seconds later – by a billowing cloud of dust-particles issuing out into the hallway.

The first to exit the cell was Tanaka. She rested her back upon the corridor-wall, although she was doubled up, facing down at the floor. Her chin was quivering, and she began to bawl uncontrollably. The others – Wolf, Boyd, Misha and Jacobson – gathered around her, embracing her and wiping her tears.

The more-than-humans heard a faint sound coming from somewhere. It was Devon White's voice, saying, "We're prayin' and cryin' with y'all, sister."

Other than for this and the show of emotion at the far end of the corridor, there was silence when the alien-girl walked over to where the President was standing.

Karéin-Mayréij took hold of Matt's hand, then that of Clairie, and – addressing those in the vicinity – she pronounced,

"Let it not be written that on this day, a great wrong was made right; for wrongs such as *his* – never can they be! At least… not in *this* reality. But now – after so many crimes, terrors and evils,"

She fell quiet for a second, and then said,

"The final test is… *over*."

To Bermuda

The arrangements for the final meeting had taken significantly more time than any of the Storied Watcher's entourage had expected, given the cardinal requirement to shield the event from the prying eyes of the *paparazzi* (there were relatively few of these on Bermuda, but the presence of even one or two would have been unacceptable), not to mention the mainstream media. Transporting the Compton refugees, for example, had to be done with the

Mailànkh Express in the wee hours of the night, and had required several trips.

Additionally, it had taken Karéin-Mayréij considerable effort simply to locate and – often to the astonishment and terror of those involved – "air-lift" her quarry, to the meeting-place. While some – like Karlie Tillman, Osvaldo Jiminez from the *Santa Esmerelda* restaurant, the remnants of the Porter family and a certain young female Air Force officer – had blanched and quailed both at the Storied Watcher's semi-godly presence, and at the prospect of being transported into the stratosphere by her, others – such as the three "NRA" hackers at whose doorstep she had appeared – positively relished the trip.

As the *Express* was left discreetly camouflaged on Bermuda during these voyages, the alien-girl had retrieved a discarded passenger-van from a New York-area junkyard, and had used her arts to quickly craft it into an air-tight vessel that could safely accommodate six or seven passengers at any given time.

Via the communications-channels provided by the White House, Karéin-Mayréij also reached out to those who she knew had been touched by the Holy *Fire* of *Amaiish*, during her time in outer space. Her invitation was enigmatic, citing only "a nice, relaxing opportunity to meet with your new brothers and sisters after the great tests that they have recently overcome".

The responses were varied. There was no answer at all from many of those contacted, while a few more (for example the Indonesian cleric) politely declined on the grounds that "we were not involved in these events, and it would thus not be proper for us to attend". However, Alan Humber, Ariel Cohen and the French novelist were all eager to come. This required the Storied Watcher to make yet more shuttle-trips back and forth, across the North Atlantic and the Mediterranean.

The response from Sergei Chkalov was far more interesting.

In a short, robustly-encrypted NeoNet-chat conversation facilitated by the hackers' tricks – and incidentally conducted entirely in Russian, which tongue the Storied Watcher had lately mastered – the former Mars mission cosmonaut advised the alien-girl that "I sincerely regret not being able to meet with you in this way, Karéin – but the conflicts that you have been faced with, in America, are not the only ones; I have had my own challenges here, specifically with Li-Ho Chen, of the People's Republic. Only by using all my own abilities, have I been able to defend Mother Russia against his machinations... so far. When you have no more need of Mikhail Grishin, please send him back here at the first possible opportunity – my country needs his powers. He will be welcomed as a hero... as will you be, yourself."

Of course, she immediately agreed to the request, albeit with the comment, "Li-Ho also is your brother, Ser-gayy... and we should not tilt at each other. I will visit him also, and try to bring peace".

But Chkalov was not finished. He added,

"And, Storied Watcher... it is my understanding that you now have taken another lover... perhaps even, a mate. Ah – but I will fondly remember our time in the *Eagle* space-ship, to the end of my days. No-one will ever be the equal of you, in my dreams. Whoever this man is, give him my best wishes... and tell him that many others, envy him greatly!"

"I will always love you, Ser-gayy," replied Karéin-Mayréij, as she wiped an aphrodisiac tear. "May the dream of me bring joy to you unto eternity, as does the knowledge of you, pleasure me! And though indeed have I taken a husband, who I love dearly – and though I have other lovers, not all of them male – I will not say, 'never again'; for I do not believe in stupid human rules of 'foreswear all others'. I will come to see you, dear friend... and again we may – ahh – enjoy each other's company."

"Those are the best words that I have heard in many months," he answered. "But please come soon... for we have much more to discuss, than making love."

Finally, the alien-girl was delayed by the need to rescue and tend to the wounds of some of those who she had met during her travels.

Foremost in the latter category were the former Presidential Science Officer Fred McPherson and Enriqué Nicandro, who had both been languishing in secret CIA holding-facilities; the men had been badly abused, so much so that Nicandro was in a near-catatonic state that the Storied Watcher was only able to overcome by using all her healing-arts. Juanita Losada and her father had also come along for the ride on this rescue-expedition; both the little girl and the Latino man were overcome with joy at seeing how Karéin-Mayréij made good on her promises.

As for McPherson, he had been repeatedly beaten so savagely that both his legs – and one wrist – were broken. He could not stand upright, and was lying in a pool of his own filth, in desperate shape, when the alien-girl located him.

Cradling the stricken man in her arms as she flew him to Walter Reed Hospital, she poured a carefully-controlled portion of her life-force upon him.

McPherson's health returned with remarkable speed. He was totally at a loss for words when his alien benefactor said, "No, learned friend – the debt is all mine own... for you helped free me from my slumber, and then you suffered on my account. But behold how I will open a universe of marvels to you... all for just the repeating of a short pledge."

During the preparations for the meetings, some of those attending had agitated for a quick take-over of one Bermuda's prestigious private clubs, on the grounds that these could easily accommodate the throng; but the alien-girl steadfastly refused these requests, on the grounds that "the New People must set an example of modesty, lest they be captured by the avarice and luxury-seeking, that taints ordinary humans".

There had been some grumbling; however, it was quickly muted when – thanks to a few discreet but very generous payments in pure artificial gold – Billings, working with a hard-pressed Hector Ramirez, managed to rent out a complex of five large apartments – plus one huge, mansion-like house – at St. Catherine's Beach, on St. George's Island.

The choice proved an excellent one on several counts, for example proximity to the airport. Some of the attendees (such as the two elder Whites, Abruzzio, Boatman, Hendricks, Kaysten, the two Presidential offspring and Minnie Chu) had elected to fly "in the conventional way" rather than take their chances in self-navigation across over hundreds of miles of open ocean.

The President had not been happy about the abrupt departure of his children, plus his FBI-director and his Chief of Staff, particularly for a trip of indeterminate length; but he had relented after much argument, along with being given a special alarm-system devised by Hendricks, the Storied Watcher and Ramirez. This – or so it was advertised – would remotely warn Karéin-Mayréij's war-children, in the event of another attack on the White House, or in the event of another crisis of equivalent gravity.

"But how do I know you're going to get back here in *time*, Karéin?" the U.S. leader had argued.

"You do not, sir," she had replied. "All is thus returned to how it had been, before my advent upon this world. However – if it is of any interest – I have done some calculations of this matter... and I can assure you that my current – ahh – 'air-speed', is no less than seven thousand of your 'miles per hour'; I labor constantly and diligently to improve upon this. I believe that this means, that no place on this planet, is more than about three hours away – and most are considerably closer than that. So unless I am somewhere like yonder South Pole when you call... I do not think that you have much to worry about."

The two Presidential offspring were present during this conversation, and Clairie sent to the alien-girl,

Oh, come on, Karéin – I can tell you're shittin' him!

You can go way faster than that!

Ah, but princelings, pleasantly responded the Storied Watcher,

When dealing with nobility, or even with someone from whom one may eventually want a favor... one always "under-promises", and "over-delivers"... does one not?

As she winked at the teenagers, Clairie giggled, while Matt's face wore a bemused smile.

"I can't *believe* this is all happening, you know," offered the daughter. "A few weeks ago I was, like, worryin' about what kind of make-up I'd be wearing. Now, I'm, like... well, *you* know."

"Perhaps you will believe better, young sister," answered Karéin-Mayréij, "When you and your brother – and the likes of Melissa, Cherie, Brent, Devon, Misha and the rest – race each other, through the very skies."

All of the New Peoples' residences on St. George's Island had excellent interior furnishings, ample space, spectacular sea-side views and easy access to the beachfront. Even at that, there was little personal space or privacy for those attending, simply because of their numbers : largely because of the Storied Watcher's distaste for "elitism", she had insisted on inviting all those whose lives she had affected, resulting in a head-count of almost a hundred humans and "more-than-humans"... not to mention three alien-powered canines.

This meant, in turn, that more than sixteen people had to be billeted in each residence, a situation that inevitably led to contention for access to bathrooms, sleeping-facilities (the Storied Watcher had helpfully purloined dozens of portable hammocks and inflatable mattresses, for this purpose), cooking-facilities (several grocery-stores along the way had been nearly cleaned-out by Billings and his troupe, as the alien-girl waited in the parking-lot, with a handy shipping-container), and so on.

Even with this, the alien-girl still had to make repeated, *ad hoc* side-trips to the Carolinas and to Virginia to replenish supplies, particularly food. Despite her best efforts, simply due to the amount that she was buying, she was eventually noticed; however, nobody in the continental United States could figure out where she was returning to. This was substantially due to false leads posted to various social networks, on the part of the NRA hackers.

As for Karéin-Mayréij's own sleeping-arrangements, she stayed in the largest of the residences; and – despite Billings' pleading – she insisted on taking her rest in the precise center of the mansion's main floor. She allowed herself but a simple sleeping-mat and pillow made out of reeds and twine, welcoming the many eager-eyed attendees who asked for permission to lie down near to her.

Over several nights, she regaled the younger ones with bed-time stories of might and magic; and when asked, "Listen, Angel Lady... these stories about, like, slayin' demons and zombie-armies is just *legends* – ain't they?", she responded with a saturnine smile, saying, "Of *course* they are legends... except that I am in them, because I was *there*... and it was by mine own hand, that these great deeds were done."

The barrage of excited questions and pleading requests for "Just one more story... *please*," became so never-ending that the alien-girl had to impose a curfew of midnight.

She was therefore usually able to close her eyes by two a.m. or so.

Taking all into consideration, the Storied Watcher's family and friends accepted the lack of creature-comforts with great aplomb. History was unfolding around them; and every one of them – even, perhaps, little "Rainbow" and her two canine companions – knew it.

There were few complaints.

All who now temporarily resided on St. George's Island had been waiting for the other shoe to drop – even her spouse had refrained from nagging the alien-girl about when the main event, was to take place. Thus it was for three days of casual exploration, games-playing, swimming, sun-tanning and general relaxation.

The beach-games proved to be a challenge due to the invisible nature of telekinesis and other similar alien-powers; eventually, Kaysten and the Storied Watcher's war-children had to be enlisted as referees, to avoid cheating at shuffleboard, horse-shoe-throwing and other contests.

The Chief of Staff came to relish his role as arbiter of disputes, as – with Vîrya I'ëà'b' adorning his arm – he became accomplished at disqualifying "impossible" croquet-shots and lawn-bowling strikes.

"But how do *we* know, that *you* know that we're using our powers, Jerry?" protested Jacobson, at one point.

"Don't ask *me*... ask 'Daughter Tornado-Diamond-Curtain'," cackled a triumphant Kaysten. "Except if you bitch at her... expect an edgy response."

Alan Humber had overheard this conversation; he ventured, "Blimey, mates... I can see I've been missin' a few things, over on my side of the Pond."

Meanwhile, Jim McGregor had been trying out his newfound fish-calling skill; but he had to abandon the project, when it was discovered that the denizens of the deep who answered the summons, were mostly large sharks.

"No, *no*," complained Billings, upon seeing the results. "The idea is that you call things that *we* eat... not things that eat *us*."

"Well... it worked just fine in fresh water," evaded the Canadian. "Ain't *my* fault, if they don't have any trout or bass, 'round here."

During this time, Karéin-Mayréij took it upon herself to re-acquaint herself with every one of the "vacationers" – as they had come to label themselves – sitting down with her human and more-than-human friends, patiently listening to their life-stories and compiling to-do lists of assistance for each person.

The only real argument – if one could call it such – was between the Storied Watcher and her younger acolytes, who were greatly disappointed in her having forbidden them from displaying their flying-skills, in front of the natives of the island.

"We seek a modicum of privacy here, dear little ones," she had informed. "Think you not that this would vanish like a morning mist, when your human brothers and sisters see you – or, better still, a dog – soaring skyward, like a sea-bird?"

The small-fry had reluctantly agreed to this, but only on the condition that "When the meeting's over… we all gonna take off, one second later".

The Council Of The Island

Finally – shortly after lunch had been had, at noon-time on the fourth day – Karéin-Mayréij traveled to each of the residences, then to the beach and indeed to everywhere that the attendees had secreted themselves. Her refrain was the same, in each place :

"Bring your cold-drink-holders, your bar-bee-cue pits, your beach-chairs and parasols, your snack-foods, forswearing mobile com-mun-ee-cators, but foremost – bring yourselves," she directed. "The time is come whereupon we should meet on top of yonder 'Fort Catherine' – the castle which looks out over the sea. We will have seclusion, as not only have I paid a handsome sum to those who own the redoubt, to have it 'closed for a private event'… but also, Wolf's two companions – under 'Rainbow''s tutelage – have agreed to guard the street-entrances to this place. We shall meet in one hour."

"Uhh, Angel Lady," commented one of the Compton refugees, "Them dogs can't talk… *can* they?"

"True… but I believe that they can make their purpose adequately clear," responded the Storied Watcher.

"Well… that's 'zactly what I was worryin' about," persisted the Hispanic man. "As in, 'they gonna make a BBQ out of anybody who tries to come up here'."

The alien-girl let out one of her typical, gently-restrained giggles and then said, "I have an, ahh, 'understanding' with little 'Boob' and 'Tube' – they have agreed to fire at least three warning-shots, first. Only then, will they sink in their fangs… but I suspect that most intruders will, ahh, get the message, beforehand. And any who are guileful enough to evade these two stalwart defenders – well, let he or she join our party, for they will have earned the privilege!"

One of the hell-hounds – fortunately out of sight of any of the usual island residents, at the time – belched a puff of smoke upon hearing this.

"One day," observed Karéin-Mayréij, in the direction of Wolf's two canines, "I shall have to teach you – his four-limbed children – something of the Ways of Ice… since you have the Ways of Fire, ahh, 'down patsy'."

Nobody felt it necessary to mention a correction.

It was mid-afternoon on the fourth day, when the group assembled in the wide-open expanse of Fort St. Catherine's stone-work roof, looking out over the Atlantic Ocean, with the fortress' antique anti-aircraft guns, cannons and revetments, in the foreground.

The Storied Watcher stood in front of the throng, with her back to the sea, while the others formed a semi-circle around her. She waited for several minutes while her hangers-on slowly got organized and deposited themselves into the available portable-furniture.

"Could those of you who can so do, please, ahh, levitate, as opposed to sitting in a chair?" she called out. "For we are short of seats for the human brothers and sisters among us."

The oddness of the request seemed even more so, when several – among these Minnie Chu, Sylvia Abruzzio and Cherie Tanaka, shrugged, retracted their legs and simulated being in a comfortable chair... with no obvious means of support underneath them.

Then – when all appeared to be suitably-ensconced – Karéin-Mayréij allowed her ethereal war-music to be briefly heard. She rose off her feet, cast a gaze to her left and extended one hand. Immediately, a wheeled cannon-assembly that must have weighed several tons, floated through the air, to land just in front of the alien-girl. She hopped on top of it and said,

"Hmm... this formidable weapon can, ahh, 'rock and roll', as do those 'roll-er-skates' that Master Curtis has told me about. I hope that it will not do so today... but if it does – you may want to clear the way, ay-sap. Or, to melt it into slag, if you are able."

"*I* can do that for ya, Karéin," quipped the bounty-hunter.

"Me first... me first!" teased Brent Boyd, to the thrill of his children.

"I see that we are not lacking in that capacity," deadpanned the alien-girl. "Surely, then... at least *one* of my objectives has thus been accomplished!"

There was a twitter of chuckling at this *bon mot*, and then the Storied-Watcher announced,

"My family – my friends – and all other of my beloved – I welcome you today to the 'Council of The Island' – a meeting among us to consider past battles, to mourn our dead and to celebrate our victories, but foremost... to look to the future. A fond remembering and – at last – a chance to say 'farewell', shall this be."

She paused for a second and said,

"There is much to say – and no doubt each of you will have his or her own questions, about what has transpired thus far... and about where we all go from here. I pledge that I will answer all of these in time, as best I am able. But for now, I would speak about my own plans... for myself, for my family, and... for this beautiful, fragile little orb called 'Earth', on which we now stand. Some of what I will say, is very – ahh – 'private'. So I trust that you will reveal it only to those who do not mean me ill. Will you agree to this?"

As one, the audience replied, "Yes, we will!"

They were now looking on with rapt attention, as she continued,

"As you all know, she who is named 'Karéin-Mayréij' vanquished the 'Lucifer' comet, at great risk to herself; that is a feat whose accomplishment I will treasure for all my days. But it did not come without a high cost. *That* Karéin-Mayréij – the one with the powers of a true god – I reveal to you now, that she is *not* me… and she is gone. None the less, she *will* return; I just do not know when. It could be tomorrow – it could be twenty years hence – it could be two millennia hence. Thus it has always been with me. I am not like you; I do not have just one 'self'. I have many… and they come and go, often without my assent. Most of these are benevolent; some are weaker, some are stronger."

Her voice lowered, and she confessed, "And I must warn you all now – there is also one 'Karéin-Mayréij' who I dread to let loose upon *any* world – but fear not, she is nowhere near you now, nor – if I have anything to do about it – will she ever be!"

Are you following this? sent Tanaka to Abruzzio.

You bet I am, responded the former JPL scientist.

Totally uncharted scientific territory.

But will she let us explore it?

For the record, sent Billings,

This ain't news to yours truly.

She told me about it, on the road, and back in Tucson… but Jaysus H Christ, I had no idea what she really meant…

"If it is of any reassurance," offered the Storied Watcher, "This recondite self – 'Black Karéin', as she has been called in ages past – has not plagued me for thousands of your years; and it takes a very special set of circumstances, to unleash her. She is under control. Do not, ahh, lose any sleep over it… oh-kay?"

There was a wave of polite, but nervous, laughter.

"Now," she stated, "We should turn to more immediate and salutary things. First among these is, I owe you an explanation about the tests which lately have occurred within yonder American empire, and then at its palace, otherwise known of as the 'White House'. Many of you have asked me about this, and – especially – about why I refrained from intervening, even when your lives or those of other innocent people, might have been at risk. Greatly was I tempted so to do; but I could not. Here is why."

The Mars Gang hung on every word, as the alien-girl explained,

"The Holy *Fire* has manifested in some of you, and its advent has thus been immediately apparent – for example *you*, brother Brent, and your, ahh, 'light-show'… or *you*, sister Cherie, and your 'shock-bolts'. Truly, these things are visible, they are most potent, and their use leaves no doubt. But the

Fire of *Amaiish* has many *other* aspects which are far less obvious – far more subtle – and often much more powerful in the long run, however counter-intuitive that may seem."

"One such art that returned to me ere the Council of The Woods," she went on, "Is the knowing of when the Fates are testing either myself, or others. I can see the nature of the test in general terms, but it is like looking at a scene through a badly-frosted window-pane. The exact details – what will happen to who, by when – these are often denied to me. Such was the case in the recent past. I knew that both Sam's and Min-nie's teams had long and dangerous journeys ahead of them, and that there would be many enemies and precarious situations for them to confront and overcome. What would have been the benefit, of disclosing this? All it would have done is to have made you all the more apprehensive –"

"Yeah, well, Karéin," interjected Minnie Chu, "That may be true... but I sure could have used a heads-up about Crowford's little nuclear Care-package, on the Airborne Command Post. I'd take the 'apprehension' any day, frankly!"

Upon hearing this, Karéin-Mayréij laughed and remarked,

"And so would have I, about the other two atom-smashing bombs, my sister... but I suppose the Gods do not have such things in their, ahh, 'play-book'. For the record... I *did* try to ask. All that I heard from the voices was, 'a great danger is on that airplane... and is in the big western city'."

"No *shit!*" joked Devon White, to more giggling.

"And there is *another* thing," expounded the Storied Watcher. "You may legitimately ask, 'If Karéin-Mayréij can see these supernatural tests in advance... why does she not intervene in them, thus to guarantee survival and success, for those involved?' And the answer is : I can tell when a peril is just an ordinary one – that is, one to be avoided or dealt with as safely as possible – or if it is an ordained one that *must* be faced at risk of one's life, for an acolyte of the Holy *Fire* to progress on his or her way towards nobility. This art affects me as well as you, and I have learned over many thousands of years past, that it is shameful and wrong – sometimes, disastrous – to evade it."

"There's your answer," whispered Kaysten, to the Russian, who nodded affirmatively.

"Thus," said the alien-girl, "This grace called me to the encounter with the 'Lucifer' object. Sam – Devon – Cherie – Brent – and, far away, dear Ser-gayy – this is one reason why I quailed, when faced with that challenge. I knew that if I should refuse the test, my own fate – and the celestial balance – would be irretrievably wounded; I would decline into a cruel, helpless, pathetic parody of the mighty, legendary 'Storied Watcher' – and I would *deserve* this calumny. Yet, I also knew that to go forward, could easily be at the cost of my own life. This is what I mean when I say, 'a test like this, cannot be evaded'. It was the same with all of you, when you set out from the

Council of The Woods. I had to retreat and pray that you would come through oh-kay; for if I *had* intervened, I would have forever crippled your own progress towards greatness and nobility."

"Well, that's all fine and good," commented Donny Wade, "But for God's sake, honey – even if you *couldn't* change it none... why didn't you just tell us all that this 'test' stuff was happenin', in the first place? Would've helped to have known that it wasn't, like, all random, I mean."

This observation was immediately supported by several others in the audience.

"Doing so might have spoiled your quest, by affecting the actions that you decided upon," parried the Storied Watcher. "I could not take that chance."

"Okay fine," grumbled Minnie Chu, "But look, Karéin... I used this 'danger-sense-skill' that you supposedly bestowed on me, and it didn't warn me of *anything* bad happening after the little – uhh – incidents, with the two nukes – the one on the plane and the one that the CIA-guy fired at it, I mean. So I told a bunch of Senators that everything was going to be hunky-dory. As the bullet-holes all over the White House will attest, that prediction was anything *but* accurate – I don't know *how* I'm going to credibly explain it to the Congress. How do you know that your 'voices' are any more accurate?"

"I just... *do*," answered the alien-girl. "And it is a different skill than the danger-sense. That one tells only of imminent perils, about a specific place or area. Did you not get a bad feeling, just before the attack transpired, on the President's palace?"

"Yeah... I sure *did*," ruefully admitted the *nouvelle* FBI-director. "The President didn't believe me. I wish he had."

"*I* screwed up, big-time, on that one, too," added Kaysten. "Sorry."

"Don't worry about it, Jerry," assured Chu, *sotto voce*. "Besides... she said we passed the test – whatever the test *was*, that is."

"It is like this," elaborated Karéin-Mayréij. "Passing a Test of Fate – for that is the proper name of what we now discuss – is *crucial*, for you all to go forward on the path towards nobility – to wit, to progress to the next levels of the Holy *Fire*. When a challenge of this type is placed in front of one, only a fool – or a coward, or both – denies it... or refuses it."

"Why's *that*, Karéin?" interrogated Saquina White. "Y'all givin' us a few more alien brownie points – or maybe a nice new gold medal or such – for gettin' past one of these-here 'tests', with our skin still on us?"

"No," responded the alien-girl, with a sudden seriousness in her voice. "It is because you *must* advance – you must become greater... wiser... more powerful. It is *vital*, in fact!"

A palpable chill went through the audience, as Sam Jacobson pressed,

"You know, Karéin... that doesn't sound too good. To *my* ears, it sounds like there's something *big* – something really dangerous, challenging, pick the right words – just around the corner. Am I right?"

The Storied Watcher looked furtively down for a second or two. Then she stared right at the former Mars mission commander and replied, "No... and yes. Beloved friend, I have searched all my arts, and I see nothing of the sort you describe, 'on the horizon'. Yet... one part of me – a little voice, way in the back of my mind – it counsels me, '*prepare* them'. I know not what for – and, mark my words – the next challenge, when and if it comes, may not be manifest for many years... centuries, perhaps. But there is *always*, a 'next challenge'! Thus it has been, since the dawn of my days. We all should be prepared – just as a precaution."

"Don't we get a little time off from being super-heroes?" asked Tanaka.

"Yeah... maybe we need a union or something," complained Abruzzio.

"I kinda thought we were more *super-villains*," maliciously offered Wolf.

"These are subjective terms," noted Karéin-Mayréij, "Though you are all 'heroes' in my eyes – and thus shall I describe you, when your peers ask me of it. But to answer the question... I would say, 'go home and be merry, and do not dwell on the future... for it will be what it will be, and there is nothing that you can do can change it, until the right time comes'. If I knew of an immediate peril – large or small – I would tell you of it, here and now. But I see none. You cannot live in fear of what may or may not happen, tomorrow, or the next day."

Worried to anxious glances were passed back and forth within the crowd; but none could think of anything more that was constructive to say; so, after another pause, the Storied Watcher continued,

"Now... as to other things. Shortly before this meeting commenced, I had a discussion with my family – Bob, Tommy, Elissha and Sayuri – about my immediate future, and how it will relate to their own. It may surprise some of you to hear that this situation – where I have many dear loved-ones close-by – is actually quite new and exciting for me. Over the many ages I can recall only one or two other occasions where I have been so blessed... and I can assure you that on *no* account, will I give it up!"

"Well," interjected Billings, "*That's* nice to hear again, this time in front of some witnesses. But you left out the part about 'I promise not to go flying off to Jupiter'... remember?"

A smiling Karéin-Mayréij threw her head back and let out a happy giggle.

"Did we say anything about *Mailànkh*, my love?" she teased.

"You *do*, and I'm coming along... even if I have to hold my breath," he answered.

"So, what I have to say on this matter, may be welcomed by some, yet it may sadden others," said the Storied Watcher. "As you know, after the 'Lucifer' incident, I happened to fall into the north-western realms of yonder 'America' empire, and from there – with Bob's help and the companionship of Tommy and of dear Whitney's family – I made my way to the 'Tucson' city, in the south-west of the empire. The rest of the story is probably familiar to you by now, but the import of it is, I could have landed in almost any place on this planet... or, indeed, bless the Gods and my luck, I could have fallen into the oceans that in fact make up most of this world's surface-area. Somehow I know that even in *that* case, I would have survived... but it would have been even less pleasant."

"She was almost *dead* when she crashed down in Idaho," whispered Chu. "Even for Karéin... I shudder to imagine what would have happened, if she had, say, ended up splashing down in the South Polar Sea."

"Yeah, but," quietly responded the nearby Ramirez, "Remember who we're *talking* about, here. You know – 'tens of thousands of years old', 'disintegrates comets for breakfast', 'laughs off hydrogen bombs'... *et cetera?*"

The *nouvelle* FBI-director nodded in acknowledgment.

"And we're talking to her as if she were a friend... a sister," she marveled, through tearful eyes. "I feel *so* lucky, to be living in these times."

"So do I, sister," offered the Storied Watcher, whose alien-powered hearing had eavesdropped on the conversation. "For – next only to a mate, a lover or a child – a trusted friend, is the most treasured thing in the universe. But back to the topic at hand. As you know, since landing on Earth, I have spent almost all my time in this 'America' place; and – with no slight meant to any who now hear my voice, especially Matt and Clairie – I confess that I have had my fill of it... and *then* some."

"*Wow,*" said Brent Boyd.

"Well," phlegmatically offered Sam Jacobson, "All things considered... I can hardly blame her."

"Over the ages," explained Karéin-Mayréij, "I have experienced many forms of government – based on different principles and ideologies – but some things, like 'corruption', 'cruelty', 'oppression', 'deceit' and, most of all, 'arrogance of rulership', seem to be common elements. Lamentably, these characteristics are all very much present in this 'United States' where most of you come from, however much the President – that is, the king – might protest otherwise. But though these things sadden and annoy me, the fact is that – despite its pretensions – your 'America' empire is but *one* ordinary principality, out of many others, on this planet. It has already had far too much of my time, and much of that has not been under happy circumstances. So I will leave this place... I will travel and live elsewhere, upon this Earth. And I will not soon return to America."

"Where you *goin'*, Karéin?" demanded an upset Compton refugee.

"Yeah," exclaimed Wolf, "For fuck's *sake*, girl – 'scuse the French, but I'm *pissed*, now – you got so much still to *do*, back Stateside! That fuckin' President's gonna go back to his old cheatin' ways, the minute you –"

"Watch your *mouth*, dude!" interrupted a glowering Matt.

"Why don't you ask your sister what it *feels* like, when I get a little hot under the collar, kid –" aggressively replied the bounty-hunter.

"Remember how it felt when you got that 'flame'-shit turned back on you?" echoed Clairie, in Wolf's direction. "Think you can take on both of us at the same time?"

"Peace... *peace!*" shouted the Storied Watcher, with her hands held out in front, motioning for silence.

She shot a glance first at Matt, and then at his sister, and said, "Now... you two need to mark my words. Did you think it was for an idle bargain, that I gifted you with the Holy *Fire*?"

"Well... sure," answered Clairie. "It was what you *said*... wasn't it?"

"Little sister," advised Karéin-Mayréij, "You and your brother are to royalty born... and you must take these lessons of guileful statecraft and games-playing, deeply to heart. Yes, indeed I *did* manipulate your mother and father – and some others – by exchanging your human lives, for the crimes inflicted on my friends and family. But I had a deeper, secondary purpose – and so must you always have when dealing with your father, or with other nobles of your empire. Namely, I set the two of you with the Holy *Fire* – thus I made you my kin, and gave you my trust – so that you could guide the President back to the path of honesty, fairness and justice, when he strays... as, be there no doubt... he will. This vital task is yours and yours alone... it falls to both of you! I will monitor how you do, from afar. Do not, ahh, 'let me down'. Do you understand?"

"Yeah... so how you like *them* apples?" sneered Wolf.

"Brother," remonstrated the Storied Watcher, "Taunt them not! Rather... lend Matt and Clairie your assistance, when they call upon you – as I expect all the rest of you who owe their allegiance to this 'United States' empire, also to do. Our two princelings are still, ahh, in 'learning-mode'. Much depends on their ability to gently guide their father – and his kingdom – towards enlightenment. But I *believe* in Matt and Clairie... and so should you."

The bounty-hunter shrugged and sighed, but did not further provoke.

"So... we're supposed to, like, run the country, behind Dad's back... is *that* what you're saying, Karéin?" pressed Clairie.

The alien-girl did not directly reply. Instead, her face wore a saturnine grin, and she winked at both the teenagers.

"I fuckin' *knew* there had to be a catch to it," muttered Matt, to the delight of several, including Wolf and most of the Mars Gang.

"What about me?" requested Kaysten. "What am *I* supposed to do, while they're – uhh – conspiring against my boss?"

"I am sure that you will figure it out, my brother," insouciantly responded Karéin-Mayréij. "But to give you an idea... Matt and Claire will need someone to negotiate with the President, in the case that he disagrees with their ideas. You are very skilled at this, Jerr-ee. I ask you to help them. Will you?"

The bewildered Chief of Staff looked hither and yon for support, but all he saw were bemused smiles.

"I guess I don't have a choice, then?" he pleaded.

"Of *course* you do," she countered. "But then the responsibility will be partly yours, should things not, ahh, 'work out'. It is to you to decide."

Kaysten leaned over and addressed the two Presidential offspring.

"We'll need to have to have a little chat, later," he said.

"No *shit!*" answered Matt. "There's no take-backs on this *Amaiish* stuff?"

"Nope," pleasantly commented the alien-girl. "You are – ahh – 'stuck with her'. If it is of any consolation… at least back in your fine white palace, you will not have to contend with any scheming wizards, witches, undead spirits, spectral beings or evil high priests… nor compete with them for your father's favor. Which is more than I can say for my own experiences, in ages past."

"Swell," complained the male teenager, as several of the more-than-humans laughed themselves silly.

Again taking control of the conversation, the Storied Watcher announced, "Bob and I have not yet decided exactly where we will go, outside of the United States – several places, like 'Switz-er-land', 'New Zee-land', 'Swee-den', 'Ta-hee-tee', 'Eye-sland' or one of the smaller islands around the world, all have their merits, on first glance – but it is possible that we will not stay permanently in any one area, and that we will move frequently. This is partly because it is our intention to live modestly and, hopefully, inconspicuously. We owe it to our children to give them as 'normal' an upbringing, as we can. We know that this will be, ahh, challenging… after all, most normal human children cannot soar like a bird, nor can they blast strong things apart just on a whim –"

As if on cue, Tommy stuck out his tongue and then fired a low-powered death-bolt at the stone floor just ahead of him, resulting in a inch-deep divot being blown out of the substance.

While chuckles went back and forth within the audience, the alien-girl wagged her finger at the boy and instructed,

"You will have to get brother Hector to help you to fill that back in, young man. This 'Bermuda' place has *rules* about defacing property, you know."

"For *sure*, Mom," smartly obliged Tommy.

"As to my own role on this planet," pronounced Karéin-Mayréij, to the intense interest of her followers, "As I have repeatedly said… I am the Earth's guardian – not her master… nor her tyrant. Mine is to *serve* the people of this world… not to *rule* them; and my first loyalty must always be to Bob, Tommy, Elissha and Sayuri. Let no-one harm so much as a hair on their heads! Matt... Clairie... may I impose upon you to have this demand communicated by your father, to the other potentates of the planet?"

"Oh... *definitely*, Angel Lady," answered the teenage girl. "After what just about happened to him, after all – I'm sure Dad will be ready to warn all those other guys."

"Yeah... but Karéin... you *do* realize that Dad can't make them do, or not do, *anything*... don't you?" remarked Matt.

"Well... *duh!*" unhelpfully commented Brent Boyd.

"I am very aware of that," replied the Storied Watcher. "But it will be easier for him to – ahh – pass on the message, than it would be for me – that is, it would save me the trouble of 'dropping in', un-announced, on a hundred or so foreign emperors and minor kings. I feel that doing that, might, ahh, 'get me off on the wrong leg' with them... Bob, did I say that right?"

"For *sure*, honey," smirked the ex-salesman. "And here I thought you didn't have a leg to stand on."

"Thank you, beloved," she offered with a warm gaze, though she clearly knew of his joke.

"I have been thinking," continued the alien-girl, "About how I will behave, now that I am a citizen of this world... yet I am not – nor shall ever be – a subject of any one kingdom. You have all seen what I am capable of –"

"Oh yeah," interjected Clairie, "We sure *have*... like half the damn Washington Monument, dropped upside-down, into Dad's front lawn."

"Impressive... wasn't it?" mentioned Abruzzio.

"You ain't just whistlin' 'Dixie'," added Billings.

"Do not worry – I will, ahh, get around to cleaning that up, in due time," pledged the Storied Watcher, with another insouciant wink, in the teenagers' direction. "But it is a modest example of what I can do, if I set my mind to it. This world has many people, and thus also has an almost indefinite number of potential demands on my time. I could not answer all these even if I wanted to; and – not only because of my duties to my family – I have no interest in becoming, ahh, 'Earth's go-fer'. Yet neither do I want to stand idly by, while people suffer undeserved, cruel fates, that perhaps I could prevent from coming about. Therefore I have decided on the following rules, governing my actions."

They all bent forward, listening with rapt attention.

The Future Burns Bright

"I will not intervene in human political, religious or ideological squabbles – including but not limited to wars," pledged Karéin-Mayréij, "Except where these may involve weapons of mass destruction that could lay waste to large parts of your world. Likewise, though I deplore the suffering caused by natural disasters – wind-storms, earthquakes, droughts, wild-fires and so on – I do not have the powers of a true God... namely, 'the ability to simply wish these things, away'. To mitigate such problems would require endless, and potentially fruitless, effort on my part; and furthermore, should I use my arts to – for example – deflect a hurricane away from one region, it would just plague another. The apportionment of such things is best left to the Gods and the Fates. Therefore, while I retain the right to help in some cases – if perchance I happen to be in the area, and a big ship with people upon it, is about to sink – you should not expect me to *always* show up... do not become dependent upon me."

"Yet," she vowed, with the sounds an other-worldly symphony somehow reverberating with each word, "I *am* the Guardian of the Earth... and not for naught, is that title. If an *unusual* catastrophe occurs – something that could not reasonably have been predicted or planned for – or one that would imperil too many innocent people, particularly children – I *swear* that I *will* do my best to help. And not only me!"

The Storied Watcher was now staring deeply at all those in the audience, at the same time.

Her dignity and presence waxed immeasurably.

She looked like a *god.*

A few of them gasped.

The realization came to many that – despite their pretensions otherwise – none of them (not even Billings), really *knew* the essence of this being.

"Today, I charge this same duty to every one of you, who now hears my voice!" she declared, with rising passion. "You are what you believe in. You become that which you believe that you can become. The Gods have blessed you – each in your own special way – with the Holy *Fire*; now go out and *use* it, for the good of your sisters and brothers! When the spirit moves you, seek out and help the poor – the weak – the desperate – the oppressed – the sick – and the hungry. Your powers will wax as you do this; for if you would heal someone, but know not how so to do, pray for this grace... and she *will* come to you. This is the gist of all nobility : to do pure good unto others. If you see yourselves in the faces of the poor, the weak and the diseased, then you are really seeing *me.* If you have served and helped one poor person without thinking of his or her caste, creed, gender or race... history – and I – will remember you kindly, for always."

"When you set out to heal," elaborated the alien-girl, "Give the highest priority to the undeservedly-afflicted young or the wrongfully-injured, over those who have lived out most of their lives already; lend the force of your life to the young, but take away pain and bestow your love and hopes for a gentle journey to the Planes Beyond, upon the elderly. For there is a natural order to the cycle of life and death, of being and non-being – you should not interfere with this, except when you descry cruelty or injustice to be present."

"But when thus you give service to your brothers and sisters," directed Karéin-Mayréij, "Take nothing but the plain shoes on your feet and the modest clothes on your back, and accept no riches or baubles as compensation... for you cannot serve both money and the Light of Heaven. Set your will upon your work, but never on its reward; for a gift is pure when it is given from the heart to the right person at the right time and at the right place, and when we expect nothing in return. The great secret of true success, of true happiness, is this : the man or woman who asks for no payment – the perfectly unselfish person – is the most wise."

"And anyway," she mentioned, "What you have taken, has been from here; what you gave, has been given here; what belongs to you today, belonged to someone else, yesterday – and it will be someone else's tomorrow; change is the law of the universe. Thus has always been the path to nobility and enlightenment, ere the first hours of the Wheel of Time! If you are grateful for the miracles that you shall work within this world... surely shall the Gods' favor, rest upon you."

The ethereal music slowly declined, as the Storied Watcher bowed her head and clasped her hands together in front.

Though they were not sitting together, both Abruzzio and Claremont wiped tears and touched the crucifixes adorning their necks.

I'm so ashamed that I ever doubted you, Karéin, guiltily thought the former JPL scientist.

Forgive me!

Do not be, sister, came the response.

Learning and growing is never easy – be that in taking one's first steps as a child, or in one's first knowledge of the Holy Fire.

You have come so far already!

If you will let me, I will guide you henceforth – for so much love and wisdom have you yet to give, for the simple people of this world!

Believe not just in me... but foremost, believe in yourself!

Abruzzio was now crying openly.

Devon White looked long at Claremont and the scientist, then at his wife. He nodded solemnly.

"I *believe...*" he whispered to Saquina.

Who – or what – are we dealin' *with here?* thought a shocked Clairie.

Like, I was just talkin' with her as if she was just a best bud –

But omigawd *–*

I think you already know what she really is, responded Tanaka.

We've known since we were last in space with her...

Search your heart, little sister...

And never forget the times that we are now living through.

"So... with the aforesaid in mind, I come now to what will – with your assent – happen in the hours and days to come," stated the Storied Watcher. "Each of you will choose to where he or she shall be transported –"

"That just on Planet Earth?" smartly interrupted Devon White. "I seem to remember, y'all sort of promised me a trip to Mars?"

"If it is oh-kay with you, and your brothers and sisters," deflected the alien-girl, "I would prefer to limit the present exercise, just to places on this world. We can discuss points 'further in the field', later. Besides… you might find a trip to *Mailànkh* to be rather unpleasant. Have you yet contrived how to use your arts, to suppress the need for certain – ahh – 'bodily functions'?"

"That'd be a 'no'," admitted the ex-astronaut. "Last time I was flyin' by myself over L.A., I still had to keep my eye open for gas stations 'long the way."

"Then," perhaps we should, ahh, 'delay' such a trip, for the meantime," requested the Storied Watcher. "For those who would just go somewhere else upon this planet, we should meet, one by one, to make the necessary arrangements. When arriving, should not make a spectacle or draw unnecessary attention, so ideally we will come to each destination with minimal noise and after dark with no fore-warning of your kin, so that we do not end up on, ahh, the 'My-Space-Tube' channels. We will combine as many trips as we can do with our existing vessels, without making voyage uncomfortable."

Many within the crowd began discussing the details of their respective trips home, between each other.

"As for my part," she noted, "I also do have some other errands to run in the America empire, before I will able to move on to other things. For example I have a tee-vee announcer in a south-western state, to whom I must make amends… there are others as well. But I would not expect that this should take a lot of time. I would like to have all the trips back home, to be done in no more than a week from now. Does this meet with your approval?"

Affirmative responses came from everywhere in the throng.

"Let me also caution you," counseled Karéin-Mayréij, "Not to immediately seek out fame and fortune by way of your association with myself, or with the Holy *Fire,* when again you return to your home-places. For so doing amounts to boasting and to personally profiting by your powers, which things are ignoble, especially if carried to extremes. A New Person should foremost be modest, setting an example for your human brothers and sisters. Rather… let fame and fortune – should they advent themselves – come to *you,* and in that case, give away the most-part, to the poor, the unlucky and the needy. How many fine meals can you eat at once, after all? How many soft beds can you lie upon? How many mansions can you be in, at the same time? I will not say – as some do – that 'money is the root of all evil'. There are many evils that have nothing to do with self-enrichment. But I *will* say that the lust for gold and fine things, paves the way for many evils. Over years untold, I have seen this proven to be true, over and over again. Fall unwittingly not into this trap!"

She shot a glance at the bounty-hunter.

"And yes, brother," she pluckishly offered, "This *does* mean that you should not seek out a 'book-dealer'. However... if one should happen to – ahh – 'look you down'... well, then... just make sure that you have them spell my name right... oh-kay?"

"Best news I've heard in, like, an hour or so, hun," happily answered Wolf, while many in the crowd guffawed.

"Meanwhile," continued the alien-girl, "Though my arts and judgment tell me that the severe perils recently encountered have been crushed – they have been driven as far away as one can expect to do, and I believe that you can go safely home – my guarantee of personal protection is to each and every one of you, and to your families too. You are exempt from the sanctions and strictures that human kingdoms might otherwise try to impose. If you, or someone who you love, are vexed by some trivial or trumped-up charge – or just danger at the hand of human beings – first contest it in the conventional way. If that fails, always trying to avoid needless harm to human beings, use your own powers to free yourselves; or call on your more puissant brothers and sisters of the *Fire*, to be saved or liberated."

"But if," she proclaimed, "Despite all this – it should come to being unjustly imprisoned, or worse – *call* upon me, and I *will* respond to you! Beforehand, you must warn those who would thus afflict you that I will be on my way, and that they should stand aside; for I will arrive in a refulgent tempest of thunder and flame, and for those who would foolishly block my way... I will take no responsibility – or blame – for what may befall them."

"*Yeaaah!*" enthusiastically shouted one of the Compton refugees, to the delight of many in the audience.

Sari, sent Billings, with a tone of great satisfaction,

Remember how – back in Tucson – I thought, "finally, the big guns are on our side?"

I know, dearest, she responded,

And do you know what?

Yeah? he asked.

You are among the – ahh – "biggest" of them.

Remember how affrighted you were, upon knowing that I could but gaze at a thing, and see it thus reduced to ashes?

Umm... that would be a "yes", for sure, he admitted.

When the same terrible art comes to yourself – and the hour is not long now – use your powers mercifully, my love...

For to destroy a thing, is far easier than to make a thing... but only by the latter, can you be a true "hero".

I love you so *much*, was all he could think to think back.

"How do we – uhh – *do* that?" asked Atasha Jones. "Call for y'all, that is?"

"*Bob* knows how," gently counseled the Storied Watcher.

"You say her name over and over again, as if you *mean* it," he disclosed. "But it's got to be her *real* name. As I found out the *hard* way, up on – or, rather, under – Amchitka."

"Wow... but y'all shouldn't let that get out too far, girl," advised Whitney Claremont. "Every second person in th' world be doin' that, every time they get a parkin'-ticket or such."

"Yeah... do you do bad dates, ex-girlfriends, bounced credit-cards and tax-collectors?" quipped the bounty-hunter.

"Lamentably, such issues do not – to my mind – amount to 'emergencies," said Karéin-Mayréij, with an arched eyebrow and a friendly wink in Wolf's direction. "Furthermore, this art will only work for people who I have personally met, and who I have adopted into my fold... and then only, when the hour is most dire. It can be fickle, too. Sometimes I hear right away... sometimes later."

Hey, sent Abruzzio,
That isn't true!
Don't ask me how *I know... but I know.*
Of course *you do, sister,* came back the reply,
While it is not a lie – the full truth of it is more complicated... I will explain it to yourself, and to a few other of my most trusted ones, shortly.

"Beloved friends," stated Karéin-Mayréij, "If you will indulge me... I have a few more modest words of advice, based on what I have learned over millennia past."

There were no objections, although Abruzzio asked,

"Karéin... do you mind if I record this?"

The alien-girl replied,

"No, of course not, sister; but above all else... record these words in your heart."

The overcome ex-JPL scientist mutely nodded.

Again, the godly presence appeared all around her while her psycho-music sounded softly in the background, as the Storied Watcher expounded,

"Brothers and sisters... do your best to affirm divine calmness and peace, and send out thoughts of love and goodwill if you would live in harmony. Try not to become angry, for anger pollutes your system. This is a principle at which I often fail – yet never will I stop trying. An insincere friend is more to be feared than a wild beast; a beast may wound your body, but an treacherous friend can wound your mind. So above all else – above your loyalties to kingdoms, causes, faiths and the like – even your affections for myself – be loyal to each other. Moreover, there is nothing more dreadful than doubt, which separates people; it is a poison that disintegrates friendships and breaks up pleasant relations. It is a thorn that irritates and hurts; it is a sword that kills. Strive to be straight with each other. This does not mean that you must do the same, with humans... although, all other things being equal, you should still try. They will distrust and fear you, and only by your nobility, charity and honesty, will you overcome this suspicion… as you must."

"And as far as the genders and the identities thereof, are concerned," she claimed, "I have noticed that human beings seem to place a great deal of importance on this aspect of being; but really the male and the female are indistinguishable… they are one. They are the universe. At the core of their mutual intermingling, the supreme consciousness opens. As the powers of your minds flourish, this truth will become more and more clear to you."

"Surely," disclosed the alien-girl, "Shall you be tested from time to time with fear, hunger or a loss of wealth and lives and fruits; but none the less be patient and give good tidings, and you will put misfortune behind you. Likewise, it could be that you dislike something, when it is good for you; and it could be that you like something when it is bad for you. But when one scorns evil – when one feels tranquil – one finds pleasure in listening to good teachings; when one has these feelings and appreciates them… then, one is free of fear."

"You have many years yet to come, far beyond the life-spans of your human brothers and sisters," she observed, with the grandeur in her voice and presence becoming simply overpowering. "Take the time that you will need to learn, what will do you well and what will do you ill. You will defend this world in ways never before envisaged… and somehow, I know that what you will do in the next years – decades – centuries, even… without this, the Earth would have had no good future at all. It is a great and solemn duty – but I *know* that you will be the equal of it. When *you* believed in *me*, that propelled me across the heavens, to the rescue of this beautiful blue world. Now I say… '*I* believe in *you!*' Each of you is a hero, in her or his own way; and your great deeds are not over – nay, they are but *starting!* Look to the future with bravery, confidence, hope and wonder… and then go out and write its story; for I will be with you, to the end of this age!"

Many within the awed, half-comprehending audience – not just Abruzzio, the Whites and the Claremonts – hung their heads, gasping and sobbing.

Their hearts were pounding.

They figured themselves as "super-humans", and – by any reasonable measure – many of them undoubtedly deserved this appellation. Yet, every person present in this place, at this time – even Billings, who knew her best – felt profoundly small – helpless – *insignificant*, compared to the shockingly powerful, ineffable – but, kindly and friendly – being who stood directly in front of them.

Even the stolid, impassive Sam Jacobson was moved, almost to tears.

Now you know, brother, came a thought to his mind,

Who you freed from that tomb upon Mailànkh.

I… I don't know what to say, *Karéin,* he attempted.

I have no words…

Sometimes, her reassuring – yet, majestic – thoughts responded,
Love is her own words.
Let her sing on your account, great friend.
Do you hear the music?
Yes, he managed.
Bob told me, "he heard an angel singing".
Now... so have I.
Thank you, Storied Watcher.

The former Mars mission commander could not look the alien-girl in the eye, any more. He stared at the floor, to avoid her gaze.

She paused for a few long seconds, clasping her hands in front, as they had seen her do, from time to time.

Her presence – though still supernaturally-potent – abated slightly.

"Finally," declared Karéin-Mayréij, "After all the twists and turns that have befallen us – as we mourn the loss of many, including Cassie's cherished husband, kind Catherine from the rest-au-rant, little Korey, stalwart Agent Kortish and our valiant, fallen brother, Sebastiàn, Mighty Prince of Venoms – we come to the parting of our ways. But it need not be a final one. You have families and lives to which to return; blessed be the Gods, now I have a family too – and I have a life to build with Bob, Tommy, Elissha and Sayuri, henceforth. I will do this... and I will treasure every *second* that I will spend upon it! We should take fellowship with our loved-ones; and perhaps in a few years, we can meet again, to embrace and – ahh – 'catch up' with each other."

Again she paused, and then concluded the Storied Watcher,

"Though the cost has been steep – and never would we do the same, had we the choice – at the end of our adventures... all is well. The tests are passed; evil is overthrown; good prevails... and we are *together*. The eternal pathway to the future, lit by the Holy *Fire* of my ancestors – who now are your own, as well – it burns ever-bright, beckoning us onward. Who will walk with me?"

She cast her gaze to the skies, as if she was searching for something.

Then – through glowing, moist eyes, with a quivering chin, the one called 'Karéin-Mayréij' – Earth's new-found Guardian, whose task would be to lead humanity into a hopeful future – looked straight at her audience.

"Beloved Brothers and Sisters of the New People... *take my hand,*" she breathed.

– Here ends –

The Future Burns Bright

and the Story of
Karéin-Mayréij's First Steps
Upon This World